THE WHERE, THE WHO & THE WHAT

A GNOSTIC SCIENCE FICTION NOVEL

J.R. MABRY

APOCRYPHILE
PRESS

Apocryphile Press
PO Box 255
Hannacroix, NY 12087
www.apocryphilepress.com

Copyright © 2025 by J.R. Mabry
Printed in the United States of America
ISBN 978-1-958061-92-3 | paper
ISBN 978-1-958061-93-0 | ePub

Please join our mailing list at www.apocryphilepress.com/free. We'll keep you up-to-date on all our new releases, and we'll also send you a FREE BOOK. Visit us today!

OTHER NOVELS BY J.R. MABRY

BY J.R. MABRY

The Worship of Mystery • Ash Wednesday

The Berkeley Blackfriars Series

The Kingdom • The Power • The Glory

BY J.R. MABRY & MICKEY ASTERIOU

The Red Horn Saga

The Prison Stone • The Dark Field

Summoners' Keep • The Red Horn

BY J.R. MABRY & B.J. WEST

The Oblivion Saga

Oblivion Threshold • Oblivion Flight

Oblivion Quest • Oblivion Gambit

CONTENTS

This book is for all those who have been
wounded by the religion of their youth.

Hear me:
The god you were given is not the true God.
There is a way out.

PROLOGUE: SOPHIA'S CHOICE

"We were a chaotic movement before the epidemic."

"We didn't *have* a mission before the epidemic."

"We always had a mission."

"No, we had a mythology. We were waving wooden swords at shadows."

"So the epidemic was a good thing?"

"There was no fucking epidemic, you moron."

"You just said it yourself—"

"It's a term of convenience to help us sync up with the consensus narrative."

"There's a significant difference of opinion on that, even among the elect."

"Don't tell me you believe that nonsense about everyone except Californians dying off. You think it was the new age crystals that saved us? Or maybe it was the smog?"

"I'm saying that maybe the Powers used a real crisis to...to give them cover."

"Everyone in every state and country is alive, unless they died of natural causes or stepped in front of a bus. Period. There was no mass extinction event."

"Despite everything we've ever heard?"

"It's the media's job to lie. It's how they control us."

"Guh...I give up."

"We get to disagree about cosmogony so long as we're on the same page about the *telos*."

"Nice parallelism. Let's set speculations aside. Did you talk to her?"

"I did."

"And what did she say?"

"She said she has chosen this young man here."

"Him? Why him? He isn't even an initiate."

"I don't know. It is not for us to question to whom she grants the spark. Our only job is to welcome them and train them when they have been revealed to us. 'Many see it being sown, but few see it being reaped,' after all."

"True enough. Has he shown any interest?"

"No, not that I know of."

"Then how are we supposed to—?"

"Watch him. Wait for an opportunity. Just...plant the seed."

"How?"

"Do I have to think of everything? I don't know. I do know he works at a bookstore."

"So he likes to read..."

"There's your *in*."

PART 1: THE BOOK OF SECRETS

O Indestructible Spirit, whoever callest to thy indestructible offspring wherever they may find themselves, we thank thee, and praise thy supreme and compassionate Gnosis for having given us the light and wisdom of the holy Valentinus. May the secrets nameless, ineffable, transcendental, and glorious, that cannot be comprehended either by the dominions or by the powers or the lower beings or by any of the mixture of the world of darkness; the secrets brought to the light of our minds by Valentinus serve as our guiding powers to the ineffable Gnosis, now and forevermore. Amen.

—*Collect for the Feast Day of St. Valentinus**

* Ecclesia Gnostica Lectionary, compiled by +Most Rev. Stephan A. Hoeller, (1975). http://www.gnosis.org/ecclesia/Ecclesia-Gnostica-Lectionary.pdf

WHAT IS OCD?

Obsessive-Compulsive Disorder (OCD) is a mental health condition characterized by recurring, intrusive thoughts and repetitive behaviors. It affects people from all walks of life, cutting across age, gender, and socioeconomic backgrounds. OCD can significantly impact an individual's daily life, causing distress and interfering with their ability to function effectively.

The defining feature of OCD is the presence of obsessions and compulsions. Obsessions are unwanted and distressing thoughts, images, or urges that repeatedly enter a person's mind. These obsessions are often irrational and out of the individual's control. Common obsessions include fears of contamination, aggressive thoughts, and a need for symmetry or exactness.

To alleviate the distress caused by their obsessions, individuals with OCD engage in compulsions. Compulsions are repetitive behaviors or mental acts that a person feels driven to perform in response to an obsession. These rituals are aimed at reducing anxiety or preventing a feared outcome. Examples of compulsions include excessive handwashing, checking and rechecking locks, and counting or organizing items repeatedly.

Although the exact cause of OCD is not fully understood, it is believed to be influenced by a combination of genetic, neurological, and environmental factors. Research suggests that imbalances in certain brain chemicals, such as serotonin, play a role in the development of OCD. Additionally, traumatic events, high levels of stress, and a family history of OCD can increase the likelihood of its occurrence.

Living with OCD can be challenging. Individuals often experience intense anxiety, shame, and embarrassment due to their obsessions and compulsions. OCD can impact relationships, work performance, and overall quality of life. Fortunately, effective treatments are available. Cognitive-Behavioral Therapy (CBT) is a common therapeutic approach that helps individuals identify and challenge their irrational thoughts, gradually reducing the frequency and intensity of their compulsions. Medications, such as selective serotonin reuptake inhibitors (SSRIs), can also be prescribed to manage symptoms.

CHAPTER ONE

Either they're running somewhere,
or unable to run away from someone;
or they're fighting, or being beaten;
or they've fallen from heights,
or fly through the air without wings.
Sometimes, too, it's like someone is killing them,
even though no one's chasing them;
or they themselves are killing those around them,
covered in their blood.
Until those who are going through all these nightmares
can wake up, they see nothing,
because these things are nothing.
—*Gospel of Truth**

---

* The Gospel of Truth: Nag Hammadi Codex I, translated by Mark M. Mattison, published in *The Gospel of Truth: The Mystical Gospel* (2018).

T he beast prowled the aisle of the church, seeking someone to devour. Its mouth was wet with gore, crimson with the blood of sinners. A low growl coming from its throat caused the stones in the floor to rumble underfoot.

Seth looked underneath the pews and saw the great feet—black, mottled with the gray of ages—move with slow, graceful precision. He felt the impact of each footfall, and smelled the stinking musk of its wet fur, sour yet tinged with the bite of myrrh.

Trying to control his breath, he moved as silently as possible to put the solid end of one of the pews between himself and the beast's line of sight. It might work for a few moments, but the beast was moving, always moving. It was a living beast, after all, and for Seth to stop, to rest, was to die. He knew the words of this catechism by heart: this animal was a hunter, and it would not be satisfied until it had devoured his soul.

He had offered the necessary prayers. He had attended the Sunday school classes. He had colored the Bible scenes. He had memorized the verses. He had gone down into the water...and still the beast was coming.

Seth scrambled once more, for the beast was near the aisle now. An offering plate clattered to the floor, filling the air with its echoing alarm. Seth froze. Then he crawled, in a mad dash for...for anywhere. Just...away. He slowly edged his forehead around the corner of another row of pews until his eyes could see the aisle. But all he saw was teeth and fur and the heaving breast of the beast, its breath hot upon him.

Seth felt his heartbeat pounding in his head, his mind flailing for an escape. But all he saw was a vision of his neck pierced through by white fangs, his rag-doll body being dragged behind him as the beast dragged him off to hell.

He turned his head away from the great, gaping maw, felt the slick of its saliva drop onto his nose and cheeks, caustic as acid. Its breath *reeked of prayers and piety, of rot and corruption, of warm and sticky blood. Seth closed his eyes and waited for the teeth to strike his neck—*

S eth felt hot breath on his cheek. Opening one eye, he saw slavering jowls merely inches from his face. The jaws opened, and a massive tongue emerged and began to lick him. He grunted and wiped the slime from his cheek. "Hello, Kush."

The dog snuffled around Seth's head and shoulders, emitting a tiny whine. "Okay, you need to go out, I get it. Give me a minute," Seth mumbled.

The sound of his phone pierced the fog of residual sleep like a lightning flash. He rolled over and fumbled for it. Without bothering to see who it was, he accepted the call. "What?"

"Dude, are you still in bed?"

"I...I thought I was in church. But...yeah."

"Look, I'm going to be there in fifteen minutes. I want you up, showered, and wearing something with a rainbow on it. It's Pride! The parade isn't going to march itself. I even have a rainbow collar for Kushy."

Seth moaned something in the affirmative and sat up.

"And don't worry about lunch, I'm bringing pizza," Angie added. "We can scarf it down before we go."

Seth squinted. The sun was higher and brighter than it had any right to be. "Pizza? For breakfast?"

"You've never had cold pizza for breakfast? What's wrong with you? And this will be hot."

"Okay."

"Shower! Now!"

"I think I hate God." Seth's eyes roamed over the crowd. It was easier to say things like that if he didn't look at her.

Angie rolled her eyes. "Okay, here we go. I'll play. Why do you think you hate God?"

Her voice was nearly drowned out by the rattle and roar of engines. Angie grinned as the Dykes-on-Bikes rolled into view in all their stocky glory, most of them shirtless with Band-Aids obscuring their nipples. Kush took little interest in the show but panted contentedly, leaning against Seth's leg and sitting on half of his foot.

"Because he wants me to live in this tiny little box."

"Who does?"

"God. Jeez, Ange, pay attention."

Angie pointed to the bikers. "Sorry. I'm a little distracted at the moment."

"I didn't think butch was your type," Seth said.

"They got fems sitting right behind them, but you'd have to actually look to see them."

Seth turned and looked at the parade. "Oh, yeah, those are more your type."

"Your type, too, I think. You were saying?" Angie prompted. She was shorter than he was, with frizzy black hair pulled back into a ponytail that made the back of her head look like a bottle brush.

"God wants me to live in this tiny little box. And I can't do it. I've tried. And I can't do it."

Angie turned and looked up at him. His sandy hair was obviously self-cut, and he had the style sense of a grunge musician. "You're doing that thing with your face again. Stop it."

"Sorry. I don't know when I'm doing it."

"It makes you look like you're trying to make your eye yawn. It makes you look like a retard."

He frowned at her. "That's not an okay word to use anymore."

"Oh, so you want to put me in a little box too, huh? Fuck that, Kojak."

"Who's Kojak?"

Angie looked back at the parade. This was a boring entry—a group of about thirty people walking together in matching t-shirts wearing leis and rainbow Carnivale beads. Their banner announced they were a gay-friendly church. Seth could see their pastor—a stout woman in a bright pink shirt with a clerical collar who looked like she would have fit right in with the bikers, tattoos and all. Kush started to clean himself.

"Besides, you don't look like you've been living in a box to me," Angie noted.

"No, I haven't. Because I can't. But I feel like he's always breathing down my neck."

"Who is?"

"God. Why can't you follow the conversation?"

"Let's see...hot pastor?"

"Again, she is *not* your type."

"I like her style, though. Listen, Seth, in case you haven't noticed, there is no shortage of distractions here. Check out the dyke on the other side there with the long red hair in the halter top and the bright red men's speedo. Just makes me want to dry-hump an avocado."

Seth looked. Angie was right. That was definitely one very hot lesbian. Seth shook his head to clear it. "Maybe we should save this conversation for another time."

"Suits me," Angie said. Then she put her index finger and pinky in her mouth and whistled so loud Seth's ears rang.

"Stop that!" Seth said. Kush's ears rose to their full height.

"I'm trying to get her attention."

"I'm tired of being scared all the time," Seth said.

"What are you afraid of?"

"God. I can't believe you can't hold a thought in your head for three seconds. God. I'm scared of God."

"So go see a shrink."

"I tried that—"

"Try another one. Or...hey, here's an idea. Actually open up to one this time. It only works if you work it."

"I guess." Seth sounded defeated.

"Dude, you are seriously raining on my parade. My *actual* parade, as it happens."

"I'm sorry, Ange. I just..." But he didn't know what he *just*. And she wasn't listening. She was ogling. "Would you be drooling all over these other girls if Sara was here?" he asked.

"Probably not."

"Why isn't Sara here?" Seth asked.

"She has to work."

"Bummer."

Angie shrugged.

Seth scowled. "Are you and Sara...okay?"

Angie didn't look at him. Instead, she kept her eyes fixed on the Bathhouse Boys, clad in skimpy briefs, doing a synchronized line dance, advertising the Jizz Factory. Twinks ran into the crowd with baskets, handing out condoms and little plastic vials of lube. Kush started to lick his penis. "Stop that," Angie said to the dog, "You'll make these boys jealous." Looking back up at the parade, Angie asked, "Can I tell you something serious?"

"Sure," Seth said. "And unlike you, I'll pay attention."

"I'm thinking of breaking up with Sara."

"What? I love Sara," Seth said, his voice rising.

"Yeah. Everyone loves Sara," Angie said. "That's part of the problem. All of my friends like Sara more than they like me."

"That's not true," Seth said too quickly. Angie turned to face him and narrowed one eye. Then she turned back to the parade.

"Okay," he corrected. "It is *kind of* true. But it's not *very* true."

"How can something be not *very* true?" Angie asked. "Either something is true or it isn't true."

She had a point. "People love you, too," he said, but even as the words escaped his mouth, they sounded lame.

"Yeah, right."

One of the Bathhouse Boys thrust a vial of lube into Seth's hands. Kush barked at the intrusion into his cozy little world. "What am I supposed to do with this?" Seth asked.

"Grease your pole, dude," the twink laughed as he bounded away. "Your girlfriend will love it!"

Seth wondered how true that was. He fought to keep the conversation on track. "Look, I'm no expert in relationships, but it seems to me that people actually *liking* your girlfriend is not a reason to leave her."

She waggled her head.

"So...what's really going on?"

She scowled. "She farts in her sleep."

Seth laughed. "Everyone farts in their sleep."

"How would you know?" she snapped.

Ouch, Seth thought. Was that a dig at his lack of romantic luck? "I've slept with people—like, all night."

"With *people*? Like more than one?"

"No. I mean...with Becky. I've slept with Becky. Once."

"That's what I thought."

"You're avoiding the question," Seth pointed out.

Angie sighed. "Okay...she doesn't really have time for me. And she smokes too much pot."

"Hmm..." Seth said.

"What do you mean, 'hmm,'?"

"Anytime there's more than one reason, none of the reasons is *the reason*," he asserted.

"That's ridiculous," she said.

"It's also true," he said. "I read that somewhere. So...what's the *real* reason? And it can't be the pot, because nobody smokes more pot than you do."

Angie kept her eyes on the parade, where a white convertible that would not have been out of place in a sixties movie rolled by. A John Waters impersonator waved at the crowd, his pencil-thin mustache obviously drawn on. Kush lay down, covering Seth's left foot with his heavy, golden body.

"Sara has this…list…of things she wants for her life. You know: Job? Check. Pet? Check. Hobby? Check—"

"Wait, what's her hobby?" Seth asked.

"She knits," Angie frowned. "Haven't you noticed? Every time she sits down, she has knitting needles in her hands, clacking away. Argh!"

"Huh, I guess. I never thought of that as a hobby."

"Well, what would you call it?"

Seth shrugged. "A nervous habit?"

"Because you're the expert on that. Maybe you should take up knitting," Angie said. "No, please forget I said that. I only need one knitter in my life."

"She has this list?" Seth prompted.

"Yeah. So. Camping trips? Check. Girlfriend? Check."

Her lips were tight, and Seth could tell she was resisting her emotions.

"What's…wrong with that? We all want things."

"What's wrong with that is that I feel like I'm just an item on her list. I feel like I'm filling a role in her head. It's like, 'I need a girlfriend. You'll do.' I don't want to just 'do.' I want someone to want me for me, you know? To really want *me*."

Seth nodded. "I get it, I think. I'm sorry."

"I mean, she's great," Angie said. "We never fight. She's kind. She's smart. She's funny. She's…great with her…tongue—"

"TMI," Seth warned.

"I just…I want someone who really wants *me*." She paused and appeared to be watching the parade, but when she spoke her voice cracked. "Is that so bad?"

Seth stepped behind her and put his hands on her shoulders, giving them a gentle squeeze. "No. No it isn't."

Angie wiped her eyes on her sleeve. "Damned allergies. How about you?"

"What about me?" he asked, blinking.

"How is it going with what's-her-name?"

He narrowed his eyes. "You know very well what her name is. I just said it."

Angie sniffed and attempted a smile. "So, you slept together, but have you...you know..."

He rolled his eyes. "What are you, eleven?"

"You don't talk about her. Do you even like her? I mean, why are you here with me instead of her?"

"She's not queer. I'm here as your ally, remember?"

"I think you're here for the boobies."

"I think you're projecting. And of course I *like* her. I wouldn't go out with her if I didn't like her." For several moments they both just looked at the parade. About forty teenagers in khaki uniforms marched in messy military style behind a banner that read, "Scouting for All."

After the last of the scouts had trailed past, Seth said, "Hey, you're always asking me what I need. What do *you* need right now?"

Angie kept her eyes on the parade route, even though there was a gap between the scouts and the next float. "Uh...I think I need a place to land when I...when I do the deed."

"You want to sleep on my couch?" he asked.

She nodded, daring to look up at him again.

"It's yours," he said. "For as long as you need it."

"Thanks," she said.

"When do you think you'll need it?" he asked.

She shifted from one foot to another. "Tonight?"

"You're going to break up with her *tonight*?" he asked, his eyebrows rising.

She looked at her watch. "We have a sex date when she gets off work. I...I'm going to tell her then. Get it over with."

"Before or after the sex?"

"There isn't going to be any sex, you idiot."

Seth gave her shoulder another squeeze. "It's going to be okay."

"No, it isn't."

"Yes, it is. I promise," he said. "After this Kush and I are going to go home. Then I'm going to clean the apartment. And I'm going to make a place for you. And I'm even going to buy you some cereal and milk."

"Almond milk, please. No cow mucus."

Seth ignored her. "And when you come over, I'm going to make popcorn and sit on the couch and watch any damn thing you want to on TV."

"Really?"

"Really."

"We should pick something psychedelic," Angie said.

"Why?" Seth asked.

"Because that pizza I brought over had mushrooms on it."

"I love mushrooms," Seth said.

"Yeah, but I added more mushrooms, *different* mushrooms, on top."

"You did not," Seth breathed.

She waggled her head back and forth, refusing to meet his eyes.

"Goddam it, Angie. That's the kind of thing you ask people about *before* you do it, not the kind of thing you spring on them. What if I had somewhere important to be today?"

"You never have anywhere important to be," she said.

"No need to rub it in. I *do* work sometimes."

"At a job you would do infinitely better if you were high," she asserted. "Do you work today?"

"No."

"Do you have anything important to do today?" Angie asked.

"No...but that's not the point and you know it."

She shrugged and looked at the parade again. A couple of leathermen on stilts walked by, holding the black-and-blue striped S&M flag between them. Kush began to snore. The crowd was too loud to hear him, but Seth felt the vibrations of the dog's mighty wheeze through the bones of his feet.

"How are you going to have a serious conversation with Sara if you're tripping balls?" Seth asked.

"I think I need to be tripping balls to work up the nerve."

"God, I hate this feeling!" Seth said.

"What feeling?" Angie asked.

"That feeling when you just drop acid—or 'shrooms, or whatever—and you know it's coming and there's no going back, and you don't know what's going to happen."

"I *love* that feeling," Angie confessed.

"That is one of the big differences between us, then," Seth said.

Just then, a string of antique cars started to pass, and Seth noticed that the sunlight reflected off the chrome with an otherworldly and incandescent dazzle. The reflected colors reminded him of the swirl of purples and greens in a pool of automotive oil, but it was shimmering like the heat rising from blacktop in summer. "Oh, shit," he said. "It's coming on. Goddam you, Angie."

"When your limbs turn to rubber, remember to just flow with it," she suggested.

"Fucking..."

And then Seth saw her. He cocked his head. A marching band was heading toward them, coming around the bend in the parade route. All of the musicians looked like they were in their 60s or 70s, with a banner proclaiming them to be the Lavender Bobcats Marching Band. The uniforms were striking—periwinkle with dark blue piping. But that wasn't what Seth was focused on. Leading the band was a majorette, her uniform crisp and smart. She looked like she was in her seventies, but time had been kind to her. Her hair was silver and hung in a bouncy bob around her jawline. Her smile was bright as the sun, and her teeth were perfect. Her white boots kicked from side to side in dramatic, exaggerated movements. She spun her silver baton over her head, catching the sunlight and refracting it to every corner of the earth in a spray of rainbow color.

"She's beautiful," Seth gasped.

"She *is*," Angie agreed.

Seth couldn't keep his eyes off her. He suspected it was because he was high, but that didn't seem to matter. His world had narrowed to a point, and she was the center and the circumference. She moved with such agility and grace and confidence that Seth found himself holding his breath. "I want to be like her," he breathed.

"I want to *be* her," Angie added.

And then, as Seth's mouth gaped, the majorette threw her head back, laughed, and met his eye. She winked.

Seth closed the drawer of cash register two and greeted the next customer. He scanned the UPC code of a paperback Western, thinking, *Don't sell too many of those.* Next to him, Travis was training a new employee on register one.

To Seth's surprise, Travis had turned out to be a patient teacher. Travis was a couple years older than him and represented a breed Seth was in danger of becoming—the bookstore lifer. His cheek piercing just looked stupid, and he wore scarves over his jeans and t-shirt attire, which Seth had to admit gave him a little flash. Seth admired his shoulder-length brown hair as much as he disdained his goatee.

The newbie was a girl named Bella, who looked no older than sixteen, with impeccable goth sensibilities. She wore black lace gloves, black lipstick, and far too much mascara. She seemed to be catching on quick.

Seth stapled a receipt to his customer's bag and handed it to him. "Thanks a lot. Come again."

No one else was in line, so he had a breather. He looked over at Travis and Bella. "How is it going?"

"Piece of cake," Bella said, looking bored.

"Hey, you wanna see something cool?" Travis asked.

"Yeah, sure," Bella said, not sounding at all like she did.

Travis grinned and winked at Seth. "Hey, St. John, where does this book go?" He held up a large paperback copy of *Frankenstein*.

Half of Seth's mouth turned up in a smile. He'd play along. "*Frankenstein: the Modern Prometheus* by Mary Wollstonecraft Shelley. We have the Dover edition in classics—row five, on the left, three shelves down, five books in, between *The Fountainhead* on one side and *Fried Green Tomatoes at the Whistle-Stop Cafe* on the other. But that there's the new annotated edition with commentary by Neal Gaiman, so we keep that in Horror—row thirteen, top shelf, fifteen books in, between Darren Shan's *Demonata* series and Clark Ashton Smith's new Arkham omnibus."

Seth smiled, every part of his mouth participating, when he saw Bella's mouth hanging open. "Fuuuuck," she said. She turned to Travis. "Can he do that with every book in the store?"

Travis chuckled. "Try him. But don't let him fool you. It's a savant thing."

"Shut the fuck up, Travis," Seth said with a laugh.

"Dude, admit it, you're fucked in the head. This is just a side effect of your superpower."

"I am not on the spectrum or anything," Seth objected. "I'm just…"

Just then the phone rang. From the blinking lights, Seth could tell it was an in-store call. Travis picked it up. "Register." He paused and listened. "No, not too busy." His eyebrows rose and he looked at Seth. "Right away." He put the phone back in its cradle.

"Rutherford wants to see you," he said. "She sounds like she's on the warpath."

"Jesus," Seth sighed. He locked his register and pocketed the key. "Okay. I'll be back. I hope."

"And Frith help you," Travis added.

Seth headed for the back. Behind him, he heard Bella ask, "Does he always walk on his toes?"

Seth grimaced but decided not to comment. When he got to the back rooms, Rutherford's office door was already slightly ajar. He paused just before reaching it, leaned against an S-panel, and took a deep breath. He knocked and poked his head in. "You wanted to see me, boss?"

Marian Rutherford looked up from her laptop. She closed it. "Have a seat." Seth did.

She was shorter than Seth, and about ten years older, with a severe black bob that projected a terrifying androgyny. She dressed like a lumberjack, grounded by her Doc Martins and adorned with a collection of silver rings in one ear.

"What's up?"

"Are you feeling okay?"

He shrugged. "Uh…sure. Why?"

She studied him. He squirmed under her gaze. "Come with me," she said, rising from her chair. She strode into the hall, not pausing to see if Seth was following. He jogged to catch up with her, and even though her stride was shorter than his, he still had to practically skip to keep up. She led him to the romance section, and turned.

"What the fuck is this?" She gestured to the wall of books.

"Uh...books?" he ventured.

She narrowed one eye. "Don't be cute with me. What's wrong with this section?"

Then he noticed. The books were arranged by color. The entire wall was a spectrum of powder-pastel colors, pinks bleeding into lavender, bleeding into baby blue. "It's...beautiful," he said finally.

"It's also unnavigable," Marian said. "Who told you to arrange the books by cover-color?"

"I...I don't know. Did I do that?"

"I told you to stock this section and clean it up. Yesterday. You don't remember that?"

"Yeah, but...I was...I guess I was kind of lost in thought."

"So you don't *remember* arranging this entire section by color?"

Seth shook his head. "No. I'm sorry. I'll...I'll fix it."

"You'll fix it on your own time. Go punch out, then get to work on it. When you get it back to where it was, you can punch in again. Does that seem fair?"

He nodded. "Yeah. Really fair. I'm...I'm sorry."

She moved closer to him and lowered her voice. "Seth, do you like it here?"

"Yeah. I do. A lot."

"You don't act like it," she said.

"I'm just..." he looked away. "It's not the job. It's...other stuff."

"Well, that 'other stuff' is affecting your job, and it's not okay. If you don't shape up, you're going to be looking for other work. Do you hear me?"

He nodded. "Yeah. I'm sorry."

"Look, you're a good kid. I like you, and I trust you. But...I think you've got some...issues. Get some help with them, okay?"

"With what money?" Seth asked, but was instantly sorry.

"What was that?" Marian asked, scowling.

"I...most of my paycheck goes for rent. I live on top-ramen. I can't afford health insurance. What kind of help am I supposed to get, and how am I supposed to pay for it?" Seth's voice was shaking, but somehow he gained the courage to hold her gaze. "If I get one bill I don't expect...I'm toast. I...feel like I'm in a well, and I can't find any handholds, and I don't know how to get out. "

"I remember that feeling," she said. "It's called 'being in your 20s.' It'll pass."

Seth didn't know how that was supposed to help. Marian put a hand on his arm. "Look, Seth. I don't have all the answers. I don't have a magic wand. You need some...psychological help. I don't know how you're supposed to pay for it. Some things you just need to figure out on your own. I'm just saying, you need to deal with it, because I can't have this—" She pointed at the bookcase. "I can't have stuff like this happening."

He nodded.

"Now go punch out and get to work."

The cashier at the supermarket was moving as slow as humanly possible. Seth had put his items on the conveyer belt, but it wasn't going anywhere anytime soon. He turned and looked at the rack of candy on the other side. A line about six deep was behind him.

His eyes were drawn to a new flavor of mint. He liked the brand, but hadn't tried this new iteration. One of the packs was askew. He reached out and straightened it. Then his finger wavered above the pack. He had touched it, and something in his brain told him that he must now touch all of them, or the "just right" feeling wouldn't happen. And it was so, so important that it happen, that he not leave the store with the unfinished feeling. He hated that feeling. Swallowing, he tapped at all the packs, one-by-one, focusing all his attention so that he would remember. Auto-pilot was the enemy, because if he zoned out, he knew he'd have to do it all again.

He paused, finger still poised above the box holding the packs of mints. He reached out for the "just right" feeling. It didn't come. He tapped at the packs again, faster this time, a grim look of desperation spreading out over his face. When he'd tapped all the packs again, the packs in the adjacent box began to exert a gravitational pull on his finger. It was as if they were saying, *Me too! We need to be tapped, too!*

He tried to break the spell by stamping his right foot twice outside of the linoleum square he was standing it. He knew it must have looked like an awkward dance move to the people behind him, but he told himself he didn't care. He tried not to look at the mints, but he couldn't stop. The packs pulled at him.

On the verge of hyperventilating, he turned and deliberately tapped all the packs in the adjacent box. He paused and waited for the "just right" feeling. It came. He almost wept with relief.

Then the box on the other side began to exert its influence. His fingers shook as he raised his hand toward it. To his great surprise, the customer behind him stepped up to him, put her hand on his, and lowered it to his side. Grabbing his shoulders, she turned him to face her. They were about the same height, but she was older. She had black hair, about shoulder-length. He thought she was pretty—very pretty, for an older person. When she spoke, her voice was soft but resolute.

"You don't need to do that," she said.

"Yes, I—"

"No, you don't. You don't actually have to touch each pack of mints. There's a voice in your head saying you do, but that voice is a liar." She pointed to the cashier. "You're up. But when you're done, wait for me, please. We should talk."

He blinked and faced the cashier. He barely registered her voice as she told him the total, and hardly noticed paying. A few moments later, the woman behind him clutched her own bag to her breast and stepped up to him. "Come outside," she said.

He felt off guard, so he simply followed her through the automatic doors. It was cloudy outside and looked like it might rain. But this was San Jose, so probably not. It would threaten, but it was not likely to make good on the threat.

The woman sat on a bench, and patted the place beside her. As he sat, she put her grocery bag on the cement at her feet. "You have OCD," she said.

"Yeah."

"Are you seeing anyone about that?" she asked.

"No," he said.

"How is that working out for you?"

He looked at his feet.

"Do you self-medicate?"

"Yes."

"Alcohol?"

"Weed, mostly."

She nodded. "And I'm guessing it helps some, when you're high enough."

"Yeah."

"But you can't always be high."

"No."

"Is it causing problems at work?"

That was too close to home. "How did you know?" he snapped.

She shrugged. "Because it always causes problems at work. It's not like I'm a fortune-teller or anything."

"Oh."

She softened and offered him her hand. "I'm Sherry."

"Seth."

"What do you do, Seth?"

"I work at a bookstore."

She nodded. "I'm a clinical psychiatrist. Do you know what that is?"

"You're a therapist."

"Yes, but I'm also a medical doctor. I treat people with problems like yours, both with therapy and with medication."

He nodded. "You think I need that?"

"Do you?"

He swallowed. "How does it work?"

"Well, if I had a patient with OCD as bad as yours, I'd first try to stabilize him through medication—to get the anxiety level down. He wouldn't have to stop smoking pot, but he wouldn't need to smoke as much or as often. Then we'd start exploring where the anxiety comes from. The OCD is a coping mechanism, a way of asserting order in a world that feels—"

"Chaotic," he finished.

"Yes. I'm guessing you know that feeling well."

"I feel like I'm grasping at threads, just trying to keep everything from unraveling."

She nodded. "I can help you do that."

"I don't have health insurance," he said. "And I can barely make my rent. There's no way..."

They sat in silence together, looking at the darkening clouds. "You know," Sherry said, "when I first started my practice, I committed myself to always having one pro-bono client. My latest pro-bono client just ended our work together."

"Did he not...didn't it work?"

She smiled, a little sadly. "*She*...moved away."

"Oh."

Sherry tore a bit of her bag away and pulled a pen from her

slacks. She wrote an address on it and handed it to Seth. "This is my office. Do you work tomorrow?"

"No."

"See me at 3pm?"

She waited. He looked at the brown paper scrap. Then he looked at her. "For real?"

She smiled more broadly this time, and touched his arm gently. "For real."

"Okay," he said. "I'll be there."

"The world isn't ending," Seth said out loud, but he didn't believe it. Visions of fire flooded his brain—of his apartment catching fire, of Kush howling as he was consumed in flame, of the entire building collapsing into smoking rubble. Seth started to sweat and felt his heartbeat racing. He clutched the edge of the kitchen counter as a wave of vertigo threatened to topple him. His knuckles were white with effort when he regained his balance.

Kush whined from his place on the couch. He knew the pattern. He knew Seth was about to leave, and he didn't like it one bit. Seth stepped away from the stove and turned in quick circles —one, two, three. Then he stamped his foot outside the circle to break the spell. He closed his eyes and willed himself to relax.

"Okay, start again," he said out loud. "Just check the damn stove, and then walk away."

He opened his eyes and looked at the first knob—it was pointing straight upward. "Check," he said out loud. He went on to the second knob. "Check." The third. "Check." Then another thought crossed his mind—he was late, and Becky would be wondering where he was. He got to the fourth knob and stopped. He'd fucked it up. He'd gotten distracted and would have to start all over again. He took several deep breaths, then looked at the first knob again. "Check." The second knob. "Check." The third knob. "Check." The fourth knob. "Check."

Slowly he backed away from the stove. He pulled out his cell phone and snapped a picture of the knobs so he could check later. There were thousands and thousands of pictures on his phone— most of them of his stove.

He breathed a great sigh of relief and turned toward the door. Then the doorbell rang. Kush leaped from the couch and began to bark. "Shit!" Seth shouted out loud. The sequence had been interrupted. He would need to start all over again. "Shit! Shit! Shit! Shit!"

He flung open the door. "What???!!!"

It was Becky. Her blonde hair looked slightly damp and she was wearing a potato sack dress that made her look heavier than she actually was. Her green eyes were wide, and she looked stricken. Kush rushed out to greet her, tail flapping madly.

Seth's shoulders deflated. "Beck, I'm...I'm sorry. I didn't know it was you. I was...I've been trying to get out of the house for a half hour."

"You're late," she said, reaching down to pat the dog.

"Yeah."

"We missed the start of the movie," she said.

Seth looked at the clock on the wall. That wasn't exactly true —it was five 'til four, but by the time they got to the theater, it would be true. "I'm sorry," he said again.

She put a hand on his arm and squeezed it. "Are you having a bad OCD day?"

"I wasn't...until I tried to leave," he confessed. "I think it's getting worse."

She pushed past him into the apartment, and he closed the door behind her. "Do you still want to do something?" she asked.

"Yeah, yeah. Let's..."

"We could stay here and get...intimate," Becky said, rubbing her index finger against his forearm.

Seth's eyes widened, looking for all the world like someone who just realized he was standing on stage buck naked. "Uh...why don't we go out?"

Becky sighed. "Okay, well...why don't we go pick up some stuff for a picnic and take a walk in the park? We can bring Kush. That always helps you."

"Which park?" Seth asked.

"I don't know. How about Happy Hollow?"

Seth nodded. "Okay." He looked back at the stove. "Uh...I've got to...you know..."

"I tell you what," Becky said. "Grab your jacket and Kush's leash and you two go stand out there in the hall. I'll check the stove and then join you. Then you can lock up and we can go."

"Okay, but first you have to check all the lights, too—in the whole house."

"Didn't you do that already?"

"Yeah, but...I might have fallen into a fugue state."

"A fugue state," Becky said, as if the notion was ridiculous.

"You never know," Seth shrugged. Then he shrank. "I'm fucking nuts, aren't I?"

"I think you have an illness," Becky said, her eyes softening. "But that doesn't mean you aren't a good person. I mean, Kush obviously loves you. He's a pretty good judge of character."

Seth flashed her an attempt at a smile, only partially successful. "Uh...and when you're done with the lights, you have to do all the candles." He grabbed Kush's leash from its hook near the refrigerator. The dog began to dance in excited circles.

"What does that mean, 'do the candles,'?" she asked.

"It means, check to make sure they're out."

"Oh. Okay."

"All of them," he said.

"How many are there?" she asked, looking around.

Seth knelt and tried to fix the leash to Kush's collar. The dog wasn't making it any easier by prancing about. "One in the bedroom, two in the bathroom, two in the living room, and one in the kitchen."

"Oh. Okay."

"And you can't just look at them, you have to touch the wicks with your finger."

"Why?"

"To make sure they're out."

"But...if they weren't out, they'd give off light. If they're not giving off light, they're out."

"But it's daytime, and you might not see the flame."

"Just to clarify, you've already done this, before I got here, right?"

"Four times," he said. "It has to be an even number." He stood up and took a deep breath. It helped a little.

"Oh, Jesus," Becky said. "Does that mean I need to do it twice? To get an even number?"

"No, no! Prime numbers are okay. So if you do it nine times, *then* you'll need to do it again."

"Oh, honey," she reached up and stroked his cheek. "Okay, out into the hall you go, both of you."

He nodded and opened the door. Kush raced out, rearing up in his excitement once he was in the hall. Becky waggled her fingers at him and closed the door. Seth wondered why she had closed it, but then realized it was probably because she didn't want him to watch her work. Kush sat and looked up at him with excited expectation. Seth began to bite a fingernail. He finished trimming it, and then bit off part of his hyponychium—the skin just to the side of the nail, at its very end. Then he bit off the other side, just to even them out. Then he chewed them slowly, feeling a momentary relief from his anxiety. Then he spat them onto his finger and wiped them on his jeans. It wouldn't do to swallow them, as that would be auto-cannibalism. That would be bad.

The door swung open again, and Becky appeared, causing Kush to leap about all over again. She closed the door behind her with a firm tug. "Okay," she said, "lock it up and let's go."

Seth handed her the leash, fitted the key in the door, and locked it. Then he locked the deadbolt. Then he rattled the door-knob, checking to make sure it was locked. He rattled it once, twice, three times, four times. But he'd had a stray thought, so he had to do it again. His left foot shot out to touch a place on the patterned floor that would reset the sequence, and he rattled the door again. Once, twice, three times, four times—

The neighbor's door flew open and Mrs. Tye's red, bloated, angry face appeared. "For fuck's sake, Seth, knock it off!"

Seth nodded and stared at the knob helplessly. He felt frozen.

"Jesus Christ," Mrs. Tye said, going back inside her own apartment and slamming the door.

"I'll check it," Becky said.

"Yes, but you gotta—"

"Do you trust me, Seth?"

"Uh...yes?"

"So trust me. I do this all the time, you know, every time I leave the house. Nothing bad has ever happened."

"Okay."

She tested the doorknob and nodded. "Locked. All good. Shall we go?"

"Okay."

She reached up and touched his cheek. "Seth, I like you. You know that, right?"

"I...I guess."

"You need to get some help."

They started to walk down the hall, toward the stairs. Kush pulled on the leash, wanting them to go faster.

"I met a therapist today," Seth said. "She said she could help me. And she'd see me for free."

Becky stopped and faced him again. "Are you going to do it?"

"I wasn't planning on it."

"Promise me you'll go." Becky's eyes searched his own. He wanted to ignore her sincerity, her pleading, but found he could not.

"I promise," he said.

───────

Seth looked up from his coffee to see Angie stumble into the kitchen, her eyes squinting to fend off the morning glare. "You slept in my bed," he said.

"Hunh?" Angie bleared.

"Becky and I went for a picnic, and then we went for dinner, and then we...went back to her place for a while—"

"Did you get any?" Angie yawned.

Seth ignored her. "And then when I got home, you were asleep in my bed. And *then*, when I woke up, you were sleeping with my dog."

"That's not my fault. The guy has a will of his own—don't you?" She reached down and ruffled Kush's golden ears.

"Coffee's made," Seth informed her.

She grunted, grabbed a mug, and slammed the cupboard door. "Sorry," she mumbled. She poured a cup from the coffeemaker's carafe and stumbled over to the table. Seth pushed a chair out with his foot.

"Sit, before you fall," he said.

"Bleh," she said. "Mornings. I hate mornings almost as much as I hate Republicans."

"Fifteen of these and you'll be right as rain." He held his cup up again.

"Fix me up with an IV. Drinking is too much work."

"You slept in my bed," he repeated. "*Why* did you sleep in my bed?"

Kush curled up under the table and tucked his nose under his tail.

"The couch hurt my back," she said.

"Aren't you the delicate little flower?" he said.

"Fuck you and the duck you rode in on."

"See? You're waking up."

"I changed your sheets."

"And then you slept on them."

"They smelled like yak sweat."

"How would you know how yak sweat smells?"

"It smells exactly like your sheets." She blew on her coffee and took a tentative sip. Her eyebrows lifted. "That's not bad. So there *is* something you're good at."

"Fuck you and the capybara you rode in on," he said.

"Capybara. Good one." She sniffed. "I feel like the epidemic caught up to me."

"Yeah, well, you look like death."

"It's good when your inner and outer realities are congruent that way, I guess."

"You slept in my bed."

"I left your pillow and some blankets out on the couch."

"Very kind." He narrowed one eye at her. For several moments they sat in silence, each sipping from their mugs. "So...did you sleep okay?"

She shrugged, avoiding his eyes.

"How did it go with Sara?" he asked.

She rocked back and forth a bit. Finally, she said, "It was horrible."

"What happened?"

"Well, first of all, when I got home, she was really busy on

some design project, and was annoyed that I wanted her attention. So...it didn't start out great. But when I finally got her to
sit down and talk to me, she crossed her arms and got really
quiet. I told her how I felt, and I could tell she was getting
angry."

"She has a temper," Seth noted.

Angie nodded, a faraway look in her eye. "Then she started
screaming at me. Then she started throwing pans."

"Throwing *pans*?" Seth asked. "As in pots-and-pans?"

Angie brushed her hair up and away from her forehead to
reveal an angry goose-egg.

"Oh. Ouch," Seth said, grimacing.

"Uh. Yeah. I just left. I just...raced for the door and left. No
packing, no clothes, no keepsakes, just my car keys and the
clothes I was wearing."

"Thus the fact that you're wearing my t-shirt."

"Yeah. Sorry."

"No worries." He took another sip. "I'm sorry, Ange." She
nodded, and her face contorted and he could tell she was struggling. "Cry," he said. "It's okay." She looked at her coffee and
nodded. A tear slid down her nose. "When I told my parents I
couldn't be part of their abusive religion anymore, they told me to
get out of their house. And where did I go?"

She sniffed. "To my apartment."

"For, like, six months. You make yourself at home here," he
said. "We're family. I got you."

She buried her head in her hands and her shoulders shook. He
rose and, leaning over, put his arms around her, resting his cheek
on the top of her head. Kush rose and wound his way around
Seth's feet, whining. When Becky stopped sobbing, Seth kissed
the top of her head and left the room, with Kush trailing after. A
moment later they returned, and Seth held up a toilet paper roll.
He set it down on the table in front of her and resumed his seat.

She tore off a wad and blew her nose. Kush lay down again, this time where he could see them both.

"Thanks," Angie said.

Seth cleared his throat. "I do want to point out that when I crashed at your place, I slept on the couch."

She tried not to laugh, and it came out as something in between a chuckle and a sob. "So how was your date with Miss Chubby?"

"Stop that. She's not chubby."

"Tomato, Tom-ah-to."

Seth gave up. "Uh...it was okay." He considered telling her about his panic attack, but decided he didn't really want to hear her opinions on the subject. "It...got off to a rough start. But once we were out and about, it was nice."

"Nice?"

He shrugged. "Yeah. Nice."

"Have you ever heard the phrase, 'damning with faint praise'?"

He frowned. "It...sounds familiar."

"Not 'it was fantastic,' or even, 'We had *such* a good time.' Just '*nice*'?"

"What's your point?" Seth asked.

Angie waved the question away. "If you don't know, I'm not going to drag it out."

"Why are you being such a bitch?" Seth asked.

"Because I have not yet finished my first cup of coffee." Angie took a sip. "What time do you have to be at work?"

"Nine-for-ten," Seth answered.

"What does that mean?"

"It means nine o'clock for a ten o'clock opening."

"Is that bookstore-speak?" Angie asked.

"Yeah. You?"

"Uh...ten-for-ten," she said. "That's cannabis dispensary-speak."

"Thanks for the translation."

"How is it going there?" Seth asked.

"I love it," Angie said. "It's the one thing in my life right now that isn't absolutely crap. And the free samples are a bonus."

"Bring some of those home, will you?"

"Have I ever bogarted my stash?"

He smiled. "Never."

She fist-bumped him. "Do you know what I wish?"

"What?" he asked.

"I wish we could both quit our jobs, move to Humbolt County, and grow weed...you know, like professionally."

"You can't keep a houseplant alive," Seth pointed out.

"Touché," she said, then lowered her voice. "Asshole."

"What?"

"You just shit all over my dream," she said.

"I wouldn't if your dream didn't integrally involve something you suck at."

"I know weed," she said.

"You don't know a pistil from a stamen."

"If you think dirty-plant-talk is going to make me hot, you're sadly mistaken."

He laughed.

"What about you, then, smart guy?" she asked. "What's your dream?"

Seth's smile faded. He looked out the window. "I...I'd sure like to not be scared all the time."

LIQUIPEDIA
THE ANSWERBOT THAT GOES DOWN SMOOTH

WHAT IS THE CODEX PANDEMIC?

The Codex Pandemic, also known as the Indonesian flu, is an ongoing medical emergency caused by coronavirus disease 2033 (CODEX-33). This virus was first documented near the city of Jayapura, Indonesia, at the tourist resort Perdamaian. Patient zero is widely considered to be Otto Skeil, a German national on vacation. CODEX-33 turned out to be significantly more transmissible than previous coronaviruses. Although Perdamaian was immediately quarantined by the World Health Organization, the virus quickly spread throughout the world. Within one year, more than a billion people had died from the disease, making it the deadliest viral disease in human history. The virus has evaded containment for thirty years, and remains a significant threat.

CODEX-33 symptoms range from mild cold-like effects to fatal respiratory failure. Most common symptoms include fever, fatigue, and respiratory conditions similar to pneumonia. Most deaths result from pulmonary edema. Transmission usually occurs through airborne droplets passed from one infected individual to another.

CODEX-33 vaccines were developed within a year of the outbreak, but the virus proved to be unusually mutagenic, and updates invariably came too late to contain new outbreaks.

Retroviral drugs such as ANTICODE can ease symptoms and reduce mortality. Early public health measures included enforced masking, lockdowns, contact tracing, and travel restrictions. Later measures included the cessation of all international travel, and many countries closed their borders.

CHAPTER TWO

This ignorance of the father
brought about terror and fear.
And terror became dense like a fog,
so no one was able to see.
Because of this, error became strong...
for they were as nothing,
this terror and this forgetfulness
and this figure of falsehood,
whereas established truth is unchanging,
unperturbed, and completely beautiful.
For this reason, do not take error too seriously.
—*Gospel of Truth**

* The Gospel of Truth: Nag Hammadi Codex I, translated by Robert M. Grant, published in *Gnosticism* (NY: Harper & Brothers, 1961).

"You're late." Dr. Sherry Teasdale stood in her office doorway. She didn't look angry. She looked concerned.

"It was...hard to get out of the house," Seth confessed. He wasn't *that* late. He stood and put aside the magazine he had been thumbing through.

"Let me guess—the stove?"

His eyes widened. "How did you know?"

"Lucky guess," she said. "Come in."

"Uh...okay." He headed for the door. She held it wide for him and shut it after him.

"Don't be nervous. Have you never done therapy before?"

"Sure, when I lived with my parents. But...it never worked."

"How hard did you work it?" she asked. When he didn't answer, she waved toward a sage-colored loveseat. "Please sit down. Can I get you a cup of tea?"

"Oh. Uh...sure."

"With caffeine or without?" she asked.

"Either is fine," he said.

A few moments later, she placed a cup on a coaster near him. It rested on a small teak coffee table. Picking up the cup, he blew on it and looked around. The room was bright and cheery. It was professional, but not clinical. Colorful, tasteful art adorned the walls. The faint scent of lavender hung in the air. Low bookshelves sported titles on psychotherapy and medical issues. He felt an urge to look at them, then a further urge to arrange them alphabetically.

"You like books?" Dr. Teasdale asked.

"Oh. Yeah. I work at a bookstore. I love them."

"What are your favorite books?"

"I like fantasy. And history. And science. And science fiction."

She nodded and picked up a yellow legal pad. She clicked a pen and made a note on it. Then she looked up again.

"But it sounds like your favorite is fantasy."

"Yeah, I guess so. It's what I look at first."

"What do you like about fantasy?"

"I guess I like the idea that there's more to the world than it seems. I...I guess I want to believe that there's magic in the world. And I like the good-versus-evil thing. In a lot of literature these days, it's hard to tell who the good guys are. That's almost never the case with fantasy."

Dr. Teasdale made some more notes. "Does that...moral clarity...make you feel safe?"

Seth cocked his head. "I never thought about it like that. I guess it does. Huh."

"Fantasy has to be doing something for you, or it wouldn't excite your imagination."

Seth nodded. It made sense.

"Your world doesn't feel very safe, does it, Seth?"

He swallowed. "No."

"Why is that? Do you know?"

"No."

"OCD is what we call a maladaptive protective mechanism. Do you know what I mean by that?"

"I think so," Seth said. "It means it's something I do to protect myself, but it doesn't really work very well."

Dr. Teasdale laughed. "That's a pretty good description. I would say that it actually *does* work pretty well, but it has side effects that are very difficult to live with."

"Okay, that's fair," Seth admitted.

"When did your OCD symptoms first start to appear?" she asked.

"A couple years ago."

"Did something traumatic happen that triggered it?"

"No, I just...it just got harder and harder to check the stove."

Dr. Teasdale scribbled on her pad. She looked up again. "So it was gradual?"

"Yeah."

She nodded. "That's normal."

"It is?"

"Yes. Think of it this way—have you ever skied?"

"No..."

"But you've seen it?"

"Sure."

"So when you ski through a valley, your skis make a groove. When you go through it again, your skis could make new grooves, but it will be easier for them to slide into the grooves that were there before. You do that enough times and it will be almost impossible to make a new groove—your skis will always fall into the same groove."

"Okay, I get that."

"Your thoughts are the same way. If you think a certain way, it's easier to think that way the next time. And soon, it's hard to think any other way. We create...grooves...in our brains." She smiled and waited.

Seth nodded slowly, his brow furrowing. "Is there any way to make it stop?"

"Yes. Yes, there is. But it won't be easy." Seth looked up at her, his forehead clouded with worry. Before he could say anything, she continued. "But living with the OCD isn't easy either, is it?"

"No."

"No. This will feel scary, but it will help. I promise you."

"Okay."

"And I'll be with you every step of the way."

"Okay."

"You need to really work this. If you want to get better, if you want to stop suffering, you have to really put in the effort."

Seth nodded again. "So what do I have to do?"

Dr. Teasdale smiled a confident smile. "We're going to try a three-pronged approach. First, I'm going to give you a prescription." She took out a pad and wrote on it. She tore it off and handed it to him. It was completely illegible. "This is for 100 milligrams of sertraline—also known as Zoloft. It's an SSRI—a selective serotonin reuptake inhibitor. Don't worry, it's not expensive. I ordered you the generic—sertraline. It will be about the cost of a tube of toothpaste. It's going to make sure more serotonin is available to your brain, and that will make you calmer—a lot calmer. It will make you feel a little bit weird at first, but you'll adjust and then you won't feel it at all—you just won't be nearly as anxious. We'll adjust the dosage as we go along until we hit the sweet spot. But you have to take it every day, and you can't skip any days. Can you do that?"

Seth pocketed the prescription. "Sure. Yeah, I can do that."

"The second prong will be talk therapy. We're going to explore your past, we're going to find out why your body decided it needed to protect you in this way. This will take time...and work. But it will help, because once you see the causes clearly, they won't have as much power over you. They'll be revealed for what they really are, and you'll be able to break away from their influence." She leaned in and lowered her voice, almost to a whisper. "Do you want to know a secret?"

"Sure."

"What is going to help more than anything else is knowledge —knowledge of what hurt you, of the reality of your past situation and your present situation. *Knowledge* will be your salvation. But no one can just give you that knowledge. You must seek it for yourself."

"Like a quest?" Seth asked. "In a fantasy novel?"

Dr. Teasdale smiled. "Very much like a quest. Think of me as your Gandalf, your guide in these strange new lands. We are going to find the treasure."

"What's the treasure?" Seth asked.

Dr. Teasdale looked concerned. "We were just talking about knowledge, remember? Knowledge is the treasure."

"Got it."

"The reason you are suffering is your brain thinks it is in a different situation than it actually is. But when you learn the truth, you will gain mastery over it."

"Like finding a magic sword," Seth asked.

"Exactly like that," Dr. Teasdale said. "How does that sound?"

"Exciting. And scary."

Dr. Teasdale closed her eyes and shook her head slowly. "It's going to be fine. This," she gestured around the room. "This is your safe space. Nothing can hurt you here. Not the past. Not anyone living. Not anyone dead."

"You sound so sure of that," he said.

"I am."

"What's the third prong?" he asked, shifting in his seat.

"Cognitive Behavioral Therapy," she said. "We need to make your thoughts jump out of those grooves you've made. We'll do this a little bit at a time. Tell me about how your OCD manifests itself—besides touching candy and checking the stove."

Seth described trying to leave the house the night before with Becky. Dr. Teasdale wrote on her legal pad the entire time. When he finished, she looked up at him and said, "Okay, here's your homework assignment. No one else can do your checking for you anymore. Only you. Okay?"

"Oh. Okay. Is that it?"

"No. We're going to work on candles first. You can check all the candles, but only once. And you can only look at them—no touching the wicks. Promise?"

"I don't know if I can do that."

"But that's why you're here. I told you it wasn't going to be easy. This is the first step to getting your skis out of the old groove. The sertraline will help with this, but it will be a couple of weeks before it really kicks in. In the meantime, we're going to jump-start the process this way. Okay?"

Seth didn't look too sure.

Dr. Teasdale softened. "Listen, Seth, the voices in your head that are telling you that your house is going to burn down, or that sudden doom is coming upon you...those voices are not telling you the truth. You can't trust them. You need to stop believing them. You need to choose...a different reality. Can you do that?"

"I don't know."

"Well. Why don't you give it a try, and let's see?"

"I don't know how I let you talk me into these things," Angie said.

Seth counted the blocks as the bus neared an all-too-familiar stop. "Thanks for coming with me."

"Your mom *hates* me."

Seth nodded. "Yeah. She does."

"It's mutual, you know."

Seth smiled. "I'm hoping that if she's targeting you, she might not score so many hits on me."

"I figured as much."

The bus groaned to a stop and with the tiny, explosive sounds of jetting air, the doors opened. Seth stepped down and turned to wait for Angie. She followed and for several minutes they strolled along the sidewalk in silence. When his childhood home came into view, Seth stopped.

"What? What's wrong?" Angie asked.

Seth swallowed. "I don't want to go."

"It's just your mom. How bad can it be? Somewhere, under all that glowering fundamentalism, she still loves you."

Seth dug his hands deeper into his pockets and said, "It's like there's this storm cloud perpetually hanging over that house. I feel like the front door is a portal to another world, a world ruled over by a dark, angry god who hates my guts. When I step through that doorway, I step into his domain. I feel like there are evil angels circling above me all the time, just waiting to pounce on me and devour my soul."

Angie put a hand on his arm. "Dude, that's intense."

Seth smiled sadly. "It is what it is."

"We don't have to go," Angie said.

Seth didn't answer. He just stared at the house.

"We can go right back to the bus stop," Angie continued. "We can go to the mall, get dinner at Dave & Buster's, play some video games. I'll even pay."

"That sounds...infinitely better."

"So let's go."

Seth didn't move. "No. Mom's expecting us...me."

"Your mother doesn't know I'm coming?"

Seth winced. "She will soon."

"Oy." She tugged on his sleeve. "Let's get this over with, you fucking masochist."

Seth took a tottering step toward the house, then another. "I wish my dad wasn't dead."

"Was he not as bad as your mom?"

"No, he was great. I mean, he was still a fundamentalist, but... he didn't hit you over the head with it every time you saw him, you know? He let me know he loved me, no matter how bad I was screwing up."

"Well, then I'm sorry he's gone, too."

Then they were at the porch. Seth sighed and mounted the two steps. He paused by the aqua-colored door. Then he knocked. He waited and heard rustling within. A few seconds later, the door snatched open.

"Seth, you're late. You said you'd be here—"

"Hi, Mrs. St. John," Angie interrupted.

Mrs. St. John glared at Angie. "Oh. You." She looked back at her son. "You didn't tell me *she* was coming. Is that mangy mutt with you, too?"

"No, just this mangy mutt," Angie said. "I'm here for moral support. He hired me through rent-a-witch."

Mrs. St. John ignored that. Instead, she frowned. "This means I'll have to cook something else, because I didn't make enough for three."

"I'm not very hungry," Angie said.

"Neither am I," Seth added.

"Oh, great," Mrs. St. John moaned. "I invite you to dinner and you—what? Spoiled your appetite on the way over here?"

"No, I just—" Seth stopped. What could he say? *No, my stomach is tied up in knots because I'm entering the Dark Domain?* "What's for dinner?"

"Meat loaf, with green beans and cornbread." Mrs. St. John actually smiled.

"*Canned* green beans?" Angie asked.

Mrs. St. John narrowed her eyes at her. "What other kind is there?" she asked. "But now I'll need to open a can of pork-n-beans. That's all right." She pushed the screen door open. "Come in, then." There seemed to be an unspoken, *if you must,* at the end of her sentence.

"Nothing like a warm welcome," Angie whispered to Seth just before he stepped into the house.

In his mind's eye, he saw the angel of death hovering an inch below the ceiling. It fixed itself above the crown of his head, and stayed with him, moving when he moved, so as to stay out of his peripheral vision. He looked up at the ceiling, and saw only the dingy once-white popcorn treatment that clutched onto every speck of dust just to mock you with it. But it didn't fool him. As soon as he looked away, he sensed the dark angel again.

Entering the kitchen, he saw several drops of wetness on the floor. One part of his mind reasoned that his mother had splashed some water when rinsing a dish. But another part of his mind knew its true origin—it had dripped from the salivating fangs of Jehovah.

His mother was a slight woman, shorter than Seth, with thin, birdlike bones that threatened to collapse in on themselves. Her hair was auburn, but streaked with gray. She wore it on the short side nowadays, which was a change from the big-hair pileups she favored in his childhood. Her face was pinched into a perpetual grimace, as if she inwardly held the entire world at arm's length like a rotten fish.

"What have you been eating? You look terrible," she said.

"Top ramen, mostly."

"Chinese food isn't good for anyone. Just look at Chinese people."

"I think ramen is Japanese."

"Don't sass me, young man."

Seth sighed. "Can I help with dinner?"

"You never lifted a finger to help me the whole time you were growing up, why should you start now?"

"Just trying to be nice," Seth said, looking at his feet.

Mrs. St. John went to the cupboard, grabbed a can of pork-n-beans, and slammed it down onto the counter much harder than she needed to. She yanked open a drawer and pulled out a can opener. Focused on her work, she opened the can, then grabbed a bowl from the cupboard. She emptied the can into it and slid it into the microwave.

Seth looked at Angie, who shook her head. Seth motioned to a seat at the table, and she sat.

Mrs. St. John looked up at Angie while she waited for the microwave. "And what have you been up to?"

"Oh, casting spells with my witch friends and trying to get

laid."

Seth felt his stomach fall so far and fast that it bruised his testicles. Mrs. St. John's lips puckered as if she had been sucking on alum. She whirled toward Seth. "You're not sleeping with her, are you?"

"With him?" Angie laughed. "Puh-leeeze. I don't fuck anything with a penis."

"You will watch your mouth in this house, young lady." Mrs. St. John pointed at her with a tablespoon. "As for me and my house, we will serve the Lord."

"Yez'm," Angie said, a wicked grin spreading across her face.

"Angie, don't provoke her, please," Seth asked.

"All right. I promise to be good so Jesus will love me."

"God will not be mocked," Mrs. St. John proclaimed, just as the microwave dinged.

"And yet, he is," Angie said.

"Angie, *please*," Seth begged.

Without another word, Mrs. St. John began to set the table. She put out the plates, napkins, and forks. Then she placed the meatloaf on a hot pad and put a bowl of canned green beans next to it. She took a half-eaten pan of cornbread from the refrigerator and set it on the table with the plastic wrap still clinging to it. Then she set the bowl of pork-n-beans down with a flourish. "Have a seat, Seth," she ordered, as Angie was already sitting.

Seth did. The meatloaf looked delicious, but the sour, musty smell of the canned green beans made his stomach turn.

"Seth, would you thank the Father for our meal?"

Seth froze. He felt the dark angel roiling just above him, just out of sight. He might have even heard him laugh. He looked at his plate and said, "I'd...rather not."

"What is your problem?" his mother asked.

"Maybe he doesn't believe in God," Angie said.

"Don't talk nonsense," Mrs. St. John snapped. "Seth, why

don't you want to offer our grace?"

"I just...don't."

Mrs. St. John rolled her eyes and sighed. "Bow your heads, then. I'll do it. Heavenly Father, we give you thanks for this meal. Bless it to the nourishment of our bodies, in the name of Jesus. Amen."

Seth realized that every muscle in his body was tense. He willed himself to relax. He shuddered.

"What was that? Are you cold?" his mother asked.

"No. I just...it was nothing."

"I can get you one of your dad's old sweaters."

"No, that's all right."

Mrs. St. John stood and reached for Seth's plate. She cut the meat loaf and put it on his plate. Then she picked up her knife and cut it into one-inch squares. Then she handed it back to him. He closed his eyes and tried to soothe himself. She reached for Angie's plate then, and dropped a slab of meatloaf onto it, then handed it back. Then she served herself. "It's your birthday next week, Seth. Would you like to have a special dinner?"

Seth looked at Angie. Angie gave him a look that said, *I'd sooner die.* "I, uh...I have plans already," he managed.

"Oh." Seth could hear the disappointment in his mother's voice. "Well, you're young and selfish. It's the way of the world."

Angie rolled her eyes and kicked Seth under the table. It was as if she was trying to break his mother's spell, to interrupt the negativity signal. He felt reassured by it. He kicked her back.

"Ouch," Angie said.

"What? What did I say?" Mrs. St. John asked her.

Angie gave her a look that Seth interpreted as, *You know very well what you said, you odiferous hedge-weasel.* Seth kicked her again. "Ouch," Angie said again. She looked at Mrs. St. John. "Mom, Seth's kicking me."

Mrs. St. John looked confused. For a long moment no one said anything. Then Mrs. St. John passed the green beans to Angie, and asked, "Seth, I haven't seen you at church in a long while. I assume you are going to a different church, then. Where are you in fellowship now?"

"I'm...not going to church right now."

His mother stopped and glared at him. "'Forsake not the assembly of yourselves together.' I'm very disappointed in you."

"I know."

"Why...*why* aren't you going to church?"

A part of him wanted to say, *I'm in recovery from church,* but he knew she wouldn't understand that. Other possible answers flooded his brain: *Because the God you worship is a demon. Because if I hear about hell one more time, I'm going to completely lose my shit. Because I think most of what your church teaches is outright nonsense, and dangerous, and destructive, and...so very, very hurtful.* But he didn't say any of those. Instead, he said, "I'm trying to figure out what I believe right now."

"'Train up a child in the way he should go: and when he is old, he will not depart from it,'" Mrs. St. John quoted.* "We raised you right, in a loving, God-fearing home. You know what's right. You just have a rebellious spirit." She pointed with her fork at Angie. "And *she* doesn't help you."

Angie opened her mouth, but Seth put his hand on her arm. She growled, but Seth didn't know if it was loud enough for his mother to hear.

"You know the difference between God's perfect will and his permissive will. God will only give you so much leash in his permissive will." Mrs. St. John narrowed one eye at Seth. "But one day he will reach the end of his patience, and then if you have not repented and returned to him, he will take your life."

"Jesus!" Angie protested.

---

* Proverbs 22:6, KJV.

"Language!" Mrs. St. John snapped at her, her fury no longer bridled. She turned back to her son. "This is not news to you, Seth. You know what the Bible says. There was a time when you submitted your stubbornness and pride to it."

"Mom, I don't want to fight. I just want to spend some time with you."

"'But if the watchman sees the sword coming and does not blow the trumpet, and the people are not warned, and the sword comes and takes *any* person from among them, he is taken away in his iniquity; but his blood I will require at the watchman's hand.'"

"What the fuck does that even mean?" Angie asked, throwing her utensils onto her plate.

"Young lady, if you cannot bridle that mouth of yours, I'm going to need to ask you to leave."

"You don't have to ask me twice," Angie said, getting up.

Seth looked at his plate. He swallowed. Then he pushed his chair back and stood.

"Where are you going?" his mother asked.

"Anywhere...that isn't here," he said. Angie reached for his hand, squeezed it, and led him to the door.

Special Agent Keira Sloane tapped on her water glass with her fingernail in a rhythmic pattern.

"Well, what do you say?" Gabe asked.

She continued to tap, staring at nothing.

Gabe passed a hand in front of her eyes. "Keira. *Keira*, have you heard a single thing I've been saying to you?"

"Huh? Oh, sorry." She waved him away. "I'm...work stuff."

He leaned back in his chair, his face melting into a mask of disappointment. For a moment, she wondered if he was about to cry. Instead, he looked at the napkin in his lap, then at the candle on the table. "Excuse me," he said. Rising from his chair, he picked his way around the crowded restaurant until he caught up with their waiter. She frowned as she watched him gesticulating. The waiter nodded, then turned his attention back to another table. Then, moving much slower, Gabe made his way back to her.

He sank into his seat with a sigh. He did not look at her.

"What was that all about?" Keira asked.

Gabe shook his head, his eyes on the tablecloth.

"Don't do this, Gabe. Don't pout. It pisses me off."

He looked at her then, and there was a hardness in his eyes that was unusual for him. "You know what pisses *me* off?" he asked. She opened her mouth, but before she could answer, he pressed ahead. "What pisses me off is that I let myself believe, however briefly, that there was something more important to you than your job."

"Gabe, I *am* my job."

"No, you're not. You're so much more than that. You're a daughter—"

"My parents are dead."

"—you're a sister—"

"I haven't seen my brothers in ten years."

"—you're a friend—"

"Name one!"

"—you're a lover." He met her eyes and swallowed. She could tell that he was allowing himself to hope again.

She sighed. *Time to nip it in the bud*, she thought. "Gabe, when was the last time we had sex?"

He took a deep breath. "April 29th."

"Four months ago."

He nodded slowly.

"Doesn't that tell you something?"

"It tells me that you work way, way too hard."

She opened her mouth again, but once more he beat her to it. "It tells me that you have no work-life balance. It tells me that I'm just not that important to you...that *we're* not that important to you."

Looking down at his hands, he bobbed his head up and down a few times, as if gathering momentum for something. Then he stood. He threw his napkin on the empty plate. He stepped around the table and leaned down, planting a soft kiss on her cheek. "Seeya, special agent." Then he turned and headed for the door.

"Gabe!" she called after him, but not loudly enough to be heard over the din of the crowded restaurant.

She stared after him for what might have been minutes or hours. Then she detected a presence at her elbow. "Madame, is everything all right?"

"Everything is shit," she said.

"Oh, I am sorry, madame."

He turned to go, but she caught his elbow. "What did he...my friend...say to you?"

The waiter looked surprised. "Did he not say? He cancelled his order for champagne—a Krug Grande Cuvée."

Keira's eyes moved quickly back and forth. "Is that expensive?"

The waiter shrugged. "There are more expensive champagnes, madame, but it is highly respected. It is about $200 for the bottle."

Keira made a face. "Why?"

The waiter turned his head and looked at her sideways. "Does madame really not know?"

"Know what?"

THE WHERE, THE WHO & THE WHAT · 55

"Apparently monsieur was going to ask you a very important question tonight. I assume it did not go well?"

"No..." Keira's voice trailed off.

"Oh, I am sorry, madame. Please allow me to bring you a dessert as a small consolation."

Keira blinked. "No. No, that's okay. Thank you."

The waiter bowed slightly and moved swiftly away.

"Isn't there something more important than your job?" Keira asked out loud.

No one answered.

———

Seth shut the cash register and looked up again. He smiled. The next customer was an older woman wearing a skirt and hat straight out of the 1960s. "I'm looking for a biography of Golda Meir," she said.

"Do you know which one?" Seth asked.

The woman looked confused.

Seth softened. "We have three. *Lioness* by Francine Kagsbrun, *Golda* by Elinor Burkett, and her autobiography, which is just called *My Life*. They're all grouped together on aisle 8, third shelf down, on the left."

"Oh. That's very helpful. Which one do you recommend?"

"I'm sorry, but I haven't read them."

"Oh. All right. Well, thank you." The woman turned and nervously wandered into the store, going in exactly the wrong direction.

There weren't any customers behind her, so Seth called out to her, "Here, ma'am, let me show you." He jogged to her side and then slowed his pace, leading her to the shelf, and pointing at it. "Feel free to peruse. Just find the one that feels best to you."

"Oh, thank you, young man. You've been very helpful."

Seth smiled and walked back toward the register.

"St. John!" Marian Rutherford shouted. Seth whirled to face his boss. "Yes?"

"Let Travis handle the register. I want you to show Belle how to strip the returns."

"Oh. Okay."

"She's finishing up her break."

"Will do." Seth headed for the break room and poked his head in. Belle was sitting under a black cloud of adolescent petulance, frowning at her cell phone. "Hey," Seth said. "When you're done, I'm supposed to show you how to do returns."

She rolled her eyes and groaned.

Seth went to the stock room and bode his time by straightening some boxes and breaking down others. In a few minutes, Belle appeared in the doorway, arms folded over her chest. Her black lace choker accentuated her glowering mascara. "What?"

"We need to do returns for the month."

"What's that?"

"It's when we can't sell a book for some reason, or they're damaged, or we just have too many of a title. The store gets a refund from the distributor." Seth grabbed a box and set it on the table in the middle of the room. Then he lifted up another one. He opened the first box wide. "This is called a mass-market paperback—"

"I know what a fucking paperback is, you idiot."

"Hey," Seth objected. "That's not okay."

Belle rolled her eyes.

Seth pulled a large paperback from the box. "Since you know everything already, what is this?"

"It's also a paperback."

"Yes, but what kind of paperback?"

Belle shrugged.

"I think you have an attitude problem," Seth said.

"I'm going to tell HR you said that," Belle answered.

Seth sighed and put both paperbacks in front of her. He pointed to the small one. "This is a mass-market paperback." He pointed to the large one. "This is called a trade paperback. We treat them differently when it comes to returns."

Belle said nothing. Her arms stayed firmly hugging her chest.

"So long as a trade paperback is in pristine shape, we send it back to the distributor. But if it's damaged—" he pulled another trade paperback from the box and with dramatic flair ripped off its front cover.

Belle's eyes widened. She looked at Seth as if he'd stabbed a kitten. "It's too expensive to ship damaged books. They're just going to be pulped anyway. So we only send back the front cover."

He picked up a mass-market paperback. "These guys, it doesn't matter if they're damaged or not." He ripped the cover from the book. "We only return the covers on all of them."

"That's...horrible," Belle pronounced.

"You are what we in the biz call a biblio-sentimentalist."

"You just made that up." Belle narrowed her eyes at him.

"Why don't you pull the covers off the mass-markets, and I'll sort the trades?"

"Okay."

"Try to have fun with it," Seth said.

"It feels evil."

"Relish the darkness," Seth said. He wanted to add, *Goth chick*, but decided HR would have an ill opinion of that.

For several minutes, they worked in silence, side by side. Belle was hesitant about ripping her first cover, but once she'd done it, she speeded up. After she'd done a short stack, she asked, "So what do we do with the paperbacks that don't have any covers?"

"We put them in the recycling bin."

"Do we have to?"

Seth shrugged. "You can keep anything you want, so long as its cover is gone. I mean, that's how I get all my books. I don't have very many that have covers. We all do that."

"Do we have to ask someone?" Belle asked.

"Nope. Just take any of these that you want. Just be careful not to rip the covers off something that isn't marked for return, or you'll be in deep shit."

"Okay. How would they know?"

"Because the computer will say we have one when we don't."

"But how would they know who took it?"

Seth turned and looked at her. "Are you seriously asking how they will know if you steal a book?"

It was her turn to shrug. "Just asking."

After several more minutes of silence, she asked. "So you only read books that are...returns?"

"Mostly. I still buy books, sometimes. But, you know, money's tight. Do you still live with your folks?"

He watched her shrink at least an inch. "Yeah."

"Well, I have an apartment, and it costs more than half what I make. I can't afford cable. I only have wi-fi because I steal it from my neighbor. I buy stale top ramen in bulk. So hell, free books? That's entertainment, right there."

She stopped and gave Seth a look that he couldn't quite identify. She had never looked at him with anything but bored disdain before, so he had a hard time reading her. At first it looked like pity, but then he thought her face might have held a glimmer of grudging respect. Before he could figure it out, she turned back to her task. She started to make a separate pile.

"Those yours?" he asked.

"Why not?"

"No reason I can think of."

"Urban fantasy, huh?"

"Something wrong with that?"

"Not a bit. I like me a good streetwise vampire romance novel as much as the next guy."

She smirked, and it morphed into a shy smile.

He noticed, but didn't say anything more.

"Do you ever get tired of it?" she asked.

"Of what?"

"Of being poor."

Seth felt like he'd been punched in the gut. "Oh, yeah. Every damn day."

"You think you'll always be poor?"

"I...I gotta make sure Travis is okay. Can you handle the rest of these yourself?"

"Oh...sure."

In the hallway, Seth took a deep breath. *Am I poor?* he asked himself. The word felt like an ill-fitting garment. He decided that if there wasn't some truth in the question, it wouldn't have stung. But it wasn't how he thought about himself.

He headed for the front, away from the rain cloud that followed Belle around.

The next morning, Seth staggered into the kitchen and started the coffee. He filled Kush's bowl, but strangely, the sound of kibble hitting the metal bowl did not rouse the dog. He put the bowl on the floor and went to find him.

He paused in the doorframe leading to the living room. Angie was still asleep, her mouth open and slightly drooling. Curled up against her tummy was his dog. Kush's eyes met his own, but he didn't move. "Comfy?" Seth asked. The lab's yellow tail beat against Angie's leg.

Just then Seth caught a flash of white out of the corner of his eye. Under the door was a note. Frowning, he retrieved it and stood up again. Written on one side, in careful cursive, was "Seth."

He recognized his landlady's writing. "Shit," he said out loud. Whatever it was, it couldn't be good. He unfolded the note and read it.

I've changed my mind about the dog. He needs to go.

Seth dropped the note and felt his knees weaken. He reached for the couch and sat on the armrest, his buttocks against Angie's head. She stirred and sniffed. "Uh…" She coughed. "What…Seth?"

He looked down at her just as she shifted as much as Kush would permit and looked up at him. "Hey…are you okay?"

Tears welled in Seth's eyes. He squatted and picked up the note again. He handed it to Angie.

"Too…early….for…symbols," Angie announced, but she took the note anyway. "Oh, shit." She looked up at him again and reached for his arm. She squeezed it. "Oh, honey, I'm so sorry."

Seth wasn't trying to stop the tears now. His throat was swollen, and his face screwed up with emotion. "What am I going to do?"

"There's only one thing *to* do," Angie said.

Seth struggled to get a breath. He felt like his lungs were too small and he inhaled until they hurt, but he still couldn't get a feeling of satisfaction. At the same time, his hyperventilation was making him dizzy. Angie noticed.

"Pain in your chest again?"

"No, can't get a breath."

"Slow down, breath more shallowly. I know, I know, it's counter-intuitive, but slow it down," she instructed.

Panic seized his brain, but he obeyed. Eventually, the panic subsided.

"We need to find a new place to live," Angie said.

"I…I can't," Seth said. "It's…I feel safe here. I can't…"

"Dude, it's either that or you lose your dog. You don't want that, do you?"

"No. No, of course not."

"Maybe you can get him certified as an emotional support animal," Angie suggested. "I mean, he is, you know."

"Yeah, but...he doesn't know any commands," Seth said. "There's no way I could get him certified."

"It's not going to help if you just shoot down my ideas," Angie said with a note of exasperation.

"Sorry. I'm sorry," Seth said. "I just..." He knelt by Kush and buried his face in his fur. Kush raised his head and sniffed at Seth's ear.

"Well, look, you don't have to do anything right this very moment," Angie said. "You have some time to figure it out. But if you want my advice, you'll start hitting the apartment lists."

Seth's face was still planted in the dog's side, breathing in the aromas of dirt, mown grass, sunshine, and comfort.

"I hab therapy ooday," Seth said into Kush's side.

"Wha...??" Angie asked. "Are you shitting me? Since when?"

"Sin a foo day ago," Seth said, his voice muffled.

"That rocks, Sethie," Angie said. "That's the perfect place to process this."

"Yeah. I gueff," Seth said. Then he began to sob.

"How is it going?"

Seth sighed and looked out the window. Dr. Teasdale waited patiently. Several minutes went by.

"I got this note this morning," Seth said. He passed the folded piece of paper to Dr. Teasdale.

"Oh, no. Seth, you didn't tell me you had a dog."

"His name is Kush. He's...he's a mutt, but he has a lot of yellow lab in him."

"And from the looks of you, you love him very much," Dr. Teasdale said.

Seth kept looking at the window, but it was blurry now. He nodded.

"Oh, Seth. I'm so sorry. What are you going to do?"

He shrugged. "I thought...maybe we could talk about that."

"Of course," she said. "Where would you like to start?"

Seth began to feel uncomfortable and kept shifting in his seat. "My body feels weird. I don't think the drugs are working."

Dr. Teasdale gave him a compassionate look. "They take four weeks to fully kick in. It's a long time to wait, I know. And the side effects will subside, too. I promise. Stick with it, okay?"

Seth nodded. "Okay."

Dr. Teasdale waited. Finally, Seth said, "Angie says I should move."

"That sounds like a good option."

Seth nodded, but didn't look convinced. "Do you know how hard it is to find a place I can afford in San Jose?"

"Hard?"

He nodded. "Plus...the idea of moving. I...It's...I can't—"

"It makes your anxiety go through the roof?" Dr. Teasdale guessed.

Seth nodded, finally looking at her. "Help me," he said.

"I'm here, Seth," she said, her face all compassion. "How are the behaviors going?"

He shrugged. "Yesterday I left the house in 15 minutes—"

Dr. Teasdale grinned. "That's half the time it normally takes. Give yourself credit for the win!"

"I guess." Seth smiled sadly. "I also didn't touch the wicks on the candles. I just looked at them."

"That is another win."

"But today...after I got the note..."

"Today was a shit show?" Dr. Teasdale asked.

Seth almost laughed. "That's...a good way to describe it."

"I'm sorry. But...it's situational. Anyone would be thrown off their game by that. Take the win for yesterday."

Seth nodded, then looked out the window again and cleared his throat. "I visited my Mom a couple of days ago."

"Oh? And how did that go?"

"It was a disaster. I shouldn't have taken Angie with me."

"Angie is your friend, right?"

"And roommate, now. She's...brash."

"Ah. So I'm guessing that she breaks some family rules."

"You could say that," Seth agreed. "It was hard to go into Mom's house. I felt like her God was breathing down my neck. It was all I could do to hold it together."

"Was it too soon to go back there, do you think?"

"Maybe."

Dr. Teasdale wrote on her notepad. Then she said, "Do you mind if we try something?"

Seth shrugged. "Okay."

"Let's explore something in your past that might have contributed to making the other night feel bigger than it actually was."

"Okay..." Seth didn't look too sure.

"Anxiety is about fear. So...can you tell me about a time in the past when you were really, really frightened?"

Seth looked down at his hands.

"Is it too scary?" she asked.

"It's not *too* scary," he said.

"Tell me about it. I promise you, once you do, it will feel like some of the pressure is off."

He looked at her then, his face uncertain. Then he looked at his hands again. "I was in high school. The youth group at our church had meetings every Friday night."

"What kind of things did you do?"

"Ice cream socials. Caroling. Revival meetings. Sometimes bands came through—Christian bands."

"Did something happen at one of these meetings?"

"Yes."

"Tell me what happened."

"The youth pastor told us it was going to be a big deal, so we should invite all our school friends. But he didn't tell us what we were going to be doing. It was...like a big secret."

"Were you excited by that?"

"Yeah, I guess. Everyone was. You know, who doesn't love a secret?"

Dr. Teasdale smiled. "So what did it turn out to be?"

"My mom drove us in our van. My friend Kyle came with me. His family was Methodist, but they weren't really church people. We were going up the long driveway to the church buildings, and some men dressed in black stopped the van. They had masks over their faces, and they were carrying guns. They had armbands on, too. I didn't recognize the symbol on them."

"That...sounds scary right there." Dr. Teasdale looked concerned.

"One of them went to the driver's side window and had a quiet word with my mom. Then another one of them opened the side door and ordered everyone out. Another man got in, he was shouting, 'You got any bibles in there?' We always had bibles in the car, and he started throwing them out the door onto the pavement. Then the second guy ordered us to start marching up to the main church buildings. He was holding his gun in a threatening way, but he wasn't...you know, pointing it at us or anything. Just... brandishing it."

"Go on," Dr. Teasdale breathed.

"When we got up to the farmhouse next to the sanctuary—"

"Was that a parsonage?" Dr. Teasdale asked.

"No. We used it for offices and the nursery, and some meeting rooms." She nodded, and jotted some notes on her legal pad. Seth continued. "The power seemed to be out. There weren't any lights on, anywhere. We were herded up the stairs to the large meeting room in the dark. Upstairs, there were candles lit. There were about thirty people there, sitting on folding chairs. They were singing—low, mournful gospel songs. 'Were You There When They Crucified My Lord,' that kind of thing. So I sat down and waited. More people kept trickling in. We just sat there in the dark and sang. Then about a half hour later, Brother Ted came up the stairs—"

"Who's Brother Ted?"

"He was our youth pastor. His father was our pastor."

"How old was Brother Ted at the time?"

"About twenty-one."

"And he was your youth pastor?"

"Yes."

"Was he an ordained minister?"

"Yes."

"Had he ever been to seminary?"

"I don't think so," Seth said, frowning.

"I see," Dr. Teasdale said, writing on her legal pad. "Go on."

"Brother Ted looked rattled—I mean, really, really rattled. His fingers shook as he approached the lectern. He gripped it and looked at us for a long minute before he said, 'Today, evil forces took over our country. Men in black uniforms arrived at our house and demanded to see my daddy. When he came to the door, they grabbed him and dragged him into the street. They forced him to his knees, and they hit him in the face. We watched from the house as the men leaned in and demanded that he renounce Jesus. He shook his head and said, "I will never renounce him!"

They pointed their weapons at him and repeated their demand. My daddy began to sing, "What a Friend We Have in Jesus." Then they shot him in the back of the head. He pitched forward onto the pavement. He twitched, and then he was still. I watched my daddy die today.'"

Dr. Teasdale's eyes were wide with horror. "Are you serious? Did that really happen?"

"Yes. Well, I mean, the fact that he told us that really happened," Seth said. "But that's not the end of it. A few minutes later, the men in black uniforms burst into the upper room and grabbed Brother Ted by the arms and hauled him down the stairs. He tried to resist, but there were too many of them.

"There was a big picture window in the room, looking down onto a lawn below. We heard shouting coming from the yard, and we all gathered around the window. We watched the men dragging Brother Ted, kicking and screaming, out onto the lawn. There was a full moon, so it was bright enough to see what was happening. They forced him to his knees and they whispered something in his ear. He shook his head back and forth, 'No!' and they threatened him with their rifles. He just kept shaking his head. And then we heard a gunshot, and we saw Brother Ted fall face-first onto the grass. He was still."

"Oh my God," Dr. Teasdale breathed.

"We just stood there, looking at him, until one of the men in the black uniforms told us to go back downstairs in a single file line. We did. In the room downstairs we just stood around waiting to be told what to do. People were crying. One of the girls was...well, she seemed hysterical. Then the sirens began. We thought the end of days was upon us."

"Where did the sirens come from?" Dr. Teasdale asked.

Seth shrugged. "I don't know. I think it was a coincidence. It was just...amazingly timed. And it scared the shit out of us."

"I'll bet. Then what happened?"

"We went outside and our parents arrived to pick us up."

Dr. Teasdale looked stricken. She shook her head. "How...how did you process that, afterwards?"

Seth sighed. "I...had a mixed reaction. Once I realized it was just play-acting, I said it was pretty cool. But while it was happening, I was really scared. I think I was embarrassed, you know, that I'd been fooled."

Dr. Teasdale just sat, staring at Seth for several long minutes. Finally, she set her notepad aside and leaned forward, resting her elbows on her knees. "Seth, do you understand how psychologically abusive that night was?"

Seth blinked. "I...think so."

"It was manipulative. It was a form of terrorism. It was an act of extremist indoctrination. It was spiritual abuse, Seth. You were abused that night."

Seth nodded. "I've never thought of it like that before."

"I'm curious...when did your anxiety begin?"

"Not long after that."

She nodded. She leaned back and picked up her notepad again. "Seth, I think you were indoctrinated with a horrific image of God—an image of God that is hateful, punishing, and abusive. It's what gives his followers permission to feel like they can act the same way." She cocked her head and waited until he met her eyes. "Seth, I want you to answer me truthfully. Don't be afraid. Just tell me the truth. Are you afraid of God?"

Seth looked out the window at the trees. He swallowed.

"How does it feel when I ask that?" asked Dr. Teasdale.

Still not looking at her, Seth said, "I don't know."

"You really don't know, or...are you scared to say?" she asked.

He didn't answer.

"I'd like you to try something," she said. "I want you to draw a picture—two pictures, actually. I want you to draw a picture of the god that was given to you as a child, and then another one of the god you believe in now."

"Do I have to?" he asked. "I'm terrible at drawing."

She smiled and shook her head, her black hair bunching at her shoulders in a way that was distractingly attractive. "The quality of the drawing isn't important. I'm a terrible artist, trust me!" She laughed, and it sounded like music to him. "What's important are the ideas in the drawing. And no...you don't *have* to do it. But...I think you've been significantly wounded. If you want to heal, we need to work together. And sometimes to make progress, you have to do things that are hard."

"That's what it means to be a grown-up," Seth said with a note of resignation.

"It sure is," Dr. Teasdale agreed. She shifted the notepad balancing on her knee.

Seth sighed, wishing they could talk about something— anything—else. "When do I do these...drawings?"

"How about right now? They don't have to be elaborate. Give yourself ten minutes for each one, and then let's look at them. Want me to set a timer for you?"

"But I don't have—"

As if anticipating his protest, she brought out a black box and set it on the coffee table in front of the loveseat on which Seth sat. Taking the lid off the box, she set a pad of drawing paper in front of him. The rest of the box was filled with colored pencils. A sharpener balanced precariously on one of them.

Dr. Teasdale took out her smartphone and tapped its screen. "Okay, you have ten minutes for your first drawing. Show me the god of your childhood."

Seth looked at the white paper in front of him. Then he got to work. He snatched up a handful of pencils, seemingly at random, and began to draw. He drew furiously, his breathing loud and labored. He was so intent he didn't notice that he was sweating.

In what seemed like no time, he heard the therapist's phone alarm sound. "Okay, quick, turn the page and start on your second drawing. Show me how you understand God now."

Seth blinked at the page. He snatched up a pencil and held it ready, as if waiting for inspiration to strike. But it didn't strike. He continued to stare at the page until the timer went off again.

"Okay..." Dr. Teasdale said. "Why don't you put both pages side-by-side?"

"But I didn't...I wasn't able to..."

"Just put them side-by-side, please. Trust me, Seth."

Seth nodded and put both sheets next to one another.

"Tell me about the first one," Dr. Teasdale invited.

Seth looked at what he had drawn. It was of a creature, but not any creature Seth knew...although it did look familiar. It looked a little bit like a bear and a little bit like a wolf. It had a huge chest and head, but no neck. Its hips and legs were tiny, like atrophied afterthoughts. A halo floated above its mangy head, but what stuck out most were the fangs—huge, pointed, and dangerous looking. They were also dripping with blood. Red gashes dripped down the page and formed a pool at the puny feet. Suddenly, Seth knew why it looked familiar. A chuckle bubbled up from his depths.

"What was that?" Dr. Teasdale asked.

"What was what?"

"You laughed. Tell me why." It wasn't a command, but a request.

"It...it looks like the Tasmanian Devil...from the Bugs Bunny cartoons...kind of."

Dr. Teasdale reached for the drawing and held it up so it was right-way-round for her. "It sure does!" she laughed. "I thought you said you couldn't draw."

"I...can't."

"This is a pretty good likeness." She put the paper back down in front of him. "Tell me about him. What is he like? What does he want from you? What makes him tick?"

"He hates me."

"Why does he hate you?"

"Because I..." Seth looked out the window. "Just because I'm me."

"That's a pretty terrible god, don't you think?"

Seth looked back at the drawing.

"He looks dangerous," she observed.

Seth thought about the dream he'd had, about the beast stalking him through the aisles of his childhood church. "He wants to kill me. And eat me."

"I am totally getting that." Dr. Teasdale wrote something on her notepad.

"But I don't have any right—"

"Seth, you have every right to your own thoughts and opinions. When it comes to what is in your own head, you don't have to please anyone—including God."

"Really?"

"Really. It is your own private space."

Seth nodded. "Okay."

"And besides...you've gone to church your entire life, at least up until last year, right?"

"Right."

"How many times a week?"

"Three."

"And at how many of those services did you hear a sermon on hellfire?"

Seth swallowed. "All of them."

"All of them," Dr. Teasdale repeated. "Seth, anyone in your position would experience post-traumatic stress. Once again what your parents did to you, exposing you to such terrorizing sermons, was child abuse."

"It was?" Seth asked.

"It was." She was firm.

"Now look at that second drawing."

"There's nothing there," Seth confessed.

"Exactly. What does that tell you?"

"I'm not sure."

Dr. Teasdale waited several seconds. Then, in a soft voice, she said, "Do you want to know what I think?"

He nodded.

"I think you don't have another image. I think you still believe in that horrible god."

Seth felt tears rise to his eyes. He brushed them away. "I...I...yeah."

"But look at him," she said, her voice still soft. "He's a cartoon character. He's a monster. In fact, that's a good name for him. He's the Monster God. Is this god really worthy of your worship, your devotion?" She tapped at the picture with one red nail.

Seth didn't answer.

"You know, you're not the first person to think that god was a monster. The ancient Gnostics thought the same. But they also thought that there was another god, beyond the Monster God, a god who was completely different from this one." She pointed at the picture again. "A god who was all loving, a god who wanted to set them free from this sorry excuse for a deity."

Seth felt a wave of vertigo wash through him. "Really?"

"Really. And they weren't the only ones. Lots of people have walked this road before. You're not alone."

"So...I don't know what to do," Seth said.

"Do you want my advice?" Dr. Teasdale asked.

Seth nodded. Dr. Teasdale picked up the picture of the Monster God and handed it to him. "Fire his ass."

Seth blinked. "I can do that?"

"Of course you can," she said confidently. She gave him an

encouraging smile. Then she tapped the blank sheet. "And that will leave you free to find out who *this* god is."

Seth nodded. "How do I...fire him?"

"You could fill out a pink slip," Dr. Teasdale suggested.

"That sounds pretty cheesy," Seth said.

"Maybe it is," she agreed, smiling. "Why don't you sit with it for a while? Maybe the way that's right for you will come to you."

"Okay," he said. "But...I don't like leaving threads hanging."

"Ah, you're a 'J'," she smiled.

"I'm a what?"

"A 'J' on the Myers-Briggs personality inventory. It means you have a hard time relaxing if something is incomplete."

"Yeah. Yeah, that's true," Seth admitted.

"Seth, our time is almost up—"

"No no, it can't be. I haven't figured out what to do about Kush."

Dr. Teasdale cocked her head. "What are your options?"

"I can move—"

"It sounds like that's a big ask right now."

"Yeah, I...can't even imagine it. It's too big."

"And other options?"

Seth wrung his hands. "I could...I could find him a new home... for now."

"Is that something you'd be willing to do?"

"It's not something I *want* to do, but I don't see any other option."

"Where would he live, then?"

Seth sniffed and wiped his nose on his sleeve. "I know this guy..."

———————

S eth stared at the table, focusing on the crumbs and several dribbles of unidentified liquid. He squirmed in his seat, looking around and grimacing. He had on a winter-patterned sweater, which was unusual both for May and for San Jose, but it was windy, and he always found it just a bit too cold in most bookstores. He rubbed at his temples, a futile attempt to assuage a headache that had been plaguing him ever since he had started the new medication.

"Oh, for crying out loud," Angie said, "Look at this mess." She wiped the crumbs off the table with her hand, but didn't venture to wipe away the spilled coffee. Angie's hair fell into her eyes. She brushed it back and glowered at the other patrons in the bookstore cafe. It was a busy afternoon, and cloudy enough to make the store seem dimmer and cozier than usual.

Seth settled the small stack of books he was carrying in his lap. Then he pulled a small packet of wipes from his pocket and scrubbed at the surface of the table. A woman at a nearby table noticed and left off in the middle of a sentence. Then, still watching Seth, she continued talking to her companion.

Once the table was clean, Seth held the wipe away from him as if it were a plague specimen.

"I'll throw it away—Jesus," Angie said, snatching the wipe from his hand and marching over to the trash can near an S-panel.

When she returned, Seth had put the books on the table and was arranging them at a right angle to his position. As she sat, she studied him, noting how the spine of every book lined up. "You're going to drive yourself crazy," she said.

"I'm already there," he said, his shoulders slumped.

"You've just got to get your mind in a different track," she said.

"That's what my shrink says...kind of. I think that's part of what she's getting at."

"Why are we at a bookstore? Aren't you sick of bookstores? What are you doing, surveilling the competition?"

"No, I'm...I just like bookstores. I feel safe here."

"Do you feel safe in a library?"

"No," Seth answered.

"Do you think that's strange?"

"Libraries smell like mold and old food."

Angie cocked her head. "Now that you mention it...I guess they do."

"Besides, I wanted to come here because they have books we don't."

"You could just order them from Ama—"

"Don't say it!" he snapped. "They're the enemy. I'd sooner be illiterate."

"That's harsh."

"I work in a local bookstore. It's personal."

"Okay, okay..." Angie held her hands up in a mock-protective pose. She pointed at the short stack of books on the table in front of Seth. "So, are those books you don't have at your store?"

"Yeah. My shrink said something about...well, I wanted to check it out."

Angie cocked her head sideways to read the spines. "Gah-noses?"

"Gnosis. The 'g' is silent."

"Huh. What's that about?"

Seth picked up one of the books and turned it over. "Well, this one is about the ancient Gnostics—you know, what they believed, what happened to them." He set it down and picked up another with a bright yellow cover. "And this one is, like, about how to do it, how they did it."

"Did what?" Angie asked.

"I'm a little fuzzy on the details," he confessed. "I mean, I haven't read them yet."

Angie frowned. "Isn't that a little...cultish?"

"It was an ancient religion."

"I thought you swore off religion." She blew her nose again.

"I did," he said, a little too quickly and a little too forcefully.

"Hey, friend here." She held her hands up again.

"Sorry, I..."

"It's a sore spot. I know." Angie crossed her arms. "You know that's why you're like this, right?"

"Like what?"

"Like...fucked up, with all your weird tics and shit. It's that fundamentalist church you grew up in. You've got...I don't know... massive religious trauma or something."

Seth met her eyes. "You and my shrink are on the same page."

"You could save a lot of money and just talk to me."

He chuckled at that. Then he looked down at the books and stacked them again, being careful to line up the spines. "I think my parents were *trying* to do the right thing, raising me in that church."

"Seriously deluded people try to do the right thing every day," she said. "And they wreak fucking havoc."

"But this stuff," Seth said, tapping the books, "it's not about religion."

She scowled. "Oh yeah? What's it about, then?"

"I think it's about...secret knowledge."

"Say what?"

"You know...the secrets of the universe. That's what Google said, anyway."

"What kind of secrets?"

"I don't know. Just...secret stuff. I mean, if I knew, it wouldn't be a secret."

"If it's published in those books, it's not a secret, either."

He shrugged. "I guess. I don't...I guess I just keep thinking there's got to be more."

"More what?"

He shrugged again. "More than...we're hurtling through space on a crusty ball of magma until we die. I guess."

"In other words, *religion*."

He shook his head. "Maybe. I had to leave the church I grew up in—"

"Of course you did," she affirmed. "Or you'd have slit your wrists by now."

"But now I just...don't believe anything, and that's..." He fidgeted in his seat. "I still want to find some *meaning* to it all." He gave her a half-smile. "Maybe I'm looking for an anti-religion."

"Huh. Good luck with that." She snapped her fingers. "Hey, I know. If you want secret societies, you could join the Rosicrucians. They come with their own sad museum full of creepy corpses. And it's local, on Park."

He almost smiled at that. "Hey, lay off that museum—it's pretty cool. And they're mummies, not corpses."

"Mummies *are* corpses, pea-brain."

"The Rosicrucians *do* need a gardener," Seth admitted. "The grounds are pretty shoddy,"

"Just don't join the Masons."

"What's wrong with the Masons?" he asked.

"They all smell like old men," she said.

"I think that's because they *are* old men," he said.

"That's it," she said. "Keep making sense." Angie took a sip of her coffee. "Uh...not to change the subject to something even more painful, but...what did your shrink say about Kush?"

Seth stared at the table. The question of Kush had been a black cloud hovering over him for the past couple of days. No matter how much he tried to ignore it, it overshadowed everything. He sighed. "I think I'll talk to Travis."

Angie frowned. "Travis? The guy you work with? Surfer dude?"

Seth nodded. "He likes Kush a lot. And Kush likes him. And maybe it can just be temporary, you know, until I feel ready to move and actually find something."

Angie folded her arms over her chest. "I can't believe you're going to just give up on the one being that loves you unconditionally."

Seth felt like she'd just slapped him. "I...I don't want to—"

"No, but you're willing to, and that's almost as bad."

Seth took several deep breaths, but couldn't seem to get a lungful of air.

"You love that dog," Angie continued. "I know you do."

"Of course I do," Seth said, still struggling, his voice cracking.

"Why not just tell your landlady to go fuck herself?"

"She'll evict me," Seth said.

"You don't know that. Do you know how hard it is to actually evict someone in San Jose? Make her try."

"I don't want to sour our relationship," Seth said.

"If making you give up your dog doesn't sour your relationship, what would?" Angie retorted.

Seth held his head in both hands, elbows on the table. The headache was reasserting itself. He felt faint.

Suddenly, Angie stood up. "Hey, I've got to go. I have a...not exactly a date. More of a chance meetup."

"If you're going to meet someone, how is it chance?" Seth asked with a humorous scowl.

"Because she doesn't know about it."

"Some people would call that stalking."

"Some people are judgmental pricks who should mind their own goddam business." She stood. "But I need to pick up some shoelaces before I go. Do you know where—"

"Fleischer's Shoes are on the other side of the mall," Seth said, not looking up from the table. "Just before you go into Macy's, on the left."

"How do you even know that? You only buy shoes at the Goodwill."

Seth shrugged. "I looked at the mall map last year."

"You're fucking spooky, Seth." She put a five-dollar bill on the table.

Seth blinked at the money. "What's that for? You already paid."

"Hey, you're letting me sleep on your couch for free. Have another latte. On me."

He eased himself off his elbows and pushed the bill back toward her. "It's okay. You can cook tonight."

"Not if you want to live. Plus, I'm hoping to be sleeping elsewhere tonight, if you get my drift." She waggled her eyebrows.

"Uh...good luck?"

She kissed the top of his head and spun away. Throwing a glance over her shoulder, she waved.

"Dental dams!" he shouted after her.

"Rather die!" she called back.

He watched her until she'd left the store. He kept thinking about Kush and he felt like he was about to suffocate. *I can't just go round and round about this,* he thought. *I need to distract myself.* He looked at the books before him. The one titled *The Violet Ray of Gnosis* looked like a cheesy new-age rip-off, with a purple, airbrushed cover featuring a heart with wings. The copy on the back was compelling, but he was repulsed by the artwork and by the fact that the author described herself as a channeler. He set it aside and picked up the next one. *The Labyrinth of the Gnostics* seemed to be half footnotes, and one paragraph in, Seth's eyes were crossed from the dense academese in which it was written. He looked at the back cover and noted that the author was a professor of ancient near-eastern religion at Georgetown whose previous books had been on the Yezidis, the Mandeans, and the Zoroastrians, whatever they were.

He set it aside and picked up the next book. It was thin, less than a hundred pages by his estimation. He couldn't tell what it was like because the book was shrink-wrapped. It was also hardcover, and apart from the title stamped in gold foil on the black cover, there was no text to give any idea of its contents. "*The Secrets of the Gnostics,*" Seth read the title aloud. He felt a thrill run up his spine. He knew next to nothing about Gnosticism or Gnostics, but he had awakened that morning with the word on his brain.

Both paperbacks were twenty dollars or more. What was curious about the little hardcover volume, however, was that it had no price tag on it.

He drained his coffee and, returning to the Religion section, he put the two paperbacks away—not where he had found them, but where they truly belonged, alphabetical by author. Then he proceeded to the checkout stand with the hardcover. He placed it in front of the cashier and asked, "Can you tell me how much this is? I couldn't find a price."

A diminutive cashier with frizzy red hair made a face as she turned the wrapped volume over in her hands. Pursing her lips, she turned to her computer and did a search. Then she did another. Then she did another. With every attempt, the furrow in her brow grew deeper. Finally she shook her head and handed the book back to him. "It's not in our system."

"Then...how much is it?"

She shrugged. "I guess it's free."

"For real?"

"There's no way to ring it up, so...yeah."

"Wow. I...I guess it was meant to be, then."

"Sure," she said noncommittally, and turned her attention to the next person in line.

Seth exited the large double doors, stepping into the merciless wind. He clutched at the book and headed for home. The curiosity became too much for him, however, and when he passed a wall in the outdoor mall that provided a natural wind break, he stopped and looked at the book again. He broke the plastic seal with this thumbnail. He slid the shrink wrap off and put it in his pocket. Then he opened the slim volume.

It was blank. He quickly turned the pages, one by one, then flipped to the end. Every one of them was blank. "What the fucking hell?" he said out loud.

A card fell out onto his feet. A gust of wind caught it up, and it tumbled end over end toward the parking lot. He ran after it and snatched it up. The card, handwritten in big red block letters read, "Thursdays 7pm. 616 Aberdeen SJ." Turning the card over, he saw what was scrawled on the back. "Yes, you."

WHAT IS FUNDAMENTALISM?

Fundamentalism is a religious or ideological movement characterized by a strict adherence to traditional beliefs and practices. The term "fundamentalism" originated in the early 20th century within American Protestantism, specifically referring to a movement that aimed to defend and promote the "fundamentals" of Christian faith against perceived modernist challenges. However, the concept of fundamentalism has since been applied to various religious, political, and social contexts.

Fundamentalist movements typically emerge in response to perceived threats to the core tenets and values of a particular belief system. They emphasize the literal interpretation of sacred texts, maintaining the authority of traditional teachings, and resisting any perceived deviations or compromises. In religious fundamentalism, scripture is often considered infallible and the ultimate source of guidance, leading to a rejection of critical scholarship and a strong resistance to change.

One prominent example of religious fundamentalism is found within Islam, where certain groups advocate for a strict adherence to traditional interpretations of the Quran and the Hadith (the sayings and actions of the Prophet Muhammad). These movements often advocate for the establishment of a society governed by Islamic law, resisting Western influences and modern cultural practices that are seen as contrary to their understanding of Islamic teachings.

Political fundamentalism can also manifest in nonreligious

contexts. Some political ideologies, such as nationalism or communism, can be characterized as fundamentalist when followers strictly adhere to a particular interpretation of their ideology and resist any compromise or deviation from its core principles. These movements often exhibit strong authoritarian tendencies and reject pluralism and diversity of thought.

It is important to note that while fundamentalist movements often arise as a response to societal changes or challenges, not all adherents of a particular religion or ideology are fundamentalist. Fundamentalism represents a specific subset of believers who emphasize uncompromising adherence to traditional values and resist accommodation with contemporary norms.

CHAPTER THREE

Those above opened to us who are below,
that we may go into the secret of the truth.
The truth is what is held in high regard, since it is strong.
But we shall go in there by means of
lowly types and forms of weakness.
—*Gospel of Philip*[*]

"Sloane!" Keira looked up from the report she was writing and saw her captain motioning to her. She scooted her chair back and speed-walked toward the glass cage he called his office. Her brown hair twirled behind her until she stopped, whereupon it draped in loose curls over her shoulders. She adjusted her glasses and shut the door behind her.

---

[*] The Gospel of Philip: Nag Hammadi Codex II, 3, translated by Wesley W. Isenberg, published in *The Nag Hammadi Library in English*, rev. ed., edited by James M. Robinson (NY: Harper & Row, 1988).

"Sit." Captain Schenck opened a file on his desk. A thin wisp of hair had been slicked back and made a valiant attempt to cover as much real estate on his head as possible.

"Where is Taylor?" she asked.

Schenck froze and looked up at her. His eyes narrowed. "Who wants to know?"

"I think I do. Sir. He's a respected part of our team, and he's well-liked. People don't usually just disappear without any notice or explanation. The whole squad is talking about it."

"They are?" Schenck turned and surveyed the squad room through the glass. He looked back at her. "It doesn't look like anyone's talking to me."

She frowned and stared at him. "Is he dead? Is he working undercover? Is he in prison? Is he in witness protection? Is his mother sick? Did he fuck up in some extravagant way that would be embarrassing to admit?"

"No comment," Schenck said.

"That's not fair," Keira said, but even as she said it, she realized it sounded whinier than she'd intended. "Every day we put our lives on the line out there for California Homeland Security. We don't get much of an outside life. We're a family here in the squad. We care about each other. And we want to know when something has happened, so that we can at least show that we care. That's not a weakness, sir, that's a strength."

Schenck sighed. "Anything I say to you is going to spread like wildfire throughout the squad."

"Are you calling me a gossip?" Keira felt heat rise in her neck.

"I'm calling you human, special agent." He leaned back in his chair and stroked his chin. "The information you are asking for is...confidential."

"Confidential to whom?"

"Confidential to you'm."

"How about I give you my list of guesses again and you can look at the ceiling when I'm close?"

"Not going to happen."

"Should the rest of us be worried?"

"About what?"

"About being the next person who gets disappeared?"

"Are you serious?"

"Hell yes, I'm serious. People don't just vanish without an explanation. This isn't Nicaragua in the 1980s. Or is it?"

"That's insulting," Schenck growled.

"Then throw me a fucking bone, boss."

Schenck shook his head. "Look, special agent, I can't tell you anything, because I don't know anything. I got word from the higher-ups—"

"What higher-ups?"

"The deputy secretary, all right?"

"John Tellerman called you on the phone?"

"No, special agent. He summoned me to Sacramento."

Keira blinked. "Oh. Wow. Okay. Please...continue."

"That's so gracious of you." Schenck emitted a sound that was suspiciously like air rushing out of the stretched nozzle of a balloon. "As I was saying... I was told that he had gotten...too close to something...something classified...and so he was being reassigned for his own safety."

"Reassigned..." she repeated. The word tasted ominous as she rolled it around in her mouth. "Did they move his whole family?"

"They did."

"And where is he now?"

"That's *classified*. Aren't you listening?"

"Wow." Keira looked at her hands, at the sore on her right thumb that she compulsively picked with her index finger. She caught herself and put her hand under her thigh, forcing the picking to stop.

"Now, can we proceed?"

"Uh...sure. Sorry boss."

"Good, because—"

"But you know, inquiring minds want to know."

"Are you through?" He pierced her with one eye.

"Yes. Through now. Very...through."

He cautiously opened the file in front of him, and turned it so that it faced her. "The CBI passed this along to us. A suspicious activity notification. They want us to check it out."

She picked up the folder, stamped with the logo of the California Bureau of Investigation. "What kind of suspicious activity?"

"It was an anonymous tip. A lot of people going in and out of a house in downtown SJ. Could be drugs—if it is, great, we can hand it off to the city."

"It could be terrorists," Keira said, flipping through the report.

"In which case, it'll land in our laps."

"It's a beautiful old house," Keira noted. "Whoever lives there has money. It could be a poker game...or a swinger's club."

"House belongs to a Terrence Basil. He's got money all right. It's all in there. We just don't know what he's doing there."

"So you want me to...what?"

"Find out. Discreetly. Ask questions. Infiltrate it—"

"You want me to go undercover?"

"Light cover. Nothing deep. Just express some interest and get the gist of it."

"How am I supposed to do that?"

"I thought you were an investigator," Schenck smiled at her for the first time. "Now get out before you ask me any more questions that could cost me my job."

Seth peered through the windows of the bus, squinting to see the house numbers. He held the card before him, saying "616" over and over in his mind. Finally, he caught one of the numbers. 1276. *Right side of the street*, he thought. *Still blocks away.*

He had been conflicted about going out. He felt guilty leaving Kush, knowing that they might not have much time left together, but soon after he got home the dog was asleep and oblivious. Plus, Seth's curiosity was piqued.

He looked up and saw a girl about his own age sitting near the side door. Her shoulders were hunched over, her long blonde hair hanging down into her eyes. She leaned as far toward the door as she could without toppling over. Then Seth saw why. A young man, perhaps five years older, was standing near her, hovering over her. He was speaking to her, but Seth couldn't make out the words. It was clear that she wasn't liking what she was hearing, though. The man wore a cruel smile, almost a sneer. He kept edging closer and closer to her, until finally, the older woman sitting next to her said, "Do you mind?" loud enough for Seth to hear.

The man took one step back, but did not so much as look at the older woman. Nor did he apologize. Instead, he kept his gaze fixed firmly on the distressed young woman. As her hair swayed, Seth saw a scarlet, irregular birthmark about the size of a quarter on her left cheek. Some might have seen it as a blemish on her beauty, but it didn't seem that way to him at all.

Seth felt conflicted. He instinctively felt like he should intervene, but every self-protective instinct screamed at him that it was a bad idea. The bus slowed, veering to the right into its next stop, and Seth saw the older woman hunch over, clutch at a handrail, and begin to get up.

Without thinking, Seth sprang out of his seat. He nearly leaped the several steps toward the older woman's place. The threatening man took another step back to let her pass, and it was clear to Seth that he intended to sit next to the young woman. Instead, Seth slid into the seat before he could get there with the speed and grace of a baseball player sliding into home. He surprised even himself.

Seth did not look at the man, but he could feel his eyes boring into the top of his head. Finally, he heard, "You stole that seat from me."

Seth tried to ignore him. He noticed that his right leg was bouncing frantically. He leaned over to the young woman and whispered, "Are you okay?"

The young woman sniffed and nodded, also not looking at the looming man. "Thank you," she whispered.

"Are you looking for trouble, asshole? I'm talking to you."

Seth forced himself to look up into the man's face. He wore a Shark's jersey, which despite being tent-like still did not hide his beer belly. "I don't want any trouble," Seth said.

"Then fucking mind your own business."

"That's...good advice...for all of us," Seth said. It felt as if it were someone else's voice and he had simply overheard it.

"You trying to say something to me, shit-face?"

Other passengers were watching now, including a woman in her mid-30s with shoulder length brown hair and glasses. She was scowling at the man, and her ferocity encouraged Seth. He looked toward the corner of the bus and noticed the closed-circuit security camera. That made him feel better, too. If this guy tried anything, at least it wouldn't go undocumented. Looking over the man's shoulder, he saw a teenager holding her phone up. She would make doubly sure. A slight smile tugged at his mouth.

He heard the ding indicating an approaching stop, and quickly swerved in his seat to see the house numbers. 672. Close enough. But if he got off the bus now, he would leave the young woman beside him to the mercy of this animal. An internal tug-of-war quickly unspooled within him. The bus slowed and then stopped. The door opened, and Seth was relieved to see the young man move toward it. He shot Seth a final glowering look. The woman with brown hair exited after him.

Seth felt a stab of panic. This was his stop—should he get out and take his chances with the bully, or should he get off at the next stop and walk? He glanced at his watch. He had some time. He'd walk.

He felt his whole body relax when the doors closed again and the bus pulled away from the curb. The young woman next to him straightened her shoulders and sat up taller. She looked at Seth, and smiled. It was a sad, embarrassed smile. "Thanks," she said.

"He was being an asshole," Seth said.

"Yeah."

"Do you know him?" Seth asked.

"No. He just started hitting on me."

"I'm sorry."

He noticed a tear slide down her cheek, and looked away, wanting to give her her privacy. He heard the electronic ding and felt the bus slowing again. He rose. "Have a good evening," he said.

"Thanks."

The doors opened and he bounded down the steps and started walking back toward the previous bus stop. San Jose was not an easy place to live without a car. Nothing was close together. The city was the very definition of urban sprawl. Fortunately, Seth knew the public transit system as well as he knew the contents of his closet. It wasn't a fast way to get around, but it was reliable.

The bus had left him by a small strip mall. He walked by an Arco station, and after waiting for the light, walked toward a group of houses shaded by trees that must have been planted fifty years ago. The houses were older, too, but they were exceptionally well tended. The yards were immaculate, and he saw only one or two houses that needed painting. He loved looking at the architecture, and despite all that distracted him, he discovered he was enjoying the walk.

Then he heard a familiar voice shout, "Hey, asshole!"

Seth looked around, and there on the other side of the street was the bully from the bus. Seth felt goose bumps rise up on his skin. He looked around for an escape route, but honestly doubted he could outrun the man, despite being slimmer.

Seth felt frozen to the spot as the man, barely looking at the traffic, began to cross the street diagonally, heading straight for him. "Oh, shit," he said out loud.

"Yeah, you—the faggot walking on tippie-toe. I've had it with pussies like you," the bully shouted, stepping up on the curb. Seth watched the man approach as the distance between them diminished quickly. "I'm sick of people telling me I'm using the wrong words. I'm tired of perverts saying 'Celebrate me! Celebrate my perversion!' Who made you the moral policeman of the universe, huh? You self-satisfied prick."

"I-I-I think you might be projecting some stuff onto me that isn't mine," Seth stammered.

"Ivy League assholes think you're better than the rest of us," the man said, now only three yards from him.

"I...look, I've never even been to college. I make minimum wage!"

"Entitled motherfuckers," he bellowed, stopping only within arm's reach of Seth. He leaned in, eyes narrowing, until they were almost touching noses.

"I wasn't trying to criticize you," Seth explained. "I was just... you were making that girl uncomfortable, and I...I had to help her."

"She wasn't in any danger, ass-bag."

"Well...I didn't know that. You're...kind of scary."

The man raised his fist and drew it back. Seth cringed and

held his hands up protectively, screwing his eyes shut. But it did no good. Seth felt the sockets of his jaw crack and felt a searing pain near his ears. He stumbled and it felt like the world was spinning. He didn't lose his feet, however. Some distant part of himself told him he should raise his fists in a boxing pose, but before he could effect such a masquerade, another blow landed on the bone surrounding his eye, spreading a sharp pain up and over the circle of his skull. Seth clutched at his face and tried to turn away from the man. Then he heard an "oof," and the sound of something heavy and meaty hitting the ground. Hands still raised, he pried open one eye and found that he was looking not at the bully, but at the brown-haired woman from the bus. She had a large tree limb in her hand, brandishing it like a baseball bat, stray twigs radiating from it like frozen flashes of lightning. At her feet, the bully writhed, holding his back.

"Oh, knock it off," the woman said. "You've got another kidney." She looked up at Seth. "You okay?"

"I don't know yet...but thanks." She was shorter than he, and her oversized glasses were appealing in a geeky way he really liked, even if she was old. Well, older. She raised the limb for another strike and waited for the bully to give her his attention. "I'm going to keep this, now that you know that I know how to use it. I want you to get up and run away as fast and as far as you possibly can. And if you ever, ever bother me, or this guy, or make unwanted advances toward young women on public transit again, I will hunt you down and bash your skull in with a brick. Now, you feel like fighting or running or rolling on the ground some more?"

With an unreadable expression on his face, the man stumbled to his knees, then got to his feet, then tottered back across the street, almost walking into the path of a passing car.

The woman put one tip of the branch on the ground and leaned the rest of it against her hip. "Let me look at you," she said.

She touched his face gingerly. "Put your hands down," she ordered. He complied but winced as she tried to spread his right eye open. "Do you want me to take you to the emergency room?"

"No, I...I don't think that's necessary."

"You sure?"

"No, but...I can't afford an emergency room."

"You don't have health insurance?" she asked.

He snorted as if that was a ridiculous notion. "I do, but my deductible is higher than my annual salary."

"That sucks," she said.

"Yeah. You get used to it."

"Which way you going?" she asked. Seth pointed.

"Me too. Want to walk together for a ways? You never know—that guy might prove to be as stupid as he looks."

"Thank you for..." he wanted to say *saving me*, but it sounded too lame. "...for your help."

"I hate bullies," she said, and began to walk. He kept pace with her, and was surprised at how fast she walked, considering her height. "What's your name?"

"Seth," he said.

"I'm Margaret. My friends call me Mags."

"Should...I call you Margaret?"

"You can call me whatever you feel comfortable with. But I like Mags."

Seth nodded. The sky had softened into a glorious orange, and the scent of blooming jasmine wafted over him.

"What do you do, Seth?"

"I work in a bookstore. Castle Books."

"Oh, yeah. It's small but I like it."

"I love it there. I...I love books."

"I know just what you mean. What do you read?"

"Fiction. Geeky stuff."

"Ah. Orson Scott Card?"

"Yeah, I love Card."

"I'm more of a Mary Doria Russell girl myself."

"*The Sparrow* and *Children of God* were great," Seth said.

"I was just wondering if you knew those."

"I tried to read another one of hers, but...not my genre."

"I get it."

"What do you do?" he asked, mostly because it seemed polite.

"I...uh...well, I'm kind of between jobs right now. I used to work...security. You know, late night stuff, at a...plant. Up in Richmond. The Chevron factory."

"Oh, yeah. I've passed that on I-80."

"That's the one."

While they walked, Seth checked the street numbers. And within a few blocks, the numbers closed in on the 600-block. He paused in front of a house, a large, looming, beautiful Victorian. "Uh...this is my stop," he said.

She looked at the house, and then back at him, and then back at the house. Her forehead bunched. "Well...huh. Me, too."

"Do you know what it's all about?" he asked.

"Not a clue," she said, shrugging. "Let's find out together, shall we?"

S eth and Margaret crossed the street toward the Victorian, brooding by itself on a large lot surrounded by twisted, leafless trees. The clouds were dark and heavy, but there was no wind. Seth remembered that his mother used to call this "tornado weather," even though there had never been a tornado in San Jose that he could recall. As ominous as the house appeared from across the street, up close he could tell it was well cared for— better than the less impressive houses a stone's throw away on either side. They mounted the gray painted steps and paused before a door that dwarfed them.

Seth looked for a doorbell but did not see one. Instead, there was a braided, ornate cord dangling from a brass socket in the ceiling of the porch. He looked at Margaret, who shrugged and pulled on the cord, resulting in the faraway sounding of bells.

A moment later, the door swung open, and they were face-to-face with a young man—red-faced and sporting a purple and black paisley vest. A shock of yellow hair was gelled to stand nearly straight upright. He cocked his head and then squinted at Seth. "What happened to you?"

"Uh...I got into a bit of a scuffle."

"So you're a troublemaker, then?" The young man raised his nose. Seth detected a mildly British accent.

"It was unprovoked," Margaret said. "I was there."

"Are you together?" The man frowned.

"No," Margaret said. "We just met on our way here."

"Huh." The young man seemed suspicious. His eyes flicked from one of them to the other. "What's the secret password?"

Seth blinked and took a step back. "Password?"

"You don't know the password?"

"I-I just found the card," Seth explained.

"Come back when you know the password, or you'll never get anywhere." The young man shut the door again, leaving Seth and Margaret alone on the porch.

"How rude," Margaret said.

Seth almost jumped with surprise when the door jerked open again. "Just pulling your chain, mates. Show me the card."

Seth produced his card and the young man examined it. "That'll do." He looked up at Margaret. "Show me yours?"

"I...I'm afraid I misplaced it. I put the address into my phone and didn't realize it was important. I must have recycled it."

He studied her for a moment, and then nodded, apparently

satisfied that this was a plausible explanation. "Well, come in, then." He swung the door wide.

Seth responded with a nervous smile, but autopilot kicked in and he stepped into the house, Margaret on his heels.

"I'm Nazz, but you can call me Nazz."

"Nazz," Seth repeated.

"'Cause it's my name," the young man added, for some reason.

"Seth," Seth said.

"Ooooo, a very auspicious name in these parts," Nazz said, waggling an eyebrow at him.

"Is it?" Seth asked.

Margaret stuck out her hand. "I'm Margaret. Call me Mags."

Nazz shook it. "Mags it is. Had a girlfriend named Mags once. Not as pretty as you."

Mags blushed at this and looked painfully uncomfortable.

"So...welcome to the Lodge," Nazz said, waving his hand around the foyer.

"Are we late?" Seth asked.

"Too near, too near, but not near enough," Nazz said. "You're here for the study group? Unless you're here to fix the cable?"

"No, I'm afraid I'd be fairly hopeless at that," Seth admitted.

"Tough luck for Mr. Basil, then. He's going to miss his *Upstairs, Downstairs* reruns. Again. Makes him testy when he can't enjoy the juxtaposition of the classes."

"The...what?" Seth asked.

"Follow me," Nazz said, then turned and walked down a corridor.

Seth waited for Margaret to go first, then followed. He reminded himself to take in his surroundings. They were in a magisterial foyer with a large wooden staircase. The floor was marble, but as soon as he entered the hallway, it gave way to polished hardwood.

The lights overhead seemed oddly dim, but the passage was navigable enough. Nazz paused by a large set of white double-doors and turned the knob on the righthand side, pushing in.

He waved Margaret and Seth through with his chin, then shut the door once they were in. Only then did it occur to Seth that Nazz wasn't here for the lecture or the study or whatever it was, but was acting as a porter. Perhaps he worked here?

Seth and Mags stepped into a large room, perhaps twenty feet square. Every wall was fitted with bookshelves, and every shelf was full. Eight people, five men and three women, were seated in a circle in the center of the room. Some were his same age while others were older. One of the men had been talking, but he left off and said, "Do please join us." He motioned to an empty seat near him, and another across the circle.

Seth felt embarrassed to be the sudden center of attention. He waited to see which seat Margaret would take, and then took the other as quickly as he could. He sat on his hands, rocking back and forth a bit to settle his nerves.

"So a gnostic is One Who Knows," the same man said, sounding as if he were finishing an uncompleted sentence.

Seth studied the man. He didn't have an accent, yet his words were oddly clipped and precise. He looked like he was in his mid-sixties, bone thin but crackling with vitality. There were deep lines etched into his face, and his thick, round glasses made his eyes appear impossibly large, like the eyes of a giant insect. He sat very straight in his chair, and was dressed entirely in black—black chinos, black shirt, and a black vest.

Seth frowned. *What is it with the vests?* he wondered.

"Knows what?" one of the women asked. She was perhaps five years older than he, with curly hair and a dark complexion. Seth wondered if perhaps she was Iranian or Afghani or Indian.

"Ah, a good question!" The man looked pleased. "The gnostic knows 'what no eye has seen, what no ear has heard, what no hands have touched, and what has never arisen in the human heart.'"

He said this with such an affected lilt that it occurred to Seth that he must be quoting from something. It was also, he noted, not really an answer.

Seth raised his hand. The man looked at him and his eyebrows rose. "Yes, Mr.—"

Seth wasn't used to being called Mister. "Seth, please. Just Seth."

"Ask your question then, Seth. Don't be shy," the man encouraged.

"Are you talking about the gnostic gospels?"

"We were not, but we certainly can." He smiled his indulgence. "Who here has read any of the gnostic gospels?"

One hand went up—an older gentleman. "Well, then, how many of you have heard of them?"

All the hands shot up now. "Excellent. And an excellent place to start." He gave Seth an approving nod. "First of all, 'gospels' is a misnomer. None of the writings in question conform to the literary genre we typically think of as 'a gospel.' The name 'gnostic gospels' is a modern contrivance, and despite its inaccuracy, it has stuck. Nevertheless, there are some points of contact between some of the gnostic scriptures and the canonical gospels. Some of them contain sayings attributed to Jesus, and some show scenes from his life, usually scenes in which he teaches someone something. But none of them are birth-to-death narratives."

"Are all of them about Jesus?" another young woman asked. She was small and birdlike, with dishwater blonde hair. Seth found he liked her look.

"No, indeed," Mr. Basil said, shaking his head. "Many people mistakenly consider gnosticism to be a form of Christianity. But this is only partially true." He opened his mouth, but then rocked back on his chair, as if a thought had just occurred to him. A playful look twinkled in his eye as he leaned forward again. "Gnosticism is a movement of secrets," he said, lowering his voice. "Secret upon secret, laid down in layers. The further you go into it, the more secrets are revealed."

"Do you ever get to the end of the secrets?" the older man asked. "I mean, do you ever know all of them?"

Mr. Basil gave him a compassionate look. "Not in this life, no. But there is no shortage of revelations to keep one on one's toes." He chuckled to himself at this. "So, here is the first of the secrets..."

Everyone leaned in closer, so as not to miss a word of Basil's *sotto voce* delivery. "Gnosticism is not a religion. It is, instead, a pan-religious movement."

"What does that mean?" asked a familiar voice. Seth quickly scanned the circle and realized it was Margaret who spoke.

"This is your first time, is it not?"

"Yes," Margaret said.

"Well, you are most welcome. When I say it is a pan-religious movement, I mean that in the ancient world there were few religions that did not have...branches, let us say...influenced by gnostic opinions. So, there were Jewish gnostics, Christian gnostics of course, indigenous Greek gnostics, Zoroastrian gnostics, and so on."

"Were there Buddhist gnostics?" a young man about Seth's own age asked.

Mr. Basil laughed at this. It was a merry sound, and Seth decided he liked the mysterious gentleman. "My dear—" he paused.

"Townes. Matthew Townes," the young man supplied.

"Thank you. My dear Mr. Townes, one could argue that *all* Buddhists are gnostics."

This got a laugh from the assembly. Seth laughed himself, although he was not sure why. Basil's assertion seemed confusing and confounding. Margaret didn't look too certain, either.

"Now I will tell you another great secret," Mr. Basil said, lowering his voice even further. Everyone leaned in, so much so that Seth wondered if they would pitch forward out of their seats. "There is no such thing as gnosticism." He leaned back, with a satisfied look on his face. He was clearly enjoying the looks on his listeners' faces.

"Come on," Ms. Singh objected. "You can't just drop something like that. You have to explain it."

"Mika, you will get nowhere on this path without patience—"

"I'm not sure I want anything to do with this path," she countered. She apparently realized she'd come across harsher than she had intended. She softened visibly. "I mean, that's why I'm here. You know, to find out about it."

"Of course. And there is nothing hidden that shall not be revealed...in time," Mr. Basil assured her. "When I say there is no such thing as gnosticism, what I mean is that, in the ancient world, no one said, 'I am a gnostic.' Gnosticism was not, as the kids say today, 'a thing.' Gnosticism is a categorical invention of 19th century academics. It is a term of convenience, an imaginary basket in which to put people and groups of people who shared... certain metaphysical assumptions."

"I don't understand," the older gentleman said, his hands clasped in front of him. In contrast to Mr. Basil, he was heavy set, with a balding head and great gray tufts for eyebrows.

"Mr...." Basil snapped his fingers.

"Jude Ash," the older gentleman said.

"Mr. Ash, a fine name," Basil said. "What do you do, Mr. Ash?"

"I'm a software engineer," he said.

"Of course you are! Every other person around here is a tech person, it seems."

Mr. Ash gave him a patient smile.

"Well," Basil continued. "What I mean to say is that Jewish gnostics did not think of themselves as gnostics, they simply thought of themselves as Jews. They were just Jews who knew some secrets that other Jews didn't. You see? And the same for Christians who knew some secrets, and Greeks who knew some secrets, and so on."

"But...were they the same secrets?" asked a young woman with bones so thin she seemed bird-like.

"In the greater part, yes, Ms. Shire." Mr. Basil's face shone in the soft light of the library. "The secrets had much in common with a very popular philosophical movement in the ancient world. Has everyone heard of Plato?"

Everyone nodded that they had. "Very good. Now what about Neoplatonism?" Some nodded, others frowned. "And Plotinus?" No heads were nodding now. Mr. Basil nodded. "You see, it's like this: In our own time we have scientific theories, such as quantum mechanics. Everyone has heard of quantum mechanics, surely."

Nods all around. "Excellent. Now how many of you have read a book interpreting the teachings of one religion or another in reference to quantum mechanics?"

"Oh, like *The Dancing Wu-Li Masters*?" Margaret asked.

"Yes, precisely, an examination of Buddhism in light of quantum theory." Mr. Basil nodded approvingly. "Does anyone have another?"

"*Quantum Christianity*?" a man who hadn't spoken yet suggested. The man was black, dressed in a suit and tie, and spoke with a distinctly African accent.

"Yes, Mr. Daniels. In fact, there are a number of books with that same name—five, at last count."

"Five?" Seth said out loud, without meaning to.

"Do you see what I mean?" Mr. Basil asked. "You can find Jewish books interpreting Judaism in light of quantum thought, as well as Hinduism, and so on. But 'Quantumism' isn't a religion —the writers of these books are simply members of their religious communities trying to understand their faith in light of this relatively new scientific understanding." He leaned back and let that sink in a bit. "Just so, the various so-called gnostics, each in their own religions, were trying to interpret their faith in terms of a philosophy that was all the rage—Neoplatonism."

There were nods all around. "And yet...not just Neoplatonism. There were certain teachings common to the gnostics of all religions not to be found in the writings of Plotinus and the other Neoplatonists. Further secrets unique to them."

"And what are those?" Miss Shire asked.

"Those...can only be revealed to those who elect to be bound to secrecy. They are, after all, *secrets*."

"So how do we...bind ourselves to this secrecy?" Mr. Ash asked.

Mr. Basil smiled. "Just keep coming back," he said. "When we think you are ready, you will be invited."

The next morning, Seth stumbled into the kitchen to discover the coffee was already made. He rubbed at his eyes and looked over at the table. Angie was dressed in a pajama top that was obviously several sizes too big for her. With one hand she held a spoon poised over a quart tub of nonfat plain Greek yogurt, and with the other hand she scrolled on her iPad. "Have you seen this horse who can do arithmetic?"

Seth poured himself a cup of the most blessed black liquid and lifted it to his nose, savoring the delicate toasted odor. "Horses can't do arithmetic," he said. "It's a trick. It has to be."

"Apple News doesn't think so. Says it's legit. Says if you tap out two with your foot, pause, and then do it again, 'Cashmere' the horse will stamp her hoof four times."

Seth heard the clack-clacking of Kush's nails on the hardwood floor as the dog sleepily wandered into the kitchen. "How about some breakfast, boy?" Seth asked. He scooped some kibble into the dog bowl. "What about if you stamp your foot three times and then seven?"

"Yep. She can add any two numbers under fourteen."

Seth put the bowl on the floor in front of Kush, who greedily tucked in. Seth collapsed into one of the chairs at the tiny kitchen table. "Okay, that's impressive. But can she do calculus?"

"Can you?" Angie asked without looking at him.

He didn't answer.

"Didn't think so. You're so judgmental of livestock."

"What?" Seth shook his head. "When have I ever said a disparaging thing about horses before, or about any farm animals for that matter?"

"At Jill's party last summer, you said you wouldn't fuck a goat."

"I did?"

"You *were* pretty wasted," Angie admitted.

"But that's not a condemnation of goats—"

"I'd take offense if I was a bearded-American."

"You lost me."

She looked up from her pad for the first time and motioned at her chin. "Beards. Goats have little beard-thingies."

"I thought those were called wattles," Seth objected.

"Turkeys have wattles. Goats have beards."

"What were we talking about?" Seth asked.

"You being anti-goat."

"I'm not anti-goat," Seth asserted. "I just don't find goats... sexually attractive."

"People ask me, 'Is Seth as vanilla as he seems?' and I always—"

"Literally no one has ever, ever asked you that!" Seth raised his voice a notch.

"Wanna bet?" Angie waggled one eyebrow at him.

Seth sighed. "Look...I have more important things to think about than sexual congress with barnyard animals...which is... gross, anyway."

"Snob."

"I am not a—"

"Speaking of animals, what about himself?" She pointed at Kush with her chin.

Seth sighed. "I haven't...I'm going to talk to Travis. Today."

"Uh-huh. I still can't believe you're going to do that."

"Do what?"

"Sell out the one creature who loves you with his whole furry being."

"I don't see what choice I have," Seth complained.

"Suit yourself," Angie shook her head. "So...where were you last night?"

"Oh. Uh..." Seth felt a momentary sense of conversational whiplash. When he adjusted, he wondered how much to say about the previous evening. "I, uh, got into a fight—"

"With who?"

"Just some guy on the bus."

Angie peered at his face. Then she leaned over the table and lifted his hair away from his forehead. Seth winced.

"Does that hurt?"

"Yeah."

She pressed on the side of the bruise.

"Does *that* hurt?"

"Yes, now stop it!"

"What was the fight about?"

"He was being a dick to this girl on the bus."

"So you followed him off the bus and said, 'Hey, my face is too pretty. Do me a favor and bust it up a bit'?"

"Not...exactly."

"Where was this?"

"On Aberdeen."

"What the hell were you doing in Willow Glen?"

"Remember, I was checking out those books on the Gnostics? I was on my way to a...a gnostic meeting. A study group... kind of."

"Are you serious?" Her forehead gathered in a frown over her still sleep-puffy eyes.

"Uh...yeah."

"How did you even find a group like that? Craig's List?"

"No, I bought...it was in one of those books. And the book was free."

"Free? Raven's Ink doesn't give books away for free."

"I know, that's what was strange. I think someone from the group just planted some books in random bookstores. It wasn't in their computer, so they just gave it to me."

"Huh."

"And inside, there was this card. It had an address and a time, and so I went."

"Without telling anyone. Geez, excellent plan. You're lucky you only got your face punched. They could have been serial killers and you'd be stuffed into a freezer right now."

Seth couldn't help laughing. "*That's* the Angie I know!"

She sniffed and smiled. "So what was it like?"

"It...there were about ten of us, I guess. And it wasn't so much a study group—I mean, we weren't focused on a text or anything —it was more of a lecture-slash-dialogue."

"Sounds boring."

"I guess it does. But it wasn't. It was...kind of fascinating."

"What was so fascinating?"

"I learned a lot about gnosticism."

"Oh, joy."

"And there was a lot about secrets."

"Did you *learn* any secrets?" she asked.

"Uh...no. They're secret. You have to...take an oath or something."

"Oh, jeez, please don't tell me you did that."

"No, but...it was cool. And so different from..."

"From your parents' church?"

"I was going to say, 'religion,' but okay, sure. And it felt...a little dangerous."

"Trust that feeling. Run the other way."

"No, you don't get it. It was fascinating."

"It sounds like a cult. Promise me you won't join a cult."

"If I think it's a cult, I won't join it. I promise."

"Why am I worried?"

"Come with me."

"Oh my god, no. The last thing I need is one more religious nutcase telling me I'm going to hell because I eat pussy."

"I get that," he said. "I really do. But...I didn't get that feeling from these guys."

"Remember this moment," she said. "So that when I say, 'I told you so,' you can tell me I was right."

Seth stared at the books on the shelf. Then he felt a hand on his shoulder. He jumped.

"Hey, little spooked, huh?" Travis edged him to the left with his shoulder and put a new stock of Clifford Simak novels on the shelf. Today he was wearing a denim jacket sporting a yellowed "Frodo Lives" button, along with the obligatory scarf. Travis peered over his glasses and spoke softly. "Dude, you okay?"

"Uh...yeah. Why do you ask?"

"I don't know, you seem...a little spacey. Rutherford asked me about it, and I covered for you, but she's on to you, man."

Seth pursed his lips and nodded. "I've been fucking up, big

time." He sighed. There was no use in putting off asking about Kush any longer. "Uh...Travis, can I ask you a weird question?"

"Sure. Anything, especially if it's weird."

"Can my—" A sharp pain shot through Seth's chest. He clutched at his chest and pressed on it.

"Are you okay?" Travis asked.

"Yeah, I just..." Seth kept pressing, but the pain did not diminish. He moved toward a chair and sat.

"Do you want me to call someone?" Travis asked.

"No, it's just...just a panic attack. I think."

"Oh. Dude. I'm sorry. Uh...what are you stressed about?"

Seth decided against the laundry list. He also gave in to the temptation to change the subject. "Do you think there's...this is going to sound stupid...secret stuff about the universe?"

"Well, that would be *most* of the stuff, wouldn't it?" Travis answered, without pausing a moment to think about it.

"What do you mean?" Seth asked, still pressing on his chest.

"I mean that what we don't know is *soooo* much bigger than what we do know. We have this little nugget of stuff we understand, and then there's everything else."

"Do you think there are people who *do* understand...well, some of it, but they're keeping it, you know...hush-hush?"

"I am one of those people," Travis said, standing up a little straighter.

"You are?"

"Oh yeah. I've done mushrooms, man. A lot. Heroic doses. I've seen things that I can't describe in words. And all of it is true."

"How do you know?" Seth asked. The pain was beginning to abate. He pounded on his chest, hoping to relax the muscles.

"Because I've *seen* it," Travis answered. "Seeing is believing."

"How do you know you weren't just hallucinating it?"

"Because it was all connected and it all made sense, you know?"

Seth was no stranger to mushrooms—even on pizza. But he had never seen what Travis was describing. But then he hadn't ever attempted a "heroic dose," and didn't particularly relish the idea, especially with his nerves. He knew he'd take the dose and spend the next eight hours panicking. "It was—" Travis put his hands on either side of his head and then pulled them apart in slow motion, making an exploding bomb noise.

"Uh...okay, that's cool. But I was wondering about, you know, secret societies," Seth pivoted.

"Like the Masons?"

"Sure."

Travis looked around and lowered his voice even further. "That's dangerous shit, bro. They run the world."

"I don't think that's true. I think it's a bunch of old men playing dress-up."

"You got that mixed up with the Catholic Church, man."

"They can *both* be old men playing dress-up," Seth reasoned. The pain was gone. He rubbed at the spot that had hurt.

Travis shrugged. "I guess so."

"Do you think the Masons know things that the general population doesn't?"

"We got a section on that," Travis said, pointing.

"I know, but if it was really secret stuff, it wouldn't be published, right?"

Travis scowled. "What's this all about?"

Seth bit his lip. He looked at his shoes. Then he made up his mind. "Last night I went to a study group. And...I think it's kind of a...gateway into a secret society."

"Dude! No way!"

"Yeah."

"Who is it? Who asked you?" Travis was bouncing on his toes.

"That's a secret," Seth said, narrowing one eye.

"Oh. Of course. That makes sense." He looked away, as if

spying something on a distant shore. Then he looked back at Seth. "Are you going to go back?"

Seth shrugged. "Probably. It was really interesting. Angie is against it, though."

"Angie is against everything."

"That. Is. True," Seth admitted.

"In my dream, that would be the best reason for going back. It's like the reverse of this dog I used to have, Rasputin. If Rasputin liked someone, that meant they were good people. If he didn't, I'd find a way out, you know? If Angie likes something, run the other way. And if she doesn't, it's probably healthy."

"I didn't know you hated her so much."

"I barely know her, dude. I only met her a couple times. But a body gets a sense, you know? She's an Eeyore."

"What?"

"We got this new personality typology book yesterday—it's in the psychology section. It categorizes people according to their Winnie-the-Pooh character. It's amazingly accurate! I understand myself soooo much better."

"Huh," Seth's eyes moved back and forth, unsure what to think of that. "I guess she *is* an Eeyore."

"See?"

"What are you?" Seth asked.

"I'm Pooh, man. And Northern Lights is my honey."

"Northern Lights?"

"It's a strain of weed, an indica-leaning hybrid. Most pleasurable. Couch-lock shit."

"Ah. And what am I?"

"You? You're a Piglet."

"What? Why am I a Piglet?"

"Because you ask a lot of questions and you're insecure."

"I am *not* insecure."

"Dude." He shook his head. "Don't try to play a playah."

"What?"

"I'm just giving it to you straight. And you did ask."

"Do you think I should do it?"

"Do what?"

"Join this...secret society. If they invite me, I mean."

"Oh! Right. Forgot what we were talking about. I copped a hit out back at break and I'm still accelerating." He leaned against an S-panel and crossed his arms. "Why is it so interesting? I mean... without revealing any secrets or anything."

"Sure. Uh...well, for one thing, there's got to be more to life than just *this*."

"Man, the odds against us evolving as we did is infinitesimally tiny. We, alone in the universe—so far as we know—have been set up for self-reflective consciousness. We got literature and music and Disneyland. We got orgasms, we got ice cream, we got weed. What more could you possibly want? Man, I am grateful to the universe for every fucking day in this pleasure-palace. Why you gotta be so cosmically greedy?"

"Cosmically—I'm not greedy. I'm just...it's not just about pleasure. Or I don't think it should be. It should be about something...I don't know, grander, more noble. I want to be part of something...important, you know? Something that matters."

"There is nothing more important or noble than a good bong hit and being doggie-style with a chick that is into you—preferably at the same time."

"I wouldn't know about that," Seth admitted.

"Chicks could be into you," Travis said. "You know, if you weren't so..."

"So what?" Seth scowled.

Travis shrugged. "Look man, I don't think it's anybody's business but yours. You wanna join a secret society? You just do fucking you."

"But what if they want me to take...oaths?"

"Well, that makes sense. You got to promise not to reveal the secrets if they're gonna tell them to you."

Seth looked at his shoes. "Yeah..."

"And they'll be brutal, too," Travis continued. "Like, 'If I reveal any of the secret shit, may you rip my beating heart out through my anus and throw me in a vat of rubbing alcohol.' That kind of thing."

"Where do you get this stuff?"

"Don't tell Rutherford, but I've been sleeping in the stock room. You wanna know what there is to do here? Read, mother-fucker. So I read all those Masonic books. I know what they make you do."

"These aren't the Masons."

"They might as well be."

"They aren't old men."

"Do they *smell* like old men?" Travis asked.

"You know what? Angie said exactly the same thing. You're starting to freak me out."

Travis ignored this. "It could be a glamour. You know, they look thirty, but inside they're wizened old farts that look like the picture of Dorian Gray. But they can't hide the fucking smell. And Old Spice is a dead giveaway. Old guys love that shit."

"I'll...keep my nose peeled."

"You do that."

"Thanks, Travis."

"I live to serve, man. And to surf. Did you see what I did there?" He punched Seth's arm.

"I saw it."

"Dude."

Seth swallowed. He had put the question off for too long. And if he thought about it, he'd just have another panic attack. Best to just blurt it out. "Can my dog come and live with you...for a while?"

Travis reared back. "Dude, what?"

"You know...my dog, Kush?"

"Yeah. He's a great dog."

"Can he...you know...stay at your place for a few months?"

"That's a big ask!" Travis complained.

"I know it is. I just...I don't know what else to do. My landlady says he has to be out...like, really soon. And I can't just take him to the pound, you know? He's my dog. I love him."

Travis nodded, his brow bunched with concern. "Dude, but..."

"Angie says I should move to a new place, but you know what housing is like right now. That's...going to take me some time." He decided not to mention the complications of moving with a raging case of OCD.

"Man, I don't know. I got my own landlord. And my roommate."

"Well, can you ask?"

Travis looked uncertain. He also looked worried. "Yeah, man. I'll ask."

LIQUIPEDIA
THE ANSWERBOT THAT GOES DOWN SMOOTH

WHAT IS GNOSTICISM?

Gnosticism refers to a diverse set of religious and philosophical beliefs that emerged in the ancient world, particularly during the first and second centuries CE. The term "gnosticism" comes from the Greek word "gnosis," meaning knowledge, as these systems of thought emphasize the acquisition of spiritual knowledge or insight as a means to attain salvation or liberation.

Most forms of Gnosticism posit a dualistic view of reality, postulating the existence of two distinct realms: the spiritual and the material. The spiritual realm is seen as the domain of the divine, characterized by light, goodness, and perfection, while the material realm is perceived as a flawed and imperfect creation. Gnostics believe that human beings are spiritual beings trapped within the material world, longing to escape its limitations and return to their divine origins.

Central to Gnostic teachings is the concept of *gnosis*, a direct experiential knowledge of the divine. Gnostics claim that this knowledge is not obtained through conventional intellectual or rational means but through personal revelation, inner enlightenment, or mystical experiences. They assert that this gnosis leads to salvation, liberation, or union with the divine and offers a deeper understanding of the human condition and the nature of reality.

Gnostic beliefs often incorporate elements from various religious traditions, including Judaism, Christianity, and Hellenistic philosophy. They frequently reinterpret biblical texts and incorporate mythological and allegorical narratives to convey their cosmological and metaphysical ideas. The figure of the demiurge, a lower deity responsible for the creation of the material world, is commonly present in Gnostic cosmologies.

Gnosticism faced significant opposition from orthodox religious authorities, particularly in early Christian groups, who viewed its ideas as heretical and incompatible with their established doctrines. Early Church fathers such as Irenaeus and Hippolytus actively criticized Gnosticism and sought to refute its teachings.

Although Gnosticism declined as an organized movement within mainstream religious traditions, its influence persisted and resurfaced throughout history, notably during the Renaissance, the Enlightenment, and in certain esoteric and mystical traditions. Today, Gnosticism continues to inspire spiritual seekers and scholars, fostering discussions on the nature of spirituality, knowledge, and the human quest for transcendence.

CHAPTER FOUR

Awaken your divinity to divinity
and strengthen your undefiled chosen souls.
—*Sermon of Zostrianos**

S eth knocked on the door of the Lodge, but this time Nazz did not greet him. No one greeted him. He tried the latch. It was open.

If it had been a home, he would not have entered. But as it seemed to be more of a public space, he tentatively pushed the door open and stepped inside. He heard footsteps in the hall and was sure he'd done the wrong thing. But then Mr. Basil's fiercely angular form appeared in shadow down the hall and waved him to come closer. "Ah! Mr. Seth. It's good that you are here. Do come in."

---

* The Sermon of Zostrianos: Nag Hammadi Codex VIII, 1; translated by Marvin Meyer, published in *The Gnostic Bible* (Boston, MA: Shambhala Publications, 2009).

Seth breathed a sigh of relief and set off down the hallway toward Mr. Basil. The older man disappeared into a doorway. Seth noted which one and followed him. He entered a warm, wood-lined study filled with bookshelves and ancient *objets d'art*. A ceremonial sword hung over a blazing fireplace; a statue of some Egyptian goddess stood sentry over a large wood-and-leather desk.

"Please have a seat," Mr. Basil said. "We haven't much time before tonight's study, but I hoped I'd get a chance to know you." He waved Seth toward two comfortable leather armchairs on either side of the fireplace. Seth sat in one, while Mr. Basil went to a sideboard and poured an amber liquid from a cut glass decanter. "Scotch? It's not a single-malt, I'm afraid, but it *is* a fine blend."

"Ah...sure." He wanted to add, "what the hell," but decided to be cautious. Mr. Basil set a tumbler in front of him. He sniffed at the scotch, and the sweet, smoky scent burned his nostrils. He took a sip, and the taste of butterscotch coated his tongue. It was heavenly.

"I'm so glad to see you back, Mr. Seth," Basil sat in the chair opposite him and gave him a warm smile.

"My last name is St. John," Seth said.

"Mr. St. John, then."

Seth grimaced slightly. Mr. St. John was his father, but he didn't renew his objection.

"What an auspicious name," Mr. Basil noted. "Of all of the evangelists, St. John is the most gnostic."

"Oh?" That was news. John had been the favorite gospel at his childhood church. He remembered them handing out tiny, powder-blue faux-leather editions of John's gospel. But he didn't remember anything gnostic about it. But then he realized he probably wouldn't know a gnostic teaching if it hit him in the face. He decided he had nothing to lose by coming clean about that. "I...I think I'm not sure what a gnostic teaching *is*."

"In good time, all in good time," Mr. Basil said. "Before we share any secrets, we...well, you need to carefully discern whether you want to *take on* the burden of our secrets."

"Burden?" Seth asked.

"Indeed. A very grave burden, and not one to be assumed lightly."

Seth's face fell into a scowl. His mind flashed on his situation with Kush. He wasn't sure he needed any more burdens. He had begun thinking of the gnostic group as more of an escape. "How so?"

"My dear boy, if and when you receive the treasure that we so solemnly protect...nothing will be the same. Everything...and I do mean *everything*...will change."

Seth's lips pursed. He didn't know if that sounded like a very, very good thing...or not.

Mr. Basil smiled then. "And we, of course, need to discern whether we can trust you with them."

"That...makes sense."

"And getting to know someone takes some time."

"Sure."

"Seth, what is it you want from your life?" Mr. Basil leaned forward in his chair, hands pressed together. What seemed strange to Seth was that this older gentleman seemed genuinely interested in what he had to say. He had his full attention. And he seemed to *care*. Seth found it appealing, unusual, and unsettling.

"I...uh...I guess I've never really thought about it. I'd like to get to a place where I'm not struggling to pay the bills every month. Poverty sucks."

"What do you do for a living?"

"I work at a bookstore."

"And what do you do when you're not at work?"

"I...uh..." Seth felt at a loss. What should he say? *I walk my dog? I watch movies with my militant lesbian best friend?* "...I hang out in other bookstores?" he finally offered. It sounded lame. *Note to self,* he thought, *get a life.*

Mr. Basil laughed. "Oh my, a man after my own heart." He looked Seth in the eyes. "Let us say you were living a bit more comfortably than you are. What then? What would make your life...*meaningful?*"

Seth's brow furrowed. He wanted to say, *I was hoping you could tell me,* but he didn't. Mr. Basil leaned back, and Seth instantly wished he had a ready answer. Surely this man had little time for an unreflective dolt.

"Don't answer just yet," Mr. Basil said. "Instead, I invite you to close your eyes and consult your heart. Ask your higher wisdom. What does she say?"

She? It was a strange request, but Seth did not object. Instead, he did as he was bid. He closed his eyes and listened. His mind was flailing, fearing that whatever this conversation was about, he was failing the test. He willed himself to be quiet. One moment he had absolutely no idea what would make his life meaningful. And then the next moment, he knew.

His eyes snapped open and a smile spread across his face.

"Ah," Mr. Basil said. "Wisdom has spoken." He grinned a strange, knowing grin. "Do tell, Mr. St. John. What would make your life meaningful?"

"The other day I met my best friend for coffee. And she had to pay. I work my ass off, and I'm still behind on my rent. And my landlady is making me rehome my dog. I want to move, but...that takes money and...resources I don't have. It isn't fair."

"No, indeed it is not." Mr. Basil's face was all compassion.

Seth's eyes took on a faraway look as he went deeper. "Plus...I feel like religion has totally fucked up my life. My parents raised me in this abusive, fundamentalist church that...I'm afraid of everything."

Mr. Basil nodded.

"My friend Angie, I've seen people spit on her and her girl-friend...former girlfriend now, I guess. But she's the kindest, smartest, most loyal friend a person could have, and it makes my blood boil."

"Yessss." Mr. Basil's grin turned into something else, something darker.

"The world is going crazy, and all our leaders can do is play petty political games, as if it was us-versus-them, instead of just us."

Mr. Basil closed his eyes, taking it in. Silence hung for several long moments. Mr. Basil opened his eyes again, leaned forward, and touched Seth on the hand. "So my boy, tell me, what is it you *want?*"

"I know that life is short. I...I haven't got long upon this earth, you know, when you consider how old the world is. So with the little bit of time I have...I want to do something that *matters.*"

Mr. Basil leaned back into his chair and steepled his fingers. "Ah. Now I know that you are in the right place."

"I am?"

"Oh, yes. You see...well, I'll tell you what. You just told me one of your deepest secrets. It is only fair that I tell you one of ours, eh?"

Seth blinked and nodded. "Okay."

"Gnosticism is, at its heart, a movement of resistance."

"Resistance?"

"Indeed."

"Resistance against...what?"

"Against the tyrants who believe it is their right—or perhaps their duty—to rule us; to tell us how to live; to tell us whom we should love—and whom we should not; to keep us from flourishing; to keep us impoverished; to keep us subservient and compliant; to enforce their petty moralities; to threaten us with imprisonment and other various hells if we do not comply.

Tyrants only rule because we fear them. Tyrants only rule because we let them, you see?"

A shudder ran down Seth's spine. "Yeah. I get that."

"The tyrannical church you grew up in probably told you that you were saved because a monstrous deity performed a violent act of child abuse against his own offspring, requiring him to be savagely murdered in order to save all of us from...what? From *himself.*"

Seth's eyes grew wide. He'd never heard it put so starkly, but that was exactly what he had been taught. He felt suddenly cold.

"But we are gnostics because we are saved, not by the blood of a slaughtered child—beastly!—but by knowledge...by wisdom...by *knowing.*"

"By knowing what?"

"Ah...well. The specifics will be for another time. But in general...in part, simply by knowing that the tyrants *are* tyrants. And that they are *beatable.*"

"I like the sound of that."

"Of course you do, my boy. *You* are one of *us.*"

Angie poured herself a cup of coffee. She yawned. "Why do I only see you at breakfast?"

"The way you scratch your ass is soooo sexy," Seth said. He was sitting at the table, scrolling through Facebook on his phone.

"Glad to hear it, because it's all you're going to get," she said. She yawned again. She sank heavily into the other chair across from him. "Did you hang out at your cult last night?"

"It's not a cult," he said.

"Define cult," she insisted.

He blinked. Kush pushed his bowl around with his nose. It still had kibble in it.

"It's a cult," she said. "Soon you're going to be wearing saffron and dancing in airports."

"I don't think it's dangerous like that. It doesn't seem...religious. It's more...occult."

"The occult isn't religious?" she asked. "I'm a witch. I know from occult. It's all *about* religion. I mean, it's *alternative* religion, but still religion."

"I haven't heard anything like that. It's more about...secrets."

"I'm going to make a bet with you," she said.

"Uh...what kind of bet?" he asked.

"When they finally tell you one of those secrets...it's going to be religious."

"You're on," he said. He took a sip of coffee and thought a moment. "Uh...what if the secret is anti-religious?"

"Define 'anti-religious,'" she insisted.

"Why are you so hung up on definitions?" he asked.

"Because if we don't have shared definitions, how do we even know what we're talking about?" she answered.

"What if it's actively *against* religion?"

"What? Like a club for compulsively secretive atheists?"

"Sure."

"As long as they're not espousing a religious system of their own, then you win."

"Okay," he said.

"Okay," she said. She gulped at her coffee.

"Doesn't that burn?" he asked. "It's way hot."

"Pain wakes me up. And the scar tissue makes my voice husky, which the girls like. Makes me sound like a three-pack-a-day smoker."

"There is nothing sexier than that," he agreed.

"Don't knock it." She cocked her head. "So...have you found a home for Kush?"

Seth sighed. He watched as Kush gave up on his bowl

and ambled over to the table, curling up underneath it, his head resting heavily on Seth's foot. "I talked to Travis about him."

"And?"

Seth shrugged. "He said he'd talk to his roommate."

"You should nudge him. Travis strikes me as a conflict avoider. You have to stay on top of him."

"You don't even know Travis," Seth objected.

"I know Travis' *type*," Angie countered. "Surfer-dude, living wild and free in the moment, allergic to responsibility.

"Yeah, okay, that's Travis."

"Text him. Text him every morning and every evening until you get an answer."

"I don't want to annoy him," Seth said.

"Jesus, you are such a people-pleaser. Do I worry about whether I annoy people?"

After a second of silence, they both laughed. The release felt good.

"Hey," Angie said, after the moment had passed. "How does Becky feel about you becoming an occultist?"

Seth sat upright. "Becky?"

"You remember—brown hair, freckles, dimpled chin, a little dumpy—"

"Hey—"

"I didn't say she wasn't cute, but you know...not possessed of *conventional* attractiveness."

"What are you trying to say?" he asked. "Are you insulting my girlfriend?"

"Is that what she is? I mean, officially?"

He moved his head back and forth. "Well, not officially. That was an aspirational statement."

"I thought so. So as you're trying to woo Miss Tubby, how is she going to feel about you becoming an occultist? You know that's a straight shot to asthma and madness, right? Not to mention consumption."

"Queen Victoria is *not* on the throne," Seth fired back. "We have antibiotics now."

She ignored him. "Have you even discussed this with her?"

He stared at his cup. "I haven't really seen her since..."

"You're so in love with this group that you forgot about her!"

"That's not true!" he objected.

"It's totally true," she returned. She affected an eerie voice, "The spirits tell me...there is no future in this relationship."

"Fuck you," he said.

"In your dreams, breeder," she said.

"Who are you calling a breeder? Just because I'm not queer doesn't mean I'm a breeder."

"We'll see. In five years you'll have little occultists running around putting hexes on people. And I'll be twenty dollars richer."

"Not gonna happen."

"You wanna bet on that too?"

"Sure."

"No way," she said. "You're in too deep already."

"I made some oatmeal," Seth said, pointing to the pan.

"Oh joy. Mush."

"I'm just saying, you are welcome to it if you want it."

She sighed. "Thanks." She took another gulp of her coffee. "Hey, what time are you off today?"

"Three."

"Want to go for a hike after? Kush would love it."

"Uh..." he squirmed in his seat.

"What? What is it you don't want to tell me?" Angie narrowed one eye.

"Iyuh...I have an appointment."

"With the fine people at your new cult?"

"Uh...yeah."

"Goddam it, Seth. I'm scared for you."

"Don't be," he said, trying to sound casual.

"Fuck that. I am." She glowered at him. "Are they going to totally take over your life?"

"No—"

"It's a good thing you don't have a penny to your name, because at least they can't get that."

"You don't know anything about them."

She leaned over the little table until he could feel her breath. "Newsflash, genius: neither do you."

"What was she thinking?" Terrence Basil asked. He put a dab of cream in his tea and stirred it. Then he leaned back in his leather chair.

"I think you underestimate him," Sherry Teasdale said, setting her teacup and saucer aside. "He's clever...and sensitive."

"We have a lot riding on this," Dr. Joshua Robinson said. He was much more portly than Basil and with a great deal less hair. He seemed uncomfortable in his own clothes. "This may be our only chance at an intercession before...before we arrive. Do we really want it riding on him? He's an unknown quantity."

"He's not unknown to *her*," Dr. Teasdale noted. "And he's less and less unknown to us. I think we need to give him a chance."

"I think it boils down to one thing—who's in charge here?" Basil said, taking a sip. It was too hot, and he made a face. At this temperature the cream was likely to curdle. Inwardly he cursed Nazz for his carelessness.

"Whatever can you mean?" Robinson asked. "It is quite clear that *you* are."

"Not at all," Basil countered. "I'm talking about *her*. She's in charge, ultimately. Do we trust her? That's the question we have to answer. If we don't...then what are we doing here? If we do, then who are we to question her?"

Robinson played with his spoon, as if he were searching his tea for trouble.

Teasdale gave a grave nod. "That's it. That's it exactly," she said. "Lady Wisdom is our mother, and she knows best."

"I wish I shared your...blind faith."

"My dear Joshua," Teasdale smiled. "Listen to yourself. Faith isn't blind, cynicism is."

"Who are you calling cynical?"

"Who is questioning our mother?" She narrowed one eye at him. "And why?"

"Don't read some nefarious plot into this, Sherry. It's just like you."

"What's that supposed to mean?" She turned in her armchair to fully face him.

"It means you see conspiracies around every corner."

"'Just because you're paranoid doesn't mean they aren't after you,'" Teasdale quoted.

Robinson opened his mouth to protest but Basil held his hand up. "No, Joshua. She's right. It's no good accusing her of having an overactive imagination. We all know Sherry has a good head on her shoulders. This is appropriate caution—"

"Accusing me of...oh, I don't know what...something rotten, you know...you call that appropriate?"

"I'm saying we do well to ask questions of ourselves, of our own motives, of our perceptions." Basil moved his hand to indicate the room, or perhaps more. "Everything is *maya*, is it not? We would be fooling ourselves not to be discerning."

"Yes, but we shouldn't run around accusing each other, half-cocked."

"I wasn't accusing you of anything, Joshua. I was only making an observation. I find your sudden fit of uncertainty...

unusual. Why isn't it proper to ask about it? Our lives are at stake here."

"We are the triumvirate in this place," Robinson's face had turned red. "We must trust each other."

"And that trust doesn't extend to her?" Teasdale pointed at the ceiling.

Robinson sighed and looked to Basil, as if for a lifeline. "I give up."

Basil smiled, reached over and patted Robinson's knee. "Let us not fall out. Our enemies would like nothing more. We have a higher purpose to pursue, and shooting each other in some kind of Mexican standoff will not help us."

"I'm pretty sure that phrase is considered racist nowadays," Teasdale noted.

"Oh, and now she's the culture police, too," Robinson said to no one in particular.

Basil clapped his hands as if to break some kind of spell, and then rubbed them together. "Friends, no more of this. We are under her care and protection, and we live to serve her. If she has chosen Mr. St. John, then who are we to quibble? Our only duty is to cultivate him."

"You make him sound like an asset," Robinson said, "like some kind of operative."

"Isn't he?" Teasdale asked.

"No, he bloody well is not," Robinson countered. "Has he taken an oath? Does he know...anything? No. And until he does, he is a prospect, nothing more."

"We need to treat him as something more than that," Teasdale said, her voice low and intentionally calm.

"And why is that?" Robinson almost spat.

"Because unlike every other prospect we have, she has her hand on him." Teasdale said this with gravity, as if it could not be disputed.

"Indeed she does," Basil agreed. "We must encourage him."

"But why?" Robinson asked. "What is so special about him?"

Basil shrugged. "I don't know. Maybe nothing. Maybe she just likes the cut of his jib—"

"Cut of his jib!" Robinson almost howled, then sank into his seat chuckling.

Teasdale gave Robinson a genuine smile at this. "I know him best, and I don't know that either. But...we are bound to find out."

"I sincerely hope we find out in time," Robinson growled.

Seth stepped down from the bus, grateful that there had been no unpleasant incidents in transit this time. He looked up at the Lodge house a block and a half away and felt his stomach wrenched by some unknown force. He knew he was feeling emotions, he just didn't know what they were. Despite giving them no orders, his feet began to move toward the Lodge as if of their own volition, or perhaps in obedience to some higher will, or perhaps destiny. He didn't know. He only knew that the house seemed to look more forbidding than when he first saw it, less like a classic Bay Area Victorian and more like the Munsters' mansion. He swallowed and let his feet carry him toward it.

As he walked, he thought. He heard Angie's voice in his head, saying, *When they finally tell you one of those secrets...it's going to be religious.* Was he running away from one form of fundamentalism only to take refuge in another? If he were, would that not be the height of stupidity? Shouldn't he know better?

But the problem was, it didn't feel the same as the religion of his childhood. *You're just fooling yourself,* the voice in his head said, sounding an awful lot like Angie. *Religion is religion. It just feels different because the window dressing is different. It feels exotic. But it's out of the frying pan and into the fire. You're escaping from one prison and running straight into another because that's the only place you feel safe.*

Of course Angie had not said those words to him, but it was exactly the dressing down he imagined...and feared. He tried to shake it from his mind, but he couldn't. *Soon you're going to be wearing saffron and dancing in airports.* Now *that* was Angie. But he doubted that assertion very much. For one thing, he hadn't seen anyone in the Lodge wearing saffron. *Vests, though...maybe,* he thought.

He shook his head to clear it. When he looked up again, the Lodge house was looming over him in all its gothic glory. He felt like there were lead weights tied to his shoes as he climbed the stairs to the broad wooden porch. He stood before the door and paused. Would Mr. Basil be here? Probably, he reasoned. He'd been there both of the other times he had visited. And Nazz? Who knew?

He didn't know what to make of either of them. Mr. Basil seemed mysterious, but somehow trustworthy. Nazz seemed simple, but with a devious undercurrent that made Seth suspicious.

He raised his hand to knock on the door, but as he did so, he heard Mr. Basil's voice in his head, saying, *My dear boy, if and when you receive the treasure that we so solemnly protect...nothing will be the same. Everything...and I do mean* everything...*will change.*

His mind flashed to Kush. Finding him a new home was not a change he wanted. And things were not going well at work. Things were not going well with Angie. Things were not going well with Becky. Things were not going well with his mother. His anxiety and OCD were off the chart. And he had no money and wouldn't until payday a week hence. His stomach rumbled as he'd not had time to boil up some ramen before it was time to leave. "How is it possible that I suck at absolutely everything so fucking hard?" he asked the door out loud.

He very much wanted things to change. He wanted *everything* to change. But the idea that everything might change also terrified him. *My life is unsettled enough as it is,* he thought. *The last thing I need is cancerous, rapid change eating every last shred of stability in my life.* The problem with change—or at least, with *this* kind of change—was that a person was at the mercy of whatever forces are "out there"—whatever that means. He was okay with change, so long as he had control over it. But he knew he didn't. And he knew he couldn't. That was what made it so, so dangerous.

He noticed that his hand was shaking, poised in a fist about an inch from the door. Slowly, he lowered it, cradling it in his other hand. Then he turned and descended the steps. *I feel faint,* he said to himself, but he knew it was an excuse. But more than anything he wanted to get home and boil up some ramen. Then he wanted to get into bed, curl up with his dog, and pull the covers over his head. Anything, just so long as he didn't have to hear any wild, troubling, uncontrollable secrets.

Just as he turned and began to walk back toward the bus stop, his phone buzzed. He pulled it out and checked the screen. There was a message from Travis: *Okay. Kush can come live with us.*

"Sloane!"

Keira poked her head into her captain's office. "Yes, boss?"

He gestured at something on his desk. "What's this?"

"What, the donut? Empty calories." She gave him an exaggerated frown.

"Not the donut, smart-ass." He picked up a folder and shook it at her. "This!"

She entered his office and closed the door behind her. She held her hand out for the folder and waited until he passed it to her. She opened it and ran her eyes over it. Then she snapped it closed again and handed it back. "That's my report."

"That's your report," he repeated.

"Yes. You asked me to do reconnaissance on the house at 616 Aberdeen. I did what you asked, and that's my report."

"Sit down," he ordered. She gave him a real frown that time, but sat without any audible complaint. He opened the file again and turned a page. "Says here you assaulted a civilian. Could that be right?"

"That's not what it says," she answered. "I wrote it, so I should know."

"You hit him in the kidneys with a stick," Captain Schenck clarified.

"He was assaulting another civilian," she answered.

"Did you ever think of drawing your service weapon and saying something like, oh, I don't know, *back the fuck off?*"

"I would have blown my cover," Keira answered.

"You were blocks away from the target," Schenck countered.

"Yes, but the guy I was defending was also going to the same place."

Schenck's brow furrowed. "Did you know that then?"

Keira squirmed in her seat and looked at the desk. "Uh...no. But it was a good thing I...you know, trusted my instincts or I would have been busted."

"Uh-huh." Schenck fixed her with an eye that could have pierced Kevlar. "How bad did you hurt him?"

"Not," she said.

"I asked Furrow to run down hospital reports, and he turned up an ER log of renal trauma. We don't know who, of course, HIPAA rules and all that bullshit. But a bruised kidney is nothing to sneeze at."

"So he'll be peeing blood for a couple of weeks," Keira shrugged. "I'd call that justice."

"Oh, you would?"

Keira detected a slight smile on her captain's face, and she felt her shoulders relax—a bit.

"So *after* you assaulted a man's kidneys with a stick, you went to the house at..." he glanced at the report again. "...616 Aberdeen?"

"Yes."

"And what did you find?"

"It's all in the report," Keira said, her voice betraying a bit more irritation than she'd intended.

"But I want to hear it from you directly." He gave her a mock-sneer. "Humor me."

Her impulse was to roll her eyes, but she caught herself in time. "It was a lecture. Just a lecture. Kind of academic."

"Political?"

"Not so as you'd notice. It was kind of historical, kind of philosophical, kind of religious. Do you know what it reminded me of? Those videos with Joseph Campbell that Bill Moyer did back in the 1980s."

"You weren't even born in the 1980s."

"My grandma was an old hippie, total New Age junkie," Keira said. "She used to play the VHS tapes of those interviews on a loop."

"Believe it or not, I'm old enough to remember those."

"Oh, I believe it," she said, before she could stop herself.

"Is it a cult?" he asked.

"I don't know. I didn't get that vibe. But so what if it is? It's not illegal to join a cult."

"Not as long as the cult stays on this side of the law," Schenck agreed. "But they have a tendency to dance on the edge of the law."

"I didn't get any red flags," Keira summed up. "In fact, I thought it was pretty fascinating. If I had an actual life, I might find myself going back for another lecture or two."

"What's stopping you?"

"When is the last time you went to church?" Keira asked him.

"My piety is none of your goddam business," Schenck answered.

"It's not about piety, it's about downtime, bandwidth."

Schenck grunted. "Who's this St. John kid?"

"No one important, just someone who happened to be in the wrong place at the wrong time. He stuck up for a girl on the bus, whom the aforementioned bully was hitting on. He followed Mr. St. John and was assaulting him...until I intervened."

"What do you know about him?"

"I ran the usual. No record of any kind. He works at a bookstore. Father is deceased. Lives with a girl, but she's not on the lease. Not sure if they're romantically involved or not. Probably."

"And he followed you to the meeting?"

"We walked together to the meeting," Keira corrected him.

"He a member of this...whatever it is?"

"No, at least I don't think so. It was his first time there, too."

"How did he hear about it?"

"He said something about a card—I don't know more than that."

"Why not?"

Keira shrugged. "I didn't get a chance to ask."

Schenck grumbled, but finally closed the folder. "Okay."

"Okay?"

"Yeah. Okay. What do you want from me?" Schenck asked.

Keira just stared at him.

"You got work to do?" he asked her.

Without another word, she stood up and left, leaving the door swinging open.

S eth stopped in front of the house where Travis rented a room. A young man Seth didn't recognize was cutting the grass with a quiet, old-fashioned push-mower, sweat staining his gray t-shirt. *That must be Travis' roommate,* he thought. Seth looked down at Kush, panting beside him. The dog was excited, if a little winded, clearly enjoying the long walk.

Seth felt his throat swell, and his jaw hurt from grinding his teeth. He forced his jaw to relax and squatted, taking Kush's head in his hands and ruffling the loose skin of his neck. "I'm really sorry about this, boy."

Kush didn't look at him. There were too many other fascinating things in this unfamiliar neighborhood. The green scent of cut grass wafted over them.

"This is just temporary. In a couple of months, when things are...better...I'll get us a new place. I promise."

Kush laid down on the sidewalk, continuing to pant. Seth stroked his fur and swallowed back on his emotion. He wiped the wetness from his eye with the back of his hand.

Out of the corner of his eye, he saw a shadow approach. Looking up, he saw Travis' roommate. His head was blocking the sun, forming a halo around him, as if to say, *here is the savior coming just in time to bring salvation.* "This must be Kush," he said, removing his work gloves and stuffing them in his back pocket.

Seth swallowed hard and stood. "Hi," he offered his hand. "I'm Seth."

"Bruce," the man said. "I'm Travis' roomy."

"So good to meet you," Seth said. It didn't ring too false.

Kush got to his feet, tail pumping, and stuck his nose directly into Bruce's crotch. He didn't seem to mind. He bent and rubbed Kush's ears. "I wish it were under better circumstances," Bruce said. "Travis told me what was going on for you, and...dude, I'm really sorry."

"Thanks," Seth said. He didn't know what else to say. But then he knew. "I...I'm really grateful to you for...taking him in. I mean, he's not your dog, your responsibility, and dogs are a lot of trouble—"

Bruce waved the comment away. "I've wanted a dog for a long time. This is a good chance to enjoy living with one with low commitment. And he's already house-broken and pretty chill, from what I hear."

"Oh, yeah. He's a couch-potato. He *will* lick you to death, though."

"I love doggie kisses!" Bruce said.

"You say that now..." Seth said, smiling despite himself.

"No, it's cool. It really is."

"Travis has my number. So if you need anything, and I mean *anything*, just call me, day or night. And if he needs to go to the vet, I'll pay for it."

"That's a good deal," Bruce said. "Hey, let me go get Travis, okay?"

"Yeah."

Seth and Kush watched Bruce walk into the house. A moment later he returned, with Travis behind him. "My dude!" Travis said, but Seth wasn't sure if he were referring to himself or to Kush. A moment later it became clear: Travis knelt and buried his face in Kush's fur, rubbing his fingers up and down the dog's sides. After about twenty seconds of this, he stood and embraced Seth.

"Thanks so much for doing this," Seth said into Travis' shoulder.

"Glad to help, dude."

"I owe you one."

"Yes, you do. Which I will delight in cashing in one day."

Seth laughed. It helped. He handed the leash to Travis. Then, hands free, he reached into his back pocket and pulled out his wallet. He took out three twenty-dollar bills and handed them to Travis.

"What's this for?"

"Kibble," Seth said.

"I figured we'd just feed him top ramen. I mean, that's what we eat."

Seth scowled at him.

"Just yanking your chain, dude!" Travis said, punching his arm. "What kind?"

"Science Diet Adult."

Travis whistled. "The fancy stuff. Okay, I'll walk down now and pick some up."

"And let me know how much you need. I'm good for it," Seth added.

"Okay, dude. Whatever."

Seth nodded. Then he looked down at his dog. His lower lip began to shake and fresh water came to his eyes. He knelt again, wrapped his arms around the dog, and laid his head on his withers. "I love you, boy." Something must have made it through, because when he pulled back, Kush licked the salt off his face.

Without another word, Seth stood, turned, and walked back home alone.

LIQUIPEDIA
THE ANSWERBOT THAT GOES DOWN SMOOTH

WHY DID CALIFORNIA SECEDE FROM THE UNITED STATES?

In 2038 the former state of California declared itself a sovereign nation, seceding from the United States of America. The reasons for this are varied, complex, and subject to some controversy, but nearly all historians agree that had it not been for the havoc caused by the Codex Pandemic, California would still be a member state of the USA.

When the Codex Pandemic struck in 2033, member states of the USA responded in very different ways. States that favored conservative politics ("Republican" or "red" states) tended toward *laissez-faire* policies when it came to confronting the Codex virus, with Florida and Alabama imposing no restrictions on their populations, nor even issuing advisories. Most other "red" states offered some sort of guidance, with Georgia and North Carolina imposing mask mandates after two years of unrestricted policies proved devastating to the population. No red states imposed vaccine mandates.

By contrast, states that favored progressive politics ("Democrat" or "blue" states) embraced restrictive policies toward the virus. Within one month of the initial announcement about the Codex virus, the Western block of Washington, Oregon, and California ordered absolute quarantines and closed their borders to all travel, allowing residents of other states and countries passage out of the states, but allowing none in. Mask mandates for all those who had to be outside their homes in public places soon followed, as did vaccine mandates. State health departments went door to door with the vaccine, accompanied by law enforcement. In California, all that refused were jailed and fined $1000 per day until they complied.

Other states accused California of "draconian measures," and when a federal court ruled its policies unconstitutional, California employed delaying tactics, moving the locus of the legal battle in a creeping arc toward the Supreme Court. When the Supreme Court ruled against California in the fifth year of the pandemic, the state declared itself a sovereign nation.

Though many decried California's actions, and many threatened war, the devastations of the pandemic rendered any kind of military response impossible. Due to the transmissibility and deadly nature of the virus, protesting states soon lost interest in California's intransigence, preferring to focus on their own internal crises.

CHAPTER FIVE

They nailed Jesus to a tree,
and he became the fruit of the Father's knowledge.
However, this fruit didn't cause
destruction when it was eaten.
Those who ate it were given the joy of discovery.
He discovered them in himself
and they discovered him in themselves.
—*Gospel of Truth**

"I'm glad you called," Becky said. "I was afraid you wouldn't."

Seth felt a stab of guilt. "No, I...It's just...there's a lot going on right now."

Becky had been a bit early, and he had still been getting

---

* Adapted from The Gospel of Truth: Nag Hammadi Codex I, translated by Mark M. Mattison, published in *The Gospel of Truth: The Mystical Gospel* (2018).

dressed. Now he had his sweatshirt tied around his waist, and his keys were in his pocket. He knew he would need to start his visual surveillance of the apartment, and he would need to focus. A feeling of dread rose up the back of his neck at the mere thought of it, and he realized that he was procrastinating.

"Yeah. The place feels empty without Kush here," Becky said. "I'm so sorry about that." She sat on the couch. Seth noticed that there was a broken chip on the couch, a fraction of a second before she sat down on it. Her pants were white. The chip had not been his, and he hoped it was not coated in nacho cheese dust. If Kush had been here, that chip would have been gone long ago.

"Yeah," Seth said. "I'm trying not to think about him, to stay busy."

"You want to talk about it?" Becky asked.

"No, I'll just..." He didn't want to say *break down and cry*, so he didn't. He looked at his hands. "I...uh...I've been going to those Lodge meetings."

Becky brightened. "Good. Do you think I might be able to come sometime?"

"Only if you want Angie bitching at you about it 24/7."

"I don't live with Angie," Becky pointed out.

"Good point. Besides, I...I don't know if I'm going to go back."

"Oh?" Becky looked concerned. "Why not?"

Seth shrugged. "It is...a little weird. And maybe Angie's right. I've been burned by religion pretty bad."

"I thought you said this wasn't religious."

"It doesn't *feel* religious," Seth affirmed. "But...what if she's right?"

"You know, there's religion and there's *religion*," Becky said.

Seth frowned. "What does that mean?"

"I mean, like everything else, it's a neutral thing that can be used for good or evil. You know, like alcohol or guns, or...even relationships."

Seth suspected there was a hidden message in there somewhere, but Becky started speaking again before he could find it.

"There's probably both healthy religion and harmful religion. I mean, it's just people, right? You have good bosses and bad bosses, good leaders and bad leaders, good communities and toxic communities. Why should it be any different with religion?"

It was a thought that had never really occurred to Seth. He had always equated religion with the brand he had grown up with. He knew there were other brands, but only now did he recognize that he might have simply been painting them with the same brush. "Huh," was all he said. His head was swimming.

"Look at me. I grew up in church. It didn't stick, but it didn't hurt me, either. It was just kind of...blah."

"What church?"

"Congregational, I think? We had a woman pastor. She was awesome. But I didn't really see what it had to do with my life."

"A woman pastor?" Seth said. He had never seen one of those and didn't realize it was possible.

"She was a lesbian, too."

Seth blinked. A woman pastor seemed odd, but a lesbian pastor seemed unthinkable. He had a hard time conceiving of a church like that. "Was she...you know...secretive about that?"

"Oh, no. Her partner came to church and everything. She was a monster at the mahjong."

Seth wasn't sure how to process that. Maybe Becky was right. Maybe there were different kinds of religion. And maybe the study group was...one of the good ones? He felt a tug of hope. But hope was an alien feeling, and he warned himself against it.

"Hey, we better get going, or the sun will be down before we get to the pond," Becky urged. They had planned to take a sunset walk around Cottonwood Lake at the Hellyer County Park, and she was right. A glance out the window revealed that the sun was lower than he'd thought.

"Okay, uh..." he said, rubbing his palms on his jeans. "You know how hard it is for me to leave the apartment, right?"

"Yeah. Do you want me to check everything for you again?" Becky offered.

"No, no," Seth held his hands up. "My therapist said I'm not allowed."

"Not allowed to what?" Beck asked.

"Not allowed to...pass the buck...the responsibility."

"Oh." Becky nodded. "Is that...good?"

"I don't know. But I'm trying to follow directions."

"Okay. How can I help?"

"Well, this is all about concentration for me. I can't be distracted. So...if you could, like, sit patiently and not say anything to me until I'm done?"

"Oh." Becky looked concerned, like she wasn't sure whether to be offended by that or not. "Okay."

Seth began by going to the bathroom to check the candle, but felt her eyes boring into the back of his head. He stopped, looked at his shoes, shook out his hands, and breathed deeply.

"What's wrong?" Becky asked.

"Uh...could you...not look at me?" Seth asked.

"Not...*look* at you?" Becky raised one eyebrow.

"You know, just...check your phone or something?"

"Okaaayyy," Becky said, pulling her phone from her back pocket.

Seth breathed several more times, then opened his eyes and started his surveillance again. He looked at the candle—but did not touch it. Then he went into the bedroom and looked at the candle there. Then he went into the kitchen and looked at the stove. He pulled his own camera from his pocket and took a picture of the knobs. Then he went to the door. "Okay," he said, "Let's go. Quickly."

Becky leaped from the couch and raced to the door. She was

not a petite young woman, and her footsteps seemed more like stompings—but Seth ignored that. He opened the door for her, then followed her out. Shutting the door behind himself, he pulled his keys from his pocket. Once more he closed his eyes and breathed in the calm. Then he inserted his key and locked the deadbolt. Then he checked it, pulling it toward himself, and pushing it back to the jamb, twisting the handle as he did so. Then he checked it again. He was about to check it again when Mrs. Tye's voice carried clearly from inside her apartment—"Fuck's sake, Seth!"

He released the knob and stepped back. Then he turned in place and smiled awkwardly at Becky. "Ready."

"Okay." She turned and went down the stairs. He followed her, noticing that, as usual, he was balancing on the balls of his feet.

A series of questions arose in his head. Did he find her attractive? He did. Did it bother him that Angie didn't? A little. But he knew he was no catch. He felt lucky that she showed any interest in him at all. Was he in love with her? He knew the answer to that, and he didn't really want to think about it.

As soon as they stepped out of the double doors onto the porch, a thought appeared in Seth's brain with the force of a small explosion. Had he turned off the lights?

"Did I turn off the lights?" he asked Becky, his eyes widening with alarm.

She shrugged. "I don't know, wh—" Then her eyes widened. "No. No, Seth. You're not going to go back up there and do it all again."

He turned and looked at the front door of the apartment building. He felt sweat gathering at his neck and in his palms. He wiped his hands on his jeans and hyperventilated. He quickly felt light-headed. "I think I have to—" He started for the door.

Becky caught his arm. "Don't."

"What?" He looked back at her.

"Don't do it. If you want to get better, don't do it. If you go back up there, to your apartment, the OCD wins. You can't let it win."

"But what if I left a light on?" Seth asked.

"Then your electric bill will be 10¢ more than if you'd turned it off." She felt in her pants pocket for something. Then she held a dime out to him.

He took it. "But what if there's a fire?"

"From what?"

"From the lights? They get hot."

"Lights are designed to work without setting anything on fire. If we stayed home, would the lights be on all evening?"

"Probably," Seth conceded.

"And do you expect the apartment would catch fire?"

"No, but—"

"No. Seth, are you extra anxious because Kush isn't here?"

Seth considered this. It certainly contributed to his dis-ease. But before he could answer, she reached up and grabbed his chin, turning his face to hers. Then she went up on tiptoe and kissed him.

"What was that for?" he asked.

"To break the spell," she said.

"What spell?" he asked.

"Whatever spell your OCD has over you," she answered.

He noticed her eyes. Her lashes on her right eye were black, but streaked with brown. Her lashes on her left eye were just black. How had he never noticed that before? "You are embarking on a new life," she said, her face serious, kind, and cautionary, all at once. "A life free from all that fear. If you go back up there, you go right back to that old life, where you're...you're a prisoner." She smiled. "Let's just go. Let's just turn around and go."

"If my apartment burns down, I'm going to blame you," he said.

"That seems fair," she agreed.

―――――――――

D r. Teasdale handed Seth a cup of tea. "It's hot," she said. "Be careful."

Seth touched only the handle and set it on the coffee table in front of him.

Dr. Teasdale leaned back into her chair and sighed deeply. "There. Now. How are you?"

"I've been a lot better," he admitted.

"Tell me about it."

"I took Kush to live with Travis."

Dr. Teasdale visibly softened. "Oh, Seth. I'm so sorry."

He nodded. "I can go see him whenever, and I know he's in a good place, but—"

"But you can't snuggle with him when you're feeling anxious," Dr. Teasdale offered.

"No. And I miss him...a lot."

"Of course you do."

"I feel like a terrible person."

"Feelings don't always tell us the truth," Dr. Teasdale pointed out. "You're a responsible person, and you made a hard choice. And you know that Kush is well-cared for. He's probably still enjoying the vacation, the newness of it all. Plus he's with someone he knows and likes, right?"

"Yeah, totally. I'm sure he misses me...at least, I hope he does."

"I know he does. It's okay to grieve, Seth. This is a loss. It's situational. Anyone would feel the same."

"Not everyone. Not everyone...loves dogs like I do."

"I'll give you that. But among dog lovers...what you're feeling is perfectly normal."

"I guess." Seth's leg began to bounce.

"Is that any better?" Dr. Teasdale asked, pointing to his leg.

"Not yet, I mean, obviously," Seth said, regretting his snarkiness immediately.

Dr. Teasdale did not seem to take offense. "How is it going with your medication? It's still too soon for us to see benefits, but how are you doing with the side effects?"

Seth closed his eyes and tuned into his body. "My body feels... a little weird. Like it's made out of some substance other than meat."

Dr. Teasdale's eyebrows rose and she wrote something on her legal pad. "What else?"

"I've been having some headaches," Seth confessed. "But they're not bad...and they pass."

"That's normal," Dr. Teasdale said. "And they'll go away. Hang in there."

Seth nodded.

"How are you doing with the CBT—the cognitive behavioral therapy?"

"You mean stopping the OCD stuff?" Seth asked.

"Exactly," Dr. Teasdale affirmed.

"Well...it's both better and worse. Yesterday I left the apartment and had a really, really strong urge to go back and check things again."

Dr. Teasdale looked concerned but hopeful. "And did you?"

"I would have, but...Becky was there, and..."

"And you were embarrassed to show her how out of control you were?"

"There was some of that," Seth confessed.

"What else was going on?"

"She talked me through it. And she was really logical."

"Was that effective?" Dr. Teasdale asked.

"It was annoying! But...she also told me that I couldn't go back in or...or the OCD would win."

"She's right," Dr. Teasdale said.

"I know," Seth agreed.

"So did you? Go back, I mean?"

There were several long seconds of silence before Seth finally said, "No."

"And did anything terrible happen?"

"No."

Dr. Teasdale nodded and gave him an encouraging smile. "Every time you don't give in to it, it will get easier."

"This is really hard," Seth said, "especially without Kush."

There were several moments of silence. Then Dr. Teasdale said, "It is."

"Sometimes it seems *too* hard."

"I get that," Dr. Teasdale said. "And you know what? At any time you can go back to the way your life was before we started this therapy. But before you give up, I want you to ask yourself a really hard question."

"What's that?" Seth asked.

"How was that working out for you?"

Seth laughed. "Now you sound like Angie."

"I think Angie and I would get along," Dr. Teasdale said. Then her smile faded. "You know, Seth, this isn't just about you."

"What do you mean?"

"I mean...this healing work you're doing. It's not just about you. I mean, it *is* about you—about you having an easier life, about you living into the best *you* possible. But it's about more than that, too. When you heal, you contribute to the healing of the world."

Seth frowned. "That sounds pretty woo-woo."

Dr. Teasdale shrugged. "Maybe it is. But any way you slice it, it's true. Your pain is part of the cumulative pain of the world. When you heal, there's a little bit less pain in the world. And that has effects that you don't necessarily see. When you make it better for you, you make it better for everyone."

Seth frowned. "Has Angie been talking to you about me being grumpy in the morning?"

"No, but...I guess that's part of what I mean." Dr. Teasdale looked like she was trying to hold back a smile.

"Making Kush go and live with Travis added to the pain of the world," he countered.

Her smile faded. "Working hard on your own healing will hasten the day you can move and bring him home."

Seth didn't look at her, but he nodded. "Promise?"

"Promise what?" Dr. Teasdale asked.

"Can you...can you promise that it'll get easier?"

"I promise." Dr. Teasdale cocked her head. "You know...I'm so glad you have Angie. And I'm so glad Becky was there yesterday. I hope you didn't take her intervention unkindly."

"No. She was right, and she was really...I don't know...sweet about it."

"You know, Seth, this is such important work, and it is such hard work. Kush may not be living with you now, but you are not alone. Angie and Becky are there. And you need people like them around to give you a reality check. What other kinds of community do you have?"

"Community" sounded like such an odd word, as if Dr. Teasdale were being translated by someone who was not a native speaker. But he was able to set aside the oddness of it and tend to the question. "There's Travis, I guess. I mean, we don't hang out much, but you know..."

"I get it—he's a work friend. You could make an effort to hang out more, which will give you the added benefit of being with Kush."

"Yeah."

"And when you're at work, you enjoy being with him."

"Yeah," Seth agreed. "It's like that. He's...he's got his own trip that he's on, you know, but...I can talk to him."

"Good. Anyone else? Any groups you're a part of?"

"Like what?"

"Oh, I don't know. It could be anything. A D&D group. A bowling league. A church or synagogue. Anything like that?"

"Oh." Seth looked out the window.

"What?" Dr. Teasdale asked. "What just happened?"

"I..." Seth wrestled with how much to tell her. Finally, he said. "I've been going to a study group."

"Oh?" Dr. Teasdale brightened. "What kind of group?"

"It's a...gnostic group."

Her face lit up. "Tell me more."

"It's...it's pretty interesting. I'm not sure what to make of it just yet. There's kind of a creepy kid there who answers the door. But I really like Mr. Basil."

Dr. Teasdale reared back. "Uh...do you mean Terrance Basil?"

"Yeah! Do you know him?" Seth asked.

Dr. Teasdale shook her head. "It's a very small world, Seth. Yes, I know Terrance. We're...colleagues, of a sort."

"So you know about the group?"

"I do. I've been a member for years."

Seth's mouth dropped open. "You're...a member of...you're a gnostic?"

"I am."

"You're not wearing a vest."

Dr. Teasdale laughed. "No, I'm at work. But when I go to the lodge...yes, I put on one of those silly vests. It's not an official thing, you know. It's just something people started doing."

"I can't believe it!" Seth's smile glowed...and then it faltered. Had Dr. Teasdale manipulated him into joining the Lodge? But he couldn't draw a direct line. She didn't know where he would go to get books, she didn't plant the blank book with the card...did she? Suddenly her compassionate smile seemed less benevolent. He shrank into himself.

"What's happening right now, Seth?"

"I...I'm not sure I trust you?"

"Why?"

"Did you *make* me join the Lodge, somehow?"

She looked troubled. "How could I have done that? I simply suggested you learn something about the gnostics. You could have simply googled them. No, you found the Lodge on your own. As far as I know, ours is the only truly gnostic group in San Jose, so I'm not surprised you found us. I mean, there's the Rosicrucians, but—" She closed her eye and shook her head, as if to say, *Don't be silly.* "Plus...if you've been told secrets, then you've taken the oaths of your own free will."

Seth nodded. That made sense. But there was a coincidence—or something—that made him uneasy. But Dr. Teasdale was speaking again. "—and like I said, it's a small world. How did you hear about the Lodge?"

"I got this book...and a card fell out—"

"Oh, that's funny. That was Robinson's idea."

"Who's that?"

"You haven't met Robinson yet?" Seth shook his head and she waved the question away. "You will. Take him with a grain of salt, though."

Seth started to relax again. It might be a scary coincidence, but it occurred to him that there might be some benefit in it. "So... can I talk to you about things that happen at the Lodge, things they tell me?"

"Absolutely. You haven't met Robinson, so I take it you haven't been initiated yet?"

"No, but Mr. Basil told me I'm one of them...of you guys, I mean."

"Do you think you'll do it?"

Seth blinked. "I go back and forth. I really like what Mr. Basil is saying. I mean, it's interesting—especially what he was telling me about gnosticism being a resistance movement."

"You like the sound of that, do you?" Dr. Teasdale smiled.

"Yeah. I do. It's...I've wanted to be part of something...important, something bigger than me, for a long time, but..."

"But I take it you're not a joiner?"

"No. Not after..." Seth looked away.

"Not after your church experience?" Dr. Teasdale asked.

Seth nodded, still not looking at her. "And Angie thinks it's a cult."

"The Lodge?" Dr. Teasdale asked.

"Yeah."

"What do you think?"

"I...it didn't seem religious at first, but...sometimes it does."

"What do you think 'cult' means?"

Seth shrugged. "Like the Moonies or the Hare Krishnas, I guess."

"Have you ever seen gnostics dancing at the airport?" Dr. Teasdale asked, one side of her lip curling up.

"No," Seth laughed. The idea seemed ridiculous.

"Seth, the word 'cult' just means a system of religious devotion. Every religion is a cult. Movements within religions are sometimes referred to as a cult. Have you ever heard of the cult of the Virgin Mary?"

"Yeah."

"It's not a derogatory term, it just means the religious devotion directed toward the Blessed Mother."

"Then why do people use it as if it were bad?"

"It has gotten that reputation, but that's a fairly recent development, only in the past sixty years or so."

"Huh." Seth felt like they were moving around an object, but not really seeing it. "I think Angie means it in the bad way—that it's dangerous for me."

"There certainly are groups that are psychologically or spiritually abusive. The church you grew up in was like that. You could call many of their methods 'cultic' in the pejorative sense, couldn't you?"

"Oh, yeah," Seth agreed.

"So let's look at that," Dr. Teasdale said. "There are several hallmarks of a cultic group—in the 'bad' meaning of that word. One of them is that they forbid anyone to question the group's doctrine. Another is that they try to control every aspect of their members' lives, including cutting off people who are deemed 'bad influences.' Another is that they have an 'us vs. them' mentality that isolates them from the rest of the world. Do any of those sound like anything you've seen at the Lodge?"

"No," Seth said.

"No." Dr. Teasdale gave him a sympathetic look. "If you did, I would be the first to tell you to run as fast as you can. But...I've never seen anything resembling religious coercion or insularity there. I wouldn't be a member if there was!"

Seth released a long, slow breath. "So...it's okay."

Dr. Teasdale leaned forward and patted his arm. "It's more than okay. It's community. It's good for you. It's exactly what you need right now—more people in your corner." She leaned back in her seat, and then moved her head as if she'd just had a thought. Then she stood and walked over to one of the bookcases. She scanned it, and then pulled out a hardcover book. It was about two inches thick, and the dust cover was the color of parchment. "This is a copy of *The Nag Hammadi Library*. Have you heard of it?"

"Yeah, aisle five, second shelf on the left."

"Ha!" Dr. Teasdale laughed. It was a musical sound, and something in Seth thrilled to it. She handed the book to Seth. He took it, feeling the heft of it in his hands. "These are the gnostic scriptures—most of them, anyway. Please take it—my gift to you, gnostic to gnostic."

"Really?" Seth asked, leafing through the book. The titles were intriguing: *The Gospel of Truth, The Apocryphon of John, Thunder—Perfect Mind*, he stopped at the *Three Steeles of Seth*.

"Seth," he breathed.

"Yes. One of the gnostic saviors. Before Jesus came, Jewish gnostics believed that Seth was the bringer of Truth."

"I...I'm not sure what to make of that."

"Why don't you read it and find out? Discover who your namesake was."

"Thank you," Seth said, clutching the book to him.

"It is like a sword," Dr. Teasdale said. "Those writings will cut you to the quick, and they will sharpen your intellect. They will challenge you, and they will make you wise."

"Hey, dude, can you hand me that spray bottle?" Travis' hand extended toward him.

Seth had been lost in thought, and it took him a minute to realize that what Travis was asking for was in front of him. He snatched up the bottle and handed it to him. "Here, let me move those for you," Seth said, and lifted the last few books from the stock shelves.

"Thanks, man." Travis sprayed the shelf down and wiped it with a red rag that looked like it had been lifted from a gas station. "You seem a little distracted...if you don't mind me saying."

"Oh. Yeah. I guess so."

"Careful. You gotta stay on Rutherford's good side. You been doing good—"

"Don't fuck it up," Seth said.

"Exactly."

"I'm just...there's a lot going on. I miss Kush..."

Travis' shoulders slumped. "You know you can have him back whenever. Just ask, man."

"I know. I just..." He sighed. "How is he doing?"

Travis shrugged. "I think he's a little depressed. He didn't eat this morning. But he's sleeping good. Snores like a motherfucker—"

"Yeah," Seth allowed himself a chuckle. "That's Kush."

"And he seems happy when one of us gets home. He's adjusting. It's going to take some time."

Seth nodded. A pain in his chest began to assert itself. He pressed the spot and took a deep breath. It didn't help. He felt suddenly dizzy. *Talk about something else,* he thought. He took another deep breath, picked up a handful of books, and started putting the books back on the shelf. "My ther—uh...someone gave me a copy of the *Nag Hammadi Library*—"

"Oh? Cool stuff," Travis' eyebrows danced. He climbed on a stepstool and handed a load of books down.

Seth took them and gingerly placed them on the worktable. It felt good to talk about something else.

"So there's this book called *The Three Steles of Seth*—"

"Which you had to read, because Seth," Travis laughed.

"Yeah. It was just a bunch of praise this, praise that. I don't know what the 'triple male' stuff means. But near the end, there was a line: 'The way of ascent is the way of descent.' I read that last night and it's kind of like an ear worm. I just keep hearing it."

"Maybe it's important."

"Do you have any idea what it means?"

Travis shrugged as he wiped another shelf. "Well, it's kind of typical mystical language, isn't it? You know, Lao Tzu says, 'The way forward is to go back,' and Heraclitus said, 'The way up and the way down are the same.' And then there's Nicolas of Cusa, who said, 'God is the coincidence of opposites.' So it's probably like that."

Seth blinked. "I'm glad it makes sense *to you*."

"You don't read much mysticism, do you?" Travis asked.

"No," Seth confessed.

"It's all about Oneness, nondualism, that kind of shit. Everything is One," Travis said, as if with authority.

"There was a lot about a capital-O 'One' in the Steles book," Seth remembered.

"So there you go."

"I'm not sure how that helps me." He handed a stack of books back up to Travis.

"Well, what are you trying to figure out—aside from this book and the thing with Kush?"

"I've been going to this study group, and I either need to go forward or back."

"Ouch," Travis made a face. "Commitment time. I hate commitment."

"*Tell* me about it," Seth said.

"What is this group?"

"It's a gnostic thing."

"Oh. So it's religious?" Travis said, looking concerned.

"Yes. No. Maybe." Seth bit his lip. "I'm not sure."

"Well, you can go forward, and see if you like it. If you don't, you can just quit. This is California. No one is going to hunt you down."

"I guess," Seth grudgingly agreed.

"So what's the issue?"

"Everyone is pulling me in a different direction."

"Everyone? I'm not."

"No, not *literally* everyone," Seth shook his head. "Angie thinks I absolutely should stay the hell clear of it. My therapist thinks it will be good for me. My mother would hate it—if she knew. Mr. Basil—"

"Who the fuck is Mr. Basil?" Travis asked.

"He's...the head of the...study group, I guess."

"I need a scorecard," Travis said.

"He says I'm already one of them."

"And you don't know what to do?"

Seth looked at his shoes. "No. I want someone to step out of an S-panel and just tell me what to do."

"Good luck with that. I've never seen *anything* come out of an S-panel that I didn't see going in."

"I know, I know."

Travis climbed down from the stepstool and leaned against the worktable beside him. "Look, the thing about being One? That means that there really isn't an *other.*"

"What does that mean?"

"It means you can poll half the population, but in the end, you make your choices alone. You're not accountable to anyone except..." He slapped Seth's chest.

"Ow," Seth said, but he noticed that his chest pain was gone.

"Don't be a pussy. What I'm saying is, we come into this world alone—"

"We don't, really."

"—and we go out alone. And all along the way, we make our own decisions. No one can tell you what to do. You have to find that inner core of aloneness and let it tell you what to do." He narrowed one eye conspiratorially and tapped his temple with one finger. "It knows what to do. It *already* knows. And so do you."

"I have no idea what you are talking about."

"And don't give an inch to the demons," Travis said, stepping away from the table and grabbing a box off another shelf.

"What demons?" Seth felt the skin on his neck bristle. Demons had been an all-to-real part of his childhood, and he thought he had left them behind.

"I mean metaphorical demons, man. There are forces inside you and outside you that seek your undoing."

"There are?"

"Of course there are. The fact that you are so torn apart over this decision—they got you exactly where they want you. You're doubting yourself. You're giving your power away to Angie and your therapist and your mom and probably me, since you're asking me about all this shit."

"I am?"

"Don't be such a doofus, dude." Travis shook his head. "The inside and the outside—they're connected. The coincidence of opposites, remember? Up and down are the same. The inside and the outside are the same."

"I'm not sure that's what nondualism really means," Seth complained.

Travis put the box down and walked directly up to Seth. He put one hand on his shoulder and looked into his eyes. "You know what to do, man. Just do it."

"I'm serious," Seth said. "Where are we going?"

"It'll ruin the surprise," Becky said.

"I promise I'll act surprised," Seth assured her.

Becky rolled her eyes. "If I tell you, will you promise to do your...checking the house-stuff and get your ass out the door?"

"Cross my heart. Hope to die," Seth swore.

"We're going to D'Virgilio's. Angie has arranged a professional whisky tasting for you."

"No shit," Seth said.

"No shit. Happy birthday, Sethins." She drew him to herself and kissed him. He kissed her back, but it was brief, and he moved away quickly. "You promised to look surprised, remember?"

"Is anyone else going to be there?"

"She asked Travis."

"She didn't ask Belle, did she?"

"Who's Belle?"

"She's a goth chick at work. Chronically depressed. She could make it rain on God."

"I don't think so," Becky assured him. "C'mon, let's go."

Just then, Seth's cell phone vibrated. He pulled it out and saw that his screen flashed "The Lodge."

"Who is it?" Becky asked. "Is it Angie? Don't tell her I told you!"

Seth punched the green button. "Hello?" He held his index finger up toward Becky. She rolled her eyes and sat down on the couch with a huff. A small plume of dust jetted from the cushions into the air.

"Mr. St. John? This is Terrance Basil. Do you have a moment to chat?"

"Uh, yes." Seth felt his pulse kick up. "Well...I mean...thank you for calling, but...why are you calling?"

"I'm calling because several students in your cohort are taking their vows tomorrow, and I wanted to know if you planned to be among them. We need to know how many people to plan for."

Seth froze. He swallowed. "Uh...do I have to say now?"

"Well, it would be convenient, certainly."

"What if I...you know...wait until next time?"

"My dear boy, you've gone as far as you can go prior to your induction. We don't induct people who aren't active, and there's nothing more to do, so...I'm afraid it's now or never. I don't mean to pressure you, and you are free to do whatever you like, but we have a way of doing things, and it *is* time for a decision."

"Oh. Uh..." Seth's mind raced. Would he always be sorry if he didn't go further? He knew he would always wonder. What would he stand to lose if he took his vows? Nothing that he could see. And he was curious. He looked at Becky, who cocked her head at him. He turned away as his stomach twisted. A part of him intuited that a choice to walk toward the Lodge was a choice to walk away from Becky. Like it or not, want it or not, he knew it was true.

"I'll be there," he said.

K eira heard her name and looked up from her desk. Special agent Tony Raine waved her toward him. She put down the pen she was holding and stood, stretching. He waved more insistently. She rolled her eyes and with a little hop, speed-walked toward him. "What's up?"

"I need a bad cop," he said.

"You got someone in interrogation?" She looked over his shoulder down the hall.

"Yeah. You free?"

"Free enough. What's the charge?"

"Just follow my lead," Raine said. He turned and strode down the hallway. She caught up with him.

"Not even a hint?"

"S-panel breach."

"Ugh. Why do you need me? It's always just some curious kid."

"He's not a kid." He paused outside a room and put his hand on the knob. "I need you because you're *scary*."

"I am?"

He narrowed one eye at her.

"Tony, that may be the nicest thing you've ever said to me."

He gave her a smile that was utterly without humor and jerked open the door.

Inside, a man sat as if at attention, both palms on the table. He was white, of average build and height, and balding. A look of defiance came into his eyes as they entered.

Raine put a file on the table and took a seat. There wasn't a second seat, so Keira leaned against the wall within kicking distance of the table, where she could see both their faces. She folded her arms and waited.

"Mr. Eric Sanders," Raine said, opening the file. "Do you know why you're here?"

"Because the cops busted my door down and dragged me here," the man answered.

"No, that's *how* you came to be here. Do you know *why* you're here?"

The man's lips grew tight, and he crossed his arms.

Raine sighed and leaned forward, putting both elbows on the table. "Look, you were caught on camera entering and leaving an S-panel. I can show you the video. Unless you're holding an electrician's union card, that's automatic jail time. There's no getting around that. I just want to know your side of it before...well, before it's too late to help you."

"And why would you want to help me?" the man asked.

"'He is armed without who is innocent within,'" Raine said. "Horace."

Keira rolled her eyes.

"Excuse me?" the man asked, his face screwing up in confusion.

"I mean...maybe you're not a criminal," Tony explained. "Maybe you're just a guy who was passing by and thought, 'I've always wondered what's inside one of these' and poked your head in. There's a million ways this could go. You could get twenty-five years, or you could go home tonight with some community service...or anything in between. So please, help yourself out. Talk to me...before I leave, and you have to talk to *her*." He pointed at Keira.

She fixed her eyes on Eric's and gave him her wickedest smile. She saw him shudder. It made her feel powerful, and she liked it.

Raine reached out and put his hand on the man's forearm. "Talk to me. Let's figure this out before things get nasty."

Keira's eyes flitted back and forth between Raine and the suspect. She watched the man's shoulders sink, his defiance short-circuiting. He swallowed.

"I've...I've heard things," he said.

"You've heard things," Raine repeated. "What things?"

"You know...theories. About the pandemic. About the S-panels. About electricians." He looked quickly from Raine to Keira and back, as if trying to gauge how his words were landing.

Raine shook his head. "I don't really follow conspiracy theories. Can you tell me more about what you've been hearing? And where you've been hearing it?"

"Online. On ten-square. They say that the virus was engineered...but it got out of hand and killed our friends as well as our enemies. And most of our own country. I mean, if there's only California left..."

"Hey, the rest of the country is still there," Raine said. "It's just not safe to travel there."

"Is everyone really dead?"

Raine shook his head. "I don't know. No one knows. No one's talking. Not even to us."

Sanders raised one eyebrow, clearly not buying this. "I just wanted to know the truth."

"You think the pandemic and the S-panels are related somehow?" Raine asked.

"Of course. It's how they get around," Sanders said, as if it should be obvious.

"Who's they?" Keira asked.

He looked up at her warily. "The electricians."

"What about them?" Raine asked.

"You're messing with me," the man said. "You know, but you're not allowed to say."

"Look, Mr. Sanders, I have no idea what you're talking about. Now do you want to help yourself out here? You need to tell me what you were doing. Please don't assume that I know anything about the theories you've been reading online. Pretend I'm coming to this cold and just *explain* it to me. Please."

The man looked down at his hand on the table and shook his head slowly. He closed his eyes. When he opened them again, he said, "Fine. I'll play your game. The electricians control everything."

"They do?" Raine's eyebrows shot up. "Like what?"

"Like the police, the governor's office, the fucking PTA, whatever needs controlling."

"The electricians?" Raine asked.

"Yes."

"To what end?"

"I don't know. That's...why I was curious."

"'Curiosity has its own reason for existence,'" Raine said. "Your buddies online don't have any theories about why the electricians are running California?"

"There's lots of theories, but not a lot of agreement on that," the man confessed.

"So, electricians are kind of like the Illuminati?" Raine asked.

"Exactly!" The man pointed at Raine and smiled for the first time.

"So...that doesn't explain why you were breaching an S-panel. You could have got yourself killed."

"Only if someone had shot me."

"Only electricians can handle power lines safely," Raine objected.

"That's not what's back there."

Raine cocked his head. "What's that?"

"I mean, there's power back there—the lights are on—but there isn't any machinery that I could see. There's just...you know...behind."

"Behind?" Raine's eyebrows bunched in confusion. "Behind what?"

"You know, behind. Behind the façade."

"The façade of what?" Raine asked.

"The world. I'm talking about the façade of the world." Sanders looked completely serious.

"The world...is a façade...?" Raine asked slowly. "So...what's behind the façade?"

"That's what they don't want us to know." Sanders looked at him sideways and nodded his head slowly, conspiratorially.

Keira let out an exasperated breath. "Oh my God, are you just going to let him go on?"

"He's making a strange amount of sense," Raine confessed.

"He's delusional! The only thing behind the S-panels is the power grid."

Sanders pointed at her. "That's what they *want* you to think."

Keira pushed herself off the wall and walked wearily to the table. "Look, Mr. Sanders, we're the feds. If there was a whole conspiracy around some façade—and I have no idea what that means—don't you think we'd know about it?"

Sanders moved his head back and forth. "Maybe yes and maybe no. It depends."

"On what?" Raine asked.

"On how much they trust you."

"And just who are 'they'?" Keira asked.

"You know," he pointed toward the ceiling. "*Them.*"

Keira looked at Raine, and he met her eyes. He shrugged. "Mr. Sanders, doesn't it stand to reason that we are *in on* the conspiracy to keep the façade in place? And that we're just yanking your chain right now?"

Sanders' face fell, as if he'd been slapped. He looked at Keira and then back to Raine. Keira almost felt sorry for him. He looked down at his hands, shoulders sagging. "Of course. Yeah. Of course you are."

Raine motioned toward the door and Keira followed him into the hall. He closed the door and turned to view Sanders through the one-way glass.

"What do you want to do?" Keira asked.

"I don't know. I don't think he's dangerous. One minute I think he's a nutcase, and another I think he's sincerely trying to piece something together, however misguided. I believe he believes it, though."

Keira crossed her arms and looked at Sanders, nodding. "Yeah. I'm kind of leaning the same way. How much good would it do to prosecute a guy like that?"

Raine shrugged. "It's a deterrent. He's not likely to go into an S-panel again after a few days in the hoosegow."

"But do we send it on to the state attorney?"

"We could let locals have it."

"S-panels are state. You can thank the electricians' lobby in Sacramento for that."

"I know, I know. But maybe trespassing?"

Keira shook her head. "The moment the California Federation of Electricians gets wind of it—and they will—"

"Fucking CFE," Raine swore. He rubbed at his eyes. "How about we turn him over to the state attorney with a recommendation for a psych eval?"

"Yeah, yeah, I like it," Keira said.

"I'll write that up," Raine concluded.

Keira nodded. She wasn't completely satisfied, but it seemed to be the lesser of two evils.

"There's only one problem," Raine said, just as she was about to walk away.

"What's that?" she asked.

"What if he's right?"

***

The door to the Lodge swung open mere seconds after Seth knocked on it. "It's you!" Nazz said. "We were laying odds on whether you'd be all-in or not."

"Really?" Seth asked. "Who's 'we'?"

"Your cohort. This way, please."

Seth noted that Nazz hadn't answered his question but didn't press it. The scent of mahogany and oil soap wafted over him as he stepped into the foyer. Nazz didn't lead him to Mr. Basil's study, but to the room the study group met in.

There he discovered familiar faces. "Seth!" Jude Ash exclaimed. The software engineer jumped out of his chair and extended his hand. Seth noticed he was wearing a plaid vest.

"Hi, Jude," Seth said. He next shook hands with Musa Daniels, whose dark features seemed more serious than ever. He waved across the circle at Lynn Shire, who bobbed her beak-like nose in his direction. Matt Townes didn't rise but nodded an acknowledgement. Seth smiled at him. "Hi, Seth," said Maria. "Hi," he answered. Mika Singh didn't rise but she offered her hand just the same. Seth shook it and took his own seat.

"There's a couple of people missing," Seth noted. "Where's Mags?"

"It seems we've been winnowed," Jude said, resuming his chair.

"Sure looks like it," Mika said. "That'll happen when you threaten people."

"I don't know what Mr. Basil said to you, but I wouldn't call it threatening," Musa countered.

"He told me it was now or never," Seth offered.

"Shit or get off the pot," Mika said.

"He...didn't use those words."

Mika shrugged, her dark eyes cloudy. "He said the same to me."

"He didn't say anything like that to me," Jude offered.

"That's because you're a Labrador retriever eager for his master to take him for a walk," Mika said.

Jude frowned, but didn't respond.

"He didn't say that to me, either, but I wouldn't be surprised or upset if he had," Maria contributed. "I mean, we've had plenty of time. If we want to move forward, there needs to be some reciprocity."

"Exactly," Jude agreed.

"Whatever," Mika rolled her eyes.

"If you're not all-in, what are you doing here?" Miss Shire asked.

"Is ambivalence not allowed?" Mika asked. "If we're not allowed to be human, then no shit I'm not all-in."

"No one is saying you can't be human," Matt said. "Stop being ridiculous."

"Who's being ridiculous?" Mika snapped. "You know who's ridiculous? The old man there in the tartan vest."

"Who are you calling old?" Jude retorted. "And what's wrong with tartan? I'm proud of my heritage. Aren't you?"

"Please," Musa growled. "You're acting like children."

"I think it's just nerves," Maria said. "We should give one another some slack."

"I think that is excellent advice, Maria," Musa agreed.

"What do you think it's going to be?" Seth asked.

"What?" asked Lynn. "The secret or the ritual?"

"Ha!" Seth laughed. It helped to break the tension. "Both, I guess."

But the others only shook their heads. Seth pulled his phone out of his pocket and glanced at it. It was two after the hour. Mr. Basil encouraged punctuality, and Seth wondered if perhaps he was waiting for stragglers. At five after, the door opened again, and Mr. Basil walked in. "So you are my initiates," he said, a sad smile playing on his face.

Seth wondered if he was disappointed that there were only six of them. But a moment later, the sadness dissipated, replaced by a patient congeniality. "I'm so glad to see all of you. You are about to embark on a great journey...and a great mystery."

"I'm ready!" Jude Ash exclaimed.

"Don't be too eager, Mr. Ash. This will be costly," Mr. Basil warned.

"Costly how?" Mika asked.

"Worlds will end," Mr. Basil said. "And I assure you, worlds do not end without tears."

Seth flashed on Kush when he said that. *So true*, he thought.

"Whose world?" Maria asked.

Mr. Basil didn't answer, but only gave her a compassionate smile.

"Are you ready?" he asked. He stood. "If you are, then please follow me."

Seth exchanged looks with several of the others. Jude stood first, clearly eager to get on with it. Mika looked troubled. Seth understood both impulses. Matt scowled, but Lynn and Maria looked hopeful. He couldn't read Musa Daniels at all.

For a moment, no one moved. Then Mika stood and nodded. The others followed suit, including Seth. They turned to Mr. Basil, who led them to the door and opened it. "This way, please," he said.

He led them down a hallway Seth had not traversed before and paused beside what looked like an antique wooden door. He opened it and waved them inside.

Seth experienced a moment of fear. Perhaps Angie was right. Perhaps they were a murder cult and Seth and his cohort were walking right into a death trap. But before his mind could complete his panicked ruminations, his body had carried him inside. The door shut, leaving them in complete darkness.

Seth was afraid to move, afraid that he might trip over something unseen, or bump into a wall. The stillness was complete. His own breath seemed impossibly loud.

Then a light blazed. It was a single lamp, hanging from a cord in the ceiling directly over a table. On the table, a long shape was covered by a sheet. Sticking out from under the sheet were two feet, their wrinkled toes pointing up at the ceiling.

Stepping out of the shadows and up to the body, Mr. Basil gently folded back the sheet, revealing a face. It was still—impossibly still—and seemed to be vaguely blue in color.

"What is this?" Lynn asked.

"It's a corpse," Jude said.

"It is indeed."

"Who is...was it?" Seth asked.

"Who is not important," Mr. Basil said. "Whoever it was is gone now. This is just an empty shell, cast off into the dirt, with all the others."

Others? Seth wondered. *Are there others?*

"Whoever has come to know the world has discovered a corpse," Mr. Basil intoned, "and whoever has found a corpse, the world is not worthy of him."

"What does that mean?" Mika asked.

Mr. Basil ignored her. "If you would be initiated into the

mysteries, revelations will be made to you, revelations you must not repeat—to anyone, anywhere, under any circumstances—under pain of death."

"Is that what happened to him?" Matt asked. "Did he tell one of the secrets?"

"No," Mr. Basil said. "He is here to...to serve as a Bible of sorts."

"A Bible?" Maria asked. Her brows knitted in confusion.

"When you swear in court, do you not place your hand upon a Bible?" Mr. Basil asked.

"Yes. To tell the whole truth and nothing but the truth," Jude said, his gray hair looking silver in the harsh light.

"Just so. There will be oaths, and oaths upon oaths. But this is the first. It is not an accident that both the words 'testify' and 'testicle' are derived from the same Latin root, *testis*. In the book of Genesis, Abraham orders his servant to grasp his testicles and make an oath."

"Ew," Mika said. "Why are you telling us this?"

"Because if you would be worthy of the secrets, you must testify yourself."

"You want us to...what?" Matt asked, "Hold someone's testicles while we swear an oath?"

"Not just someone's," Mr. Basil said. He pointed at the corpse with his chin. "His."

"Gross. No," Mika said.

Jude's face became solemn, and he nodded. "Now?"

Mr. Basil bowed slightly.

Jude stepped toward the corpse, and as he did so, Mr. Basil drew the sheet off completely, exposing the nakedness of the dead man's body. The hair of his chest seemed ghostly and insubstantial. His pubic hair was matted, a bird's nest swaddling the withered orchid of his genitals.

Seth saw Maria take a step back. Lynn held her hand in front of her face to obscure her view. Musa's face was utterly unreadable. Mika turned her back to the body.

But Jude stepped up to the corpse, his face almost glowing. "I...I'll do it. What do you want me to do?"

Mr. Basil watched the older man intently. "Reach forth your right hand and cup his testicles in your fingers."

Jude reached for the corpse's organ and, pushing the flaccid penis aside, thrust his fingers between the legs until the testicles rested in the cup of his hand. He looked up at Mr. Basil, his fascination undiminished. "Now what?"

"Repeat after me: I, Jude Ash...of my own free will and accord... in the name of the God above all gods...and in the presence of these witnesses...do hereby most solemnly and sincerely promise and swear...that I will ever conceal and never reveal...any of the secrets, arts, parts, point or points...which may be imparted to me by this Gnostic fellowship..."

At every pause, Jude repeated the phrase, his voice strong and resonant and resolute. Seth felt a chill run through him, and goosebumps broke out on his arms.

"And all this I solemnly, sincerely promise and swear..." Mr. Basil continued, "with a firm and steady resolution...under no less penalty than that of having my body severed in two...my bowels taken from thence and burned to ashes...the ashes scattered before the four winds of heaven...that no more remembrance might be had...of so vile and wicked a wretch as I would be... should I ever, knowingly, violate this obligation...so help me God."

For a moment, all was still, as if time had frozen. Mr. Basil reached for Jude's hand and removed it from the corpse's crotch. Then he clutched the hand in both of his own. "Now I call you brother," he said, looking deep into Jude's eyes. "And there is nothing hidden that will not be revealed to you."

Seth saw Jude's eyes shining with tears in the harsh light of the lamp over the body. He brought his other hand to clasp both of Basil's own, and for what seemed like a long time they looked at one another.

It felt to Seth that they were experiencing a kind of homecoming, and he felt his heart ache. He had not felt that kind of belonging since he had been a child in his parents' church, and a deep and primal part of him longed desperately for that feeling of safety, of holding, like the swaddling of his soul in the warmest and rarest love.

"That's it—I'm out of here!" Mika said. She made for the door and swung it open. Then she ran. Seth heard her footsteps receding into the hall.

Mr. Basil sighed. "One person is a child of Wisdom, and another person is a child of death." He let go of Jude's hand at last, and the older initiate stepped away from the body. Jude reached into his vest pocket and pulled forth a handkerchief. He wiped his eyes and blew his nose. Despite Mika's disruption, it still felt like a holy moment.

The others seemed frozen, whether by the shock of what they had witnessed or by the sacrality hanging thick in the air, Seth could not tell. Perhaps none of them could.

"Okay, I'm in," Seth said. He stepped up to the body. He lifted his right hand and looked at the tiny penis and the wrinkled scrotum of the body before him. With a shaking hand, he reached into the cool depths between the corpse's legs and gingerly cupped the testicles. Then he looked into Mr. Basil's eyes and held them.

"Let's do this," he said.

PART 11: THE BOOK OF REVELATIONS

Be strong, for you are the one to whom these mysteries have been given, to know them through revelation, that he whom they crucified is the first-born, and the home of demons, and the stony vessel in which they dwell, of Elohim, of the cross, which is under the Law. But he who stands near him is the living Savior, the first in him, whom they seized and released, who stands joyfully looking at those who did him violence, while they are divided among themselves. Therefore, he laughs at their lack of perception, knowing that they are born blind. So then the one susceptible to suffering shall come, since the body is the substitute. But what they released was my incorporeal body. But I am the intellectual Spirit filled with radiant light. He whom you saw coming to me is our intellectual Pleroma, which unites the perfect light with my Holy Spirit. —*The Apocalypse of Peter**

---

* "The Apocalypse of Peter," translated by James Brashler and Roger A. Bullard, published in *The Nag Hammadi Library in English*, rev. ed., edited by James M. Robinson (NY: Harper & Row, 1988).

LIQUIPEDIA
THE ANSWERBOT THAT GOES DOWN SMOOTH

WHAT ARE S-PANELS?

"S-panels" is a colloquial abbreviation for systems panels, which allow electricians access to the local electrical infrastructure. After terrorists repeatedly attempted to sabotage the electrical grid (and succeeded in Bakersfield in 2035, leaving hundreds of thousands without power for weeks), electrical equipment in all public buildings was relocated behind S-panels to restrict access. Only licensed and guilded electricians have access to S-panels. Domestic electrical work is routinely left to licensed but non-guilded contractors.

CHAPTER SIX

Within Unity each one will receive themselves,
and within knowledge they'll purify themselves
from multiplicity into Unity,
consuming matter within themselves like fire,
and darkness by light, death by life.
—*Gospel of Truth**

Seth climbed the stairs to his apartment, his key at the ready. Without thinking, he moved it toward the lock, but the door was already slightly ajar. He scowled, pushed the door open, and went inside.

The lights were on, but dimmed. There was a bottle of whiskey on the coffee table, alongside two small mason jars, one

---

* The Gospel of Truth: Nag Hammadi Codex I, translated by Mark M. Mattison, published in *The Gospel of Truth: The Mystical Gospel* (2018).

of them containing half a finger of the spirit. Seth stooped and picked a brassiere off the floor. "Goddam it, Angie," he said.

He sighed and turned toward his bedroom. He reached for the doorknob, but then he saw the violet post-it note at eye-level: "I met someone. Fucking her. You get the couch tonight."

"Goddam it, Angie," he said again.

He turned back to the living room, and noted for the first time that his pillow and a fresh blanket were stacked on the couch. He hated to admit it to himself, but that was thoughtful of Angie, especially in the heat of passion. Still, it didn't make up for usurping his bed or using his bed for...

If you got laid, you wouldn't bat an eye, the voice in his head informed him. He wondered if that was true. He suspected it was.

He picked up the mason jar with the remaining whiskey and knocked it back. Then he went to bed.

"I already poured your coffee," Seth said, pushing it toward her. He glanced down and saw Kush's bowl in its usual spot. There were still a few stray kibbles in it. He sighed.

Angie blinked, her hair a tangled mass of snakes. She smacked her lips and fell into the chair like a dropped sack. She reached for the cup and brought it to her nose, sniffing. "Oh, delicious elixir of life."

"You slept in my bed. Again," Seth said. "With someone else."

"Yeah, well, there's no privacy on the couch."

"It's gross," Seth said.

"I'll wash the sheets," Angie said.

"It's just the idea of it," Seth said.

"What? Of girl sex?"

"No, of *any* sex. In my bed. That I'm not...having."

"You're just jealous."

Seth knew it was true because there had just been a voice in his head telling him that. Hearing it out loud felt like a condemnation. He decided to change the subject. "I did it."

"Did what?"

"I took the oath."

She closed her eyes and shook her head. "Oh, Jesus fucking Christ, Seth. Why?"

"I wanted to know the secrets."

"And what were they? Wait, don't tell me, *they're secrets.*"

"They didn't tell me any secrets—yet. I just took the oaths."

She glowered at him. "Oh my god, you're loving the suspense."

He wondered if that was true. He suspected it was. The whole thing was a little spooky and a little exciting. He realized that probably wasn't an accident. *Am I being manipulated?* the voice in his head asked. He suspected he would not like the answer to that one, so he dismissed it.

"You know what the worst part of this is?" Angie asked.

"What?"

"You're the one person in my life I can truly be open with. And, I think, I've been that person for you..."

Seth looked down at his coffee, a feeling of dread welling up from the pit of his stomach.

"...and now there's this whole part of your life that you have to wall off, that you have to hide from me." She bit her lip and sniffed. "There's an...it's an intimacy thing...and we can never really have that again."

"That's not true," he objected, but he didn't meet her eyes.

"Yeah. Yeah, it is."

They sat in silence for several minutes. Seth shifted in his seat and looked at the table. "I...I'm sorry, Ang. I...I never thought of that."

"Too late now."

Was it? Seth wondered. He could just not go back. He might have sworn an oath, but they hadn't told him anything. If he never went back, if he never heard any of the secrets... He heard his bedroom door open down the hall. "Your friend is up."

"She's not a friend," Angie said.

"What's her name?" Seth asked.

"Uh...I didn't ask," Angie said. "We just met, you know, at the Pelican."

"Jesus, Ang. How do you do it?"

"See? Jealous."

A black-haired woman with wilder bed hair than Angie's stepped into the kitchen wearing a t-shirt and gray boxer briefs. Then she noticed Seth. "Ah!" She tugged her t-shirt down to cover her underwear. Then her face contorted in confusion. "Seth?"

Seth was sitting bolt upright now. "Mika?"

"What the fuck are you doing here?"

"Uh...I live here. You slept in my bed. What are *you* doing here?"

She turned to Angie. "*He's* your roommate?"

"It pains me to admit it, but yes," Angie responded. "Uh...I take it you two know each other?"

"Yeah, she..." Seth paused, wondering how much to say. "She's in my gnostic study group. She...left last night before taking the oath."

"I wasn't going to touch that dead man's cock!" Mika almost shouted.

"Say what?" Angie gasped, looking at Seth.

"So you just left and...went to a gay bar?" Seth asked.

"I was upset," Mika explained. "It was...upsetting. You didn't think it was upsetting?"

"Suddenly this study group sounds a lot more interesting," Angie said, almost giddy.

"And you just fucked the first girl you saw?" Seth asked.

"Not the first! I liked her look," Mika glanced at Angie and smiled.

"Tell me more about the dead cock?" Angie pleaded.

"Did you touch it?" Mika turned back to Seth. "Did you hold his...cold blue balls in your hand?"

Angie turned to Seth, her eyes wide.

"Uh..." Seth looked from one to another, wondering how much he was allowed to say. He decided that there was nothing he might add that wasn't already on the table. "Yeah. I did."

"Figures," Mika said.

"What does that mean?" Seth asked.

"Like, dead balls?" Angie asked.

"Just...men," Mika almost spat.

"What the fuck, Mika?" Seth asked.

"So, was there really a dead body?" Angie asked both of them.

Mika looked at Angie. "Yes. A dead body."

"And you were supposed to do...what to it?"

"Cup its balls in our hands and swear an oath," Mika said.

"No shit," Angie breathed. She turned to Seth. "Did you do that?"

Seth felt like a trapped animal.

Angie laughed. "Oh my god! Of course you did." She turned to Mika. "I like you."

Mika looked momentarily confused, but then softened. "I like you, too."

"Wanna go at it again?" Angie asked. "Because all of this dead cock talk has really got me hot."

"Sure," Mika said.

Angie rose, took her hand, and led her out of the kitchen. Mika let go of the t-shirt, and Seth watched her gray bottom waddling away. "Hey!" Seth shouted after them. "That's my bed!"

When Seth approached the door to the Lodge, it was clear that something was going on inside—something big. He knocked on the door and waited. After nearly a minute had gone by, he knocked again, this time much more loudly. Then he jumped as the door swung open swiftly.

"There you are," Nazz said, narrowing his eyes. "I thought maybe we'd scared you off." He was wearing a brown corduroy vest, and his hair seemed wilder than usual. His eyes were also a little bit bleary, as if he were drunk or maybe high.

Seth stepped toward the threshold, but Nazz blocked his way. "Not so fast. Now that you're an initiate, you should be able to figure out the password."

Seth frowned. "Password?" He had cupped the balls. He figured he should be done with this nonsense now. But he didn't say that. Instead he simply said, "Okay."

"Where was wisdom found?"

Seth had no idea what to answer or what Nazz was looking for. He felt his palms start to sweat. His mind raced back over the study sessions, searching for something Mr. Basil had said that might give him a clue. *Calm down,* he told himself. *Reason it out.* He forced himself to relax. He played the question out in his mind again. Then again.

Then it struck him as odd that Nazz did not ask where wisdom *is* to be found. *Was* implied the past tense, a completed action. Then his eyes went wide. "Nag Hammadi?" he asked.

Nazz smiled. "We accept different answers to this question from initiates at different stages of their ascendancy. But...that is an acceptable answer. Enter." He stood out of the way and held the door wider.

"Thanks," Seth said. Once inside the foyer, he was surrounded by a crowd of people milling about. It was a party atmosphere— some people held glasses of wine and some cradled bottles of

THE WHERE, THE WHO & THE WHAT · 183

beer. People stood in small groups of three or four, talking in animated tones, clearly glad to be there. Some were dressed up—a loud, gregarious, large man sported a yellow polka-dotted bow tie that seemed particularly festive. But many others were dressed casually, as Seth was. Nearly all of them wore vests, of wildly different patterns.

Nazz had perched himself on the first landing of the large staircase, surveying the scene and presumably listening for the door. Seth picked his way through the crowd and climbed to the first landing.

"So, big night," Nazz said.

"Is it? I mean, I guess it is. But I don't know why."

He was hoping Nazz would give him a clue, but instead the young man asked, "How's it been, new initiate and all?"

"Uh...okay, I guess. My best friend is giving me hell about...you know, being part of...whatever this is."

"You ain't told this friend anything, 'ave you?" Nazz narrowed one eye at him. His hair stood almost straight up. Seth wondered just how much hair gel was required to achieve such a feat.

"I don't know anything," Seth reminded him.

"Course you don't," Nazz said. "That'll change, though."

Seth nodded. "Uh, Nazz, who are all of these people?"

"Initiates, like yourself."

"That's...a lot of people."

Nazz shrugged. "I guess. We've had more."

"Is that Nicholas Cage?"

Nazz squinted. "Looks like it. Time has not been kind."

"Are all these people...are they from here? I mean, Nic Cage doesn't live in San Jose, does he?"

"No, they're from all over the state...if you can call it that."

"What does that mean?" Seth asked.

Nazz winked at him. "They're here, same as you are, for the swearing in."

"I thought we already did that," Seth said.

"There are oaths upon oaths," Nazz said.

"Huh." A hundred questions ricocheted through Seth's head. He lit upon one. "Did all of these people...uh...hold a corpse's balls?"

Nazz smiled and looked Seth in the eye. "You have a good time tonight, yeah?" He slapped Seth on the arm and walked upstairs.

"Where are you going?" Seth asked.

"Playstation," Nazz said.

"Oh." Seth heard a door shut above him, and turned back to the scene before him. He spied Jude and Maria, but before he could make his way to them, Mr. Basil walked into the foyer and clapped his hands several times until the hubbub died down. "Welcome, everyone. I am Mr. Basil. I will be your host this evening. Please join me in the dining room."

Seth suspected he was speaking about the large room the study group met in, and as he followed the excited stream of people, he discovered he was right. Chairs had been set up—not in a circle as before, but in neat rows with an aisle down the middle.

Seth took a seat near the back of the room. All assembled, the crowd wasn't as large as he initially thought. He estimated there were perhaps sixty people. He looked for Nicholas Cage, but from the back couldn't pick him out. He did, however, see the other members of his cohort who had taken vows. Lynn caught his eye and waved at him.

Murmurs quieted as Mr. Basil glided to the front of the room. There was a small lectern set up, and he settled himself behind it as if it were a comfortable easy chair. He gave the room a welcoming smile. "I am so pleased to see you all. This is the largest class we've had in nearly ten years. It does not auger a turning of the tide, but it does hearten me that our cause is far from lost."

Cause? Seth wondered. *What cause?*

"I welcome you to the California Master Lodge. I am glad to see people from both the Sacramento Lodge and the Los Angeles Lodge. Thank you so much for making the journey. I hope one of the things you take away from this gathering is the fact that you are not alone. We have brethren all over. There is no major city you can visit where we do not have a presence. You will not lack for food or shelter or any other assistance, no matter where you go."

A murmur rippled through the room. This was, apparently, a boon that no one had considered, and it was met with over-whelming approval. A few people even clapped. When silence was restored, Mr. Basil continued. "We have teased you all with the promise of secrets. Those promises were not in vain, I assure you. But you will not learn any of them tonight—" A low moan emerged from the crowd, but Seth sensed it was good-natured. "What I want to do tonight is to give you an instruction—a cate-chism, of sorts, the oldest in the gnostic tradition." Seth saw many people sit up straighter at this news. "Who can tell me who Valentinus was?"

A couple of hands went up. Mr. Basil pointed to a young African-American woman. "Please stand, Ms.—"

"Day, Ariel Day," she said.

"Please tell us, Ms. Day, who was Valentinus?"

"He was an ancient gnostic teacher. He probably wrote *The Gospel of Truth*. And he was almost elected Pope."

Mr. Basil smiled broadly. "That's fine, Ms. Day, please be seated. Ms. Day is quite correct, although a bit of clarification is in order. In the second century, when Valentinus was teaching, there was no office of the papacy. Valentinus was, however, narrowly defeated for the office of the Bishop of Rome. That office would evolve into the papacy in good time, but it was not so while Valentinus was living." Seth saw Ms. Day shrink in her chair.

186 • J.R. MABRY

"Nevertheless, Ms. Day, you have the facts in hand, and I thank you." Ms. Day's spine straightened again at this. "Can you imagine how the Christian tradition might have evolved differently if Valentinus had triumphed in his election? The mind boggles."

This got a chuckle from many in the room. Seth found himself smiling as well.

"Do read *The Gospel of Truth*, if you have not already," Mr. Basil said. "We will be studying it, but please do not wait to acquaint yourself with it. It is not a true gospel, of course—what I mean is that it is not a narrative of the life of Christ. It is, instead, more like a sermon, or perhaps an essay. Nevertheless, it is a powerful teaching, and it will enrich your souls to read it."

Mr. Basil clasped his hands behind his back and began to pace. After two times across the width of the room, he paused and looked up at the assembly. "What is gnosticism about?"

"Secrets?" someone ventured.

Mr. Basil laughed. "One might think so, my friend, but no. Secrets are necessary, but only for your protection and mine—and everyone's, really. But no, secrets are instrumental, not foundational. Anyone else like to hazard a guess?"

"Um...resistance?" a middle-aged man with shocking red hair suggested.

"Ah! Good, I see you've been paying attention. You are close, but not there yet. We only need resistance, because we do not have...*what*?"

There was a low rumble in the room, but no hands went up. Mr. Basil stepped around his lectern until he was nearly on top of the front row. Everyone leaned forward, and in a whisper, Mr. Basil let one word drop: "Freedom."

A wave of twitters rolled through the room. Mr. Basil held his hand up until silence once more prevailed. He took a step back and raised his voice. "Freedom! *That* is the core of our movement.

Valentinus said, 'What makes us free is the knowledge—the gnosis—of who we were, of what we have become, of where we were, of what we have been thrown into, toward what we are speeding, of what we are being freed from, of what birth really is, and of what rebirth *really* is.'"

There was another murmur in the room. Several people hastily tried to capture what Mr. Basil had said on notepads, or by typing into their phones. Seth didn't understand a bit of that, but it seemed important. He felt a shiver run down his spine at the word "rebirth," however, and it resonated dissonantly with childhood memories of being "born again." It was the first hint of religious language, and Seth heard Angie's warning in his head again about getting involved with a cult.

But Mr. Basil was speaking again, so Seth set his thoughts aside. "That is an excellent question, Mr. Davies, and all in good time." Seth cursed himself for missing the question, and willed himself to focus. "What I have just recited is a course of study in itself. When you go back to your home Lodges, it is the answers to these questions that will be imparted to you. The answers to these questions are the secrets for the sake of which we took our oaths. The answers to these questions will lead you to freedom...and to the struggle against this present darkness, against wickedness in high places."*

No one said a word. Seth heard neither rustle nor cough from the assembly. He realized he was holding his breath. He forced himself to breathe.

"That is enough teaching for tonight. Tonight is for fellowship and food, and perhaps a bit more wine than is good for us. And since this is California, I assume there will be some smoked libations as well—please partake of those out on the porch." This got a smattering of laughter from the crowd. "Tomorrow, those of you

---

* Ephesians 6:2.

who have travelled will be initiated into the first of the mysteries. Those of you who are members of the local Lodge—I will see you on Thursday, at our usual time. The only difference is that Mr. Nazz will direct you to the temple rather than this, our accustomed room."

He stepped behind the lectern again and smiled warmly. "Now, I would ask if there are any questions, but then we would be here all night." A bigger laugh erupted from the crowd. Mr. Basil held a hand up, as if conferring a benediction. "And so I give to you instead this promise: You are invited into the exalted and perfect light. When you enter it, you will receive glory from those who can give it. You will receive thrones from those who bestow them. You will receive fine robes from those who make them. You will be washed by those who can truly cleanse you. And you will become glorious in the extreme. You will become like you were in the beginning, back when you were light."* He lowered his hand and stepped out from behind the lectern again. "Go now and sow your pleasure. Tomorrow you will sow your salvation."

Keira frowned at her computer. How to start? *Let's go with the obvious,* she thought. She typed in "S-panels conspiracy theories" and hit the return button. Then she whistled. 43,582 pages. That would have been nothing before the epidemic, but for what was left of civilization, it was a lot.

Her eyebrows shot up at the sight of a page claiming to be a history of S-panel conspiracies. She clicked on it and gasped. She had no idea if the page were comprehensive, but it certainly looked it. A glance at the menu grouped the theories by type:

---

* Adapted from "Trimorphic Protennoia," from *Suppressed Prayers* (Harrisburg, PA: Trinity Press International, 1998), p. 141.

Alien Portal Theories, Government Spying Theories, Political Theories, Religious Theories, and Secret Society Theories. A second menu arranged the individual theories in chronological order of emergence.

She clicked on Political Theories, and was met with a new menu containing twelve individual theories with such names as "Antifa Theories," "Democratic Theories," "Freedom League Theories," "Republican Theories," and more. She clicked on "Democratic Theories" and discovered that instead of containing theories originating with the Democratic Party, it contained theories *about* the Democratic Party. She clicked on "Social Control" and was met with a page of dense text. It was heavily hypertexted, with links to original, historical conspiracy posts and even archived news sources. There were also numerous photos depicting people allegedly involved, those perpetuating the stories, and key events both alluded to and speculated about.

The main gist of this theory seemed to be that the Democrats were using S-panels to record and document instances of hate speech, or the voicing of any opinions not sanctioned by the "radical left." The history alleged that evidence obtained through the recording equipment in the ubiquitous panels was responsible for egregious violations of civil liberties.

As she read, Keira found herself growing more and more uncomfortable. She realized that it wasn't because the theory was so crazy, but because it seemed so plausible. How had the left-leaning media obtained so much video footage of people voicing unpopular opinions, footage that inevitably led to someone getting cancelled? She had always assumed that it was through cell phone recordings, but now...

Only then did she notice that she was hunched over her computer screen, her eyes mere inches from the text. She forced herself to back up, pushing her rolling chair back from her desk. "Whoa, Nelly," she said out loud.

She looked around the room and it looked suddenly strange to her. Were her co-workers stealing glances at her? She shook her head. *Those are dangerous ideas,* she thought, glancing momentarily back at the screen. She pushed herself up, out of her chair. "Coffee," she said.

Keira picked up a file that she had been neglecting and headed for the break room. She had a terrible habit of reading while walking. Once, while on an errand in San Francisco, she had been engrossed in a novel and had nearly stepped into an open manhole. It had made her a little more careful since...but only a little.

Her mind kept wandering to the conspiracy theory she'd been reading about, and she wondered how she would read them all without being turned into a raving lunatic. She forced herself to focus on the file. Barely looking at what she was doing, she poured herself a cup of coffee. Still holding the coffee pot, she tried to turn the page, and ended up spilling hot coffee on her forearm and wrist.

"Shit!" she yelled, dropping the carafe. It shattered on the linoleum floor. She tossed the file aside and snatched at a tea towel. She wiped her arm and inspected it. It was red, but did not appear to be welting. "Dodged a bullet," she whispered to herself. Inwardly, she cursed her carelessness.

Just then Tony Raine came through the door and froze, coffee cup in hand. He looked at the shattered glass and his face fell into an instant glower. He then took in Keira, and the way she was holding the towel on her arm. "Jesus, Sloane. You're just a little tornado, aren't you?"

"Fuck you, Tony."

He picked his way around the shards to avoid stepping on them and sidled up to her. "How bad is it?"

"Not too. I'll be all right."

"I have some aloe vera gel in my desk..." he offered.

"Of course you do," she rolled her eyes.

"Do you want me to get it?"

She hated being indebted to him for anything, but she sighed. "Sure. Can't hurt."

"Okay. And I'll call janitorial."

"That's...great of you, Tony. Thanks."

"Don't mention it."

"I've been reading about those S-panel conspiracies."

"Y'know, Gore Vidal said, 'I'm not a conspiracy theorist—I'm a conspiracy analyst.'"

"That may be the only thing Gore Vidal and I have in common," she said.

"And...what's your conclusion?"

"I think they're addictive."

"There are recovery groups for people who get sucked into them." He scratched the back of his head.

"I believe it."

"Uh...Schenck was looking for you," Raine offered.

"When?"

"Just now."

"Dammit. Okay. Thanks."

Tony exited the little break room. Keira threw the tea towel onto the counter and picked up the file again. She put it on the table and quickly reassembled the pages into the right order.

Raine stuck his head in the door again. "Here you go," he said, tossing her a small tube of bright green gel.

She caught it and, opening the cap, squirted a blob into her right palm. Then she rubbed it gingerly onto her left arm. "Thanks," she said, tossing the tube back.

"Anytime. And the janitor is on his way."

Keira nodded and scooped up the file. As she walked, she opened it again and found the place where she'd left off. Using her peripheral vision, she navigated to Schenck's office, and pushed the door open with her elbow. Her eyes still scanning the file, she said, "You wanted to see me, boss?"

When she heard nothing, she finally looked up. The office was empty. She turned and scanned the squad room. She still did not see the chief. She glanced down at his desk and considered leaving him a note. Then she saw a post-it with "SLOANE?" written on it in big block letters. It was affixed to a yellow file folder.

She stepped up to the desk and reached out for the folder. Then she stopped and looked around again. No one was watching her, and Schenck was still nowhere to be seen. She opened the folder and noted it was stamped "Confidential." She should have snapped it closed right then, she knew, but her curiosity had been whetted. It was, after all, what made her a good investigator. She read the first line, then the second. Then her eyes went wide. "What the holy actual fuck?" she breathed.

Seth put the key in the lock to his apartment, but once again the door was open. He steeled himself for what he'd find and stepped in. Angie smiled up at him from the couch where she was sitting cross-legged, a nearly full bowl of popcorn in her lap.

"Hey, sunshine," she said. "How's cult-life?"

"Fuck you," he laughed and plopped down beside her. "What's this?" he asked, pointing to the grainy, black-and-white movie on the TV. "Is that Godzilla?"

"Yeah."

"The sound is down."

"Yeah. I was using They Might Be Giants as the soundtrack. Then the album ended and I forgot to turn it back on again."

"Huh...where did you get the idea?"

She shrugged. "It just seemed obvious." She handed him the

bowl and he grabbed a fist full of popcorn. "Oh, hey, you got a notice from the power company. You have to pay your bill in person this time or they're going to turn out the lights."

"What? Why?"

She shrugged again. "Ask the man. They probably just want to give you a stern talking-to, you know, put the fear of God into you. Why don't you just pay your bills on time?"

"Are you...opening my mail?" Seth asked.

"It looked important," Angie said without a hint of guilt.

Seth sighed. Then he leaned forward and corrected the angle of the coffee table, restoring it to its proper place directly in line with the couch.

"You know, sometime when you're out at your cult, I'm going to move all the furniture so that nothing is at right angles with anything else. And then I'm going to watch you blow a gasket."

"You are a cruel person."

"I know you say that with love." She snatched up a handful of popcorn. "So what did you do at your Gnostic group to— ...Oh, wait, I forgot. It's a *secret*."

Seth shut his eyes and shook his head. "We didn't do anything secret. It was an inter-regional gathering. There were people there from all over the state."

"Ah. Impressive. Did they all cup the balls?"

"You've got to let that go," Seth said.

Just then the phone rang. "Why do you still have a land line?" Angie asked. "That's so...20th century."

"I thought I needed it for the DSL."

"DSL? What is this, 2006?"

The phone was on its third ring. "Will you please pick that up before I miss it?" Seth asked.

Angie reached over to the table next to the couch and picked up the receiver. "Hello?" she said.

"You could have just handed it to—"

"This is Angie, his witchcraft-practicing lesbian roommate." Angie's eyes widened. Then she handed the phone to Seth. "It's your mom."

"Holy—" he said, and caught himself. He closed his eyes and centered himself, and then put the receiver to his ear. "Hello, Mom."

"Why do you hang out with that horrible, horrible girl?" his mother's voice chided.

"She's my best friend," Seth asked.

"You need new friends. Christian friends. That one will lead you straight to perdition."

"Mother—"

"You're not having sex with her, are you?"

"What? No! She's—"

"Because a girl like that will give you scorpions."

"I think you mean crabs," Seth corrected her.

Crabs? Angie mouthed.

"There are no crabs in the Revelation of John. Only scorpions," his mother said firmly.

"Mom, why are you calling so late?"

"Is it late? I've been baking."

"Who are you baking for?" Seth asked.

"You know how your father loves those little toads-in-the-hole."

Seth opened his mouth to say, "Dad's dead," but closed it again. He felt adrenaline surge through his body.

"I want to know when you're coming over. I have some plants to hang and I can't get your father to do it."

"I...maybe Saturday? In the morning?"

"That will be fine, dear. I'll make pancakes."

"Oh. Okay."

"Are you going to church?"

"Uh..." Seth froze.

"I know you're not going to our church, because *you are not there*."

"I...uh...I'm in a Bible study group," Seth lied.

Angie's face screwed up into a mask of disbelief as she shook her head. She threw a piece of popcorn at him.

"What denomination?" His mother grilled. "Is it a Bible-believing church? It's not the Episcopalians, is it? Because those homosexual Catholic-wannabes are all marching straight into the lake of fire."

"Mom, please." Seth dropped his forehead into his hand.

"I'm waiting," she said.

"It's a...they're seekers," he said.

"Oh! We have a couple of seeker-churches in our region. That's just fine. Just make sure you avoid any of those liberal social justice churches. If you hear 'social justice' from the pulpit, you just get up and run as fast as you can, because that's a Satanic agenda."

"Okay, mom. I haven't heard anything about social justice yet."

"Let's keep it that way. Your father and I are both praying for you."

"Okay," he said.

"See you Sunday," she said.

"Saturday," Seth corrected her.

"You could come to church with us on Sunday," she said.

"But I'm not. I have to work," he lied again.

"Remember the Sabbath and keep it holy," she said.

"I'll see you Saturday," Seth said and handed the phone back to Angie.

Angie dangled the phone as if it were a soiled diaper. "She's still talking," she pointed out.

Seth motioned toward the phone's cradle and Angle put the receiver in its place.

"Well, that was invigorating," Angie said.

Seth's right eye had begun to twitch. He sighed. "She...tonight she thinks my dad is still alive."

"Oh...you know, she didn't seem that bad when we went for dinner," Angie noted.

"No. That was a good night. Tonight is...not a good night."

"She seemed sharp as a tack."

He nodded. "It's later. You know."

"Sundowning?" Angie asked.

"I think so. I mean, I'm not an expert..."

"No, I get it. It's a thing that happens."

"The thing is...she's not any better this way. She's horrible whether she's all there or not," Seth said, looking at his shoes.

"Her world is a very unsafe place," Angie said.

Seth nodded. "You know, it's bad enough already. You don't need to provoke her."

"She won't remember it tomorrow," Angie said with a shrug. "Let a girl have her fun."

That was probably true.

"Bible study group?" Angie asked. "That's stretching it a bit, don't you think?"

"It's not too far off," Seth said.

"I thought you said it wasn't religious," Angie narrowed one eye at him. Seth opened his mouth to say something, but Angie interrupted him. "You can't have it both ways."

Seth closed his mouth. "I'm really worried about her."

"She shouldn't be living alone," Angie said.

"No."

"She'll burn her house down some day, making puff pastries at three in the morning," Angie said.

"That's exactly what I'm afraid of."

"And she's skinny as a bird," Angie pointed out. "Who eats all that stuff she bakes?"

"She says my dad does," Seth said.

"Your dad who's been dead for, what, ten years?"

"Yeah."

Angie cocked her head. "Who *does* eat all that stuff?"

"I have absolutely no idea," Seth confessed.

———

S eth was only two knocks in when the door swung open.
"Hi!" Becky said.

Seth smiled, but was surprised by how sad he felt. "Hi."

"Come in, come in," Becky waved him into her flat.

Instantly her cat, Bo, began to rub himself against Seth's legs. He leaned over and gave the cat a quick rub.

"I'm so glad you could come over," she said. "Do you want a beer?"

"Uh...sure. A beer would be great."

She trotted into the kitchen and Seth took a seat on the couch. Bo jumped up and began to turn circles in his lap. He finally stopped, looking at the kitchen, where Becky had disappeared, leaving Seth staring at his freckled cat anus.

When Becky emerged, carrying two beers, he finally nudged Bo to the ground. Becky sat next to him and handed him one of the bottles.

"Thanks," he said, accepting it. He took a swig, pleased by the spicy, nutty flavor of a brown ale. "Becky...I'm sorry I haven't been around."

"I was a little worried," she confessed. "I thought maybe you'd met someone."

"I don't work that way," he said. "If I was interested in someone else, I'd...I'd break up with you first, before, you know... going out with them." He meant that to sound comforting, but it didn't come out that way. It sounded more like a prophesy than a hypothetical.

"Oh," she looked down at her hands.

"What I mean is that...no...I'd never do that to you." He tried to manage a comforting smile, but was afraid he was only making it worse.

"That's okay," she said, in a tone that clearly wasn't. She swallowed. "Angie said you were...in a study group."

"Uh...yeah."

"Something occult."

"Did she say that?" he asked. "Because I wouldn't call it occult. It's gnostic—"

"Oh, yes, that's it! That's what she said. Sorry." Several awkward moments passed. "So, tell me about gnostic...stuff."

"Uh...I don't know very much, really. Just that 'gnostic' means 'knowledge,' and there seem to be a lot of secrets."

"What kind of secrets?"

"I don't really know. They haven't told us any yet."

Her brow furrowed. "These study sessions don't sound very exciting."

"Oh, they're actually good. Fascinating, really," he countered. "We just...haven't gotten to the good stuff yet, I don't think."

"But when you do..."

"Uh...it will be a secret."

"Can I come? To the study group?"

Seth didn't look at her, but felt her eyes on him. "I'm not sure that's a good idea."

"Why not?"

"Because I don't think you're really interested in gnosticism."

"How do you know?"

"Well...can you define it?"

"Can you?" she returned.

He couldn't. He felt heat rise up his neck. "It's an-an interfaith movement. It talks about liberation through knowing."

"Knowing what?"

"I...well...I don't know."

"Why don't you think I'd be interested? It's something we could do together."

"I don't—"

"I love philosophy and religion," she went on. Her yellow page boy bounced as she moved her head back and forth.

"It's not very religious," he said.

"What is it you think is so fascinating about it?" she asked. The question wasn't aggressive, it was curious, almost sweetly so.

"Well, I...when I left my parents' church, I left the whole Christianity thing behind. And I think that was healthy...for me, anyway. But..." he looked around the room, as if hunting for something. "Then I didn't know what my life was for. I feel like I've just been spinning my wheels, working in the bookstore, not... doing much. Making minimum wage. Barely making rent. Life seems kind of...hard, pointless, meaningless."

Becky looked troubled. "I'm sorry you feel that way. I thought that maybe we...you and me..."

"Oh, this...this doesn't have anything to do with you," Seth said. Her shoulders deflated. *Way to go, Ace,* the voice in his head congratulated him. *I literally cannot say anything right.*

"So...you're hoping this...gnostic thing can give you...what? Meaning?"

He shrugged. "Maybe."

"Why them? Why that? Why not, I don't know, Transcendental Meditation?"

"Because I hate meditation. It's boring." He made a face like he had been served lima beans. "I don't know if there's anything there, really. I just...I'm starting to look. And you don't get on a plane to start searching. You just start looking where you are, right? I'm just exploring, and this came across my path. It's no big thing, it's just...compelling, I guess. And promising."

She nodded. He wondered if she really did understand. "'Life sucks and then you die,'" she quoted. "That's kind of my worldview."

"Yeah, mine too," he said. "And pretty much everyone I know. And I can't go back to my parents' church, that's not only hopeless, that's...I don't know, it feels actively evil, you know?"

She nodded, a little sadly, it seemed to him. She hadn't grown up religious, but he sensed she was trying to understand.

"So, I just want to find more than that, more than 'life sucks and then you die.' And I don't know if I will find it, I'm just...I'm looking."

Becky reached over and took his hand. "I'll support you in that...if you'll let me."

"Really?" he asked.

"Really," she said.

A part of him felt relieved. Perhaps he hadn't completely bunged it up after all. On the other hand, he liked Becky, but he knew he wasn't in love with her. It was only a matter of time, but... *This is fine for now,* the voice in his head said. He wasn't at all sure that was true. A prick of guilt irritated him. *If you aren't serious about her, cut her loose,* the voice in his head said.

"That's great," he said. He put his arm around her shoulder and leaned his head against her.

———

"I need to duck in here," Angie said, pointing to the door of a thrift shop.

"Oh. Sure," Seth agreed. Angie opened the door and then held it behind her until Seth entered. "What do you need?"

"A new jacket," she said. "You can help me pick it out."

"Okay," he said.

She wound her way to the women's section and cast around for the coats.

"Over there," Seth said, pointing. She made a beeline for it and began to sort through the stock.

Seth loved the way thrift stores smelled—like the dusty pillows in the guest room at his grandma's house.

"I think it's criminal that people pay fifty dollars for a new pair of pants when you can get exactly the same thing here for ten bucks," Angie said.

"No argument here," Seth agreed. "I buy all of my clothes at these places."

"You'll wear it and you'll like it," a woman said at the next rack to a teenager who must have been her daughter.

"It's lame," the girl said, folding her arms.

"God hates stuck up princesses that talk back to their mothers," the woman said.

"Well, I hate God," the girl said.

The woman slapped the girl so hard that everyone in the store stopped and looked. Time seemed frozen.

"Bitch!" the girl shouted, and stormed off.

"Come back here right now, young lady," the woman said.

"That woman has lost already," Angie said.

Seth noticed his fingers had begun to shake, and he started sweating.

"Dude, your eye is doing that thing," Angie said.

"I...I gotta go over here," Seth said.

"You said you'd help me pick out a coat," Angie complained, but Seth was already striding past row after row of chrome-coated racks, putting as much distance as he could between himself and the mother-daughter conflict.

He held the furthest rack in both hands and steadied himself. He closed his eyes and breathed deeply in and out, in and out, willing his nerves to settle. Eventually, he felt his shoulders relax and his fingers stopped trembling. When he opened his eyes again, he blinked, not registering what he was looking at. Then he knew.

"Vests," he said out loud. He cocked his head and began to sort through them, one after another. Most were either too gaudy or too plain. Then he found a muted paisley print that was mostly navy blue. It was smart. It was almost elegant. It had some style, but it wasn't flashy.

He pulled it off the rack and tried it on. He walked to the mirror and saw how it hung over his t-shirt. The navy pleasingly contrasted with the orange of his shirt, and the fit was perfect. He pulled it off and looked at the price tag. Three dollars.

He folded the vest over his arm. The mother and daughter were forgotten. He held his head up high and headed for the cashier. When he sowed his salvation, he would be properly attired.

WHAT IS A SACRAMENT?

A sacrament is a sacred and symbolic religious ritual that is considered to have a profound spiritual significance. It is a tangible and visible expression of invisible grace, believed to be instituted by a higher power, and practiced by various religious traditions. Sacraments play a crucial role in the spiritual lives of believers, serving as a means of connecting with the divine and receiving blessings.

In Christianity, sacraments are believed to convey spiritual benefits to participants. The Catholic Church recognizes seven sacraments: Baptism, Confirmation, Eucharist, Reconciliation (Confession), Anointing of the Sick, Holy Orders, and Matrimony. Protestants generally only recognize Baptism and Eucharist as sacraments.

The fundamental characteristic of a sacrament is its dual nature. Each sacrament consists of both a physical component, known as the "matter," and a spoken or enacted element, known as the "form." The matter involves the use of physical elements such as water in Baptism or bread and wine in the Eucharist, while the form encompasses the specific words or gestures spoken or performed by the celebrant.

Sacraments are seen as acts of divine grace, initiated by a higher power and facilitated by religious leaders or ministers. Through sacraments, the faithful believe they receive divine blessings, forgiveness, spiritual nourishment, and a deepened relationship with the divine. They are seen as powerful conduits for experiencing and expressing faith and for participating in the redemptive work of God.

The significance of sacraments extends beyond the individual participant. They are also seen as acts of communal worship and unity, binding believers together in a shared religious experience. Sacraments often involve the participation of the faith community, reinforcing the sense of belonging and the bonds of fellowship among believers.

CHAPTER SEVEN

Do not wash yourselves with Death.*
—Sermon of Zostrianos

Angie watched the new customer closely, trying to size him up. He looked tentative. Lots of them did. She put on her most appealing smile and sauntered over to him. "Hey, big guy. This your first time?"

The "big guy" was shorter than she was, and nearly jumped out of his skin at the sound of her voice. He looked around as if planning his escape.

"Hey, chill out. We're all friends here. Let me help."

The young man's eyes flashed like a caged animal's. But then he visibly relaxed. "This isn't anything like I thought it would be."

"Your first time to a cannabis dispensary?"

---

* The Sermon of Zostrianos: Nag Hammadi Codex VIII, 1; translated by Marvin Meyer, published in *The Gnostic Bible* (Boston, MA: Shambhala Publications, 2009).

"Yeah."

"And you didn't expect it to look like the Apple store?"

"No. I thought...I don't know what I thought."

"Maybe some hippie place with sawdust on the floor and dreamcatchers hanging in the windows dangling over the crystals?"

"Something like that. Seedier, maybe."

"I get it. Relax, though. Weed's legit now." She placed a reassuring hand on his elbow. "Tell me what you're here for—medicinal or recreational?"

"Uh..." He looked sheepish again. "Recreational?"

"Great!" she said, a little too chipper. "Do you know what kind of strain you want?"

"Strain?"

Whoo boy, she thought. *Okay, time for Weed 101.* "Do you want a bright, energetic buzz? That's great for creativity and getting a lot of shit done around the house—good daytime weed, too. Or do you like a heavy, relaxing high? That's really helpful with anxiety and can put you to sleep. Or you could do something in the middle—something euphoric but not sleepy, you know?"

"Um...that sounds good—the last one."

"Excellent. Over here, then." She led him to a counter where there were about twenty varieties on display. "You want to check out the ones with a green dot beside them—those are hybrids. Every one will have a different effect, of course, and they can differ quite a bit. I really like White Widow and Gorilla Glue, but if it's your first time, I highly recommend Blue Dream. It's a great entry-level strain. Can I set you up with an eighth of that?"

"Sure, that sounds...great." The kid looked so grateful he might cry. He was certainly more relaxed, which was something the Blue Dream would only help with. "Do you need some rolling papers? We have a two-for-one sale going on."

"Sure, okay."

She tossed two packs of raw hemp rollers into the bag with the canister of Blue Dream. "You let me know when you're ready to upgrade to a pipe or a vaporizer. A dry-herb vaporizer will save your lungs."

"Okay...I will."

She took his credit card, and a moment later handed him a receipt. She gave him another bright smile. "You come back anytime. And let me know what you think of that. If it doesn't do just what you want it to, let's talk some more and I can make some other recommendations."

"Thank you so much," he said, taking his purchase and walking out a good deal more confidently than he came in.

"Another job well done, Angie," Angie said aloud to herself. Then she saw someone she wasn't expecting, someone else who looked distinctly out of place.

Angie walked up to her. "Becky? I didn't know you were into weed."

Becky whirled at the sound of her voice. *Is everyone jumpy today?* Angie wondered.

"Oh, Angie. I'm so glad to see you."

Angie frowned. "Is everything okay?"

Becky looked down. She was pretty, but her blonde braids made her look like a chunky St.-Pauli-Girl. *She'd do better with a buzz cut and some tatts,* Angie thought. *But maybe that's just me.*

"Can we talk?"

"Well, I'm at work...but I have a break coming up. Let me see if I can take it a little early."

"I can wait."

"Let me see." Angie speed-walked into the back. "Hey, Sid, can I take my break a little early?"

Sid had a sandwich halfway to his mouth. He put it down, frowning. "Now?"

"Yeah, if that works for you."

He looked at his sandwich, then back up at Angie. "Yeah, okay."

"Thanks a bunch. I owe you one."

"You owe me three, last time I checked."

Angie flashed him a smile and spun back out onto the floor. She caught Becky by the hand and led her outside. She kept going until she was on the side of the building. She fished a cigarette out of her pocket and pressed a tiny bubble of black hash into its tip. Then she lit it and inhaled deeply. She closed her eyes and savored the sweet and savory mixture of the tobacco and hashish. When she let it out, she felt everything in her relax. "Okay, that's better. You want a drag?" She held the cigarette out to Becky, but the young woman shook her head.

Angie slid down the side of the building and sat cross-legged with her back resting against it. Becky did the same, smoothing her dress over her knees. "What's on your mind?" Angie asked.

"Have you seen Seth?"

"Every damn morning," Angie said. She touched Becky on the arm. "Are you okay? You seem depressed."

"Seth hasn't called me in days. We had kind of a hard conversation. And then...nothing. I thought about going to the bookstore—"

"*Not* a good idea. Bad place for a scene," Angie noted.

"Yeah." Becky looked like she might cry.

Angie took another drag. As she blew out the smoke, she said, "Becky, if you're worried that Seth is interested in another girl... he's not."

"I...no, I didn't think that. I know he's going through a lot of stuff right now. I know he's really grieving Kush. And his OCD is..." Becky shook her head. "It's scary."

"You know what scares me?" Angie asked. "That fucking study group."

"Oh. The gnostic thing."

"Yeah. Did he tell you about fondling some guy's balls?"

"What?" Becky's hand jerked to her mouth. "What are you talking about?"

"So...I'm guessing that's a no."

Becky shook her head. "No wonder he didn't want me to go with him."

Angie laughed, but then caught herself. "Sorry. I can't believe you'd even think about getting involved with that crazy cult."

"Is it a gay thing?" Becky asked. "Because that would actually explain a lot. He...just doesn't seem very interested in sex."

Angie cocked her head. "How...not interested?"

"Like, as in...we've never had any."

"Hoo boy." Angie shook her head. "Trust me, Seth is a zero on the Kinsey scale. There's not a gay bone in that boy's body. Trust someone with impeccable gaydar. But...I didn't think he was a fucking virgin."

Becky looked at her shoes. "Now I feel like I've said something I shouldn't have."

"Don't worry about it. I've razzed him for less."

"Please don't tell him I told you."

"I make no promises, especially if I'm high. Have you called him?" Angie asked.

"I left a message...maybe two. I-I don't want to crowd him...it might push him away."

"You're being *way* too passive, girl," Angie said. "I'd slap him around if I was you."

Becky looked horrified.

"Look, I'll feel him out, okay?" Angie offered. "I'll ask him how things are going with you two, and see what he says. How's that?"

"Would you?"

"Of course. I could even slap him around a bit, if you like."

When Seth stepped into the Lodge's dining room, Jude Ash leaped up from his seat to greet him. Seth wasn't expecting a bear hug, but he didn't resist it.

"So good to see you! Wasn't Tuesday great? So many people!"

Seth waved at Lynn, who bobbed her head in greeting, reminding Seth of one of those plastic birds with a test-tube body that sticks its beak in a glass of water before springing up again. He held his hand up to Musa Daniels, who gave him a strained smile. Matt ignored him, but Maria waved at him with cheery excitement.

"Well, we'd have another person here if we didn't have to touch dead genitals," Seth noted. He thought about telling them all about finding Mika at his home after the ceremony, but decided against it.

"Heh," Jude laughed nervously. He wiped his palms on his jeans and did not look Seth in the eye. "Yeah. That was...weird."

Seth sat. Their chairs were arranged in a circle. A short table stood in the middle of the circle. Jude sat down next to Seth and pointed at the empty chair. "I guess that's for Mr. Basil."

"I guess so," Seth said. He looked around and marveled at how large, how empty the room seemed. His mind flashed on two nights ago, how it had been nearly full, bursting with life and excitement.

His thoughts flitted to Kush. He wanted so much to go and visit him at Travis', but he knew the dog needed time to adjust and settle in. It wouldn't be good to upset him right now. He needed to do what was best for Kush.

Seth heard the squeak of a door's hinge and looked over his shoulder. Through a single door opposite the double doors came a man about Jude's age. He looked strangely familiar, but Seth could not place him. His almost white hair was billowy and bushy. His mouth was jowly, as if he were part bulldog. He was heavy-set, but not fat. The words "big boned" appeared in Seth's mind. He wore casual slacks, a blue button-down-collar shirt, and a brown tweed jacket with leather patches at the elbows. He was carrying a bowl of water in one hand; a towel was draped over his wrist. In his other hand, he held a taper set into a brass candle holder.

"You!" Matt said.

The man met Matt's eyes and halted. He smiled. "Yes, me!" He continued his way to the empty chair and set the bowl, towel, and candle on the table before them. Then he sat.

"I know you," Jude said.

"We are all, unfortunately, intimately acquainted," the man agreed.

"But you're not dead!?" Maria breathed.

"No, thank God," the man said.

Seth cocked his head like a dog. Then it hit him. This man was the corpse. It was this man's testicles he had cupped when he swore his oath.

"You weren't dead the other night, either!" Lynn exclaimed.

"Assuredly not," the man agreed.

"But how...you...it...they were so *cold*," Lynn's nose twitched as if she'd stepped into a fish market.

"Oh my God, yes. The boys were cold indeed. I had to soak my crotch in ice water for twenty minutes before I climbed upon that table, and even then I kept an ice pack between my legs until just before you stepped through the door."

Seth's mouth was open, but he could find no words.

"But you seemed so *dead*," Jude breathed. "You were...blue."

"Makeup," the man said.

"You were so *still*!" Jude added.

"Decades of meditation," the man countered.

Jude shook his head, finally speechless.

"This is your first lesson—" the man said, holding forth one finger, "—everything is not what it seems."

Seth felt a chill run through him. The idea that he had held this man's—this living man's—balls repulsed him. *I'm not gay,* he thought. There had been nothing even remotely erotic about it when he thought the man was dead. Now that he knew the man wasn't, he didn't know what to think about it. He felt dirty.

"I am Dr. Joshua Robinson. I will be your catechist."

"Cata-what?" Matt asked.

"Teacher," Robinson said. "For your spiritual instruction."

Seth felt his heart sink into his stomach. *It doesn't seem...religious,* he remembered himself saying to Angie. *But she was right,* he thought. *Here it is.*

"I didn't think this was religious," Seth said.

"He speaks!" Dr. Robinson waved his hands toward Seth. He dropped his hands and considered Seth, not unkindly. Finally, he said, "Young man, *everything* is religious, in one way or another."

"I don't know what you mean," Seth said.

"Truth cannot be comprehended. It can only be hinted at, pointed to. As the Gospel of Philip tells us in verse 59, "Truth did not come into the world naked, but through symbols and images. We cannot apprehend it any other way."

"Uh...what do you mean by images?" Maria asked.

Dr. Robinson looked mildly surprised. "Images—metaphors, symbols...and stories, of course." Maria nodded, and Dr. Robinson continued. "Religions are stories we tell ourselves to help us make sense of the world. Our lives are given purpose and meaning when we understand our little stories—our own little lives—in the context of a bigger story, a cosmic story—the narrative offered by the religion we are committed to. Even if you are an atheist, you are still telling yourself a story about the universe, how it got that way, and your place in the whole—and that too is a religious story, whether you want to admit it or not."

"Okay..." Seth wasn't convinced, but had to admit it was a compelling vision.

"We gnostics also have a story. It is...complex, but you'll get the gist of it soon enough. It is, however, almost an anti-story. It is the complete inversion of the story most religious people in the state have grown up with."

Seth liked the sound of that. A part of him had felt betrayed—first by the revelation that the corpse was alive, and then by the sudden introduction of religious language. But now he was intrigued again, so he set aside his objections for the time being. If this was the total inversion of the religion he grew up with, he wanted to know more about it before rejecting it outright. He had, after all, come this far...

His thoughts were interrupted by movement. Dr. Robinson leaned over and scooted the table between them a little closer to himself. Then he reached into the pocket of his tweed jacket and withdrew a lighter. He lit the candle, saying, "The master did everything by means of a symbol—baptism. No one can see himself in a mirror—or reflected in a bowl of water—without light. Nor can you see by the light without water or a mirror. For this reason it is necessary to baptize with two things—light and water."* He replaced the lighter in his pocket and pulled forth a small, dark amber vial. "I will tell you a parable, and will enact a mystery," he said. "God is a dyer." He unscrewed the top of the vial and held it over the water. "Just as those good dyes—what they call 'true' dyes—become one with those things being dyed, so it is with those things God has dyed."† He tipped the contents of the vial into the water. Instantly, the water swirled with billowing clouds of brilliant purple. A few moments later, the clouds had dissipated, leaving the whole of the bowl a deep,

---

* Gospel of Philip, 60, 67.
† Gospel of Philip, 37.

placid color. "Because God's dyes are eternal, we are changed forever when we are dipped in those colors."

He rose and took up the bowl, holding it close to his chest. He moved to stand behind Jude. Seth looked at Jude. His eyes were closed and his face serene. His hands rested in his lap, almost as if he were meditating. "Receive the first mystery," Dr. Robinson said. Dipping his hand into the bowl, he released a handful of water over Jude's bald head. Lavender-colored water raced over his ears and down his cheeks. Jude took a deep breath, clearly savoring the moment. "Amazing," he said. Holding the bowl in one hand, Dr. Robinson placed his other hand on Jude's head and closed his own eyes. Seth assumed he was either praying or perhaps psychically transmitting some ineffable property into Jude's being.

Then the moment passed. Dr. Robinson removed his hand. Jude opened his eyes, and they were shining. Robinson gave a shallow bow, and then moved to stand behind Seth's chair. One voice in Seth's head said, *I'm out of here*, but his body did not move. Instead, Seth mimicked Jude's behavior. He closed his eyes and waited to see what would come.

"Receive the first mystery," Dr. Robinson said again. Then Seth felt water running into his hair and down his neck. Then he felt the weight of Dr. Robinson's hand on his head, and felt a heat radiate throughout his head. Then the pressure lifted, and Seth felt momentarily dizzy. He was glad he had been sitting down.

Seth looked at Maria on his other side. She did not look relaxed, but she did not protest. Nor did any of the others. At last, Dr. Robinson set the bowl back down and then moved the table back to the center of their small circle.

"I *felt* that," Lynn said.

"Savor that, for not everyone does," Dr. Robinson said. "The orthodox say that their sacraments are efficacious whether you feel something or no. But we gnostics place a great deal of import on personal experience. If you don't feel anything, how do you know anything has happened? No, the experience means a great deal."

"But what if I didn't experience anything?" Seth asked.

Dr. Robinson shrugged. "This is a symbol of a mystery that will be complete by the end of our time together. I dare not disparage anyone's experience, certainly not Ms. Shire's," he gave Lynn a nod. "But I suggest we set your question aside until our time is finished, and then I'll invite you to ask it again. Will that be all right?"

"Sure," Seth said.

Dr. Robinson opened his mouth, as if to begin an oration, but then paused. He glanced sideways at Seth. "And did you not...feel anything?"

Seth swallowed. "I...I think I did. It was warm."

"It is different for everyone," Dr. Robinson said, nodding. "But for a first mystery, warmth augers well."

Seth had no idea what that meant, but he didn't inquire. Dr. Robinson pulled a remote control from his inside jacket pocket. Pressing one button with his thumb, the lights dimmed. The candle seemed to flare, bathing everything in its warm, yellow glow. Then Seth heard a high-pitched whine, and a light splashed on the wall nearest Dr. Robinson. He moved so as not to obstruct anyone's view. An image resolved on the wall—a star field. But the stars were moving, as if a camera were panning over the sky. The camera slowed and finally came to rest on the glorious spectacle of a nebula that looked vaguely like the fingers of a hand extended in blessing. Dr. Robinson cleared his throat. "This is the Helix nebula." The picture shifted to what looked like an elaborate space station. Seth frowned as he tried to take in its enormity. It consisted of ring upon ring of white tubing, all connected with gray columns that looked strangely classical. He tried to count the rings, but before he even got halfway, Dr. Robinson spoke again. "This is the *Cibus Dei*. It is a multi-generational starship that has been en route for more than a hundred years. This is the first great mystery, sisters and brothers. The *Cibus Dei* is our home. We are not on earth, and we never have been."

"Whaaa..." Matt said. Seth looked over at him and saw his jaw slack. Seth frowned, not sure whether Dr. Robinson was joking, or if perhaps it was another fake-out.

The picture vanished, leaving them bathed once more in candlelight. Then the lights came up again, but not as brightly as before.

"I know this is a great shock, and you won't want to believe it," Dr. Robinson said, resuming his seat. "And that is fine. We gnostics are freethinkers, so you must weigh the evidence for yourselves. But as you ponder this mystery, I ask you to pay attention to a few things." He leaned forward, looking them in the eye, one after another. "Pay attention to the sky. It is too close. The physics are off. Watch some old movies by John Ford, or perhaps *Laurence of Arabia*, and compare the sky you see there to what you see outside. It is simply *not right*. Second, pay attention to distances. Cities are too close together. It should take an hour to drive to San Francisco...but it doesn't. The scale is off—not by a lot, but by a noticeable degree, if you're paying attention to it."

Seth scowled. It was a joke. It had to be a joke. He felt something in his hair and instinctively reached for it. His hand came back wet, and that surprised him momentarily. He had forgotten all about the dying ritual, the baptism, whatever it was.

"Finally, consider S-panels. They seem like a normal thing, yes? It's how electricians access the grid—at least, that is the story they tell us. Have you ever wondered why it is so difficult to become an electrician? People have noted that they hold a position of outsized esteem in our society, and indeed they do. Read your literature. Prior to 1950 or so, electricians were peers not of doctors or lawyers, but of plumbers and contractors. Also, look at any litera-

THE WHERE, THE WHO & THE WHAT • 217

ture prior to 1950—do you see any mention of S-panels? You do not. Nor will you see them in movies. Only in media after 1950 do they make an appearance. Consider one more thing, if you will. The year is 2065—but have we made any significant scientific progress in the past fifty years? We have not. Is that not strange? And I'll tell you why that is." His voice lowered to a whisper. "We are out of range." He leaned back again and explained. "Previously, scientific discoveries, medicine, even literature and the arts, the recent developments on earth could be transmitted to us, could be incorporated into our own media. But now...now we are frozen in time, dependent upon only such novelty as we can generate ourselves. And the powers-that-be," he looked menacingly at the ceiling. Then he looked back down, directly into Seth's eyes, "don't want us to evolve too far away from what they consider earth-normative."

He sat back in his chair and sighed. "And I know you do not believe any of this, my friends. Mr. Ash, I'm sure even you have your doubts. But let that be. Go and explore the world—such as it is—with fresh eyes. Because what I have said to you cannot be unsaid. Now that you have heard it, you cannot unhear it. The world has changed forever now, and you cannot undo it. God's dyes are eternal, and we are changed forever when we are dipped in his colors."

Keira's teeth were on edge and her leg bounced as she waited in the cold, empty room. When the door swung open, she jumped to her feet. "Sit down, special agent," Sloane said to her.

"I want to know why you've taken my gun and my badge from me," she said.

"Sit *down*, special agent."

Glaring, Keira took her seat. "I want to know why I'm being punished."

Sloane shook his head and sneered. "That's funny. I want to know why you were rifling through a file on my desk marked 'confidential.'" He folded his hands in front of him, his suit jacket sleeves looking too short for his arms.

"I wasn't 'rifling' through anything," she said. "That's a loaded word, and you know it."

"Oh. I'm just putting a negative spin on it?" Sloane asked.

"Yeah. Yeah, you are."

"So, you were not helping yourself to a confidential file on my desk?"

"I went to your office to look for you," she explained slowly. "And I saw the file. I was curious."

His eyebrows jumped. "Does curiosity give you national security clearance? Because I thought only HSA could do that."

"We *are* HSA."

"And there's a chain of command. Intelligence is on a need-to-know basis, and different people have different levels of clearance. You know this, special agent. Stop playing dumb."

Keira looked at her hands. "Curiosity makes me a good investigator."

"Curiosity is one factor in the makeup of a good investigator. Another is the ability to respect authority."

Keira bit her lip. "I didn't get much of a look at it."

"That's not an excuse."

"What I don't understand is why some Star Trek scenario has a top-secret wrapping," Keira said.

Sloane sighed. "Look, this can go one of two ways. I can refer you to Internal Affairs for an investigation into why you knowingly violated national security—"

She interrupted him. "What's the other option?"

"The other option is I bump your security clearance, pretend none of this ever happened, and read you in."

"I got ten years with HSA, chief," she said. Her voice quavered, and she fought to master it. "Ten more and I can retire. I don't want to lose my pension."

"You should have thought of that before you opened Pandora's box," Sloane growled. Several moments of silence followed.

"So...what are you going to do?" Her own voice sounded hopeless to her. She felt pathetic.

Elbows on the table between them, he buried his face in his hands and massaged his temples. "My first choice would be clocking you on the side of the head with my service pistol."

"And what's your second choice?" she asked.

"I was torn between choosing you or Gray for this...security bump. I was leaning toward Gray."

"Why?"

He shrugged. "Because I *trust* him."

A knot twisted in her stomach.

"But he's also a pain in the ass who talks too much," he added.

She looked up, grasping after a straw of hope.

"But your little...indiscretion has forced my hand." He folded his hands and put them down on the table. "The fact is, special agent, you are good at what you do. And you're smart. And you don't get on my nerves...usually."

"Are you saying that...what? You're going to recommend me for this new...whatever it is?"

"It's nothing new to HSA. It'll only be new to you. You'll still work out of this squad, you'll just be...doing things that require a higher security clearance—*if* I can trust you. Can I trust you?"

"Of course! Yes! I mean...look chief, I'm sorry I looked at that file. It won't happen again. I promise."

"I believe you. But the fact is, your punishment will be that you will have to do this again...and again...and again. Because your life is about to change."

"I'm up to it, chief," she said, forcing her face into a mask of courage and certainty.

"You'd better be," he said.

Seth paused at the door of his mother's house and closed his eyes. He focused on the bottoms of his feet, and felt his body respond with mild relaxation. He took several deep breaths until he started to feel dizzy. Already, he felt the Monster God looming. His mind flashed on the image of the starship Dr. Robinson had showed them the night before—rushing headlong into the unknown night, toward...what? He felt a wave of vertigo, so he opened his eyes and steadied himself on the door jamb.

He knocked. He waited as he heard his mother's footfalls approach. The door swung inward, and his mother was there, looking up at him. "There you are. You're late."

"Sorry, Mom. The bus—"

"It's always someone else's fault, isn't it?" She turned and walked away, back into the house, leaving the door open.

Seth sighed again and entered, shutting the door behind him. He followed his mother to the kitchen where some plants were arrayed on the food prep island in the room's center.

He cocked his head at the sight of them. Some were lush and green. Others were clearly dead—and some were fast on the way.

"Here's some coffee," his mother said, setting a cup down on the table.

"Uh...thanks. I don't have a lot of time, though—"

"Of course you don't. Drink your coffee."

He sat and lifted the cup to his nose. His mother knew he drank it with milk, but she didn't believe in putting milk in coffee

—something she justified with some reference to the book of Leviticus. He sipped at it and grimaced. It was over strong and sour. He put it back on the table.

"How are you?" he asked.

"What's that supposed to mean?" his mother asked.

Seth didn't know how to answer that. She had intuited something true, it seemed—he was hoping to divine more than what just a pleasant greeting might reveal. He coughed and said, "Well, *I'm* doing okay, I think." It was a lie, of course. He wanted to burst forth with everything he had heard at the Lodge—to be an excited child again, telling his mom what had happened at school, hoping she would share in his awe, his wonder, in the incredibility of it all.

But he knew better than that. First, he had taken an oath. Second, it was a very strange revelation to come from what his mother understood to be a Bible study. Third, whatever support, whatever sympathy, whatever love he might once have hoped for from his mother, he knew that he would not receive it now. He had strayed too far from the idealized image she had in her head of who he *should* be, and she would forever punish him for that, regardless of what he might ever do or say or accomplish.

He felt the weight of the Monster God pressing down on him, distorting and perverting every felicitous emotion or connection or relationship that might ever have been possible under this roof. He saw how the heaviness of her god had crushed his mother's soul, and had nearly done the same to him. He felt a sudden sharp pain stab at his lungs, and he found it hard to breathe. He clutched at his chest and took several shallow, shuddering breaths.

"What?" his mother asked. "What's wrong?"

He wanted to say, *Your god is too heavy; he's smothering me.* But instead he said, "It feels like a heart attack."

"Don't be ridiculous," she waved his words away. "You were

always so dramatic." She stood and walked over to the plants. "I'd hang these myself, but the stepstool shakes."

Seth punched his chest, trying to get whatever muscles were seizing to relax. He focused on his breathing, keeping it slow, and making each breath a little bit deeper than the last, ignoring the searing pain that came with each expansion of his lungs.

"Are you paying attention to me?" his mother asked.

He nodded. He wanted to ask her about his father, to see if she was still delusional. Against his better judgment, he said, "Why didn't you ask Dad to hang those?"

She turned on her heel and pierced him with her eye. "You are a wicked, wicked child."

That didn't tell him much that he didn't already know. He still didn't know how present and together his mother was. She was, after all, asking him to hang plants that were clearly as dead as his father.

"Okay, where do you want this one?" he held up one of the plants that was actually living.

"You can't wait to be away from me, can you?" his mother asked.

It was tempting to answer honestly, but instead he simply raised the plant a bit higher, as if asking her to focus. "You can put that here," she pointed to a ceiling hook by the sliding door leading to the backyard. Balancing the plant's pot on the tips of his fingers, he guided the eye formed by the tops of the pot's plastic tines over the hook, and then stopped it from swinging.

He picked up another one, this one also green and lovely.

"Outside, on the porch."

Seth nodded and moved toward the door, plant perched on his right hand. With his left he slid the door back and stepped out. "Where?" he asked.

She huffed and followed him out. "I swear, you can't button your shirt by yourself." She pointed to a hook and turned back inside. With practiced calm, he raised the plant and settled the loop over the hook.

Then he returned inside. He picked up one of the dead ones. "And this?"

"In here," she said. He followed her to the hallway leading into the bowels of the house. She stopped at the door to his father's study. His eyebrows rose in surprise. She pushed open the door, and Seth gasped.

Items that he recognized as belonging to his father were arranged in careful, precise rows that covered nearly every inch of the floor. The tops of every piece of furniture, too, displayed his father's effects, each piece at right angles to every other. He saw arrangements of pens and pencils, fishing lures and weights, ancient-looking marbles, and stacks of what looked like receipts. Tools had been tacked to the walls, often held by twist-ties attached to pushpins. Next to each grouping, a verse from the Bible had been scrawled with a wide sharpie in what was obviously his mother's hand.

He stepped in, mouth agape, and turned a slow circle. He stopped when he saw his father's desk. Arranged in a neat row were nearly a dozen dead rats, their tails darting into free space like a conductor's batons, frozen by rigor.

"Just hang that there," his mother said, pointing at a hook in the ceiling to the immediate right of the desk.

"Oh, Mom," Seth breathed. A voice in his head said, *These dead rats are hurtling through space*, but he tried to ignore it. "Mom, what are you doing here?"

"What do you mean? God has called me to be a homemaker, and I am faithful. I keep a clean house, young man, and don't you forget it. The nerve, bringing that filthy girl in here. I know you're having carnal relations with her."

Seth didn't have the wherewithal to argue. With shaking hands, he hung the plant. Then he stared at the rats.

"Come on," his mother said. "There's more. Even when you get tired of it all—the loneliness, the disappointment—somehow, there's always more."

"Let's bring this meeting to order," Mr. Basil said, placing a snifter of cognac on the small table next to his chair. Drs. Robinson and Teasdale were already seated. A fire crackled in the fireplace ironically, beating back the chill of overeager air conditioning. He turned to Robinson. "How did our current cohort take to the first revelation?"

The fingers of one of Robinson's hands had been resting on his face, but he waved those fingers toward the ceiling. "As well as they ever do. Some with fascination. Some with incredulity. Others...it's hard to tell."

"Well, let's talk about the fascinated first," Basil said. He reached beside his chair and pulled up a leather notebook. He flipped it open to a letter-sized pad of lined paper. He then removed a fountain pen from the notebook's clip and unscrewed the cap.

"The most trusting would definitely be Jude Ash," Robinson said. "He is, as they say, 'all-in.' I could tell him the continent of Australia was made of tubers and he would agree."

"But I'm guessing Mr. Ash isn't the shiniest apple in the basket," Mr. Basil posited.

"Decidedly not."

"Any others?" Dr. Teasdale asked. She, too, was taking notes.

"Musa Daniels," Dr. Robinson said.

"Oh, yes," Mr. Basil said. "Nigerian fellow."

"That's the one. He's serious, and he's sharp. He may be the most well-educated of the current crop. And he did not bat an eye."

"Good, good," Mr. Basil said. "That one could be useful. What does he do?"

"He is a Licensed Clinical Social Worker."

Mr. Basil's eyebrows rose and he turned to Teasdale. "We should groom him to be your successor, perhaps?"

"Who are you calling old?" Dr. Teasdale narrowed one eye at him.

Mr. Basil chuckled and took another sip of his cognac. "Others?"

"Matthew Townes is not quite openly hostile," Robinson said. "But he definitely has a chip on his shoulder."

"Let's keep an eye on him. Is there any reason to suspect that he should be...disinvited to continue?"

"I haven't met Mr. Townes," Dr. Teasdale said, "But I suggest we give the first revelation time to do its work. Once Mr. Townes starts to notice things, he may have a change of heart. We've seen it before."

"Indeed we have," Mr. Basil agreed. "All right, let's give him some time, but reassess before we advance him to the second revelation." He made a note. "Any other hostiles?"

"I would not call Ms. Shire hostile," Dr. Robinson moved his head back and forth, as if trying to weigh his opinion toward one side or the other.

"But?" Teasdale asked.

"But...she is an excellent critical thinker. It is going to be hard for her to make the leap. But again, we should give her a bit of time."

"We'll watch her, too," Basil made another note.

"Can we talk about the elephant we seem to be dancing around?" Dr. Teasdale asked.

"Oh. Him," Dr. Robinson said.

"Yes, him," Dr. Teasdale said.

"Just because he's your favorite—"

226 · J.R. MABRY

"Let me stop you right there, Joshua." Mr. Basil pointed a lazy finger at the catechist. "Need I remind you that he is *her* favorite? I doubt our dear Dr. Teasdale would take as much of an interest if she had not directed us to him."

Teasdale nodded and turned a scowl toward Robinson. "And what do you have against him?"

Robinson shrugged. "I suppose it's just that I haven't seen anything...especially remarkable about him. Not even vaguely. It seems strange that—"

"That twelve blue-collar Judeans changed the world?" Dr. Teasdale asked. "That a 12-year-old girl was asked to host an Aeon? The Pleroma chooses whom it wills. It isn't our place to question its favor."

Robinson shook his head. "I just wish I could see it."

Mr. Basil cocked his head. "Have you truly no idea why Mr. St. John might be helpful to our cause, Joshua?"

Robinson shook his head. "He pays attention. He is not stupid. He seems kind to his cohort. But he also seems a bit of a Nervous Nellie."

"I'll just check the DSM-V for a description of that diagnosis, shall I?" Dr. Teasdale smirked.

Mr. Basil turned his gaze on the psychiatrist. "And what about you, Sherry? Do you have any idea why Mr. St. John might be...exceptional?"

She looked at the pad of paper in front of her. "I am bound by doctor-patient privilege not to reveal anything about Mr. St. John's mental state, but I can tell you that I concur with most of what Joshua has said."

"Most?" Mr. Basil asked.

"Yes. Most. You see...I think I do know why he might be...extraordinary."

Mr. Basil had been slouching in his chair, slowly succumbing to the cognac and to gravity in equal proportions. "Oh, yes? And why might that be?"

"Instead of telling you about it, I think perhaps a demonstration would be more effective," Dr. Teasdale said.

"What kind of demonstration?" Robinson asked.

Normally Seth would have resented having to go downtown to pay the power bill in person, especially on his one day off. But this day was not like other days. This day, he *knew*. Dr. Robinson's words had been echoing in his head since the moment he had woken up. He had been numb the night before, not sure what to make of the startling revelation. But today, in the daylight, he couldn't stop looking around.

Waiting at the bus stop, his eyes went to the sky. He squinted, trying to see as high as he could. Did the clouds look...off? Could they really be projections? Was there actually an elaborate sprinkler system up there to simulate rain? He brought his gaze down to the horizon, hoping to get a sense of perspective, but the buildings blocked his line of sight.

He looked at the concrete below his feet. *What is under it?* he wondered. Dirt, sure, but how far down did it go before one hit a floor of hardened steel? And below that...the emptiness of space?

He shook his head to clear it. *This is crazy,* he thought. He almost said it out loud, but there were other people standing at the bus stop. He didn't want them to think *he* was crazy, too.

But he couldn't shake it. After the bus arrived, he kept searching the street, glancing up at the sky, trying to find some visible evidence that what Dr. Robinson had said was either just fucking with his head, or...somehow true. Or perhaps something in between? He had no idea what that could be, but just acknowledging that there could be another option made him feel a little bit better.

He suddenly realized that the large, African-American woman on the bus next to him was glaring at him. Then he noticed that his leg was bouncing. He put his hand on his knee and willed it to stop. He looked back toward the woman, who half-smiled and silently mouthed, *Thank you.*

Seth flushed, and looked back out the window. The more he looked at the sky, the less real it looked, but he didn't know if that was actually true or just his imagination. He suspected he was highly suggestible, and he didn't trust himself. A shudder ran through him, and he noticed he had begun blinking compulsively. Again, he willed his body to stop.

He didn't mind his compulsions when he was alone. But he hated bringing attention to himself in public. A bouncing leg was one thing—a full-blown facial tic was another. One was simply annoying, the other was a source of morbid curiosity—a curiosity he did not welcome.

He exited the bus at his stop and walked toward the Pacific Gas & Electric office. It was located in San Jose's tiny business district, and it was only eight stories tall. It was the first time it had ever occurred to him that there were no skyscrapers in the city. Why was that?

He frowned as he pondered the question. He navigated to the proper office on autopilot and got in line. While waiting, he pulled out his phone and typed in the question, *What is the tallest building in San Jose?* The Miro building, at 28 floors. But it was mostly residential, according to Google, and he doubted he could get in above the first couple of commercial floors.

But even the eighth floor of the PG&E building might yield him a different perspective, he reasoned. Soon it was his turn to be served. Angie had been right. They wanted to give him a warning, and he assured them he would not be late again. Then he paid the bill—in cash, as requested—and was dismissed, not unkindly.

He wandered into the lobby, and his eyes were drawn to the high ceiling. When he looked down, his eyes lit on the elevators. Without thinking, he went toward them. He pushed the button to the eighth floor. Others crowded in behind him, pushing buttons for their floors of choice. One woman balanced a cardboard tray filled with specialty coffees. Seth looked up to avoid making eye contact with anyone.

A couple of people exited on the second floor, including an elderly gentleman with a cane. The rest of the passengers exited on the third floor, leaving Seth alone. He sighed, relieved to be alone again. The elevator moved to the fourth floor and the doors opened again, but no one got in or out. Seth pushed the button for the eighth floor again, and the doors closed. But the elevator did not move.

He frowned at the panel. The number "8" was lit up. And then it went out. He pushed the button a third time. It lit up again, but after about fifteen seconds, the light went out. The elevator remained exactly where it was.

Seth pushed the button for the sixth floor this time. Again, the number lit up, but then went out after a short time. Seth pushed the button for the fourth floor. The number lit up and the doors opened. He stepped out into the hallway.

The floor seemed to be deserted. The placard holders by the doors were empty, announcing the presence of nothing and no one. He opened one of the doors and looked in. He was met with an empty expanse of carpet lit by the ambient light coming from a far wall made entirely of glass.

He walked to the window and pressed his face against it, looking up. He was four stories higher than he had been, but he knew that was not very high. The sky looked no different than it had from the ground. He sighed and turned back toward the door.

He shut the door behind him and walked down the hallway. A snake of wires hung from a dislodged ceiling panel, wrapped in a segmented skin of aluminum. He shifted to his right, hugging the wall to avoid contact with the spray of copper erupting from its end.

The place smelled of nothing. He slowed when he heard whistling. He paused at a corner, and pressed his eye to it. He briefly saw the back of a man as he walked into a restroom. Seth moved quickly into the hall, expecting to go past the restroom without being seen.

Questions tickled at his brain. What was he hoping to discover? He'd gone as high as he could, and it hadn't answered any questions for him. He was not, so far as he could tell, any closer to the sky. Everything was normal. Was Robinson bullshitting him? Playing with him? To what end?

He cast a glance at a leather electrician's bag near the wall of the corridor. It was open, revealing its secrets. Looking up, Seth saw something he had never seen before: an S-Panel slightly ajar. It was swung nearly closed on its hinges, but the clasp bolts were undone.

Like all S-panels, it was five feet tall and almost three feet wide, hinged to one side, with two locking clasp bolts at its top and bottom right hand corners. It was metal, painted off-white with an eggshell finish.

Tentatively, Seth reached out and grabbed the lip of the panel, pulling it toward himself, pulling it open. He held his breath, and felt his blood racing in his ears. The electrician could return from the restroom at any time. He heard Dr. Robinson's voice in his head, *Look at any literature prior to 1950—do you see any mention of S-panels? You do not. Nor will you see them in movies. Only in media after 1950 do they make an appearance.*

He moved to the opening and peered in. He saw another hallway inside, its walls and floor a gleaming light gray. He heard a scuffling sound from the direction of the bathroom and froze. If he were caught, the electrician could report him. There would be a fine—probably more than his monthly paycheck, or so he feared.

Without thinking, he ducked his head and entered the panel.

The light was brighter in the hallway within. He blinked as he looked both ways. The hallway went a good distance in both directions, with little to break the monotony of it. He chose a direction and just started walking. He passed several doors on either side. They all looked like S-panels, although he noticed that some of them had two clasp bolts, while some only had one.

He realized he should have grabbed a bolt key out of the electrician's bag, but that was unrealistic. He didn't even know what one looked like. He tried one of the one-clasp doors, but it wouldn't budge. With a start, he realized that if the electrician—no, *when* the electrician—locked up the S-panel in the PG&E building, he would be trapped.

Am I still in the PG&E building? he wondered. The hallway seemed longer than the building was wide. He looked back in the direction he had come. A loud clank startled him, and he whirled to see an S-panel swinging open about 30 yards down the corridor. Without thinking, he ran back toward the panel through which he had come. He heard voices behind him, commanding him to stop. Glancing over his shoulder, he saw a man—not larger than himself—dressed in what looked like a white jumpsuit. Another was just behind him. They were running toward him.

He put his head down and ran as fast as he could. As he got closer to the S-panel, he saw that it was still ajar. He threw his weight against it, and felt its considerable mass give even as pain tore through his shoulder. He heard an "oof," and jumping over the lip at the bottom of the panel, exploded into the PG&E building's carpeted hallway. Out of the corner of his eye, he saw the crumpled form of the electrician on the floor—he'd no doubt knocked him off balance when he forced open the panel.

But he could see the electrician was still moving, even if he was also stunned. Seth did not slow down. He raced for the elevator, and punched at the down button, but he couldn't just stand there and wait to be caught. He cast around for the stairway and saw the sign. He raced for it, hit the door's horizontal bar, and leaped down the stairs, taking two at a time.

He didn't slow down until he hit the streets. He wiped sweat from his eyes and forced himself to walk slowly, to blend into the casual pace that was the norm in San Jose. But his heart was still racing, and he fought the urge to break into another run. Instead, he looked at the sky—the impossible sky. With every glance he was more convinced that it was too close. Like an alpha dog asserting dominance by hovering over the shoulder of a lesser dog, it pressed down upon him, looming, smothering, threatening.

He knew that feeling well, and he hated it.

WHAT ARE SOME GROUPS WITH GNOSTIC CONNECTIONS?

Throughout history, various groups have claimed Gnostic origins or exhibited connections to Gnosticism. One such group was the Manichaeans, founded by the prophet Mani in the third century AD. Manichaeism blended elements of Gnosticism, Zoroastrianism, Buddhism, and Christianity, proposing a cosmic dualism between light and darkness. The Manichaeans believed in the imprisonment of divine sparks within the material world and emphasized the importance of salvific knowledge for liberation.

Another group with Gnostic influences was the Cathars, who flourished in Western Europe during the 12th and 13th centuries. The Cathars held a dualistic worldview, considering the material world to be inherently evil and the spiritual realm pure and good. They believed in the existence of a hidden God and sought to escape the cycle of reincarnation through ascetic practices and the pursuit of knowledge.

In more recent times, the Theosophical Society, founded by Helena Blavatsky in the late 19th century, drew upon Gnostic concepts and incorporated them into its teachings. Blavatsky's Theosophy emphasized the acquisition of hidden knowledge and the belief in a spiritual hierarchy guiding human evolution.

Furthermore, certain modern esoteric and occult movements —such as the Masons, Rosicrucians, Martinists, the Hermetic Order of the Golden Dawn, and Thelema—also display Gnostic influences. These groups have incorporated Gnostic ideas, symbolism, and rituals, emphasizing the pursuit of inner enlightenment and the exploration of hidden truths.

In addition, neo-gnostic churches arose in the late 19th and 20th centuries, many as part of the independent sacramental movement (aka, independent Catholic movement) derived from the Old Catholic and other Roman Catholic or Orthodox schisms. The earliest of these would be the church founded by Jules Doinel, but neognostic Catholicism reached its greatest influence under Bishops Stephan Hoeller and Rosamond Miller.

While these groups may differ in their specific beliefs and practices, they all share a common thread of seeking spiritual illumination through the acquisition of secret knowledge. Their Gnostic origins or connections demonstrate the enduring influence of Gnosticism throughout history and its continued resonance in various religious and philosophical movements.

CHAPTER EIGHT

In this way, the Word of the Father goes out in all,
as the fruit of his heart and an expression of his will.
But it supports all. It chooses them
and also takes the expression of all,
purifying them, returning them
to the Father and to the Mother,
Jesus of infinite sweetness.
—*Gospel of Truth**

"Wait, where are we going?" Seth asked, rubbing at his shoulder.

Angie dropped the clothes she was folding on the couch and put her hands on her hips. "Out," she said. "For my

---

* The Gospel of Truth: Nag Hammadi Codex I, translated by Mark M. Mattison, published in *The Gospel of Truth: The Mystical Gospel* (2018).

birthday. You're not the only Gemini on the planet, you know."

"Oh," Seth said. "I...I'm sorry...I...it slipped my mind."

"Of course it did. And what's wrong with your shoulder?"

"I...no, nothing. It's fine. Uh...I don't have a present for you."

"Of course you don't." She sighed and picked up one of his t-shirts from the pile on the coffee table, folding it. "Just go have a good time with me. Get me drunk and drive me home and put me to bed. That's your present to me."

"Oh. Okay. I can do that. I can't pay, though."

She closed her eyes and shook her head. "You truly suck as a friend."

He plopped himself on the couch.

"Don't sit on my underwear!"

"Sorry." He moved to the floor. "And I'm sorry...about being a sucky friend."

She rolled the top of a pair of socks—hers. A slight smile brushed her lips. "Well, if you weren't, I wouldn't be able to enjoy this delicious feeling of moral superiority right now."

"That's my other gift," he said.

"Thank you. It's just what I've always wanted!" she mock-exclaimed.

He smiled a little sadly and their eyes met and softened. Finally, he looked away. "Where are we going?"

"Sushi Pirate. Where else?"

"Great!" he said, brightening. "When do we leave?"

"As soon as you help me finish folding our laundry."

Seated at the counter, Seth watched the elaborate sushi dishes float by him on tiny pirate ships. Angie already had three plates in front of her. Seth had none.

"What the fuck are you waiting for?" Angie asked, her mouth full of California roll.

"Uh...are they all raw?"

"Do not tell me you haven't had sushi before."

"Okay...I won't tell you that."

"No, knucklehead, they are not all raw. Here, try this." She dipped a piece of California roll in soy sauce and held it up to him on her chopsticks.

"What is it?" he asked.

"It's crab meat—cooked crab meat—cucumber, and avocado, dusted with sesame seeds. Try it."

Seth opened his mouth and let her feed it to him. "Oh. Okay. That's good."

"Of course it's good. Here, let's grab you one of those," she reached for a plate of California roll as it floated by and placed it in front of Seth. "And one of these," she snagged a more plain-looking preparation.

"What's that?" Seth asked.

"Oshinko—it's vegetarian, it's a kind of pickle. It's good, don't worry. Aaaaaand, one of these," she snagged another plate.

"And what is that?"

"Inari," she said. "It's sweet rice inside a tofu scrotum—I know how you like you some scrota. It's like dessert."

"You are never going to let that go, are you?"

"What? You cupping a dead man's balls? Not on your life. At your funeral, I am going to lean over your casket and say, 'No cupping balls for you anymore,' and I'll cackle."

"And *I'm* the one who sees the psychiatrist," Seth said.

"Mix a little of the green horseradish into your soy sauce," she said, "then dip it."

Seth did as instructed and quickly decided that sushi was both strange and amazing. He put another piece into his mouth and chewed, looking up—straight into the eyes of the sushi chef. He was scowling.

Seth froze. "What?" He turned to Angie. "What am I doing wrong?"

She looked at him. "What are you talking about? Nothing."

"Then why is—" he pointed at the sushi chef with his chopsticks, but the chef was now at work on another roll.

"Why is what?" Angie asked.

"He was...looking at me," Seth said.

"That's allowed. He probably wanted to see if you were enjoying his handiwork."

"But he didn't look happy...at all."

"Dude, his girlfriend probably just broke up with him. Everything is not about you. Chill."

Seth swallowed and looked around. An older woman was looking at him. She looked away as soon as he met her eyes. She was eating alone at a table. She sipped her tea.

He looked to the other side, and once more met the eyes of another patron. He, too, did not look pleased. But he didn't look away. He turned the page of a newspaper in front of him without looking at it. Seth felt a chill run through him and turned back to the sushi stream in front of him.

"What's wrong with you? You look like you've seen a ghost."

"People are looking at me," Seth said.

Angie turned in her seat and frowned. "What is up with you tonight?"

"I...what do you mean? It's not my fault that people are looking at me." Although he suspected that wasn't true. If he hadn't gone through that S-panel, would people be surveilling him? He doubted it very much.

"You're being paranoid," Angie said.

"Just because I'm paranoid doesn't mean—"

"Yeah, yeah, save it," Angie waved his cliche away. She narrowed her eyes at him. "Are you off your meds?"

"No!" Seth protested.

"Are you sure? You're not just saying that?"

"No. I haven't missed a dose. Look, this isn't me. People are really looking at me and...it's freaking *me* out." He hunched his shoulders and leaned into his plates.

"You are freaking me out. I think you're just feeling guilty about Kush. Lighten up. We're supposed to be having a good time."

"Tell that to the people following me," Seth said.

"Oh, now people are following you?" Angie asked.

"I think so."

"Why?"

Seth met her eyes, then looked away. He blinked. "I...I can't say."

"Does this have something to do with your little cult?" Angie asked, her voice darkening.

Seth ate one of the inari, but didn't really taste it.

"When do you see your therapist next?" Angie asked him.

"Uh...day after tomorrow."

"Promise me you'll tell her about this...people looking at you and following you," Angie said.

"I'm not sure I can."

"What's going to happen?" Angie asked, her voice rising. "Are the gnostic police going to come after you?"

"I...I don't think so," Seth said. "But I made a promise."

"The promise doesn't include the slippery slope of mental instability, dude. If you need help, you need to get help. I'm sure even your fellow vest-wearing cult members don't want you to descend into gibbering madness."

"How do you know about the vests?" Seth asked.

"I have eyes! Few categories of clothing exceed vests in sheer dorkery. I saw you buying that vest at the thrift store, and I saw you wearing it to your latest cult meeting. Give me some fucking credit!" Angie said. Other patrons stopped to look at her, and she lowered her voice. "Nice vest, by the way, as dorky apparel goes."

"Thanks," he said. "Do you really think it's okay to talk to my therapist?"

"Of course I do," she said. "Everything you say to her is confidential. How are they going to know?"

"Uh...I don't know. Cameras?"

"Wow. Okay, 'Cult members have installed cameras in every therapist's office in the state, film at eleven.' Do you even hear yourself?"

Seth blinked. "I'm...scared."

"Good," Angie said, putting her hand on his arm. "Because I'm scared *for* you."

Dr. Sherry Teasdale crossed her legs and sighed. She gave Seth a reassuring smile and said, "How are you?"

Seth opened his mouth, but did not know where to begin. "I-I found out something...disturbing...and I don't know how to deal with it," he finally managed.

"Tell me about that," she said, writing on her notepad.

"I...I'm not sure I'm allowed. I mean, it's a secret," he said.

"Everything you say here is confidential," she said.

"Absolutely?" he asked.

"Well, unless you tell me you plan to hurt someone or yourself. Or if you reveal that you've abused minors or the disabled or the elderly. Then I have to break confidentiality." She gave him a compassionate look. "Do any of those apply?"

"No," he said firmly. "No, they don't."

She nodded. "Then everything you say is completely private—just between us."

"But...I'm afraid that if I tell you...you'll think I'm crazy."

"I promise I won't think that. I think you're a person reaching out for help, and nothing you say can change that."

Seth wasn't sure how he felt about that answer. It wasn't untrue, but.... He fidgeted on the green leather couch and scratched at his neck. He noticed that his eye was twitching. He wondered if Dr. Teasdale had noticed.

But she didn't say anything. Instead, she waited patiently, gazing at him with quiet attention. It was a little bit unsettling.

"Do you think Mr. Basil would mind?"

"Do I think he would mind if he knew you were talking to me?" Dr. Teasdale clarified.

"Uh...yeah."

"No, I don't think he would mind. In fact, I know he wouldn't. He has referred several initiates to me when they've had trouble... assimilating the revelations."

"Oh." Seth nodded, his eyes focused on something far away. "Okay, then."

"So, what would you like to talk about?" Dr. Teasdale asked.

His first impulse was to talk about Kush, but it felt like beating a dead horse. Then he thought about talking about everyone looking at him in the sushi restaurant, but rejected that—he didn't want Dr. Teasdale to think he was paranoid on top of being OCD. He decided on the big question that wouldn't let him alone and scared him the most. "Can we talk about the spaceship thing?"

Dr. Teasdale smiled and nodded. "Let's talk about that."

"It seems...far-fetched."

"It does," she agreed.

"I mean, this ship would have to be...huge."

She nodded. "It is."

"I don't think there's enough metal on earth to—"

"It's not metal," she said.

"It isn't?" he asked.

"No. It's rock. It's a series of warrens burrowed into an asteroid."

Seth blinked. "It is?"

"It is."

"But Dr. Robinson—"

She rolled her eyes. "God. Robinson." She shook her head and smiled. "Did Dr. Robinson show you a picture of a starship?"

"Yeah—"

She shook her head. "It doesn't look like that. Robinson used to show people a picture of the real *Cibus Dei,* but since it just looked like a rock, people had trouble believing it."

"So we really are on a spaceship, but it doesn't look like the one Dr. Robinson showed us?"

"No. I mean...that's correct."

"But why...how...?"

"Gnostics have always been more about symbol than reality." She shrugged. "The spaceship he showed you is a good symbol for the real thing. It's just not a *photograph* of the real thing. Does that make sense?"

"Yes, but why are gnostics more interested in the symbols?"

"Because we believe they're more real than the things they signify."

Seth frowned. "I don't get it."

Dr. Teasdale's eyes went to the ceiling and she bit her lip. Then she looked down and smiled. "Here you go. Take love, for instance. We gnostics think the *idea* of Love is stronger than any particular love affair. Wouldn't you agree that that's true?"

Seth wasn't sure. He said so.

"Well, how stable are love relationships?" Dr. Teasdale asked him. "I mean, relationships end all the time, don't they?"

"Sure," Seth agreed.

"But is there ever a time when there isn't love in the world?" she asked.

"No," he said.

"There you go. And that's true of any other idea or symbol you can name."

"Huh," Seth said. He wasn't sure what he thought about that. He would need to think it over.

"So I went to pay my phone bill, and I saw an open S-panel," Seth confessed.

Dr. Teasdale's eyebrows sprang up. "Oh?" she said, sitting up straighter in her seat. "Tell me more."

"So, I went inside. And it was...a really long hallway. Very... industrial. And it seemed bigger than the building I was in—longer, I mean. And someone saw me, and I ran."

"Someone?"

"Yeah, like, someone who worked there. I ran, and they chased after me. But I was faster." He said the last with a bit of pride.

"That was...very lucky." Dr. Teasdale looked worried.

"What's wrong?" Seth asked.

"I'm not sure. Is there anything else?"

"Yeah. I feel like, everywhere I go, someone is watching me."

"Who?"

"I don't know...people on the bus. People in this sushi restaurant I went to a couple of nights ago. I...I can feel their eyes on me. And sometimes I catch them. And some of them don't even look away! They're...scowling. It's scary."

Dr. Teasdale nodded, looking a bit frightened herself. "Seth, you need to be very, very careful."

"Oh?"

"If they're onto you...it could be bad for you."

"What do you mean?" Seth asked.

She set her notepad aside and leaned forward, resting her

elbows on her knees. "Listen, I'm taking my therapist hat off right now. I'm just speaking to you gnostic-to-gnostic now."

"Okay."

"The S-panels lead to the inner workings of the *Cibus Dei*. Now that you've seen it, you have empirical proof that what you were told at your baptism is true—even if it doesn't look like that dolt Robinson said. But...Seth...it's not good that they know that you know...or even that you suspect. You need to keep a very low profile."

"Should I stay away from the Lodge?"

"No, I think you need the Lodge more than ever. Just...be discreet. Cover up when you're going out—"

"But it's hot," he said. "This is San Jose."

"It won't kill you to wear a hoodie," she said.

Seth nodded.

"And keep your nose clean. Don't give the authorities any reason to detain you. Do you hear me?"

"Do the authorities...know?" Seth asked.

"That depends," she said.

"On what?" he asked.

"On what authorities you're talking about."

"Well, if he had any doubts before, he doesn't now." Sherrie Teasdale placed a bit of cheese on a cracker and popped it into her mouth. "Where did you get this cheese, Terrance? What is it?"

Mr. Basil ignored the latter question. "Why do you say that—that he has no doubts now?"

"Because he went through an S-panel." She licked the salt off of her fingers.

"He what?" Robinson spluttered.

Mr. Basil's eyebrows lowered, giving his eyes a dark look. "Whyever did he do that?"

Teasdale shrugged. "Why do people climb mountains? Because it was there. Because it was open. Because he was curious. Because we told him an outlandish, impossible story and he wanted to see if it was true."

Mr. Basil slumped down into his chair and passed a hand over his face. "Do we need to relocate?"

Dr. Teasdale's face fell, finally serious. "I don't think we do. Nothing connects him to us—"

"Not yet, perhaps," Mr. Basil noted.

"We don't know that," Robinson said.

"No, we don't." Mr. Basil, hands steepled, rubbed the tips of his index fingers against his lips, his eyes moving back and forth quickly. "Was he seen?"

"He was chased, but they didn't follow him out of the S-panel."

Mr. Basil shook his head. "This is too dangerous."

"Or...it's an opportunity," Dr. Teasdale said. "Remember what we talked about last time? He has a gift. I've seen it, obviously she sees it. Now it's time for you to see it."

"He's a liability," Robinson said. "We should cut him loose."

Mr. Basil shot him a hard look. "*You* try explaining that to her, after the fact."

Robinson squirmed in his seat.

"I think his value outweighs whatever danger he poses," Teasdale said. "Test him. We came up with a plan last time. Do it."

"We brainstormed ideas last time," Basil corrected her. "That's not the same."

"Look, no one has come snooping yet," Teasdale argued. "We have some time. *Test him.*"

Basil took a deep breath, then with a groan hoisted himself to his feet. He walked over to a black, rotary telephone on the desk and picked up the receiver. "Number?"

"You have the number," Teasdale said.

"I know, but I don't feel like looking it up. Can you just give me the number, please?" There was irritation in his voice, and Teasdale fished for her cell phone without further complaint. She found the number and related it to him. He dialed it.

"Mr. St. John, how are you?" Basil said. His eyes bounced from Teasdale to Robinson as he listened. "Good, good. Say, do you have a minute? I have a...a favor to ask." A few moments later, he continued. "We have been...I'm sorry to say...burgled."

His eyebrows rose at whatever he was hearing. "Yes, yes, they broke in last night, apparently. When I came in this morning, it looked like a tornado had hit the place." He listened for several moments, then said, "They did, yes. Priceless artifacts of historical and religious value. Quite unsellable, I'm sure. No one would know what they are. It's a shame, really, a waste." He listened as Seth spoke, then answered, "Another gnostic group...?" A smile broke out on his lips and Robinson stifled a laugh. "I hadn't considered that, but...yes, I suppose it's a possibility."

Teasdale helped herself to another cracker.

"Well, that's why I'm calling, really. I know that you work in a bookstore and probably have some skill in organizing books—" He cocked his head. "Yes, no doubt, no doubt. That's exactly why I thought of you. I wonder if you would be able to come over and assert some order, here? Until we clean it up, I can't be sure exactly what's been taken."

Basil nodded. "Well, exactly. We have many valuable volumes, to be sure." Basil brightened. "Splendid. Could you come tonight? Our insurance company is pressuring me for an inventory." He looked at Robinson and Teasdale and shrugged. Robinson gave him a thumbs up. "I'm ever so grateful to you, Mr. St. John. I'll see you tonight. Six PM? Fine then." Basil hung up the phone. He turned to Teasdale. "I hope you're right, as I'm about to sacrifice the order of my sanctuary."

"I'm right that we need to test him," Teasdale said, reaching for another cracker.

"I suppose, I suppose." He sighed.

Robinson rose from his seat and headed for the door.

"Where are you going?" Basil called after him.

"To drown my sorrows."

"Drown them some other time. Right now I need you to help me bust this place up."

———————

Becky knocked on the apartment door and waited. She heard movement within, straightened her dress, and smiled. When the door opened, her smile faded.

"You could *pretend* to be happy to see me," Angie said.

"I'm sorry. Uh...is Seth ready?"

Angie frowned. "Seth's not here."

Becky's shoulders fell. "What?"

"He had a Lodge meeting tonight."

Becky looked at the floor and bit her lip.

"Did you...have a date tonight?" Angie asked.

Becky nodded, hot tears springing from her eyes.

"Why don't you come in?" Angie asked, opening the door wide.

Becky didn't move at first, but then she crossed the threshold. Then she stood there, arms crossed, head down.

"Hey, I just ordered a pizza, and there's no way I should eat the whole thing by myself." Angie pointed to the pizza box on the coffee table. "Help me out by having a slice? You can eat your disappointment before it eats you."

"I'm not hungry," Becky said.

"I'm going to grab you a plate and a napkin in case you change your mind," Angie strode off to the kitchen and returned a moment later, setting a plate and paper napkin on the coffee table next to the pizza box. Then she sat down and patted the space beside her.

Without looking at her, Becky moved to the couch and sat with a heavy sigh. Angie put a hand on her thigh and patted it. "I wish I had known. It's not like he keeps a calendar hanging in the kitchen with his daily events written on it."

"It's not your fault," Becky managed.

"No. I just...I'd help if I could, though," Angie said. "You're a good person, and you deserve better."

Becky said nothing at first. The pizza smelled wonderful, but the idea of eating made her feel physically sick. She sniffed and wiped her eyes.

Angie picked up her own plate and nibbled at a half-eaten slice. "He's been acting like a real shit lately," she said.

Becky nodded, but then asked, "Not just to me?"

"No. To everyone. He gave away his dog, for Christ's sake! I'm seriously scared for him," Angie admitted.

"Me too." Becky leaned back and slumped into the couch. She uncrossed her arms and looked at the ceiling.

"It's the cult he's joined," Angie said. "They're messing with his head somehow. He's become a lot more anxious since he started going. He thinks it's helping him, but it's not. And he's also become a really secretive little shit."

Becky nodded, still looking at the ceiling.

Angie put her slice down again. "Can I ask you a personal question?"

Becky looked at her briefly and nodded again.

"Why do you like him? I mean, he's not what I'd call sexy. And he doesn't seem to have a romantic bone in his body. So...what is it you find attractive about him?"

For a long minute, Becky didn't answer. Then she cleared her throat. "When I was little, my dad took me to the pet store to pick out a puppy. They had a new litter in, labradors, black. They were so, so cute, you know? I was in heaven, petting them and playing with them. My dad wanted me to get this male—he was strong, and curious, and didn't seem to be afraid of anything. And he was cute as a button. But when he asked me which one I wanted, I pointed to this female, the runt. She had a wounded paw, and she was limping. She was also really shy, kind of cowering in the corner. My dad tried to talk me out of it, but I was insistent. And she was...she was the best dog I ever had."

Angie pulled up her knees and rearranged herself cross-legged on the couch. There was a thoughtful look on her face. Finally she said, "So you're saying...what? That Seth is your wounded puppy?"

Becky nodded. "I seem to collect them."

Angie reached for one of Becky's hands and held it. "You're a good person," she said again.

"I don't know about that," Becky said. "I just know that it's partly the fact that he's so...damaged...that makes me like him. But sometimes I wonder if he's...if he's too damaged, you know?"

"Yeah."

Becky let go of Angie's hand and fished in the pocket of her dress for a tissue. She blew her nose and wiped at her eyes again. "He's been really...preoccupied lately."

"Have you noticed that he's been more anxious, too?"

"I guess so. I haven't seen much of him, and that's..." She swallowed. "I used to feel like I was a priority for him. But now..."

Angie looked at her knees.

A few minutes of silence passed. Then Becky asked, "Why is he your best friend?"

Angie grimaced. "Because he's the only person I know who doesn't judge me."

"He worships you," Becky said.

That made Angie laugh. "I doubt that. But he lets me insult him and he doesn't chuck me out on my ass." She shrugged. "It's what passes for intimacy in my life."

Despite herself, Becky smiled at this. "Thank you for being such a good friend to him."

"I could say the same," Angie said.

"I feel lost and helpless. It's like he's farther and farther away every day."

"Yeah," Angie agreed. "It's exactly like that."

"I just want to shake him," Becky said. "I just want to wake him up."

Angie nodded. "Me, too. So...and here's the question I've been asking myself...are you willing to risk your relationship with him to get him some help?"

"What relationship?" Becky asked. Angie narrowed one eye at her and waited. After a few moments, Becky added, "Anything. What do you have in mind?"

When Seth arrived at the Lodge, the front door was already ajar. He frowned and after a few moments of hesitation, pushed the door open. The foyer was empty. He shut the door behind him.

"There you are!" A familiar voice called to him. He looked up to see Mr. Basil striding toward him. "My dear boy, thank you so much for coming so quickly. You have no idea what the day has been like."

Seth had never seen Mr. Basil look so disheveled. His black hair hung in sweaty—or oily—strands, and he exuded a forced cheeriness that Seth found distressing. He snatched at Seth's hand and gave it a quick pump.

"There was a robbery?" Seth asked.

"They were definitely looking for something. Some things were taken. We're still doing an inventory, but you will definitely help with that."

"How?"

"Well, I believe that some of the items that may have been stolen are, well, books. And until we can see what we have—"

"You don't know what you don't have," Seth finished.

"Well, precisely."

Seth nodded and Mr. Basil touched his elbow and steered him toward his office at the end of the short hallway. As Seth crossed the threshold, he gasped. There was no book on any shelf—all were in piles on the floor, many lying open. An ornate screen lay in a pile among paintings and objects d'art. One window had been smashed, hurriedly covered over by cardboard. Chairs had been overturned, and Mr. Basil's ornate desk lay on its side, legs extending into space. On one wall a large hole had been torn into the drywall. "What was that?" Seth pointed to it.

"That was a safe, hidden behind a painting of the death of Hiram Abiff."

Seth stepped into the room, but there were few patches of the oriental rug not covered by detritus. He carefully stepped from patch to patch, until he found a spot big enough to turn around.

"My first impulse was to put as much right as I could, but the insurance company told me not to touch anything until the police had documented it," Mr. Basil informed him. "You just missed them."

"The front door was open," Seth said.

Mr. Basil rolled his eyes. "I asked them to shut it behind them. Argh!"

Seth had never seen Mr. Basil in an unguarded moment, and the Lodge master seemed to notice. "I'm...I'm sorry. It's...been a very trying day, and I am not at my best."

"I totally get it," Seth said. "Is it okay to touch things now?"

"It is. I'll get Nazz down here—if I can prise him away from his video games—to help me with the furniture and artwork. Then we'll be able to start the inventory. We'll leave the books to you, if you don't mind?"

Seth shook his head. "How do I know where anything goes?"

Mr. Basil looked momentarily sheepish. "I…admit, the organization of the books was…idiosyncratic. I knew where everything was, but no one else would be able to find a thing, I fear. If there is a bright spot to this whole affair, it's that the library—what's left of it—might be properly sorted for once." He gave Seth a sad smile. "You don't mind, do you?"

"I'm glad to help," Seth said, giving him a compassionate nod. He looked around at the books again. "Is there any particular system you'd like to use? Dewey decimal or perhaps the Library of Congress Classification system, or chronological, or alphabetical, or maybe something that simply makes intuitive sense, by subject?"

"The latter will do splendidly, I think. If you just put the books like-with-like, grouped by subject, in some kind of recognizable order, I think that would be best."

"Okay," Seth said. "I'll get to it."

Mr. Basil left the room, and Seth stepped to a pile and began to line all the books up in neat, straight rows, spines up so he could see them all at a glance. A few minutes later, Mr. Basil returned with a sullen Nazz in tow, wearing a plaid vest. Mr. Basil pointed to the desk first and they picked their way over to it.

"Oh, and Mr. St. John, please let me know if you need anything," Mr. Basil said.

"Well, I missed dinner," Seth said. "So maybe in a couple of hours…pizza and some Coke?"

Mr. Basil grinned and for a moment even Nazz looked pleased. "Of course. You and Nazz can argue about toppings."

"Seth." Mr. Basil gently shook Seth's shoulder. Seth blinked, bleary, and picked his head up from the table. Dim light was coming through the windows. An empty pizza box to his left reeked. Seth sniffed and rubbed at his eyes. Nazz was nowhere to be seen, and it occurred to him that, unlike himself, the doorkeeper had the good sense to go to bed.

He squinted up at Mr. Basil, who smiled and gently set a cup of coffee down in front of him. "Oh my god, thank you." Seth cradled the cup in both hands and sipped at it. It tasted like roasted heaven.

"I want to thank you for all your hard work. This is...superb." He waved his arm around the library. "You'd almost think we'd never been robbed."

"It was fun, actually," Seth said. He yawned and stretched and scratched the top of his head. His stomach rumbled.

"I'll ask Nazz to whip up some eggs," Mr. Basil said. "How does that sound?"

"Oh. Uh...is he up? Don't get him up if he isn't up," Seth said.

"Oh, he's up. He made the coffee."

"Oh. Then...sure."

"Lovely. I'll be right back." Mr. Basil strode from the room. Seth took in the warm, paneled study, and felt a swell of pride. It did look very good—better than it had before, somehow. Just then it occurred to him that Mr. Basil had called him by his first name. Or had he dreamed that? No, it had happened, he was sure. He wasn't sure why that felt important, but it did. It suggested an intimacy that Seth hoped was real.

Seth gulped greedily at the coffee, grateful that it was not too hot to drink. He had finished half the cup when Mr. Basil returned. "We'll have breakfast for you at the kitchen table in about fifteen minutes. Does that sound all right?"

254 • J.R. MABRY

"That sounds great," Seth said.

"In the meantime, I wonder if we could go over a short list of very valuable books—the ones worth reporting to the insurance company. If you could just point out where they're likely to be, it will help orient me to how you've arranged the books as well."

"Yeah, sure," Seth said with a tired smile.

Mr. Basil looked at the list in his hand. "Hollingdale's *Interlinear Hermes Trismegistus?*"

Seth nodded and without looking at the bookshelves, said, "Fourth bookcase from the left, third shelf, sixteen books in—grouped with other works on Hermeticism. I arranged the books by esoteric genre in chronological order of each movement's appearance. Within each section, books are alphabetical by authors' last names. Of course, I can change that if you'd prefer the books to be arranged by year of publication."

Mr. Basil's face was hard to read. He blinked and seemed uncertain what to say. Finally, though, he found his voice. "Oh. Uh...no, no, that system of arrangement will do very nicely. Thank you, Seth."

Seth felt a rush of warmth fill his chest at being called by his first name again. He gave Mr. Basil an even broader smile. He watched as Mr. Basil went to the fourth bookcase and laid his hand upon the third shelf. With his other hand, he pulled a thick leather volume from the shelf and examined it. "It appears to be undamaged," he said with satisfaction. With a note of hesitation —or perhaps wonder—he replaced the book and looked at his list again. "A.E. Waite's *The Way of Divine Union*, first edition?" He looked up at Seth hopefully.

Seth sipped again from his coffee and, again without looking, said, "Fifth bookcase, fifth shelf, twenty books from the left, grouped with other Victorian Occult Revival movements. I subdivided that section in chronological order of appearance— Blavatsky and other Theosophical authors, Mathers and the

Golden Dawn, Crowley, and the Fraternity of the Rosy Cross. I put Waite with the FRC material, since that was largely his movement. It has a cracked spine."

Mr. Basil had already moved to the bookcase and in seconds had pulled the book. "That was already there, I'm afraid, so no harm done."

"That's good," Seth said.

Mr. Basil put the book back in its place and turned back to Seth. There was an odd look on his face that Seth did not understand. Much seemed to be happening behind the Lodge master's eyes, but he had no idea what it was. Mr. Basil bit his lip and looked down at his paper again. "One more, dear boy. Iain Gardner's *The Kephalaia of the Teacher.*"

Seth sniffed and wiped his nose on the back of his hand. "I gave pride place to the books on Gnosticism, bookcases one through three. Bookcase one is ancient Jewish, Christian, and Pagan Gnosticism, bookcase two is late antiquity and medieval Gnosticism—so, Manicheanism, the Bogomils, and Cathars, among others—and bookcase three is Neo-gnostic revival movements and transpersonal interpretations, starting with Jung, of course."

Mr. Basil coughed. "Of course."

"*The Kephalaia* is Manichean, so second bookcase, first shelf, sixteen books in."

Mr. Basil checked, but this time he did not pull the book from the shelf. Instead he just turned and stared at Seth.

"I wasn't sure where to put Freemasonry at first," Seth said, "but finally decided to create a section for graded fraternal orders —I put the Alchemical Wedding there, I hope you don't mind. There didn't seem to be enough material to warrant a special section for fictional movements."

Mr. Basil began to laugh. It started as a chuckle, but then became full-throated and free. Seth's forehead bunched in confusion. He'd never seen Mr. Basil's composure crack in this way, and it confused and concerned him. Yet he couldn't help smiling. Finally, Mr. Basil sank into a chair across the table from Seth, still chuckling into his hand.

"Is it...okay?" Seth asked.

"It's...more than okay, dear boy."

"I was thinking that perhaps I could make some section markers, but I didn't know how you'd want that done. It's so nice in here, I didn't think post-its were really appropriate."

Mr. Basil said nothing, but his eyes were shining as he simply stared at Seth.

Seth shrank a bit. "What?" he asked. "What did I say?"

"Nothing," Mr. Basil answered. "And...everything. You've done...an amazing job here, Mr. St. John. I'm...I'm very grateful to you and..." His eyes drifted to the ceiling and Seth could tell he was thinking.

"And...?" he prompted.

Mr. Basil just shook his head. "She was right. She was right, and I did not see it."

"Uh...who was right?" Seth asked, feeling lost.

Mr. Basil met Seth's eyes. "This will be more help to me than you can know. Thank you."

"You're...welcome," Seth said, once more grateful for such special attention from Mr. Basil.

"Breakfast will be ready," he said, getting up from his chair. Seth nodded and rose, bringing his cup in hopes of more coffee. But before they left the room, Mr. Basil put a hand on Seth's shoulder. "Mr.— Seth, I am very impressed by your...organizational skills. I wonder if perhaps we may call upon you for...greater service?"

Seth shrugged. "Like what?"

"That discussion is not...let us say, it is not ripe yet. But you are willing?"

"Is it like this?" Seth motioned toward the bookshelves.

"It is, in a way. In a way. Come, Nazz will become...annoyed...if we don't strike while the eggs are hot."

K eira looked at the time on her phone. Schenck was late. It wasn't like him. "Make sure you're on time," he'd said. "Make sure you wear a uniform," he'd said. When she'd asked him what for, he'd chuckled a bit and said only, "People will ask fewer questions."

So here she was, on time at the office and in uniform. The last time she'd worn it was at the funeral of a fellow agent. She'd washed it twice, but it still smelled like some kind of toxic plastic.

Then she saw Schenck walking toward her from the direction of the elevators. "Sorry, Sloane," he said. He was out of breath and clearly sweating. "I, uh...it took longer to get clearance than I thought."

"Clearance for what?" Keira asked, hands on hips. "I thought the security clearance went through."

"It did. This is for...something else. A ride...of sorts."

"Where to?" Keira asked.

"You'll see," Schenck said, turning back toward the elevators.

Keira affected her best James Cagney impersonation. "'We're going to take you on a bit of a ride, see? But we ain't gonna tell you where, see?' Nope, nothing suspicious about that. Are you going to blindfold me, too?"

Schenck actually laughed. "If we actually *were* the mob, we'd have picked you up on the street and shoved you into an unmarked van."

"That's no end of comfort," Keira said. The elevator doors opened, and they both got inside. To Keira's surprise, her boss did not select a button for their intended floor. Instead, he fitted a key into a small, 2x2-inch metal panel above the keypad. It was the same brushed metal as the sides of the elevator, but the keyhole was visible inside a raised metal button. He turned the key and opened the panel. Inside was a black plastic pad about one inch square. Her eyebrows rose as he placed his thumb on the pad. An electronic chime sounded.

Their office was on the top floor of the building, so Keira was shocked when the elevator went up. Her brows furrowed and she looked at Schenck. He kept his eyes facing forward, steadfastly ignoring her gaze.

"There's another floor?" she asked.

"Need to know," he answered, still not looking at her.

"Is this part of the increased security clearance?" she asked.

"Part of it."

She nodded and faced the doors. The elevator slowed to a stop and the doors slid back, revealing a hallway much like the one they had just left. Schenck exited and waved at her to catch up. She did. A man was walking toward them, his eyes on his phone. As he passed, he said, "Schenck."

The chief nodded and said, "Stephens."

The hall ended in a left turn, and Schenck took it. He paused in front of an S-panel. He pulled his keys from his pocket again and began to count through them.

"What is this?" Keira asked.

"It's an S-panel."

"I can see that it's an S-panel," Keira countered. "Why are we standing by an S-panel?"

"We're going in," Schenck said.

"What?" Keira asked. "Neither of us are electricians. Do you want us to get thrown in jail? We aren't authorized to breach S-panels."

"You are now." He pulled a key off his ring. "Hold out your hand."

She did. He placed the key in her palm. She stared at it.

"Open it," he said.

"Is this a trick?" she asked. "Or a test?"

"It is not a trick or a test," he said, his face impassive.

"Would you tell me if it was?" she asked.

"Probably not," he confessed. "But it isn't."

"So you're not going to arrest me if I open it?"

"No, I will not," Schenck promised.

"Will guild agents leap out of hidden doors and drag me away?"

"Well, you never know," he deadpanned, "but it's highly unlikely."

She took the key in her right hand and pushed it into the lock. "I'm trusting you, chief."

"You should. And I'm probably the only person you should trust. No matter what you find, I want you to come to me first. If anyone contacts you or wants to work with you, you clear it with me, first. Do you understand?"

"Yeah..." She was not liking the sound of this at all.

He pointed to the lock with his chin and gave a nod upwards that Keira took to mean, *Get on with it.* She turned the key and heard a deep, resonant click. It swung toward her unassisted. "I've never seen one of these open before," she said.

"Most people haven't. Electricians usually use screens when they go in, so no one can see them do it."

She reached for the door and pulled it open further. She peered into the panel and saw a hallway of sorts. It looked industrial, its walls painted white, interrupted here and there by pipes and ducts.

Schenck gestured toward the opening. Keira gave him a look that said, *Are you sure?*

He nodded and gestured again. She stepped through.

LIQUIPEDIA
THE ANSWERBOT THAT GOES DOWN SMOOTH

WHAT IS THE GREAT SILENCE?

"The Great Silence" refers to the phenomenon of gradual disengagement between nations and states due to the absolute quarantine in some places and the rapid mortality caused by the Codex virus in others. During the first few years of the pandemic, internet connections kept areas isolated by the virus in touch with others, but as mortality soared in much of the world, electronic infrastructure suffered, and in many places collapsed altogether, especially in developing countries and the southern United States.

As Absolute Quarantine Areas (AQA) succumbed to martial law, the internet in many countries and some states cut ties with the wider internet and established intranet systems limited to users within their borders. Phone service was also limited to within provincial boundaries. This was a hugely controversial move in California, as millions of people lost instantaneous contact with loved ones in other states and countries. Email between isolated places still trickled through, but it took progressively longer for international and interstate messages to be exchanged. Pac Bell claimed that a substantial electronic backlog was responsible, but by 2040 all internet communication outside California ceased.

Explanations from Sacramento blamed the collapse of governmental systems in other places, lauding the California National Guard's ability to keep order and, in 2045, to return power to civilian authorities.

Conspiracy theories abound, however. Some theorists blame

the Great Silence on the actions of a secret "deep state" cabal bent on isolating and controlling California's substantial natural and human resources. Others offer extraterrestrial or occult explanations. None of these "alternative" realities provide any substantiating evidence, however, and the general consensus is that, among all the nation-states of the world, only California managed to escape the total collapse of civilization.

CHAPTER NINE

For this reason they who have been troubled
speak about the Anointed One (Christ) in their midst
so that they may receive restoration
and he may anoint them with the ointment.
The ointment is the pity of the father,
who will have mercy on them.
But those whom he has anointed
are those who are whole.
—*Gospel of Truth*[*]

A ll day at work Seth felt a growing disquiet that, by the end
of the day, threatened to consume him. There had been
something about organizing Mr. Basil's library that

[*] TThe Gospel of Truth: Nag Hammadi Codex I, translated by Robert M. Grant, revised by Willis Barnstone and Marvin Meyer, published in *The Gnostic Bible (Boston, MA: Shambhala Publications, 2003).*

had given him a calming feeling. It was as if asserting order on something on the outside effected a corresponding order within. All day he found himself volunteering for tasks that involved organization in a desperate attempt to keep the anxiety at bay. Perhaps it was the lack of sleep, perhaps it was the fact that he couldn't shake the feeling that someone was watching him, or perhaps it was the stark violence done to the Lodge library, but by the end of the workday his anxieties had overwhelmed his ability to suppress them.

Finally at home, Seth discovered he could not sleep. He had selected his most calming Indica and had smoked nearly the whole joint. He was sweating, rocking back and forth, two fingers in his mouth. He heard a door open, but didn't look toward it.

"Oh. You're home." Angie stepped into the living room, dressed in boxers and a t-shirt. Her hair was mussed, and she was squinting at the light. She stopped. "What the fuck are you doing?"

Seth didn't respond. Instead, he continued staring at the carpet in front of him, at exactly 144 Boston Baked Bean candies arranged in a grid. "I can't get it right," he said. His voice was thin, twisty, and high, like he was about to cry.

"What the fuck is *my* candy doing on the *floor*?" Angie yelled.

Seth kept looking from one bean to the next. "I can't get it just right. I can't make it...perfect."

"Make what perfect? What the fuck are you doing?"

But it was clear what he was doing. She watched him nudge a bean this way, then another that way. He was trying to make all 144 beans equidistant from one another, like a square Chinese checkers board, but further spread out.

"You are so buying me another box of Boston Baked Beans, dude," Angie said, sitting cross-legged on the couch behind him.

Seth didn't respond. Instead, he nudged another bean, then another.

"Uh...I feel stupid asking this...but why is it important to make all my beans so perfectly...arranged?"

"Because..." Seth stopped. He swallowed. He kept looking at the beans, searching for anomalies.

"Is it because you feel out of control?" Angie asked. "And you're trying to assert some kind of order?"

Seth wondered about that. It made sense. But he also knew it wasn't rational. He felt compelled. "I can't...*not* do it," he finally explained.

"Seth, what happened?" Angie asked.

"What do you mean?"

"I mean, you're a nervous guy at the best of times, but you're not usually...this lost."

"I'm not lost. I know exactly where I am," he said.

"And where is that?" Angie asked.

"In my apartment. In the spaceship."

Angie cocked her head. "Uh...spaceship? What spaceship? Spaceship...earth?"

Seth looked up suddenly, and there was terror in his eyes. "I... I'm sorry I said that. I wasn't thinking."

Angie's brows knit together and she hugged one knee. "But you did say it. And I want to know what you meant by it."

"I...I'm not allowed to say."

"Is this a cult thing?"

He looked away, back to the beans. "I got some...news, I guess. Tonight. It...it shook me up a little."

"I can see that. What news?"

"I'm..."

"Let me guess. You're not allowed to say?"

Seth nodded.

Angie sighed. "Wow. I remember a time when we could tell each other everything. I miss that time."

Seth nodded again. "I know."

"Are they worth it? These secrets?" Angie asked.

"They're...big. I wish I didn't know them."

"So stop going, before you learn more things you wish you didn't know," Angie reasoned.

Seth knew this made sense. But he also knew there was no going back. He couldn't unlearn what he had heard. And he knew there was more to be revealed. He dreaded it, and at the same time, he lusted for it.

"Becky came by earlier," Angie said. "Apparently, you two had a date."

Seth's head whipped toward Angie, and he scooted where he could see her more easily. His eyes were wide. "Oh, shit."

"Oh, shit is right. So do you discard people now, too? Or just dogs?"

Seth cringed. It was a low blow. He studied the pattern of Boston Baked Beans in front of him. "I should go get him."

"Don't you dare," Angie warned. "You abandoned him and Travis stepped up. It's not fair to take them away from each other now."

"He's going to come home sometime...when I move."

"I'll believe it when I see it. Besides, you're changing the subject. We're talking about Becky."

"You're the one who brought up Kush!" Seth complained.

Angie ignored him. "I saved your ass, by the way."

"What? How?" Seth asked.

"I filled in for you. What are friends for?" She smiled.

"What does that mean?"

"Let's just say that little lady left here feeling satisfied for the first time ever. Apparently, your tongue skills suck."

"You did not," Seth insisted.

"Of course not. Becky's too innocent to allow a big bad wolf like myself to root at her hedgehog. But I did have to talk her down. She was pretty upset."

"Shit," Seth said.

"Hey, Mr. Clueless, I've got some real news for you—not cult news, actual news. If you don't snap out of it, you're going to lose that girl. She deserves better than what you're giving her right now—a lot better."

"I...I know."

"You've either got to open up to her and start paying attention to her, or you need to let her go...preferably before she dumps you. It'll hurt less if you do it, and I speak from experience. It will hurt less for her, too."

"Why is that?"

"Because she'll have the comforting knowledge that, for the first time in weeks, you're being honest with her."

Seth felt a chill go through him. "I can't balance both of these worlds," he confessed. "I can't keep them from..." he gestured at the Boston Baked Beans, "...you know, touching each other."

"Yeah, heaven forbid things should touch. Or people."

"You don't understand," he said.

"Nope. You got that right," she agreed.

"I don't want to hurt anybody," he asserted.

"So...someone is making you hurt everyone who cares about you against your will?"

"It's just...it's more than I can manage."

"Because...spaceship?"

Seth looked up and met her eye. She held it.

"Yeah," he said.

"Where the hell are we?" Keira asked.

"Behind," Schenck answered.

She followed him through a labyrinth of tight hallways, all of them brutally industrial. She quickly lost any sense of direction, and decided to simply trust her boss. "What do you mean 'behind'? Behind what?"

"Behind what everyone thinks of as 'the world,'" the chief answered.

"What does that even mean?"

"You'll see." He stopped at what looked like a service elevator. Removing his wallet, he fished a card from its guts and waved it in front of a black plastic panel to the right of the brushed silver doors. Instantly, they opened, revealing a very ordinary-looking elevator. They stepped in. Schenck entered a code on a keypad and the doors closed. The elevator started to ascend.

"Is this part of the office?" Keira asked. "Because I thought we were on the top floor."

"We were."

"So how...?" Keira scowled at him. He ignored her. The elevator kept going up...and up and up.

Finally, it stopped. The doors did not open. Schenck turned to her and looked her in the eye for the first time. Whereas just moments before his expression had been stony and unreadable, it was now full of emotion. His eyes were moist and he worked his mouth in a way that betrayed an attempt to master himself.

"Special agent, you have been granted a new security clearance."

"I...yeah, you told me that."

"I think you do not fully appreciate the...the real-world implications of this."

"Okay..." Keira shifted from one foot to another, not liking the sound of this.

"After we're done here, I want you to take a couple of days off. Don't come back until Monday."

She shook her head. "What the hell? Did I do something wrong?"

"And I want you to see a therapist," he said. "A—a therapist with clearance."

"Are you serious?" she asked, hands on hips. "How can you give me a promotion in one breath and in the next punish me? This makes no sense."

"Keira, listen to me. This isn't punishment. This is...care. I care about you, and I need you to take care of yourself."

"Okay, this is getting weird. Is this going to be a sexual harassment thing?"

Schenck held his hands up in a warding gesture. "No, no— God, I don't mean it that way. I mean it in a good-boss kind of way. This is going to...shake you up, and I want to make sure you're...'properly resourced,' as they say in HR."

"You're really scaring me now," Keira said.

He nodded, still holding her eyes. "Good. Hold that thought."

He waved the card over another black panel to the right of the doors. They slid open. "Come with me," he said, stepping out.

"Right behind you," she said, shaking her head.

They stepped into yet another featureless hallway. Aside from ducts and the occasional pipe, there was absolutely no concession to anything but stark utilitarianism. *How hard would it be to hang a picture?* she wondered.

Schenck paused by another door, and waved his card again. Keira heard a click and he pushed the door open. She stepped into what looked like a laboratory environment. Several people were wearing either lab coats or blue coveralls, and they all stopped what they were doing and stared at her. Schenck ignored them and strode quickly to an office. He knocked and waited. He must have heard something from within because he turned the knob and pushed his head inside. "We're here. Yes, she's with me. We're going to go see the sky."

See the sky? Keira mouthed. She looked around the room again.

Seven people were still standing stock still, staring at her. "Take a picture—it lasts longer," she snapped.

Slowly, one by one, they turned back to their work.

Schenck closed the door again and turned to her. He opened his mouth, but before he could speak, she said, "I'm getting a serious *Stepford Wives* vibe."

"This way," he said, and began toward a far door.

She felt the eyes in the room boring into the back of her head as they walked. Schenck waved his card in front of yet another panel and the door opened. Inside, she saw only an industrial stairway. Without a word, Schenck began to climb. "What the hell?" Keira whispered as she followed him.

It was hard to gauge how many flights they ascended, since there were no landings, no exits, no discernible floors. Finally, out of breath and surprised at her chief's stamina, they reached what was clearly the top. Yet again, Schenck waved his card and a door clicked open. He pushed it wide and held it for her. She stepped out into—

"Fuuuuuuck," she breathed. She didn't notice the door closing behind her. The only things she could see, the only things she had eyes for, the only things that mattered were the stars.

It truly did look like the sky. It surrounded her on all sides save the floor. Everything around her was dark, but the sky itself was brilliant, shockingly aflame. She had never seen stars so bright, so vivid, so...close. Her mouth hung open and she turned around and around, slowly taking it all in.

When she was a girl, her father had taught her all the major constellations. She still enjoyed picking them out—it made her feel close to him. But she did not recognize these stars. They seemed well and truly random. And what was even more shocking was that they seemed to be moving. They were moving past her, almost too slowly to notice. But she did notice.

She turned toward the sound of Schenck's breathing. The

radiance from the stars lit his features in high relief, throwing a blueish cast over them. "Chief, what on earth...?"

"We're not *on* earth, special agent."

———

"And?"

Mr. Basil looked up from the scotch decanter and looked at Dr. Teasdale. "And?"

"We can't even start a meeting properly without you launching into it cryptically?" Robinson complained.

"Have it your way," Teasdale waved away her question.

Mr. Basil finished pouring his scotch and took his seat. "There. Is everyone settled?" Robinson nodded his agreement and Teasdale raised one eyebrow. "Very well. Doctor?" He turned to Teasdale.

She rolled her eyes. "Did he pass your test?"

"Who?" Robinson asked.

"Don't be obtuse, Joshua," Teasdale said, not bothering to control the edge in her voice.

"Must be that time of the month," Robinson said to Basil.

"That is insulting," Teasdale snapped. "And beneath you."

"Children," Mr. Basil said, holding his hands up in a conciliatory gesture. "Kindness and grace."

Robinson grumbled something into his brandy snifter.

Dr. Teasdale cleared her throat. "How did Seth St. John do regarding the task you assigned him?"

Mr. Basil nodded before looking at her. "I wouldn't have believed it, but...he has a remarkable facility."

"Doesn't he, though?"

"What facility is that?" Robinson asked. "The only facility I've seen is the ability to stay awake in class and ask questions that are not too stupid."

"Then you haven't been paying attention," Teasdale answered. "Maybe you should only have one brandy before class."

"Now who's being insulting?" Robinson glowered.

"Enough!" Mr. Basil barked.

Both Robinson and Teasdale shrank a bit in their chairs. "Dr. Teasdale is quite right, Joshua. Mr. St. John is...a treasure. I now see why she has singled him out."

"Or at least one reason," Dr. Teasdale added. "He contains multitudes."

"As do we all," Mr. Basil conceded.

"What makes you think so?" Robinson asked.

"There was not one book left upon a shelf when you left, Joshua," Mr. Basil explained. "Mr. St. John came in and in one night organized the library—much more comprehensively and intuitively than it ever had been done before."

"*Remarkable*," Robinson said, with a distinct note of sarcasm.

"And once done, he was able to identify the exact location of any book I named, straight down to the case, shelf, and number of books left to right, without looking."

"Every book?" Robinson asked.

"Every book. I suggest you test him yourself."

"Perhaps I will. But what I don't understand is the utility of this...parlor trick."

"Don't you?" Mr. Basil asked.

"No indeed," Robinson admitted.

Mr. Basil turned back to Dr. Teasdale. "Sherry, I wonder what you think of another test?"

She cocked her head. "Such as?"

"Such as...let us see if Mr. St. John's talent extends to cartography."

S eth shook Jude's hand and took a seat in the dining room of the Lodge. The room was lit with candles, and the air almost crackled with energy, mood, and magic. Jude was wearing a brown corduroy vest with a button missing and a 3-inch trail of tan thread hanging from where it had been. It seemed a little sad, but Seth said nothing.

All day he had been edgy and nervous, but seeing his cohort calmed him somehow. Musa leaned back in his chair, arms folded over his chest, staring off into space. Seth waved, but he seemed lost in his own world. Lynn returned his wave, almost bouncing in her seat. Maria had on a new pair of glasses. They seemed too large for her face, which Seth found kind of sexy. Matt was seated next to her, dressed in parachute pants and a concert t-shirt with an open plaid flannel shirt over it. His face was fixed on a paperback. Seth squinted and read the title: *The Divine Invasion* by Philip K. Dick.

"Is that good?" Seth pointed at the book.

Matt shrugged. "Define good."

Seth frowned at such obtuseness. "Uh...okay. Are you enjoying it?"

"I guess. It's gnostic," Matt said, which did not answer either of Seth's questions.

"So how are you all dealing with the...the ship thing?" Seth asked.

"Fucking freaky, isn't it?" Matt asked, looking up from his book for the first time. "It's like a dream come true. I always wanted to go to space, and now...here I am. I didn't even have to pass a physical. It's amazing, you know? Nothing really changed, except my mind."

It was as if someone had flipped a switch, as the normally surly Matt now seemed positively chatty. Seth cleared his throat. "I...uh...went through an S-panel. I saw the inside...of the ship."

"You did not!" Matt said, almost leaping from his chair. "What was it like?"

It was Seth's turn to shrug. "It was boring. Like being in an industrial plant or something."

"Oh." Matt looked disappointed. Seth wondered if he had imagined Robby the Robot from *Forbidden Planet* roaming the halls.

"What makes you think it was the inside of the ship?" Maria asked.

"Because it was longer than the building I was actually in. So the building was...well, there was some kind of illusion to it, you know?"

"I keep looking at the sky," Jude confessed.

"Me too!" Maria and Seth shouted together. Then they both laughed.

Just then the side door opened, and Dr. Robinson entered. He was wearing a black pinstriped vest with matching trousers. He carried a candlestick and a stack of papers. "Greetings, initiates," he said cheerfully. Walking over to them, he placed the papers and candlestick on the floor. Retrieving a small, low table, he placed it in the middle of the circle of chairs. Once in place, he put the candlestick on top of it. Then he moved a chair into place, and put the papers underneath the chair. Then he sat with a satisfied sigh. "Sorry, it's been a busy day."

Seth smiled at him, thinking about Dr. Teasdale rolling her eyes at the mention of his name. Robinson seemed less intimidating after that, somehow. "Tonight, we introduce you to the light of chrism. It is the second of the holy seals."

"What are the seals?" Musa asked.

"The orthodox call them sacraments," Dr. Robinson replied. "But to us they signify—and effect—initiatory stages."

"Stages on the way to...what?" Lynn asked.

Dr. Robinson smiled patiently. "Enlightenment. And liberation."

Lynn scowled, clearly not satisfied with this explanation. "Liberation from what?"

"That, my dear young lady, is what tonight's catechism is all about."

She nodded and seemed to relax a bit.

"First...how are you all doing?" he asked.

Matt shrugged. "Fine. Why?"

"The first revelation is often the hardest. It tends to turn one's world upside down, and many initiates have trouble assimilating the information."

"No, I thought it was cool," Matt said.

"*Cool*," Robinson repeated blackly. He sighed.

"I had a hard time," Maria said.

"I kept looking at the sky," Jude said again.

"That is very common," Dr. Robinson smiled. "We desperately want some kind of...objective verification of such an...altered reality."

"I believe it," Seth said. "I went through an S-panel."

Dr. Robinson reared back. "Did you, now?"

Seth nodded and looked to Maria for support. He liked the way she smiled at him. He felt encouraged.

"And what did you see?"

"Not much. Just...a long hallway."

"Were you noticed?"

Seth nodded. "I ran and they chased me. Some men. In coveralls."

"How is it that you are with us tonight, young man?"

"I run fast?" Seth suggested.

Dr. Robinson's lips pulled back in his first genuine smile of the evening. "I'll bet you do." He turned back to the group as a whole. "What Seth did was very dangerous. You don't want to be targeted. The best thing we can do is to stay under the radar. The authorities think we're just another new age mystery school. We want to keep it that way."

"My therapist mentioned 'the authorities,' too, when I told her about it," Seth noted.

"Your therapist? You told your therapist our secrets?" Dr. Robinson's face darkened.

"She's an initiate," Seth said. "Dr. Teasdale?"

"Oh, yes. Right. *Her.* I didn't—" Dr. Robinson paused, thinking, and as he did so his face looked even darker. "Well...it's good you have someone to talk to, I suppose."

He leaned back and closed his eyes, as if willing himself to relax. "Please join me. Jesus said, 'I am the light which is above all things. I am the All, from me all things have emerged and to me all things have been revealed. Split the wood, and I am there; lift the stone, and you will find me there.'"*

Seth frowned. He'd had an excellent grounding in the Bible in the church of his youth, but he'd never read that one.

But Robinson continued, "Let us become aware of the divine presence, within us and around us."

Seth closed his eyes, but he wasn't sure what he was supposed to do. He waited quietly.

Robinson finally said, "Amen," and Seth repeated it automatically. He shrank a bit. No one else had said, "Amen" with him.

Dr. Robinson rose from his seat and went to the back of his chair. Then he struck a dramatic pose and began to sing:

> First there was one, there was one God,
> And then it split into two,
> Then it split into seven, and then into twenty-two.
> All of them were emanations,

---

* "The Gospel of Thomas," logion 77.

like Will and Life and Power,
Then comes your hostess,
the emanation with the mostest,
the emanation of the hour:

Sophia, Sophia, it's her fault that we're here
Sophia, Sophia, she caused this vale of tears.

Seth's eyes went wide, and he reared back in his seat. The song was loud, fast, and brash, like a Broadway show tune, and Dr. Robinson acted it out with obvious relish.

She gave birth without her consort,
it was a naughty thing to do
She started out in heaven,
and she ended up in poo.
And the being she gave birth to,
well he wasn't very nice—
He had the head of a lion,
and he wanted sacrifice.
He thought he was the only god,
and don't think that you're bent
If you think he sounds familiar:
he's the god of the Old Testament.

He's Yaldobaoth, he's Saklas,
and sometimes Samael.
He created all the archons,
and he made this earth a hell...

Dr. Robinson stopped, in what was obviously mid-verse. He opened one eye, and a broad grin spread across his face. He sighed. "Well, that's enough of that. I'm guessing you didn't catch all of that, so it's time to back up and tell the story in more detail. How does that sound?"

Seth looked at Jude, Lynn, Musa, Maria, and Matt. They all looked like they were about to burst out laughing. Then Lynn did laugh. "That was...unexpected," she said.

"Yes, well, I could go on, but I won't." Dr. Robinson resumed his seat. "I'm going to tell you a story. You can understand it literally or metaphorically—it's all the same to me. All of it is true, but no images we can conjure can possibly describe the reality of it. It is all shadow play."

Seth did not understand the bit about shadows, but he let it wash over him and continued to focus.

"This story comes from a gnostic gospel called *The Apocryphon of John*. It is a...complex work, some might even say psychedelic. What I will tell you now is a streamlined version, just the highlights. But I encourage you to read it for yourself to digest all of the nuances at your convenience. You'll find it in any collection of the Nag Hammadi manuscripts. Barnestone's *The Gnostic Bible* has the most readable version, Bentley's *The Gnostic Scriptures* is the most scholarly." He waved his hand in the air as if to dismiss his last point. "But that is neither here nor there. These are the important details. Are you ready?"

Seth noticed that he was leaning in toward Robinson—they all were.

"Once upon a time, there was only God—the true God, the God of light and life and wholeness, at peace in the Pleroma, which means 'the fullness.' This God was in the business of emanating, dividing himself into lesser beings, beings that circumnavigated him in harmonious orbits, each assigned their own archetypal provenance. These emanations were formed into mated pairs—we call these syzygies. The syzygies in the furthest orbit from the Source were a couple you might have heard of:

Christ and Sophia, or, translated into English, Anointing and Wisdom."

Seth dimly remembered that "Christ" was the Greek word for "anointed." But he had never heard the word "syzygy," and already he was struggling to keep up. He frowned and listened even more intently.

"Sophia got bitten by curiosity, and so she left the Pleroma to explore. She found herself in our universe, in chaos. But alas, poor girl, she had left no trail of breadcrumbs, and so could not find her way back home to the Pleroma."

Dr. Robinson looked genuinely sad, his lips growing pouty and his eyes soft. He shook his head. "Poor, poor Sophia. But she was a clever girl. She knew that what God did all day was emanate, and so she reasoned that she might be able to reach God by imitating God. Er..." Robinson gave them a conspiratorial look. "...this is dream-logic, so just go with it, please." He leaned back again and continued. "So she emanated a being, a spiritual being, like herself. But because she had produced it without the other half of her mated pair, the being she gave birth to was malformed. He was called 'Samael,' which means 'the blind god.' She told her son about the Pleroma and her longing to go home, and about the glory of the true God, but Samael said to himself, 'Mother keeps talking about this other god, but I'm the only god I know of. So, forget about this other god—*I'm* going to do what gods do.' And so Samael created the earth, and then from his own being he emanated the archons—evil angels who govern the earth, who surround it and guard it.

"And then he made Adam and Eve and placed them in a garden..."

Seth's eyes went wide again as he felt a familiar panic trickle through his head and neck. He felt like Robinson had just grabbed hold of the world and yanked it sideways. He needed to process what his catechist had said, but Robinson was already speaking again.

"...told them that he was the only god, that they must worship and serve only him. And then he instructed the archons not to let the souls of Adam and Eve or their children escape when they died, but to return them to the earth for an endless cycle of reincarnation and slavery. You see, he had created a prison planet—the earth—and he longed to keep his creations captive forever."

He paused, and looked at each of his students in turn, no doubt assessing their reactions. Seth looked at his classmates; they seemed as stunned as he was. Jude looked like he'd been slapped. Musa's face was unreadable. Maria's mouth was open—as was Lynn's—and Matt's forehead was bunched and his lips tight.

"Are we supposed to believe this?" Lynn asked.

"'Believe' is a problematic word," Dr. Robinson said, with a slow shake of his head. "This is myth. To us gnostics, myth is more important than history. History often lies, as it is always written by the victors, as you know. But myth? Myth *always* tells us the truth."

Lynn looked troubled. Seth wondered if they would again lose another classmate. But she stayed, crossing her arms and slouching down in her chair.

Jude leaned forward, his surprise having shifted to fascination. "How did Sophia feel about what her son had done?"

"Ah! What an excellent question," Dr. Robinson said, "and very pertinent. Sophia saw what Samael had wrought and was horrified by it. She took compassion on Adam and Eve and placed within them a part of herself—a spark of true divinity, something Samael did not possess. As the evangelist Philip wrote, 'The soul of Adam came from a Spirit whose partner is Christ. The spirit given to him is his Mother, and it filled his soul.'* So now there was a part of Adam and Eve that was greater than their creator. This spark longed for the fullness of the Pleroma, for the infinite light, for freedom. It was something Samael could not control."

"I feel that spark," Jude said.

"Of course you do." Dr. Robinson's face became momentarily beatific, kind. "You would not be here otherwise."

"I've always felt it," Jude added. "I just...never knew what it was."

"And what does your heart tell you now? Does what I am saying resonate with that experience?"

"Like nothing I have ever heard before," Jude said, almost worshipfully.

Dr. Robinson nodded in a way that was both reverent and not-at-all surprised, as if this was something he had heard before, perhaps many times.

Robinson leaned forward and continued. "But Sophia was not the only one moved to pity. The true God, viewing these events from afar, from the Pleroma, also felt for them, and he sent an emissary, a...well, a secret agent, if you will...to intervene. He sent Sophia's mated pair, the Christ, to put things right. So the Christ traveled into the space that Samael had carved out for himself—our universe—and, taking the form of a serpent, he entered the garden and confronted Adam and Eve—"

"Christ is the snake??!!" Matt exclaimed.

"Indeed. The snake is the ancient symbol for healing. Why do you think we have the caduceus? Just look at any medical logo—there it is."

Matt blinked. This time it was his mouth hanging open.

Robinson nodded. "This is even attested to in the orthodox scriptures. In the book of Numbers, the Israelites complained of

---

* "The Gospel of Philip," logion 71.

the hardness of life in the desert, and so Samael sent a plague of serpents to bite and afflict them. So Moses made a bronze statue of a serpent on a pole, and raised it up. Anyone who gazed upon it lived, and anyone who did not...did not."

"I never understood that weird story," Seth confessed. He still didn't.

"Yet in the gospel of John, the most gnostic of all the orthodox writings, Jesus makes a connection between himself and that serpent. He tells Nicodemus, 'just as Moses lifted up the serpent in the wilderness, so must the Son of Man be lifted up.' Christ and the serpent are one." Dr. Robinson leaned back and let that sink in.

"What did the Christ-Serpent say to Adam and Eve?" Maria asked.

"Oh! Quite right, quite right. I get distracted." Robinson leaned forward again and continued. "The serpent told them, 'That being who tells you he is god? He is a liar, a pretender to the throne. He is nothing but a demonic tyrant, whose goal it is to keep you imprisoned here for eternity—you and your children. But there is a way you can escape from him...' And he told them the secrets they needed to know in order to slip past the authorities—the archons—when they died, so that they could return home to the Pleroma."

"But what about poor Sophia?" Maria asked.

"The Christ tried to persuade her to return with him. And a part of her did. Our mythology says that there are now two Sophias—the redeemed Sophia who returned to the World of Light, and the unredeemed Sophia, who could not abandon her son and also hoped to minimize the damage he would do."

"Wait, she divided in two?" Matt asked, "Like mitosis?"

Dr. Robinson laughed. "I suppose, yes, something like that. Again, this is myth. It is symbolic of the dualism that we are

THE WHERE, THE WHO & THE WHAT · 283

trapped in. That is the prison, after all, or at least it is a main feature of our prison."

"I'm confused," Seth admitted. "What does this Christ-Serpent have to do with Jesus?"

"Another excellent question." Robinson pointed at Seth. "The serpent was the first theophany—"

"What does that word mean, 'theophany'?" Musa asked.

"It means a divine appearance," Robinson said, with a hint of annoyance. Seth half expected him to say, *What do they teach young people in school these days?* but instead he turned back to Seth. "Adam and Eve benefited from the Christ-Serpent's ministry, but they did not pass this secret knowledge on to their children—and thus human beings have been in bondage ever since. But the True God is compassionate, so he sent the Christ to us again—but this time in the form of a man."

"Jesus?" Maria asked.

"Yes, Jesus," Robinson smiled at her, "our kind Lord."

Seth felt something squirm in him and he shifted in his seat. Robinson noticed. He cocked his head at Seth and asked, "Does it make you uncomfortable when I say that?"

"Uh...a bit. Why?"

"I was going to ask you the same question." Robinson waited.

"Because religious language makes me...I grew up religious—very religious."

"Ah," Robinson nodded. "You suffer from religious trauma."

Seth blinked. "I've never heard that term, but...yeah. I guess I do."

Robinson nodded slowly, his face kind. For the first time, Seth thought he might like him. "Seth, have you not guessed? The god you grew up with is not the True God. The god you grew up worshipping is Samael, the blind god."

Seth felt his blood turn cold. "The god you were given is a false god. He is no god at all, but in fact, a deformed demon. His only wish is to keep you enslaved. He wants you to deny your passions, to hate yourself. But there is good news here—there is another God, the True God of the Pleroma. And this God calls you into healing and wholeness and light, and what is more, gives you everything you need to escape the monster god Samael. That is why you are here. It is why you came to us. There is, within your soul, that spark of true divinity given to us by Sophia—and that spark longs to escape...to go home. I can see that longing within you. It is real. It is strong. It is true. You can trust it. You know what I am talking about, don't you?"

Seth felt like he was watching himself from afar. He watched himself nod, his eyes fixed on Robinson's.

"I know you do. All of you." He smiled at Matt, Lynn, Musa, Jude, and Maria then, too.

A few moments of silence passed. It turned into a minute. Seth was surprised that he didn't feel uncomfortable. Instead, it felt full, quiet, sacred.

Finally, though, Maria broke the silence. "Can you tell us more about Jesus?"

"Oh, yes. You must not believe the false god's lies about him. He is no one's son, and certainly not Samael's. That was just Samael's attempt to get 'ahead of the story,' and change the narrative. The Christ is a spirit being and has nothing to do with matter. Matter is the creation of the demiurge—"

"The what?" Matt asked.

"Oh, I am sorry, that is a technical name for Samael, the false god. It means, 'lesser power.' Matter is the creation of Samael. It is evil and corrupt. What has light to do with darkness? Nothing at all. So, the Christ could not really have been a human being— that's nonsense. He would not sully himself so. Instead, he is a pure spirit, and he only *appeared* to us as a human being. As the Gospel of Philip says, 'Jesus tricked them all, for he did not reveal himself as he really was, but instead appeared to them so they could see him. He appeared to all of them in a way they could understand—to the great, he seemed to be great, to the small, he seemed small, to the angels, he seemed to be angelic, and to people, he seemed to be human."

"So Jesus wasn't *really* human?" Seth asked.

"No. There are some funny stories about this, actually," Dr. Robinson said. "Some ancient gnostics said that Jesus could piss, but could not defecate."

"What?" Lynn asked, her face bunching up in confusion and amusement.

"It's true, they said this," Robinson confirmed. "And some said that on the cross, Jesus laughed, because the soldiers thought they were hurting him. But he had no body to hurt!" Robinson grinned. "This is the meaning of the resurrection. Not that a dead body got up and walked around again, but that you cannot kill a being of pure spirit. It was not Jesus who died on the cross: it was the lie that Samael had told the world, the lie that made them as blind as he was. As the Gospel of Philip also says, Jesus is called 'the one who is spread out. Jesus came to crucify the System.'

"What do you mean by 'the System'?" Maria asked.

"The word in Greek is *kosmos*, which is often translated as 'the world.' But that does not mean the planet. It means the corrupt web of lies and tyranny that governs the planet. It has exactly the same pejorative meaning as it does in our vernacular, as when you say, 'The System is corrupt.' I am talking about political systems, religious systems, the systems of cultural taboos and norms enshrined in every culture. I'm talking about the conceptual web of ideas that keep the vast majority of human beings asleep and subservient and enslaved to the demiurge."

Seth's head swam and he felt faint. "I think...I need to lie down," Seth said. Trembling, he scooted himself off the chair and lowered himself to the floor. Robinson leaped up to help, but Seth had safely navigated by himself. He spread out his arms and legs like the Vitruvian man, trying to hold onto the earth and staring at the ceiling. He realized he was hyperventilating and tried to slow his breathing down.

"It is...a lot," Robinson said, kneeling by him. The older man felt his forehead, and then, apparently satisfied, patted his arm before rising again and resuming his seat.

"Are you okay?" Lynn asked.

"I...think so. Just a little dizzy."

"This is a lot of information," Dr. Robinson said. "I have often wondered if perhaps we ought not break up the revelations and offer them in more...digestible portions." He sighed. "But the problem is that it is all one big story, and one part is connected to every other part, and it doesn't make a lot of sense unless you have all the parts."

Maria nodded, her eyes large and her face grave.

Musa, however, looked troubled. "But...you said this was just myth, right? It isn't real."

"You are confusing myth with legend," Robinson answered him. "A common mistake. Legends are fiction. Myth is truth."

"Like, historically true? I mean, there wasn't really an Adam and Eve, right?" Matt asked, his voice rising with incredulity.

"History is not important," Robinson said. "The story tells the truth of the matter, whether it happened just that way or not."

"So what *did* happen?" Musa asked.

"In our culture, we want history to play out like a movie," Robinson said, growing impatient again. "But it doesn't. There is no objective witness, no camera. Instead, history is like a dream, seen through the cultural and personal filters of billions of subjective souls, each with their own internal stories and biases and delusions. No one knows our history. But we can share the dream."

"This makes no sense to me," Musa said.

"It does to me," Maria said.

"Me, too," Seth said from his place on the floor. "It makes sense of everything I've ever wondered about in my life. It makes too much sense. It makes so much sense that I...feel like someone hit me on the head with a hammer."

Robinson nodded. "Yes...that was how it was for me, too."

A few moments of silence passed. "So how did Jesus' coming, the...the second theophany...how did it help us?" Maria asked. "I don't really get that part."

"Well, unlike the orthodox—who are enslaved to Samael's lies—we do not believe that we are saved by believing the right things. We are saved by knowledge—that is what 'gnostic' means, one who is saved by knowledge. And the Christ, in the form of Jesus, came to give to us, in these latter days, the very same secrets he imparted to Adam and Eve when he met them in the form of a serpent. He gave them the knowledge of their true situation, and the secret knowledge they would need to escape it. He gave the very same information to the apostles, who have handed it down to us."

"But none of that is in the Bible, right?" Matt asked.

"No. The Bible is the product of Samael's church, not ours. The apostles did not write down the secret teachings—"

"Because they're secret!" Lynn exclaimed.

"Just so," Robinson said, smiling. "They only passed them on orally, from teacher to student."

"And that's what you just did now...for us," Seth said, although it was not a question.

"Yes. I have given you the lesser mysteries—I have told you the truth of our situation. We are enslaved in Samael's System. But I have not told you the greater mysteries...I have not told you how you can escape that System. That will be for another time."

"Oh, thank god," Seth said, without thinking.

"Which god?" Matt asked.

Dr. Robinson smiled at this. "That is actually a very astute question. When you read the gnostic scriptures, that question must always be on your mind. You can only tell by context which god the author is referring to—sometimes it is the demiurge, and sometimes it is the True God. And sometimes...it's hard to tell."

"That sounds confusing," Seth said.

Robinson shrugged. "It is. But how is that different from any scripture? It's why we study them, so we can gradually understand them better. The trick is to understand the crisis the author is writing to address."

"Is scripture only written to address a crisis?" Maria asked.

Robinson winked at her. "Always and only. Understand the crisis motivating the writing, and you understand the scripture."

"Huh," Seth said. He would need to think about that, too. In fact, he suspected he would need a few weeks to process all he had just heard.

But Dr. Robinson was in motion now. He reached into his pocket and pulled out a lighter. He lit the candle on the small table in the middle of their circle. He put the lighter back in his pocket and pulled out a round metal box, like a tiny hatbox, about as big as a large man's thumb. It was gold in color; its top and bottom were about the size of a quarter. He held it up. "This is chrism—it is oil set aside for a sacred purpose. 'The master did everything by means of a symbol—baptism and anointing... A pearl which is cast down into the mire is not despised, nor if it is anointed with oil is it more valued. Rather, it has great worth to its keeper at all times. So it is with the children of the True God.'* A soul thrown into matter is no less precious to God. Nor can the Christ increase that which is of inestimable worth. Yet let this oil be for you a sign of the wholeness that is already in you, the original gift of Sophia. And let it also be a sign of the light you have just received, which has revealed to you for the first time your true

---

* "The Gospel of Philip," logion 41.

situation. For only when you know the truth can you be free. You have just been given knowledge, which is always salvation. For whomever has been anointed has everything, held in promise. Receive the second seal."

With this, Robinson unscrewed one side of the object, revealing what looked like a yellowed wad of cotton. Holding the first object in one hand, he held the other over it in a gesture of blessing. Eyes closed, Robinson nevertheless turned his face toward the ceiling and prayed, "It is fitting for you at this time to send your son Jesus the anointed to anoint us, so we can trample on snakes and the heads of scorpions and all the power of the demiurge, since Jesus is the shepherd of the seed. Through him we have known you. And we glorify you: Glory be to you, the father in the son, the father in the holy church and in the holy aeons. From now on he abides forever in the perpetuity of the eternal realms, until the untraceable eternal realms of the eternal realms."*

Opening his eyes, Robinson brushed his thumb over the cotton and knelt beside where Seth lay. The young man seemed to shrink into the carpet, not sure what was coming. Robinson smiled reassuringly and pressed his thumb to Seth's forehead. Seth felt him make the sign of the cross. Then the older man looked into his eyes—deep into his eyes, as if he were trying to catch a glimpse of his soul. "Soul and spirit are constituted of water and fire,"† Robinson said, still holding his gaze. "There is water in baptism, but there is fire in chrism. ‡ Water is used to wash, but oil is used to seal." Then Robinson slapped him—hard.

"What the hell?" Seth protested, his hand going immediately to his cheek. "What was that for?"

The look in Robinson's eyes was confusing, because it was still

---

* Adapted from NHX XI 2; 40, ii ff, quoted in *Suppressed Prayers* (Harrisburg, PA: Trinity Press International, 1998), 97-98.
† "The Gospel of Philip," logion 58.
‡ "The Gospel of Philip," logion 22.

compassionate. "It is to remind you that such terrible knowledge does not come without price. The life you knew is over. The life you have now will be hard. But it will also lead to glory." With that, he stood up and gave Seth a reverent bow, then moved on to Maria. He performed the same ritual for her, but she was ready for the slap when it came. Then he did the same for each of them, every time repeating the same words.

Then he pulled a handkerchief from his back pocket and wiped the oil from his fingers. He put his right hand into the pocket of his vest and pulled forth several chains. He sorted them out, and Seth saw that there was a medal of some kind dangling from each of them. Pulling one of the chains free, he placed it over Jude's head, then Maria's, and so on around the circle as he spoke:

"You can now properly be called 'Christian'—not as the followers of the demiurge would have it, not Christian because you follow a false Christ, but Christian because you are anointed. As you may have guessed, the word 'Christ' and the word 'chrism' are related. Christ simply means 'one who has been anointed.' The Gospel of Philip says, 'The name of Christian is welcomed with anointing, in the fullness and energy of the cross, which the apostles call the union of opposites. For once anointed, one is not just a Christian. One is the Christ.'"* He paused, then knelt and put the final chain around Seth's neck, saying, "*You* are Christ now."

Seth swallowed and reached up to feel the medal. Holding it out where he could see it, he squinted at it. It held the unmistakable image of a serpent draped over the horizontal beam of a cross.

---

* "The Gospel of Philip," translated by Jean-Yves Leloup & Joseph Rowe, p. 97.

WHO IS SOPHIA?

Sophia is a significant figure in Jewish, Christian, and Gnostic religious traditions. While interpretations and depictions of Sophia may vary across these traditions, she is commonly associated with divine understanding, spiritual insight, and the embodiment of feminine wisdom. "Sophia" derives from sofia, the Greek word for "wisdom."

In Jewish tradition, Sophia emerges in Midrashic literature as the personification of Torah, who delivered the Law to Moses, and dwells among the Jews as the wisdom to stay faithful to it. In Kabbalistic tradition, Sophia is often equated with the concept of Chokhmah, one of the ten sefirot (emanations of God) in Kabbalah. Chokhmah represents the highest form of wisdom and is regarded as a channel through which God's wisdom is revealed to humanity. In Jewish thought, wisdom is highly esteemed and regarded as a fundamental aspect of the divine nature.

Drawing on Proverbs 8:22-31, Christian theology emphasizes her role in creation and as a guide for righteous living. Early Christian theologians understood Sophia to be synonymous with "the Word," the preincarnate Christ who would eventually be born as Jesus of Nazareth.

In Gnostic traditions, Sophia takes on a complex and multifaceted role. In Gnosticism, Sophia is seen as an emanation from the divine realm who becomes entangled in the material world. In some Gnostic myths, Sophia is portrayed as an aeon, a divine being or spiritual entity, who unintentionally brings about the creation of the flawed physical universe. Her fall from the divine realm and subsequent redemption are central themes in Gnostic cosmology.

The significance of Sophia within these religious traditions extends beyond her role as an abstract concept or personification of wisdom. Sophia serves as a symbol of the divine feminine, highlighting the importance of feminine qualities in spiritual and philosophical pursuits. She embodies the integration of knowledge, insight, and compassion, inviting people to seek divine wisdom and develop a deeper understanding of the divine nature.

CHAPTER TEN

We shall enter into the wisdom
of those who have known the truth.
Those who have awakened
to the truth cannot abandon it.
The System of the Pleroma is strong.
A small part of it is what broke loose
to make up the world.
What encompasses everything,
the realm of all, did not
come into being. It was.
—*Treatise on the Resurrection**

---

* Treatise on the Resurrection: Nag Hammadi Codex I, 4 translated by Malcolm Peel and Bentley Leyton, revised by Willis Barnestone, published in *The Gnostic Bible* (Boston, MA: Shambhala Publications, 2009).

The next day at work went by in a blur. Several times Seth realized he was staring off into space, usually when someone was talking to him and he hadn't noticed. Going back to the break room to get a cup of coffee, Travis came up behind him and put a hand on his shoulder. "Hey, dude. You okay?"

Seth realized just how tense his shoulders were and willed them to relax. "Yeah. Yeah, fine. Just...distracted."

"Hey, if it's about Kush, he's doing great. We're having a gay old time."

"I...I'm glad to hear it. I mean, I do worry about him, but right now, I'm—"

"Girl stuff?"

"Uh...no. That's a problem, too, though. I've been so distracted, I haven't..." He trailed off. He needed to talk to Becky, before it was too late to save...whatever it was they had.

"Dude, you can't even finish sentences. What's up?"

As soon as Seth released the carafe of coffee, Travis snatched it up and filled his own cup.

"Uh...I can't really talk about it."

"Well, you better talk about it with someone, because Madame Beast just asked me what was wrong with you."

"Do you think she'll fire me?" Seth asked, panic sneaking into his voice.

"I don't think it's that bad yet, but you know...she's got her eye on you."

"Shit," Seth said. "Yeah, yeah, okay. I'll...snap out of it." He didn't know if that was something he could really do, but he could certainly make an effort.

Travis returned to the floor with his steaming cup of coffee, and Seth sat at the break table. He pulled out his phone and texted Becky. "Can we talk tonight?"

He stared at the screen, waiting. Then he saw the flashing ellipses, and he knew she was typing. Then the ellipses disappeared. Whatever she had typed, she had erased and started over. Inwardly, Seth was relieved he did not see the initial message. But eventually, the ellipses appeared again, and a new message sprang into view.

"Okay. I'll meet you at your place after work. Dinner?"

"Sure," Seth wrote. "In or out?"

"Out," she responded. "On me."

"Sounds good," he wrote. He put his phone back in his pocket, relaxing a bit. Maybe their relationship wasn't unsalvageable after all.

H e managed to get through the workday without any further fugue states. As soon as he got home, he got into the shower, but instead of feeling good, he was overwhelmed with the feeling he was being watched. He looked around, searching for cameras, but there were none. He looked at the ceiling and the word "archon" appeared in his mind.

"Archons," he said out loud, then instantly regretted it, as if simply speaking the name would invoke them. One part of his brain recoiled against the myth Dr. Robinson had revealed to him. He recognized this as the rational part, and he knew that the story was crazy. Believing it was crazy. But another part of his brain had relaxed when he heard it, almost emitting an audible "yesssss," as if, for the first time, he had heard a story that made all the pieces fit together. And this latter part of his brain, the part that resonated so deeply with the gnostic myth, was the greater part. He had no idea why it felt so right, he simply knew that it did. He hadn't known why he had distrusted institutions or authority so much...but the story explained it. Archons were behind it all, and they did not have his best interests in mind. He hadn't known why he had feared the god of his childhood faith, why he had quit the church as soon as he was on his own and not compelled to attend...but now he did. The god of the New Song Christian Fellowship wasn't a god at all, but a demon bent on his slavish devotion, on his perpetual imprisonment, on his blind and mindless obedience.

The thought that there was another God, a True God, out beyond the jurisdiction of this prison planet, a God who truly loved him and wanted the best for him and who wanted to liberate him from the System made every tense muscle in his body melt into peace. He didn't know how he knew it was true. His soul just knew.

He grabbed a towel and stepped onto the ragged blue bathmat, drying himself. He caught a glimpse of himself in the foggy mirror and found the sight strangely ethereal. "I am a Christian," he said to his reflection. Inwardly, he squirmed. He went further. "I am Christ." He blinked, then looked deeply into his own eyes. Yes. Yes, there was truth there. He felt the rightness of it in his bones. He was anointed. Something had shifted. He had the knowledge, and it had changed him.

As he dressed, he still felt plagued by the feeling that alien eyes were upon him. Powerful eyes. Malevolent eyes. It was no longer an intuition, but a fact. There were forces outside of him that loathed his newfound knowledge, who hated the fact that he knew and knew that he knew, who had turned from his overlord to his enemy.

He looked at the clock. Becky would arrive in a half hour. Just enough time to check the apartment. Making sure he had everything he needed—phone, wallet, antacids—he went to the kitchen and took his evening dose of psychiatric medication. Then, satisfied that he was ready to walk out of the door, he began his check of the apartment. First he checked that all lights were out. Then he walked to every room and touched the wicks of every candle, just to make sure they were out. Then he came to the stove and, putting all other thoughts from his mind, studiously checked each knob. He felt his body temperature rising and his breath quicken. He willed himself to relax and started again. This time he got through all five knobs without an intrusive thought, and waited to see if the "just right" feeling would visit him. It did. He breathed a sigh of relief and withdrew his phone. He snapped a quick picture of the stove—just in case he worried about it later— and stepped into the hall, locking the door behind him. Then he headed down the stairs. He would wait for Becky on the front stoop, now that his apartment was properly sealed behind him.

B ecky was quiet as they walked to the restaurant. She was acting hurt, shyer than usual, and sad. Seth shrank into himself, pricked by guilt, becoming quiet himself. They completed their walk in silence. They sat in silence, they perused their menus in silence, and they avoided looking at each other until their orders were taken.

Once the waiter had walked away, however, Seth cleared his throat. "Uh...can we talk about the other night?" Still not looking at him, Becky nodded. "Look, Beck, I'm really, really sorry. I...you know I go to the Lodge on Thursday nights, and I just totally spaced when we made plans."

"You seem like you're in space most of the time," Becky said.

Seth felt a cold chill run through him. "You don't know how right that is," he said, then instantly regretted it.

"What does that mean?" she asked. Now she was looking at him, her face bunched in hurt.

He briefly panicked. "Oh, uh, I just...I'm agreeing with you. I've...been pretty spacey lately. And-and I'm sorry. I'm just..." He trailed off. What could he say? What should he say? He decided it might be best to be as truthful as he could. "I...uh...I'm learning a lot of...a new spiritual perspective. And it's kind of thrown me for a loop. I...I'm trying to assimilate it, and process it and stuff, and it's...it's kind of kicking my ass."

"So stop," she said.

He shook his head. "I..." He wanted to say, *I can't*, but that didn't feel right. Finally he said, "I don't want to."

"But it's obviously not helping you. You're...how are you doing at work?"

Seth looked down at the tablecloth. "Uh...not good."

"I didn't think so. I ran into Travis yesterday at the food co-op, and he's worried about you."

Anger flashed in Seth's eyes. "You guys...talked about me?"

"Of course we talked about you," Becky said, a little heat rising into her voice. "We're concerned about you. We...we love you." There was the hurt in her eyes again.

A part of Seth recoiled at Becky's use of the word, "love," but the rational part of his brain reminded him that she was not speaking in a romantic context. He forced himself to relax. "I know. I'm sorry. I'm sorry about a lot of things. I'm sorry I made you feel...like I didn't care about you." He paused, and the silence between them was so thick and heavy that he couldn't bear it. "Because I do," he blurted out, "care about you." He managed a weak smile, and met her eyes for a brief moment. Then he looked away again, his shoulders falling. "I suck. I'm sorry."

"What I don't understand," Becky started, "is why this Lodge thing is something you only want to do by yourself. If I went with you, we would be able to talk about it, and you wouldn't have to shut me out. There wouldn't need to be...secrets. And...maybe it would bring us closer together."

"You don't understand. And I'm not sure I could explain it. But...it's not a hobby. It's something that either calls to your soul or it doesn't." He wasn't sure where those words had come from, but they sounded right.

"And how do you know that what you're learning wouldn't call to me, too?"

"Uh...I don't," he confessed.

"But you're just going to shut me out anyway, on the off chance that I'm too stupid to 'get' whatever it is you're doing?"

"No, no that's not it at—"

"Because that's exactly how it sounds," Becky said.

"That's...that's not what I think," Seth insisted.

Becky crossed her arms. Just then the waiter breezed in, setting a steaming plate in front of Becky. Then he set one in front of Seth, and the powerful, delicious odor of pork medallions marinated in an apple cinnamon sauce on a bed of wild rice wafted over him. The waiter left, but Becky did not seem to notice the plates. She just kept staring at Seth.

"I want you to tell me one of the things," she said.

"I...what things?"

"Don't play stupid. You know exactly what I'm saying. I want you to tell me one of the secrets."

Seth blinked. He had picked up a fork, but it was still suspended in air. "You know I can't...I can't do that."

"You'll do that, or I will get up and walk out right now, and you will never, ever see me again."

"Becky, that's...it's not fair."

"I'll count to three. One..."

Seth put the fork down. He started to sweat. "Becky, I took an oath."

"Two..."

"On pain of death. You don't understand."

"Three." She looked him in the eyes. Profound sadness radiated from her. She nodded and pushed her chair back, standing up.

"Becky, please don't—"

"Goodbye, Seth."

Seth swore under his breath. "Okay, okay, just...sit back down."

Becky looked at him warily, but sank back down into her seat. "You're going to tell me one of them?"

Seth looked around. Was anyone looking at him? No. Everyone around him seemed to be engaged in their own meal, their own conversations, utterly oblivious to his presence. He looked back to Becky. "If I tell you one thing, do you promise, promise, promise you won't tell another living soul?"

She nodded gravely. She looked relieved, her eyes softening, glistening.

"Okay, then. I...here goes." He leaned over the table and looked straight into her eyes. He whispered, "We are not on earth."

"We're not?" she asked.

"We're not."

Her eyebrows rose and her lips pursed. "So...uh...where are we?"

"We're on a multi-generational starship. This environment is crafted to make us *think* we're on earth. But we're not."

He leaned back and watched her. She stifled a laugh. "You're bullshitting me, aren't you?"

"No, I—"

Her eyes flashed with anger. "Goddam you, Seth. I trusted you. And I...I gave you a chance. I..." She stood. "I can't believe you think so little of me. Goodbye Seth. Have a good life."

"I t's worse," Seth said. "It's a lot worse."

"What's worse?" Dr. Sherry Teasdale asked, writing something on her notepad.

"The OCD. I...I've been zoning out."

Dr. Teasdale looked concerned. "Why do you think that is?"

Seth looked at the swaying tree out the window. A long silence passed. "Do you think that tree knows it's in space?"

Dr. Teasdale looked out the window too, but looked quickly back to Seth. "All trees are in space. It's just the size of the vehicle that differs. So...no. I don't think so."

"But the soil only goes so far down. It would hit metal."

"It would hit rock. The *Cibus Dei* is constructed inside an asteroid. And hitting rock is something that trees do with astounding frequency in the wild."

Seth looked at her then, and his shoulders fell. "Are you making fun of me?"

"No, Seth. I'm sorry. That came out sounding more sarcastic than I intended."

Seth nodded. "I'm used to sarcasm. I live with the queen of sarcasm."

"How is it going, living with Angie?"

He shrugged. "She gives me a lot of shit."

"About what?"

"About letting go of Kush...and about the Lodge."

"Oh?"

"Yeah, she says I've been duped by a cult."

"What do you think?"

His eyes moved back and forth, but did not look at her. "I...I don't know. There are things about the Lodge that scare me. I wasn't ready for the...the religious stuff. But everything Dr. Robinson said seems to be true—"

"Except for the photo of the actual *Cibus Dei*," Dr. Teasdale reminded him.

"That seems insignificant," Seth said, "like whether things in a myth happened exactly like the myth says, or if it's just telling you the core truth in a fanciful way."

Dr. Teasdale smiled. "You've been paying attention."

"Of course," Seth said.

Dr. Teasdale wrote something on her pad. Then she looked up and gave him an unhurried smile.

"I love her—Angie, I mean," Seth said. "She's my best friend. I don't like arguing with her. She says the Lodge has come between us, that we didn't used to have secrets from each other."

"Do you think that's true?"

"Yeah." Seth looked down at his hands. "Yeah, I do. And I hate it."

Seth thought of telling her about accidentally letting "spaceship" slip with Angie that night when he had been so compulsive, but couldn't bring himself to confess that he'd revealed one of their secrets. What if she told Mr. Basil? He didn't want to get booted from the Lodge. So he kept that as a secret of his own. He hoped she couldn't tell.

"What? What just happened?" Dr. Teasdale asked.

Seth felt a moment of panic. Then his brain hit on something he could substitute. He relaxed a bit. "I...uh...Becky broke up with me."

Dr. Teasdale wrote this down. "I'm so sorry to hear that. What happened?"

"She...Angie has been talking to her. About the Lodge. And... she didn't like the fact that I have to keep secrets from her, either."

"I see." Dr. Teasdale's face grew a bit graver. Or perhaps she was just concerned. "How did it happen?"

"We were going out to dinner. And she...she told me she didn't like the secrets. And...and I guess when she didn't get the response she wanted, she stormed out. She broke up with me."

"What response do you think she wanted?"

Seth couldn't meet her eyes. He didn't want to let on that he'd let a secret slip to Becky any more than that he'd let one slip to

Angie. He cleared his throat. "I...I guess she wanted me to stop going to the Lodge, too."

"Have you spoken to her since then?"

"No."

"When was this?"

"Last night."

Seth felt her eyes on him. It felt like they were boring into him. "Seth, I am sorry."

"Yeah." He shrugged.

"Do you love her? Becky, I mean? I know you love Angie, but do you love Becky?"

Seth frowned. He didn't know the answer to that. He liked Becky. He liked spending time with her. He liked snuggling on the couch with her. She was funny and kind and a little bit sad, which Seth had always found intriguing.

"You're taking a long time to think about that," Dr. Teasdale noted.

"I like her," he said finally. "But I'm not in love with her."

"I'm not surprised to hear that."

"Why do you say that?"

"Because you led with your conflict with Angie rather than your conflict with Becky. You care more about Angie."

That was true. He did. He liked Becky, but he needed Angie. He had no romantic feelings for Angie—she was like a sister to him. But he knew that he loved her, probably more than any other person alive. Slowly, Seth nodded.

"I feel like my world is...unraveling." Seth played with a bit of fuzz on his jeans.

"Your girlfriend left you," Dr. Teasdale said. "You are experiencing painful conflict with your dearest friend. You have just discovered that you are not on earth... How many seals have you received?"

"Two. Baptism and Chrism."

"Right. So you have also learned that the Creator is an evil monster and that you have a spark of true divinity inside you that longs to escape the powers and principalities that govern the prison of this universe. You are now part of a hunted band of subversives and freedom fighters who must hide their true motives lest the authorities intervene and disappear you...or worse. Tell me again why you might be a little bit stressed?"

Seth laughed at this. "Well, when you put it like that..."

"I think what you are experiencing is perfectly normal. *Anyone* would be stressed. You are trying to assimilate a lot of very disorienting information, and at the same time you have a good deal of interpersonal upset. It's a *lot*, Seth."

He nodded. Somehow, hearing that felt oddly affirming. He realized just how badly he needed the reality check. But then another thought occurred to him. "So...what if the new god—the True God, I mean, in the Pleroma—what if he's just as bad as Samuel?"

Dr. Teasdale's face softened into a look of sincere compassion. "Oh, Seth. You've been stung, so it's hard for you to trust. I think that's normal, too. This is just something you'll...you'll have to take a leap of faith."

"That's the hardest thing of all," Seth mumbled.

"I believe it," Dr. Teasdale said. "And because of that you will live with a higher level of ambient stress until you *are* able to trust. There's no avoiding it. You just will."

He nodded again.

"And things will settle down in your personal life. Trust me. The sting of the breakup will fade, and Angie will adjust to this new...dynamic in your relationship."

"Do you think so?" Seth asked.

"I know so." Dr. Teasdale gave him a reassuring smile.

"But you've never met her. She's...fierce."

Dr. Teasdale laughed. "Good! You need a little ferocity in your life." Her smile faded and she became more serious. "We do need to get a handle on your OCD, though. You can't give into it."

"That's hard," Seth said.

"I know it is. But you have to do this. I understand that you have to check the stove...that's prudent. But you only get one shot at it. Check it, and check it good, and then let it go." She pointed her finger at Seth. "You may not check it twice. Say it back to me."

"I may not check it twice."

"Good man. Same with the candles. Same with the lock. And the same with...well, anything else your OCD decides to fixate on. Got it?"

"I don't know if I can."

"You can. You have to. You can do this, Seth."

"Why do you think so?"

"Because you're already suffering. And you don't want to suffer more, do you?"

"No."

"Also, remember your heritage now, as a gnostic. 'For freedom have you been set free.'* OCD is just another kind of bondage. You can't let it win."

Keira stared at her coffee cup. "The little fucker was right," she said out loud, remembering Eric Sanders, the man who insisted the world is a façade. *What did he call it? The behind,* she thought. *Well, fuck if there isn't a 'behind' after all.* She picked up her coffee cup and looked at it as if she had never seen such a thing before. *This cup is in space. I'm in space. I have always been in space...*

A hand passed in front of her eyes. She did not immediately

---

* Galatians 5:1.

react. She did, however, blink and lean back a little. Then she looked up and saw Tony Raine hovering over her.

"Sloane, you okay?"

At this, Keira burst out laughing. And it was not a chuckle, it was not polite. It was a deep, unhinged belly laugh. When it subsided, Tony's eyes were wide with what looked like fear, and he was backing away from her. "Jesus, Sloane," he said.

"Oh my God," she said, still chuckling. "I am soooo not okay."

Raine continued to back up, until at about eight paces, he turned and almost sprinted away. Keira sighed and laid her head on her arms, which were resting on the top of her desk. She continued to stare at the cup. *The cup holds coffee the way the starship holds people,* she thought, *...and cars...and buildings and parks and historical landmarks.* Suddenly she sat up straight. "Wait," she said out loud, then completed the thought internally. *How can historical landmarks be historical? They have to be replicas.*

Yesterday she had felt like Schenck had pulled the rug out from under her and knocked her entire world on its ass. But the more she thought about it, the more upsetting it became. Even the thought of historical landmarks being fake completely fucked with her concept of reality. After someone punches you in the face, even a slight jab further can feel more consequential than it otherwise would. And she felt pummeled.

"Sloane!" Schenck's voice rang out over the squad room. She sighed again and lifted her head from her arms. She smiled at him sleepily and got up, wandering over to his office. He scowled at her as she wove her way uncertainly toward him. He held the door and moved out of her way, indicating a chair. She sat.

Still scowling, he made his way behind his desk and lowered himself into his chair. He did not take his eyes off her. "Special agent, are you drunk?"

She sat bolt upright and scowled back at him. "What? Don't be an idiot."

She saw Schenck bristle, and she added, "Sorry, boss. You're not an idiot. I'm just...maybe I'm the idiot. I feel stupid."

He cocked his head and leaned on the elbows on his desk. "How so?"

"I...all these years, I've been duped. What kind of investigator am I?"

"You can't blame yourself for that, special agent. The verisimilitude is very good."

"It is. But now..." She looked away, out his window. She stood and walked over to it, resting one hand on the glass. "It's like when someone points out a continuity flaw in a movie. You didn't notice it before, but you can't stop noticing it every time you watch it after that. You can't unsee it, you know?"

She looked back at him and saw that he was nodding. She turned back to the window. "I can't unsee what I saw."

"No."

"And now...none of it looks real."

"And that is freaking you out." It was not quite a question.

"Yeah. Oh, yeah."

"Special agent, I told you to take a few days off. Why are you here?" He paused for a moment, but before she could answer, he opened the drawer to his right. He rummaged around in it until he found what he was looking for. He extracted a white business card and held it out to her.

Keira frowned and moved toward him, accepting the card. "Dr. Sherry Teasdale," she read. "A shrink?"

"She's on retainer for DHS, and yes, she's got clearance. I want you to take a day at the spa, maybe get a mud bath up in Calistoga. Drink a little bit too much wine in Sonoma with your girlfriends."

Keira's eyes narrowed. "I'm about a diphthong away from assaulting a superior officer."

Schenck ignored the threat. "Then when you're relaxed as a wet noodle, go see Dr. Teasdale."

"Is that an order?" she asked, pocketing the card.

"It is."

"If you're directing my activity, how is it a day off?" she asked.

He narrowed one eye at her, but the edge of his mouth curled up, revealing a flake of humor. "You drive a hard bargain, special agent. All right, all right. It's on the clock. But you do all of it, do you hear me?"

Keira nodded. "Under protest."

"So noted. But your protest doesn't count for much. You're out there at your desk demonstrating the investigative powers of an eggplant. I need your head in the game. And if I need to shrink it to achieve my ends, that's just your rotten luck. Am I clear?"

"Clear as toast, sir."

He narrowed both eyes at her. "You freak me out sometimes, Sloane."

"I have that effect on people, sir. It's my superpower."

He made a brushing motion in her direction. "You're no good to us here today. Get lost. Go play, and play hard. Then see Dr. Teasdale again before you come in on Monday. At 10am Monday morning, I want to see you at your desk, clear-eyed, focused, and ready to work. Do you understand me?"

"I do."

"Do you have a boyfriend?"

Keira bit her lip. "No."

"Uh...a girlfriend?"

"No!"

"One of those non-binary jobbers?"

"Not that it's any of your business, but no. Why?"

"I just wanted to let you know that you could bring him... them...whatever...along. The spa and hotel are on the Department. Meals, too."

"Really?" Her eyebrows shot up.

"Really."

"Well, too bad I don't have a plus-one, then."

Schenck shrugged. "You might get lucky. Lots of lonely people in the northland."

"This conversation has taken an uncomfortable turn," Keira said.

"Fine. Get out of here," Schenck said, pointing toward the door.

---

*S*eth *looked down at Kush. The dog was wearing sunglasses and a purple t-shirt that said, "End Bi Invisibility." The gay pride parade was raging all around them. Seth looked around for Angie, but couldn't find her. He pulled on Kush's leash and started to scan the crowd for her. The street was crazy crowded, and Seth realized just how hard it was going to be to find her. "Angie!" he shouted, but his voice was drowned instantly by the cheers and laughter and thumping house music crowding the air.*

Kush pulled, pausing to sniff the butt of another dog. Seth pulled him away and kept searching. He hadn't noticed her walking away. She hadn't told him she was going anywhere. His face clouded as he became worried. A tingle of panic rose up within him.

Just then a fresh cheer assaulted the air. Seth whirled toward the street to see...her. The majorette's steps were high and exaggerated, but they were also enthusiastic—an energy that was infectious. A smile broke out on Seth's face as he recognized her. "You..." he said, and suddenly the air seemed to be charged with multicolored, refracted electricity.

Her silver hair bounced as she marched, her grin so wild and wide that it seemed to reflect the whole sky. Her shiny white boots flashed in the sun, always in motion. Her baton whirled above her head, and in her other hand was another baton. A third hand spun yet another baton, and the three batons interpenetrated and moved through the whirling circles of the others, a dancing astrolabe, wheels within wheels within wheels.

Within the blur of the whirling, Seth saw all the spheres of heaven, and he suspected that if he could look long enough, he would understand all the mysteries of the universe, the seen and the unseen. And he wanted to, desperately.

He dropped Kush's leash and walked toward her, all thought of Angie and his dog fading with the crowd noise. It was as if he and the majorette were the only two beings in the cosmos. He froze as she turned her face from the heavens...directly toward him. She winked.

He woke with a start, her beautiful, ancient, joyous face still powerfully present in his mind's eye. He looked to his left, at where Kush used to sleep, and saw only the dent in the mattress made by years of the dog's nesting and rest. He felt a familiar ache in his chest, but this time it wasn't only for the dog.

Angie stared at the aqua-colored front door. Then she took a deep breath and knocked on it. She heard the sound of footsteps within, and the door opened a crack. A single eye appeared, about level with Angie's own. "It's you," said the eye. "What do *you* want? Is Seth with you?"

"Hi, Mrs. St. John. No, Seth isn't with me. Can we...can we talk?"

"About what?"

"About Seth. There's...there's something you need to know."

The eye narrowed. "You're pregnant. You're living in sin with my son and now you're with child."

Angie closed her eyes and shook her head slowly, barely

keeping a grip on her temper. "I'm not sleeping with your son, and I'm not pregnant."

"Then what is it?"

"Can I just come in, please?"

The eye looked her up and down. It was clearly not happy. But the space between the door and the frame widened until the whole of the little woman was visible. "Come in, then. But no blaspheming. God will hold me responsible for what happens under my roof."

"Fine," Angie said, and went in.

She led her to the kitchen, and waved toward the table. Angie froze as she took in the room. On the food prep island ten or more rats were lying in a row. They were clearly dead, the black beads of their eyes sightless. There were wooden dowels emerging from their anuses. Angie stared, her face contorting with disgust. She moved toward the island for a closer look. The rats' little paws had been sewn to their chests, and then a tiny yellow sign had been sewn onto their paws, as if each rat was holding its sign up for all to see. On each one of the little signs was a verse of scripture: "Rejoice in the Lord always," said one, and then in smaller type, a scripture reference. Another said, "I can do all things through Christ." Another said, "Joy comes in the morning."

"What the hell?" Angie asked.

"What did I tell you about blaspheming?" Mrs. St. John snapped.

"I...sorry...just...what...uh...are you doing here?"

"There's a craft fair at church. The taxidermy school in Fremont practices on rats, and they're cheap by the dozen. I'll put them on little stands—you know, it's a 'pretty.' Cheers up the house."

Angie blinked.

Mrs. St. John picked one of the rats up by the stick and moved it up and down like a hesitant puppeteer. Its sign said, "My grace is sufficient for you."

"Hi, Miss Angie," Mrs. St. John squeaked in a cartoon voice. "Did you know there is joy in Jesus?"

Angie blinked, unable to move. Or speak.

Mrs. St. John put the rat back in its place. "The glue is still drying on their little behinds. Do you think I should glue googly eyes over their old ones?"

Angie shook her head.

Mrs. St. John harrumphed, then turned toward Angie. "Do you want some coffee?"

Angie found her tongue. "Uh...I can't stay. I just...I need to tell you about something."

Seth's mother waved her toward a chair. Angie inspected it before sitting, afraid to touch anything.

The older woman sat without hesitation and picked up a coffee cup already there. "All right. What did you want to talk to me about?"

"I'm..." She was about to say, *worried about your son*, but she had new worries about the mother. "I think Seth has...joined a cult."

Mrs. St. John almost dropped her coffee cup. She was able to set it down without too much spillage, however. "I'm sorry? What does that mean?"

"I'm saying that...when we were here last time...Seth lied to you. He isn't going to a Bible study. He's going to a...some kind of gnostic group. He joined it."

"What does that mean, gnostic?"

"Look...I don't really know. I just know it's religious, and it's not the kind of religion you...well, that you would approve of."

"Is it a Bible-believing church?"

A pained look crossed Angie's face. "I'm going to go out on a limb here and say no."

Mrs. St. John's face twisted into a persimmon of contempt. "I knew it. You have led him astray, you Jezebel."

Angie didn't know what a 'Jezebel' was, but it didn't sound nice. "Fuck you, granny. I told him *not* to join it."

"Language!"

Angie's hand flew to her mouth. "Okay. Sorry."

"How could this have happened?"

Angie shrugged. "He wanted a religion that didn't make him feel like sh—" Angie caught herself. "—like crap."

"We don't say that word in this house."

"Poop?"

"We do not say that word in this house either!"

"Excrement?"

"That is acceptable."

"Fine. But I think you just missed my point."

Mrs. St. John ignored her. She looked down at her hands, her head moving back and forth in a slow, steady 'no' motion. "Where did I go wrong?"

Angie knew the question was rhetorical, but she couldn't help herself. "Do you want a list?"

Mrs. St. John looked her in the eyes. It was not a kindly look. "Just what do you want? Why are you here? Other than to smear my son's name."

"I'm not smearing anyone," Angie protested. "I'm worried about Seth. And I thought you might be worried, too."

Mrs. St. John's face softened, and she looked away. "I still don't know what you're up to."

"I want us to work together to help him."

Mrs. St. John did not look convinced. "Be ye not unevenly yoked together," she quoted.*

Angie wondered if the older woman said everything in such

---

* 2 Corinthians 6:14, KJV.

cryptic terms. *No wonder Seth is so bug-fucked,* she thought. She cleared her throat. "I thought that maybe we could stage an intervention."

Mrs. St. John sat up straighter in her chair. "I'll talk to my pastor. He is an experienced deliverance minister."

"What is that?" Angie asked.

"He does exorcisms."

"No, no, no," Angie said, holding her hand up between herself and the older woman. "Let's not go off the deep end. Let's just get the people he loves most in a room with him at one time, and let's tell him how we...how we love him, and how we're concerned for him, and how we want to help him. How does that sound?"

It was Mrs. St. John's turn to blink. Her forehead bunched as she thought. "Where would you do it?"

"How about here? You could ask him to come over and...fix something, maybe?"

"You want me to lie to him. 'For what has light to do with darkness?'"

"It's not a lie if what you want fixed is...him."

That gave Mrs. St. John pause. She looked down at her hands again. "Who else would be coming?"

"I thought we could ask Becky—"

"Who is Becky?"

"Really? Seth hasn't told you about Becky?"

"No. Who. Is. Becky?"

"No need to get testy," Angie complained. "Becky is Seth's girlfriend....was Seth's girlfriend. I don't know if they're still together or not to be honest."

"Is he sleeping with her?"

Angie lied. "I don't know!"

"I thought he was sleeping with you!" Mrs. St. John almost shouted.

"Ew! No! Don't be gross," Angie said. "We're just friends."

"Friends who live together," Mrs. St. John spat.

"That doesn't mean we're sleeping together."

"You put a man and a woman under one roof and it's only a matter of time," the older woman insisted.

"That's ridiculous," Angie said. She held her hands up in a "time-out" gesture. "Let's...stop. Just...stop."

Mrs. St. John cocked her head. Angie continued. "Let's stay focused on what we're here for: helping Seth. Do you want to host the intervention or not?"

Mrs. St. John's eyes moved back and forth. Finally, she said, "I suppose...that would be okay."

Angie relaxed visibly. "Thank God."

"Thou shalt not take the Lord's name in vain, young lady!" Mrs. St. John scolded.

———

Seth stepped to the curb from the bus and started to walk toward the Lodge. He looked at his feet, and found his stride was time and again interrupted by the effort to not step on the cracks or dividers in the sidewalk. Thoughts battered at his brain about what would happen if he *did* step on a crack—disfigurements, illnesses, Angie's death...

He forced himself to look up, to admire the sky. *The unreal sky,* he reminded himself. The knowledge that all of nature was artificial robbed him of the ability to take solace in it. Instead of soothing him, it was just another reminder of his situation. And yet he was not devoid of hope. The memory of the majorette conjuring the spheres of the heavens flashed through his mind, and he felt strangely content.

He climbed the stairs of the Victorian and reached for the bell. But before he could ring it, the door swung inward. Nazz grinned at him, wearing a green corduroy vest. "You're early."

Seth adjusted his own vest. "Yeah. Well, with public transit—"

"Mr. Basil would like a word with you."

"Oh." Seth blinked. "Okay." He was proud of his work on the library, but now he wondered if perhaps Mr. Basil had found some fault with it.

"Go right in," Nazz asked, heading for the stairs and undoubtedly, his X-box.

"Thanks."

Nazz turned back to Seth at the first landing. "Hey, some night when you don't need to go straight home, come up and challenge me to a game of 'Call of Duty.' I have 'Vanguard' and 'Black Ops: Cold War,' so take your pick."

"Oh. That's great. Cool, yeah. Thanks."

Nazz waved at him and climbed the rest of the stairs back to what Seth imagined as his lair.

Seth looked at the hallway leading to Mr. Basil's office and took a deep breath. Then he squared his shoulders and began to walk, silently counting his steps as he went by fours. *One, two, three, four; one, two, three, four; one, two...* He stopped at the door to the office and knocked.

"Come in," came Mr. Basil's voice.

Seth pushed open the heavy mahogany door. Mr. Basil was seated behind his desk, reading. He looked up, and setting the book on his desk, rose to meet him. "Ah, Mr. St. John, so glad to see you. Please sit down."

They both sat, and Mr. Basil gave him a smile that was either compassionate or concerned. "Once again, I want to thank you for your wondrous efforts putting our library back in order. Truly above and beyond."

Seth discovered he had been holding his breath. "So...you didn't find anything wrong with it...or any books where they shouldn't be?"

"No, don't be silly," Mr. Basil waved away his question. "Some of your placements were novel choices, but once I thought through the logic of them, I discovered I quite agreed with you. So...bully for you!"

Seth breathed a great sigh of relief. Then there was a pause that became more uncomfortable as it went on. Finally, Mr. Basil leaned forward in his chair and placed his elbows on his knees, clasping his hands before him. "Mr. St. John, I just wanted to check in, as they say. There is a lot to...assimilate, and I want to know how *you* feel you are doing. How would you say your catechesis is going?"

Seth cleared his throat. "It's...uh...it's okay, I guess. It's...it *is* a lot to take in. I'm...I guess I'm rolling with it."

Mr. Basil nodded, not looking convinced. "Dr. Robinson tells me you are an eager and attentive student."

Seth felt a warm glow well up in him. "He does?"

"He does. And he is not someone who gives his praise liberally."

"Well, I'm surprised to hear that, but...I'm glad he thinks so."

"Do you agree? *Are* you an eager and attentive student?"

"I think so. Yes, sir."

He gave a half smile. He tapped his book with his fingers absently. "How are you...coping with the revelations of the seals?"

Seth opened his mouth to say, *Not well*, but he thought better of it. "I'm...adjusting."

"Really? Are you being entirely honest with me, Mr. St. John?"

Seth looked down. "I'm struggling. My OCD is...crazy right now."

"I am not surprised. You know, the seals are difficult for all of us. It takes a while to get your sea legs again."

"Sea legs?" Seth was confused.

"It's an idiom, perhaps out of fashion. Forgive me, I am old." He smiled. Then he sighed. "It means getting back to normal after a new variable is introduced. Some people have more trouble than others. We want to make sure you have the help you need to navigate your...new reality."

Seth scowled. "Has Dr. Teasdale been talking to you?"

He looked away. "Ah yes, Sherry. I'm so glad you have her to support you. But I want you to know that we have other resources at your disposal as well. If you need some time away, we have a retreat center near Mendocino where you can find some green, some quiet, some time to put your inner world back in order."

Seth thought that sounded marvelous. "How expensive—?"

"There is no cost. And we will provide your meals as well. And if you need bus fare, you need but ask."

"But...work—"

"We also have doctors among us who will provide you an excuse. Or medical assistance." Mr. Basil opened his drawer and pulled out a 3x5 card. Then he snatched a pen from the cup on his desk and began to write. "Here is a referral to a physician who is also an initiate. She'll be very happy to talk with you and help you with any health needs that Dr. Teasdale cannot attend to."

He handed the card across the desk to him. He took it. The writing was a scrawl, but readable. He put the card in the pocket of his vest.

Mr. Basil opened an old-fashioned day planner on his desk and glanced at something. Then he smiled. "Ah, you're to do the third seal tonight. Are you excited?"

"I...don't know. To be honest, I'm scared. If it's anything like the first two—"

"Don't be," he waved Seth's concern away with a swipe of his hand. "I think you'll find this one quite pleasurable. You'll meet *her* tonight."

"Her?" Seth asked.

"Her."

WHAT IS EUCHARIST?

The Eucharist, also known as Holy Communion or the Lord's Supper, is a central sacrament in Christianity, particularly within Catholic, Orthodox, and many Protestant traditions. Derived from the Greek word "eucharistia," meaning thanksgiving, the Eucharist is a ritualized act of commemoration and participation in the death and resurrection of Jesus Christ.

The origins of the Eucharist can be traced back to the Last Supper, an event described in the New Testament Gospels, where Jesus shared bread and wine with his disciples, instructing them to do the same in remembrance of him. The Eucharistic meal became a central element of early Christian worship, symbolizing the sacrificial death of Jesus and his ongoing presence among believers.

The theological understanding of the Eucharist varies among different Christian traditions. According to Catholic doctrine, the bread and wine used in the Eucharist undergo a transformation known as transubstantiation, where they become the actual body and blood of Christ while retaining the appearance of bread and wine. This view is based on the interpretation of Jesus' words at the Last Supper: "This is my body" and "This is my blood."

In contrast, many Protestant traditions hold to the doctrine of consubstantiation or sacramental union. They believe that Christ is mystically present in the elements of bread and wine, without necessarily endorsing a literal transformation.

During a Eucharistic service, the bread is consecrated and

distributed to the faithful, often accompanied by the recitation of prayers and hymns. The wine, or in some cases, grape juice, is likewise consecrated and shared. The act of consuming the consecrated elements is seen as a means of receiving spiritual nourishment and uniting with Christ and the community of believers.

The significance of the Eucharist extends beyond its commemorative aspect. It is understood as a means of grace, a tangible encounter with the presence of Christ that fosters spiritual growth and deepens the bond between the individual and the divine.

While practices and theological interpretations may vary, the Eucharist remains a fundamental and unifying ritual in Christianity, symbolizing the central message of Christ's sacrificial love and the ongoing communion between God and humanity.

CHAPTER ELEVEN

I am the real voice. I cry out in everyone,
and they recognize it, since a seed lives in them.
—*Three Forms of Thought**

A s Seth entered the ornate, paneled dining room, he was pleased to see his fellow classmates. All were vested, and they each gave him a smile as he entered, even Matt. Jude rose and gave him a bear hug. Maria gave him a hug as well, although it was brief and reserved in comparison. Still, he felt well welcomed, and sat at his place in the circle with an excitement that even 180 milligrams of anxiolytics could not quell.

---

* Trimorphic Protennoia: Nag Hammadi Codex XIII, 1, translated by John D. Turner, revised by Willis Barnestone, published in *The Gnostic Bible* (Boston, MA: Shambhala Publications, 2009).

Maria looked around the circle at each of them. "How are you doing...with it all?" she asked.

"You mean the revelations?" Matt asked.

"Yeah."

For several moments, no one said anything. Finally, though, Seth managed, "Rough." This elicited both knowing and compassionate looks from the others.

"How so?" Maria asked.

"Anxiety, mostly," Seth confessed.

Nods greeted this. Seth looked at his feet. His shoes were scuffed in places he didn't remember making contact with the ground.

"A month ago, I was just an animal on a planet," Jude said. "Now, the air is filled with these...dark spiritual powers. I feel like Chicken Little. The sky is...well, maybe not falling, but it's...heavy."

Matt nodded. "It's heavy. That's for sure."

Everyone looked at Matt, and he squirmed, apparently feeling that more was being asked of him. "Look, I don't know if I believe any of this stuff. In fact, I'm sure I don't. But the spaceship thing... I think I *do* believe that. And that's crazy. And if I believe that, then why is the whole...demiurge and Sophia opera that Dr. Robinson sang about any crazier? I mean, I think it *is* crazier, but that's what I'm thinking about, you know?"

Again, there were nods all around. "How about you, Maria?" Jude asked. "How are you coping?"

"Mr. Basil recommended I see a therapist—"

"Dr. Teasdale?" Seth blurted out, rocking forward on his chair.

Maria's eyes widened and she smiled. "Yes! How did you know?"

"Oh, uh..." Seth sat back in his chair again. "She's my therapist, too."

"It's so helpful to be able to talk to someone about all this stuff," she said. "I mean, other than you guys, who can I talk to? And I'm someone who processes out loud. Obviously." She pursed her lips and her eyes moved back and forth sheepishly.

"Yeah," Seth said. "It helps."

"Well, I don't see a shrink," Jude said, "but I think *this* is helpful. Why don't we get together, on not-Lodge nights? You know, to talk like this?"

Matt looked skeptical, but Maria brightened. "Brilliant!" she said.

"It'll be hard to find a time," Matt said.

"Sundays at three," Maria said.

Matt blinked. "That would be...fine, I guess."

"Yeah," Seth said.

"I'm in," Jude said.

"See?" Maria asked. "That wasn't so hard. Where?"

"We could meet at The Universal Bean," Seth suggested.

Maria looked momentarily pained. "It's a pretty public place to be talking about this kind of stuff."

"True," Seth conceded.

"My place," Jude said. "You can all come to my place. It'll give me an excuse to clean it up."

"That does not sound promising," Matt opined.

"No, it'll be fine. And I'm a block away from the light rail," Jude said. "I'll give you my number, you can all text me—with your names, please—and I'll put together a text group and send you the address."

Everyone pulled out their phones as Jude rattled off his number. Just as Seth pocketed his phone again, the door swung open, and Dr. Robinson entered. He was dressed all in black, for some reason—a black shirt, black pinstriped trousers, and a matching vest. He gave them a perfunctory smile and quickly moved to take a seat in the small circle. "Good evening, initiates."

There was a small rumble of mumbled responses, but Dr.

Robinson did not seem to notice. "Tonight, we embark upon the third seal—"

"Please, no more," Maria moaned. "I'm still reeling from the first two."

Dr. Robinson smiled. "Don't worry. This one is not so difficult."

"That's what Mr. Basil said," Seth interjected.

"Oh. Talked to Mr. Basil, did you?" Dr. Robinson narrowed his eyes at Seth. He did not look happy about it. Seth wondered just how fraught the internal politics of the Lodge actually were. Before Seth could think of how to answer, Robinson continued. "Tonight, I introduce you to some...let us say, aspects of worship in our esteemed Lodge." He paused to let that sink in.

"Who are we worshipping?" Matt asked, with clear suspicion in his voice.

"The True God, of course, Mr. Townes. We worship the Fullness, and the aeons who minister to him...and us."

"Sophia?" asked Maria.

Dr. Robinson broke out into a sincere smile. "Oh, yes."

"Goody," Maria said.

"First, I will teach you a creed. Then I will teach you to pray. Then you will employ both of these as you receive the third seal."

He paused again, and Seth saw tentative nods all around.

"Excellent," Dr. Robinson said. "So, first the creed. If they say to you, 'Where do you come from?' what will you say?"

No one answered. Finally, Matt said, "San Jose?"

Dr. Robinson looked amused. "You will say, 'We come from the light.' Try it with me. Where do you come from?"

"We come from the light," the students responded, more or less in unison.

"Good! Now, when they ask you, 'Who are you?' what will you say?"

"I'm guessing 'Seth St. John' is not the right answer?" Seth ventured.

"Indeed not. You will say, 'We are its children, chosen by the True God.' Let's give it a try. Who are you?"

"We are its children, chosen by the True God," the students intoned.

"Well done. There is one more. When they say to you, 'What is the sign of the Fullness in you?' what will you say?"

No one spoke, nor ventured a guess or even a joke. Finally, Dr. Robinson supplied the answer. "You will say, 'It is motion and rest.'* Now you try. What is the sign of the Fullness in you?"

"Motion and rest," they all responded.

"Very good," Dr. Robinson replied. "Now let's try the whole thing." He put all three questions to them again, and they responded with the proper answers. Afterwards, he said, "This is the where, the who, and the what of the gnostic faith. Everything that we are about is summed up in this creed."

"Yes, but what does it even mean?" Matt's question sounded like more of a protest.

"As you go deeper into the mysteries, its significance will crack open like an egg, and its meaning will flourish like a blossoming tree, sowing its good fruit in your souls."

"That is a hopelessly mixed metaphor that tells me absolutely nothing," Matt complained.

"Give it time," Dr. Robinson smiled patiently.

"And now will you teach us to pray?" Maria asked. She seemed genuinely eager.

"Indeed—"

"Oh, good," Maria said, almost giddy. "Because I've never really gotten the whole prayer thing."

"Consider yourself lucky, then," Dr. Robinson said, "for it

---

* "The Gospel of Thomas," logion 50.

means that you have not communed with evil. For what has light to do with darkness?"*

A solemnity fell upon them. Even Matt seemed subdued. Dr. Robinson cleared his throat. "I invite you all to close your eyes. I am going to ask you to vividly imagine something, a person—"

"Sophia?" Maria asked.

Dr. Robinson ignored her. "Just...close your eyes, please. Now imagine you are floating in space—"

"Outer space?" Matt asked.

"Yes," Dr. Robinson replied.

"How will we breathe? What will keep our blood from boiling?" Matt asked.

"I am not asking you to go outside the *Cibus Dei*, I'm just asking you to imagine it."

"But not imagine my lungs exploding?" Matt asked.

"That...doesn't happen, but yes, just imagine that you can float in space unaided, and that you are." Seth suspected Dr. Robinson was struggling to control his temper. "Are you all floating in space now?"

Seth nodded slowly.

"Excellent. Now imagine a being floating toward you. She's far away at first, but she is coming near to you. She is translucent, yet she is shimmering with light. Her hair is the color of starlight, and her dress trails after her like a comet. Can you see her?"

Amazingly, Seth did. Very clearly. He gave another slow nod.

"Good. This is Sophia. She is the mother of the soul. Soon, she will be your mother as well. Now speak to her—it doesn't matter that sound doesn't travel in a vacuum," Dr. Robinson said quickly, obviously anticipating another of Matt's objections. "She will hear you. Say to her, 'Holy Sophia, please give to me a measure of your light.'"

---

* 2 Corinthians 6:14

Seth did as instructed. He could sense her presence, but could not see her. He could see the stars behind her. And he could see that she was there. And her hair was...yes, the color of starlight. But her face was a blur. Then, to his great surprise, he heard her speak. "I can and I shall," she said. He did not hear her voice with his ears, but in his head. Her voice was sweet, and it was kind. Seth felt as though this being might feel affection for him, might even *love* him. He wasn't sure what to do with that.

But then he remembered that he was only imagining this. But it was very vivid, perhaps too vivid. "Are you real?" he asked the being.

"I am as real as you are," she replied. "Which is to say, completely and not at all."

"What does that mean?" Seth asked.

"It means that everything is contained in the All. All things come forth from the All. All things return to the All. Fullness is their true nature, and their separateness is a delusion which brings suffering."

Seth had his answer, but was no closer to understanding anything. As if it were very far away, he heard Dr. Robinson's voice again. "Now thank her for granting you an audience, and return to our circle."

"Thank you," Seth said, not wanting to leave her presence. He sensed her warmth, and then the blur that was her seemed to swim away. Seth opened his eyes and found himself once more seated in the circle.

To his surprise, Dr. Robinson sat completely still, saying nothing. No one else moved either, or spoke. Seth shifted in his chair and cast his eyes down. His mind was racing, flashing images of the Holy Lady he had just beheld. *That was prayer?* the voice in his head asked. It was like no prayer he had ever experienced. If he had, he would never have doubted his faith. *Perhaps everything Dr. Robinson has been saying is true,* he thought. *The religion I was raised with is a sham...* But he knew that already. *...and maybe this is the real thing.* A chill ran through him, and in spite of himself, he shuddered.

Then Dr. Robinson moved. He reached under his chair and pulled out a rough chalice made of pottery. Then he brought forth a small plate. Leaning over once more, he lifted a small cloth bag. Undoing its drawstring, he drew forth from it a small loaf of bread —not much bigger than a dinner roll—and placed it on the plate. Then he lifted a very small bottle of wine, the kind you get on airplanes, Seth recognized. Dr. Robinson twisted the top off the bottle and poured its contents into the chalice. He replaced the bag under his chair, sat up straight and took a deep breath.

"This is the third seal," he said. "Eucharist. It is the lesser seal of union, the gate into the garden, which points to the greater seal of union."

Seth had no idea what this meant, but he didn't object. To his great surprise, no one else did either, although he saw Matt glowering, his arms folded over his chest.

Dr. Robinson raised his arms up, holding his hands level with his ears, his palms facing outward toward them. Seth had once seen a Catholic priest on television hold his hands in the same position. Then, in a loud, sonorous voice, Dr. Robinson began to speak again.

"What praise and what offering or what thanksgiving shall we name as we break this bread, but you, alone, Jesus?" he intoned. "We praise your name of Father which was spoken by you. We praise your name of Son which was spoken by you. We praise your entering the door of our world. We praise your resurrection shown to us through you. We praise your way. We praise your seed, the word, the grace, the faith, the salt, the inexpressible pearl, the treasure, the plough, the net, the greatness, the diadem, the one who for our sake was called Son of Man, the truth, given to us, the rest, the knowledge, the power, the commandment, the freedom of speech, the hope, the love, the liberty, the refuge in you."*

Seth felt barraged by the flood of symbols, coming too fast for him to take in or sort out. He willed himself to relax and simply let the imagery wash over him. He closed his eyes and felt a peace pass through him.

"For you alone, Lord, are the root of immortality and the fount of incorruption and the seat of the aeons," Robinson continued, "you who have been called all these things on our account, so that we, when we name you through them, may know your greatness, which at present is invisible to us, but can be seen only by the pure as it is portrayed only in your humanity."†

Dr. Robinson leaned over and picked up the bread, holding it before him. "In the earliest days of this dark world, our Mother Sophia placed within the first man and woman a spark of true divinity. Holy Mother, we ask you to place that same spark in this holy meal tonight, so that those of us who eat of it may receive the Fullness, even in exile." He placed the bread back on the plate. He then made the sign of the cross over the bread and cup. "Come, gift of the Most High! Come, perfect compassion! Come, fellowship with the male! Come, holy power. Come, knower of the mysteries of the chosen! Come, you who contend for our nobility! Come, treasure of glory! Come, darling of the mercy of the Most High! Come, Silence, you who reveal the mighty deeds of the whole greatness! Come, you who unveil the hidden things and make the secret manifest! Come, hidden Mother! Come, you who are manifest through your deeds and give joy and rest to all who are joined with you! Come and partake with us in this eucharist

---

* "Acts of John" 109, quoted in *Suppressed Prayers* (Harrisburg, PA: Trinity Press International, 1998), pp. 107-108.
† *Ibid.*

which we celebrate in your name, and in the love feast at which we are gathered together at your invitation."*

Dr. Robinson paused, bringing his hands together in an attitude of prayer. Then, much more solemnly and quietly, he said, "And for the gall which you drank for our sakes, O Christ, may the gall of the demiurge around us be taken away. And for the vinegar which you drank for us, may our weakness be strengthened. And for the spitting which you received for our sake, let us receive the dew of your goodness. And because of the reed with which they struck you for our sake, let us receive the perfect house. Because you received the crown of thorns for our sake, let us who have loved you be girded with a crown that does not fade away. And for the linen cloth in which you were wrapped, let us be girded with your unconquerable power."†

Dr. Robinson's voice cracked. Seth looked up and saw that his eyes were brimming. "And for the new tomb and burial, let us receive renewal of soul and body. And because you rose and came to life again, let us come to life again and stand before you in righteous judgment."‡

Dr. Robinson took a deep breath, and wiped at his eyes with his sleeve. Then he picked up the chalice and plate and held them out to those assembled. He turned, looking them all in the eyes one by one and saying, "May the grace which was before all things, inconceivable, ineffable, fill your inner self and multiply in you her wisdom, by sowing the grain of mustard seed in the good earth."§

---

* "Acts of Thomas" 106, quoted in *Suppressed Payers* (Harrisburg, PA: Trinity Press International, 1998), p. 106.

† "Acts of Thomas" 158, quoted in *Suppressed Payers* (Harrisburg, PA: Trinity Press International, 1998), p. 107.

‡ *Ibid.*

§ Irenaeus, *Against Heresies*, Book I, 13:2, quoted in *Suppressed Prayers* (Harrisburg, PA: Trinity Press International, 1998), p. 105.

"And now, initiates, starting with Maria and proceeding clockwise, come to the table and partake of this holy meal. Like this." He broke off a small piece of the bread, and dipped it in the chalice. Then he held it, dripping, up to heaven. Closing his eyes, he waited, although Seth could not tell for what. Then he lowered the bread into his mouth, chewed, and swallowed. He held his arm out to Maria, and motioned toward the table.

She stepped forward and did as he had done, even holding the bread up before eating it. And so did they all. When it was Seth's turn, he stepped up to the table and took up the bread. It was rougher bread than he was used to and hard to break. He did it, though, and, careful not to wet his fingers in the wine, dipped one end of the little piece he held. Dutifully, he held it up, and as he did so, he felt a presence wash over him. He almost staggered, but caught himself. He felt suddenly cold. Then an audible voice whispered in his left ear. *Her* voice. "This is the Fullness, given to you. The One is in you, and you are in the One." Seth's eyes snapped open, and he wavered. He saw the bread above him, one end stained purple, and it came back to him where he was and what he was doing. He lowered the bread into his mouth, chewed, and brought the Fullness into his belly for keeps.

K eira crossed her legs. Then she uncrossed them. Then she twisted sideways in her chair. Then she sighed.

When the door to the waiting room opened, she leaped to her feet. The psychiatrist's eyebrows shot up at the sight. "Well, aren't we eager?" she laughed. She offered her hand. "I'm Dr. Teasdale. You can call me Sherry."

"Uh...Keira Sloane," Keira said.

"California Homeland Security, right?" Dr. Teasdale asked.

"Yes. State Protective Service."

"Always good to know who's signing the checks," Teasdale said.

Keira gave a nervous laugh. "So...how do we do this?"

"Never been in therapy before?" Teasdale asked.

"No," Keira said.

"Not to worry. It's almost painless. Come on in." Dr. Teasdale opened the door to her office and motioned Keira to follow.

Keira took a deep breath and crossed the threshold.

"Would you close the door, please?" Dr. Teasdale asked.

"Sure." Keira pushed it closed until she heard a click.

"Please have a seat. Anywhere you like," Dr. Teasdale said.

The room was small but uncluttered. There were a few tasteful pieces of art on the walls—watercolors of a Paris skyline. Keira saw a couch and two matching chairs that looked both comfortable and stylish. "Where do you usually sit?" she asked.

"I usually sit there," Dr. Teasdale pointed at the chair nearest the window.

Keira warily lowered herself into the other chair. She clasped her hands, then unclasped them, then clasped them. "Sorry," she said, and put her hands underneath her thighs.

"No need to apologize," Dr. Teasdale said, taking her seat. She opened her notepad and wrote a few quick lines. Then she looked up at Keira and offered her what seemed like a genuine smile. "Please relax. This is a safe space to say absolutely anything. Nothing you say here will ever be repeated outside this room. And I'm not here to judge you or categorize you or pathologize you. I'm here to help, mostly by listening and asking questions. How does that sound?"

"Aren't you a mandated reporter?" Keira asked.

"Sure, but I doubt you're going to confess to child or elder abuse, are you?"

"My mom makes me crazy," Keira said.

"Ever hit her with a lamp...recently, that is?" Dr. Teasdale asked.

"No."

"So we're good then, yeah?" Dr. Teasdale almost laughed.

Keira found herself chuckling...and her stomach muscles relaxing a bit.

"So my work is a little different," Dr. Teasdale said. "Most therapists can't prescribe medicine and most psychiatrists don't do talk therapy, but I do both. By training I am a psychiatrist, so I'm a medical doctor who specializes in the treatment of mental illness. But I also do psychological counseling, like a psychotherapist. I find the combination of talk-therapy and medication to be the most effective method, as I can really get to know and monitor my clients."

"Uh-huh." Keira said. "Mental illness, huh?"

"Don't let that scare you," Dr. Teasdale said, her voice tinged with compassion. "Everyone struggles psychologically. Life is stressful. Have you ever felt anxious? Or depressed?"

"Sure," Keira admitted.

"Then you're human...and normal...and you're in the right place. People don't always come to me because they're sick. Sometimes they come as a prophylactic."

"What do you mean?" Keira's face bunched up in confusion.

"I mean they use our time to process the...well, the bumps in the road so they can stay in balance."

"In their lives, you mean?" Keira asked.

"Exactly."

"So I'm not crazy?" Keira asked.

"Do *you* think you're crazy?" Dr. Teasdale asked.

"Well, if you'd've asked me that two weeks ago, I'd have said no. But now..."

"Well, let's talk about what's happened since then. Your

referral said you've just been bumped up to a level 6b security clearance," Dr. Teasdale said, not quite a question.

"Yes."

Dr. Teasdale cocked her head. "So you've...seen."

Keira looked away and nodded.

"Tell me about what you saw," the doctor said.

"My boss—"

"Do you mean your referring officer, Captain Schenck?" Dr. Teasdale asked, making some notes.

"Yeah. He took me up an elevator—which is crazy because we were already on the top floor—but it just kept going up...and I don't know how that's possible. And then when we got off, we...it was kind of like a factory floor and kind of like a laboratory. And then I saw stars."

Dr. Teasdale kept writing. "Stars," she repeated.

"Yeah. A lot. Of stars. Not...familiar stars."

"No." Dr. Teasdale kept writing. After a few minutes she stopped and looked up, catching Keira's eye. "And then?"

"And then the Captain told me we weren't actually on Earth, but on a big starship of some kind...out in space. And then he took me back to our office and told me to come see you."

"And when was that?"

"A couple of days ago."

"And...how are you doing?" Dr. Teasdale asked.

Keira's eyes darted back and forth. "I don't know. I mean...is he fucking with me? Or is this a test of some kind? I mean, I'm here seeing a psychiatrist, right? So if I agree—'Oh yeah, sure, we're on a starship'—do I fail the test and they cut me loose because...crazy?" Keira was gesturing wildly with her hands. "Or if I don't agree—'No, Captain Schenck, I think you're full of shit'—do I fail the test for questioning my superior officer? I'm afraid to move one way or the other, because I don't know what's going on!"

Dr. Teasdale nodded. "I totally get how that's stressful."

"Do you?"

"I do."

Keira shook her head and crossed her arms. "I don't know which way is up."

"What do you think about the starship idea?" Dr. Teasdale asked.

"I think it's fucking lunacy!" Keira barked. Then her hand went to her mouth. "I'm sorry...I should control my emotions."

"Not here," Dr. Teasdale said. "Here you can be as expressive as you like. Just don't shoot the therapist."

"No...of course."

"What if we really *were* in space?" Dr. Teasdale asked.

"Do *you* think we're in space?" Keira asked.

"What I think isn't important," Dr. Teasdale answered.

"But I want to know," Keira said. "Because I...I don't feel like I have any moorings."

Dr. Teasdale looked down at her pad and sighed. "I...found it hard to believe, too. But then I saw it for myself, and...and I really struggled with it. It took a while, but I...adjusted. And then I devoted my life to helping other people...adjust."

"So...all the people you see are...people who...have *seen*?"

"Not all, but...many. My government contract constitutes a significant part of my practice," Dr. Teasdale said.

"So, you help people...like me...who find out about the...spaceship thing...adjust?"

"Yes," Dr. Teasdale said. "It's why we're here right now. This is what I do." She waved her hand around the room as if showing it off.

"So...other agents.?"

"Sure...and scientists and engineers and software programmers and operations managers and...anyone else who works...*behind*."

Keira sat up straighter in her chair. "That's what Captain Schenck said...I mean, that was the word he used. I didn't get it then. Behind. Behind what?"

"Behind the illusion that most people live under...that we're on earth, that we're not hurtling through space in a starship."

"As in 'behind the curtain'?" Keira asked.

"Sure, if you like."

"You're serious about this?" Keira shook her head incredulously.

"I am."

"And you're not bullshitting me?"

"No."

"And if I say, 'Sure, we're on a spaceship right now,' I'm not going to get fired?" Keira asked.

"Well, you might get fired for something else, but not for believing that we're on a starship, no."

"Because that's not crazy," Keira almost wailed.

"No, it isn't crazy. It's the truth," Dr. Teasdale said.

"And just when did this starship launch?" Keira asked.

"In 2035," Dr. Teasdale answered.

"That was fifty years ago," Keira asked.

"Yes, and we're still living exactly like we were in 2040. Don't you think that's strange?" Dr. Teasdale asked. "I mean...science had been moving along at a pretty good clip, and then suddenly... it didn't. Why would that be?"

"Why would science stop at 2040 if the ship launched in 2035? That doesn't make any sense," Keira asked.

"Sure it does," Dr. Teasdale said patiently. "Because by 2040 we were out of range. So scientific advances were reserved for whatever we could come up with on our own."

Silence descended on the room like a thick wool blanket. Keira found it hard to breathe. She gasped for air.

"Put your head between your knees," Dr. Teasdale told her, in a kind but commanding tone. Keira leaned over and felt the blood rush to her head. Her breathing slowed. After a few seconds, she slowly sat upright again.

"Okay..." Keira said, wiping sudden water from her eyes. "Uh... okay. So...we're in space...we're on a starship. Why?"

Dr. Teasdale gave her a sad smile. "The answer to that, Special Agent, is a level of security clearance you don't yet have."

———

Seth approached the park with hesitant steps. As soon as he saw Travis' wild hair, he pulled the hoodie up over his face and turned toward the nearest large tree. Reaching it, he leaned against its far side. He took a deep breath, and peered around it until he could clearly see Travis again.

And not just Travis. Kush.

Travis threw a frisbee and Kush took off after it. The dog snatched it up and then raced back toward Travis, but instead of bringing it to him, he halted about nine feet from him and crouched, his head low and his butt high in the air, tail wagging madly, daring Travis to come after it.

Seth felt an ache in his chest begin to stir. He rubbed at the spot, but smiled despite the painful, conflicted feelings coursing through him. Kush had played that same game with him so many times.

On the one hand, Seth was relieved to see the dog looking so happy. Travis looked happy, too—not put-upon, not resentful, but genuinely enjoying caring for his dog. Seth felt grateful that the arrangement seemed to be working out.

At the same time, he missed Kush terribly. There was a huge empty space in the bed every morning when he woke, and an awareness of that absence persisted throughout the day. He hated himself for banishing the being he loved more than any other living creature.

Is this how the Monster God feels, sending people to hell? he wondered. He shook off the thought. Kush was not in hell, he reminded himself, not even close. The dog was happy. Seth was sure Kush missed him—yet he was not in pain, he wanted for nothing. Here he was, laying down in green pastures...

Seth sighed and bit his lip. He swallowed back on the emotion swelling in his throat. Then he felt a peaceful presence descend on him. It calmed his nerves, and the ache in his chest released its clutch. He wondered if it was the sertraline asserting itself, but he knew it was not. It was her...Sophia. Wisdom. Here she was, surrounding him, filling him, supporting him, comforting him. He breathed a brief prayer of thanks to her. Then she was gone.

During her visitation, he had tipped forward until his forehead rested against the tree. He put both hands on the rough bark and pushed himself away, until he was fully upright again. He put his hands on his heart and took a deep, calming, healing breath.

Will she always be there now? he wondered. He hoped so, with a desire so intense it felt desperate.

He peered around the tree again and watched his friend and his dog play. He still felt sad, but it was not debilitating—instead, it was a rich sadness, full of pathos and beauty. Under his breath, he blessed his friend and his dog. Then he headed toward home.

"They have received the third seal," Robinson reported.

The fire crackled in the fireplace. Although the days were still hot, the evenings were becoming unseasonably chilly.

"Did anyone see her?" Mr. Basil asked. "I mean, *really* see her?"

"I didn't ask," Dr. Robinson admitted. Mr. Basil grunted his displeasure. Robinson defended himself. "It won't do to foster any kind of spiritual one-upmanship among the initiates."

Dr. Teasdale laughed. "I love the irony, since we're always being accused of being spiritual elitists by the orthodox."

Mr. Basil was not amused. "I'm particularly interested in knowing if Mr. St. John experienced a vision of her."

"I'll find out," Dr. Teasdale promised. "If he did, he'll no doubt bring it up in session."

"I don't think we can wait that long," Mr. Basil said. "We need him for reconnaissance." He pronounced it the British way, with the emphasis on the third syllable rather than the second. "We draw near, and despite our best efforts, we still don't have a complete map."

"We have the Altrigger drawings—" Robinson began, but Basil cut him off.

"Which have been shown to be inaccurate, putting the lives of pneumatics at risk. Eckhart died because of Altrigger's mad scribblings."

"Eckhart couldn't find his way out of a bathroom with an accurate map," Robinson shot back.

"Let us not speak ill of the dead," Dr. Teasdale interceded. Both men were becoming heated, and someone needed to speak sense. She secretly enjoyed the role. "What's done is done. The important thing is that we learn from our mistakes and not repeat them."

Mr. Basil shifted in his seat and grumbled. He turned his head toward Teasdale. "And what do you think? Is he ready?"

"I think he's...fragile," she answered. "He's under a lot of stress, and the medication has still not fully kicked in. Plus, we'll need to make adjustments once it does."

"Why should we hang our hopes on someone who is mentally ill?" Robinson asked.

"People who live in glass houses, Joshua!" Teasdale almost

burst out laughing at the absurdity of his question. "How long have you struggled with depression? And yet here you are, on the triumvirate."

"Yes, but I'm not going into a combat situation," Robinson groused. "I catechize. It's *safe*."

"None of us are safe," Mr. Basil said, with a finality that broached no disagreement. He turned back to Teasdale. "So you're against it, too?"

"No." She cocked her head thoughtfully. "No, I'm not. I just...I wish we had more time for him to stabilize, and to...well, to solidify his identity as a gnostic. He's still very green."

"Do you think he would be willing?" Mr. Basil asked.

"He thinks the world of you, Terrance," Dr. Teasdale said. "He'd jump off a cliff if you asked him to."

"That is no comfort," Basil said. "It's too very like what we would be asking him to do. Do you think he is able?"

"I suppose it depends on what ability you're asking about," Dr. Teasdale responded. "If you mean, 'Is he able to do the reconnaissance?', I'd say yes. We've all seen what he was able to do with the library. But if you mean, 'Is he able to remain calm in stressful situations, think on his feet, demonstrate the needed prudence to avoid detection or recognition—'"

"Yes, yes, yes," Mr. Basil waved the rest of her sentence away. "Let's take them one at a time. We all agree he has the native talent for the work?"

"Yes," Teasdale responded.

"I suppose," Robinson conceded.

"What about remaining calm under fire?" Mr. Basil asked.

"He's a train wreck," Robinson said.

"Why in the world would you think that, Joshua?" Dr. Teasdale asked. "Has he said or done something in your class that leads you to think so? Or is this just your prejudice? And if so, where is that coming from?"

Robinson did not answer right away. He glared at her. Mr. Basil prompted, "Yes, Joshua. You seem to have it in for Mr. St. John. I'd like to know why."

"It's a feeling," he said. "I trust my gut."

"It's certainly your dominating feature," Dr. Teasdale grinned.

Robinson scowled at her. "Lowering yourself to personal insults, Sherrie? That's not like you."

"Oh, lighten up, Joshua. I've earned the right to tease you now and then."

He grunted, slid down into his chair, and steepled his fingers.

"What of prudence?" Mr. Basil asked.

"His ruling emotion is fear," Dr. Teasdale said. "A legacy of his orthodox upbringing. He's been sorely wounded by the demiurge—"

"Who hasn't?" Robinson interjected.

"—so he's developed coping strategies in order to stay safe. I would say he is hypervigilant. It's one of the things we're working on."

"Don't we want him to be hypervigilant?" Mr. Basil asked.

"I have two roles here, Terrance, and they are not always in harmony," Dr. Teasdale responded patiently. "I'm here to assess his readiness to enter into her service, of course. But I'm also a mental health professional who wants to reduce the amount of suffering in his life. But I can assure you that, under pressure, he'll revert to his default mode. He's not going to lose his vigilance just because I'm treating him."

Robinson did not look so sure, but Mr. Basil nodded. "Plus, there's her. She has faith in him."

"So do I," Dr. Teasdale said. "He's a good kid."

"Joshua? What say you?" Mr. Basil pierced Robinson with his eyes.

"I say no," Robinson said. "He's still too much of an unknown factor. If he's captured, he'll give away the game."

Mr. Basil leaned forward, placing his elbows on his knees. He sniffed. "Well, I always prefer it when we can make decisions by consensus. But it looks like we will have to admit failure and default to democracy. It's two against one, Joshua." He turned again to Dr. Teasdale. "Sherrie, let's get him ready."

As they approached the house, Angie saw Becky shiver and hunker down into her coat. "What's wrong with you?" Angie asked. "It isn't even cold."

"I get cold when I get nervous," Becky said.

"A little weed would take care of that," Angie said.

"The cold or the nervousness?"

"Yes. Weed is the answer to everything. I've got a joint. You want to hit it before we go in?" Angie asked, holding the joint up.

"Uh...I'll pass, but thanks."

"Suit yourself." Angie put the joint back in the breast pocket of her shirt.

"So this is where Seth grew up?"

"Yeah, from about seven on." Angie looked at Becky sideways. "Are you telling me you haven't been here before?"

"No," said Becky.

"So you haven't met his mother?"

"No," said Becky.

"Oh, boy. Well...gird your loins."

"What does that mean?" asked Becky.

"You'll see soon enough. And...O my God, he didn't introduce you to his mother?" Angie shook her head. "You were so right to dump him."

Becky stopped. It took Angie a couple of steps to notice. When she turned around, she saw that Becky's shoulders were shaking.

Angie went to her and put a hand on her shoulder. "Are you...okay?"

Becky shook her head and wiped her eyes. "I'm sorry."

"No. I just...what did I say? Was it about dumping Seth?"

Becky nodded. "I...oh, God. I love him."

Angie pulled her into a hug. "So do I. That's why we're here."

After a long timeless moment, Angie let go and held Becky at arm's length. "That doesn't mean he isn't a little shit sometimes. Often."

Becky uttered something in between a laugh and a sob. "I know." She pulled a travel packet of tissues from her coat and blew her nose. Angie gave her some space.

Once Becky had put the tissues away, Angie asked, "Are you going to be okay?"

"I think so."

"Come on, then. We need to orient before Seth gets here."

Becky nodded, opened her mouth and eyes wide and took a deep breath. Then she fanned her face with her hand. "Let's do this."

Angie took her hand, gave it a gentle squeeze, and led her to the aqua door of Seth's mother's house. Letting go of Becky's hand, she knocked. She heard footsteps inside and the clacking of the deadbolt sliding open. Then the door opened quickly inward.

Mrs. St. John was standing there dressed in a shapeless muumuu, her hair in curlers.

"Hi, Mrs. St. John," Angie said. "This is Seth's...ex-girlfriend, Becky."

Mrs. St. John looked confused. "I don't like you," she said to Angie. "Why are you here? And why is there a hippie in my living room?"

Angie looked past Mrs. St. John and saw Travis looking like a treed squirrel. He waved nervously. She waved back. "We're staging an intervention for Seth." Mrs. St. John still looked confused. "Your son, Seth," Angie reminded her, an edge creeping into her voice. "He's going to be here any minute."

"Why? Why is Seth coming here?"

"Because you told him you had a lamp that needed fixing, or some such thing. But really, we're going to confront him about the cult he joined."

Angie saw Mrs. St. John's eyes flare, and like a slot machine landing on all three picture wheels, saw the recognition click in. "Oh. Yes. Seth's father will be..." She looked behind herself. "Come in, come in, don't just stand there. You'll let the flies in."

Becky gave Angie an uncertain look, but Angie stepped inside with a confident step, almost pushing past the older woman. Angie strode into the living room and gave Travis a perfunctory hug. "Hey, dude," she said.

"Hey, dude," he answered. "Hey, Beck."

"Hey, Travis. Thanks for coming."

"It's the least I can do for my main man at work."

"Mrs. St. John, can you get some coffee or tea started?" Angie asked. "And if you have any cookies you can bring out—"

"Well you don't ask for much," the older woman said, hands on hips.

"You did agree to host," Angie reminded her.

Mrs. St. John let out an exasperated huff and stormed off to the kitchen.

"Is she always like this?" Becky asked.

"You caught her on a good day," Angie whispered. "So...thank your lucky stars. But she can change on a dime, so be on guard."

Becky nodded, looking more uncomfortable than ever.

"Thank God you're here," Travis said. "She was grilling me about who my personal lord and savior is. I don't think she wanted to hear Krishna." Suddenly Travis' eyes grew wild and he pointed behind the young women. "What the hell is that?"

Angie turned and saw a taxidermied rat standing erect on two feet, held in place by a dowel reaching up into its anus and down to a round wooden stand. The rat was holding up a sign that read, "The Lord hates the wicked."

"It's a church craft fair thing," Angie explained. "Just roll with it."

"It's fucking creepy," Travis whispered.

"Language!" Mrs. St. John shouted from the kitchen.

"How the hell did she hear me?" Travis asked, looking almost as nervous as Becky.

"I heard that!" Mrs. St. John called again.

"I don't have a good feeling about this," Travis said. "It's like that Lilliputian dude Glum on 'The Adventures of Gulliver' on the Banana Splits show, you know? 'We'll never make it!'"

Angie scowled her incomprehension, and Becky looked equally lost at sea.

"I'm just saying," Travis added for some reason.

"How's Kush?" asked Angie.

"Oh, he's good, he's good," Travis said, brightening. "Poops a lot, though. Amazingly big poo—"

"So what's the plan?" Becky asked. "Seth'll be here any moment."

"Dude is preternaturally prompt," Travis agreed.

"I guess I'll take the lead," Angie said. "I'm his best friend, and I think I have the best idea of the kind of group he's joined."

"How gnostically literate are you?" Travis asked.

Angie ignored him. "The most important thing for you two to do is just back me up. We have to present a united front."

"But what if dude makes a good point? You have to give a dude his props," Travis objected.

"Not tonight you don't," Angie said, her voice brooking no dissent. "If we don't hang together tonight, we lose him—you know, to the cultists."

"Not all gnostics are cultists," Travis objected.

"Whose side are you on?" Angie asked, raising her voice.

"I am on Seth's side," Travis said, with unexpected push-back. "And I think there's another side to this."

"Look, if you can't back me up on this, then I need you to leave," Angie said, her eyes fierce.

Travis held up his hands. "Just trying to be the voice of fucking reason here."

"Language!" Mrs. St. John called from the kitchen.

"How does she do that?" Travis asked.

Mrs. St. John strode into the living room, bearing a tray loaded with cans of soda and a loaf of banana bread. She set it on the coffee table and straightened up again, putting her hands on her hips. "If you children can't converse without potty mouths, you can all just go home. 'As for me and my house, we will serve the Lord.'"*

"Sorry, Mrs. St. John," Travis said.

Mrs. St. John turned on Becky. "And just who are *you*?"

"I'm Becky."

"I told you," Angie said, "she's Seth's ex-girlfriend."

Mrs. St. John looked confused. "I thought he was sleeping with you," she said to Angie.

"Not if you fu—not if you paid me," Angie said.

"I knew it. You're a prostitute. You have that look," Mrs. St. John sneered.

"Can you not tell the difference between whore and dyke?" Angie shook her head.

Mrs. St. John ignored her. Turning to Becky she said, "So he's sleeping with you? But you're so...dumpy."

Angie gasped and instinctively reached for Becky, putting her hand on her elbow. She watched Becky's face work out her feelings, and her eyes brimmed. "That's enough, Mrs. St. John," Angie

---

* Joshua 24:15

said. "I don't care who you are or how high-and-mighty you pretend to be, that was a mean, hurtful thing to say, and you owe Becky an apology."

Mrs. St. John flashed Angie a wicked look. "How dare you speak to me in my own—"

Travis stepped in between the two women. "Mrs. St. John, Jesus is here. Jesus is always here. He's here when we need him, and he's here when everything is fine. He's always watching, and he's with us now. How do you think Jesus feels about what you just said to Becky?"

Mrs. St. John blinked. Angie watched her face soften. Then she raised her chin. She turned to Becky. "I'm sorry I said you were...a little heavy. I'm also sorry that you're a whore."

Travis planted his face in his palm. "Suddenly everything about Seth makes sense."

Just then there came a knock on the door. Every head in the room jerked toward it. Angie touched Mrs. St. John on the shoulder. "Okay. Don't let on until you get him in this room."

Mrs. St. John sniffed and pushed past her. Angie turned to the others. "Sit, sit."

Becky sniffed and snatched a tissue from a box on the coffee table. Angie sat next to her. "Are you okay?"

"Yeah, just...Travis is right. No wonder Seth is...so Seth."

Angie patted her knee. "I know. That's why he needs us."

"To think I might have had her as a mother-in-law."

"You dodged a bullet," Angie agreed.

She heard Seth's voice down the hall. "Why couldn't it wait until the weekend?" He stepped into the living room and stopped, wavering as he took in the scene. "What the...?"

Angie stood. "Hi, Seth. Have a seat. We need to talk."

"What is this?" Seth asked.

"Banana bread," Mrs. St. John said, entering from behind him. "I know how you hate the zucchini. It has pecans."

Seth looked from one face to the other, his brow growing dark.

"Sit," Angie commanded. Seth sat, as did Mrs. St. John. Angie took a deep breath. "Seth, we're here because we love you—"

"Not in a gay way," Travis interjected.

Angie ignored that and continued. "—and we're concerned about you. *Really* concerned."

"Is this because of the Lodge?" Seth asked.

Angie nodded.

"Why is it any of your business?" Seth snapped.

"It isn't," Becky said. "You're right. You get to be religious...in any way you want. But if what you're doing is hurting you...I think we get to say so."

"How the hell is it hurting me?" Seth demanded. His hands were balled into fists, and one knee was bouncing.

Angie pointed to his knee. "Your anxiety and OCD...it's gotten worse since you started going to the Lodge. If it was helping you, it would be better. But it's not. I think it's...aggravating whatever else you have going on."

Mrs. St. John cleared her throat. "Seth, this tramp you live with is trying to convince me that instead of going to a Bible-believing church, you've joined a cult. You tell her she's a liar and a whore. You would never turn your back on Jesus that way, even if you are sticking your weenus in little-miss-dumpling over there."

Angie put her hand on Becky's back and stroked it. "That's not helping, Mrs. St. John," she said, her voice soft and firm. "Seth, can you honestly say you are suffering less now than before you started going?"

Seth glowered at her, his lips taut and thin. "There's no causal relationship—"

"I don't think you're being honest," Angie said. "With us or maybe even with yourself."

"Look, there's a lot you don't understand," Seth said.

"So explain it to us," Becky pleaded.

"I can't," Seth said.

"Because...secrets?" Angie asked.

Seth looked down at his hands and his shoulders deflated. "Yeah."

"Secrets are poison," Angie said. She'd heard that once in a twelve-step meeting, back when she was going to meetings.

"Secrets are sometimes necessary," Seth countered.

"That's just an excuse," Angie said.

"That's the truth," Seth said.

Angie pursed her lips and shook her head. She felt at a total loss.

"Hey Seth," Travis piped up. "Is that group you're going to Sethian anti-cosmic gnosticism or Valentinian unitive gnosticism?"

Angie shot Travis a glare that could pierce metal, but Seth looked relieved at the sharp left turn. "It's, uh...we read both kinds of scripture, but we definitely lean Valentinian."

"Oh. Valentinus rocks," Travis said, flashing him a thumbs up. "Gospel-of-fucking-Truth."

"Language!" Mrs. St. John snapped. Then under her breath, she muttered. "Jesus save me from the hippies. And the whores."

Angie sighed. They weren't getting anywhere. She had hoped that the combined show of force would shock Seth into some self-awareness, but it was clear that he was dug in.

"Hey, man," Travis said. "I think gnosticism is cool and all. And we could talk about it for hours, but...Angie really cares about you and she's worried about you. I understand how you might feel defensive right now, but...man, you gotta speak to the love. There's a lot of love in this room for you right now. I'm your bud and I am leveling with you. If you don't speak to the love, you're going to feel like shit when you leave."

Angie felt a shift in the atmosphere. Even Mrs. St. John did not object to Travis' language. Angie looked at Seth, her eyes pleading. Despite herself, her eyes grew wet and her throat swelled. "I do love you, Seth." Her voice squeaked with emotion.

Seth met her eyes. She saw him relax. The anger and tension on his face melted into something like tenderness, maybe even pity. "I'm sorry, Ange," he said. "I'm sorry I've been neglecting you, that I've been so busy. I'm sorry I've had to keep secrets from you. I'm sorry I've made you worry." He looked over at Becky. "I'm sorry, Becky. I...I haven't been honest with you. I like you a lot, but...I'm not in love with you. And I'm sorry if I led you on. I kept hoping my feelings would catch up to us, you know? But they didn't. And then I just got so busy that..." He stopped and looked down at his hands again. They were clasped so tightly in his lap that his knuckles were white.

"What about me?" his mother demanded.

Seth turned to look at her. Angie saw anger flicker on his face again, but it was only for a moment. "Mom, I'm sorry I can't believe in your god any more. I think the god you worship is demonic. I think he's evil, and he makes his followers do evil things. The way you treat Angie, what you just said to Becky, the over-the-top judgmentalism my whole life. It isn't gnosticism that made me into an emotional train wreck, it's the Monster God you worship."

Mrs. St. John's eyes grew wide, and she leaped to her feet. "Get out!" she shouted, pointing toward the door.

Seth cocked his head. "What?"

"Get out! You are dead to me. You just walk straight into hell, if that's where you want to go, you and all your devil-friends." She glared at all of them. "Out. Out! OUT!"

Awkwardly, they stood. Becky rushed to the door. Seth met Angie's eyes and a wordless understanding passed between them. Travis kept his eyes on the coffee table. "Uh...can I take some of this banana bread?"

Mrs. St. John snatched the taxidermied rat from the end table behind her and began to swing it, striking Seth on the side of the head, spinning it and bringing it around for another swing at Travis.

Seth howled and Angie pushed him toward the door. Nearly tripping over one another, they ran through the door Becky had left open. Travis came up behind them. They stood in the front yard, in the moonlight, in the chill, in the silence, looking at one another. No one said anything. Travis stood outside the circle, looking in. "I brought the banana bread," he said, holding the loaf out in his bare hands. "I expected her to come after us and say, 'Bring back that banana bread, you little shit,' but she didn't."

Angie ignored him. So did Seth and Becky. Angie looked to Seth with brimming eyes. "Seth, I—"

He held up his hand. He was the very picture of calm, but his voice quavered as he spoke. "I know...you did this because you care about me. But...you also betrayed me—all of you."

"Seth, I—"

"You colluded with the enemy!" He pointed at his mother's house.

"She cares about you, too...in her own twisted way," Becky said.

"I can't live with people I can't trust," Seth said. "When I left home, I swore...never again." He looked straight into Angie's eyes. "And I can't trust *you*."

Angie felt tears welling up, and her throat grew tight. "Seth, is it worth it? Is whatever you're getting at the Lodge worth alienating the people who really love you?"

That stopped him. He looked at his feet and swayed back and forth, as if buffeted by the wind. But there was no wind. "Don't come home," he said to Angie. "Come tomorrow when I'm at work and get your things. Leave the key on the table."

He turned and walked away into the dark.

WHO WERE DONNY & MARIE?

Donny and Marie is an American entertainment duo consisting of siblings Donny Osmond and Marie Osmond. In the 1970s and early 1980s, they achieved great popularity through their music, television, and live performances. Donny and Marie became a cultural phenomenon, leaving a lasting impact on the entertainment industry.

Donny Osmond, born in 1957, began his career as a child performer with the Osmonds, a singing group composed of his brothers. He became a teen idol with hits like "Puppy Love" and "Go Away Little Girl," captivating fans of all ages.

Marie Osmond, born in 1959, also started her career as part of the Osmond family. With her powerful voice and stage presence, she achieved solo success with songs such as "Paper Roses" and "Meet Me in Montana," excelling in various genres.

In 1976, Donny and Marie created their television variety show, "The Donny & Marie Show." The program showcased their singing, dancing, comedy sketches, and guest appearances by celebrities. Their chemistry and charisma captivated audiences, leading to a successful four-year run. Their signature song was "I'm a Little Bit Country, I'm a Little Bit Rock'n'Roll," which they performed on every show, interspersed with jokes.

In their later career, Donny and Marie headlined live performances in Las Vegas and embarked on concert tours, impressing audiences with their energy and stage production. Their shows featured a blend of their individual hits, duets, and entertaining banter, solidifying their status as a dynamic duo.

Members of the Church of Jesus Christ of Latter-Day Saints, they became the most famous Mormons in the world, and presented an appealing and wholesome image that reflected well on their faith. Donny Osmond died in 2034 at the age of 77 of the Codex virus. Since Marie died after the Great Divide, nothing is known of her end.

CHAPTER TWELVE

Those who are asleep live each in a private world;
those who are awake live in one great world.
—*Heraclitus*[*]

"Musa, Seth, thank you so much for coming, especially after a full day of work." Mr. Basil swung his office door wide and shook hands with the two initiates. "Please have a seat. Can I offer you a scotch?"

"No, thank you," Musa Daniels said, sitting in one of the armchairs near the fire.

"I'll take one," Seth said, sitting in another chair near Musa. "What kind?"

"Ah. Bruichladdich." Mr. Basil poured two glasses and handed

---

[*] Adapted from John Burnet's *Early Greek Philosophy*, chapter 3, Fragment B89 (UK: A. and C. Black, 1908).

one to Seth. "It's not expensive, but for an everyday scotch it's very good. Are you a scotch man, then, Seth?"

"It sure beats gin all to hell."

That made Mr. Basil chuckle. "Don't like the juniper berries so much, eh?"

"Makes me gag."

Mr. Basil sat. "I suppose you're wondering why I've asked you in."

Musa and Seth glanced at one another. Both nodded.

"The leadership team has met, and they've singled the two of you out for...special service. You both have exceptional abilities that make you valuable assets for the gnostic project."

Seth felt a prick of pride race through him. He sat up a little bit straighter. He looked over at Musa again, but found the man scowling. Mr. Basil seemed not to notice.

"We have succeeded in mapping out some areas of the *Cibus Dei,* but to be honest, we haven't even scratched the surface. As you may have guessed, the ship is massive, as is the supporting infrastructure. Maps of the illusion, the Disneyfied planet earth, we already have, but what we need are maps of the support structures behind—"

"Behind what?" Musa asked.

"Behind the S-panels," Mr. Basil said.

Seth stiffened. "I...I've been there."

Mr. Basil nodded. "We know."

Seth wondered how Mr. Basil knew. Then he realized that Dr. Teasdale must have told him. He wasn't sure how he felt about that.

"We are hoping you will go through an S-panel again—many times, probably—and bring us back accurate maps of what you find there."

"They chased me out," Seth said, his voice rising. "I barely escaped."

"That was chance. This time, you'll be prepared. We will plan everything out. We know when the guard shifts change. We know where the cameras are—"

"How can you know that if you don't know the ship?" Musa asked.

Mr. Basil shrugged apologetically. "We know where the cameras are in the areas we know."

Musa was still scowling. "What you're saying is that you can get us where we're going safely, but when we actually get to the place that you need a map of...we're on our own."

Mr. Basil nodded reluctantly.

"But what if we're caught?" Seth asked. "Or we bump into an electrician?"

"You may need to subdue an electrician."

"Are you crazy?" Musa asked, a little too loudly. "You want me, a black man in...well, what I *thought* was America...you want *me* to attack an electrician? That carries the death penalty."

"A lot more people will die if you don't," Mr. Basil said.

"What do you mean?" Musa asked.

"There are two seals yet to be broken, two revelations in which you have yet to be initiated. 'There is nothing hidden that will not be revealed.'"

"This is bullshit," Musa said.

"Mr. Daniels, please. Bear with me. We are all risking much to do this work. I am risking everything to lead this resistance. You are both at risk because of your involvement. There are powers that would like nothing better than to snuff us out. Those powers are the enemy...not me. But you are right about the...'bullshit,' as you call it. It is the agenda of the powers that is bullshit."

Musa did not seem assuaged.

Seth's mind raced. A voice in his head said, *This is it. This is what you were born for. This is your life's purpose.* Something shifted within him, and the shift felt *right*. "I'll do it," Seth said.

Mr. Basil's eyebrows rose. Musa looked at Seth as if he had been betrayed. "Seth—" he started, but Seth interrupted him.

"No, I'll do it. This is the right thing. I'm sure of it. And I'll be good at it. I...remember things."

"Indeed you do," Mr. Basil nodded approvingly. He looked back at Musa. "Are you sure you won't reconsider, Mr. Daniels?"

Musa looked from Seth to Mr. Basil and back to Seth. Then he shook his head, slowly and sadly. "No, Mr. Basil. I have much respect for you, and I think what you are doing is good. I am willing to serve our goals in many capacities, but this...this I cannot do."

Mr. Basil nodded in resignation. "Very well then, and I quite understand. I cannot walk in your shoes just as you cannot walk in mine. I honor your decision. But given that decision, will you please excuse us, so that Mr. St. John and I can discuss his first mission in private?"

Seth found the look on Musa's face impossible to read. He had become as rigid as stone. The man rose, cleared his throat, and then strode from the room.

Mr. Basil took a sip of his whisky and smiled at Seth. "That was...unexpected."

"He's scared," Seth said. "I would be, too."

"But...you are volunteering for the same assignment as he...?"

"But I'm not black. If I get caught...it would be worse for him," Seth admitted. "You know that."

Mr. Basil seemed to soften. "It's too bad. He's the sharpest mind I've seen in a while."

Seth wasn't sure whether that was a slight to him, but decided to let it go. "So what do we do?"

Mr. Basil placed his drink on the end table and rose, circling to the desk. He snatched up a thumb drive and tossed it to Seth.

"What is this?" Seth asked.

"It's the parts of the ship we know. They're arranged on a grid that corresponds to points in the seen world, what we call the Disney field. As you'll see, there are vast sections that are unmapped. We just want you to start filling in the gaps."

"Is there a part you want me to start on first?"

"There is, actually. There's an S-panel in the men's restroom of the Ferry Building in San Francisco. We have no idea what's behind it, and we think it might contain some command operations. We need eyes in there. We need to know the terrain."

"The Ferry Building...that's where the big farmer's market is, right?"

"Yes. You'll need to do it at a time just after opening or just before closing—sometime when the rest-room traffic is low so you can get into the S-panel without being seen."

Seth nodded.

"When might you have some time in the next day or so?" Mr. Basil asked, opening up an old-fashioned day planner.

"Um...I'm off tomorrow."

"Good," Mr. Basil said, writing in his calendar. "Training is at 10am."

———

Angie knocked on the door and waited. She heard nothing coming from within, and her shoulders slumped. She'd just turned to go when the door opened. She whirled to see Becky in a bathrobe, her hair wet.

"Ay! I'm sorry to get you out of the shower," Angie said.

"It's okay," Becky said, her face softening. "Come in."

Angie scooted up the step to the apartment's door and went in. She shut the door behind her and followed Becky, who was scrubbing at her hair with a towel. "I was done anyway. I was just standing there using up all the hot water for no reason."

"Except that it feels good," Angie said.

"Can I get you something to drink?" Becky asked.

"What do you have in the way of hard liquor?" Angie asked.

Becky's lips pursed and moved sideways. "Cabernet blanc?"

Angie made an involuntary face, but covered quickly. "Sure. In a tumbler."

Becky laughed and went to the kitchen. She returned with a large red-wine glass filled nearly to the brim with the white wine. She set it on the coffee table and pointed to her hair. "I'm going to go deal with this while I can still avert catastrophe."

"Yeah, of course," Angie agreed, sitting on the loveseat in front of the wine.

Becky trotted off to her bedroom and shut the door. Angie sighed. "It's bad enough alienating your only friend," she told herself out loud. "It's humiliating having to rely on friends-of-friends." She reached for the wine glass and downed half of it in one draught. She made a face as it went down. "*That* is headache material."

She stood up and began to pace the room. She paused by a bookshelf and leaned over to read the titles. *Lady Chatterley's Lover, The Jungle, Man's Search for Meaning*, the *Norton Anthology of American Poetry*, a white leather-bound Bible, the first three Chronicles of Narnia, *Sense and Sensibility*, and what must have been a full set of Nora Roberts.

"Huh," Angie said. "No William S. Burroughs. What am I getting myself into?"

She considered turning on the television and scrolling through Becky's watch list, but before she could breach that privacy, the bedroom door opened again, and Becky emerged, wearing pink pajamas adorned with yellow duckies.

"I have a pair like that," Angie said, pointing at the pajamas, "except they're black and they have skulls all over them."

"So...not like these at all," Becky said, with a touch of humor in her voice. She turned and went to the kitchen and returned a moment later with her own glass of white wine—a more modest serving in the proper glass. "Cheers," she said, holding her glass out.

Angie picked up her glass and duly clinked it. She took another swig and set it down again, swishing the sour liquid through her teeth.

Becky sat cross-legged on the floor. "So what's up? I guess you want to talk about...last night?"

"Don't you?" Angie asked.

Becky looked away. "I'm not sure. I guess so. I've spent most of the day avoiding thinking about it. Whenever my brain gets close to it, I...recoil. It's like an electric shock."

"I've been sticking my finger in the socket all day," Angie confessed. "But...that's not the only reason I'm here."

Becky cocked her head. Her still-damp curls fell over her shoulders and it occurred to Angie how pretty she was. Angie looked down at her hands.

"I...uh...need a place to sleep. Preferably one that isn't my car."

Becky's eyebrows shot up. "Did you sleep in your car last night?"

Angie couldn't meet her eyes. She rubbed her finger along the rim of the glass.

"Oh, Angie," Becky said. She rose and moved around the coffee table, sitting on the loveseat next to her guest. "Of course you can sleep here."

"I just...I can't go back to Seth's, you know? I guess a part of me feels guilty," Angie confessed.

Becky chuckled.

"What?" Angie asked.

"I don't know...I guess, I didn't think you *felt* guilt. You're so..."

"Bitchy?" Angie supplied.

Now Becky laughed. "*Not* what I was going to say."

"You didn't have to," Angie said.

"You stay with me as long as you need to," Becky said.

"Are you sure?" Angie asked. "I'm incredibly annoying."

"Let's make a deal. When I annoy you, you tell me. And I'll do the same for you. And that way we'll nip it in the bud before any resentment sneaks in."

"Yeah, that sounds way too grown-up for me. It also sounds like nagging."

"Let's just give it a try." Becky nudged her with her shoulder.

Angie sighed. And then she collapsed in on herself, her shoulders shaking with sobs.

"Oh, honey," Becky said, putting her arms around her. She held her until the shaking stopped. Angie drew away and wiped her eyes on her coat sleeve. "I'm sorry."

"Don't be sorry," Becky said. "I love him, too."

"But you're not crying," Angie said.

"That's because I'm numb," Becky said. "I'll take my turn, I'm sure."

"It's fucked up."

"It sure is."

"Where do you want me?" Angie asked, changing the subject. "Here?" She pointed to the loveseat.

"Are you kidding? It's way too short. You'll get a kink in your neck."

"It would not be my first kink," Angie joked. "If you have a couple of extra blankets, I can sleep on the floor."

"Don't be silly." Becky stood up and waved her off the couch. "Come on. Help me change the sheets. You can sleep with me. It doesn't make any sense for me to sleep in a perfectly good queen-sized bed while you sack out on the floor."

"You're not afraid I'll try something?" Angie asked.

"I trust you. Besides, I don't think I'm your type," Becky said.

"How do you know?" Angie asked, following her.

"Not enough piercings, for one. And being straight, for another."

"You have your good qualities, though," Angie conceded.

A s usual, when Seth knocked on the door of the Lodge, Nazz answered. But instead of opening the door wide to let him in, the young man exited and locked the door behind him. "I'm supposed to meet Mr. Basil," Seth complained.

"Nope. You're supposed to meet me," Nazz flashed him a smile that seemed insincere with a little "gotcha" thrown in. Nazz walked briskly toward the street. Seth threw a glance over his shoulder at the Lodge house, but followed Nazz just the same.

"Are you sure?" Seth called.

"Sure as snails," Nazz answered.

Sure as snails? Seth mouthed.

Nazz stopped by a bright red Toyota Corolla that had seen better days. He unlocked it the old-fashioned way, with a key, and climbed in. Leaning across the passenger seat, he unlocked the other door, which opened with an audible groan of complaint.

Seth paused for only a second to take in the ripped upholstery and the layer of potato chip bags on the floor. With a sigh he heaved himself into the seat and planted his feet on top of the trash, swinging the door closed behind him. It didn't seem to close just right, but he guessed that was the best it could do.

Nazz started the engine which, to Seth's surprise, roared to life without complaint. "Where are we going?"

"You'll see," Nazz said. He signaled his intention and pulled out onto the street.

Seth felt the silence in the car swell until it was almost unbearable. Finally, he managed, "Uh...how long have you been... a gnostic?"

"Ever since I was a wee babe," Nazz said in a faux Scottish accent.

"Wait, you were raised in this..." he started to say "cult" and was momentarily taken aback at himself.

"Whatever this is?" Nazz completed his sentence and laughed. "Yeah. You haven't put it together yet?"

"Put what together?" Seth asked.

"That your precious Mr. Basil is my dad?" Nazz asked.

"Mr. Basil is your *dad*?" Seth's voice rose several pitches.

"Why is that such a shock?"

"I don't know, I just..." He looked over at Nazz, to see if he could divine a resemblance. Nazz' hair was so wild that it threw him off. He still couldn't really see it. Nazz was a short young man, after all, and Mr. Basil was almost impossibly tall. "And your mom?"

"She's in jail," Nazz said. "Or prison, rather."

Seth's eyes went wide. "Prison? Why?"

Nazz glanced over at Seth with a positively wicked smile. "For doing what you're about to do."

Seth felt a trickle of ice race down his spine. "How long is she in for?" he asked.

"Hard to say," Nazz answered, his eyes back on the road now. "Supposed to be fifteen years, but you know how it is. They can always drum up new charges."

Seth didn't know what to say to that. The rest of the ride passed in silence, but it wasn't awkward, it was simply grave.

Finally, however, Nazz pulled up in front of a warehouse in an industrial park. Without a word he got out and walked toward the door. Seth followed. The younger man unlocked the door and flipped on the lights. Seth looked up and saw that large lamps amply illuminated the entire space. Looking down, however, he couldn't see very far. He was in a very small vestibule, bounded on all sides by six-foot partitions, just like you'd see separating one desk from another in a large office building.

"This way," Nazz said. He went through the only opening in the room dividers into another partitioned space, this one even smaller. One of the partitions here, however, held what was clearly an S-panel, or at least a mockup of one. Nazz walked up behind him. "Open your hand," he said.

Seth turned to face him and hesitantly brought his palm up. Nazz fished in his pocket and pulled out a key fixed to a generic-looking keychain. Seth examined the key. It was a strange shape—the part that fitted into the S-panel was round, which made sense, as the hole in the panel's access plate was the same shape. All around the circle of the key were tiny indentations at irregular intervals. The keychain was simply a plastic tab that read "Mort's engine and body repair" in gold lettering that was flaking off.

Nazz pointed at the S-panel. "You go in there." He pulled out his phone and pushed a button. He held it up so Seth could see—he had opened a stop-watch app. "You have exactly fifteen minutes. If you're late, you fail. You can be early, though, no worries there. But once you're back, you need to draw a map of the terrain. And it needs to be accurate."

"And if it isn't?" Seth asked.

Nazz shrugged. "You fail. No skin off my nose."

"And what if I fail?"

"Then I guess someone else gets to do this job."

Seth wondered if perhaps that wasn't a good idea. A sudden pain stabbed at his chest, and he pressed on the spot. Then he started punching it.

"What are you doing?" Nazz asked.

"Nothing. I'm...I have chest pains sometimes."

"So you hit yourself?"

"I'm trying to make the muscles relax."

Nazz rolled his eyes. "If you have a heart attack in there, you fail," he said.

"Thanks. I kind of figured that."

Nazz punched at his phone. "Go."

Seth looked at the key in his hand.

"Time's a-wastin'," Nazz prodded.

Seth crossed the short distance to the S-panel—it looked exactly like an actual S-panel—and inserted the key, which turned easier than he had expected it to. The panel swung toward him effortlessly. He pulled it open further and stepped inside. "Do I shut it again?"

"Yes!" Nazz called.

Seth pulled it toward him and heard a soft click as the latch caught. There was a keyhole in exactly the same place on the back of the panel. Seth nodded and turned.

He was surrounded on all sides by the six-foot partitions, covered in brown fabric. Having actually been inside an S-panel before, he wondered that there wasn't more attention given to verisimilitude, but dismissed the thought. *Work to do*, he told himself.

He could go in two directions, and chose the path to the left at random. The panels were, as he had expected, arranged to form a maze. The path was blocked by a panel, but there was an opening to his right, which he took, discovering a switch-back leading him back toward where he'd started, but one level deeper into the maze. It took a turn to the left, then another turn to the left. Then it dead-ended.

He turned and sprinted back to the opening. He cursed himself for not setting the timer on his phone so he'd know how much time he had left. He found the back of the S-panel again and kept going, this time to the right. It came to a left-hand turn and then went deep. He turned left again and stopped. The path opened out into a small room. At the far side of the room was a table, adorned with red paisley drapings. It was dim in the little room formed by the partitions, save for two large candlesticks burning at either side of the table. And sitting on the table between them was a woman. She was living—her eyes were open, and she blinked. But she did not look at him or acknowledge him in any way. She was also entirely nude. The woman's hair, shining gold in the candlelight, spilled over her shoulders, obscuring her breasts from view. He did not recognize her, but she was so arrestingly beautiful that he could not move.

She seemed frozen, sitting completely still, like one of the gold-painted mimes standing motionless at a tourist attraction. With cautious steps, he moved toward her. He reached out his hand to touch her shoulder, but then pulled back. She had not invited his touch. His arm fell to his side.

Seth wavered a bit. She was the last thing he'd expected to see, and it took a moment to adjust to the surreality of the scene. He shook his head to clear it and moved toward the only other opening in the partition walls, but threw another glance over his shoulder at the woman. She was still unmoved.

He exited the little room and turned left as the pathway gave him no other choices. This time the path went for some distance. He jogged down it, almost unable to see it in the dim light spilling over the tops of the partitions. He tripped and went sprawling. Feeling around with his hands, he discovered there had been a blanket in his path. "Dammit," he swore under his breath. He got up and started running again.

He stopped when he heard a hiss.

He pulled out his phone and with his thumb flicked on the flashlight. In front of him, in the corner as the passage opened to the left, was what could only be a possum. Its breathing was labored, and its eyes were wide. One leg was caught in a trap, red gore trailing from it. The little beast strained in his direction, little jaws snapping at him, specks of foam dotting his mouth.

Seth froze. Should he go back? Should he try to release the creature? Should he try to jump over and hope he didn't get bit? And was that thing...rabid?

He backed up and prepared to sprint. He ran as fast as he could, leaped into the air, and sailed over the snapping jaws of the possum. But he realized in mid-flight that he wouldn't be able to correct his trajectory. The possum was in a corner where the path changed directions, so he'd aimed to clear the edge of the partition furthest from the beastie. But he couldn't stop his momentum and crashed into the partition forming the far wall of the path.

To his surprise, the brown cloth covering the partition softened the blow somewhat, but he still went down hard. The partition pitched into another partition behind it, and that one struck another, creating a rapid succession of muffled crashes.

Seth struggled to his feet, cradling his head, which had taken the brunt of the blow. He watched as section after section of partitions toppled like a dim row of brown dominoes.

"Time's up!" Nazz' voice carried over the partitions behind him, blessedly still standing.

"Goddam it," Seth swore. He turned and followed the path out. When he reached the little room, the woman was still there, still sitting stock still. He barely glanced at her, however, and pressed on to the S-panel. He had no trouble picking his way back, and inserting the key into the panel lock, he climbed over the lip of the panel and shut it behind him.

Nazz was there, of course, grinning at him. Seth wanted to wipe the smile off his face with his fist, but instead he only glared. "I broke your maze," Seth confessed.

"Not the first time," Nazz said, with an air of righteous satisfaction. "I'd ask you how you did, but you clearly sucked so hard there's no point."

Seth saw a chair over by the door they'd entered and he went to it. Sitting, he put his head between his knees and took a deep breath.

"You light-headed?" Nazz asked.

"No, just angry and trying to get a grip," Seth answered.

"Don't take it so hard. Did you think this was going to be a fucking cake walk?"

Seth didn't know what he'd expected, but it wasn't this.

Somewhere in the distance, Seth heard crashes and voices. "What's going on?" Seth asked.

"They're resetting the maze for you," Nazz said.

Seth shook his head.

Just then the S-panel opened and the woman who had been sitting on the table stepped over the lip of the panel, wearing a white terrycloth bathrobe. "Hey, Nazz."

"Hey, Sheila," Nazz called over his shoulder.

She didn't acknowledge Seth's presence, but walked past them to the door they'd used to enter the warehouse space.

"Who was that?" Seth asked.

"That was Sheila. Don't you listen?"

"But why was she—"

"Did she slow you down?" Nazz asked.

"Uh...yeah."

Nazz shrugged, as if that explained everything. "They're going to take about a half hour to set it up again and change it around. In the meantime, why don't you practice?"

"Practice what?" Seth asked.

Nazz went to a small table Seth hadn't noticed before and picked up a clipboard. He walked back to where Seth was sitting and handed it to him. Seth took it. The clipboard held graph paper, but there was nothing on it. Nazz handed him a pen. "Draw what you saw."

"You want me to draw...her?" Seth asked.

"Don't be stupid," Nazz almost spat, a chink appearing in his too-cheery demeanor. "Draw the path."

S eth hadn't yet knocked on the door when Jude pulled it open. "Come in!" he shouted, all gregarity. He turned and seemed to expect Seth to follow him in. Seth did, shutting the door behind him. He wished he didn't have to be here. He was still smarting from his failure the day before. The image of Sheila sitting motionless on the altar, clothed in candlelight and nothing else haunted him. He saw her every time he closed his eyes. He didn't know if he wanted to try the maze again—to do it better—or never see anything like it again.

"Everyone else is here," Jude shouted over his shoulder. "We were laying odds as to whether you'd show."

"Yeah...the bus," Seth said. He suspected everyone else had cars—most people did in Silicon Valley. In San Jose, public transit was a neglected afterthought.

He turned the corner and saw his entire cohort of initiates waving at him—even the normally surly Matt. Despite his feelings, he couldn't help but smile. Everyone seemed genuinely glad to see him. It made his heart feel warm, which only confused him further.

"There's chips and salsa and my special curry guacamole on the coffee table," Jude pointed. "And Matt brought beer—it's in the fridge."

"There's also wine on the counter," Lynn added, "just in case you aren't a Philistine."

"Hey, it's *craft beer*," Matt objected. "It's not like I brought Budweiser. Sheesh."

Lynn moved over to make space for him on the couch. He shot her a grateful smile and sat.

"Anyway, I didn't see a damn thing," Matt said.

Maria turned toward Seth and explained, "We were discussing the exercise we did to visualize Sophia."

"Oh. Sorry to interrupt," Seth lowered his head.

"Don't be silly," Lynn said.

"What about you, Seth?" Musa asked. As usual, his voice carried more gravity than most and all eyes turned to Seth. He looked around, feeling caged. He wished he'd heard what others had said first. He decide it was okay to say so. "Uh...before I spill my guts, what did the rest of you see?" He tensed, waiting for the reaction to this. He needn't have worried.

"Fair point!" Lynn said, pointing at him. "I saw her. She looked just like Stevie Nicks."

"Didn't see a damn thing," Matt repeated.

"I didn't either," Jude said, looking sad.

Maria cocked her head. "I couldn't see her, but I could feel her."

Seth nodded. "I couldn't make out her face. She was...blurry. But she was there."

"She looked *just* like Stevie Nicks," Lynn insisted.

"I suspect this is a case of inculturation," Musa pronounced.

"What does *that* mean?" Matt asked.

"It means that every culture beholds the unmanifest in the clothes of its people," Musa said.

Matt frowned. "In English, maybe?"

"Baruch Spinoza said that triangles would picture God as triangular. We all see our deities in our own image. For instance, if you go into the home of a Scandinavian Lutheran family, what color is Jesus?"

"White," Maria said, nodding. "With blue eyes and blonde hair."

"Exactly." Musa nodded.

"And if you go into a Mexican house, Jesus looks Mexican," Maria added.

"Just so. And if you go into the house of a Korean Presbyterian?" Musa posited.

"Jesus would be Korean?" Jude asked.

"Of course," Musa answered. "So to me, the holy mother Sophia did not look like...Stephie N—"

"Stevie," Lynn corrected.

"To me she appeared as Oshun," Musa finished.

"Who the hell is Oshun?" Matt asked.

Musa turned his face to him, looking just a bit too patient. "She is the goddess of beauty, of love, of the river. She wears white and gold and coral. Sophia was dressed in just this way when I saw her. And her face was clear to me. It was the face of my own people."

"I thought you were a Christian," Lynn looked confused. "I mean...before you found the Lodge."

"The rest of the world does not put such firm boundaries between religions as you Americans tend to do."

"Wait, how could you have been born in Nigeria?" Matt asked. "It would have been cut off by the epidemic before you were born."

"I never claimed to have been born in Nigeria," Musa said. "I was born in Fremont. My parents were both from Nigeria, and I grew up in a Nigerian church that other Christians might find... mmmm...syncretistic. It was an...insular community."

"So you've never been to Nigeria?" Matt asked.

"I have not. There is a special sadness that comes with being forever cut off from your true home. Perhaps..." and he sighed, "... this is why the gnostic teachings speak to me so. I long for home, and find this place to be...oppressive at times."

There were nods all around and everyone grew quiet.

Matt interrupted the silence. "Here's what I don't get. Is all this stuff we're learning mythology or is it supposed to be true?"

"Who says mythology isn't true?" Musa asked.

"What do you mean?" Matt asked. "Mythology is the definition of not-true!"

"Then I believe you have a very anaemic understanding of mythology," Musa said.

"How so?" Maria asked, her lips curling up in a smile. She seemed to be enjoying the possibilities posed by the subject.

"Myths are stories that make sense of our lives. Whether or not they are rooted in history or legend is irrelevant."

"Wait, how can whether something really happened or not be irrelevant?" Matt asked, a bit of heat entering his voice.

"You are not listening to me," Musa said, all patience. "I did not say that whether something happened is irrelevant. I said that whether it happened or not has no bearing upon whether it should be classified as myth. Myths are as likely to be historical as not. Myth has a functional definition, not an ontological one."

"You lost me there," Matt threw his hands up.

"I get it," Maria said. "Myths are stories that are useful to us. Some of those stories really happened and some of them didn't. Either way, the stories are still important because we use them to make meaning."

Musa nodded.

"I like that," Maria said.

"Okay, that was very academic," Matt objected, "but it didn't address my actual question. Are the stories Dr. Robinson is telling us true or not?"

Musa shrugged. "I can attest that they have been successful in making meaning in my life."

There were nods all around. Seth found himself nodding as well. "And I saw her," he said. "Maybe not her face, but I saw her.

It wasn't just in my imagination. There was something real going on."

"But that's the definition of a gnostic, yes?" Lynn asked. "A gnostic is one who knows because she has experienced it for herself. She doesn't just accept what other people tell her."

"'A man with experience is not at the mercy of a man with an opinion,'" Musa quoted. When others looked confused, he added, "L.H. Hardwick," but it didn't seem to help much.

"I've seen her," Lynn said. "And she looks like fucking Stevie Nicks."

This made everyone laugh, including Musa. "Yes," he said, the smile still lingering on his face. "I have seen her too."

"So does that make me not a gnostic?" Matt asked.

"I think that is a question for Dr. Robinson, surely," Musa said. "You should write it down."

"I don't need to fucking write it down. And I don't like you all pretending that you're more 'spiritual' than me."

Lynn moved forward to sit on the edge of her seat and turned to face him. "Now who's making up stories, Matt? No one here is claiming to be more spiritual than you are. No one. If you feel insecure, then fucking take responsibility for it. Moderating our feelings is what big boys and girls do."

Matt's eyes grew big. He opened his mouth to object, but then seemed to think better of it. He sank down into his seat, momentarily subdued.

"I saw her," Seth said. "In fact, I think she visited me. I was feeling sad, and then...I felt her. And I felt...better."

"Oh, Jesus," Matt said. "Here we go. Therapeutic emotional crap."

"Matt," Maria said, in a voice that was even and compassionate. "They're not saying they're better than you...or me. They're just telling us what they experienced. I didn't see her, either, but I don't blame them for that. You shouldn't, either."

"I think they're making it up," Matt said.

"Why would we do that?" Lynn asked. "We didn't know that you hadn't seen her. I know I'm surprised—and relieved—to discover I'm not the only one. I think your anger is misplaced."

Matt did not look at her. Instead, he rose, crossed the room, and headed for the front door. Everyone jumped as he slammed it behind him.

"Okay...that was unnecessary," Lynn said.

"Give him time," Musa said. "He is feeling left out."

"I guess I am, too," Maria said.

Seth considered bringing up his dream about the majorette and her spinning batons, but decided against it. It was only a dream, after all, and what did it have to do with anything they were discussing? He didn't know. He suspected it did, but didn't know how.

"Were you able to see her face?" Musa asked.

"I don't...I don't remember," Lynn said, cocking her head and frowning. Her lips got pouty. "Now that you mention it..."

"I couldn't make out her features," Seth said. "They were kind of a blur."

"That was my experience, too," Musa nodded, his face grave.

"Perhaps it will get clearer in time," Maria suggested. She looked thoughtful. "I wonder how I can meet her...?"

"Why don't you ask her?" Lynn asked. "I mean, what can it hurt?"

"You mean, like, pray to her?" Maria asked.

"Yeah, exactly," Lynn said.

"I would feel pretty weird doing that," Maria admitted.

"This is all pretty weird," Seth observed.

No one disputed that.

When Keira got to her desk, there was a post-it note stuck to her chair. "My office."

She looked up at Schenck's office and saw him through the glass, hunched over a file. She frowned and made her way over. She knocked on the door, then opened it before he responded.

"You wanted to see me, chief?"

Schenck looked up and seemed to take a moment to adjust. "Yeah. Yeah, come in. Shut the door. Sit."

Keira did as instructed, in order. She put both palms between her knees and waited. Schenck shoved a file across the desk to her. "I have a case for you."

She picked up the file and opened it. A photo of a blonde, middle-aged woman with a pageboy cut looked up at her.

"Her name is Eileen Caraway. She's an electrician."

"Yeah? So?"

"All right, maybe I should say *was* an electrician. She's dead."

"How?"

"Coroner says a blow to the back of the head."

"Any leads on the perp?" Keira asked.

"Whoever it was has access to an S-panel."

Keira's eyes went wide. "Really?"

"Really."

She scowled at the file. "You don't suspect me, do you?"

Schenck cocked his head. "Say what now?"

"Okay, okay. Just checking. New girl with the roller-skate key and all."

"We've got the scene taped off, but local police can't go near it. I want you to investigate."

Keira nodded. She closed the file and stood. "When—?"

"You still here? Crime scene is getting cold, special agent."

"On my way, sir."

Schenck looked down at his stack of papers and sighed. The

audience was over. "Thanks, chief." Keira let herself out and headed for the elevators.

Half an hour later she was at the crime scene—a local television studio belonging to the CBS affiliate. The big networks had been atrophying since the early 2000s, but there were still some holdouts. NBC and ABC were gone, but CBS had somewhere along the way figured out how to conquer streaming, and had rediscovered the power of local, nonpartisan news.

The entrance to the main office was unobstructed, and except for the presence of three police cars one wouldn't be able to tell that anything was amiss. Once inside, she flashed her badge at the front desk and was pointed toward a hallway on the right. She walked just fast enough that she wasn't quite jogging, picking up the trail quickly by following the bright yellow police tape.

A uniformed cop moved to intercept her, but she proffered her badge again. "I'm Special Agent Sloane. What do we have?"

He studied the badge and CHS ID card. He looked at her face, then back at the card. Then he nodded and moved the tape for her. "ME took the body, but nothing's been touched other than that. It's in back, in the computer room."

Computer room? Keira wondered. She stepped through the door and instantly understood what he meant. This was definitely where the IT guy did his stuff. The walls were lined with racks holding various sizes and shapes of electronic equipment. And there, on the far side of the room, just where you would expect to see an S-panel, there it was, its door swung open into the room.

The sight of an open S-panel still felt odd to her, as if something was fundamentally not right with the world. *Understatement of the year,* she thought. She pulled a couple of blue nitril gloves from her pocket and put them on. She pulled her phone from her slacks and unfolded the larger screen. Then she accessed her case files and looked at the photos the CHS forensics team had uploaded. The victim had been pretty, older than Keira by about ten years. She was wearing a white lab coat. A pool of blood gathered around the top of her head.

She didn't see any blood in this room, which could only mean that it happened *inside*. She poked her head into the panel and saw the blood about two yards from the door. The forensics team had marked the outline of the body on the floor with blue painter's tape. Keira stepped over the lip of the S-panel and into the narrow, industrial hallway behind. She knelt by the outline and studied the blood. It had begun to dry, but what struck her was that it wasn't smeared. She realized how careful the ME's team had to have been to move the body without causing any distortion to the blood pattern, and she had to give them props.

She looked down the hallway in one direction, and it seemed to go on forever—much longer than the building on the outside did. She turned and looked in the other direction. This hallway seemed to end at about the same place as the front of the building. She heard a ping and looked at her phone again. Prints were in. She glanced at the summary—no prints from anyone not authorized to be there. Which only meant that whoever had broken in had worn gloves...either that or the killer was a coworker. She checked the security cameras just as the feed came through. Cameras twelve and fourteen were apparently broken. "Of course," she muttered. But the feed from camera thirteen was there. She pushed on the icon and waited for it to launch.

There were only a few seconds of the perpetrator. She watched someone she assumed was Ms. Caraway walk into view, her back to the camera. *The hair is right, at least,* she thought. She counted to seven before another figure entered the frame. This seemed to be male, wearing an open hoodie from which a dark shock of hair stuck out at an odd angle. She couldn't make out the face at all from the camera's perspective. "No, that would be too easy," she mumbled. The intruder was dressed in dark colors, except for one thing—a paisley vest.

LIQUIPEDIA
THE ANSWERBOT THAT GOES DOWN SMOOTH

WHAT IS THE DIFFERENCE BETWEEN ATHEISM AND AGNOSTICISM?

Atheism and agnosticism are two distinct positions regarding the existence of deities or a divine being. While both atheism and agnosticism relate to the domain of belief, they address different aspects of the question and adopt different stances.

Atheism refers to the absence of belief in any gods or deities. An atheist, therefore, is someone who does not hold a belief in the existence of a divine being. Atheism can take various forms, including strong atheism, which asserts that gods or deities do not exist, and weak atheism, which simply lacks belief in gods due to insufficient evidence or convincing arguments. It is important to note that atheism does not necessarily imply certainty or a denial of the possibility of gods, but rather a lack of belief in them.

On the other hand, agnosticism concerns knowledge and claims that the existence or non-existence of gods is inherently unknown or unknowable. Agnostics, or agnostic atheists, acknowledge the limitations of human knowledge and assert that it is impossible to ascertain the existence or non-existence of a divine being definitively. Agnosticism does not negate the possibility of gods, but rather emphasizes the uncertainty surrounding their existence.

It is worth noting that atheism and agnosticism are not mutually exclusive. Many atheists also identify as agnostic, as they recognize that the existence of gods cannot be proven or disproven definitively. In this sense, agnosticism can be seen as a position on knowledge, while atheism is a position on belief.

Furthermore, it is important to differentiate between atheism and religious skepticism. While atheism relates specifically to the belief in gods, religious skepticism encompasses a broader skepticism towards religious claims, rituals, and institutions. Skepticism can be seen within both atheistic and agnostic frameworks, as individuals critically examine and question religious beliefs and practices.

CHAPTER THIRTEEN

You have come not to suffer but to break your fetters.
Break free, and what has bound you will be broken.
Save yourselves so that the spiritual part of you
may be saved.
—*Sermon of Zostrianos*[*]

T hrough the bus window, Seth watched the streets of downtown San Jose pass before him. He didn't mind time on the bus. It was good thinking time. He had the back of the bus to himself, so he was alone with his thoughts. He was still smarting from this morning's catastrophe—at least that was how it felt. *I let myself get too puffed up,* he thought. *I thought I was some kind of superspy who was going to totally nail it for the*

---

[*] The Sermon of Zostrianos: Nag Hammadi Codex VIII, 1; translated by Marvin Meyer, published in *The Gnostic Bible* (Boston, MA: Shambhala Publications, 2009).

cause...and I completely fucked it up. He felt a surge of shame. It was a familiar feeling.

His cell phone vibrated. He pulled it out of his vest pocket and frowned at the junk mail text. Then he navigated to the group text message Mr. Basil had sent out earlier that afternoon: "Fourth seal tonight, initiates."

So much seemed unreal now. He felt like things were slipping away from him. He hadn't missed any work yet, but he knew his head was not in the game when he was there. More and more the Lodge was becoming the center of his universe. He wasn't sure whether that was a good thing. Angie was certainly clear on that issue. His heart sank as he thought of her. She had been his best friend for years, and it seemed impossible that something could come between them. After all, how much of her bullshit had he put up with? And she couldn't just give him this one thing? He ground his teeth at the thought of it.

And not only had he lost Angie, he had lost Kush and Becky, too. The body count was piling up. *How can I really believe that none of it is my fault?* Seth wondered. He began to wonder if he actually did believe that.

The bus pulled over at his stop and he got up. He swung down the steps and almost sprinted toward the Lodge. He ascended the porch steps and the door swung open before he could even knock. "Knew it was you," Nazz said, wearing a leopard-print vest.

"How did you know it was me?" Seth asked.

Nazz didn't answer that. Instead, he said, "You're almost late."

"'Almost late' means 'on time,'" Seth snapped. He was tense, he realized, and it was making him snippy. He forced himself to relax and wondered if he needed to ask Dr. Teasdale for a larger dose of his medication.

"Pops taught me that if you're not ten minutes early, you're late," Nazz said. Seth assumed he was referring to Mr. Basil, and he couldn't believe anyone would refer to the esteemed man as

"Pops." But Nazz was his son, so he assumed there was a lot of unseen baggage in that relationship. There always was.

"You know the way," Nazz said, heading back upstairs.

"Am I the last one?" Seth asked.

"By my count."

Seth nodded and made his way to the dining room. Pushing open one of the double doors, he saw a familiar sight—Jude, Lynn, Mika, Musa, Matt, and Maria were already seated in the circle, talking amiably. Jude waved at him, breaking out into a large smile. Seth saw something out of the ordinary in his peripheral vision and glanced toward the windows. A table was spread with a large assortment of items—crystal vases, stacks of magazines, books, toys, figurines, and much more. It looked like an over-stuffed table at a yard sale. After one more glance at the table, Seth took one of the two empty chairs.

Matt and Maria were in the middle of what seemed like an intense discussion, so they didn't acknowledge him at first, but Musa gave him a nod and Lynn squirmed in her seat in mock-excitement at the sight of him. "How are you?" she asked.

"Hanging in there," he said. It wasn't much of an answer, but it had the benefit of being both vague and true. "You?"

"I'm just so jazzed about the next seal," she said, squirming again. She vibrated her head which somehow made her seem even more birdlike.

Seth heard a door open and looked toward the sound. Dr. Robinson entered, in matching vest and tie. He closed the door behind him and strode toward the circle of initiates. From one hand hung a black cauldron, and in the other were a long-nosed barbecue lighter and what looked like a miniature baseball bat. He moved toward his chair, and stepping past it, placed the cauldron on the floor in the middle of the circle. He placed the small bat and the lighter into it and settled back into his own seat.

"Let us take a moment to align ourselves with the Real," he

said, closing his eyes. Seth did the same. Dr. Robinson's voice was gentle but powerful. "Feel outward, into space. Feel your way past the archons, out until you meet her. Let her enfold you, embrace you, caress you."

Seth did as instructed. He imagined himself soaring beyond the clouds, toward the stars, beyond any satellites or spiritual powers...and then he saw her. She was before him as certainly as Lynn was, across the circle. It was not like a fantasy or a dream. There was a reality to it that unsettled him. But although her body, ghostly as it was, was in sharp focus, her face was still blurry. She reached out for him with open arms. He sank into them, and felt them close around his neck, his back. He nuzzled into her soft, warm bosoms. It did not seem awkward or odd or erotic in the slightest. It felt maternal, in a safe way Seth had never experienced. It occurred to him that being held by her was healing something deep within him, something he could not articulate. He sank into her and felt himself utterly held. He sighed and felt his throat start to swell with emotion.

When Dr. Robinson recalled them into the room, he wiped his eyes on the back of his hand. He hoped no one noticed, but when he looked up at Dr. Robinson, he found the older man staring straight at him, a confused look on his face. Seth sniffed and turned his attention to the cauldron in the middle of the circle.

Dr. Robinson cleared his throat. "Tonight, initiates, you will be introduced to the fourth mystery, a seal of great power. This is the seal our gnostic forefathers called 'Redemption,' but I like to call it the mystery of liberation." Seth's eyebrows rose. Liberation sounded good. Dr. Robinson continued. "Look back over your life, and at all the various aspects of your life now. What is it you need —or have needed—to be liberated from? Take a moment to think about it."

Seth looked around the circle and saw his fellow initiates with furrowed brows, interiorly studying their lives. Seth looked down at his feet and forced himself to do the same. He felt the resistance and recognized it. With effort, he pushed past it.

He had felt liberated when he had moved out of his parents' home. He loved his father and missed him, but had to admit he'd felt liberated when he had died, for there was one less set of eyes looking at him with judgment. He'd even felt liberated when he took the plunge and cupped Dr. Robinson's testicles. He shuddered at the thought, and it occurred to him how surreal it was to now be sitting under the doctor's tutelage. *And what do I need to be liberated from now?* the voice in his head wondered. His mind flashed on Angie and her nagging and interfering, but there wasn't really enough energy around it. It was an irritation, not bondage. Next he thought of Becky and how he wanted to be liberated from her expectations. They weren't technically together now, but he only felt half free for some reason that he couldn't quite parse. But again, there wasn't much energy there. He thought about work, about the grinding poverty he lived with day in and day out, trying to live in the Bay Area on minimum wage. There was energy there. He felt the resentment and the bitterness and the anger and the helplessness rise up within him. He thought for a moment he'd found the thing, but then his mind flashed on the dream he'd had on the morning of the parade: the beast pursuing him through the aisles of his parents' church, slathering jaws snapping at his heels.

"All right, please open your eyes if you have closed them, and share with us what you need to be liberated from."

"The patriarchy," Maria said. Dr. Robinson nodded and waited.

"Racism," Mika said.

"Well, before I found this group, I would have said environmental catastrophe," Musa said.

"And now?" Dr. Robinson asked.

There was an odd look in Musa's eyes that Seth couldn't read.

Distrust, perhaps, or contempt. "And now I think it must be gaslighting."

Seth saw Dr. Robinson roll his eyes and sigh. "Any others? Matt?"

Seth looked over at Matt. The young man was staring at his shoes. "I'm an addict. I don't care what it is—alcohol, NyQuil, kava kava, weed, passionflower, mushrooms, coffee, kratom, cough syrup, salvia divinorum, dagga weed—hell, I'll even lick the poison off an amazonian toad if it'll get me high. Anything to make me feel...different from how I feel when I'm...normal."

Dr. Robinson nodded, and it seemed to Seth that there was real compassion in his eyes. He turned to Lynn. "Ms. Shire?"

With uncharacteristic bitterness, Lynn said, "From propaganda, that constant barrage of spin we get in the media."

"Seth?"

All eyes turned to him. He cleared his throat. "From the god my parents gave me."

A cold silence descended over them. Seth felt uncomfortable and looked up at Dr. Robinson. Had he said something wrong?

But the doctor was nodding gravely. "Thank you. Thank you all. You are all familiar, then, with bondage of one sort or another. Allow me now to put these...oppressions...into a larger, more cosmic context. As you were told at your second seal, Samael the demiurge has created a prison planet. He has surrounded it with his evil angels, the archons." He looked at Seth. "This is the god your parents gave you, my boy." Seth felt a chill run from the top of his head down to his calves. He shuddered involuntarily. Dr. Robinson continued. "Samael's intention is to keep us all captive, to..." he looked at Musa now, "...to gaslight us into thinking that he is good and that he only wants the best for us." Seth looked at Musa and saw the grave man nod almost imperceptibly. "It is he who controls the media," Dr. Robinson looked at Lynn. Next he looked at Maria and then Mika.

"And among the evils he and his archons propagate are sexism, racism, homophobia, hatred and prejudice of every variety. They are the source, the fountainhead of all that is evil and corrupt. They are the authors of suffering."

He paused and let that sink in. Then he pulled several sheets of paper from his vest pocket and unfolded them. "I have here a bit of scripture—the ninth logion from the Gospel of Philip. Can someone volunteer to read it?"

Musa Daniels put his hand out, and Dr. Robinson passed one of the sheets to him. Musa cleared his throat and read in a dignified, sonorous voice, "The archons wanted to deceive humankind because they saw that we were related to goodness. They took the name of 'goodness' and applied it to those who were not good, so that by means of names they might deceive people and keep them mired in evil. And then, as if doing us a favor, they referred to good people as evil! They knew what they were about: they wanted to take free people and make them into slaves forever."

Dr. Robinson nodded gravely. "Thank you, Mr. Daniels. Redemption is the seal that liberates us from Samael's control. It doesn't matter what we believe—doctrine is quite beside the point for gnostics. We cannot let the powers that are above us vanquish us. Instead, we must vanquish them. We do this by freeing ourselves of their power over us. We refuse to be conquered, and we conquer the authorities by soaring outside their very narrow sphere of influence. But we do not do this by might of arms, or by treachery, or by coercion of any kind. We do this work internally. It is only in our own minds that we are prisoners. It is only because we believe the lies that we are in any way subservient. This work is accomplished by the gift of wisdom, of knowing who we really are, whence we come, to whom we actually belong, why we are here, and where we are going. This knowing is both intellectual and spiritual. It is both acquired and bestowed. It is something we do—in this sacrament, this mystery.

But it is also something that is done in us...something that *she* does in us."

Seth saw several nods around the circle. *We're getting the hang of this,* he thought. Dr. Robinson held aloft another sheet of paper. "Would someone be so kind as to read logion sixty-eight of Philip's gospel?"

Maria held her hand up. Dr. Robinson handed the paper around the circle to her. She sniffed, straightened her spine, and began. "There were three places of offering in Jerusalem: the one that opened to the west was called, 'the holy'; the one that opened to the south was called, 'the holy of the holy'; the third, which opens to the east, was called, 'the holy of holies' where the high priest entered alone. Baptism is like 'the holy' place, Redemption is like 'the holy of the holy' place."

"Thank you, Miss Shire. Now—"

"So what happened to the second and third seal?" Lynn interrupted.

"I'm sorry?" Dr. Robinson asked, cocking his head.

She studied the paper. "The scripture said that Baptism was like the holy place, and Redemption is like the holy of the holy place. So what about Chrism and Eucharist, the second and third seals? And what seal is the holy of holies?"

"Ah...I understand now. I believe the author is trying to give us a sense of just how important these particular seals are. This is not to disparage those not mentioned. It is an analogy, a metaphor."

"You can only sail a metaphor until the wheels come off," Matt interjected.

That elicited a chuckle from Dr. Robinson. "Quite. As for the holy of the holies, I'm afraid that is a seal yet to come."

That seemed to satisfy Lynn. Dr. Robinson sat up straighter in his chair and said, "In your first seal, we told you a third of the truth, and you were set free, but only in part. In your second seal, we told you another third of the truth, and you gained yet more freedom. This night I will tell you the whole of the truth, and you will be set free indeed." He held up the final piece of paper. "Do I have a volunteer for another logion? One hundred and four, this time."

Seth reached out for the paper, and Dr. Robinson handed it to him. Seth's eyebrows rose. It *was* long. He swallowed and started in. "As long as their inward parts are hidden, most things in this world live and are preserved. If those parts become visible, they usually die, as in the case of a man whose guts are exposed. As long as his guts are hidden, he lives. If they are exposed, or pulled out of him, he dies. It is the same with a tree: as long as its root is hidden it will flower and thrive. But if its roots are exposed, it withers. This is how it is with anything born in the System, not just concerning the things that are revealed, but regarding those things that are hidden as well. For as long as the root of evil is hidden, it is strong. But if it is noticed, it is destroyed. If it is revealed it will perish. That is why the Word says, 'Already the axe strikes the roots of the trees!' It will not just cut it down—whatever is merely cut will grow up again. Instead, the axe goes down into the ground until the root is dug up. In this way Jesus tore out all of the roots of this place, whereas others had only partially succeeded. Let each of us dig up the root of evil in our own hearts, and tear it out. It can be dug up if we recognize it. But if we do not see it, it takes root deep in our hearts and brings forth its fruit in us. It becomes our master, and we are its slaves. It seeks to imprison us and forces us to do things we don't want to do, and prevents us from doing those things we know we should. It is only strong until we recognize it. Only when it is hidden does it drive us. Ignorance is the mother of all evil, and is dependent on confusion. Those who have sprung up from ignorance are not real, never were, and never will be. Yet real people will be made whole when the whole truth is revealed. In a way, truth is like ignorance:

So long as it is hidden it rests in itself, but when it is revealed, people recognize it. They honor its power over ignorance and confusion, and it sets them free. As the Word says, 'You shall know the truth and the truth will make you free.'* Ignorance results in slavery, but knowledge makes us free. If we know the truth, we will find its fruits growing in our hearts. If we join with it, we will be made whole."

"Thank you, Mr. St. John," Dr. Robinson gave him a shallow bow. He pointed to the cauldron. "Behold the instrument of your liberation, initiates."

"A cooking pot?" Matt asked.

"A crucible," Dr. Robinson responded.

"Explain," Matt said. It was more of a command than a request, making Seth feel uneasy.

"Of course. Tell me what you have learned about Samael, the demiurge."

Mika looked thoughtful. "He is the creator of this world. And he made the archons. And he's trying to keep us in prison."

"Indeed. But he is not just the maker of this world, but of this whole region of space. The Wholeness in its inscrutable mercy hollowed out a space within itself for duality, for illusion, for Samael to hold sway—but only for an appointed time."

"Why?" Lynn asked.

"That we do not know." Dr. Robinson's response was both quick and unguarded.

"So he isn't just the god of the earth, but of, like, the galaxy?" Lynn repeated what she had heard.

"Just so," Dr. Robinson said. Seth nodded, and saw others doing so as well. His heart raced and he felt a cold chill, anticipating the new revelation. "We are speeding toward him even now," Dr. Robinson concluded.

---

* John 8:32

Seth heard a gasp from someone in the group. Lynn said, "Is that why we're on the *Cibus Dei*? We're going toward the demiurge?"

"Yes."

"Why?" she asked. "Don't we want to escape him?"

"Why yes, we do. But that is because we are gnostics. Those out there," he waved toward the window, "they don't know anything of what is really happening around them. They are ignorant, and their ignorance is their prison. It is the powers—the archons and those who knowingly serve them—that put us on this ship, and steer us on our course."

"But why?" Maria asked.

"Philip tells us in his forty-third logion," Dr. Robinson said. "God eats people, so people are sacrificed to him. Before humans were sacrificed, they used animals, but there was nothing divine about those they sacrificed to."

Seth blinked. "What does that mean?"

He saw Musa's eyes grow large. "*Cibus dei*," he said. "The food of god."

Dr. Robinson closed his eyes and nodded his head slowly.

"Oh my god," Musa said, his face a mask of horror.

"What?" Jude asked, looking from one initiate to another. "What am I missing?" Seth wondered the same thing.

Musa looked at Jude. "We are the offering. We are the sacrifice. This ship, and everyone on it, will be eaten by the demiurge." He looked at Dr. Robinson. "Am I not right?"

Dr. Robinson nodded again, this time with his eyes open. "That is the truth of it. We are speeding toward our doom at very nearly the speed of light. And we are almost there. And when we arrive, Samael will open his jaws and consume us entire. It will slake his thirst for blood and will keep him sated for eons."

"But why?" asked Jude.

"Because he is hungry. And because the powers on earth want

to live. It has always been thus with the demiurge. People sacrificed their enemies, they sacrificed their spotless lambs, all so that Samael might be sated and not consume *them*. They gave this monstrous god an offering in exchange for their own lives."

"But they have no right to sacrifice us!" Lynn objected.

"Tell that to all the lambs, to all the doves, to all the goats whose lives were stolen from them on altars all over the earth throughout countless ages. They did not consent. Their lives were captive, and then they were stolen, and the demiurge feasted upon their blood. And their blood bought time for those who held the knife."

"That's horrible," Seth said.

"It is indeed," Dr. Robinson agreed. "But sacrifices are fewer and fewer and the demiurge grows weak. So we have been sent—this ship a spotless lamb, an innocent victim—to redeem the lives of many."

Seth felt his guts rumble. He felt impossibly cold. He wondered if he were going to be sick.

"I don't know if I believe this," Matt confessed.

"We have to stop it," Jude said.

Dr. Robinson turned toward him. "My dear Mr. Ash, what do you think we are doing here?"

Seth's nausea passed and he felt a hope welling up within him. "That's why I'm being trained to do reconnaissance," he said. "We're mapping the spaceship so that we can...stop them before we reach the demiurge."

"That's right. You have all been given assignments, and each and every one of them is essential to our mission. We are the resistance. We alone stand against the archons. We alone seek to liberate humankind and all that we love from the tyranny of these cosmic powers arrayed against us. If we are ever to be free, it will be up to us. To all of us. To you."

Seth felt a wave of shame roll through him for not taking his training more seriously. He hated himself for his pettiness, his self-pity. It had felt like a game. And now it...didn't. He longed to get back to it, to do better, to master it. Indeed, it seemed that nothing else mattered.

"But first," Dr. Robinson said, "before you can liberate anyone else, you must free yourselves. You must become free of the power of the archons in your own little lives."

The words *your own little lives* echoed in Seth's head. It felt like an insult at first, but he realized just how true it was. They were confronted with cosmic evil. His own life was small. It was inconsequential, pathetic even. He realized in that moment how very little his own life mattered. *I'll be a sacrifice, all right, but not to the demiurge,* he thought. *I'll do it for the world...for life.*

"And how do we do that?" Matt asked.

Once more Dr. Robinson pointed at the cauldron. "You will burn your ties to them."

"What kind of psychodrama shit is this?" Matt asked.

"I would caution you to guard your tongue, Mr. Townes," Dr. Robinson said, his voice suddenly icy. "This is not a psychological trick. This is a sacrament, the fourth great seal. As the Neoplatonists have so ably explained, a symbol participates in the thing symbolized. What you do to the symbol, you do to the reality. You aren't just changing something in your mind, you are changing it in reality with a capital 'R'—the spiritual reality, the only reality that is *not* illusion."

Matt crossed his arms and narrowed his eyes. Seth had not heard such an explanation before, but something in his soul leaped at the truth of it. Dr. Robinson rose and walked toward the windows. He gestured toward the large table, laden with odds and ends. "I ask you now to peruse the items we have assembled here. You'll find religious symbols, books, statues, and a wide assortment of magazines. Take some time to pour over them, and pray for our Holy Mother Sophia to guide you. Look for an item that represents the power that the demiurge holds over you. Look for a symbol of your oppression. If you don't find it among the items collected here, find an image from one of the magazines. There is a box under the table with construction paper, scissors, and glue sticks if you would prefer to make a collage—"

"What is this, kindergarten?" Matt snapped.

"Far from it," Dr. Robinson said, with obvious annoyance. "This is the second most sacred rite in our tradition. I ask that you respect it. I did not instruct you to make a collage, Mr. Townes. I only said that you may." He turned his attention back to the group. "Take as long as you need. This is holy work. If you find your object or image straightaway, I invite you to meditate on it, on the ways you have been dominated and controlled and wounded by Samael and his archons. This is not abstract, my friends. This tyranny is personal. This is the night we acknowledge that this is not simply a myth we are working with like some Jungian analyst. This is the night when you make yourselves free women and men—truly free, for the first time in your lives."

Seth felt a chill melt from his shoulders down to his hips, a chill that made him shudder. He nodded. He understood the gravity of it. It felt deeply, profoundly, dangerously right. Dr. Robinson waved toward the table again. "Please," he said.

Hesitantly, they all got up and moved toward the table. It did indeed feel like a yard sale, Seth mused, as they stood shoulder to shoulder and poured over the contents. Seth was first drawn to the statues—Shiva dancing in a hoop of flame, about the size of his fist; a pottery Star of David, fired a brilliant blue color; a crucifix; a terracotta goddess figure, sporting a bulging belly but no eyes; and many more that he didn't recognize. He picked up a brass statue of a dog, a Boxer, posed to look both regal and strong. His heart instantly leaped, and he suddenly remembered the musty smell of Kush's fur. His heart hurt, and he pressed on his chest.

He glanced over and saw Maria already looking through the magazines. Lynn was holding up a Barbie, stroking its hair with a faraway look in her eyes. Musa and Matt just glared at the table, not touching anything. Seth moved to the right and found a pile of medals and medallions—some military, some Masonic, some from law enforcement, some from various recovery groups. He sorted through them, but nothing called out to him. He remembered to connect with Sophia and closed his eyes. Once more he saw himself floating in space and felt a deep calm descend on him. Then she floated into view, a ghostly blur that nevertheless filled him with peace.

As the warmth of his connection with her flooded his heart, he opened his eyes again. He moved next to the books. There were two large stacks, the taller one leaning precariously. He tried to straighten it, but almost ended up toppling it. When it finally came to rest—still listing—he turned his head sideways and began to read the spines. *The Koran, The Bhagavad Gita,* Marx's *The Communist Manifesto,* Kierkegaard's *Fear and Trembling,* Camus' *The Stranger,* a collection of Buddhist sutras, Elie Wiesel's *Night,* Jung's *Memories, Dreams, and Reflections,* Calvin's *Institutes,* C.S. Lewis' *The Lion, the Witch, and the Wardrobe,* the AA *Big Book,* Dr. Spock's *Baby and Child Care,* and at the very bottom, a black leather-bound Bible—the Revised Standard Version with concordance.

Seth felt like he'd been punched in the gut. Dr. Robinson said he'd know it when he found it, and he had no doubt. Carefully, he snatched the books four and five at a time from the leaning stack and made a new stack on the floor until he reached the bottom. He picked up the Bible, put it at his feet, and replaced the books, evenly distributing them to both stacks this time, so that neither looked likely to topple. Then he picked up the Bible and studied it. It was old—its leather cracked and the black worn off in places. The gilt lettering was still readable on the cover and spine, however. There was a zipper starting at the top of the spine and running around the edges to the spine's bottom, but some of the black fabric had pulled loose from the covers. Carefully, he unzipped it, and opened it at random. *Serve the Lord with fear, with trembling kiss his feet, lest he be angry, and you perish in the way; for his wrath is quickly kindled,* he read. "This is the book of the Monster God," he whispered.

"What was that?" Maria asked.

"Oh...nothing. I think I found mine." Closing the Bible, he wandered back over to his seat. His hands were shaking, and he realized he was about to do something his childhood church would consider deeply heretical, perhaps even apostatizing. *Well, okay,* he reasoned. *I am an apostate, aren't I?* When he was a child, to call someone an apostate was almost as bad as calling them a communist or a homosexual. He considered embracing the term, claiming it for himself. "I am an apostate," said out loud.

"Who told you that?" Dr. Robinson was leaning back in his chair like a fifth grader, so much so that Seth wondered how badly the rotund man would be hurt if he toppled over backward. But he didn't fall. He did smile, however, and it was the first time Seth could remember Dr. Robinson showing any warmth toward him. He wasn't sure he liked it.

"Who told me...that I was an apostate?"

"Yes," he said.

"My church...when I was growing up."

"And are you?"

"Well, I think my church was worshipping the demiurge, so... yes, I'm an apostate from the religion that had me fooled back then."

Seth had a hard time reading Dr. Robinson's eyes. He seemed to be seeing something that Seth could not. "What did you find?" he asked.

Seth held up the Bible. "Revised Standard Version. It was the translation we used most at our church when I was a kid."

"Not the King James?"

"Some of the older people used the King James," Seth conceded. "But newer translations like *The Living Bible* were frowned on. Everyone could agree on the RSV." Seth realized as he said it that it rhymed. He shared a smile with Dr. Robinson, another moment that felt both strange and unprecedented.

"It is a good choice," Dr. Robinson said. "It will be powerful."

Seth nodded. "I'm getting that."

"What does she have to say?" the older man asked.

"She winked at me," Seth said.

Dr. Robinson's eyebrows shot up. "Did she, now?"

Seth smiled again, but inside he felt sad. He felt like he had during his break-up with Becky. There was the same feeling of dread as well. He wondered at that.

"You might ask her about it, just to be sure," Dr. Robinson suggested, "while the others are still choosing."

Seth nodded his assent and closed his eyes, unconsciously clutching the Bible to his breast. He imagined himself once more floating in space. For a second he wondered if he would ever meet her anywhere else, but he forced himself to focus. *Don't mess with what works,* the voice in his head told him.

For several moments he seemed to be alone, hanging like a piece of detritus against a brilliant sea of stars. Then she floated into view. She wore a flowing dress with trailing sleeves that made her seem vaguely gypsylike, but once again her face was a blur. He felt himself swoon from a rush of emotions he could not identify. *Hello, my love,* her blurry lips said. He heard the voice in his head.

Hello, Seth thought back. Her smile told him she had received his message. He held the Bible out to her. She looked down at it, and when she looked back up, her eyes were sad. She nodded. *My* son is a bully, and his followers use his book like a club. *I'm sorry you've been hurt.*

Thank you, Seth thought. *It's okay.*

No, it isn't, she countered. *There is nothing okay about what has happened to you...or what is happening to you...all of you.*

Seth did not dispute this. *Is it all true?* he asked. *I mean, everything Dr. Robinson has been saying?*

She cocked her blurry head, a motion that Seth took for pity. She nodded gravely. *It is as true as your cultural and linguistic metaphors can convey. The way Joshua words things is not how I would word them, but they are not much less accurate for all of that. It is true enough.*

Seth nodded. He wasn't sure he understood exactly what she meant, though. *So is your son—he's the demiurge?*

Yes. Samael. He is the blind god. As she said it, she looked even sadder.

And our ship...the Cibus Dei*...we're being offered as a sacrifice to him, so that he won't...I don't know...hurt the people on earth?*

Yes, she confirmed. *All of this is true. Your blood is being offered to slake his thirst. It will buy time for the children of Eve, just as the sacrifices to Moloch did in ancient times.*

Moloch? Seth asked.

Another of his names, she explained. *Samael, Moloch, Ialdabaoth, Saklas, Nebro, Satan, Ahriman...every people has its own name for him.* She looked down toward his feet. *He is my shame.*

It's not your fault, Seth said, although he had no idea if that was actually true or not. *It can't be,* he added hastily.

But it is, my love, she said. *The Fullness permits it, but it was my own...stubbornness...that set everything into motion.*

Could the Fullness stop it? Seth asked.

Of course, she said.

So isn't it the fault of the Fullness? Seth wondered. *I mean, doesn't it share in some of the responsibility?*

It permits it for a time, she said cryptically. *But soon duality will run its course, and all things shall share once more in the Fullness. You must learn to live in that time...and this, both at once.*

How do I do that? he asked.

You are already learning, she said, her voice soft with compassion. *You must be fearless, because my son's days are numbered. He cannot win in the end. All will see through his illusion in time. You must not let him scare you any longer. You call him the Monster God, and so he is. But you can also pull his fangs out if you are brave...if you do not give in to fear.*

Do you know *me?* Seth pleaded. *I'm scared all the time. Fear is my middle name. I have an anxiety disorder.*

That is why you must have courage. You must feel the fear...and prevail just the same.

But I'm...I'm nobody, Seth protested.

Not true, Sophia countered. *You are* mine.

A disembodied voice broke into the conversation. "Mr. St. John?"

Seth's eyes snapped open. All of the initiates were back in their seats. Seth wondered how long he had been talking with the Holy Mother. He decided it didn't matter.

"Sleep on your own time," Matt snapped.

Seth opened his mouth to protest, but Dr. Robinson held up his hand. Seth frowned but kept silent.

Dr. Robinson rose, moved the cauldron from the center of the circle, and strode to the small table they often used for an altar. "Give me a hand with this, will you, Jude?"

Jude leaped up and together they lifted it over Jude's chair, setting it in the middle of the circle. Then Dr. Robinson waved Jude toward his seat again, and put the cauldron on the table. Reaching down, he took up the long-nosed grill lighter, dipped the tip of it into the cauldron, and pulled the trigger. It clicked and a spark leaped into the air. There must have been some kind of oil or accelerant in the cauldron, because fire instantly shot up toward the ceiling. Seth involuntarily jerked back, and he saw Musa almost topple over in his chair. Seth laughed, but quickly stifled it. He realized it must be a reaction to the stress, but it still seemed inappropriate.

Soon the fire settled, forming a much smaller but consistent blaze. Dr. Robinson stood as close to the flames as he dared. He raised his hands toward the ceiling, and began to intone in a loud voice: "You are what you are, you are who you are!" He turned his face to the ceiling and paused, as if waiting for some secret communion to be consummated. Then he continued. "Your great name rests upon me, O uncreated, you who are whole, you who are within me and all around me. You who are visible to everyone, and I see you. Now that I know you, I am mingled with the unchanging. I am armed with the armor of light; I have become light! The Mother tends to us because of the splendid beauty of grace. Therefore, I have stretched out my hands. You have placed the circle, the image of wholeness, within my breast, the shape of the aeons in light, which no darkness can touch. I shall declare your glory truly, for I have known you."

Then Dr. Robinson closed his eyes and sang, "*Sou ies ide aeio ois*. O aeon, aeon, God of silence!" Speaking again, he said, "With all that I am I honor you. You are my place of rest, O Son *es es o e*, the one without form, who raises up we mere humans and purifies us into your own life, according to your eternal name. The incense of life is in me, and I offer it up for the peace of the saints."* With this, Dr. Robinson tossed something into the fire. Seth couldn't see what it was, but immediately thick smoke with a delicious, pungent aroma began to rise from the cauldron and fill the room.

---

* "Gospel of the Egyptians," from *Suppressed Prayers* (Harrisburg, PA: Trinity Press International, 1998), p. 97.

Robinson looked at each of them in the circle, pausing to make eye contact, and for the first time Seth felt some kind of kinship, some connection with the catechist. "My spiritual children," he said, now speaking to them. "Much has been revealed to you, and much more is yet to be uncovered. Everything will be revealed, not for your sake alone, but for the sake of all humankind. Increase your faith, and the faith of others will increase as well. Without her, you have no hope against the powers, the archons. But their power can be broken. Once their power over you is severed, she will be able to intercede for you. She will reproof the archons, so that you cannot be seized. If they try to seize you, she will overpower each of them. Remember the things I have spoken, and let all that holds you in bondage be food for the fire."

He gestured toward the flaming cauldron. "Please tell us about the item you have chosen. Make a conscious connection for us between it and the power the demiurge has over you, and then destroy it. This is the fourth seal, whereupon you become, for the first time in your lives, truly *free* women and men."

Without any further hesitation, Lynn stepped forward. In her hands she held what looked like a black-and-white ad from a 1950s magazine. She held it up and showed it around the circle. It depicted a father sitting in a reclining chair. A woman with perfectly coiffed hair bent near him, handing him a pipe. A young boy was running from behind with a pair of slippers, and a slightly older daughter stood at the ready with a newspaper. The headline read, "A Man is King of His Own Castle."

Lynn turned it so she could see it again, and a look of distaste soured her face. "This represents the patriarchy—the power that men assume for themselves over women solely because they have penises. The demiurge calls himself 'Father,' and everything about his religions perpetuates sexist injustice—all of them." She threw it into the fire, and it was quickly consumed.

Musa stepped forward next. He held up a familiar Sunday

School picture of Jesus. He had blue eyes and feathered brown hair, like a 1980s fashion model. Musa sneered at it. "When you worship this image, you worship whiteness. The real Jesus was dark, a Palestinian. For me, this reveals how white people have deified themselves, have made themselves out to be gods, a most unholy apotheosis."

Seth didn't know what "apotheosis" meant, but he felt profoundly uncomfortable just the same. Musa threw the picture on the fire. The wooden frame took a few moments to catch, but soon the fire had leaped up a couple of inches, and Seth heard a satisfying crack come from the cauldron.

Maria stepped up next. She held up what looked like a grandfather clock made for a dollhouse. Seth leaned in and saw that its hands were painted on, making it permanently four o'clock. "I've worked in corporate America for twenty years now. A couple of years ago, I got sick. Everyone told me I was crazy...but I wasn't crazy. I literally could not get out of bed for days at a time. Eventually I realized that I had allowed myself to buy into a system that demanded more and more work in less and less time. I drove myself so hard that I...collapsed. Which means, as far as the System is concerned, I'm a person without value now, because I refuse to drive myself into the ground. I choose spaciousness. I choose naps. I choose silence. I choose listening to my body. I choose health and healing."

"What is the sign of the Fullness in you?" Dr. Robinson asked her.

"Movement and rest," she said. Seth felt goosebumps sprout up on his forearms.

She placed the tiny clock into the cauldron, turned, and returned to her seat.

Matt stood and stepped up to the fire. In his hand was a belt. "My father beat me until I was sixteen. That was when I finally hit him back. But when I was growing up, a week didn't go by that he didn't hit me." He pointed to his right clavicle. "He broke that when I was four." He pointed to his left forearm. "He broke that when I was six." He pulled his hair back from his forehead to reveal a scar. "He did that when I was ten. Fifteen stitches." He pointed to his back. "I only have the right kidney. The other one..." Seth looked up to see Matt's eyes brimming. Matt, the tough guy, was on the verge of breaking down. He sniffed and mastered himself. "I know I'm an asshole sometimes. I'm sorry. I just...I don't trust people in authority. People who presume...to know what's good for me, I guess. Fuck them, right?" He threw the belt onto the fire. "I choose to not be afraid of assholes anymore. Ever. And that includes archons."

Seth saw Dr. Robinson smile slightly and nod his assent.

Jude stepped forward next. In his hands was a flag of the Republic of California, sporting a brown bear chasing a red star. "I'm tired of our government lying to us. I mean, they lied to us about being on earth, right? Didn't we deserve to know that we were on a starship? I think so. I'm tired of stolen elections and crooked politicians and spin doctors and everyone else stuck in the swamp." He threw the flag onto the flame. It must have been made of nylon, because it melted rather than burned. Seth recoiled at the smell.

Dr. Robinson must have noticed, because he sprinkled more incense into the cauldron, which didn't actually help. It just made the air thicker and harder to breathe.

Nevertheless, Seth stepped up to the cauldron. "For the first twenty years of my life, I served the demiurge. I worshipped him. I obeyed him." He held up the Bible. "I believed this. Not anymore." Unzipping the Bible, he opened it and tore the first few pages from it. He tossed them into the fire. Then he tore a few more. Then a few more.

He didn't know how long it took, but page by page he dismantled the entire book while the others looked on with respectful silence. Finally, left only with the spine and the zipper attached at both ends, he threw that into the cauldron as well. He didn't know what he expected. When he was a child, he had heard a story about a woman in his church burning a Ouija board because the pastor said it was demonic. When she put it on the fire, she said she heard it scream. He half expected the Bible to scream as he fed it to the flames. But if there was any screaming, it was only in his head. He stepped back to his seat.

Dr. Robinson took a deep breath and said, "Be strong, daughters and sons of the Fullness, for the archons, who are your enemies, have made war against you, but you have prevailed over them. You endured, and you destroyed the power your enemies have over you. Death will tremble and be angry, not only he himself, but also his fellow world-ruling archons. But she shall appear for a reproof to the archons. And she shall reveal to them that you cannot be seized. If they clutch at you, then she will overpower each of them. Remember the things I have spoken and let them go up before you."

PART III: THE BOOK OF SALVATION

Awake, brethren, you chosen ones,
on this day of the salvation of souls...
When the time for the perfection of the Son of Man
had come, all the demons knew it.
And the lord of the sinful doctrine...
covered himself in deceit.
And the demons took counsel with each other.
The twelve thrones above were disturbed.
Poison flowed down on the lower creation,
upon the sons, and the chalice of death
was prepared for him.
—Manichean Crucifixion Hymn*

Then the apostles worshiped again saying,
"Lord, tell us: In what way shall we fight
against the archons, since the archons are above us?"

---

* http://www.gnosis.org/library/crucihymn.htm

Then a voice called out to them
from the appearance saying,
"Now you will fight against them in this way,
for the archons are fighting against the inner man.
And you are to fight against them in this way:
Come together and teach in the world
the salvation with a promise.
And you, gird yourselves with the power of my Father,
and let your prayer be known.
And he, the Father, will help you
as he has helped you by sending me.
Be not afraid, I am with you forever,
as I previously said to you when I was in the body."
Then there came lightning and thunder from heaven,
and what appeared to them in that place
was taken up to heaven.
—The Letter of Peter to Philip[*]

---

[*] Letter of Peter to Philip: Nag Hammadi Codex VIII, Translation by Frederik Wisse, edited by John H. Sieber, published in *The Coptic Gnostic Library* (Leiden: Brill, 1991).

WHAT IS MYSTICISM?

Mysticism, derived from the Greek word "mystikos," meaning "hidden" or "secret," is a broad concept that encompasses various spiritual practices, beliefs, and experiences across different cultures and religions. It refers to the pursuit of direct, personal experiences with the divine or ultimate reality, often involving a deep sense of connection, union, or transcendence beyond ordinary human consciousness.

Characterized by a sense of mystery and awe, mysticism is not limited to any specific religious tradition or dogma. It has been explored and embraced by individuals within Christianity, Islam, Judaism, Hinduism, Buddhism, and other faiths, as well as those who identify as spiritual but not religious. Mystical experiences are deeply personal and subjective, defying easy description or categorization.

Mystics often seek to transcend the limitations of the rational mind and explore the depths of the spiritual realm through practices such as meditation, prayer, contemplation, chanting, and ecstatic rituals. These practices are intended to quiet the mind, open the heart, and cultivate a heightened state of awareness, leading to a direct experience of the divine or a profound sense of unity with all creation.

One common aspect of mysticism is the belief in the existence of a hidden or inner reality that lies beyond the surface-level appearances of the world. Mystics often emphasize the importance of intuitive knowing, inner guidance, and direct experience as opposed to relying solely on intellectual understanding or religious doctrines.

Mystical experiences can range from moments of profound insight and illumination to ecstatic states of bliss, union, or even encounters with the ineffable and transcendent. Such experiences are often described in metaphorical or symbolic language, as they involve encounters with realities that are beyond the ordinary grasp of language and reason.

Throughout history, mystics have played a significant role in shaping the spiritual landscape of humanity. Their teachings and writings have inspired countless individuals to embark on their own spiritual journeys, seeking a deeper understanding of themselves, the world, and the divine.

It is important to note that mysticism is a deeply personal and subjective pursuit, and interpretations of mystical experiences can vary widely. While some view mysticism as a path to personal enlightenment or union with the divine, others see it as a means of gaining insights into the nature of reality or finding meaning and purpose in life.

CHAPTER FOURTEEN

It is not divinity or blessedness or perfection;
rather, it is something unknowable. Not that it has this,
but it is greater than blessedness and divinity and perfection.
It is not perfect, but greater.
It is not infinite or limited by another, but greater.
It is not corporeal and is not incorporeal.
It is not large and it is not small.
It is not quantifiable, not a created thing.
It is not something that exists, which people can understand,
but something greater, which no one can understand.
—*Vision of the Foreigner**

---

* Vision of the Foreigner: Nag Hammadi Codex XI, 3, translated by Marvin Meyer, published in *The Gnostic Bible* (Boston, MA: Shambhala Publications, 2009).

"Hey, dude." Travis carried a box of new releases—hardcovers—into the back room and eased them onto a shelf.

Seth didn't respond. It was that time of the month—returns day. He was ripping the front covers off the books that hadn't sold. After, he'd ship the covers off to the distributor for credit.

Travis sighed and walked over to him. He leaned against the worktable and tried to catch Seth's eye. Seth resisted this, keeping his focus strictly on the paperbacks in front of him.

"Hey, man, I get it. The people you trusted most ganged up on you," Travis said. "I know it doesn't feel like we were trying to help but...we really were."

Seth said nothing. He ripped off another cover and sent the paperback spinning toward one of the boxes on the table.

"And that Angie chick is...well, she's really persuasive, you know? To tell you the truth, I was afraid she'd kick my ass if I didn't go along with it."

That might not be far from the truth, Seth thought. Despite his best efforts, he felt his resolve crumbling. Travis hadn't organized the intervention—Angie had. But it was still a betrayal, and it still stung. Part of his brain told him to grow up and get over it. Another part of his brain told the first part of his brain to go fuck itself.

"Look, I know you're mad at me, and...well, I get it. I really do. I'd probably feel the same way. But we've got to work together here. Plus, we share a dog. And...even if you don't still consider me your friend, I still consider you mine. And I hope you can forgive me some day."

Seth stopped. He looked into Travis' eyes. And then the tears came.

"Hey, little dude. I'm sorry. I didn't mean to make you feel worse." Travis put his hand on Seth's shoulder and gave it a feeble squeeze.

Seth pulled him into a hug and held on tight as the sobs gushed out of him.

"Woah. Okay. Whatever you need, man. I got you."

Travis rocked him back and forth a bit until the sobs subsided. As Seth drew back, Travis said, "You okay, man?"

Seth didn't know. "They gave me a job to do. It was a training, really."

"Wait," Travis said, gently pushing Seth to arm's length to see his eyes. "Who's they?"

"The Lodge. The...gnostic group."

"Uh-huh. They gave you a job..."

"And I was training for it."

"What kind of job?" Travis asked.

"I can't tell you that," Seth said, looking away.

"Okay. Secrecy is part of the bag. I get it. So you were training for a big, secret job."

"Yeah," Seth said. He wiped his nose on the back of his hand. "I...uh...I fucked it up. Big time."

"I'm sorry to hear that, Sethie. I really am. But...you know, that's why you do training. To learn, you know, to practice and shit, to get better."

"I didn't expect to suck this hard at it."

"I wonder if you're being harder on yourself than you need to be."

Seth considered this, and all he could see was Nazz rolling his eyes, feigning patience. He hadn't done any better at his second attempt.

"Wasn't there any part of it that you did good at?" Travis asked.

He had. He'd drawn a flawless map. But he'd timed out both

times. *Not good enough,* the voice in his head told him. "Yeah. Part of it was okay."

"So focus on that. You got more practice sessions coming up?"

"Yeah."

"You'll do a little bit better at every one of them."

"How do you know?" Seth asked.

"Because that's how practice works."

Seth wondered if Travis might be right, but he didn't want to let himself off the hook that easily. He'd fucked up and he needed to suffer. Then he heard a voice in his ear—her voice. "Who told you that?" she asked.

His eyes snapped open.

"Woah, dude. What just happened?" Travis asked.

"I heard her."

"Who?"

Seth looked off to the side, shaking his head slowly. "You...you wouldn't understand."

"Now I'm starting to feel insulted. I think most people wouldn't, you know, but there's a good chance I would."

Seth looked at Travis sideways. *That might be true,* he thought. "Sophia. Holy Wisdom. I heard her voice. Just now."

"Dude! Are you shitting me...or hallucinating...or is it, you know, gnosis?"

Seth knew he wasn't shitting anyone, but he wasn't sure about the other two. "It's not gnosis," he said. "It might be a hallucination...but I don't think so."

"Well, tell her I'm a big fan."

Seth sniffed and one side of his mouth turned up in a smile. "Okay." But then he looked back down. "And I've lost my dog. And my best friend. And my girl."

"I get it, dude. It sucks. But...Becky? She wasn't really your girl, was she? I mean, she's nice and all, but is she your soulmate, dude? I mean, really?"

Seth knew the answer to that. He didn't want to say it out loud, but he knew.

"And as for Angie. Yeah, that sucks. But you get close enough to a bottle rocket like that and you're eventually going to get your fingers burned."

Seth blinked. He wanted to take offense, to object, to say that Travis hadn't earned the right to say something like that. But he knew that his friend was just being square with him. And besides...he also knew he was right. Seth sighed.

"Uh...dude...what are you doing?" Travis picked up the pile of covers Seth had ripped off.

"Returns. It's the Friday before the end of the mon—"

"No, I get that. I mean, what are you *doing*?" He held up one of the covers.

"I don't know what you're—"

"Dude, this book came out last week," Travis said. He started flipping through the covers. "Oh, man. This...this is selling. And this..." He tossed the covers down and shook his head. He looked over at Seth. "Dude. This is not good."

Seth picked up the covers and began to flip through them. An icy wash of terror splashed down his back as he realized what Travis was saying. These were not the return books.

"Did you grab the wrong pile?" Travis asked. "Dude, there's a couple hundred of these." He pointed to the other stacks of covers. "Most of these are new, man."

Seth felt his Adam's apple drop into his bowels. He felt light-headed. "I gotta..." His vision became snowy. Then he went down.

———

Joshua Robinson stepped under the awning of the bus stop and looked around. No one was in earshot. He fished out his cell phone and dialed it. A few moments later, he heard the hiss of static, a couple of clicks, and then a distant voice. "Hello?"

"This is JT," Robinson said.

"Where are you?"

"Outside. It's a safe place."

"Is there anyone around?"

"No one close enough to hear me."

"Anyone watching you?"

"No, not that I can see."

"Report."

Robinson watched a woman walk across the street, following her with his eyes. "Basil seems to have found a pet."

"What do you think?"

"I think he's unremarkable."

"Is he at least intelligent?"

"He's so exceedingly average that I'm having trouble keeping my opinions to myself."

"Does Basil suspect anything?"

"I don't think so. No."

Robinson turned and saw a man looking at him. He stiffened, but the man looked away and began walking.

"Why is he giving this one special attention?"

"He's convinced that she has...singled him out."

"Have you asked her about it?"

"She doesn't talk to me the way she...allegedly talks to him."

"Basil is in his position precisely because he has a facility for that sort of...mystical congress."

"Yes, but I sometimes wonder if his mystical messages conveniently favor his own opinions of things."

"Are you suggesting that he's not accurately reporting her revelations?"

"I'm suggesting that he's suggestible, and that none of us are beyond fooling ourselves."

"Why do you think Basil is so keen on him?" the voice asked.

"Apparently because he's good at organizing books."

"You're joking, surely."

"I wish I were."

There was silence on the other end. The voice gave an inarticulate groan. "You realize that he might see this as betrayal, JT."

"I call 'em as I see 'em," Robinson reported.

"How many seals has he received?"

"Four."

"That's...pretty advanced. How is he coping with them?"

"In class he seems fine. Teasdale has confidence in him for some reason."

"So are you the outlier in your...mistrust?"

"Does that make it any more unwarranted?" Robinson asked.

"It doesn't...unless it does."

"Thank you for the vote of confidence."

"Have you told Basil how you feel?"

"I have. He is unmoved."

"Is it possible you are projecting some antipathy onto him that isn't rightly his?"

"It's always possible," Robinson growled.

"Do you plan to undermine him?"

Robinson didn't answer right away. "Should I?"

"Your confidence in him is that low?"

"I think we can find better."

"Do you have someone in mind?"

"We have another fellow, Musa. Basil is working on him."

"And you have confidence in him?"

"I have *more* confidence in him. He's smart, and he knows his own mind."

"The other does not know his own mind?"

"The other is a reed blown by the wind," Robinson almost

spat.[*]

"What are you asking for, JT? Are you suggesting that we intercede?"

It was Robinson's turn to pause. "I'm not asking for anything. I'm just reporting the facts."

"As you see them."

"Of course. That's what you ask me for, isn't it?"

Silence. Then, the voice cleared its throat. "Very well. Keep me updated."

"Always."

At the sound of the knock, Schenck looked up from the file on his desk. "Yeah?"

Keira opened the door a crack. "Hey, boss. Can I run something past you?"

"You got something on that S-panel breach?"

She opened the door and let herself in. Then she gingerly shut it behind her and sat in one of the two chairs facing the Chief's desk. She leaned forward and whispered, "I don't know."

Schenck leaned over his desk, rocking forward on his elbows. He lowered his own voice to a sandpaper wisp. "Why are we whispering?"

Keira sat back. "No...reason."

"You feeling all right, Sloane?"

"I'm fine, sir."

"Spit it out. I have work to do here."

"The video. I can't stop thinking about it."

"I thought there wasn't enough for a positive ID," Scheck said.

"There isn't, but...the vest won't leave me alone."

---

[*] Matthew 11:7

"It *is* odd, I guess. Especially with jeans."

"I keep watching that one clip, over and over. And...there's something familiar about it."

"Like what?" Schenck raised one eyebrow.

"I can't put my finger on it. But...remember a couple of weeks ago you had me check out a secret society over on Aberdeen?"

"Yeah. That was the CBI tip we got on suspicious activity, right?"

"Right. It turned out to be a harmless religious gathering. Classes on gnosticism."

"Whatever that is," Schenck tossed out. "I'm hearing 'so what?' bounce around in my head. Oh, look, it came out. So what, special agent?"

"So, several of the people there were wearing vests. Not a lot of them, not most of them, but...more than one. I thought it was kind of an eccentric affectation at the time, and the fact that there were a couple of them was just...odd. 'But who knows?' I thought at the time, 'There could be a high preponderance of drama geeks that are drawn to this kind of religion,' you know?" She shrugged. "But maybe it's more than that. Maybe..."

"Maybe someone from that group is responsible?" Schenck asked.

"Yeah. And then there's that nagging familiarity to the way this guy moves...like I've seen it before. But I can't remember where or when."

"Maybe another visit is in order," Schenck suggested.

"That's what I was thinking, but...should I just go to another class, or—"

"This is a murder investigation, Special Agent," Schenck said. "I don't see any reason for pussyfooting around. Get an isolated screen shot of that vest and go to whoever is in charge over there. Ask him if he's seen it before. Then..." He twisted his head. "Special agent, is there any reason why I'm telling you how to do your job?"

"Because I think it makes you feel useful."

Both of Schenck's eyebrows soared.

"Sir," Keira added.

Schenck harrumphed. "Get it done, special agent."

"But sir, don't you think it might spoil whatever element of surprise we have? I mean, isn't it best if they don't *know* we're investigating?"

"Once again, this is a murder investigation. It's not necessarily a bad thing if we rattle them," Schenck pointed at her. "It might shake something loose."

Angie paused outside the door of Professor Julia Lowery, shifted her bag on her shoulder, and raised her hand to knock. But she couldn't bring herself to do it. Every step of the way across the Santa Clara University campus had felt like an incursion into enemy territory. She found herself surrounded by what she assumed to be happy-happy rich kids, and it made her flesh crawl. She lowered her hand. "This is a mistake," she said to herself, and turned to go.

Just then the door swung open. "Oh!" said a woman's voice. Angie turned, cringing. A woman in her mid-forties was framed in the doorway, a quizzical look on her face. She was short—about the same height as Angie. She had wavy black hair and looked like she might be part Hispanic or Native American, or maybe even Indian.

"I'm sorry," Angie said.

"Don't be." The woman smiled. "Are you...one of my students?" She cocked her head.

"No," Angie said. "I just..." Angie reached into her bag and drew forth a battered trade paperback, titled *Gnostics: The Misunderstood Christians.* "You wrote this, right?"

The woman glanced at the paperback. "Yes," she said. "In my youth. It's kind of embarrassing now."

Angie paused, not sure how to take that. The woman must have noticed, because she leaned in and with a conspiratorial air, whispered, "I've gotten better at writing since."

Angie nodded.

"Did you want to talk to me about...something?" the woman asked.

Angie felt frozen between weeping and spilling her guts to this woman and turning and running away as far as she could get from this palace of privilege. Before Angie could muster an answer, the woman swung the door wide. "Come in. I'm Julia."

As if drawn by a magnet, Angie was pulled inside. Dr. Lowery pointed to a chair across from her desk. "Please have a seat. I'm sorry I don't have tea or anything to offer."

Angie shook her head.

"What's on your mind?"

"Is this...an okay time?" Angie asked.

"It's a fine time. I was just on my way to the cafe to boredom-eat a biscotti, so you actually saved me. The conversation may prove to be more nourishing."

Angie wasn't sure what to make of that. But the woman was friendly and warm and not at all pretentious as she'd feared. She allowed herself to relax just a bit. She held up the paperback. "I've been trying to read this."

The woman rolled her eyes. "'Trying' being the operative word, I'm sure. At that time, I thought you had to write in academese in order to be taken seriously. I'm sorry to put you through it."

"There's some...weird stuff in there," Angie said.

"Do you mean the gnostic teachings?" Dr. Lowery asked.

Angie nodded. "I'm not sure I get it."

"That's because they're almost impossibly Byzantine," Dr. Lowery chuckled.

Angie didn't know what "Byzantine" meant, but she put that aside. "Can you, like, give it to me in a nutshell?"

"That is nearly an impossible task." Dr. Lowery sighed and shook her head. "There were a number of gnostic movements in the ancient world, but they all had a few characteristics in common. One is that the creator of the world is evil—"

Angie's eyes went wide. "Really?"

"Yes. That's the demiurge I write about. He has created this earth as a prison, and is keeping us all enslaved to him."

"Okay..." Angie's thoughts flashed to Seth's descriptions of the god he had been raised with. She thought back to their dinner with his mother. He had paused at the door, afraid to go in. His voice echoed in her head, *I feel like the front door is a portal to another world, a world ruled over by a dark, angry god who hates my guts. When I step through that doorway, I step into his domain. I feel like there are evil angels circling above me all the time, just waiting to pounce on me and devour my soul.*

"That's terrible," Angie said.

Dr. Lowery shrugged. "Well, it does make sense out of some thorny theological questions."

"Such as?" Angie asked.

"Such as why would a good god allow so much evil and suffering in the world? Especially if he has the power to stop it."

"Unless..." Angie whispered. "Unless *god* is evil."

"That's right. The gnostics taught that there was another god, though, out beyond our universe—a god of love and light and wisdom, who wants to help us escape from the evil god's clutches."

"How?" Angie asked.

"Have you ever seen *The Truman Show*?" Dr. Lowery asked.

Angie frowned. "That old movie with that goofy guy?"

"Jim Carrey, yes." Dr. Lowery smiled. "He's not very goofy in that movie, though. Did you see it?"

Angie nodded. "A long time ago."

"You might want to watch it again. This guy Truman is living in an artificial reality—"

"He's on TV all the time, but doesn't know it!" Angie remembered.

"That right. He's being kept in the dark. But once he figures out that he's being watched, manipulated, he's able to escape."

"He was in a dome or something..." Angie offered.

"That's right. And he was able to get out of it...but only because he gained knowledge of his true situation."

Angie's eyes moved back and forth, trying to piece it all together. Dr. Lowery continued. "That's why they're called 'gnostic.' *Gnosis* is the Greek word for 'knowledge.' The gnostics believed they could escape from their prison because they were given knowledge that they *were* in prison."

"So Seth thinks he's in prison?" Angie asked.

Dr. Lowery cocked her head. "Who's Seth?"

"My friend. He's...he's been going to a gnostic study group. And I'm worried about him."

Dr. Lowery began to laugh. She moved her hand as if waving away Angie's words. "Neo-gnostic groups. They're harmless."

"They are?" Angie asked.

"There aren't any actual gnostics around, not anymore," Dr. Lowery explained. "Of course, there are groups influenced by the gnostics, like the Masons and AMORC. But anyone calling themselves 'gnostic' these days is only gnostic in the Jungian sense."

"I don't know what that means," Angie confessed.

"Have you heard of Carl Jung? He was a pioneer of transpersonal psychology."

"Okay, yeah. Archetypes, right?"

"That's right. He thought the gnostic teachings were an early form of psychotherapy. In his interpretation, the demiurge is our own ego."

It was Angie's turn to cock her head.

Dr. Lowery seemed to notice. "What I mean is that we all have a little tyrant in our heads—you know, the one shouting 'Me!' and 'Mine!' and 'I'm such a piece of shit!'"

"Oh, yeah, I know that voice," Angie said.

"Jung thought that voice was shaping how we see the world, that we're prisoners in a world of our own making. And we need to search beyond that voice to a higher source of wisdom, one that tells us the truth about ourselves—that we're lovable, that on some level we're still whole."

"That's...beautiful," Angie said.

"Yeah. And of course the neo-gnostics dress all of this up in catholic ritual and give themselves grand titles like Tau Basiliedes and so on. But it's all harmless fun."

Angie nodded. "You really think there's nothing to worry about?"

"Not from a neo-gnostic group. They don't take the cosmology—"

"I'm not sure what that means in this context," Angie said, holding up her hand.

"I mean their theory of the universe—the actual prison, the demiurge being an actual demonic god—they don't take that stuff seriously. They're all just metaphors for interior psychological processes."

"Really?"

"Really." Dr. Lowery smiled. "I did my dissertation on neo-gnostic movements. It was a fascinating study."

"Okay," Angie said, standing up. "Thank you."

"This might help," Dr. Lowery said. She stood and went to her bookcase. She pulled a paperback from it and handed it to Angie.

Angie took it and looked at the title: *Neo-Gnostic Movements, Ancient and Modern.*

"I think that might help put your mind at ease," Dr. Lowery said. "I just recently reworked that from my dissertation. It's much easier reading, I promise."

"Thank you," Angie said.

"My pleasure. It was lovely talking to you."

Angie moved toward the door, but then stopped and turned back. "If I have more questions—"

"My office hours are Friday afternoons from 1-4pm. Drop by any time during that timeframe."

Angie put the book in her bag and hugged herself. "Good. Thanks."

"I can't do this," Seth said.

"Can't do what?" Dr. Teasdale asked. She cocked her head and gave him a compassionate smile.

He wasn't sure he liked that. It seemed to border on placation, or patronization, or pity, or...something. He looked away. Outside, the branches of a tree swayed in the yellow, hazy, late afternoon light.

"Any of it. I can't fucking do *any of it.*"

Dr. Teasdale leaned forward. "Okay, Seth. Breathe. Take a deep, big breath and hold it. Now let it out...slow...slow..." He did as instructed. He did feel a little better, but only a very little. "Now, sit back and close your eyes. Imagine her floating up to you—"

"But I can't see her face—" he objected.

"Never mind that. Your eyes are closed, remember? Just feel her put her arms around you."

He forced himself to be still, to focus, to use his imagination.

And then he did feel her arms. Not Dr. Teasdale's, but Mother Wisdom's. He felt her breath on his ear, her breasts behind him, her arms encircling his chest, holding him close, quieting every jangled nerve within him.

"There now," Dr. Teasdale said. "You feel better, don't you? I can tell you do."

Seth nodded.

"You can do this anytime, you know. She's always there for you."

"But...she's got to have better things to do with her time."

"It's the System saying that, Seth. It's the System that tells you that 'time is money,' and that productivity is more important than relationships. Sophia is all about relationships. She loves you deeply, she cares about you, and there's nothing more important to her than holding you...right now...and any other time you need to feel her close to you."

"I...want to believe that—" Seth began, but Dr. Teasdale cut him off.

"Don't believe it. Belief is too high a bar. Just choose to trust it. That's all."

A switch turned in Seth's head. Yes, trusting was easier than believing. It still took effort, but unlike believing, it was an achievable goal.

"Just stay nestled in her arms for now while we talk," Dr. Teasdale instructed. "I have a feeling that this whole session will be easier if you lean on her. Come to think of it, that's true of most things." Seth's eyes were closed, but he could tell she was smiling. He took a deep breath. He felt calm, peaceful, *held*.

"You just received the fourth seal, yes?" Dr. Teasdale asked.

"Yeah. Redemption," Seth said. "Although it seems like a strange title."

"Why is that?"

"I don't know. The word has a lot of baggage from...my old religion."

Dr. Teasdale's face softened. "It's hard to untangle it all, isn't it?"

"Yeah."

She nodded compassionately. "Well, the way I think of it is this. To redeem something is to buy it back. To make an exchange. Like you redeem a coupon. It doesn't trigger you when I say that, does it?"

He shook his head.

"In the Rite of Redemption you made an exchange, too. You bought back your own power. You took it away from the archons and you owned it for yourself...maybe for the first time."

Seth nodded. "Is that what happened?"

"What do you think happened?"

"I think I destroyed the symbol of...of the power that the demiurge held over me."

"Is destroying the symbol the same as destroying the symbolized?" Dr. Teasdale asked.

Seth blinked. "I...I'm not sure."

"'The Lord did everything in an image,'" Dr. Teasdale quoted.

"The Gospel of Philip," Seth said.

Dr. Teasdale smiled—a broad, bright smile. "Yes! Exactly so. Images...symbols are all we have to work with. But they are more powerful than our culture gives them credit for."

"Dr. Robinson told us that symbols participate in what they symbolize," Seth said.

Dr. Teasdale nodded.

"It feels like a leap of faith," Seth said.

"Is that hard?" Dr. Teasdale asked.

"I kind of wish I felt something," Seth admitted.

"Feelings are a fine tool, but they are terrible masters," Dr.

Teasdale reminded him. "They are not terribly reliable. They don't always tell us the truth."

"I wish I knew what the truth was," Seth confessed.

"That is a lifelong struggle," Dr. Teasdale said. After a few moments of silence, she shifted in her chair. "Let's go back to what you said when you first came in. You said, 'I can't do any of this. Tell me one thing that you feel like you can't do."

Seth looked down, adjusting to the change in topic. "Well, I apparently can't keep a girlfriend."

"I'm confused," Dr. Teasdale said. "Did she break it off or did you?"

Seth wanted to take offense, but he felt too warm and comfortable. "No one did," he confessed.

"Well then, have you been avoiding her or has she been avoiding you?"

"She sends me a text every day," Seth said.

"Do you answer?"

"No." Seth squirmed, but Sophia tightened her embrace. He relaxed again. "She betrayed me."

"She and Angie?"

"Yes. And Travis."

"Who is Travis?"

"He's my friend from work. Kush is staying with him right now."

"Oh, yes. But...betrayed how?"

"They ganged up on me...you know, staged an intervention."

"Intervening because...?"

"Because Gnosticism," Seth said.

"Oh." Dr. Teasdale seemed taken aback. "And how was that?"

"It was fucking uncomfortable. And annoying. And...kind of devastating, actually."

"I can well believe it." Dr. Teasdale sighed. "Well, Seth, I don't agree with them that you needed an intervention. There's a war on and you're a soldier and they don't have the security clearance to really know what's going on."

Seth nodded. "I know that."

"But I also think that what they did, they probably did out of love for you...not because they wanted to undermine you."

He knew that, too. But he didn't want to admit it.

He changed the subject. "I totally fucked up at work."

"How so?"

Seth wondered for a moment if she was going to bring him back on track, but she seemed to flow with it. He continued. "I pulled the covers off of about two hundred brand new books. I was doing returns, but...I wasn't really paying attention."

"Oof," Dr. Teasdale said. "That had to hurt."

"Yeah," Seth agreed.

"What did your boss say?"

"She didn't say anything. Yet. She told me to go home, clear my head. She said we'd talk tomorrow."

"Okay, nothing like the Sword of Damocles hanging over your head."

"Yeah," Seth agreed. "I'm living in total, agonizing dread just waiting for it."

"I get that. Have you asked her for help?"

"What? Rutherford?"

"Is that your boss?"

"Yeah."

"No, I meant Sophia. Have you asked her for help?"

"No, but...how?"

"Just tell her how you're feeling. Ask her to help you."

"Is she going to change Rutherford's mind?"

"I don't know," Dr. Teasdale admitted. "But I do know that whatever happens, you'll feel more supported. You can ask Sophia to go into your boss's office ahead of you, too, to prepare the way. You can ask her to carry your worry and your anxiety—"

"I can?"

"You can."

"That sounds...crazy."

"No, it isn't crazy. It's just...well, it's the love of a mother, from a mother who knows *how* to love."

Unlike some mothers I know, Seth thought. "Does everything come back to Sophia?"

"On this side of the veil...yes."

"And on the other?"

"On the other, there will be no distinction between you and her...or you and the True God...or you and anyone else. All will simply be...the All."

"How will I know it's the All, if I'm just enveloped in the All?"

"Do you want to be conscious of the All?" Dr. Teasdale asked.

Seth thought that he did, but then it occurred to him that he might not be able to handle it. Would it break his tiny mind? He didn't know. "Would I...go crazy?"

"No...it's only the tyranny of the demiurge, of dualism that makes you think so. You'll be fine. Some gnostics think that you'll be so absorbed into the One that all memory of being a seemingly separate being will simply fade away. Others think that you'll retain enough 'you-ness' to know and enjoy being part of the All."

"What do you think?" Seth asked.

"I honestly don't know. I think I'd prefer Door Number Two, though."

"Me too," Seth said.

"How are you doing with the medication?" Dr. Teasdale asked. "It's been long enough now that you should be feeling some of the effects. Are you feeling any different?"

Seth moved his head back and forth. Did he feel any different? "The OCD isn't as bad," he said. "It's way easier to leave the house now."

"Good," Dr. Teasdale wrote something on her notepad. "I'm so glad to hear that. And the anxiety? Are you calmer?"

"I think so. It's not that different from weed, in a way."

Dr. Teasdale smiled. "What do you mean?"

"I mean, what I like about weed is, after you smoke it, it feels like someone just draped a warm blanket over your brain, fresh from the dryer."

Dr. Teasdale laughed. "That...is an excellent description."

Seth's eyebrows shot up. "You've...smoked?"

"Please. Do I look like a Puritan?" Dr. Teasdale shook her head slowly.

"Huh," Seth said. "I was not expecting that."

"Anyway, you were saying how weed was like an SSRI."

"Oh, yeah. Well, it kind of feels like that blanket is there all the time, now. If I stop to pay attention, I can feel it. It's a lighter-weight blanket, but it's still warm ad soft."

Dr. Teasdale was scribbling furiously. "That's excellent, Seth. I'm going to raise your dosage a bit, and maybe the blanket will get a bit thicker."

"Sounds good to me," Seth said. He looked down at his feet. He sighed.

"What just happened?" Dr. Teasdale asked.

"Ah...well, I just realized I was avoiding talking about the Big Thing."

"It seems like we've talked about a lot of big things. So...what big thing are you *not* talking about?"

"I appear to totally suck at being a gnostic spy."

At this, Dr. Teasdale burst into laughter. Seth shrank. "What?"

"No, no, it's not you. It's...the way you put it." She wiped her eyes. "Okay, Seth, why do you think you suck at being a gnostic spy?"

"Nazz took me to do a training course. I tried it twice. Both times I timed out."

"It's a training course, Seth. That's the place where you're *supposed* to make mistakes. It's how you learn."

"I guess. But Nazz—"

Dr. Teasdale made a raspberry sound and waved him away. "Nazz. Jesus."

Seth looked back and forth. "What am I missing?"

Dr. Teasdale sighed. "Nothing. Nothing. I am guarding my tongue. Let me guess—Nazz is not the most patient teacher?"

"I would not say so, no," Seth agreed.

"I don't know why he..." She trailed off and shook her head. Seth wondered who the "he" was in her incomplete sentence, and suspected it might be Mr. Basil. "Go on, please, Seth."

"I fucked up. That's all there is to it."

"And how did you do on the map portion?"

Seth shrugged. "Okay."

"Define okay. Did Nazz give you a percentage?"

"No. But he said it was perfect. Both times. At least, as far as I got."

Dr. Teasdale smiled. There was a sad look on her face...or was it pity? Seth couldn't tell. She leaned forward and placed a hand on his knee. He felt a jolt of electricity rush through him at her touch. "Seth, that means you're doing great. It means you're able to do exactly what Basil and the other leaders are hoping you can do."

"But—"

"The timing will come. It's why you practice." She patted his knee. "You are blind to your own powers, Seth, but you must trust that they are there. She has her hand upon you."

"Do you really think so?"

Dr. Teasdale sat back. "I know so. And more importantly, Basil does, too. You can't let Nazz' snottiness derail you. He's a little shit who doesn't have a fraction of the talent you do, and he knows it. All his nastiness is just jealousy." She leaned back.

"Goddam it, I said the quiet part out loud. You didn't hear that, did you?"

"Not a thing," Seth confirmed.

Teasdale chuckled. Then she sat upright, and it seemed to Seth that she'd had an idea. She rose and went to the bookcase. She took down a copy of *The Nag Hammadi Library*—

How many copies does she have? Seth wondered

—and flipped through it. Looking satisfied, she sat back down, crossed her legs and handed the book to Seth. "Can you read this part...and this part aloud?" she asked.

Seth took up the book and settled it in his lap. He began to read. "'I am the first and the last. I am the honored one and the scorned one. I am the whore and the holy one. I am the wife and the virgin. I am the mother and the daughter...I am knowledge and ignorance. I am shame and boldness. I am shameless; I am ashamed. I am strength and I am fear. I am war and peace. Give heed to me.'"* Seth looked up. "I don't get it."

"Do you know who is speaking?" Dr. Teasdale asked.

"No, who?"

"It is Sophia, Mother Mystery herself. Now read it again."

He did. This time gooseflesh erupted on his arm. He looked up. "I still don't...what is she saying?"

"She's saying that she is the coincidence of opposites," Dr. Teasdale said. "And you are her son. Just like her, you are full of contradictions. You can be a failure...and a victor. You can struggle...and triumph. You can be clueless and filled with gnosis. The idea that you have to be perfect is a lie of the demiurge. You don't have to be anything other than what you are, right now. Good, bad; smart, stupid; sick, well...these are all labels that we put on things. In reality, everything is one. In truth, there are no distinc-

---

* "Thunder, Perfect Mind," from *The Nag Hammadi Library*, translation by George W. MacRae.

tions. There just is what there is, without judgment, without blame. So stop beating yourself up over something the demiurge pulled out of his ass."

Seth couldn't help laughing at that. He realized that was why she had said it, to shock him out of his resistance to what she was saying. It worked. "I get it," Seth said. "It's like a video game. There's no way you're going to reach the top level the first time out. You have to work and die and try things and die and get crazy and die a hundred times before you figure it out."

Dr. Teasdale nodded. "Yes. And that's why you've got to make this mistake in training. Because out there—" She pointed to the window. "*That* isn't a game."

WHAT IS CATTLE PROG?

Cattle Prog is widely considered a sub-genre of progressive rock. Progressive rock, also known as prog rock, emerged in the late 1960s as a subgenre of rock music that pushed the boundaries of traditional rock conventions. Characterized by complex compositions, virtuosic instrumental performances, and a fusion of various musical styles, progressive rock aimed to explore new horizons in music. Bands such as Pink Floyd, Yes, Genesis, and King Crimson pioneered the genre, incorporating elements of classical music, jazz, folk, and psychedelia into their sound. Progressive rock often featured lengthy and intricate compositions, experimental arrangements, and thought-provoking lyrical themes. It remains influential, inspiring subsequent generations of musicians and captivating listeners with its expansive and adventurous approach to music.

Cattle Prog, a relatively recent sub-genre, expands the list of prog rock fusions to include country, bluegrass, and western styles. Most musicologists agree that the movement began in Bakersfield, California in the early 2030s with a cluster of bands including Face Like a Horse, Chaps Chaps, and The Lysergic Cowboys. The style is generally played on traditional instruments, such as acoustic guitar, mandolin, fiddle, and pedal steel, although typical prog conventions such as mellotron choir and electric guitar are often part of the mix.

Against all odds, the sub-genre became a dark horse movement, due in part to the placement of the song "Crafty Bastard" by The Lysergic Cowboys in the popular film, *The Stranger Game* (2032). Other bands copied the sound and to date there are more than two dozen active Cattle Prog bands in California, according to *The Corral*, a Cattle Prog fan blog.

CHAPTER FIFTEEN

The rich become poor and kings are overthrown.
All changes. The world is an illusion.
Why do I seem to shout?
The resurrection has nothing of this character.
It is truth standing firm.
It is revelation of what is,
and the transformation of things,
and a transition into freshness.
Incorruptibility floods over corruption.
Light rivers down upon the darkness,
swallowing obscurity.
The pleroma fills the hollow.
—*Treatise on the Resurrection**

---

* Treatise on the Resurrection: Nag Hammadi Codex I, 4 translated by Malcolm Peel and Bentley Leyton, revised by Willis Barnestone, published in *The Gnostic Bible* (Boston, MA: Shambhala Publications, 2009).

K eira turned the coffee pot upside down, catching the last few bitter drops in her cup. It was now a little more than half full, and cold. She looked over at the gold coffee packets, and then back at the carafe, weighing the benefit of warm, fresh coffee over the effort needed to produce it.

Before she could come to a decision, her phone buzzed. She pulled it from the pocket of her chinos and glanced at the screen. "FINANCIALS ARE IN," it announced.

Snatching up her half cup of cold, embittered coffee, she carried it out to her desk. She punched at her keyboard and watched her computer screen blaze to life. Then she logged on to the California Homeland Security site and pulled up the forensic accountant's report.

She started with the man at the top, Terrance Basil. According to his tax records, he officially worked for a non-profit called The Pleroma Trust. She squinted at the word, "Pleroma." *What the fuck does that mean?* she wondered. She did a quick search and clicked on the entry from UCLA Languages. "Greek, meaning, 'that which makes full,' or 'fullness,'" she read aloud. "In Christian theology, the totality of the Godhead is resident in Christ. In Gnosticism—" She caught her breath. Then she continued, slower. "—the All, in which is contained the totality of God, aeons, syzygies, and all other divine powers. In Valentinian Gnosticism, the entirety of the nondual universe."

"Okay, that fits, I guess," Keira whispered. She felt a cold chill run through her. She kept reading. In the previous year, Mr. Basil had made slightly more than the national average, a figure that was consistent for nearly twenty years of employment. An older generation of detective would have looked for offshore accounts, but those had not been accessible since the contagion. There was still a field for it on the report page, but Keira had never seen one that wasn't blank. She pulled up his bank statement report. No large sums had been deposited in any connected account. Mr. Basil received a monthly direct deposit. If he received any other funds, there was nothing to indicate such. His tax records indicated that his housing was supplied by his employer, which bumped his total compensation, but not to the point where one could consider him rich. Comfortable, yes, but it was clear that Mr. Basil did not have an extravagant lifestyle. No large sums in, no large sums out. There was an annual vacation—often to Yosemite—and there were business trips. None of these raised any red flags for the accountants. Nor would they for her.

"All right, if not Mr. Basil..." She turned to other Pleroma employees. She pulled up a report on a Joshua Robinson. His job title was listed as "catechist." She had to look that up, too. "A religious teacher." Robinson made significantly less than Basil, but supplemented his income by teaching Philosophy and Religion at The Transpersonal Counseling Institute in Palo Alto. His combined income was greater than Mr. Basil's, even accounting for the housing, but again, he was not what Keira would consider rich. She pulled up his other records. Again, there had been no large transfers. There was nothing out of the ordinary.

She pulled up more linked reports, which seemed to be for the directors and catechists of Lodges located in Los Angeles, San Diego, San Francisco, and Sacramento. None seemed out of the ordinary. "Damn," she sighed, leaning back in her chair.

"'S'matter?" Tony Raine asked, apparently on his way to the break room.

She shook her head. "Just got the forensic reports on the Lodge leadership."

"Anything?"

"Not a damn thing."

"Maybe you're looking too high," Raine said.

She cocked her head. "What do you mean? Forensics didn't flag anything, on anyone."

Tony shrugged. "Maybe it isn't about the money."

"Then what's it about?"

"I don't know. Religion makes people do weird things."

"I guess." She didn't really see how it fit.

"'With or without religion, good people can behave well and bad people can do evil; but for good people to do evil—that takes religion,'" Raine recited.

"Who said that?"

"I wish I had. But I think it was Steven Weinberg."

"Huh. So if it's not about money, how do we track..."

"Have you checked out the connections? Known associates, contractors, former employees."

"What, and run full forensics on each of them?"

Raine shrugged, nearly tossing his coffee. He noticed and licked a spilled drop off of his thumb. He smiled sheepishly. "First, just check out the list. Do you want me to help?"

She wouldn't mind, but she wasn't going to give him the satisfaction of saying so. "No, it's okay. I just...needed a break to get over my initial discouragement, I guess."

"'Be strong, saith my heart; I am a soldier; I have seen worse sights than this.'"

"Who the fuck said that?"

"Homer, the Odyssey."

"What, do you just sit around all day memorizing aphorisms?"

"No, what, are you crazy?" He looked offended. "I fucking read, Sloane. You should try it sometime." Shooting her a final black look, he resumed his journey toward the breakroom. A moment later, she heard an irritated grunt. "Who the fuck took the last bit of coffee without making more?" he yelled.

She slunk down into her seat and ran a search on known

associates for Terrance Basil. With a bored expression that bordered on sleepy, she read down the list of unfamiliar names. Then her eyes went wide, and she jerked herself up straight. "Fuck!"

Tony's face appeared at the breakroom door. "What?"

Keira ignored him.

"You did this, didn't you?" He held up the empty carafe.

She continued to ignore him. She could only stare at the name in the middle of the list, glaring out at her as if it were lit by neon. "Sherry Teasdale," she said.

The hairs on Seth's neck stood at attention. He looked around and saw Belle leaning against the wall next to the other cash register, arms folded over her flat chest. Her Doc Martins were crossed, her too-black bangs were hanging into her face. Through them her heavily-mascaraed eyes were staring at him. She blew a bubble, popped it, and continued chewing her gum, somehow all without disturbing her black lipstick.

"What?" Seth asked.

"You scare me," Belle said.

"What? *I* scare *you*? What are you even talking about?" Seth asked.

"The way your brain works. It's...creepy. You're like one of those savants who can't string four words together but can play a piano concerto by Mozart flawlessly."

"Gee...I'm not sure how to feel about that," Seth opened one eye wider than the other. "And I don't play the piano."

"I said it's *like* that," she said. "Or have you not heard of similes?"

"Just...stop looking at me, please. It's creeping me out."

"We creep each other out, then. Mutually assured creepage." But she didn't stop staring at him. She blew another bubble.

Then the phone rang. She picked it up. "Registers," she said. She looked at Seth again, her painted-on eyebrows rising on her forehead. She hung up.

"What?" Seth asked.

"I think you know what."

Seth sighed. "Might as well get it over with." He locked his register, fitted the bungie holding the key around his wrist, and headed for the back. *Dead man walking*, the voice in his head announced. As he passed aisle after aisle, he tried to rehearse what he was going to say to Marian Rutherford. But nothing was coming.

Without remembering how he got there, he found himself outside her door. He raised his fist to knock, but before he touched wood, her voice called from within. "Come in." He pushed the door open and stepped inside.

She put aside the paper she had been studying and looked up at him. "Sit," she said. Placing her elbows on her desk, she steepled her fingers and watched him. Seth sat. Instantly, his leg began to bounce. He started to sweat.

She pulled a box from somewhere near her feet and put it on the desk in front of her. Then she started pulling torn-off paperback covers from the box, one after another. She covered every possible inch on her desk with them, and then began a second layer. Seth felt like a perp in an interview room, being forced to look at photos of his crime scene, his victims.

His vision began to go snowy, and a roaring began in his ears. He blacked out.

W hen he came to, he was staring at the ceiling. "That was very dramatic," Rutherford said.

"What happened?" Seth asked.

"You fainted...apparently. Sorry I didn't have a swooning couch for you."

Seth suspected he was being mocked, but was too disoriented to take actual offense.

He felt his heart raging in his chest. He tried to sit up, but was struck by a dizziness that laid him out flat again.

"Can we just talk like this?" Seth asked.

"You want to talk?" Rutherford asked.

"That's what you wanted to see me about, yeah?"

"No. I don't need to talk. Do you need to talk?"

"I don't..." Seth didn't know how to respond. He closed his eyes to keep the room from spinning. "I think I'm having a panic attack."

"Poor baby. Or maybe you just felt I needed a little more drama in my life this morning, eh?"

"I don't know what you're talking about," Seth confessed.

"Well, let me help you make sense of it, then." She stood over him, hands on her hips. He could see up her nostrils, which looked porcine and cavernous from that angle. "You're fired."

"I'm..."

"Look, St. John, I've given you a lot of slack. I've been very patient. Surely you see that."

"Well...yeah." He had to concede it. He'd been distracted, that was for sure.

"I've given you plenty of warnings. But you just cost the company about $4500 in lost sales. Now I could take that out of your check, but I won't. Instead, it seems to me that a good shaking is in order. So consider this your shake. And I hope you get your life in order. Now go, clean out your locker, and bring me back the key. Do you need a security guard escort, or can I trust you not to torch the place on your way out?"

"No, I'm...fine," Seth confessed.

"Okay, then." Rutherford said, hands still on her hips. "Any day now, St. John."

"Travis called me," Angie said. She stared at the ceiling, but it was dark and the only thing she could see was an acute trapezoid of light thrown through the window by a streetlamp.

"Oh?" Becky turned over to face her, gathering a wad of bedclothes up to her chin. "How is Kushie?"

"Kush is fine. It's Seth he's worried about."

Becky's eyes grew wide. "What happened?"

"He said Seth got fired today."

Angie felt the bed shake and looked over to see Becky up on one elbow. "What?"

"That's what he said," Angie affirmed. "He said he really fucked up at work, and they fired him."

"What did he do?"

"I don't know," Angie said. She watched Becky slide back down to the bed.

"Poor Seth."

Angie said nothing. "Do you know what we'd be doing if I were still living with him?"

"Um...no..." Becky said. From the hesitancy in her voice, Angie could tell that the question made her nervous.

"Relax. I have about as much romantic interest in Seth as I do in a stinky sock."

"I know. Sorry..."

"We'd be eating chips and salsa and watching a Godzilla movie and smoking waaaayyy too much weed."

"That sounds pretty good," Becky admitted.

"It's what he needs...it's what he'd need. I wonder who's smoking him out now?"

"What if no one is?" Becky asked.

Angie turned on her side to face Becky. "That's what worries me. I feel like I'm falling down on the job."

"You mean, the best friend job?" Becky asked.

"Yeah."

"You've done all you can do."

"Have I?"

Becky didn't answer at first. Finally, though, she said, "I think you've done all he'll let you do."

Angie didn't know how to answer that. So instead, she said, "I went to see a religion scholar."

"You did? I mean...*you* did? You might as well say you went to a white-power rally."

Angie laughed out loud. "I know. I just...I wanted to know more about that group—"

"The gnostic group?"

"Yeah. She said—"

"The religion scholar was a woman?"

"Yes. Why does that surprise you?"

Becky was silent for a few moments. "I don't know. I guess I just assume that..."

"That religion is a man thing?"

"I mean, isn't it?"

"In some religions, sure," Angie conceded. "But not all."

"Anyway, what did she say, this scholar?"

"She said that gnostics don't take any of their teachings seriously."

"That doesn't make any sense," Becky said. Angie could almost hear her frowning. "Why would they bother with it?"

"I can't figure it out. I mean, obviously it means something pretty serious to Seth. And from what I understand, I can see some of the appeal. I think he's trying to heal from the damage his mom and her nutso religion has done to him."

"I think so, too," Becky agreed. She laid a hand on Angie's arm and gave it a squeeze. "But he doesn't want our help."

"Apparently not," Angie muttered.

"I hate myself for thinking this, but..."

"But what?" Angie asked.

"Maybe it's time we let him go."

Angie was silent. She watched the trapezoid of light on the ceiling, looking like the reflection of a shining city bearing the impossible architecture of a Lovecraftian universe. "What would that look like?" Angie finally asked.

"It would look like you getting a new best friend. It would look like me getting another boyfriend. It would look like us... moving on."

"We're sure as shit failing the Bechdel test now."

"That's it. We can set a new goal. No talking about men."

"Seth's not a man," Angie said.

"What do you mean he's not a man?"

"He's just a scared little kid."

"Back for more punishment, eh?" Nazz asked. Today he was wearing a plaid vest, and his hair seemed to not quite be cooperating. *Even Nazz has bad hair days,* Seth noted. Nazz swung the door wide.

Seth entered. He was sweating and short of breath. The nearest bus stop to the warehouse was nearly a mile away and he had been speed walking in an effort to not be late. He had almost succeeded. "Thanks," he said. He excused himself to find the restroom. He splashed water on his face and tried to catch his breath. When he found Nazz again near the mock-up S-panel, he was feeling almost like himself.

He fished in his pocket for the key and held it up for Nazz to see. Looking bored, Nazz held up one finger and navigated on his phone—finding the stopwatch app, Seth assumed. Having apparently found it, Nazz looked up and nodded. "Go," he said.

Seth took a deep breath, fitted the key into the S-panel, and turned it. He expected a click, but this time it seemed stuck. He turned it harder, but was afraid that the key would break off. S-panel keys were probably rare, so he withdrew the key, pocketed it, and walked away from the panel as quickly as he could, back toward the restroom. Then he turned and faced Nazz. "How'd I do?"

"Flying colors, Ace," Nazz said, making a note on his phone. "Okay, let's try it again." He made a quick call on his phone and said, "Normal position again, please."

Seth took his place near the panel again and heard a faint *click* from the other side. Nazz worked at his phone for a few seconds, then looked up and nodded again. "Go."

Seth fitted the key, and this time it turned smoothly. Before stepping in, however, he pulled a stocking mask over his face. Then he went in.

The maze was different this time. He knew it would be. He sprinted to the end of the hallway, and saw that it branched two ways, left and right. He chose the left and jogged it, slowing down only for the switchback turns. It dead-ended, and he retraced his steps, a bit faster this time. He passed the original "T" leading back to the S-panel and kept going. He rounded a corner and once more found himself in what he had come to think of as the "temple." The woman was there again, naked on the altar. He didn't slow down this time, but simply jogged past her. "Hey, Sheila," he threw over his shoulder.

"Way to go, sweetheart," she called after him.

He caught sight of a wad of blankets and leaped over them. He came to another "T" and once more took the left-hand path. After two turns to the right, the narrow hallway opened up into what looked like a clean room. Two people in hazmat suits looked up and turned toward him.

Seth stopped and turned back, running full tilt the way he had come.

"Hi, again, Sheila," he said as he blew by her altar.

"Doing great, Seth-baby," she responded.

He retraced his steps to the S-panel, and by the time he reached it, he had the key out and ready to insert. He did so and swung it open. He closed it behind himself and in a single fluid motion, locked it again.

He pulled the ski mask from his face and noticed that he was panting. Nazz was nodding, making a note on his phone. When he was finished, he pointed to a pad of paper. Seth knew what to do. In less than three minutes, he had sketched the pathways he had travelled, including the dead ends. He paid attention to scale, and even included the number of steps.

He handed the paper to Nazz and waited. Nazz studied the paper and smiled. "100%," he said. "Take five while we set up again."

Seth allowed himself a deep breath and felt a rush of satisfaction. *Maybe I can do this,* he thought. *Maybe I can do this after all.*

Angie waved at a customer, who waived back with some uncertainty. *School teacher,* Angie thought. She picked her way through the glass-paneled designer shelves until she was standing next to her. The customer was about ten years older than Angie, with long brown hair gathered in back with a sage green scrunchie. She wore glasses that made her eyes seem bigger than they probably were, almost like a manga character. "Can I help?" Angie asked.

"Can you, like, make recommendations?"

"Of course," Angie flashed her best smile. "That's why I'm here. I'm a certified medical cannabis educator." It was almost true. She'd done the training but had let her certificate lapse.

"A couple of years ago I was in a car accident," the woman said. "It really messed up my back."

"Pain?" Angie asked.

The woman nodded. Her big eyes appealed for help.

"I'm so sorry," Angie said.

"There's just so many strains," the woman said, "and I don't know anything about them. I don't know where to even start."

"I've got you covered," Angie placed a compassionate hand on her arm. "Tell me more about your situation."

"Well, I'm a sub at Wi—a high school—"

Nailed it, thought Angie.

"And so I need to stay awake. But if I sit for too long it just gets excruciating without...some help."

"I totally get it. As an analgesic, Cannabis is thirty-five times more powerful than aspirin. It's good medicine." The woman nodded. Angie pressed further. "Okay, tell me about the pain. Is it sharp or dull?"

"Kind of both. When it shoots, it's sharp, but then it just aches."

Angie nodded. "Okay, here's what I'm going to recommend. To stay awake and alert, you'll need a strong sativa. But sativas aren't the best for pain. So I'm going to recommend a hybrid that will give you the best of both worlds."

The woman's eyebrows shot up. "Okay..."

"This way," Angie passed through the rows of glass shelves to a display panel containing a well-lit and beautifully arranged variety of cannabis flower. "This right here, the one with the big

448 • J.R. MABRY

nugs, that's Black Jack. It's a cross between Jack Herer, a strong sativa—very bright, very energizing—with Northern Lights, which is an indica-leaning hybrid that's great for pain." She leaned in closer. "It's also euphoric as fuck, so that's an added bonus."

The woman's hand shot to her mouth as she giggled. She was cute, but Angie put that out of her head. She was too old for her, she was a customer, and she was a *teacher*. Three strikes.

"But here's the problem," Angie said. "We don't have this strain in a vape cartridge—and those are only approximations anyway. And gummies don't get that granular. You can get an indica gummy or a sativa gummy or with some brands a hybrid gummy, but they're not going to get as specialized as you need. I suggest you buy an 1/8 of this, grind it up, and put it in a cup of vodka for a week. Then, strain it out and put it in a dropper bottle. When you're not at work, experiment with your dosing. Start with three drops and increase it until you find the sweet spot that eases your pain, but leaves you able to work well. And you'll probably work better and be in a better mood."

The woman's eyes were glistening. "Thank you. Thank you so much."

"You're so welcome. And everyone responds differently, so if the Black Jack doesn't do it for you, come talk to me again and we'll reassess. It's just like with regular medicine, it's a bit of trial and error. But we'll do you right."

The woman give Angie a hug, which prompted an involuntary, "Oh!" The woman headed for the cash register.

Angie followed, crossing to the back of the counter.

Evelyn and Dave were stocking, arranging the brightly colored jars in little pyramids.

"—he was totally nuts," Evelyn said. "I don't know what he was on, but it seriously scared me. I mean, he's got kids—little kids!"

"Did she call a 5150 on him?" Dave asked.

"Excuse me," Angie said. "I need a jar of Black Jack."

"Oh. Sure," Dave tossed her one. She fumbled but caught it.

"You could have just handed it to me," she objected.

"What would be the fun in that?" Dave asked. He turned back to Evelyn. "Anyway, you were saying?"

Angie turned to the register, keeping one ear open on the conversation behind her.

"I told her to. Her therapist told her to. Shit, I think her priest told her to, but did she listen? No."

"How long will she be...you know, in the ICU?"

"Hell if I know. Fuck, I'm just glad she's alive."

On autopilot, Angie took the schoolteacher's credit card and completed the sale. She put the jar of weed into a plain brown paper bag and stapled the receipt to the top. "Don't open that until you get home, in case you get pulled over for something."

"Thanks." The woman snatched up her bag and with a bit of swagger in her step, headed for the door.

"And let me know how it goes!" Angie called after her.

The woman turned and waggled her fingers at her.

Evelyn had gone to the back room, so Angie sidled up to Dave. "Uh...I feel stupid asking this, but what's a 5150?"

Dave frowned at her. "Do you live under a rock?"

She rolled her eyes. "For the sake of argument, let us say that I do. What's a 5150? And stop being a jerk."

"If you think someone is a danger to themselves or others, you can call the cops and ask them to pick them up. They put them in a psych ward for seventy-two hours so the docs can decide if they should go home again or...you know...be admitted for treatment."

"Huh. How did I not know about this?"

Dave shrugged. "It's common knowledge."

"Don't be a shit," Angie said. "And...can just anyone call the police and ask for a...a 5150?"

"I think so—"

Just then Evelyn arrived, holding an open box of spliffs. "5150?" she asked.

"Yeah," Dave said. "Can anyone call one in?"

"Now, yeah," Evelyn said. "Not before the pandemic, though —back then it had to be a therapist or a cop, I think. But you know, when we got cut off, people freaked out."

Angie nodded, feeling a strange power fill her body.

Evelyn set the box on the counter and opened it. "New Cherry Pie samples from Harvest Sun. Here, take one before the customers snatch them all up."

"Don't mind if I do," Angie said, pocketing two.

K eira climbed the steps to the Lodge. She smoothed out her slacks and took her badge out of her pocket. She put the tote bag she was carrying on the ground. Then she knocked. After a few moments, she heard footsteps. A young man she recognized answered, a thick shock of stiff black hair pointing diagonally from his head. He held the door only wide enough to fill the space with his own body. "Yeah?"

She flipped open the wallet that held her badge and raised it to his eyes. His brows leaped as he read it. "Holy shit. What do you want?"

"I need to speak to Terrance Basil. Is he here?"

"Uh...just a minute." The young man slammed the door and she heard his footfalls fading away. A minute later or so, she heard them returning. He opened the door again, wider this time. "This way, please."

She nodded, picked up the tote bag, and stepped in. She felt a wave of fear and wondered if she should have brought Raine with her as backup. *Too late now,* she thought, trying not to think of someone leaping out of the shadows and smashing in the back of her skull. *Happy thoughts*, she reminded herself.

The kid led her down a wood-paneled hallway to a large, heavy door that must have been solid oak. He knocked, but without waiting for a reply, swung the door inward. He motioned her in.

"Thanks," she said, crossing into the room. Terrance Basil was seated behind a sturdy wooden desk. He stood. She recognized him as the lecturer from her previous visit. He rose and crossed to meet her. She was surprised at how tall he was. He loomed over her as he offered his hand. She shook it and he waved her toward a chair. She put the tote bag on the ground beside the chair, and as she sat, she did a quick visual surveillance of the place. Bookshelves lined pretty much every wall, and they weren't cheap bookcases. They were built especially for the space. *That's impressive,* she thought. A plate of stained glass hung in a window. Another window, however, was boarded up. In a room of such perfect opulence, it stuck out like a hot dog on a plate of caviar.

She showed Mr. Basil her badge and replaced it in her pocket. "I'm Special Agent Keira Sloane, California Homeland Security."

"I wish you'd introduced yourself properly the last time you were here," he said. "It doesn't get us off on a very good foot."

"We were following up on a referral from the CBI. They got a suspicious activity tip about the house."

Mr. Basil rolled his eyes. "The neighbors do not like the fact that we have people coming in and out all the time. I can't tell you how many times the police have been here wondering if we were selling narcotics."

Keira allowed herself a smile at this. "Yes, well, it didn't hurt that you have a zoning exemption. After your lecture I told the CBI that you were mostly harmless. "

It was Basil's turn to smile. "Ah. That's a relief...I think."

"I actually found your talk to be very intriguing. If I wasn't such a workaholic, I might have come back."

"You would have been most welcome," Mr. Basil said. He spread his hands. "You still are."

"Well, thanks. But I'm not very religious."

"Funny, neither am I," Mr. Basil responded.

She liked him, she realized. She liked him a lot. It didn't mean that she trusted him, but if he'd said, *Fancy a pint and a game of darts?* she wouldn't have said no.

"To what do we owe the pleasure today?" Basil asked. "Surely you have not come to confess past surveillances?"

"No," she agreed. She opened the tote bag and drew from it a large ziplock bag. There was writing on the bag. She passed it to Mr. Basil. "Do you recognize this?"

She watched his eyes as he reached for the bag. He turned the bag over to the side with no writing. Then he froze momentarily. Was she imagining it, or had a bit more color just drained from his already-ashen complexion? A moment later and his poker face was once more firmly fixed. He handed the bag back to her. She almost didn't need to ask the question again. She had her answer. But she asked anyway. "Do you recognize it?"

"No, I'm afraid not. Should I?"

Liar, she thought. "The wearer of that vest is guilty of murder...of an electrician."

She knew that he knew she was watching him, but there was no disguising his reaction now. He ran his fingers through his hair and changed his position in his seat. "That's a serious crime," he said.

She wanted to say something snarky about stating the obvious, but she kept it professional. "It happened while the murderer was breaking into an S-panel." *Seriouser and seriouser,* she thought. The alarm on his face was oddly satisfying. She decided to lunge while she had him off balance. "What can you tell me about your relationship with Dr. Sherry Teasdale?"

She watched his face explore a number of expressions, from discomfort to alarm to irritation and finally anger. But then he closed his eyes, and she watched his shoulders collapse. His face became searching, then serene. When he opened his eyes, he was composed and calm again.

"We are a registered charity and we have nothing to hide. Our membership records and finances are a matter of public record."

It was true. Keira hadn't needed a warrant to obtain the financial records. Everything appeared to be on the up-and-up...at least on paper.

"Sherry has been a valued member of our Lodge for nearly twenty years," Basil continued. "She is a dear friend. And she has taken her turn serving in our leadership. She's on the triumvirate council now, in her second year of a three-year term. She served a prior term about twelve years ago as well. Why do you ask?"

"Let's just say I thought it odd that she works both for you and for us."

"I don't think she works for CHS, does she?" Mr. Basil asked.

"She's under contract with Homeland Security for psychiatric services."

"Ah, I see what you mean." He shrugged. "I really don't know what to tell you, special agent. She might be a Zen Buddhist or an Episcopalian, but she's not. She's a gnostic. It's not a crime."

"No, but something doesn't smell right," Keira said.

"I fear I cannot tutor your nose." Mr. Basil looked away, and she saw beads of sweat forming on his brow. "Ms. Sloane, if you are investigating S-panel breaches, you must have a very high security level indeed."

It was such an odd thing to say that Keira was caught off guard. She narrowed her eyes and cocked her head. She waited.

Mr. Basil rose and began to pace behind his desk, back and

forth in the small space, acting like a very tall caged cat. "Since your security level is high, there's no need for secrets between us," he said. He stopped in front of one of the bookcases and leaned over, as if he were reading the spines.

She waited.

"Tell me, special agent, do you know the name of the ship we're on?"

Keira froze. It was her turn to blanche. Basil turned to face her, and there was the tiniest gleam of satisfaction in his eye.

"What...ship?"

"Oh, come now, special agent. The starship. Do you know the name of it?"

She realized that she didn't. It had never occurred to her to ask.

"You don't, do you?" he asked. Hands behind his back, he walked back behind his desk at an unhurried pace. "You know that we're on a starship, but you don't know what she was christened. When that bottle of champagne crashed against her hull at her commissioning ceremony, what was the name stenciled on the side? Surely you must know that she has a name, this vessel."

Of course it would. She shook her head, unable to tear her eyes away from Basil's face.

"Let me ask you another question," he said, resuming his seat. He had her on her back foot now and knew it. His demeanor exuded a renewed confidence. "Do you know *why* we're on a starship?"

He paused. His eyes bored into her own. It was her turn to fidget in her chair. She didn't know, and she could tell that he knew that. He looked down at his hands, resting on the desk. "We must be going somewhere, yes? We must be going for some purpose, yes? Otherwise, why the expense? Why the trouble? Why all the...subterfuge?"

She didn't know the answers to any of those questions, and

the fact that she didn't know them tore her up inside. *You're a detective,* a voice in her head accused. *How can you not ask questions? How can you not be curious? Or did you just not want to know?* "It's...it's a good question," she conceded.

"Which?" he asked.

"All of them."

He moved his head back and forth. "But that is not an answer. It is merely an opinion about my questions."

"No," she agreed.

"No, what?" he asked.

"No, I don't know," she confessed.

WHAT IS LOVE MYSTICISM?

Love mysticism, also known as bridal mysticism or mystical love or the mysticism of love, is a spiritual concept that explores the transformative power of love in transcending the boundaries of individual identity and connecting with the divine or ultimate reality. Rooted in various religious and philosophical traditions, love mysticism delves into the profound and mystical experiences that arise from the depths of love and its potential to unite the lover with the beloved.

Love mysticism is found across cultures and has been explored within the context of different religious traditions, such as Sufism in Islam, Bhakti in Hinduism, and Christian mysticism. It encompasses a range of experiences and practices that seek to deepen one's relationship with the divine through the path of love.

At its core, love mysticism recognizes that love is not merely an emotion or a human attachment, but a transformative force that can lead to union with the divine. It emphasizes the fusion of the human and the divine through the intensity and selflessness of love. In this mystical journey, the lover seeks to dissolve the ego and transcend the limitations of individual identity, ultimately merging with the object of their love, which can be a person, a deity, or the divine essence itself.

Practices within love mysticism vary, but often involve acts of devotion, contemplation, prayer, and ecstatic experiences. These practices are intended to cultivate a state of love that transcends the ordinary and merges with the divine. Love mystics often express their experiences through poetry, music, and art, using metaphors and symbolism to convey the ineffable aspects of their encounters with the divine.

Love mysticism explores the profound interconnectedness between human love and divine love, seeing them as inseparable and intertwined. It recognizes that love is a universal force that binds all of creation and offers a path to spiritual awakening and enlightenment.

It is important to note that love mysticism is a deeply personal and subjective experience, and interpretations may vary. Some may view it as a metaphorical or symbolic expression of the longing for union with the divine, while others may approach it as a literal and transformative journey of love.

CHAPTER SIXTEEN

The savior swallowed death. You must know this.
He laid aside the perishable world and made
himself into an imperishable aeon, raised himself up,
and swallowed the visible with the invisible.
—*Treatise on the Resurrection**

"Why are there nothing but cans of black beans in here?" Becky asked, her head in the cupboard.

"Beats me," Angie answered. "But you know what they say: Legumes abhor a vacuum."

"Well, we have to buy groceries sometime. We can't keep eating pizza every night." Becky sighed, and, walking back to the

---

* Treatise on the Resurrection: Nag Hammadi Codex I, 4 translated by Malcolm Peel and Bentley Leyton, revised by Willis Barnestone, published in *The Gnostic Bible* (Boston, MA: Shambhala Publications, 2009).

table, took a slice from the box. It was big enough that she needed two hands. She sat down and watched with alarm as a strand of melted cheese broke loose and began to stretch toward her right breast like a descending spider. She flailed her other fingers to try to snag it, but she had run out of hands and it was clear that if she used either hand to snag it she'd lose the whole piece. "Goddam it," she said as the grease stained her blouse.

"Is that grease on your boob or are you just happy to see me?" Angie asked.

"I'm serious," Becky said.

Angie was halfway through a piece of her own, but she didn't care what kind of mess she was making—and so of course was making no mess at all. "Uh-huh."

"I'm going to get as big as a house," Becky said.

"But it's easy and delicious," Angie said.

"That's not an excuse," Becky answered.

"It's a reason."

Becky looked at her pizza like it was suddenly made of something inedible. She tossed it back in the box.

"More for me!" Angie said.

"Have you ever been overweight?" Becky asked.

"Never," Angie said.

"I hate you...and your kind."

Angie closed her eyes and exaggerated the enjoyment of her next bite. "Mmmm..."

"You suck."

"No, *you* suck, breeder. I lick," Angie answered.

Becky laughed. "I did not see that coming."

"I could make a joke about that, too—"

"No, that's all right. We're eating," Becky objected.

"*I'm* eating. You're staring at your food with disdain."

"Fine." Becky picked up her slice again and took another bite. "God, that's good."

"That's what I'm saying," Angie said, her mouth full of pizza. "I heard about something today...something I didn't know about."

"What's that?"

"Do you know what a 5150 is?"

"Yeah," Becky said. She put down her slice again and picked up a napkin. She licked it and began dabbing at the grease spot on her blouse. "It's a psychiatric hold."

"And anyone can call one in," Angie said.

"Yeah? So?"

"I'm thinking...maybe I should call one in...you know, for Seth."

Becky's head snapped up, her hand holding the napkin frozen in mid-air. "What?"

"I know he's seeing a therapist, but...maybe she's not objective, you know? Maybe she's in on it."

"In on what?"

Angie shrugged. "I don't know...the whole gnostic thing? I had a friend who was part of this really abusive church—kind of like the one Seth grew up in. And she started...she got suicidal. So her parents took her to a therapist. But get this—they took her to a *Christian* therapist."

"There *are* Christian therapists. What's your point?"

"She was in on it. She was trying to reinforce the same bullshit that was making her depressed in the first place!"

"Do you have any evidence that his therapist is 'in on it'?" Becky asked.

Angie put her slice down. She looked at her feet. "I had a dream..."

"Oh, Jesus," Becky said. "I can't even believe you."

"I'm just saying, what if she is?"

"You're just making shit up now."

Angie sighed. Maybe she was making it all up. She bit her lip.

Becky reached for a large wax cup that sloshed with ice

when she moved it. "Besides that, I thought we said we were both going to let this go. What happened to our resolution about making this an apartment Alison Bechdel would be proud of?"

Angie kept staring at her feet. "So, I haven't told very many people about this..."

"About what?"

"I didn't graduate high school because I was on heroin. I was a mess back then. I was a punk chick—"

"And you're not now?"

"I had the spiky hair, dog collar, the whole mascara nightmare. And my girlfriend turned me on to the H. At first we just snorted it, like cocaine. It was awesome. I've never felt so good, you know? Then we started smoking it. But the high kind of... degenerated over time. So we started with the needles."

"Holy shit, Ange." Becky tossed the wadded napkin on the coffee table.

"I know. I woke up one morning and my girlfriend was cold... dead. We were in a junk house, you know. So I just ran."

"Oh, Ange." Becky reached over and moved a strand of black hair out of Angie's eyes.

"I ran to Seth's place. I knew he had a crush on me, but...I also knew that he was a good guy."

"You didn't sleep with him, did you?"

"No! Where did that come from? Like I would ever. Besides, I was in too rough a shape. But he took me in...put me to bed... cleaned up my vomit and my shit until I got clean. I owe him my life, Beck."

Becky nodded, her eyes starting to brim. "Why are you telling me this? I mean, I'm glad you are, but...why?"

"Because he could have sent me away. He could have yelled at me for being such a dumb shit. He could have let me walk when I was crazy during my detox. But he didn't. It was tough love, but it was *real* love, you know? I don't know if I've ever experienced real love before Seth...or after."

Becky nodded. "But I don't see what that has to do with the whole 5150 thing."

"You don't?" Angie looked hurt. "He did the hard thing, and he saved me. Don't you think I should return the favor?"

* * *

Keira sat at her desk and stared into space. Tony Raine waved his hand in front of her eyes. "Anyone home?"

She shook her head. "Uh...yeah." She opened her mouth and *Tony, did you know we are on a starship?* almost came out. She closed her mouth again. "I'm fine."

"You don't seem fine. What's going on with you?"

"I'm fine. I'm just...thinking. It's how you solve cases. You should try it sometime."

"Yikes. Feels like I just tried to take a bone from a terrier."

"I'm not a fucking terrier. I'm a Doberman."

Tony's eyebrows rose on his head. "Are you? Listen, you want to talk, I'm here. If you don't want to talk, that's fine, too."

Keira deflated. "I'm sorry..."

"Wrong time of the month?" Tony asked.

"I will kick your fucking ass, moron," Keira said.

Tony held up his hands. "Whatever. I'm just getting coffee. Boss says he wants to see you, though."

"Why didn't you just say so?" Keira snapped, but he'd already turned his back to her.

She sighed and with an effort got to her feet. Feeling like she had lead weights velcroed to her shoes, she headed for Schenck's office.

What she couldn't fathom was how Basil had known about the starship. That information was top secret. There was only one explanation. She kept hoping she'd uncover something that would change her mind, something that would straighten out the tangles, but she kept coming back to the same conclusion over and over.

Keira stuck her head in Schenck's office door. "You wanted to see me?"

Schenck's coffee cup froze halfway to his lips. "Well if I did, now I regret it. You look like hell." He set the cup down.

"Yeah, well..." She stepped inside, but hugged the wall. "I've been chasing my tail all night."

Schenck pointed at her. "That I'd like to see."

"Was that...sexual harassment?" Keira asked.

"Will you stop with the sexual harassment threats? Get your mind out of the gutter, special agent. I mean that you're entertaining in the same way that a cartoon dog is entertaining."

Keira wasn't sure about that. "Deputy Dawg," she said.

That made him laugh. "Okay, how's the S-panel predator?"

"Is that what we're calling him? What—or who—is the prey, exactly?"

"You tell me. Goddam it, Sloane, just give me a fucking update before I get hauled away by HR or keel over from starvation."

Keira opened her mouth to say, "Fat chance of that," but Schenck pointed at her again and narrowed one eye. "Watch yourself."

Keira sighed. "We've got a male in a vest. We've got clean-as-a-whistle financials—"

"Too clean?"

Keira shrugged. "I'm not an accountant, and the forensics guys didn't say there was anything suspicious—only that there was nothing illegal."

"So you got nothing."

Keira looked back and forth. Then she shut the door behind her and sat down.

"Uh-oh," Schenck said.

"So I had their financials run—" Keira started.

"Who's 'they'?" Schenck asked.

"The people on staff, over at that Lodge."

"And?"

"All clean."

"You're killing me, Sloane." He pressed the heel of his hand against his right eyebrow. "You done? Because I got a call—"

"There was one person on staff who...I didn't expect."

Schenck closed his eyes and slowly shook his head back and forth. "This is like trying to dig out a goddam splinter. Who? Who didn't you expect?"

"My therapist," Keira said.

One of Schenck's eyebrows went up. "Your therapist? The one we sent you to?"

"Yeah. Dr. Sherry Teasdale. She's under contract with CHS, and...she's on staff with the gnostic Lodge."

"But it's a religious thing, right?" Schenck asked.

"Yeah, but—"

"Last I heard we still had freedom of religion in California."

"So you just think it's a coincidence that Dr. Teasdale is a member of this gnostic cult?"

"I don't see anything wrong with it. My grandpappy was a Rosicrucian and my father was a 33rd-Degree Mason and a Shriner to boot, fez and all. My nephew is a Thelamite, whatever the fuck that is. People get to choose their religion. Even vest-wearing religions."

"That's not all," Keira said.

"Jesus, what now?" He picked up his coffee cup and took a sip.

"I interviewed the leader at the Lodge. He knows...about the starship."

Schenck choked, sending brown plumes of joe arcing through

the air. Keira did not flinch, but wiped the coffee from her face and hands without comment.

"How does he know about the starship?" Keira continued. "I mean, he'd have to have a high-level security clearance, right? Or..."

Schenck raised his eyes to hers. Coffee beaded at the tip of his chin and fell, further staining the papers on his desk. The air reeked of burned beans. "Teasdale?"

Keira shrugged. "She has the clearance. She's on his payroll. He knows something he shouldn't know. How else...?" She left the sentence unfinished.

"Jesus' mom on a pony," Schenck swore.

"*Now* do you think there's something fishy here?" Keira asked.

"Pick her up," Schenck said.

Keira nodded and rose. She headed for the door but paused just at the threshold. Turning back, she said, "You know, let's hold off for a day."

"What?" Schenck asked.

"I have a therapy appointment with her tomorrow. Let's preserve the element of surprise."

Angie put her car in "park" and picked up her phone. 911. Just three simple numbers. That would do the job. She stared at the keypad and sighed. "Tough love," she said out loud. A voice in her head said, *He'll thank me for this one day,* but it sounded like hollow bullshit even before it finished its sentence. "Oh, Seth. Why do I fucking care so much?"

Why *did* she care so much?

Because he *cared so much,* the voice in her head said, and this time, the voice rang with Truth.

And because you love him, the voice continued. *And because he'd do it for you.* Truth.

Would he? She knew the answer to that. He would. He'd risk everything to save her, even from herself. What she was doing for him was no different.

Her hand paused over the phone, and her index finger began to shake. She punched at the "9." *But what if you're wrong?* the voice asked. She lifted her finger from the keypad. *Wrong about what?* she asked her internal voice.

Wrong about everything, came the answer.

It wouldn't be the first time, she conceded.

So...what kind of person would that make you, if you destroyed his life over something that exists only in your own head?

It would make me a singular kind of shit, she answered firmly.

Truth, the voice confirmed.

But what if I'm not? she pressed.

Are you really willing to take that chance? the voice asked.

A moment later, Angie found herself pounding the steering wheel, yelling into the empty car, "WHAT DOES LOVE WANT FROM ME?"

Silence. She took a deep breath and then let it out slowly. She felt her throat thicken with emotion.

If you feel this uncertain, this lost, how can you take the chance? the voice asked.

"I'm going bat-fucking crazy," Angie said out loud.

She looked down at her phone and hit "1."

She jumped then, as a bus barreled by, hitting a pothole with a loud "pock" sound. On the side of the bus was a poster for a movie, "Girl, Don't Do Me Wrong"—a comedy crime caper starring two African American actors that she didn't recognize.

Girl, don't do me wrong, the voice in her head repeated. *This is a sign.*

"Oh, it's definitely a sign," Angie said out loud. "It's a sign on the side of a fucking bus and it means *nothing*." Bullshit.

Angie screamed and beat her fists on the steering wheel again. Then she picked the phone up from where it had fallen into her lap and hit the last "1."

"911, please state the nature of your emergency."

"Hi, I'm—" Angie began, but just then a homeless man stepped in front of her car. He gave her a look of profound compassion. Then he closed his eyes, and shook his head slowly.

"Uh...never mind...the cops are here...already." She hung up. Would they trace her phone call for daring to use up their operator's time without actually reporting anything? Panic stabbed at her. It was the system—it was capable of anything.

Angie heard a thud and looked up. The homeless man was nowhere in sight. "What the fuck?" Angie asked. She hadn't looked down for more than a couple of seconds, and now he was gone. But where? She scanned around her car, looking through all the windows. There were no buildings close enough for him to run to, let alone shuffle toward at the gait he had been moving at.

Then her eyes widened, and she got out of the car. She circumambulated the car counterclockwise, seeing nothing around the back or the sides. When she reached the front of the car, she let out a yelp. The man was lying in front of her car, apparently passed out.

She knelt by him and felt his neck for a pulse. It was there, but he seemed to be sleeping soundly. Had he fainted?

She ran back to the car and grabbed her phone. She punched at "911" again, and when the operator answered, she said, "Hi, I just called. I thought the cops were coming to help, but they...I don't know, they must have been on their way somewhere else." It was a lie, but who cared? It would cover her butt. "Ah...a man just...collapsed...in the street...in front of my car. He's unconscious. Can you send an ambulance?"

Keira flipped through the pages of a magazine in the waiting room—*Dog Fancy,* from 2038. It wasn't quite tattered, but it had seen better days. Keira was not particularly interested in dogs, and the pages barely registered. Instead, she was preoccupied by the realization that she was holding her body differently than on past visits to Dr. Teasdale. Whereas before she had felt tentative, out of place, insecure, today she felt confident and exhilarated. She had shifted Dr. Teasdale from a room in her head labeled "authority figure" to one labeled "suspect," and it made all the difference.

Her head jerked up when she heard the door open. Dr. Teasdale poked her head out and said, "Keira? Come on in."

Keira tossed the magazine back onto the coffee table and stood, straightening her slacks. Then she strode to the door. Dr. Teasdale held it open for her, and she entered, taking her usual seat. Dr. Teasdale picked up her notepad and settled herself. She gave Keira a friendly, professional smile and asked, "How are you doing?"

"Pretty good," Keira said, nodding.

"That's good to hear," Dr. Teasdale said, making a note. "There's something different about you today."

Keira shrugged. "I think I'm...coming to terms."

"With what, exactly?" Dr. Teasdale asked.

"You know...the situation," Keira said.

"I think it would help if you said it out loud," Dr. Teasdale said.

Keira rolled her eyes. "Okay...I think I'm coming to terms with the fact that I have lived my whole life on a starship."

Dr. Teasdale gave her a compassionate look. "I hear that. What makes you think you're coming to terms? What has shifted?"

"It just…makes sense of a lot of things that…didn't before. I mean, the pandemic. We're not allowed to travel outside California. That made sense, keeping Californians safe from contagion, but what I never understood was why we couldn't talk to people in other states or other countries on the telephone or over P2P. The fact that we're light years away…now it makes sense. I mean, why did it take weeks or even months to get an email reply? And then, when I was in high school, even the email stopped. And the reasons they gave seemed like bullshit to me, even at the time. Something about satellite interference from China? Come on. That's something you sort out in days, it doesn't make for a permanent situation."

Dr. Teasdale's brows were high, and her lips pursed as she made notes.

"So…that helped, I think. When I can put things in order, I get calmer. And this…it should completely freak me out—and it kind of did—but it also put a lot of things in order that…weren't before. Am I making sense?"

"Total sense," Dr. Teasdale said, not looking up from her notepad as she scribbled away.

"But there are still things that don't make sense," Keira said.

Now Dr. Teasdale looked up, and with a kind smile asked, "Like what?"

"If we're on a ship, the ship must have a name. I mean, every ship has a name, right? What is the name of *this* ship?"

Dr. Teasdale's eyes grew wide. "What a good question. Have you asked your boss?"

Keira shook her head. "No…but would he know?"

Dr. Teasdale shrugged. "He might. But maybe he never thought to ask."

"Do you know?"

Dr. Teasdale cocked her head. "Where is this coming from?"

Keira looked away. "It's just simple curiosity. I mean, I'm an investigating agent. It's my job to know things, and when I don't know things, I find them out. So now that I know I'm on a starship, I'm curious about it. Nobody balks at knowing the name of the state they live in. Why should the name of the ship be a secret? I mean, any more than the ship itself is a secret?"

"That's a fine question," Dr. Teasdale asked.

"But you're not going to tell me?" Keira asked.

"I'm not sure it's my place to tell you."

"But you do know?" Keira asked.

Dr. Teasdale looked wary. She gave a slow nod. "I know."

"Is it...I don't know...above my clearance level?"

"That's a question for your superior, not for me," Dr. Teasdale said. "But I don't think it's any more secret than the ship itself."

"Would you tell it to me? The name?" Keira asked. She watched Teasdale's eyes flit back and forth as she thought. The psychiatrist uncrossed her legs and crossed them the other way. Keira enjoyed making her sweat. She reminded herself not to smile.

"My better judgement tells me you should ask your superior officer about that. But...I don't see what harm it can do. The name of the ship is the *Cibus Dei.*"

"Seebus Day?" Keira's brow scrunched. "Is that Irish or something?"

"It's Latin, actually," Dr. Teasdale said, dropping a chuckle that was probably intended to normalize the tension in the room. It didn't work. "It means 'The food of God.'"

"The food of God? What the fuck does that mean?"

Dr. Teasdale shrugged. "Maybe it's just a name."

"No, no. I can tell by how wigged out you are. It's not just a name. It's not random."

Dr. Teasdale closed her notebook and raised her chin. She started to cross her arms, but stopped, clasping them on top of her notebook in her lap.

"I was also wondering...*why* are we on a starship?"

Dr. Teasdale reared back visibly, still watching Keira, but turned her face slightly away. The doctor cleared her throat. "What have you been told?"

"Nothing. Just that we are. But we must be here for some actual reason. I mean, the expense, the trouble... What is this all about?"

"That is a most excellent question. And the answer to *that*...I am *not* permitted to divulge."

"Really. Because Terrance Basil thought you might be able to tell me."

Dr. Teasdale leaped to her feet, wavering a bit back and forth as her notebook clattered to the floor. "Have you spoken to Mr. Basil?"

"Yeah. I spoke to him. I asked him if he thought it was in any way improper for a psychiatrist on the CHS payroll to also be on his payroll...the payroll of the Lodge, I mean."

Keira watched the details of every muscle in the doctor's face. The poor doctor looked like a trapped rabbit. Then she watched her relax—an obvious effort of will, and only partially successful.

"I'm sorry," Teasdale said, resuming her seat. "You surprised me."

"Sorry about that," Keira said, adding in her head—*not.*

"I think this conversation has become too much about me, and I'd like to keep the focus on you," Dr. Teasdale said, sounding imminently reasonable.

"But here's the thing—I'd really *like* to talk about you," Keira countered. "And you can answer my questions here, or you can answer them downtown. So...what would you prefer?"

"Is this an interrogation?" Dr. Teasdale asked.

"It is if I have to put you in cuffs and take you to the CHS for a formal interview. Or we can just sit here and talk." Keira flashed her an insincere smile. "Your choice."

Dr. Teasdale sighed. "Fine. What do you want to know?"

"Why are we on a starship?"

"I can't tell you that," Dr. Teasdale said.

"You can't or you won't?" Keira asked.

"I suppose...technically...I won't. That information is, I'm afraid, above your clearance grade."

"The name of the ship isn't, but the reason the ship is going where it's going is too classified for me?"

"That's correct," Dr. Teasdale answered.

"But not for you?" Keira asked.

"That is also correct." Dr. Teasdale had regained her composure and was all business. "You are free to ask your superior, however. Perhaps he will see fit to raise your clearance."

Keira doubted that. *Need to know,* Schenck would say. Hell, maybe he didn't even know. "There is a reason we're on a starship, right?"

"For our purposes here, we should treat that like one of the great existential questions," Dr. Teasdale said. "Why are we here? What is the purpose of life?"

"Ah," Keira nodded. Her right hand was knotted into a fist. She forced it to relax. "Don't you think it's odd that a psychiatrist on the CHS payroll should also be employed by a fringe religious group under investigation?"

"There are some errors in fact in that question," Dr. Teasdale said. "First, I am not on the payroll of CHS. Many years ago I was approached by CHS for a special program to provide care for agents and other employees, for which I did extensive training and received a security clearance that is renewed every two years. But I bill them as an independent contractor." Keira opened her mouth to object, but Dr. Teasdale held her hand up and continued. "Second, my religion is not a concern of yours, nor of CHS. It does not enter into my work, and I am protected by the first amendment of the US Constitution, which, I will remind you, is still considered the law of the land in California—even in *this*... alternative California."

That elicited a thought Keira hadn't had before. "Oh. So there is still...another California...a real California on planet Earth?"

Dr. Teasdale scowled at her, as if she was an idiot child.

"I guess that makes sense," Keira asked.

"I think our time is over," Dr. Teasdale said, standing.

"I'm not so sure about that," Keira said, not getting up.

"Are you arresting me?"

Keira didn't answer immediately. The truth was, she wasn't sure.

"And if you are," Teasdale continued, "on what grounds? Being religious?"

"No," Keira answered, but knew her answer was not clear.

"I have another client in ten minutes and I need to...collect myself," Dr. Teasdale said, opening the door.

"We'll talk again soon," Keira said.

"I look forward to it," Dr. Teasdale said.

Angie paused at the hospital reception desk. "I'm here to visit Anthony Morrell, please."

The volunteer smiled looked up at Angie, and then frowned. *What, do I have a booger?* Angie wondered. But she figured it was probably the blue streaks in her hair and the nose ring that elicited such antipathy. It often did in norms.

The woman's demeanor took on a professional chill. "Name?"

"Anthony—"

"Your name," the woman interrupted her with edgy impatience.

"Oh. Angela Brega."

The volunteer wrote out a name tag with a wide Sharpie. She

peeled it from its backing and handed it to Angie. "Through the center hallway to the elevators, fourth floor."

"Thanks," Angie said. She speed-walked toward the elevators, and once inside bounced on the balls of her feet until the elevator stopped. She glanced down at her name tag, on which the volunteer had also written a room number. 467. She quickly read the signs and turned right.

It only took a few minutes to find the room. The door was wide open. She knocked, but poked her head in before receiving an answer.

A bone-thin African American man lay in the bed, staring at the television mounted high on the wall of the small room. The sound was off, but the subtitles were on. He looked down as she entered, and then scooted himself up in the bed when he realized she wasn't a nurse.

"To what do I owe the honor?" he asked.

Although in much different circumstances, Angie remembered the man. She moved to his bedside. "Hi, Mr. Morrell. My name is Angie. You...passed out in front of my car."

"Oh..." Anthony looked away, as if embarrassed. "I suppose I should thank you for not running over my ass."

"Sure. You're welcome. But I wasn't moving, so it wasn't likely."

"Lucky for me." Anthony looked at her sideways. "Why are you here?"

Angie shrugged. "I just wanted to see if you were okay, I guess."

"This a white guilt thing?"

"Fuck you. It's a 'some guy collapsed in front of me, and I want to see if he's dead yet' thing."

Anthony smiled. "Okay. Good answer, Angie." He pointed at her. "I like you."

476 · J.R. MABRY

"The jury is still out on you," Angie said. She pulled up a chair. "So why did you collapse?"

He shrugged. "Don't know. I wasn't drunk—I don't do nothin' to desecrate the temple, you know what I mean?"

Angie had no idea whatsoever, but she wasn't going to let him know that. "Uh-huh."

"They done some tests. I'm still waiting to hear."

Angie nodded. "Well, I'm glad to see that you're awake, at least."

"At least there's that. It was kind of scary. Felt like my vision was just going fuzzy. And then I felt real dizzy. And the next thing I know, I'm in the emergency room with needles in my arms."

"That sucks," Angie said.

"Damn right it does."

The room fell silent, and as the silence deepened, Angie felt more and more uncomfortable. She had no idea what to say. What did she have in common with this man? What did she have to offer him, or he to her? She couldn't think of a single thing.

She rose. "Well, I guess I'll let you rest—"

"Fuck rest. I'm bored out of my everloving skull."

Angie hesitated.

Anthony sighed. "But I guess you got better things to do."

"I don't really." She hadn't intended to say that. It just fell out. Now she felt trapped.

"Good. Besides, it don't look like you're the kind that just give up on people. Have a seat, weird white girl, and tell me about yourself. You got a cloud hanging over you, and it ain't raining on my account."

Angie sat. Was she that transparent? And just how much should she say? On the other hand, who else did she have to talk to, other than Becky? And she already knew what Becky thought. "I have a friend who's...going off the deep end."

"Off the deep end how?" Anthony asked. He reached for a pink sippy cup and held it to his mouth.

"He joined this cult, and then he, like, started getting really busy and distant. We tried an intervention, and now he's not speaking to us...to me. And I don't really know what to do about it. I was thinking of calling a 5150 on him—"

Anthony made a face. "Ouch! That's a sure-fire way to end a friendship."

"I know." Angie's shoulders sank.

"How do you know this...cult is harmful?"

"Aren't all cults harmful?" Angie asked.

"What makes a religion a religion and a cult a cult?" Anthony asked.

Angie blinked. "Uh...harmfulness?"

"No," Anthony said. "Size." He pointed at her. "If it's got a lot of people, it's a religion. If it's only got a few, it's a cult. Ain't no other difference."

Angie didn't know what to make of that. "But don't cults—"

"Sounds like you're judging one small religious group by comparison to another. That's called the fallacy of false equivalence."

"What do you mean?"

"I mean, both Jesus and Hitler had mustaches, right? That don't mean their teachings were the same."

Angie nodded. "So you think maybe...it's not a dangerous cult?"

Anthony shrugged. "What the fuck do I know about it? I'll tell you one thing, though. A smart guy named Herbert Spenser once said, 'There is a principle which is a bar against all information, which is proof against all arguments, and which cannot fail to keep a man in everlasting ignorance—that principle is contempt prior to investigation."

Angie blinked. "Uh...okay. Where did you hear that?"

"The AA Big Book, the font of all wisdom."

"I thought you didn't drink or anything."

"I don't...now."

"Oh." Angie looked down at her hands. "So...what does that mean?"

"I think it means that before you judge your friend any more than you already have, you ought to check it out."

"I've been reading up on it—"

"Fuck reading about it. Go experience it."

"Are you serious?"

"If you read about it, all you're going to get is someone else's opinion on it. Why not form your own opinion?"

Angie nodded. "Go to the Lodge?"

"The Lodge?" Anthony asked. "You mean the Gnostic Lodge, over on Aberdeen?"

"Yeah," Angie said, her eyes widening.

Anthony laughed. Then he laughed some more.

"What? Why is that funny?" Angie asked.

"Oh, girl. Just go. Ain't no one gonna hurt you there. And they got some tasty snacks. Just...be sure to wear you a vest."

Seth bent to grab a handful of grapes from the refrigerator. Then he heard a thump. He looked up, then looked around. Everything seemed normal. Then he heard it again. He realized it wasn't something falling over, but someone knocking slowly and softly. He frowned and headed for the door. He opened it a crack.

His eyes sprang open. "Mr. Basil!" He pulled the door open wide. "Uh...come in, come in. I...wasn't expecting you."

Mr. Basil gave him a kind smile and entered. Seth shut the door behind him.

"Sorry about the mess." He waved him toward the couch.

"Can I get you a beer?" Seth winced. Was it too early in the day to offer him a beer? It was barely after noon.

"A beer would be lovely."

Inwardly, Seth heaved a sigh of relief. He sprinted back to the fridge and pulled out a couple of Anchor Steams and popped the caps off them. Then he walked quickly back to the living room and handed one of them to Basil.

The tall gentleman took it with an expression of thanks. As Seth sat on the floor nearby, he wondered at how surreal it was to have Mr. Basil in his living room. The man seemed to fill the place up, his knees, bent stork-like, higher than his pelvis. He looked like he was more folded into the couch than sitting on it.

"I would have come by the Lodge," Seth said.

"There is no Lodge. Not anymore," Mr. Basil said.

"What?" Seth asked, almost dropping his bottle of beer. "What, was there a fire, or—"

Mr. Basil held up his hand. "No, nothing like that. The house is still there. We just...we can't use it. We've been found out. The CHS is sniffing around, and I'm afraid we're exiles until...well, until they stop."

Seth looked down, his eyes darting back and forth as he thought through the implications of this. "So..."

"We'll use the warehouse as our base of operations. Just please don't bring a cell phone when you go there. And go by a circuitous route."

Seth nodded. So using the Ryde app was out, not that he used the expensive service often.

Mr. Basil gave him an encouraging smile. "It'll be fine. We've survived scrutiny in the past. We just need them to believe that, at heart, we're just a kooky cult."

Seth didn't know how to respond to this. Was it a joke?

"Fortunately," Mr. Basil continued, "that's close enough to the truth that it isn't hard to play the part. Next week I'll start a lecture series at the Rosicrucian Museum on 'Gnosticism and Popular Culture.' It should be fun."

Seth nodded. "Can I help, somehow?"

"Well, as it happens, that is why I am here. But before I go into that, I want to know if you're ready for your final seal."

Seth froze. Every seal had been devastating in its own way. And this last seal, he knew, was the greatest of them. Did he really need the rug pulled out from under him again, and in a potentially much more dramatic fashion? *I'm barely holding it together as it is*, he thought. His leg started to bounce.

"Yes," he heard himself saying, although his voice sounded distant, as if it were coming from someone else. "Yeah, I'm ready."

"Good. Tomorrow night, then, at the Warehouse. Eight o'clock. And you can't be late."

"No, of course not."

"Good. I'm glad you're taking your final step with us, Seth, because...well, you're going to need it for what I'm about to ask of you."

"Okay...?" Seth asked warily.

"You asked if you could help. Well...Nazz has given me your reports, and you've made quick improvements. And your maps are flawless."

The compliment helped Seth to relax a bit, although his leg continued to bounce like a jackhammer. "Uh...thanks."

"It's true, dear boy. And I think you're ready." He cocked his head and fixed Seth with one slitted eye. "So how about it? Are you ready to go through the S-panel again? For real this time? For us?"

Seth felt sweat seep through his skin, almost as if someone had turned on a faucet. "I...uh...I didn't expect it to come so soon."

"Yes, well, the...investigation has upset our timeline. Plus, our astronomers insist we're getting close—"

"Close to what?"

"Close to *him*."

"The demiurge?"

Basil nodded, closing his eyes. He took a deep breath. "I know it's scary, but there's only three ways this can go." He held up one finger. "Either we succeed and turn the *Cibus Dei* around—" He held up a second finger. "—or we die trying—" He held up a third finger. "—or we do nothing and all die in the belly of the great beast himself."

Seth had not heard their situation spoken of in such stark or pithy terms. He felt a bit of vertigo. He nodded slowly. When put like that, what choice did he have?

"I'll do it," he said.

"How the hell did I let you talk me into this?" Becky asked.

"Relax. I'm not even sure what 'this' is," Angie answered. She leaned back in her seat, resting her knees on the steering wheel.

"So that's the Lodge?" Becky asked. "It's a nice house."

"It seems to be a very, very empty house," Angie noted. "But this is one of the nights I know Seth goes."

"So...what happens here?"

"Fuck if I know," Angie said. She looked at a hangnail that was bugging her. She chewed at it, but it didn't help.

"So what's the plan?"

"I don't really have a plan."

"Are you going to confront him on the way in?" Becky asked.

"I don't have a plan," Angie repeated.

"You're just going to wing it?"

"Exactly."

"Are you planning to go in?"

"Maybe."

"Is that why you have a vest on?"

"Maybe. I got one for you in the back seat. You'll have to brush the lint off."

"Ugh. I'm not going in."

"We'll see."

"Why am I even here?" Becky asked.

"Because you're as interested in stopping...whatever this is...as I am."

"I'm not sure that's true..." Becky objected.

"And because stakeouts are boring, and you're entertaining."

"Gee, thanks," Becky said. "I'll have my agent invoice you for my time."

That made Angie grin, but she didn't take her eyes off the Lodge.

"What happens if I have to pee?" Becky asked.

"You're wearing a skirt, what's the problem?" Angie asked.

"What?"

"Drop your drawers in here, then squat by the side of the car. Who's gonna see? Skirts are your super-power."

"Gross," Becky said. "I bet you'd actually do that."

"Me? Never. Wouldn't wear a skirt to save my own life."

"But you'd pee outdoors?"

"Done it a million times."

"Why do I not doubt that?" Becky asked herself, out loud.

Angie glanced at the car's media panel. "6:50," she said. "Something tells me it ain't happening tonight."

"Well, give it more time. Maybe being fashionably late is, like, a gnostic thing."

Angie grunted. Just then a rusted Toyota Corolla turned onto the side street and slowed down near the Lodge. It parked, and a couple wearing vests got out. They pointed at the Lodge, and then talked to one another.

"I've got to do something about my hair," Becky said.

"Shhhh!" Angie said. Her window was already rolled down, but as they were parked on the other side of the street, Angie was too far away to hear what the couple were saying. They each pulled out their phones and scrolled. Then they hastily piled back into their car and pulled into the street.

"Hold on," Angie said, pulling a hard U-turn and barreling after the Corolla. Angie was careful to keep a good half-block behind them. Once on El Camino, however, she drew closer so as not to be stuck behind any lights. Once she had to run the yellow to keep up, but she stayed with them.

They drove for eighteen minutes before pulling into the parking lot of a warehouse in an industrial district. There were few spaces left, as the lot was nearly full. But Angie found one near a far corner of the building.

"Where are we?" Becky asked.

"Still in San Jose," Angie said.

"Actually, East San Jose by now," Becky said.

"Fine." Angie reached into the back seat and grabbed a vest. She tossed it in Becky's lap. "Put this on."

"What? Why?"

"Because whatever is going on is probably already going on, and we're missing it."

"So? We found them, right? Isn't that what you wanted?"

"What I want is to find my friend and find out whatever fresh hell he's gotten himself into, so that I can get him out. Now, you coming or am I flying solo?"

"Holy flying Jesus," Becky said. She gave forth a great "oof" and opened the passenger door. Once on her feet, she put on the vest. Its bright green pattern clashed with her chiffon skirt and cream blouse. "This looks ridiculous."

"That's the fundamental nature of vests," Angie said. "You'll fit right in." Angie's own vest was cracked black leather, and it went well with her black jeans and Doc Martins.

"You got me a sucky vest on purpose."

"Oh my God, listen to yourself," Angie rolled her eyes. "Boo-hoo, my vest doesn't match my blouse. Don't you think there are more important things to whine about?"

"I'm not whining," Becky objected.

"You're totally whining. You're whining so bad you're whinging."

"I don't even know what that means," Becky admitted.

"It means exactly what you're doing right now." Angie headed for the back of the building.

"They're going that way," Becky pointed at the couple they'd followed, now rounding the corner at the front of the building.

"Which is exactly why we're going this way. By definition, you don't break into a building by going through the front door."

"I don't think that's true. You can break into the front door if it's locked."

"Are you through yet? Can I focus?"

"I hate you," Becky said.

"And we've only been living together a little more than a week. Congratulations, you've lasted longer than most of my girlfriends."

"I'm not your girlfriend."

"No kidding. I'll bet you don't even give head."

Becky seemed stunned into silence by this, and Angie suppressed a smile. Rounding the corner, out of sight of the parking lot, Angie noticed three entrances, one each by the corners of the back of the warehouse, and one large loading dock with a rising corrugated door. Angie walked directly to the nearest of the regular-sized doors and tried the handle. Locked, of course. Reaching into her vest, she pulled out her kit.

"What the fuck is that?" Becky asked.

"What does it look like? It's a Dangerfield set. Best there is." Angie said, kneeling so that the knob was at eye-level to her.

Untying the strings of her kit, she selected a triangle pick and inserted it into the keyhole. Closing her eyes, she felt around until she'd divined the contours of the tumbler. Then she gave the pic a twist, and with a bit of pressure, she felt the handle turn.

"Oh. My. God." Becky held the sides of her head in her hands in imitation of Edvard Munch's "The Scream." "I'm going to spend the rest of my life in jail."

"Stop being such a drama king, Nancy," Angie said, holding the door open.

Becky just stood there. "Fine. Look, I'm going in now," Angie said. "You can come or not. Suit yourself. Just know that when this door closes, it's locked again."

Angie went in. She smiled as she heard Becky bustle in behind her. "We are so, so dead," Becky whispered. Angie held up her hand to stop her. Then she put her finger to Becky's lips. She leaned in and whispered, "Stay close."

WHAT DOES "TABOO-BREAKING" REFER TO IN TANTRA?

Tantra is a spiritual and philosophical tradition that originated in ancient India and has spread throughout various cultures and religions over time. Rooted in Hinduism and later adopted by Buddhism, Jainism, and other belief systems, tantra encompasses a diverse range of practices, rituals, and beliefs aimed at spiritual growth, self-realization, and the union of the individual with the divine.

The term "tantra" is derived from the Sanskrit word meaning "loom" or "weave," symbolizing the interwoven nature of existence. Tantra seeks to embrace and integrate all aspects of life, including the physical, emotional, and spiritual realms. It recognizes that all experiences and energies can be pathways to enlightenment and liberation.

Central to tantra is the notion that the divine resides within each individual and can be accessed through various means, including rituals, meditation, yoga, breathwork, and sexual practices. Tantra views the human body and its experiences as sacred and strives to transcend dualistic perceptions of good and evil, embracing the unity and interconnectedness of all things.

Breaking taboos in tantra refers to the intentional exploration and transcendence of societal, cultural, or personal restrictions within the context of tantric practices. While tantra encompasses various taboos and guidelines aimed at spiritual growth, some practitioners may choose to challenge these boundaries as part of their journey towards self-discovery and liberation.

One aspect of breaking taboos in tantra involves challenging societal norms and expectations related to sexuality. Tantra acknowledges the transformative potential of sexual energy and encourages individuals to explore their sensual and sexual nature in a conscious and mindful way. This may involve practices such as sacred sexuality, conscious touch, or ecstatic experiences that challenge traditional beliefs and attitudes towards sex.

Another aspect of breaking taboos in tantra relates to defying cultural or religious restrictions that hinder personal freedom and self-expression. Tantra recognizes that societal norms and conditioning can limit an individual's potential for spiritual growth. By questioning and challenging these restrictions, practitioners may strive to reclaim their authentic selves and embrace their unique desires, identities, and expressions.

The breaking of taboos in tantra is not about reckless or irresponsible behavior, but rather a conscious and intentional act aimed at expanding one's consciousness, pushing boundaries, and questioning societal conditioning. It involves a deep understanding of the underlying principles and a willingness to explore and confront limitations in order to experience personal growth and transformation.

CHAPTER SEVENTEEN

Jesus said, "I tell you the truth, no one will ever enter
the kingdom of heaven because I ordered it,
but rather because you yourselves are filled."
—*Secret Book of James*[*]

W hen Seth stepped into the warehouse, it was transformed. The brown room-dividers were nowhere in sight, and the space was lit by candles, creating the appearance of a vast cathedral rising to heights untouched by the flickering light. The intoxicating aromas of frankincense and myrrh filled the air, lending an even more surreal feeling to the cavernous space. There were many milling

---

[*] The Secret Book of James: Nag Hammadi Library, Codex I, 2, translated by Marvin Meyer, published in *The Gnostic Bible* (Boston, MA: Shambhala Publications, 2009).

around, talking in groups of two here, three there, four over yonder. All were dressed in simple white robes that were nearly— but not quite—translucent.

Before Seth could approach anyone, however, he saw a familiar figure striding toward him. He froze as he realized what he was seeing—Dr. Teasdale glided over the cement floor on bare feet, her white robe billowing behind her, the outlines of her areolae visible through the thin fabric, along with the dark inverted triangle of her pubic hair. His mouth hung open as he stared at her. She didn't seem to notice, however, and caught him up in a hug that felt, all at one time, too intimate and completely unerotic. "Seth, I'm so glad to see you," she said. "Are you excited?"

He didn't know how to answer that. He was becoming aroused, but he wasn't sure that was what she meant.

"It is your final seal, after all," she continued. "Remember what our Lord said: 'There is nothing hidden that will not be revealed.'* Tonight, there will be no more secrets." She grabbed his arm before he could respond, and slipping her own through it, she guided him toward the left side of the room, away from the confluence of candles. "The vestry is over here—well, our makeshift vestry. Normally, we'd be at the Lodge, but...gnostics are nothing if not adaptable." Having reached the side of the room, she led him to a door. "Just through there you'll find a place to change. Tell them you'll need the initiate's vestments—it's a little different from the plain robe most people will be wearing. Well, it *is* a regular robe, but they'll fit you with a dalmatic to go over it, too."

Seth opened his mouth to ask, "What's a dalmatic?" but Dr. Teasdale had already opened the door and shooed him inside. She shut it again without salutation. Inside, a harsh industrial fluores-

---

* Luke 8:17

cent light hung from a set of chains, one of the rods sputtering a protest punctuated by flickering. A moment later, a young man Seth didn't recognize entered, carrying a large cardboard box.

"Oh, hullo," the young man said. "I don't know you."

"No," Seth agreed. "I'm Seth."

"I'm Asa. So good to meet you." He set the box down, then turned and bounced on his toes. He grinned and extended his hand, exuding a buoyant enthusiasm that reminded Seth of Kush. "You must be here for a robe! Are you a celebrant, an acolyte, an initiate, or a congregant?"

"Uh...an initiate," Seth said, shaking his hand.

"You don't sound too sure," Asa said in a teasing tone.

"You know, every one of these has been...a bit of an adjust-ment," Seth confessed.

Asa laughed, a sound that seem to be coming from the bottom of a deep well. "Tell me about it! Not to worry, though. Tonight is the last of them, and the best. And what's more, it'll make sense of everything that came before."

"Promise?" Seth asked.

The young man put a comforting hand on Seth's shoulder. "I promise."

Seth nodded. The young man held out a robe, exactly like the one that Dr. Teasdale had been wearing. It wasn't completely white, but flaxen, with light brown hatchwork. It felt rough to his fingers and had a surprisingly satisfying heft.

The young man opened another of the boxes and rooted around. "Back at the Lodge, all of these are in their proper draw-ers. This is a sacristan's nightmare."

"Is that what you are? A sacristan?"

"I am! You should volunteer for a season. It's a great education in liturgics. I rotate off next year, but I'm thinking of re-upping, because I just really geek out over it. Ah, here it is." He pulled a folded garment from the box. Unfolding it, Seth saw that it

492 · J.R. MABRY

sparkled like gold. The young man held it up to his own robe, tucked just under his chin. "Lovely, eh?"

"Uh...yeah," Seth agreed. The garment was similar to a stole, but instead of two ribbons running parallel down the body, it was one panel that covered the middle of the body, from the neck all the way down to the knees. The gold, he saw now, was stitched into a pattern that reminded him of Victorian needlework. Whoever had made this had put hundreds of hours of work into it. The young man held it out to him.

Hesitantly, he took it and put it on. But the dalmatic flummoxed him. "How do I?"

"So, at the top, you see there's a big oval. That drops over your head. This flap goes in front, and this flap goes in back. Here, let me help you put it on." There were no sides to the garment, so Seth didn't have to raise his hands. But he held his head still as Asa lowered the garment onto his shoulders. He straightened the front panel and then motioned Seth to turn. Apparently, the rear panel needed no adjustment. "That looks great," Asa said.

"Okay," Seth said. He had no idea what else to say. He pointed to the door, "Can I—"

"Oh, no. Once you're vested, you have to remain hidden until the start of the ceremony. Follow me and I'll take you to the green room." He smiled conspiratorially and whispered, "It's not really green. Not even the one at the Lodge." He seemed to think this was a great joke, but Seth wasn't sure he got it. "Besides, Dr. Robinson wants to do some instruction."

"Ah. Okay." Seth felt relieved to hear that. A little context and a few rubrics would be very welcome indeed.

It turned out that the green room was nearly at the other side of the warehouse, and Seth felt his spirits rise with the ambient conviviality on display. Unlike the other seals, which had been administered in a solemn but casual manner, this one seemed likely to be highly liturgical, and yet there was undeniably a carnival atmosphere gathering.

Seth shook his head as they approached an elaborate stage. At its center, draped with gauzy, golden material, was a low stone altar. Gold fabric matching his dalmatic hung from high poles straight down to the stage floor—seven of them, evenly spaced, as if the stage itself was an altar and these were seven gigantic candlesticks.

Asa circumambulated the stage and approached a door set behind it. "Here you go. Break a leg."

"Uh...thanks." Seth entered the room, and saw a familiar sight —several of his cohort gathered around Dr. Robinson. Robinson looked up and gave Seth a patient smile—too patient?

"Ah, Mr. St. John. We've been waiting for you."

Definitely too patient, Seth noted. Dr. Robinson was dressed in the same simple robe everyone else was wearing. Among his cohort gathered here were Lynn, Musa, Maria, and Jude, all in dalmatics as he was.

"Let us pause a moment to make contact with her, for this is truly her night," Dr. Robinson said.

Seth quickly dragged an empty chair into the circle and sat. He closed his eyes and concentrated on his breathing. He noticed the jangled edges of his nerves quivering painfully. He willed them to be still. He noticed all the tension in his muscles, and he willed them to relax as well. Soon his breathing was slow and deep. He turned his attention further inward, and at the same time, projected himself outward—into space, into the place where *she* was.

And she was there. Once more, her face was obscure, but he knew her. He felt himself engulfed in warmth, in light, in comfort. In his ear he heard a whisper: "Tonight, you will be mine."

It might have sounded ominous, but it didn't. It sounded romantic, thrilling.

At the sound of a tiny Tibetan bell, Seth's eyes snapped open. He watched as Dr. Robinson set the bell—two bronze disks held together by a leather strap—on the floor beside him. He sniffed and looked at each of them in turn.

"We gnostics generally put people into three categories. You might be thinking, 'that's very Platonic,' and you would not be wrong. But whereas Plato divided society into Gold for the rulers, Silver for their administrators, and Brass for the working people, gnostics divide them into different categories.

"First, there are the Hylics, those who have no soul. They are simply animate matter, and when they pass, all that they are simply returns to the earth. These are people who have no spiritual inclination or interest.

"Next we have the Psychics, those who have an animal soul. These are they who have an interest in spiritual things, whose minds have been pricked by Wisdom. Just as sand enters an oyster and is transformed into a pearl, Psychics have been selected by Wisdom and wounded by her. By means of that wound they were impregnated with a soul. That soul continues to develop as they grow in knowledge."

Maria's hand went up.

Dr. Robinson looked surprised to have been interrupted. "Um...yes, Ms. Gonzales?"

"Are you saying that none of us are born with a soul?"

"That is correct," Dr. Robinson affirmed.

"But we grow a soul?"

"You *can* grow a soul," Dr. Robinson said. "But it takes attention and effort." He gave her another of his patient smiles. "Perhaps you've noticed?"

Maria looked perplexed, but then it seemed like something clicked. Her face relaxed and she nodded.

"What happens to the souls of Psychics when they die?" Jude asked.

"Well, that depends upon whether they have cultivated good or evil in their lives. If evil, then what little soul they have gathered dissipates and they return to the earth, much as the Hylics do. But if they have cultivated good, then their soul endures and is granted another body by the archons."

"So they reincarnate?" Jude clarified.

"Yes," Robinson affirmed.

"But they're still prisoners of the demiurge?"

"Yes."

It was Jude's turn to nod and look thoughtful.

"Finally, there are the Pneumatics. These are they in whom Sophia has placed the spark of true divinity. They alone are given the secret knowledge needed to escape the archons. They alone are truly free. They alone will escape their prison and return to their true home."

"And what are we?" Seth asked. He didn't know where the question came from. It just tumbled from his lips.

"Right now, you have cultivated your animal soul. You are all Psychics. But this is not to be disparaged. Some of the greatest spiritual heroes of humankind have been Psychics—Socrates, the Buddha, St. Paul, Lao Tzu, Einstein—all of these were Psychics and they were lights in the darkness of this dire world."

He paused and let that sink in. Seth didn't like hearing that he was only a Psychic, or only possessed the soul of an animal. His mind flashed on Kush. It wasn't so bad being compared to him, was it? Kush was the most soulful being he knew.

"But don't despair. Tonight, you will receive the final seal. Up until now, you have received only knowledge. Knowledge is good, but it is not perfect. Tonight, however, you will receive not knowledge, but wisdom. What you gain tonight will not be something you could learn from books; it is not something that can be described in words. It can only be experienced. Knowledge is of the mind, but wisdom is of the heart. Tonight, your hearts will be impregnated by Holy Wisdom. Tonight, you will experience the coincidence of opposites. Tonight, all twoness will collapse into one. Tonight is the great and original tantric rite that will erase duality and place within you a spark of true divinity."

"Just like Eve and Adam," Lynne breathed.

"Exactly so," Dr. Robinson said, looking genuinely pleased for the first time. "This night you will experience the planting of the seed of the Word in your soul. As Meister Eckhart said, 'A pear seed grows up into a pear tree, a nut seed grows up into a nut tree —but a seed of God grows into God, to God.'* And in Thomas' gospel, Jesus said, 'I will give to you what eyes have never seen, what no ear has heard, what hands have not touched, and what has never arisen in the human heart.'† You will receive that gift tonight."

Seth felt the hair on the back of his neck rise, and a chill shook his entire frame.

Dr. Robinson put his hand through a slit in his robe and withdrew a folded piece of paper. "Listen to what Philip says in his gospel: 'Right now what we have to work with is this physical creation. Some say, "The powerful are held in high regard, while those who are weak are invisible and scorned." The truth, though, is just the opposite: those in high regard are actually weak and inferior, while the unseen are powerful and honorable. Mysteries are revealed through images and symbols. The Bridal Chamber, however, remains hidden; it is the holiest of all holy things. In the beginning, a veil concealed how the demiurge governed creation, but being torn away, the things within are revealed, and this house will be left behind, or even destroyed. Thus the demiurge will flee from here, but it will not enter the holiest of holy places,

---

* *Meister Eckhart: The Essential Sermons, Commentaries, Treatises, and Defense*, translated by Edmund Colledge and Bernard McGinn (Ramsey, NJ: Paulist Press, 1981) p. 241.
† "Gospel of Thomas," logion 17.

for it cannot unite with the Light and the Fullness. Instead, it will be beneath the wings of the cross, and held in its arms. This shall be our salvation when catastrophe floods them. If someone in the tribe is a priest, he can enter the curtain with the High Priest. But the curtain was not torn only at the top, allowing access to those above, nor was it only torn at the bottom, permitting access to those below. Instead it was torn from top to bottom, allowing all, the high and the low alike, access to the secret Truth. This is truly excellent and mighty! We shall enter through these "weak and despised" symbols. They are indeed weak in the presence of the glory of the wholeness that they bring forth. But there is glory that surpasses glory, and power that surpasses power. Therefore those who are whole open to us the secrets of Truth. And those who are the holiest of the holy revealed themselves, and invited us into the Bridal Chamber.'* Tonight, this prophesy will come true in your own experience, in your own person...in your own body."

Seth saw nods all around. Dr. Robinson stood. Just then came a knock on the door. A woman Seth did not recognize poked her head in. "Two minutes," she announced, and withdrew again. Dr. Robinson waved them over to the door. "We're going to enter single file. Just follow me, and sit where I sit. Once you are seated, look up. You'll see that everything happens beneath the shadow of the cross. This is symbolic and important. Jesus came to crucify the system. In this ritual, this is exactly what you will be doing."

There was another knock and the door flew open. With hands crossed in front of him, Dr. Robinson walked slowly and solemnly out of the room. Seth followed directly after him, and he saw the others behind him out of the corner of his eye. Dr. Robinson immediately turned right down the hallway, and then left into the open warehouse space. All was dark, save for a thousand flick-

---

* "The Gospel of Philip," logion 105.

ering candles. Seth blinked, trying to adjust to the lack of light while not losing sight of Robinson. Fortunately, there was little in his way. Dr. Robinson walked in front of the first row of seats to stage right, and at the corner of the stage, turned left. There were two rows of empty chairs. Dr. Robinson went to the end of the row and sat. Seth sat next to him, and Lynne sat on his other side.

While the others were walking toward their seats, Seth noticed for the first time that the assembly was singing a chant.

There are three places of offering in the Holy City
the one that opens to the west is called "the holy"
—all may enter there, for it contains no mysteries.

The one that opens to the south
is called, "the holy of the holy."
The one that opens to the east
is called, "the holy of holies"
—there the high priest enters alone.

For us, Baptism is "the holy" place,
For us, Redemption is "the holy of the holy"
—for us, the Bridal Chamber is "the holy of holies"

Baptism brings forth resurrection
And Redemption ushers one into the Bridal Chamber
—the Bridal Chamber leads us
to something we cannot imagine.

The curtain is rent from top to bottom,
so that those of us who are below may ascend.
—Lord, make us one and liberate us

from the tyranny of this world. *

T here was no tune to this chant that Seth could discern. It was mostly sung on a single note, with some variation at the end of the lines, although the pattern of these notes eluded him. All were seated by the time the last note of the chant faded, echoing throughout the cavernous space.

Then all stood. Seth jumped to join them, as did his fellow initiates. Another chant was begun, but it seemed to be in another language, and Seth could not divine its meaning. He only then noticed that there was a broad center aisle, and from the rear of the room a figure was striding slowly and confidently toward the stage. Seth looked back and saw who it was—Mr. Basil.

His face was serene, hands steepled in prayer at his chest as he walked. He wore the same flaxen robe that everyone else did, but over it was a much larger, much more ornate vestment that looked a bit like a pancho. It matched the shining gold fabric of his dalmatic, only there was more of it. Seth recognized it as being very much like what he'd seen Catholic priests wear at mass.

Seth's head turned to follow his progress down the aisle. Now he was parallel to Seth's row, now he was past it, ascending the steps to the stage. He walked to the stone altar—the stage's only ornament—and bowed to it. Then he walked around it, and stood at the far side, facing the congregation.

"Peace be with you," he intoned.

"And with your spirit," came the sung response, all on one note.

Assuming a rich, resonant voice, Mr. Basil spoke, echoes reverberating strongly throughout the chamber. "You sons of men,

---

* Adapted from "The Gospel of Philip," logion 68.

repent and you, their daughters, come hither! Leave the ways of this corruption and approach her, and she will enter into you and will lead you out of annihilation! She will bestow wisdom upon you in the ways of truth. You shall not fall victim to corruption, nor to annihilation. Hearken to me and be saved, for I proclaim the grace of God among you!"*

"Holy Wisdom, come!" the congregation responded.

"Tonight, four of our sisters and brothers in the resistance tradition pass from illusion to reality, from darkness into light. Tonight the veil which is pulled over every eye at birth will be lifted from them, and they shall behold what they truly are. Now they are Psychics, but soon they will be Pneumatics, for they are passing from knowledge to experience, from theory to known fact, from bondage to liberation. This is the rite of union! This is the rite of revelation! This is the rite of freedom!"

"Holy Wisdom, come!" the congregation cried out as one.

"Let the great and holy rite commence, and may the spirit of Holy Wisdom be visited upon all who celebrate and on all who witness."

"Holy Wisdom, come!" the congregation shouted.

At this, Mr. Basil stood off to the side. Seth saw a young woman dressed in the flaxen robe and adorned with a gold sash worn sideways, hanging from her left shoulder to her right hip, where it was fastened in some way that Seth could not determine. She held a book, bound in red leather and embossed by gold symbols that Seth did not recognize. She opened the book and began to read in a loud, melodious voice.

"A reading from the Gospel According to St. Philip: 'Everyone who goes into the Bridal chamber will be born in the light. They are not born from ordinary intercourse, which occurs in the dark,

---

* "Odes of Solomon," Ode 33, from *Suppressed Prayers* (Harrisburg, PA: Trinity Press International, 1998), p. 103.

where any light they kindle is eventually put out. But the sacrament of this Union occurs in broad daylight—though not the kind of daylight that ever dims. Anyone who becomes a child of the Bridal Chamber shall receive the Light. And anyone who does not receive it here will not be able to receive it there. But those who do receive it here will be invisible to the archons and unstoppable. Nor will anyone be able to disturb them, even if they are friendly with the System. And when they leave the System, since they have already received the Truth through images, the System is transformed into the eternal realm, which is for them wholeness. And this is how it is revealed to us: not hidden in the darkness of the night, but rather in perfect daylight.'"* She closed the book and shouted, "The word of truth for a people of truth!"

"Amen!" the congregation responded.

Then began another chant. Hearing rustling behind him, Seth looked over his shoulder to see that someone else was processing. His eyes widened as he saw who it was.

"Sheila?" he asked out loud. Fortunately, it was not loud enough for many to hear him over the chanting. But it was indeed her, he could see that, even if he could not clearly see her face. A white veil had been pulled over her face, held in place by a garland of flowers. But that was all she wore. Below the veil, she was completely naked. He recognized the shape of her breasts from when he had seen her during his practice runs through the maze.

She wasn't a fashion model's ideal of perfection. Her hips were wide, and he could see the ripple of cellulose on her thighs. But Seth still found her beautiful.

She moved without hurry, without shame, as if she had indeed found an antidote to the curse imposed by the demiurge in Eden—a curse that demanded a fig leaf, clothing, and embarrassment at the mention of any and every bodily function.

---

* "The Gospel of Philip," logion 107.

Every eye was on her, and yet to Seth's great surprise, it didn't feel awkward or creepy. Instead, it felt healthy and proud and strong. *What is happening?* the voice in his head asked. He didn't know, but he didn't want it to stop.

Sheila processed directly to the stage, but before ascending the steps she turned and looked Seth straight in the eye.

"Oh, shit," he whispered.

The chant stopped, the echo fading after many seconds. Sheila held out her hand to him. "Wisdom bids you come. Do you bid Wisdom come as well?" she asked.

Dr. Robinson leaned over and whispered into his right ear. "Say, 'I do,' loudly enough that we can all hear you."

"Uh...I do!" Seth shouted, jumping a bit at the loudness of his own voice.

Sheila grinned and winked at him. He reminded himself to look at her eyes rather than at her breasts, and he nodded. As if watching himself from afar, he saw his hand rise to meet hers. Her fingers curled around his, and she drew him away from his seat, toward the center aisle.

"Let us become as our ancestors were, naked and without shame."

"Uh...okay."

He froze in horror as she knelt down and grabbed the hem of his robe. She drew it upwards, exposing him to all the world. His hands rose of their own accord above his head as she drew the robe up and off of his shoulders.

The surreality of it all made him stagger, but she clutched at his hand again. She led him to the stairs, but stopped before taking the first step.

A new chant struck up, this one in English, a call and response. *"If the female and the male had not been separated, there would be no death,"* sang one choir to Seth's left. From the right side of the room, a second choir responded, *"Separation is the origin of death."**

Sheila placed her foot upon the first step, pulling him up with her. The choir on the left continued. *"This is why Christ came, to heal that ancient separation."* The choir on the right answered, *"To make all things right by uniting them again."* Sheila and Seth stepped up to the second stair. *"And all those who died because of this separation,"* sang the choir on the left, followed by, *"He will give them life again through union,"* on the right.

Sheila and Seth took the final step now, onto the stage. Seth was keenly aware that hundreds of people behind him were now staring at his buttocks. *Is there a smear of shit on my butt?* the voice in his head asked, nearly hysterical. He weighed how bad it would look to reach back with his free hand to check, but decided it would only make things worse.

Now both choirs sang together, in unison. *"The female unites with the male in the Bridal Chamber. Those who have been joined in the Bridal Chamber can never be separated again."*†

Sheila led him to the altar. Then she turned and scooted up onto it, facing the congregation. A new chant began, but it was in a language Seth did not recognize. He'd seen Sheila in this pose before, of course, but now she looked radiant. He wondered if it had to do with the lighting, but suspected it was something about how she was holding herself, how she was feeding off the emotions of the congregation. The air was electric with energies Seth did not understand.

Sheila reached out and grabbed his arm. She tugged on it until he stumbled toward her. She kept pulling him until he was standing in front of her, her knees squeezing at his hips. Her eyes shone with what seemed to be an almost ethereal light. Her lips

---

* "The Gospel of Philip," logion 70.
† "The Gospel of Philip," logion 70.

twitched, then she smiled, then she looked at his mouth and pulled on him again. As their lips touched, the chant behind them was punctuated by hoots and catcalls. Sheila grinned, but didn't let him go—she just pressed her smiling mouth harder onto his.

He was fully erect now, and embarrassingly aware of that fact. Sheila's arm circled his back and drew him in—closer, closer, until his penis was rubbing against her abdomen. It felt good...too good. He'd never been this close to a woman before, this intimate, not even with Becky. It wasn't that she hadn't invited it. It was just that he had never felt comfortable.

He was far from comfortable now, yet there was a passion rising in him that even his self-consciousness could not quell. The kiss somehow came to an end, and Sheila pulled back just far enough to look into his eyes. "I'm not me," she whispered. "I'm her. And you're not you. You're the Christ. When I look at you, I'm going to see him. When you look at me...you need to see her. Can you do that?"

Seth blinked, but he nodded. His mind raced, trying to process all of the strange, charged inputs flooding into him at once. *There are hundreds of people watching me,* the voice in his head said. But the only person he wanted to focus on was Sheila. *Not Sheila,* the voice reminded him. *Not Sheila,* he repeated to himself.

He closed his eyes and remembered the last time he had met with Sophia. He pictured the star-dappled canopy of deep space, and then he felt her presence. Her arms embraced him, and she was suddenly before him. He still could not make out her face, but it was undeniably her. "You need to see yourself as separate so that you don't bump into the furniture," she whispered in his ear. "But you are not separate. It's part of the illusion that you live in. I bring you now into Truth. You think we're different people, but we're not. Enter me and be One again." He wondered who was doing the whispering, really. Was it Sheila? But it didn't sound like Sheila's voice. Also, he was pretty sure he wasn't hearing it through his ears. He also didn't want to open his eyes, as he was afraid it might break the spell. Instead, he reached for Sophia, found her, and pulled her body as close to his as was humanly possible.

Far away, he detected some fumbling, and realized that someone—Sheila? Sophia?—was guiding his hardness into softness. He pushed and felt a merging that set his brain afire. He tightened his arms around her—whoever she was—pulling and pulling, until she seemed to pass into his chest. Then a shuddering began in his cock that rippled out until all of his members were shaking. He grunted and groaned involuntarily, pushing himself deeper and deeper into union. He was becoming One.

His orgasm erupted like a bomb in his brain. Time stopped. In slow motion, he saw her, but not from without. He saw through her eyes, and beheld her own ethereal body as his own. He lifted his hand, and lo! Her hand moved. But then he noticed the stars, and he couldn't tell if they were outside of her, or inside of her. He decided he didn't know, and it didn't matter.

He also had little time to consider it, for now, in a timeless, eternal moment, he saw everything that was. He saw the True God in the heart of the Fullness, the source of all whose center point was everywhere and whose circumference was nowhere.* He saw the infinite aeons dancing arm-in-arm with their mates in eternal ecstasy, circling the cosmic center. He saw—and was, and knew that he was—another aeon, the lonely Christ, forever pining for his exiled mate. All was suffused with a light so brilliant that the cumulative luminescence of a million suns could not approach it. The deepest reaches of space were brimming with brightness.

And then he saw the shadow.

It was just a pocket, like an isolated cyst on a healthy body,

---

* "Liber XXIV Philosophorum" by Marius Victorinus.

filled with corruption. It was surrounded by love, and held in grace, and permitted to persist by the patient kindness of the One. It seemed tiny, a flake of bitterness at any moment in danger of being swallowed up by the savory and the sweet. The defensive backs of the archons were turned against the radiance to ward it off, to keep their embattled portion of space in darkness.

And then he saw *him*: in the center of the shadow, like the tiny mirror opposite of the True God, the demiurge writhed in gibbering anguish. He was blind, lashing out at all who dared approach, snatching at a nearby star with a desperate, unquenchable hunger.

Seth felt the one overriding emotion and quality radiating from the True God at his back, and that quality was love. Before him, however, was Samael, whose overriding emotion and quality was fear. It was terror that drove him, Seth realized, and terror by which he ruled. He saw that the whole of the shadow, the only home he had ever known, was ruled by terror, a feeling he knew all too well, a feeling that short-circuited his brain in every moment of every day. And he saw that it was small. It wasn't love that was in danger of being snuffed out, as the religion of his youth had insisted. It was fear that was in danger of being enveloped, invaded, and transformed by love.

It was a knowledge too wonderful to be true...but it was true. It was too terrible to contemplate—how cruel was the lie, the illusion that had deceived him and so many. But now that it was exposed it seemed not so much terrible as desperate...imperiled... pathetic. He felt compassion welling up within him, not only for himself, but for the whole imprisoned race of humanity, for the beguiled galaxy groaning for its liberation,* and even for the gnashing, deformed godlet at the center of the shadow.

Now you know, she whispered within him. *Now I know,* he

---

* Romans 8:22

answered. And he also knew that this knowledge was his salvation. He could never unsee what he had just seen. All of Dr. Robinson's stories paled in comparison to this knowing. *This is gnosis,* Seth thought, and he knew that it was true. All of it. And that he was no longer separate from it. The illusion had been broken. He was a fear-driven loser no longer. He was the All, he was Light, he was the Fullness, he was Christ, he was Sophia, he was the True God radiating Love throughout infinite worlds. He was all of it, including the cyst that marred his too, too perfect body.

"That sounded good," whispered a voice in his ear. He opened his eyes and saw *her*—Sheila yes, but lurking behind those hazel pupils the intelligence of Sophia. Differences were arbitrary now, he saw that clearly. They were functional, practical, but not reflective of underlying truth. He suddenly understood a distinction between conventional reality and ultimate reality. Conventional reality was tugging at his sleeve, but it could never again dictate who he *was*.

"Hi," Seth said, smiling. His eyes were glazed, and tears wet his cheeks. Sheila opened her mouth and licked the salty water from his face. He wasn't expecting it, but it felt sexy and hot, and he realized his penis was still deep in her belly.

She pulled him deeper into her. "No rush, love."

"No rush," he repeated. He was slowly becoming aware of his surroundings. People were cheering, applauding. He even heard noise makers sounding, the kind friends sometimes brought to New Years parties.

Then he heard a voice, rising above all the jubilant noise, a voice he knew—and the last voice he expected to hear. "What the fuck, Seth!?"

He pulled out of Sheila and turned to face the voice. "Becky?"

She was dressed in a yellow skirt and an off-white blouse, and for some reason she was wearing a hideous vest. And she was striding up the aisle directly toward him.

"What the fuck?" she repeated. "You wouldn't get it on with me, in the privacy of my apartment, but what, you don't mind going at some slut in front of an audience? What the fuck is wrong with you?"

Seth blinked, not knowing how to respond. A silence had descended on the congregation, and it seemed for a moment as if he and Becky were the only ones in the room. "Hi, Beck," he said. His voice sounded weak, even to him. His penis, flaccid now and hanging heavily over his scrotum, dripped cum and began to shrivel.

She stopped at the stage and stared up at him. "What the hell are you doing? Who are these people? What is going on?"

"It's...kind of a long story," he offered.

"So this is the precious secret you couldn't tell me? You're fucking people in public? Is that what gnosticism is all about?"

"Uh...actually, this is the first time," he said.

"I don't fucking believe you," Becky said, her voice cracking and tears beginning to roll down her cheeks. "I would have *loved* you."

"I do love you," Seth said. "I know that now. Not the way you wanted, but really—"

"Don't even try...don't even go there...just shut the fuck up," she brayed, her hands flapping in frustration.

"I'm sorry, Beck. I'm sorry you had to see this. I'm sorry you had to find out this way."

"Would I *ever* have found out if I hadn't been here?" she yelled.

"Well...no, probably not."

"You would have just strung me along while you screwed people on, on, on...on *stage*?" she wailed.

"Um...I didn't really think it through. Maybe?"

"I thought you were a good guy, Seth St. John. I really did. Holy shit, did you have me fooled." She sniffed, turned on her heel, collected her dignity, and retreated as quickly as her legs could carry her.

Before Seth could react, Mr. Basil had taken the stage. Sheila was still seated on the altar, legs spread for all to behold her fullness. Seth felt momentarily faint and completely mortified. His moment of transcendence had been punctured by Becky, and he felt his nakedness keenly. No nightmare he had ever had came close to this. He wondered what he should be doing or where he should be standing. He contemplated covering his privates, but realized there was no point and it would only make him look more ridiculous.

But to his great relief, Mr. Basil shook out a fresh flaxen robe and walked over to him. He raised it over Seth's head and lowered it over him. Then he took the gold stole off his own neck and placed it over Seth's. When Mr. Basil spoke, it was booming and forceful, strong enough for those at the furthest reaches of the warehouse to hear. "'The powers cannot perceive those who are clothed in perfect light, and so they cannot seize them. You have now put on the perfect light in the sacrament of union.'"*

The congregation cheered again, a roar punctuated by clapping and whistling. Mr. Basil held his hands up to quiet them. "We have others to bring into Union this night." He waved Seth to his chair. With shaking legs, and having never been so grateful for a robe in his life, Seth teetered to the stairs. Suddenly hands were grasping at his arms, and Dr. Robinson was there, supporting him as he descended the stage.

"This way, my boy," Robinson said, sounding more compassionate and encouraging then Seth had ever remembered.

Seth lowered himself to his seat with a grateful sigh. Then he looked up at his cohort. Lynn was gone. Musa's eyes were huge and wet. "I...I think I'm...I can't do this," Maria said. She stood and

---

* "Gospel of Philip," logion 69.

turned into the aisle. Then she ran for the exit. No one pursued her.

"Mother!" Jude shouted, standing up. "I'm coming, Mother!" He raced for the stage. In a state of numb detachment, Seth watched as an acolyte pulled his robe from him, revealing a hirsute body and thick middle. His penis, however, was already erect and prepared for the ritual.

Seth couldn't watch, however. He lowered his eyes and tried to recollect every fragment of memory from his experience. It had been so vast, so timeless, so...everything. The only thing he could do was to let it wash over him again. But it was more distant in memory. Still, it made him question everything—who he was, what his life was about, what mattered and what didn't, what was real and what wasn't. One thing he knew: He no longer had any doubts. He had seen the True God in his Fullness. He had seen Christ and Sophia. He had seen the demiurge. And he had seen just how infinitesimal he was...except that he was more than he had been. He was no longer confined within the boundaries of his brain. He was all that is, including *her*, including Samael, including worlds uncountable and unnamed.

He realized he was hyperventilating and was starting to feel faint. He slowed his breathing and hugged his chest. Soon he began to feel normal again. He swallowed and looked up at the stage, just in time to see Mr. Basil lowering a fresh robe over Jude's body, followed by another gold stole.

Seth looked over at Musa, but the large black man was unreadable. His face was grave and hard as granite. Dr. Robinson motioned him toward the stage, but Musa glowered at him. "No," he said. Then he stood and with slow dignity that seemed to Seth to be tinged with sadness, moved into the aisle and walked away from the stage.

"Goddamn it," Dr. Robinson swore. Then he looked at Seth. "You. Get up there." He gestured toward the stage.

Seth was about to protest, but his legs were already moving. Not knowing what he was doing, what was expected, or what would happen, he once more ascended the stairs and walked toward where Jude and Mr. Basil were standing. With one hand on Jude's shoulder, he raised his other hand until Seth was near and rested it on his shoulder as well until they were in a huddle. "Since our other initiates have opted out, I would like to ask the two of you to assist me as we celebrate Eucharist."

Seth had few resources left, either to process what was happening or to object. In a daze, he moved toward the altar. Mr. Basil held his hand out to Sheila, who smiled at him and took it. He helped her to her feet, and led her off the stage. Then, as he was walking back to the altar, he motioned to someone Seth could not see. A moment later, two acolytes came forward with baskets about the size of a file box. Mr. Basil turned to one of them and took the basket from him. The acolyte removed the lid and stepped back. Mr. Basil turned to Jude. "Please put the bread on the altar. You too, dear boy," he said, with a nod toward Seth.

In what seemed like slow-motion, Seth reached into the basket and pulled forth husky, rustic loaves of bread. When they'd emptied the basket, there were six loaves grouped together, more or less in the center of the altar.

Then Mr. Basil reached for the other basket, but did not yet remove the top. Instead, he placed it on the altar before him and addressed the congregation. "Peace be with you."

"And with your spirit," they responded.

"Lift up your hearts," he exhorted them.

"We lift them up to the Fullness," they replied.

"Let us give thanks to the True God," he invited them.

"It is right to give our thanks and praise," they agreed.

"It is right and a good and noble thing, always and everywhere to give thanks. We praise your name of Father, which was spoken by you. We praise your name of Son which was spoken by you. We praise your entering our world. We praise your resurrection in us. We praise your way. We praise your seed. We praise the Word, the grace, the faith, the salt, the inexpressible pearl, the treasure, the plough, the net, the greatness, the crown, the one who for our sake was called Son of Man. We praise the truth, given to us, the rest, the knowledge, the power, the commandment, the freedom of speech, the hope, the love, the liberty, the refuge in you."*

He lifted the lid off the basket and set it aside. Then, without being touched, the basket *moved*. Seth jumped and took an involuntary step backward.

Mr. Basil continued. "We remember, O Christ, when you first came to us. When we were lost in ignorance and darkness, believing the lies of the god of this world,† you sought us out and found us. In the form of a serpent, you slipped unseen through the prison that held us, and you gave to our mother and father the secret, the knowledge, the gnosis that would set them free."

With that, Mr. Basil picked up the basket and turned it upside down. Seth jumped again as he saw a mass of small, slithering black snakes descend upon the bread.‡

"All that you touch is transformed," Mr. Basil said, raising his voice for all to hear. "All who eat of you and drink from your mouth become you."§

Seth watched the snakes sliding over the hills of bread, finding the plains of the stone altar, and finally drop, one by one, over its side onto the floor.

"Come, gift of the most high! Come perfect compassion!

---

* "Acts of John," 109, from *Suppressed Prayers* (Harrisburg, PA: Trinity Press International, 1998), p. 108.
† 2 Corinthians 4:4
‡ Epiphanius, *Panarion* 1:37:5:6.
§ Adapted from "The Gospel of Thomas," logion 108.

Come, fellowship with the male! Come, Holy Spirit!"* He made the sign of the cross over the bread and the remaining snakes.

Then he looked up at the congregation. "And now I bid you: Come, knowers of the mysteries of the chosen! May the grace which was before all things, inconceivable, ineffable, fill your inner self and multiply in you her knowledge, by sowing the grain of mustard seed in the good earth."†

Mr. Basil reached down and took up one of the loaves of bread. Shaking the snakes from it, he handed it to Seth. "Go stand over there and give it to the faithful as they come up." He pointed to a spot just in front of the altar, not far from where Seth had been standing when he had performed the ritual of the Bridal Chamber. But obviously, he would be facing the other direction this time, toward the congregation.

He did as he was bidden, taking up the bread and walking to the designated spot. Not long after he got into place, he saw Jude taking his place near him, just to his left. But instead of bread, Jude was holding the largest of the snakes. He held it just behind the head, so that it could not strike him. He held it at chest height, with its head pointed toward the congregation.

Then Seth noticed that people were filing from their seats and up the stairs. The first of the communicants approached him—a young man not much older than he. Instinctively, Seth tore a piece of bread from the loaf and put it into the young man's outstretched hands.

The young man put it into his mouth, closed his eyes, and mumbled a brief prayer that Seth could not hear. Then the young man moved to where Jude was standing, and, clasping his hands

---

* "Acts of Thomas," 50, from *Suppressed Prayers*, p. 106.

† Irenaeus, "Against Heresies," I:13:2, from *Suppressed Prayers* (Harrisburg, PA: Trinity Press International, 1998), p. 105.

behind his back, leaned in and kissed the snake on the mouth.[*] Then he turned and walked out of Seth's sight, presumably to another set of stairs to descend and resume his seat.

By then the next communicant was in place and she cleared her throat. Seth fumbled with the bread, but managed to break a piece off for her. He kept his attention on his duties from then on. He'd stopped trying to make sense of it all, and instead was simply focused on not embarrassing himself further.

After about ten minutes, the large loaf he was holding was exhausted, but to his surprise, an acolyte was standing by with another loaf. He received it gratefully and resumed distribution of the sacrament. After what seemed like an hour or more, the last of the communicants filed past.

Wearily, Seth tottered back to the altar, holding the shredded remains of a loaf. He set it on the stone slab and then just stood there. Mercifully, Mr. Basil approached and broke off a piece of bread, holding it out to him. Seth held his hands up as he had seen the others do, and watched as Mr. Basil put the bread in his hand. He stared at it, as if forgetting momentarily what he was supposed to do with it. But eventually he brought his hands to his mouth and received the bread, chewing the hard nutty crust and its doughy interior. It was delicious, and he found he wanted more. There were still some scraps on the altar, but he didn't know if it was proper to take them for himself. But then Mr. Basil held out his own hands, and Seth was instantly glad he hadn't followed his impulses. He broke a piece off one of the scraps for Mr. Basil and placed it in his hands. Then Jude was standing next to him, still holding the snake. Mr. Basil motioned with his head toward Jude, and Seth instinctively broke a piece of bread off and held it up to Jude's mouth. Jude received it gratefully and held forth the snake. Mr. Basil bowed to the snake, then moved in for a

---

[*] Epiphanius, *Panarion* 1:37:5:7.

kiss. Then Jude turned the snake to face Seth. Seth blinked. The snake blinked. Its tongue shot out and was immediately withdrawn.

Why should I kiss a snake? the voice in his head asked.

Because it's not just a snake, it represents Christ, another voice answered.

But it isn't Christ, the first voice objected.

How do you know? the other voice asked.

His brain recoiled at the absurdity of it. Was he really considering the idea that the snake before him was Christ? It was more likely a symbol of Christ. *Just as Moses lifted up the serpent in the wilderness,* he heard in his head, *so must the Son of Man be lifted up.** Jude was still holding the snake up to him. Without thinking about it further, Seth jutted his head forward and pecked his lips against the snake's head. He had half expected the snake to bite him, and was grateful when it didn't.

Mr. Basil then took the snake from Jude and held it forth for Jude to kiss. This Jude did without hesitation, with a look of fascinated rapture on his face. *Jude is an idiot,* the voice in his head asserted. *So what does that say about me?* the other voice asked.

The congregation was buzzing as Mr. Basil gathered what snakes he could and returned them to the basket. He held his hands up and everything became quiet again. "Where did you come from?" he asked, his booming voice echoing in the vast hall.

The congregation answered, shouting in unison, "We come from the light!"

"Who are you?" Mr. Basil shouted back.

"We are its children, chosen by the True God!" the congregation responded.

"What is the sign of the Fullness in you?" Mr. Basil shouted.

---

* John 3:14

"Motion and rest!"* the congregation shouted back, followed by hooting and whistles.

"Our kind Lord told us, 'When you strip yourselves naked without being ashamed, and take your garments and put them under your feet and trample them like little children, then you will look upon the child of the One Who Lives, and you will become fearless.' You are now beyond duality, dark and light, beyond right and wrong, beyond good and evil. Let your transgressions be signs for you of your blessedness." At this he held his hand up and made the sign of the cross. The congregation responded with a roar, and there was suddenly a flurry of motion throughout the warehouse.

Almost as one, the congregation pulled their robes off, standing naked together in the candlelight. Then they turned to one another and began to kiss, fondle, and caress. Before Seth was able to completely understand what he was witnessing, it had turned into an orgy.† Seth, whose first and only sexual experience had been earlier that same evening, found himself witness to a vast sea of undulating, writhing, copulating bodies. Moans and ecstatic shrieks punctuated the air. Catching motion out of the side of his eye, he looked over and saw Jude, bent over nearly double, his robe falling over his head and covering his face while a naked Mr. Basil thrust himself into his anus, grunting in obvious pleasure.

Seth jumped when he felt a tap on the shoulder. Whipping his head around, he was shocked to see Dr. Teasdale before him. She was naked, too, her brown hair falling in rings around her shoulders. She sidled up to Seth and reached down to grab the hem of his robe. She pulled it up and over his head, leaving him once

---

* "The Gospel of Thomas," logion 50.
† Epiphanius, *Panarion* 1:26:4:5

more exposed. Then she reached down and began to massage his penis.

"You shouldn't...you're my—"

"Seth, don't you see the purpose of this ritual? Right and wrong cancel each other out here. The duality between them is erased. All is One. Come, be one with me." He felt her mouth twitch against his and he mashed his lips onto hers. He closed his eyes, surrendering to both flesh and spirit.

LIQUIPEDIA
THE ANSWERBOT THAT GOES DOWN SMOOTH

WHAT ARE CONSPIRACY THEORIES?

Conspiracy theories refer to explanations or beliefs that propose secret, often malevolent, actions carried out by powerful individuals or organizations, aimed at manipulating events or suppressing information for their own gain. These theories typically challenge the widely accepted mainstream narratives and posit alternative explanations that involve hidden agendas, covert operations, or cover-ups.

Characterized by their speculative nature, conspiracy theories often lack substantial evidence and rely on conjecture, speculation, and cherry-picked information. They often attract a fervent following of individuals who feel marginalized, mistrustful of authority, or seek to make sense of complex events. The allure of conspiracy theories lies in their ability to provide seemingly logical explanations for perplexing or unsettling occurrences, offering a sense of control and comprehension in a chaotic world.

Conspiracy theories have a long history, spanning various domains such as politics, science, and popular culture. They range from well-known theories like the belief that the moon landing was faked, claims of widespread voter fraud during elections, the existence of a secretive global elite manipulating world events, or more recent examples such as the belief that S-panels are portals to alternate universes. The internet and social media have played a pivotal role in disseminating and popularizing conspiracy theories, allowing ideas to spread rapidly and enabling like-minded individuals to connect and reinforce their beliefs.

While some conspiracy theories have been proven false or unsubstantiated, a few have turned out to be partially or entirely true. Historical examples include the Watergate scandal or the Tuskegee syphilis experiment, where conspiracies were unveiled through investigative journalism or government inquiries. These cases highlight the importance of critical thinking, scrutiny of evidence, and the need for reliable sources of information to differentiate between genuine conspiracies and baseless speculation.

Conspiracy theories remain a topic of debate and concern due to their potential negative consequences. They can erode public trust in institutions, sow division, and promote hostility toward marginalized groups or individuals. Additionally, conspiracy theories may divert attention from genuine societal issues and impede collective efforts to address them effectively.

CHAPTER EIGHTEEN

Jesus reveals it to her
after taking her aside on the mountain,
praying, producing a woman from his side,
beginning to have sex with her,
and then partaking of his emission,
if you please, to show that
"Thus we must do, that we may live."
And when Mary was alarmed and fell to the ground,
he raised her up and said to her,
"O you of little faith, why did you doubt?"
—*The Questions of Mary**

* "The Questions of Mary," quoted by Epiphanius, *Panarion* I:26:8:2-3, from Wilhelm Schneemelcher, *New Testament Apocrypha*, Vol. 1 (Louisville, KY: Westminster/John Knox, 1990), pp. 390-391.

Angie opened the door to Becky's apartment and found her roommate on the couch, curled up in the fetal position, her cheeks wet and her eyes red. "You were right," she croaked.

"That's not a sentence I hear very often," Angie said, sitting next to her and putting a hand on her thigh. She rubbed it with atypical tenderness. "Um...what was I right about?"

"About Seth and that...cult. You were right about everything, and I didn't... I'm sorry I didn't really get it, or get on board with it. The intervention, I could have been..." She trailed off.

Angie made some shushing noises and continue to stroke her leg. "It's...okay. I didn't know it was that bad until tonight, either. Uh...how did you get home?"

"Ryde."

Angie nodded. "I'm glad you left when you did, because it only got worse."

Becky looked at her for the first time, widening one eye in disbelief. "How could it get worse?"

"After you left, they...well, let's see...another guy—big Bubba kind of fella—fucked the woman on the altar. Nothing like sloppy seconds."

"Jeez," Becky shook her head. She was lying down, so it was more like grinding her hair against the couch.

"Then they dumped a basket of snakes over some bread and then everyone lined up to eat the bread and kiss the snake."

"You're shitting me," Becky said.

"God's honest truth. Seth passed out the bread," Angie said, her face grave and without a hint of her usual mischief.

"O my God," Becky moaned.

"And then they all got naked and had an orgy."

"That part you're making up," Becky said.

Angie shook her head. "I wish I was." She held up her phone.

"I have video, in case you want to see it. They just pulled off those white robes and started going at it with whoever was around. And then when the guys started cumming, they pulled out and creamed into their hands, and then they held their hands out to each other and they licked it up—girls, guys, it didn't matter. Everyone got them some cum."*

"Augh! Gross!" Becky covered her head with her arms, as if she couldn't hear any more.

"And then they sang a hymn," Angie said. "And that was it."

"If I didn't know you...I wouldn't believe it," Becky confessed.

"Yeah, well ordinarily I wouldn't vouch for myself as the most reliable narrator, being a pothead and all, but I wasn't high tonight—I only wished I was. Speaking of which, where the hell is my vaporizer?"

"It's charging," Becky pointed to the desk.

Angie rose and crossed to the desk, unplugging the vaporizer. She checked the chamber and, satisfied there was still enough herb for a viable hit, turned it on to begin heating. As she waited, she leaned against the desk.

"Did anyone see you?" Becky asked.

"I don't think so, but I had to get out of there," Angie said. "I haven't had that many cocks waving in my face since I did lighting at a photo shoot for a gay bathhouse in Berkeley called the Jizz Factory. Just what do you see in penises, anyway?"

Becky ignored the question, sitting up but looking like she was clutching the sofa cushions for dear life. Her hair was matted and her nose was running. "Shit, Angie. What did we just see?"

"Something we weren't supposed to, that's for sure."

"How could Seth have gotten involved in something like that?"

"One step at a time, I imagine," Angie said. The vaporizer

---

* Epiphanius, *Panarion* I:26:4:8

vibrated, indicating that its desired temperature had been reached. She took a long drag on the mouthpiece and let the steam out slowly. "You know what bugs me is that we were there, watching the rest of his life, for each and every one of those steps. And we didn't do anything until it was too late."

"You tried. You organized that intervention."

"It was a disaster," Angie said, taking another hit.

"But you tried."

"Yeah. I don't think there are consolation prizes for when your loved ones get brainwashed."

"No," Becky admitted. "So what do we do?"

Angie shrugged. "I'm getting high. You want some?" She held the vaporizer out to Becky.

"What the hell," Becky said, rising from the couch and snatching it up. She took a long drag and started coughing. "I thought there was no smoke with this thing."

"There isn't. But even the steam can be harsh if you're not used to it," Angie said. "Just go a little easier."

Becky took another drag—slower and shallower this time— and handed the vaporizer back to Angie. "That's enough."

"No kidding. For a lightweight like you? That's plenty. You might want to lie down again."

Becky waved her warning away. "What do we do?" she asked again.

"I'm not sure there's anything we *can* do," Angie said. "He's in pretty deep. I mean, obviously..."

"So what do we *do*?" Becky asked a third time.

Angie crossed the room and sat next to her. "I think...we grieve."

"Where's your hoodie?" Nazz asked.

Seth froze. "Hoodie?"

"You're here to gear up. How are you planning to hide your face?"

"Um...ski mask? I have one."

"Better do both." Nazz went to a chipped fiberboard wardrobe in the supply room of the warehouse and pulled out a grey sweatshirt with a hood. It looked a size too big for Seth, but that was probably an advantage. The less they could tell about his actual frame, the better. He handed it to Seth.

"Thanks," Seth said. He pulled on the hoodie, and then felt at his pocket to make sure the ski mask was there. It was.

"I think that's it," Nazz said. "Stay put. The old man wants a word with you."

Seth nodded and Nazz left the room. Seth checked his pulse and found it slightly elevated, but not too bad. The sertraline was doing its job, he was relieved to see. He wasn't panicked, and was only slightly anxious. *Situationally appropriate anxiety*, the voice in his head labeled it. He didn't question it.

His thoughts drifted to Dr. Teasdale. Sherry. He felt his loins stir just thinking about her. Would it be different between them now? Of course it would be. *How could it not?* he wondered. But how? Would she refer him to another therapist, so they could... what? Be lovers?

The door snapped open, and Mr. Basil walked in. He motioned to a plastic chair and Seth took it. He sat in another like it and crossed his legs, leaning back. "Well, my boy, how are you doing?"

"I'm okay," Seth said.

"This is the real thing," Mr. Basil said. "You're not nervous?"

Seth shrugged. "A little. I think I should be. This is dangerous. And important."

Mr. Basil shifted, and his face became thoughtful. "Something's changed, Mr. St. John."

Seth nodded. "It's all true. I saw it. In the ritual. I saw...him. The enemy. I saw her. But I saw...everything else, too. And I mean *everything.*"

Mr. Basil nodded. "You are a Pneumatic now."

"I guess I am," Seth agreed, as if acknowledging his age.

"A word of advice before you go," Mr. Basil said. "Lean on her. Before you go into that S-panel, connect with her. Feel that connection and hold to it tightly the whole time. That way, when she whispers to you, you'll hear it. You are not doing this alone. And if you try to do it alone, you'll fail. Take her with you. She will be your eyes and ears, much more so than you can perceive on your own."

Seth nodded. He would not have believed such a thing even last week. He would have thought it wishful thinking, or an entertaining fantasy. But now...now it was as real as his own fist.

"Go with Wisdom, my boy. And come back to us."

Seth walked past the S-panel, his eyes moving back and forth, scanning for cameras. Oddly, he saw none. That was unusual, as most panels were monitored. *Must be why they picked this one,* he thought. At the end of the hall, he went into the men's room and emptied his bladder again. He knew it was nerves, but he kept feeling like he had to pee. Leaving the restroom, he headed back to the S-panel. This time someone was coming. He hunkered down into his hoodie and kept walking. The woman coming toward him was almost yelling into her phone, something about an "idiotic stunt" that was "totally out of place at a wedding." She passed and he kept walking to the end of the hall.

He pushed open the door to the stairwell and let it close behind him. He pressed his face to the tiny window and waited until the woman turned a corner. Then he opened the door again and headed once more toward the S-panel. This time he was alone, and with swift, practiced movements, he had the key out of his pocket and into its socket, turned it, swung the panel outward, stepped inside, and locked it again.

He took a deep breath and looked around. *That's it,* the voice in his head said. *I'm Behind. There's no excuse for being here. You get caught, you go to jail.* He held his hand up in front of him. To his amazement, it was steady. He took courage from that.

Behind looked a lot like it had last time he had been through a panel. The corridor he was in was industrial, with wires and ducts running the length of the space as far as he could see. He knew the area he was to map, and he looked for visual cues that would alert him that the S-panel was near. He found a red turn wheel on one of the ceiling ducts almost directly adjacent to the panel. That would do.

He turned right and strode as quickly as he could. It was cold back there, and he realized there wasn't the need to heat the spaces Behind since they were rarely visited. He realized that it must take a lot of energy to warm a ship of the *Cibus Dei*'s size given the absolute zero of space, and it made sense that they'd cut corners where they could. Suddenly grateful for the hoodie, he made sure that it was blocking the view of his face from the sides as he walked.

He noted everything he passed—hallways stretching off to the left, electronic panels, and breaker boxes. Up ahead, he saw the corridor was about to dead end. He went the length of it, then turned and speed-walked back to the first corridor on the right. He turned and kept walking.

Slowly, the map was forming in his mind. It connected to

parts of the map he had studied, and now he was filling in missing bits. He felt a thrill at this: it reminded him of scratching the silver film off of lottery tickets as a child, revealing the hidden numbers.

The corridor branched in three different directions. Seth didn't hesitate. He took the right-hand corridor, intending to run it out and then return, in order to be systematic. But he knew it was not necessarily a workable plan, since he had no idea how far the right-hand corridor would go, how deep, how vastly it would branch into new labyrinths.

He felt mildly satisfied when it dead-ended at a steel door. The door had a tiny window with what looked like chicken wire inside the glass. Seth's eyes widened as he saw someone heading toward the door. He had his head down, checking something on a tablet. Seth plastered himself against the wall near the door's hinges so that, should the man open the door, the door would hide him. Involuntarily, he closed his eyes as the door swung out. The man had pushed it hard, and it very nearly bumped Seth's nose—but not quite. As Seth watched the man stride away from him down the corridor, he reached out and grabbed the handle, just in time to stop it from closing.

Poking his head inside the door for a quick look, he withdrew and processed what he'd seen. It was a large room, with a ceiling at least three times the normal height. Rows and rows of computer mainframes populated the room, grouped in what looked like "neighborhoods." He imagined it as a 1/20 scale city— Tokyo, perhaps, waiting for Rodan or some other *kaiju* to unleash its wrath.

But there were people there, too. Men and women, dressed in white lab coats. None had seen him, he didn't think. But he didn't want to push his luck. Inserting his fingers so the door couldn't close, he allowed himself a long look through the glass. A set of stairs led to a second level, where there were offices. Lab techs or scientists or whatever they were were ascending and descending the stairs to the upper level.

He knew this was a major find. He knew this room—a data control center of some kind—was not on any of their existing maps. This had been here all the time, and they...they did not know.

"What the fuck are you doing here?" a voice behind him asked.

Seth whirled, feeling surprise and shock and shame, all at once—at having been careless, at having been seen, at having been caught. He let go the door and heard it click behind him. Instinct took over, and stepped backwards into the corridor to be clear of the little window. The man coming after him was larger than he, balding, with angry, intense eyes that threatened to pin him to the spot.

Seth looked at the corridor behind the man. Should he run for it? The man was sure to raise the alarm. He reached into his lab coat and pulled out a hand-held transceiver. Seth once more looked behind him and feigned surprise. The man whirled to look behind him, and as soon as he did, Seth clasped his hands together and hit him at the base of the skull with everything he had. The man let out a quiet "oof" sound and collapsed. He wasn't unconscious, however, and began to rock back and forth, trying to regain his feet. Seth grabbed the radio and hit him on the head with it, over and over. Blood sprayed out over the walls, over Seth's clothes, over his hands.

As soon as the man was still, Seth shoved the radio into the pocket of his hoodie and ran.

He knew exactly where he was going. The map hovered in his brain in perfect detail, and in what seemed like too short a time he was once more at the S-panel. He wiped the blood from his hands onto the hoodie and inserted the key.

Once outside, he locked the key again and headed directly to a

530 • J.R. MABRY

nearby bathroom—a unisex one-seater with a baby changing table. He felt lucky not to have passed anyone in the hall. Nor was there anyone in the bathroom. He locked the door and looked at himself in the mirror. He knew that if he just fled, he would be chased—especially covered as he was in blood. Praying that the man he attacked would not be found immediately, he hoped he had a little bit of time. He washed the blood from his face. Then he cleaned off the radio as best he could, and fastened it to his belt as if it belonged there. Then he removed the hoodie and threw it into the trash.

His hair was a bit wet, but it would dry. He took a deep breath and went into the hallway. A young woman was walking toward him holding a sheaf of papers. Glancing up, she smiled at him, and kept walking. He gave her a nod and, trying to find a balance between nonchalance and full-out running, headed for the elevator.

His heart rate was racing, but he wasn't panicking. He felt no desire to avoid stepping on cracks or count the tiles as they passed beneath his feet. Why was his OCD completely at bay? Shouldn't he be completely freaking out? But he wasn't. He took it as a gift—a gift from her.

He somehow avoided bouncing on the balls of his feet as he waited for the elevator to arrive. When it did, he got on and hit the button for the lobby. The ride down seemed like it took an eternity. But he heard no alarm. The radio on his belt was silent. He pulled the hood off his head, and felt at his face. His heart sank as he realized he had forgotten to wear the ski mask.

He stifled his panic. The elevator doors opened and, as casually as he could, he moved out into the lobby. He passed unnoticed through the revolving door and out into the bright, fake, San Jose sun.

"We've got a smear of blood here, Simmons," Keira said, pointing at the back of the S-panel. She was ambivalent about the presence of the forensics team while she was reviewing a crime scene. On the one hand, she could point out the nonobvious aspects she wanted processed. On the other hand, they were underfoot and in the way.

Her left nitril glove wasn't seated properly and she tugged on it, hoping it would settle into a better fit. "Take me to the body," she told one of the forensics team members—a lithe blonde sporting a ponytail she was too old to wear. Keeping Pony Tail in her peripheral vision, she kept her eyes on the carpet. "Careful!" she called out. "Blood."

Pony Tail froze in place. "Simmons!" Keira shouted. "Blood!" She waited until the young man could reach them. "When you're done, follow us and collect anything you find on the floor."

"You bet," Simmons agreed. He was a wiry, gnomish man about her own age, prematurely bald and wearing Coke bottle glasses. He was good at what he did, and inwardly Keira didn't want anyone else touching the scene. That wasn't her call, though. They were all well-trained and there was a lot to process.

"Let's go," Keira said, biting back on her tongue to avoid calling the woman with the ponytail "Barbie." "Uh...what is your name?"

The blonde woman rolled her eyes. It was then that Keira realized she was also chewing gum.

"What?" Keira asked.

"We've worked on scenes together for four years," the woman said.

"Have we? Jeez, I'm a prick," Keira said. The woman did not disagree.

"I'm Carol Mukherjee."

"Mukherjee? Sounds Indian. You look like you're from Uppsala."

"My husband is Punjabi. His parents immigrated before the pandemic."

"Ah," Keira said.

"Which you would know if you took any interest in the people around you."

"Point taken," Keira said, not really wanting to get into it. Then she kicked herself because she'd already forgotten the woman's first name. She sighed and returned her focus to the case.

After several turns and about a half-mile of corridors, they stopped. At the far end of the hall, a man lay face down in a pool of blood. The back of his head was matted with gore. The man was still. The man was dead.

Keira made another attempt to get her left glove to fit right and squatted near the body, careful not to smear any of the blood spatter. Out of habit, she felt for a pulse, but there was nothing. "Any sign of the murder weapon?" Keira asked.

Ms. Mukherjee shook her head, forcefully enough to pummel both cheeks with the bob of her ponytail. She blew a bubble. When it popped some of it stuck to her nose. Nonplussed, she removed it from her nose and put it back in her mouth with all the nonchalance of pushing a lock of hair from her eyes.

"Definitely blunt force trauma," Keira said. She pulled back what was left of the man's hair and saw a few jagged edges of skull fragments. "What do you think it was?"

"You're asking me for my opinion?" Ms. Mukherjee asked. "Because it's more likely that I'm hallucinating."

"Let's say for a moment that I am," Keira said, not taking the bait. Truth was, gum aside, she liked Mukherjee's pluck.

"It's not deep enough for a tire iron or rebar," Ms. Mukherjee said. "It looks like a brick to me."

Keira nodded. But there were precious few bricks in the bowels of the ship. Then she noticed something poking out from under a flap of skin. She pulled a pen from the pocket of her slacks and gingerly lifted the flap.

"Hey, Mukherjee. Do you have some tweezers?"

Amazingly, the woman did. She passed them to her. Keira received them without thanks and grasped the edge of the mysterious something. It came loose without complaint and Keira held up what looked like a piece of black plastic, a semi-circle with irregular ends, about the length of her pinky fingernail.

Keira stood and held it where Mukherjee could get a good look. "What do you think?"

The blonde woman leaned in and squinted at the item. "Looks like a broken rheostat."

"What, like a volume knob?"

"Yeah, maybe from a radio...a walkie-talkie or something."

"Bag it," Keira said.

The woman pulled out a plastic bag without complaint and held it open. Keira dropped it into the bag, and handed it to her. "He's ready for the ME," Keira said. "Did you get photos of the spatter?"

"Not yet." She snapped her gum.

"Don't let anyone near here until you do," Keira said.

"Aye-aye."

Keira narrowed one eye at the woman, but didn't reply. Instead, she did her best to retrace her steps, being careful not to step on any blood. She got lost once, but found her way back quickly. As soon as Simmons was within sight, he called out. "We got the security footage. It's ready on your phone."

Keira nodded and pulled her phone from her back pocket. It was always a pain in the ass to sign into the encrypted network, but after a few minutes she was successful and began scrolling through the sector's security feed. Oddly, there were no cameras on the S-panel. That had been made law a couple of years ago, when the incursions had started, but given limited budgets and local priorities, the law had not yet been completely implemented. That anyone wanting to breach a panel would pick one that was unmonitored was a no-brainer, and Keira cursed the state-city gridlock that gave rise to a whole host of problems. She wondered why the people who ran the ship, who must in some shadowy way hold the puppet strings of the state government, allowed such localized rebellion. It was a mystery.

Pulling up the feed for the next camera along the hallway, she fast-forwarded through it, stopping whenever someone darkened the frame. And then she saw it...him...her, whoever it was. The frame looked male, she decided. He was wearing a gray hoodie pulled up to cover his face. There was nothing special about the way he walked...or was there? He seemed to walk forward on his feet—not exactly on his toes, but not touching his heels, either. He seemed to balance on the balls of his feet, which made him lean farther forward than most people. The way this person walked reminded her of something, but she couldn't place it.

She noted the time stamp and followed the figure from one camera to the next. "Damn," she said, as, even after three cameras, the man's face was still obscured. Then the man disappeared. "Do you mean to tell me that there's no camera on that door back there?" she said out loud. She meant the door just outside the mainframe room, the site of the murder. But it seemed that was the case. "Holy shit," she swore. Leaning against the wall of the corridor, she slid down, the top of her head lowering like a barometer measuring her hope.

Then she jerked upright and jumped back onto her feet. Coming back, the man's hood had been thrown back and his face was exposed. She paused the feed and zoomed in on his face.

"Holy shit," she said again. "Is that Seth?"

S eth looked at his leg. It wasn't bouncing. There was no pain in his chest. He didn't feel any compulsion to count the ceiling tiles. But when the door to Dr. Teasdale's office opened, he still jumped to his feet and stammered. "Uh...h-hi..."

Dr. Teasdale gave him a kind, professional smile. "So good to see you, Seth. Come in."

Seth dragged his fingers through his hair, straightened his jacket, looked at the floor, and headed for the door. As soon as it shut behind him, Dr. Teasdale waved him toward his usual chair. Lowering his head, he complied.

Dr. Teasdale sat, pulled her notepad into her lap, and gave him a compassionate look. "You seem dejected, Seth."

"I...uh...I'm not sure where we are," he said.

"Where we are?" Dr. Teasdale cocked her head.

"I mean..."

"Oh," Dr. Teasdale said. She nodded. Was she blushing? Seth wondered if it was just his imagination. "Something you need to understand, Seth, is that...well, it's like Vegas, I suppose. What happens in ritual space stays in ritual space. What happened between us at the ritual is just a celebration of the essential oneness of all things. It isn't personal, and it certainly isn't romantic. If you continue with us, you'll have lots of...experiences of oneness."

Seth bit his lip and felt his throat swelling up. *Don't cry, don't cry, don't fucking cry,* he told himself. "I feel...sad," he finally croaked.

"Ah. You started to have some feelings...for me?" Dr. Teasdale asked.

Seth looked away. He nodded.

"Oh, Seth, I'm so sorry. I didn't mean to mislead you. But I want to be clear: I like you and respect you. I even admire you. But I'm not in love with you, and the idea of any kind of relationship between us, outside of this room, is impossible."

"But the Lodge—" Seth began.

"Is a place for worship. Please don't get the wrong idea about anything that happens there. We can't be friends, and we certainly can't be any more than that. I'm your therapist, and this is a completely professional relationship."

"But...we had sex!"

"Seth, I do understand why this might be confusing. But we didn't 'have sex.' We both participated in a ritual held by our spiritual community. That is all."

"So we're...church friends?"

"What do you mean by 'church friends'?" Dr. Teasdale asked.

"You know...people you are friendly with at church, but don't hang out with otherwise."

Dr. Teasdale chuckled. "That's a very creative framing for it. I'm not going to assent to it, but I think maybe you're not far off."

"I get it," Seth said, knotting his fingers.

"Do you?" Dr. Teasdale asked. "Because if your feelings are too strong, maybe it's best if we don't work together. I can refer you to someone that I really trust. And they're 'in the network,' if you take my meaning."

"No," Seth swallowed and took a deep breath. "I want to... continue. I can...it'll pass. It always does."

"What always does?" Dr. Teasdale asked.

"You know...feelings."

Dr. Teasdale nodded. "They're like waves on the ocean. They roll in and if you wait a bit, they roll out again. You can always count on that."

Seth nodded, forcing himself to look her in the eye.

"How is the OCD?" Dr. Teasdale asked.

"That's what's...that's something I don't understand," Seth said.

"Tell me about it," Dr. Teasdale made a few notes on her pad.

"I...uh...ever since the ritual, I didn't, I haven't...you know."

"Slow down, Seth. Take a few deep breaths. Then explain it to me as if I were a child."

Seth nodded. He took several breaths. Then he cleared his throat. "Before the ritual, I was...doing better. The medication helps. But I was only about 50% there. I was still having obsessive thoughts, still having compulsions. But after the ritual..."

"After the ritual?"

Seth shook his head. "Nothing. I feel...calm. I mean, I was nervous coming in here because...I didn't know how things were going to be between us and I was afraid that, you know...what would happen is what happened."

"That's situational, not chronic," Dr. Teasdale said.

"Yeah. I understand that."

"Tell me about your other symptoms."

"That's just it, there...there aren't any."

"No counting?"

"No."

"No chest pains?"

"No."

"Your leg isn't bouncing, either?"

"No."

Dr. Teasdale made a note, then looked up at Seth with a knowing smile. "Why do you think that is?"

Seth shrugged. "I have...no idea."

"Why don't you tell me about what happened during the ritual—not the...eucharistic sharing at the end, but the ritual of the Bridal Chamber?"

Seth cast his mind back, and it was as if he was there all over again. Feelings and perceptions flooded his brain, so much so that he felt dizzy just thinking about it. "I saw it all. I saw her, I saw the Pleroma—the Fullness. I saw how everything is held in the True God, contained within him, held in love. And I saw a little pocket of...I don't know, darkness or shadow. And in the middle of it, I saw a creature of...he was thrashing, full of rage. He had this beak that snapped out at anything and everything that got close to him. I saw that Earth was in that pocket. And so is the *Cibus Dei*, except that we're...we're heading right for him."

Dr. Teasdale nodded, her face suddenly very serious, a look of wonder in her eyes. "You are truly a Pneumatic now, Seth. The archons have no hold over you anymore. You have achieved gnosis."

"I didn't do shit," Seth said.

Dr. Teasdale laughed at this. "No, you're right. It's a gift. But you have to cooperate to receive the gift. And *you have the gift.*"

"I don't feel like I deserve it," Seth said.

"You don't. None of us do. It isn't about worthiness. It's about love. It's about grace. She loves you and chose you and called you by name. And she touched you and brought you out of your prison."

Seth nodded. "Uh...speaking of prison..."

Dr. Teasdale's eyes snapped up from her notepad. "Yes?"

"I...went on an assignment yesterday."

"Oh?"

"I figure I mapped out about a half-mile of...the Behind...that hadn't been mapped before."

"That's wonderful!" Dr. Teasdale brightened.

"But...I was seen," Seth looked away. He swallowed. Internally, he debated whether he should mention that he had neglected to wear his ski mask.

Dr. Teasdale lowered her chin, but her eyes did not move from him. "By whom?"

"There was a huge...computer room," Seth explained. "I was

looking in the window, and he came up behind me. We...struggled. He had this radio. He was about to call someone. I grabbed it and...I hit him with it."

"You hit him?"

"I...I think I might have killed him."

Dr. Teasdale's eyes were wide now—wider than Seth had ever seen. "Where is this...radio now?"

Seth pulled a gallon-sized ziplock bag from the pocket of his jacket. The inside was smeared with blood, but it was easy to see the military-issue walkie-talkie. "Do you want it?" Seth held it out to her.

He expected her to protest, to tell him to take it away, to get rid of it. But to his surprise, she reached out and pinched the far end of the bag, holding it like it was a rotten fish. She gingerly lowered it to the coffee table. "That...is going to be more useful than you know. We haven't been able to unscramble their communications...until now, that is. That's excellent work, Seth."

Seth's mouth opened, then closed again. He'd expected a tongue-lashing, a warning, something. Anything but this. "What...what are you going to do with it?"

"I'll take it to Basil. He'll know how to best use it to our advantage."

Seth nodded. "You'll tell him that I—"

"I'll tell him everything."

Seth wondered momentarily how that fit into the whole "confidentiality" promise, but decided to let it go. He didn't need to keep any secrets from Mr. Basil. For some reason, he trusted the man.

"I've never killed anyone before," Seth said.

"You don't know that he's dead," Dr. Teasdale said.

Seth shrugged. "I'm pretty damned sure."

"Okay," Dr. Teasdale said, visibly changing tracks. "So how do you feel?"

"Bad."

"Can you say more about that?"

Seth jumped to his feet and raised his voice. "I killed someone, damn it!"

"Shhhh...the walls aren't *that* thick," Dr. Teasdale warned. "Sit."

Seth sat again. Dr. Teasdale sighed. "Just...tell me about your feelings. Don't assume I know what you're feeling."

"Okay." Seth let out a long breath. "I keep playing it over and over in my head. What could I have done differently, you know? But every other possible outcome would have ended up with me in jail."

"Is it possible that it was necessary?"

"How was it necessary? It was nothing but self-preservation."

"It is war, Seth. Don't you think it's expected, even necessary, that there are casualties in war?"

"Yes, but he was just—"

"Besides, he was just a Hylic," Dr. Teasdale said. "He didn't have a soul. He was...nothing much more than an animal."

"How do you know that?"

"You aren't born with a soul. You have to grow one. The man you killed, he was a scientist, wasn't he?"

"Yes," Seth conceded.

"So he probably wasn't religious, which means he most likely was not a Psychic. And he's not one of us, so he's definitely not a Pneumatic." She shrugged. "It's sad when a dog dies, but...it's just a dog, isn't it?"

Seth blinked. He felt a chill descend from his shoulders on down and he saw Kush in his mind's eye. Was he just a dog? No. No he wasn't. He was *his* dog, and it was different. Seth swallowed and refocused. "How do you *know* he wasn't one of us? I mean, *you* work for them, and you're one of us."

Dr. Teasdale's face softened. "It's true, and it's...possible. But it's not very likely. Look, Seth, I admit I'm favoring the likelihood over the possibility. I'm also trying to put this into a manageable context for you. He most likely was not a Pneumatic. There's a larger chance he was a Psychic, and if so, that's unfortunate. But again, it's not likely. Most probably he was a Hylic. And it's still tragic, and I understand why you feel bad. I guess I'm just saying, it's not as bad as it could have been, and you should cut yourself some slack."

Seth didn't know how to process any of this. He stared at his knee. It was still. It was like an alien knee, not his at all. *What happened to my knee?* the voice in his head asked.

"And another thing," Dr. Teasdale said. "Don't fool yourself by thinking 'But he was a civilian.' This was not collateral damage. He worked on the other side. He was an enemy combatant. He is trying to kill us all. You killed an enemy soldier. There's a proper response for that, you know, and it isn't guilt, it isn't censure, and it sure isn't jail. It's a fucking medal, and in my book, you just earned one."

Seth felt his shoulders deflate. What Dr. Teasdale was saying was comforting, to be sure, but only if he let himself believe it. He wanted to believe it. He just didn't know if he *did* believe it.

"Seth, where did you sleep last night?"

Seth snapped out of his reverie. "What?"

"Where did you sleep?"

"I...oh...uh...at home, of course."

Dr. Teasdale closed her notebook and gave him a grave look. "You killed someone and then you went home?"

"Y...yes." Seth kept his eyes trained on her but moved his chin back. "What?"

"Seth, they'll be looking for you now. If they weren't before, they sure will be now. You can't show your face. You can't go home. You need to ditch your phone—buy a burner if you absolutely need to have one—go without if you can."

"But—"

"Seth, listen to me." Dr. Teasdale scooted to the edge of her seat and with her elbows firmly on her knees, held his eyes. "You didn't do anything wrong, but you have struck a blow that our enemy cannot ignore. We will do everything we can to protect you, but make no mistake: You are now a hunted man."

LIQUIPEDIA
THE ANSWERBOT THAT GOES DOWN
SMOOTH

WHAT IS A FAG HAG?

"Fag hag" is a colloquial term that refers to a woman who forms close friendships or social connections with gay men. This term, while primarily used in the LGBTQ+ community, is not universally embraced and has garnered both positive and negative connotations over time. It is important to note that the use of this term can be perceived as derogatory and offensive, as it reduces women to a supporting role based on their association with gay men.

The origins of the term "fag hag" are unclear, but it is believed to have emerged in the mid-20th century. Some suggest that it originated as a derogatory term used to denigrate women who associated with gay men, while others argue that it was reclaimed by some women as a self-identifying term that celebrates their close bonds with gay friends.

Fag hags often share common interests with gay men, including fashion, pop culture, nightlife, and advocacy for LGBTQ+ rights. These relationships can provide mutual support, understanding, and companionship. Gay men may appreciate the empathetic perspective and nonjudgmental attitude that some fag hags bring to their friendships.

While some women embrace the term "fag hag" and view it as a badge of honor or a term of endearment, others find it offensive and objectifying. Critics argue that it perpetuates stereotypes and reduces women to accessories or mere extensions of gay men's lives.

In recent years, there has been a growing recognition of the need to move beyond labels and stereotypes. Many now prefer more inclusive terms, such as "ally" or "friend," to describe women who form meaningful connections with gay men. These terms emphasize equality, respect, and the shared pursuit of social justice.

It is important to respect individual preferences and to use language that promotes inclusivity and understanding. As attitudes and perceptions evolve, it is crucial to engage in open and respectful dialogue to foster greater acceptance and appreciation of diverse relationships within the LGBTQ+ community and beyond.

CHAPTER NINETEEN

Be seekers of death, then, like the dead who seek life,
for what they seek becomes apparent to them.
And what is there to cause them concern?
As for you, when you search out death,
it will teach you about being chosen.
—*Secret Book of James**

K eira slipped the safety off her service pistol and gave the signal. The tactical team leader nodded. A man in military black swung a handheld ram at the door. A loud "crack" echoed through the stairway and hall as the door erupted in a shower of splinters. "Go! Go!" the team leader shouted. Keira pressed in right behind them.

---

* The Secret Book of James: Nag Hammadi Library, Codex I, 2, translated by Marvin Meyer, published in *The Gnostic Bible* (Boston, MA: Shambhala Publications, 2009).

"State agents!" she shouted, a message that was repeated by many on the team.

"Clear!" a member of the tactical team shouted. Another said the same.

It was a small apartment. It only took seconds for the team to ascertain that the place was empty. Keira holstered her pistol and walked up to the team leader. "Thanks, Danny," she said.

"No problem, special agent. That's what we're here for. Just glad no one got hurt."

Keira nodded.

"You got it from here?" Captain Daniel Preston asked.

"Yeah, yeah. Leave me Dewey and Pico, just in case he comes home, will you? Just as long as it takes us to do the search and forensics work. Three hours, tops."

"No problem. And they can call for their own pickup."

"That's perfect, thanks."

Anders Pico walked up to them, his rifle hanging to one side. "Forensics just pulled up."

"'Bout time," Keira said.

"Let's move out!" Preston shouted. He had a quick word with a couple of his men, and in moments, all but two of them were rumbling down the stairs.

"Don't touch anything," she said to what remained of the tactical team.

"We know the drill," Pico answered. "You want us to guard the door outside, stay out of your hair?"

Keira frowned, not sure if Pico had just used an offhand idiom or was making a sexist dig. She decided to let it go. "Outside would be great, Sergeant."

The two men in black tactical gear exited the apartment and closed the door behind them. Keira savored the silence. Dust motes hung on a ray of light piercing through a rip in the drawn shades. She watched them float, weightless, aimless, free. She felt herself relax.

She sighed and looked around the room. It seemed like a typical bachelor's apartment. Band posters adorned the walls, most with tattered corners, testament to their having been hung and torn down more than once. The air reeked of old pizza boxes and burned popcorn. The couch cushions sagged, and a swollen tuft of cotton burst through a hole in the right armrest like the pus of an infected wound.

Keira took gloves from her pocket and put them on, stretching them until they fit closely enough to be functional. If they were capable of interstellar travel, she was sure there had to be a way to make gloves out of latex or nitril or whatever that actually went on easily.

She looked under the couch, which yielded only a fluffle of quivering dust bunnies. The carpet was dotted with felled popcorn shards. She looked up as the door opened. Simmons and Mukherjee stepped in, field cases in both hands. Mukherjee blew a bubble. "So this is where the terrorist lives. Looks about right."

"At least it's not his mom's basement," Simmons countered.

"This is California. There are no basements," Keira answered.

"Figurative stereotype," Simmons explained.

"What are we looking for?" Mukherjee asked.

Keira stood. "I don't know. We only know he killed someone, and he lives here, and we don't know where he is. So we're looking for evidence of terrorist activity, weapons, explosives, chemicals, links to anyone who might know his location."

"On it," Simmons said. He pointed to the kitchen table and they both set their cases on it and flicked open the fasteners.

Keira tried to stay out of her team's way as they processed the apartment, but even as she did so, she did her fair share of poking about. She didn't see any weapons. There were video game consoles and an old laptop in Seth's bedroom. A pile of dirty clothes had begun to mildew. Aside from cleaning supplies under the sink, there weren't any chemicals to speak of. There was plenty of evidence of cannabis, but no other drugs, certainly nothing illegal. There were, however, a lot of books, most of them with their covers ripped off, which seemed strange. She was looking through one of them, an illustrated guide to occult symbols, when Mukherjee walked up behind her, blowing a bubble that came perilously close to snagging her hair. "Watch that!" Keira warned.

"*Occult Symbology*," Mukherjee read. "Are we arresting people for entertaining medieval metaphysics now?"

"No, I just...why don't any of these books have covers?"

"He must work at a bookstore," Mukherjee said, shrugging.

"Why?"

"I used to work at a bookstore. When they pulled books for return to the publisher, they didn't actually return them. They ripped the covers off, and returned those. The rest went into a bin for the employees. After a week, anything that wasn't snagged went into the recycling bin."

"That's...really helpful," Keira admitted. "Thanks."

"No problem. It might be the most helpful thing we've found."

"Clean?"

"So far. Lots of prints, but we won't know anything from those until tomorrow." Mukherjee stepped toward one of the fiberboard bookcases and turned her head sideways to read the spines. She pulled one from the shelf. "Why does a red-blooded American boy have a book of lesbian erotica?"

"Don't red-blooded American boys love to see girls getting it on?" Keira asked.

"Yeah, but that's just the thing. This isn't porn. It's literature," Mukherjee said, flipping through the paperback. "It's more romance than porn. Most men would find this boring as fuck."

"Maybe it isn't his?" Keira wondered aloud.

"Looks like there's someone else living here," Mukherjee said.

"Really? How do you know?"

"Tampons in the bathroom."

Keira's eyebrows shot up. "Okay. Good find."

Mukherjee froze. Keira noticed. "What?"

She turned the erotica paperback around so that it was facing Keira. "This is his handwriting," she said.

Keira leaned over and squinted at the text. "It's just a bunch of numbers and letters."

"Exactly. Looks like a password to me."

Mr. Basil sat heavily on the dusty loveseat. The small side-room in the warehouse was crowded with odds-and-ends, betraying the room's true function. Dr. Robinson scowled at his phone, while Dr. Teasdale's gaze seemed far in the distance as she swung her crossed leg back and forth lazily.

"All right," Basil said. "Let's talk about the shit-show that was our ritual the other night."

"Why do you call it that?" Dr. Robinson said, stuffing his phone into his vest pocket. "The faithful seemed edified and energized."

"In case you didn't notice, three-fifths of our initiates walked out," Basil said, his voice dripping with testy poison.

Robinson shrugged. "Self-selection. They weren't worthy, or they weren't ready to become Pneumatics."

"I have another theory," Basil said, his eyes hardening. "It's clear to me that if they had been properly catechized, we would not have lost them."

"How dare you?" Robinson snapped, his voice rippling with outrage.

"If they had been properly instructed, they would have known what they were about to experience, and they would have been ready for it."

"I'm— I'm— I'm shocked, Basil. Really!" Robinson blustered.

"It's never happened before," Basil said. "So we know that you *can* properly catechize people. Why didn't you do it this time?"

Robinson reared back, but was strangely silent.

Dr. Teasdale leaned in, looking grave. "That's a very good question, Joshua. Why *did* you change your curriculum?"

"My work is not subject to *your* oversight," Robinson objected.

"Me? No," Basil agreed. "And Sherry? No. But the both of us together can kick up some dust, Joshua. Now answer my *fucking* question."

Mr. Basil rarely swore, and he saw a shadow of fear flit through Robinson's eyes. But the catechist stood his ground. "I don't answer to you."

Mr. Basil sighed. "Do you want to know what I think?"

"No, as a matter of fact," Robinson answered.

"What's that, Terrance?" Teasdale asked.

"I think that this is exactly what you had planned," Basil said slowly, "but the person you hoped to scare off stuck the course."

"Seth?" Teasdale asked.

Basil gave her an affirmative glance. "You beastly motherfuck-er," Teasdale spat at Robinson.

"Lies," Robinson said.

"I don't think so." Basil shook his head. "I think you expected Musa to stay and Seth to run."

"And what of the women?" Teasdale turned on Basil. "Don't they enter into it?"

"Collateral damage," Basil said without looking at her. "Musa was Joshua's pet, and Seth his scapegoat. But your plan backfired, it seems."

"Nonsense!"

"And now we've lost most of our current cohort, and some

very promising recruits indeed," he said, with a bow of acknowledgement in Teasdale's direction.

"I don't have to stand for this," Robinson said, standing.

"No, but you'll answer for it," Basil said. "Sit down."

Robinson looked confused. Basil was the senior member of the triumvirate, but he rarely issued commands. Slowly, Robinson lowered himself to his seat again.

"I want to know, Joshua, and I want to know *now*: why did you change your curriculum?"

Joshua looked away, but remained silent. The three of them sat in the discomfort for what seemed like far too long.

Finally, Teasdale cleared her throat. "We have a larger problem to discuss."

Basil turned his face to her, but Robinson continued to look away.

"Seth's latest assignment had...complications."

"What kind of complications?" Basil asked. "And how do you know? He hasn't reported to me yet."

"I've just come from a session with him," she said. "I'm not surprised he hasn't been in touch, Terrance. He's scared. He feels like he failed you, but he didn't. He found something, something important. He can fill in a large block of our missing geography. But he also found the mainframe...or at least *a* mainframe."

"You're joking." Mr. Basil's eyes widened, and a touch of a smile visited his lips.

"No, but..." Teasdale let out a long breath. "But he was caught and attacked. He...fought back, and he won. He killed one of the computer technicians."

Both Basil and Robinson were staring at her now. Robinson's mouth was agape.

"Killed?" Basil asked.

Teasdale nodded. "It was self-defense, but I'm sure Homeland Security won't see it that way."

"Egad," Basil breathed. "Is he alright? Mr. St. John, I mean."

"He's shook up, but he's fine. But you should talk to him, Terrance. He's in rough shape, emotionally."

"Of course, of course."

"Except...I told him to ditch his phone and not to go back to the apartment," she said. "So I'm not sure how you'll get in touch."

"When is your next appointment with him?"

"Three days from now."

"That's too long."

"It's not safe for him to go to work, or back to his apartment," Teasdale said. "So if I were to hazard a guess, I'd say he'll come here to sleep. So...stay put. He'll come to you."

"Do you think so?"

She shrugged. "He's on the outs with his best friend and his girlfriend and his mother. Aside from sleeping on a park bench... he's going to come here."

Basil nodded. "Okay then, I'll wait." He turned to Robinson. "You see? You had no right to doubt him. We've been looking for that mainframe room for decades. Now we know exactly where it is."

"If you can trust him," Robinson said.

"The only person I don't trust right now is you," Basil said. He watched Robinson's shoulders fall, but the catechist's face remained hard as rock. "And I'm still waiting for an answer. I know you have it in for Mr. St. John. I just didn't realize your hatred for him was so extreme that you'd risk a whole cohort in order to undermine him."

"You know nothing," Robinson spat.

"Look me in the eyes, Joshua, and tell me that you did not intend to undermine Seth St. John."

Robinson met his eyes, but said nothing.

"What did he do to you, Joshua?" Teasdale asked him.

"We need someone smart and stable, someone we can depend on," Robinson said.

"Yes, we do," Mr. Basil agreed. "And you've just proved to me that it isn't you."

Robinson jutted out his jaw. "Your affection for him blinds you—both of you. You think that he's an asset, but he's not. He's just proven every intuition I have had about him. He is a liability, now more than ever."

"Really, Joshua," Teasdale retorted. "The depth of your antipathy for him is staggering."

"He has just proven that it is well deserved. He *was* just a spy—very well, we all are. But now he is a murderer. And anyone associated with him is at risk. We need to distance ourselves from him, and that right quick." He leaned in and looked Basil in the eye. "If we don't, he will surely drag us down with him when he is caught. We will be strung up as accomplices." He leaned back. "As indeed we are."

"We all knew the risks when we assumed our covenants," Basil said.

"And we're intelligent enough to know when the risk has become too great." Robinson glanced at Teasdale, then back to Basil. "It won't do to coddle him. We have crossed a line. They are looking for him now. If they find him, everything we have built will come crashing down."

"What are you saying?" Teasdale asked.

"I'm saying that he needs to be...eliminated."

"Excuse me, Joshua, are you suggesting that we have Mr. St. John killed?" Basil asked.

The two men stared at one another for a timeless moment. "That is exactly what I am saying," Robinson said.

"He just uncovered some of the most important intelligence we've had in a great while, Joshua," Teasdale said, "at great risk to himself. That kind of performance is to be lauded, not punished."

"Hear, hear," Basil chimed in.

"So you won't even consider it?" Robinson asked. "Not even to protect all that you've built? Not even to protect yourself? You wouldn't do it for *her*?"

"*She* isn't suggesting we kill one of her darlings, Joshua," Basil said.

"I'm not the only person who feels this way," Robinson said.

Basil cocked his head. "What are you saying?"

"I'm saying that there are others, those to whom we all answer—"

"Dr. Robinson, are you telling me you have gone over my head?" Mr. Basil's eyes narrowed.

Teasdale leaped to her feet. "Get out!"

Groaning, Robinson got to his feet as well. "Gladly. I think our...partnership is at an end. If you will not protect yourself, I must do what I consider prudent for me and mine."

"Are you resigning your role in the Triumvirate?" Basil asked.

"Effective immediately," Robinson said. He offered his hand to Basil.

Basil did not take it. "You heard her. Get out."

Finally feeling safe, Seth pulled his hood off as he walked toward the warehouse. His heart ached, and he couldn't stop thinking about Dr. Teasdale. *Sherry*, he corrected himself. *No,* he decided, *Dr. Teasdale.* It wouldn't do any good to harbor unrealistic hopes. It would only cause him more pain. He knew that, and yet it was hard not to fixate on what might have been...what could be if only she would—

"What the actual fuck, Seth?"

He stopped and whipped his head around. Out of the midafternoon shadow of the building stepped Angie.

"What are you doing here?" he snapped.

"Walk," she said, pointing toward the road.

He hesitated, but finally turned toward the road and started walking. She fell into step beside him. "So, you eat cum now," she said.

"What?" He stopped.

She pointed to the concrete in front of them and kept walking. He caught up to her. "You know, I always thought you were the male equivalent of a fag hag," she said, shaking her head. "How could my gaydar be so far off?"

"What? I'm not gay," he objected.

"Oh, right. You're not gay, but you eat cum," she continued.

"I have no idea what you're talking about," he said.

"Sure, you don't," she replied.

They walked in silence for several seconds. Finally, she said, "I saw you."

"What do you mean?" he asked.

"Becky and I. We snuck in the other night. During your little... 'church service.' We saw you get it on with that chick on the altar, in front of everyone."

He stopped again and faced her. "Wait, I know Becky was there, but...you saw that, too?"

"Yeah. I stuck around until the spermophagial picnic started. Then I was out of there."

"Oh, shit," Seth said.

"So...what the fuck?" Angie asked. "I mean, I love a good fetish as much as the next dyke, but...Jesus and mango on a stick, dude, that's seriously fucked up. I took you for a vanilla sex kind of guy, you know. I figured whatever Becky put out would be right up your alley, but man...you had me fooled."

"It isn't about sex," Seth said.

"Really? Because it sure as hell looked like it was all about sex to me."

"Not at all. It's...it's like Tantra."

Angie scowled. "What's like Tantra?"

"What we're doing."

"What does Sting doing fuck-all not to ejaculate while he's humping Trudie have to do with whatever I saw here the other night?"

"Who the hell is Sting?"

"Ancient pop reference. Answer the question."

"You can't understand," Seth said.

"Wait? I can't understand?" Angie put her hands on her hips. A vein on her forehead swelled. "Why? Because I'm too stupid? Because you refuse to explain? Just why can't I understand, Seth?"

"Because you're a Hylic."

"What the fuck does..." She stopped and cocked her head. "Oh. I read about that. Hylics are the lowest humans on the totem pole. Are you saying I don't have a soul, Seth?"

He nodded.

"And you're, what, one of the spiritual elites at the top of the pole? What are they called, Hydraulics?"

"Pneumatics," he corrected her.

"Oh, that's rich—you elitist bastard. So I'm, what, just a mutt? Dispensable, just like Kush?" He opened his mouth, but couldn't think of any way to respond. She pointed at the street ahead of them again. "Walk."

He walked.

"You broke her heart, you know. Becky. She would have married you, if you'd asked."

"I didn't ask."

"No shit. Instead, you publicly humiliated her."

"How— Never mind. It's not worth arguing with you about it."

"Because I'm just a Hylic," Angie stated.

"No, because it wasn't like that and you know it. I didn't

intend for her to be there. I didn't try to humiliate her. She went where she wasn't supposed to go...and so did you. I'm sorry if she was humiliated, but I didn't want that to happen."

"It happened," Angie said.

"I get it," Seth said.

"Do you not see how crazy this is yet? And what was that, some kind of Satanic ritual?"

"It's not crazy, and no...it's just the opposite. It's a ritual that breaks through the illusion of the demiurge and allows you to experience the oneness that really is."

"That really is what?"

"That really is...what everything really *is*."

"Does that make any sense, even to you?"

"Of course. I've never been more sure of anything in my life."

"And we're still on a spaceship?"

Seth nodded.

"You're making my brain hurt."

"So stop trying. Just...pretend I'm dead."

"How can I pretend you're dead?" Angie almost yelled. "You're alive, and you're my best friend and...and I love you."

They stopped again. Seth reached out and pulled her into a hug. She returned it. While they embraced, he said, "'Do not think that I have come to bring peace to the earth; I have not come to bring peace but a sword. For I have come to set a man against his father, and a daughter against her mother, and'...and a guy against his best friend."*

"Who said that?"

"Jesus."

"Fucking Jesus."

"Hey—"

---

* Matthew 10:34-36

Angie pulled away again. "You can't tell me that Jesus has anything to do with what I saw the other night."

"Jesus has *everything* to do with what you saw. He and Sophia are mated pairs—"

"Syzygies," Angie corrected him.

He cocked his head.

"What?" Angie said. "I may be a spiritual lowlife, but I read. And I've been reading a lot about your...freaking ancient mystery cult."

"So you know about the demiurge?"

"Yes, you asshole, I know about it...him...whatever."

"Do you know his name?"

"Which one? Samael? Nebro? Saklas? Ialdabaoth?"

Seth's eyes went wide. "You...you *know*."

"It's not like it's a secret. Liquipedia is a thing."

"You...you could be a Psychic," Seth said.

Angie scowled, and then brightened. "Oh, you don't mean with crystal balls and tarot cards, do you?"

"No."

"Was that a compliment?"

"I was just saying the truth. You know a lot. Maybe you aren't a Hylic after all. Maybe, you've grown..." He trailed off.

"Were you about to say, 'Maybe you've grown a soul?' 'Cause if you were I'm going to punch you in the head."

"Okay, I wasn't going to say that," Seth insisted.

"Liar."

Despite himself, Seth smiled. Angie took his arm and pulled him along. "You could join us," Seth said.

"Oh, great. Listen, if I wanted to gobble cum I'd have chosen a very different life path."

"That's not all there is to it," Seth said.

"Oh, that changes everything, then," Angie said with faux chipperness. "Sign me up."

"Don't make fun," Seth said.

"How can I do anything else?" Angie said. "It's low-flying geese and I have a baseball bat."

"That may be the most convoluted metaphor I've ever heard."

"I try to earn my keep," Angie said.

"Angie, what you saw the other night...you didn't see what I saw."

"You mean I wasn't staring into the face of that slut on the altar while you were pounding her? No. No, I didn't see that. She was pretty hot, though."

"Her name is Sheila."

"Noted."

"Anyway," Seth continued, "the ritual worked. I...broke through—"

"Broke through what? Sheila's hymen? Because I think that happened a *looooong* time ago."

"No, I broke through the illusion of duality. I saw...everything, just as it is—"

"A new lens prescription can do that too, and there's a lot less semen involved...normally."

"You don't get it. I saw the demiurge. We're heading toward him. If we don't stop this ship...then we're going to end up a sacrifice to him."

"Wait a minute," Angie said. "Are you saying that the spaceship is headed toward this demonic god?"

"Yes."

"And what happens when we reach him?"

"He eats us."

"He eats, what, the whole ship?"

"Yes."

Angie stopped again. "Is this a metaphor, too?"

"No," Seth said, looking as serious as he had ever been. "It's a literal fact. I saw it."

"You saw it, while you were screwing Sheila?"

"Yes."

"How did you see it?"

"In a vision," he said.

"Oh, Christ-pissing-blood—"

"So I know it's true...everything they've told me."

She put her hand on his shoulders and shook him. "Dude! Read my lips: mental suggestion. They told you that's what you would see, and so that's what you saw!"

"No," he said. "It was more real than anything I've ever experienced. It's more real than you."

"Wow. Just...wow."

"I know, it's a lot to take in," Seth said, his voice compassionate.

"You have no idea," Angie said.

"I think I do."

"No. No, you don't." She started walking again. "So you and your cum-eating club over there, your *mission*—can I call it a mission?—is to bungle up the works of the spaceship so that... what? So that we don't reach the monster-god?"

"Yes."

"And what will happen to us?"

"I don't know. We'll have to turn around. I guess we'll go back to earth. But that's not the point. The point is that we can't feed the demiurge."

"Because that would be bad," Angie said, her voice dripping with sarcasm.

"Very bad," Seth agreed.

"If you want to do freaky rituals, why can't you just love Mother Earth and be a witch like me?"

"Because we're not on Mother Earth."

"And you really believe that?"

"Of course," Seth said.

The walked in silence for a while longer.

"I don't think we can be friends anymore," Angie said.

"I understand," said Seth.

"**W**ake, up, my boy." Mr. Basil's voice was soft and kind. It floated first into the dream Seth was having, but soon nudged him out of sleep and into waking life. He felt the man's large hands tousling his hair. He opened his eyes and saw Mr. Basil smile. "I'm sorry you had to sleep here."

Seth jerked up. Where was he? Then he relaxed. The room began to look familiar again. It was the small storage room at the warehouse—his only safe space. "Sorry," Seth apologized.

"Don't be," Mr. Basil said. "You seemed to be having a pretty active dream."

What had he been dreaming about? Seth snatched at the wisps of images, but they flew from his grasp.

"How are you?" Mr. Basil asked.

"I don't know yet," Seth stretched. "Too groggy."

"This might help," Mr. Basil reached behind him and picked up a paper coffee cup with a plastic lid.

Seth sat up and melted with gratitude as he accepted the cup. "Oh my God."

"You're welcome. I brought one for me, too." Mr. Basil had been squatting, but now he sat cross-legged beside Seth on the floor. For several minutes they blew on their coffees and took hesitant sips. "Sherry—Dr. Teasdale—said that you broke through at the ritual," Mr. Basil began. "I mean, we always hope that will happen, but one never knows."

Seth nodded, cradling his cup so that the steam wreathed his face. "I've never been more sure of anything in my life. I mean...I saw it, Mr. Basil. I saw all of it. I realized yesterday that this isn't a faith for me anymore. When you've seen it, it just becomes fact."

Mr. Basil nodded. "That is the essence of mysticism. It's the direct experience. Religions are the rules and laws and rituals built around enshrining someone else's mystical experience. This is...different."

"Oh, yeah." Seth sniffed. The steam from the coffee was making his nose run.

"I have some bad news," Mr. Basil said.

Seth met his eyes. "What?"

"Dr. Robinson has resigned his position on the Triumvirate. He is no longer...with us."

"What does that mean?" Seth asked.

"It means that he is against us."

Seth frowned. "And what does that mean?"

"Joshua never believed in you...not the way I or Sherry did...or indeed, as our Holy Mother did."

"I could tell. He always seemed...suspicious," Seth said. "It felt like he was always hoping I would fail."

"That perception is not wide of the mark," Mr. Basil admitted. "But I'm afraid it's worse than that. He thinks you are a sufficient danger to the cause that we should have you killed."

Seth reared back, almost spilling his coffee. Had he heard right? "What?"

Mr. Basil closed his eyes and nodded gravely. He opened them again and reached out his hand, placing it on Seth's arm. "He is alone in this. At least none here agree with him. Certainly I do not, nor does Dr. Teasdale."

"So...what does that mean?"

Mr. Basil sighed. "I don't know. I just think you deserved to know. You need to be careful. Joshua may decide to take matters into his own hands."

Seth looked down at his knee. It wasn't bouncing. His

breathing was slow and regular. "I...I'm homeless. I've lost everyone I love. I killed a man. The police are looking for me. And now my teacher is going to try to kill me. Why aren't I curled up like a pill bug?"

"Maybe Dr. Teasdale's medication is working?" Mr. Basil suggested.

"Maybe," Seth conceded, but he knew it was more than that. He looked up at Mr. Basil. "Why are you here?"

Mr. Basil sighed. "Well, there's not a simple answer to that. For one thing, it's the only safe place for me, too, at the moment. But as to why have I awakened you to this audience? For one, I wanted to see how you were doing. As you say, you've been through a lot." He smiled. "But I have also come to ask you about an assignment."

"An assignment? Why aren't you just...assigning me?"

"Because the danger is..." Mr. Basil looked away. "This isn't something I can just tell you to do and expect you to do it. It's something you must choose to do...because you might not come back from it."

Seth looked down at his hands again. "What is it?"

"First, you'll need to get rid of your phone—"

"Oh, yeah," Seth said, "Dr. Teasdale already told me to ditch it."

"Did you?"

"Uh...not yet."

Mr. Basil fished a tiny black phone out of his pocket. "Here's a burner. Trade with me, and I'll dispose of it."

Seth blinked uncertainly at the nondescript phone in Mr. Basil's hand. "C'mon, they can trace the one you have. We need this place to be safe."

Seth nodded and handed him his phone. He put the burner in his pocket.

"Now...the job," Mr. Basil said, taking a deep breath. "There's one section we've been unable to map—many sections, of course, but we have reason to think that there's a reason this one hasn't been mapped. Anyone else who has tried it has not returned."

"Oh. Okay," Seth said.

"The access point is in Sacramento, at the Pacific Gas & Electric building...should you decide to go, that is."

"How will I get there?" Seth asked.

"Caltrain," Mr. Basil said.

Seth nodded. "Okay. When do I leave?"

"Tell me what you have," Schenck said, swirling cold coffee around in his mug.

Keira sat opposite her boss and sighed. "Not a whole hell of a lot."

"That's not what I like to hear."

"I know, I know..." Keira looked out the window. For the millionth time in the past month she marveled at how real the sky looked.

"I thought you got a laptop," Schenck prompted.

"We did. And we got into it, too. We found the password written in a book of lesbian erotica."

Schenck's eyebrows shot up. "Okay, I wasn't expecting that. Tell me something else that will unseat my expectations."

"The internet searches are what you'd expect for a kid in his twenties—a lot of porn, looking up restaurants, that kind of thing. And then there's the gnosticism."

Schenck frowned. "Come again?"

"Remember that group you had me check out, the suspicious activity notification?"

"Oh, yeah." Scheck raised his chin, obviously searching his memory. "The cult."

"Exactly. It was a gnostic cult. It's…interesting stuff."

"Is there a point lurking around?"

"Sorry, chief. His internet searches included a lot of gnostic myth, history of gnosticism, and gnostic-influenced movements."

"So he's into this stuff. So?"

"Remember I told you about the vests?"

"Yeah…"

"The earlier S-panel breach—"

"The first murder, you mean? The woman, Vera Brennan?"

"Yeah. The murderer wore a vest."

Schenck cocked his head. Keira continued. "And now this one —the computer scientist, Taussig—the murderer, Seth St. John, he's part of the same group."

"Seems like a raid of this cult's HQ is in order."

"We're too late for that. They've abandoned the Victorian they were meeting in. Sherry Teasdale is in the wind, too."

"Shit. So where are they now?"

Keira shrugged. "That's what I'm trying to figure out."

"And no clue on the computer?"

"None."

"Sounds like you know what you've got to do," Schenck said. "I don't want you distracted. I want you to find Mr. St. John before he kills again."

Keira nodded.

"Anything else?"

Keira stood, but then she sat back down again.

"Yeah?" Schenck knocked back the rest of his coffee. He made a face.

"When I was talking with Dr. Teasdale, she asked me a question that's been nagging at me. She asked me if I knew *why* we are on a spaceship."

Schenck's eyes darted to his left, then to his right. They did not come back to Keira's own.

"Is there a question for me here, special agent?" he asked.

"It's a good question, don't you think?"

"Yeah, it's an excellent question, and well above my pay grade," Schenck said.

"Are you saying you don't know *why* we're on a spaceship?"

"That's exactly what I'm saying," Schenck said. "That's the thing about classified information. It's generally need-to-know."

"Are you telling me the truth?" Keira asked. He still wasn't looking at her. She slammed the flat of her hand onto his desk, making a loud "crack" sound that spun his head toward her.

"What was that for?"

"To get your attention," Keira said. "And I wanted you to look me in the eye when you answered."

Schenck glowered and shifted forward, resting his weight on his elbows. His eyes bored into hers. "I do not know why we're on a spaceship."

"And you aren't at all curious?" Keira asked.

"Of course I'm curious," Schenck replied. "But I'm also a loyal soldier. When and if I need to know, someone smarter and with more authority that I have will tell me. End of story."

"And you don't think that maybe the reason we're on a spaceship might have something to do with why a bunch of rebels are breaking into S-panels?"

"No, I don't. I think that's a leap, special agent. Who put such an idea into your head?"

"Sherry Teasdale."

"Did you ever consider that she might be trying to throw you off the trail?"

Keira deflated a bit. "Actually...no." She narrowed one eye at him. "Don't you feel betrayed?"

"By who?"

"By the woman you told me to trust?"

"I think we have a possible security breach," Schenck said. "Which, in an operation as large as ours is, sounds like Tuesday."

"Are you covering for her?" Keira asked. "Or are you covering your own ass, since you were the one who recommended her?"

"I don't like your tone, special agent," Schenck said. "And I don't find this line of inquiry helpful. Leave it."

"Wait, am I a dog?" Keira asked. "Don't you think I should follow the facts wherever they lead me?"

"Of course you should...to a point. There are larger security issues at play."

"And who gets to say which issues are more important?" Keira asked.

"In this office?" Schenck asked. He slapped the desk himself. "I do."

D r. Robinson stepped down from the bottom step of the bus and stumbled, bashing his knee on the curb.

"You all right, buddy?" the bus driver called.

"Fine, fine," Robinson said. Heat rose to his face as he stood up again. He balanced on his left foot as he tested his right ankle. There was some pain, but it wasn't too bad. He limped away from the bus stop, his pride having received the greater injury.

It was night, and aside from a motorcycle roaring by, it was quiet. Robinson took a cell phone from his pocket and dialed.

"Yeah?"

"It's Dr. T," Robinson said.

"I can read a screen."

"Are you...in a secure location?" Robinson asked.

"Do you mean are CHS agents pounding on my door, or do you mean is this conversation private?"

"Um...both, I suppose," Dr. Robinson answered.

"Yes, then."

"You're sure no one can hear you?"

"Just a sec."

Robinson heard some scuffling, a bump, some cursing, and a rattle as the phone was picked up again. "We're safe."

"Okay, then. I have some news for you. I...uh...quit."

"Quit what?"

"The Triumvirate."

There was silence on the other end. Then, "No shit?"

"It's true. So...Basil hasn't said anything about it?"

"No, but it's not like he tells me anything anyway. What happened?"

"We had a...disagreement."

"About? Or is that confidential?"

"It would be, except..." Robinson looked around. His pulse quickened as he did so. He had the feeling he was being watched, but there was clearly no one around. He coughed. "Are you there?"

"I'm here, doc. You were about to tell me why you quit when you went into a fugue state."

"I didn't..." Robinson sighed. "We disagreed about a Mr. St. John."

A laugh erupted on the other end of the phone. At first it seemed genuine, but as it continued it was clear it was exaggerated. "Whoooo....let me guess: He's creaming his jeans over him, and you're not so sure?"

"That's a fair assessment," Robinson admitted.

"And the lady doc?"

"She sides with him."

"Ouch."

"Indeed."

"And so that's it? You're just out?"

"I left before it came to blows."

"Wise. He has a mean right hook. I know this from experience."

"I don't doubt it."

A silence fell between them. A bus went by, the noise of its passing making speech impossible anyway.

"Are you on the street?"

"I am."

"Anyone around?"

"No. I'm sure of it," Robinson said, but he still couldn't shake the feeling that there were eyes on him. *Of course there are,* he reminded himself. *They're just not human eyes.*

"So what now?" the voice asked. "Does that mean you're on the outs with all the leadership?"

"I still report to the Canon-to-the-Ordinary, but I'm not sure how long that will continue, now that I no longer have an official place in the hierarchy."

"Have you spoken to Tau Valens?"

"I have never spoken to Tau Valens. Have you?"

The voice snorted. "Not likely."

Robinson sniffed. "You never know. Strange bedfellows."

"Hey, was that a homo-bash right there?"

"Not much of one. Keep your wig on," Robinson warned.

"You sure like to walk close to the edge. I think you get a kick out of pissing off absolutely anyone you're talking to."

"That may very well be," Robinson judged. "But I don't need you to be my therapist."

"As if. Uh...just curious—what *do* you need me for?"

"I wanted to assess whether your antipathy for Mr. St. John was a match for my own."

"Are you asking me if I hate his guts?"

"Um...quite."

"Hmm...I don't like him, but I don't hate him, either. He's kind of boring."

"I didn't ask whether you wanted to hold hands at the roller rink," Robinson snapped.

"What *are* you asking?"

"Are you going to make me come right out and say it?"

"Oh. Well, I'm not recording anything."

"Good to know." Robinson said through gritted teeth. "Look, maybe this was a mistake. I should—"

"No, no, doc. Hang in there. You just surprised me is all. Are you looking for...what? An accomplice?"

"Something like that, yes."

"To...perhaps take a certain young initiate out of action?"

"Something like that."

"Temporarily or permanently?"

"Either one, I suppose, but with a strong preference for the latter."

"And let me guess, you'd like me to handle the dirty work?"

"Something like that," Robinson said again.

"Huh. What's in it for me?"

"Well, I was hoping you'd enjoy twisting the knife, but I misjudged your level of...disaffection."

"Oh, I'd enjoy twisting the knife, all right," the voice said. "But it isn't Seth I want to hurt."

"Your father?" Robinson couldn't help smiling.

"Only if I could see his face when he hears the news."

"I'm sure a clever lad like yourself could arrange that," Robinson said.

"Count me in," Nazz said.

WHAT ARE SECRET SOCIETIES?

Secret societies, also known as clandestine organizations or covert fraternities, are exclusive groups characterized by their secrecy and restricted membership. These societies operate outside the public eye and often maintain rituals, codes of conduct, and symbols that are known only to their members. While the term "secret society" can evoke intrigue and mystery, it is important to note that not all secretive groups engage in nefarious or illicit activities.

The origins of secret societies can be traced back to ancient times, with examples found in various cultures and civilizations. These groups served a variety of purposes, including religious, political, philosophical, and social objectives. Secret societies often provided a space for individuals to share and explore esoteric knowledge, engage in intellectual discourse, or uphold certain values or traditions.

Membership in secret societies is typically selective and requires initiation rituals or rites of passage. This process serves to establish trust, loyalty, and commitment among members and helps maintain the secrecy of the organization. Secret societies may have hierarchical structures, with different levels of initiation and knowledge reserved for higher-ranking members.

Throughout history, secret societies have been associated with conspiracy theories and rumors of clandestine activities. While some secret societies indeed engaged in political intrigue or subversive actions, it is essential to distinguish between genuine historical evidence and sensationalized claims. Notable examples of secret societies include the Freemasons, the Illuminati, and the Skull and Bones society.

Today, secret societies continue to exist, often reflecting the interests and aspirations of their members. Some focus on charitable or philanthropic endeavors, while others may have more esoteric or spiritual aims. The secrecy surrounding these societies can contribute to a sense of exclusivity and camaraderie among members.

It is important to note that the term "secret society" is sometimes used colloquially to refer to groups or organizations that maintain a degree of secrecy or privacy without engaging in secretive or malicious activities. These may include social clubs, professional associations, or private societies with restricted membership.

CHAPTER TWENTY

The adversary spies on us,
lying in wait for us like a fisherman,
wishing to seize us,
rejoicing that he might swallow us.
For he places many foods before our eyes,
things which belong to this world.
He wishes to make us desire one of them
and to taste only a little,
so that he may seize us with his hidden poison
and bring us out of freedom
and take us into slavery.
—*Authoritative Teaching**

---

* Authoritative Teaching: Nag Hammadi Library, codex VI, 3. Translation by George W. MacRae, published in *The Nag Hammadi Library* (San Francisco, CA: HarperCollins 1990).

As the train slowed to a stop, Seth watched his knee. It wasn't bouncing. He also wasn't grinding his teeth. And the knot in the pit of his stomach had untwisted. And yet he knew he was about to embark on his most dangerous mission—Mr. Basil had said so. He marveled at his own sense of calm. He felt like he was inhabiting an alien body—not his, but still strangely familiar. It was a much more comfortable place than he was used to.

The other passengers rose and began reaching for their hand-bags, briefcases, and backpacks. Seth waited until the line at the doors had diminished before rising. He didn't have a bag. He had intentionally brought nothing that might slow him down.

Sacramento was not unlike San Jose in that it was sprawled out. No place was walkable from any other place. If one didn't have a car, one was at a distinct disadvantage. But Seth was used to public transit. He pulled up his 411 app and entered the address of the building he was headed for. It was only two bus rides away.

Forty-five minutes later, Seth stepped out into the early after-noon sun and found himself enjoying the heat. Sacramento was famously hot in the summertime. As the summer had passed, so had the heat in the South Bay, yet here in the north the asphalt still bubbled and felt soft beneath his sneakers.

He crossed Florin Perkins Road and looked up at the massive Pacific Gas & Electric building. It seemed oddly lopsided, with an ornate doorway and façade adorning the left half of the building, the right half looking like an enormous stone box. A large parking lot was about a quarter full, the cars baking in the heat. He heard a whine and turned to follow it.

A small white dog scratched at the window. It had been left open a crack at the top, enough for Seth to pass his fingers in. It didn't occur to him that the dog would object to the intrusion, and indeed, the dog seemed to be delighted. But his fingers were warm—too warm.

The dog's eyes were fixed on him, dark tear stains forming elliptical circles under the brown of its pupils. Seth felt torn. *The dog is none of your business,* a voice in his head reminded him.

Yet the dog is trapped, as much a prisoner as every other soul on this ship, another voice countered. *Don't I have a duty to do something about that?* Indeed, wasn't that what he was there for?

"Hey! Get away from my car!" a woman shouted at him.

Seth started a bit, but felt a calm descend on him quickly. He smiled at the woman. "I'm sorry," he said. "Your little guy looks hot."

"Back away or I'll pepper spray you," the woman said, fumbling in her purse.

Seth raised his hands and backed away from the car, a smile still fixed to his face. "I'm not trying to steal anything. I just love dogs. Honest. And I'm glad you're here. I'm glad he's going to be okay."

Seth turned, stuffed his hands into his pockets and made a beeline for the front door. He didn't look behind him again, but heard the car door open and close.

He breathed a sigh of relief and knew that he'd just dodged his first bullet of the day.

His right hand closed on the S-key. Somehow just touching it made him feel safer. He knew this was ironic, but it didn't matter. He avoided eye contact with those he passed, heading straight for the elevators. According to his instructions, he hit the button for the top floor—the fourth floor. He counted three seconds and hit it again.

When the elevator door opened, he found himself in a nearly empty office. No one paid him any attention as he strode with feigned confidence to the end of the hallway, then turned right.

He noted the S-panel to his left and paused. He turned and looked behind him. No one was coming.

This time he made sure he had his ski mask with him. He pulled it from his back pocket and drew it over his head. Withdrawing the key, he slipped it into the panel and was relieved that it turned easily.

He shut the panel behind him, feeling it settle into place with a pleasing click. His pulse quickened, but he felt otherwise calm as he chose a direction at random. Counting his steps, he reached the end of a corridor, noting the unmarked doors to either side.

He paused at the corner and listened. Voices...and they were growing louder. He looked at the doors behind him and tried one of them. It was locked. He leaped to another, and it too was locked. The voices were laughing and he could make out their words, although he wasn't really listening. He tugged at the handle of the third and final door, and was relieved when it gave. Pivoting inside, he closed it behind him, keeping the handle turned so that it would make no noise.

There was no light on in the tiny room, but he had noticed shelves with what looked like printer paper, paper towels, and toilet paper. He waited until the voices faded. The ski mask felt hot on his head. The area around his mouth had become wet. Closing his eyes, he breathed deep until his pulse slowed.

Then he opened the door again and looked around. No one. He stepped out of the storage room and closed the door behind him. Then he set off at a jog in the direction he had been going.

He marveled at how clean The Behind was. *Who dusts in here?* he wondered. But it made sense that cleanliness was important for the efficient workings of a starship. What further amazed him, though, was the fact that all the people who worked Behind must live normal lives among the Deceived, always keeping their secrets—presumably from their own families. He wondered how much they really knew, and how much they themselves were the deceived.

He turned left at a T in the corridor, but it dead-ended at a large security door requiring a key card. He noted that mentally, and turned back. But before he got very far, he decided to try the door. What could it hurt? He ran back and set his hand on the handle. Just as he'd expected, it didn't budge.

Just as he let go of it, he heard an interior latch click. He dove for the space on the wall next to the hinges just as the door swung open. Safely behind the opening door, he watched as someone in a hazmat suit walked away from him down the corridor. The figure pulled off the hood, revealing a head of long, curly black hair.

Seth glanced at the door and saw that in a couple of seconds it would latch again. As quietly as he could, he leaped to the other side of the doorway and stuck his hand in the gap. The door came to rest against it soundlessly. He stood still until the woman in the hazmat suit turned a corner.

He peered past his fingers into the secured area. If there was a reason a hazmat suit was necessary in there, he wasn't sure he wanted to go. A voice in his head told him there was enough at stake to risk it, and he couldn't think of a legitimate counterargument. He couldn't tell much about the space beyond through the sliver he had to look through, but it seemed to be empty of people.

He pulled the door wide enough to pass and went inside. He pulled off a shoe and left it wedged so the door couldn't lock behind him. Then he pulled the burner cell from his pocket and opened the camera app.

He was relieved to see that he had cell reception—that meant that everything he photographed would be automatically loaded to the cloud. Even if he were to be caught, whatever he found would still be available to Mr. Basil. But there seemed to be nothing of substance in this room. Lining one wall, he saw a couple of banks of mainframe computers and a tangled mass of IT equipment.

Seth swiftly crossed the room and entered another corridor. This was lined with windows, looking in on several very large rooms in either direction. He ducked, hoping to stay enough out of sight not to be noticed. The top of his head, however, bobbed along at the bottom of the windows as he crab-walked sideways. Then he stopped.

The second room the windows overlooked was vast. Filling its immensity were large machines, the utility of which completely evaded Seth. As quickly as he could, he snapped pictures. It took several to cover every part of the room. A bright LED panel caught his eye. It included several continually fluctuating numbers; beside them were various signs. The words meant nothing to him, all except for one: speed.

Engines, the voice in his head said. *You're looking at the engines.*

He zoomed in on the LED panel and snapped a couple of pictures, just to be sure. Then he continued down the corridor, continuing to stay low. It dead-ended at another security door.

It was enough. It was big, and Seth knew it. Again, he focused on his breathing to calm himself, stuffed the phone into his jeans, and crawled beneath the windows back to the first security door. There, he paused only long enough to put on his shoe. Gently easing the security door closed, he turned. Then he ran.

Angie knocked on Seth's door. There was no answer. She waited a few more minutes, just to be sure. Then she slipped the key from her pocket and unlocked the door.

Inside, she felt a wave of nostalgia. There was the ratty couch where she and Seth and Kush had watched an endless parade of *kaiju* movies, the same couch she had slept on for weeks. There were still popcorn crumbs on the carpet near the coffee table.

She sat on the couch and bit her lip. The emptiness of the apartment triggered something in her—a loneliness she had been holding at bay. "Oh, Seth," she said out loud. It wasn't the loss of this place that made her sad. It was the loss of him.

Sighing, she rose and went to the kitchen. She fished a brown paper grocery sack from between the refrigerator and the counter and walked down the hallway to the bathroom. She threw her toothbrush into the sack, plus the few of her toiletries still there. Next, she moved to the bedroom and waded through the hamper, pulling out her clothes and stuffing them into the sack. She paused when she came to one of Seth's T-shirts, one that she really liked. She shrugged and threw that into the bag as well.

Picking up the bag, she headed for the living room again. Then she heard a "click." She froze and listened. She heard the door close. She hugged the wall of the hallway. She did not want Seth to find her there. She walked backwards slowly, toward the bedroom, holding the bag as still as she could to keep it from making any noise.

Once inside the bedroom, she set the bag on the bed and looked around. If it was Seth, how could she escape? If she was lucky, he'd head for the bathroom—she could sneak out once the door was closed. But if it wasn't Seth...

She shook her head. Who else could it be? It wasn't Becky, it sure wasn't Travis, and if Seth had other friends, Angie didn't know about them. Maybe someone from the Lodge? If so, how would that go, if they found her here? She could just tell them the truth. She had a key, after all, and she wasn't taking anything that wasn't hers—except for the t-shirt.

To her surprise, a woman's voice called out, "Hello? Is there anyone here? This is California Homeland Security." Angie's face furrowed into a deep frown. CHS? *What the fuck?* Angie mouthed.

Without thinking, Angie raised her hands and called, "In the bedroom." Then she waited. She heard footsteps in the hall. Then a shadow loomed in the doorway. Then the light turned on.

Angie lowered one hand to shield her eyes until they adjusted. A woman in her forties filled the doorframe, pistol drawn, looking as sexy as Angie's wettest dream in tight khaki chinos and a button down shirt, her blonde hair cut short.

"Who are you?" the woman asked.

"Angie. Who are you?"

"Special Agent Keira Sloane."

"Can I see some ID?"

Without her gun hand wavering, the woman fished into the back pocket of her chinos and pulled out a wallet. Letting it fall open, Angie saw a gold badge.

"Your turn."

Angie put her hand into her own pocket and pulled out her driver's license. The woman leaned toward her and took it. Glancing quickly between the license and Angie's face, she tossed it back at her. "What are you doing here?"

"What are *you* doing here?" Angie asked.

"I'm investigating a crime," the agent said.

"I'm collecting my stuff since my roommate kicked me out."

"Is your roommate Seth St. John?" the agent asked.

"Yeah," Angie affirmed. "Wait...what did he do?"

"I'm not at liberty—"

"Oh, Jesus, what the fuck did he do?" Angie asked, lowering her hands.

"Do you know the whereabouts of Mr. St. John?" the agent asked.

"No, we're...we're not really speaking right now."

The agent scowled at this, and turned her head slightly sideways. "Why don't you come into the living room and have a seat?"

"Why don't you put the gun down?" Angie suggested.

"Don't try anything," the agent said. "I'm a quick draw."

"Noted," Angie said. She was relieved when the agent slipped the pistol into the holster at her hip. *God, she looks tasty enough to just lick her face*, Angie thought.

"C'mon out," the agent said, waving her toward the living room.

Angie slipped past her and walked down the hallway. "What did you say your name was?"

"Special Agent Keira Sloane."

"Keira. I like that."

"Thanks," the agent said, sounding sincere. Once in the living room, she waved Angie toward the couch. The agent, however, continued to stand.

"What did he do?" Angie asked again, sitting in her usual spot.

"I'm not at liberty to reveal the details of an ongoing investigation," the agent said.

"Does it have something to do with that gnostic Lodge?" Angie asked.

The woman's eyes widened. "It may," the woman said. "What do you know about it?"

"More than I want to," Angie said. "And not enough, apparently." She looked away. "Jesus, Seth, what have you gotten yourself into?" She shook her head and looked back at the agent. "He used to be so...normal, so milquetoast, you know? Then he...I don't know, he started going through some kind of existential crisis. 'Why am I here?'" she moaned in an exaggerated, mocking tone. "'What is the meaning of my life?' That kind of bullshit. Drove me nuts." The agent nodded, but said nothing. Angie continued. "Then he started reading books on gnosticism, and then he started going...there. And that's when things started to get weird."

"Weird how?"

582 • J.R. MABRY

"He was always my best friend, ever since high school. We never had secrets from each other...not until now."

"Were you lovers?" the agent asked.

Angie responded with a raspberry. "Please. He's got one too many penises for me."

"Ah," the agent said, but she smiled. "But you were staying here?"

"I broke up with my girlfriend. Seth let me crash here for a few weeks. Then we...he started getting all secretive and shit and I wouldn't shut up about it, and...next thing you know, we're not speaking to each other." Angie felt her throat swell up, and she wiped her eyes on her sleeve.

"I can see how hard that was for you," the agent said, her voice tinged with compassion.

They sat in silence for several seconds. Then the agent said, "What can you tell me about Seth's interest in S-panels?"

Angie reared back. "What? I don't know nothing about no fucking S-panels!" She shook her head. "Are you shitting me? S-panels? Holy fuck, this is worse than I thought."

"Did you ever see him with an S-panel key?"

"No!" Angie almost yelled.

"Did you ever hear him talk about S-panels?"

"No," Angie said, "Except, you know, to acknowledge their existence, like you do."

"But nothing out of the ordinary? No talk about breaching them?"

"Hell no. Fuck no."

"You're sure?" the agent asked.

"I'm totally, 100% fucking sure," Angie said. "Jesus, Seth!"

The agent seemed to be thinking. Then she pulled a card from her breast pocket. She leaned over the coffee table and handed it to Angie. It was a typical business card, with a gold foil stamp of the CHS badge on the left half of it. "This is my card. If you think of anything else, please let me know. If you see anything or notice anything, please let me know. I'm not trying to hurt Seth. I'm... he's in over his head and I'm trying to protect him...maybe from himself."

Angie nodded as she stared at the card.

"Call me, okay?" the agent asked.

"I will," Angie said.

Seth waved and a familiar red Toyota Corolla rolled up to the curb. Seth opened the door and climbed in. "Thanks for the ride," he said.

"It's the least we can do," Nazz said. "How did it go?" He pulled away from the Tamien train station and onto LeLong Street.

Seth was still buzzing from the adrenaline, but his hands were steady. "In and out without any snags."

"That's why we practice, right there," Nazz said, nodding with approval. He pointed to the cupholders on either side of the stick shift. "Hey, I stopped at 7-11 on the way. Got you a Coke."

"Oh, thanks," Seth said. He picked up the waxed paper cup and took a tentative sip through the straw. He had always thought of himself as a Dr. Pepper guy, but he liked a Coca-Cola well enough. He was ordinarily wary of fountain drinks as they often didn't taste like they were supposed to. As he feared, this one had an odd taste to it. He put it back in the cup holder without comment.

"I think I found something—something important," Seth said.

"Oh?" Nazz asked, turning right on West Alma.

"I think I found the engines."

Nazz looked over at him with wide eyes. "No shit."

Seth pointed ahead of them. "Eyes on the road."

Nazz obeyed, and Seth thought he looked suddenly pale. "Uh...tell me more."

"Access is in the PG&E building, just where I was sent. How did they know?"

Nazz shrugged. "I don't think they did. It was just an unmapped area."

Seth frowned. "Well, they must have suspected, since they hadn't found the engines yet and they considered this a high-priority section."

"I couldn't tell you," Nazz said. "Did you get us a map?"

"I drew it on the train," Seth said.

"Are you crazy?"

"The car was almost empty," Seth said. "No one saw me."

"There are cameras in those cars."

"I didn't see any," Seth said, sounding not-so-sure.

"Jesus," Nazz swore.

"What?" Seth asked. "It would just look like...I don't know, architectural drawings, or like I was laying out a new kitchen or something. I didn't label anything."

They drove in silence for a few blocks. Then Nazz asked, "Don't like the soda?"

Seth didn't want to seem ungrateful. "It's okay. I'm not a big fan of fountain drinks."

"Huh. Try to do a guy a favor."

"Sorry, man," Seth said. "It was thoughtful. Thank you."

Nazz looked down at the drink, then back to the road, scowling.

"Look, Nazz, I know you don't like me—"

"What are you talking about?" Nazz asked.

"You know exactly what I'm talking about. Whatever shit you and your dad have going on, I somehow got in the middle of it, and that's the last thing I wanted to do. Anyway, I'm sorry if I hit a nerve or stepped in a big pile of dog shit. I didn't mean to."

"Whatever."

"I mean, maybe we don't have enough in common to be friends, but...I mean, we're on the same side, right?"

Nazz' eyes stayed glued to the road. He said nothing.

"Anyway, if I hurt you somehow, I didn't mean to. I'm sorry. Can we at least be cordial colleagues?"

Nazz' fingers tightened on the steering wheel, hard enough that his knuckles were white. Seth began to wonder if he was doing more harm than good. "Okay, let's just leave it alone. But if you ever want to talk about it, I'm totally down with that."

Nazz still didn't look at him, but his clenched jaw nodded curtly. He picked up his Coke and drained it noisily.

"You want mine?" Seth asked.

Nazz didn't answer.

***

"Beck, are you awake?"

Becky turned over and yawned. "Yeah. You're home late."

Angie slipped into bed and faced Becky, their noses about three inches apart. She could smell Becky's sweat, and it smelled good.

"I went to Seth's place to pick up some of my stuff."

"Oh?"

"I ran into a state agent, CHS."

Becky's eyes widened. "At Seth's?"

"Yeah. Seems he's gotten himself into some trouble."

"What kind of trouble?" Becky asked.

Angie briefly recounted her conversation with the agent.

Afterwards, the two women lay together in silence for a long moment. Finally, Becky said, "Well, shit."

"Yeah. I told you he was going off the deep end."

"But why?"

"I think that's what the agent was trying to figure out."

"Yikes. Do you think...we'll be implicated?"

"What? How?"

"I don't know...guilt by association?"

Angie thought about it. "I don't see how. Besides, she—the agent, I mean—she didn't seem suspicious, just...intent on finding Seth."

"And what happens to him if she does?"

Angie shook her head.

"I wish I'd never heard of that fucking Lodge," Becky said.

"Becky, I'm surprised at you! Language!" Angie giggled.

Becky didn't smile. "I mean it. I wish I'd never heard of them. I wish...I wish *he* hadn't."

"I know." Angie stared at Becky's eyes. She wasn't her type, but she was pretty and smart and caring. She understood now why Seth liked her.

"What do you think the...the draw was, for him? What was the attraction?"

"He said he felt like his life didn't have any meaning," Angie remembered. "I guess they gave it to him."

"I wish he could have found it...with us," Becky said, her voice tinged with sadness.

Angie reached out and stroked her head. "I know." Withdrawing her hand, she sniffed and said, "I wonder...Seth's always been a goody-two-shoes. It's one of the things I love...loved...to tease him about."

"I can see why he's an easy target," Becky admitted. "He's kind of Charlie Brown."

"O my god, he *is* Charlie Brown!" Angie slapped her shoulder.

Then she looked thoughtful again. "Maybe this is his way of breaking bad, of finding...I don't know...wholeness. Embracing his inner bad boy...finally. Maybe it's about finding his freedom. I know how I felt when I finally admitted to myself that I liked girls. Maybe it's the same for him."

"Maybe..." Becky's voice trailed off.

"I wish there was something I could *do*," Angie said.

Becky looked thoughtful. Then she said, "You *did* take that video."

"Video?"

"Of the ritual," Becky reminded her.

"Oh, yeah. I blocked it out."

"You did not," Becky said.

"Yeah, but I don't want to look at it again."

"You don't have to. Just...upload it. Post it to Facebook or something. Expose them."

"The Lodge?" Angie asked.

"Yeah. I mean, nobody knows they're doing this weird shit, right?"

"I called that agent and told her about it—and about the warehouse," Angie said. "That's something."

Becky propped herself up on her elbow. "Okay, but is that enough? Who knows how many other lives they've ruined? Why not bring them down? If you ask me, it's payback time."

Angie looked at the ceiling, but nodded. She liked the sound of that. A lot.

Becky blinked. "I wonder...if *I* like girls."

Angie's forehead bunched into a confused frown. "What?"

"You said you found your freedom when you admitted you liked girls. Maybe...maybe I like girls, too."

There was a moment of awkward silence, then Angie burst out laughing. "If I were drinking milk, it would have just spit out my nose."

"What?" Becky asked.

"Girl, you are the straightest bitch I have ever met."

"I can't be girl-curious?"

Angie's eyes narrowed. Then she rolled into Becky and pressed her lips onto hers. She held them there for a long moment, then she rolled away. "Feel anything?"

"Um...yes."

"Huh. Well, maybe you're bi."

"Maybe I am," Becky said, her voice quavering.

"Are you okay?" Angie asked.

"I think this is a bigger deal for me than it is for you," Becky said.

"Hey...I see that. I'm sorry," Angie said, her eyes softening. "I just never...dude, you just came out to me and I wasn't supportive. I really am sorry."

"I don't know if I came out—"

"You totally came out." She reached out and took Becky's hand. Becky squeezed it.

"Can you...can you kiss me again?" Becky asked.

"Beck, I don't think I'm your type...and I don't think you're my type. Let's not start something that can't go anywhere. Besides, we're good roomies."

"I know. I'm not...I'm not saying, 'Let's be girlfriends,' I'm just saying...I trust you and...and I'd like to try it."

"You know what will happen, right? I'll be thinking this is a casual fuck, and you'll fall in love."

"No..."

"That's exactly what will happen," Angie said. "I know...I've been there...on both sides of it."

"I won't. I promise. Just..." Becky rolled over and lay on top of Angie.

"Oh. Okay, then," Angie said. Then she parted her lips and kissed her deep.

"**O**n what authority do you have it that people actually get up this early?" Tony Raine asked, popping a potato chip into his mouth.

"How did you get to be a special agent when you're so goddam whiney?" Keira responded. The sun was just coming up, the first pink slivers of light intruding on the slate gray sky. The industrial park seemed utterly deserted, and except for a single car in the parking lot, the large warehouse in front of them was dark and quiet.

"How did you even know about this place?" Tony asked, reaching for his coffee.

"Go easy on that or you'll ruin our stakeout asking them if you can use their john."

"You bought it. Answer the question."

"I got a text message this morning from the former roommate of our person-of-interest."

"The dyke?"

"Jesus, Tony. What century do you live in?"

He shrugged. "It's your case. I haven't memorized the *dramatis personae*."

"It was a good bit of luck, running into her at his apartment. I didn't expect it to shake something loose, but it did."

"Did you threaten her?"

"What? Fuck, Tony, what do you take me for?"

"A mean-ass bitch that would make me crap my pants if I met you in a dark alley."

"Awww...you really know how to sweet-talk a girl."

"Something's happening," Tony said, pointing at the warehouse.

"Thanks for helping out today, Seth," Jude said.

"No problem. I'm actually looking forward to it—I need to get out." Seth held the door for his friend. "And thanks for picking me up."

"No problem."

"Plus, it's not every day that you move," Seth added.

"You'd be surprised how quickly your friends disappear when you say, 'work day,' and promise pizza."

Seth laughed. "No I wouldn't."

"How did your last assignment go?"

"In and out without a hitch. And I think I found something... something big."

Jude's eyes widened. "Really? What?"

"I don't think I should say just yet. But it's big."

"Man, I so envy you. Total fucking spy!"

"We all serve."

"Yeah, but I fold newsletters and put them in envelopes. It's only half as exciting."

That made Seth laugh. He put his hand up to slap Jude on the back, but before he touched his friend, Jude's legs folded out from under him and he crumpled to the ground.

"Jude, what the fuck?"

Blood began to pool beneath Jude's head.

Seth felt a bee sting his ear. Without thinking, his hand went to the spot, and came back with blood. Instinctively, Seth dropped to the ground, just as a tiny plume of dust shot into the air just a few feet in front of him. Then he felt a scale of force he had never experienced before that pitched him face-first into the asphalt. Searing pain raged through the left side of his body, and he struggled to get air.

He heard a roar above him, and within seconds, a black sedan screeched to a halt just behind him. He felt hands on his upper arms, hands beneath him, hands scooping him up. He seemed to hover precariously on empty air, and then he smelled the warm, acidic balm of leather, his face pressed into it, sliding along it. He melted into it, and as he did so, heard several metallic *ping* sounds. And then, as if surrendering to the gravity of a nap, everything went black.

WHAT ARE DARK GODS?

Dark gods, also known as malevolent deities or gods of darkness, are a recurring theme in mythology, folklore, and various religious traditions. These entities are often depicted as powerful supernatural beings associated with evil, chaos, destruction, and other negative aspects of existence. While the concept of dark gods varies across cultures, their portrayal generally represents a contrast to benevolent deities and embodies the darker aspects of the human psyche.

In many mythological traditions, dark gods are personifications of forces that oppose order, goodness, and harmony. They are often associated with death, underworlds, and the shadows that lurk in the human subconscious. Examples of dark gods can be found in various pantheons, such as the Greek deity Hades, the ruler of the Underworld, and the Norse god Loki, known for his mischievous and disruptive nature.

The worship or veneration of dark gods has been present in certain cults and secretive practices throughout history. These practices often involve rituals, sacrifices, and acts that challenge societal norms. Some individuals are drawn to the mysterious and rebellious nature of dark gods, while others see them as representations of the darker aspects of human nature that need acknowledgment and integration.

It is essential to recognize that the concept of dark gods does not imply an absolute malevolence or an endorsement of evil. Rather, they represent a fundamental duality that exists in many belief systems, reflecting the complexity of human experience. The existence of dark gods raises questions about the nature of divinity, the balance between light and darkness, and the role of these entities in the cosmic order.

While dark gods are often portrayed as antagonistic figures, they can also serve as catalysts for personal growth, transformation, and introspection. Some individuals seek to understand and integrate their shadow selves by exploring the symbolism and teachings associated with dark gods.

The interpretation and significance of dark gods vary across cultures and belief systems. They continue to fascinate and captivate the human imagination, serving as a reminder of the multifaceted nature of the divine and the eternal struggle between opposing forces within the human psyche.

CHAPTER TWENTY-ONE

The father was not jealous.
What jealousy, indeed,
can there be between him
and his members?
*—Gospel of Truth**

ngie pushed the button on her mouse and waited as the video loaded. She had already loaded it to Clikr and now she waited for it to load to ViewTube. She felt a momentary stab of conscience. She had already betrayed her friend once, and now here she was, doing it again. Only this time, she was posting porn featuring his skinny ass, on platforms the whole world would see.

---

* Adapted from The Gospel of Truth: Nag Hammadi Codex I, translated by Robert M. Grant, published in *Gnosticism* (NY: Harper & Brothers, 1961).

It had been Becky's idea, but that didn't matter. She was the one doing the deed.

The thought of Becky distracted her. For a straight girl, she had certainly seemed eager. And while fumbling and inexperienced, she had navigated her way around girl parts well enough. She felt another twinge of guilt, since she knew there was only one end to that story. Becky might be bi, which was fine, but there was nothing she could do—save a total makeover that included pube-shaving, piercings, and a major attitude adjustment—that would make her anything resembling Angie's type. Added to that, she wasn't dyke enough, she wasn't inked enough, and she wasn't heroin-chic skinny, either. She was a sweet, pudgy girl who might be able to find Angie's clit, but would never find her heart. Angie sighed as she realized the truth—she'd done a piss poor job of finding *anyone* who completely fit the bill, thus far.

A *ding* alerted her that the video had finished uploading. Angie clicked in the title field and typed "Ritual Sex Orgy at San Jose Gnostic Lodge." In the keywords field, she typed every raunchy term she could think of, and threw in "free gift" and "giveaway" besides. Who cared how people got to the page, just so long as they did? Once there, who could resist a peek? *Well, maybe Becky,* Angie thought, which only cemented her fears.

Her hand hovered over the "enter" key that would launch the video out into the world. *It's for his own good,* the voice in her head reassured her. *But I could just send it to that hot state agent,* she argued. *What fun would that be?* the other voice countered. It was hard to argue with that.

She could still send a link to the agent. She would. Right after she posted links on Facebook and Instagram and Reddit and CycloPOD.

She hit the button.

"Cup of coffee, special agent?" Tony Raines held a cup out to Keira.

The past twelve hours had been a lysergic blur of hospitals, inter-agency phone calls, long-winded explanations to faceless higher-ups, and concern for her suspect. She took the cup from him, mumbling something like thanks, and looked through the window at Seth St. John. A bullet had entered his back, clipped his clavicle, and exited the front of his chest. He was damned lucky it hadn't shattered a bone or punctured a vital organ. Surgery had wrapped in under two hours, and he'd been sleeping for six.

"You want to try waking him?" Tony asked.

"What? And get on the bad side of the doctors?" Keira asked.

"Ooo, is that the voice of prudence and propriety I hear? Who are you and what have you done with Special Agent Sloane?"

"Fuck you, Tony."

They both grinned, standing side-by-side at the window, looking in on the sleeping young man.

"He's a good kid," Keira said.

"How the fuck do you know? He killed a top-level computer tech."

"I met him," Keira remembered. "The first time I went to the Lodge. This asswipe was hassling a girl on the bus, and Seth there put himself in harm's way to make him stop."

"So...he's a *chivalrous* murderer?"

"Later the guy came after him. I had to hit him in the kidneys with a tree branch."

Tony's eyebrows shot up. "So...just a normal day on the job."

Keira nodded her agreement to that. "We talked. You get a sense of people, you know?"

"'I looked the man in the eye. I found him to be very straight-forward and trustworthy. I was able to get a sense of his soul.'"

"Exactly," Keira nodded. "Who said that?"

"George W. Bush, talking about Vladimir Putin."

"You're an evil son of a bitch, Tony."

"Aphorisms don't lie."

"But you can make them mean anything you want them to," Keira said.

Tony waggled his head back and forth. "Yes and no."

"'Innocent until proven guilty,' remember?" Keira said.

"Are you saying you're too close to this to be objective?"

"What? Not even. I met the guy—once. There's no 'close' there. Just a gut feeling. I trust my gut."

Tony felt at his own bulging stomach. "I loathe mine."

"You could cut down on the donuts."

"Clichés are clichés because they're true."

"Is that a syllogism or just you being stupid?"

"Would it matter?"

Keira's phone buzzed. She pulled it from her pocket and, being careful not to spill her coffee on her screen, punched the answer button, then speakerphone. "Sloane," she said. "I'm here with Raines."

"How's our suspect?" Schenck's voice growled.

"He's out of surgery and resting comfortably."

"Have you been able to question him yet?"

"Unless he talks in his sleep, I don't see what good it would do."

Schenck grunted. "The search is finished. They're cleaning up now."

"What did they find?"

"Uh...let's see..." She could almost hear him putting on his glasses and picking up a file. "...some ceremonial gear, a massive slew of office partitions, for some reason. Oh, and get this: a fake S-panel."

Keira's head jerked toward Tony. "What the fuck?"

"It's not a smoking gun, but it strongly suggests they might have been training for S-panel breaches."

"Okay, okay, that's something. Anything else?"

"Just a bunch of empty rooms. Found a couch your boy might have been sleeping on. He was in the wind, right?"

"Yeah. That makes sense of why we found him so early. Any sign of the shooter?"

"We found shells on the roof. .22 caliber."

"So a sportsman, not a pro."

"Sure looks like it. He might have been shooting to kill, but he didn't really have the gear for it."

"Did a number on the big guy," Keira said.

"That would be one Jude Ash, another suspected member of this so-called Lodge."

"I saw a red Corolla speeding away," Keira offered.

"Yeah, we got that from your initial report. We've got an APB out. Nothing yet."

"Okay, okay, boss, thanks."

"There's one more thing."

"What's that?"

"I'm not sure how to describe it. I sent you a link via email. Check it out and let me know what you think."

"Okay, will do."

Tony reached for her coffee as she hung up on the call and navigated to her email app. She found Schenck's message right on top, and clicked on the link.

A ViewTube page bounced up, with the title, "Ritual Sex Orgy at San Jose Gnostic Lodge." The video, already autoplaying, showed what appeared to be the bare buttocks of Seth St. John pounding away at a naked woman seated on what could only be described as a religious altar.

"What the fuck is that?" Tony asked, peering over her shoulder. "Some Satanic ritual?"

"Let's find out," Keira said, not able to take her eyes off the screen.

Seth's eyes opened on an unfamiliar room. There were several beds, but he seemed to be the only person lying in one. A pain in his chest made him look down. A PICC line was fixed just above his right breast. On his left were bandages. Now that he was focusing on it, what had been a dull ache rose in intensity.

Looking around, he saw a man in aqua scrubs puttering about the room. Seth opened his mouth, but only a croak emerged.

The man whipped around at the sound, and smiled. "Hey, sleepyhead." He walked over to Seth's side and checked his PICC line. The man was in his mid-30s, tall and lean, with a bleach-blond buzz cut. He had a scar that bisected one eyebrow. "How are you feeling?"

"Like hell," Seth croaked.

"I'm not surprised. I'm Terry. I'll be your nurse for this shift."

Seth tried to nod with his eyes. It was only partially success-ful, but it hurt too much to move.

"Where am I?" Seth managed.

"You are in the Vacaville State Detentional Facility. We just call it 'Vaca.' That means 'the cow,' in case you didn't know."

"Huh," Seth responded. "So...I'm in jail?"

"That's more right than wrong. Vaca is kind of jail for VIPs. Better conditions, and much better health care. I've worked in the state prisons, so I can tell you that from experience. I don't know how you rate, my friend, but you should feel lucky that you do."

"I'm lucky I'm in jail?"

"Uh...what I mean is, if you have to be in jail, this is definitely the one you want to be in." He pulled out his phone and his thumbs danced over its face. "I just told the special agents that you're awake, so they'll be in to talk to you soon."

"What's soon?"

"Sometime today. Are you hungry?"

Seth shook his head.

"That's okay. But you let me know when you can handle it. For today, you'll get your dinner through your IV."

Seth nodded. "Why am I in jail?"

"You don't know?"

Seth was quiet. Then it all came rushing back. "Oh," he said. "Um...how is Jude?"

"Jude?" Terry asked, smiling. "I don't know anyone named Jude. I know the Beatles song. That's it, though. Sorry."

Seth looked down. Something to ask the agents. He made a mental note to do so. "I'm sleepy."

"Well, sleeping is the best thing you can do. I'll wake you when the agents get here, but it could be hours."

"Okay. I think I'll pray."

Terry patted his arm. "That's good for you, too. And if you need anything, I'll be right here. If you don't see me, I'm just in that little office over there." He pointed. "I can hear you, though. Like I said, you'll get good care here."

"Thank you," Seth said. He watched as Terry strode to his office. He kept the door open.

Seth shut his eyes. He longed to feel Sophia's presence. He wanted to be embraced by her, to feel her maternal comfort surround him. He reached out for her in his imagination. He saw himself floating in free space, and he called for her.

To his great relief, he saw her float into view. Her face was still obscured, but he knew it was her. He held his hands out, expecting her to pull him to her.

Instead, though, she just floated. In normal space, she would have seemed to be a few yards away. Her vague face was darkened, and she rose to the point where she was looking down on him.

"What?" Seth asked. "What's wrong?"

The Holy Mother said nothing. She just stared, the flowing train of her dress rippling in a breeze that couldn't possibly exist in space.

"Are you angry with me?" Seth asked. "I didn't mean to get shot. I was trying...I was really trying. I thought I was doing good." He dropped his eyes. "But I did let you down. I did get shot. And Jude got shot. Is Jude alive? Is he okay?" He looked up at the Holy Mother hopefully. Her blurry face just stared down at him.

After what seemed like an eternity, she finally spoke. "Why are you trying to hurt my son?"

Seth cocked his head. "Your son?" Who was her son? The answer bubbled up through his brain fog. *The demiurge.* But wasn't Sophia trying to undo the demiurge? Wasn't she on their side?

"What do you mean?" Seth asked.

"Why do you refuse him the offering that is his due?" Her voice was terse and icy.

"I don't—"

"You have your food. Why deny him his?"

"I'm not—"

But he was. He was working with the other gnostics against the demiurge, trying to subvert the sacrifice of the whole of California, trying to cheat him out of the flesh, life, and souls of 40 million people, every dog and cat, every chicken and wild turkey, every zoo animal, every fish in San Francisco Bay. They were his intended food, his propitiatory sacrifice. They were his by right, by offering, by the consent of every human on earth trading California lives for theirs. He could only imagine how the people of earth had sacrificed, what resources and expense had been deployed, only so that their descendants could live. They were there by the consent of untold archons, who arranged all things for the good of the insatiable and bloodied maw of their god.

Yes, he was trying to stop that. But Sophia had always been in favor of the interruption of the sacrifice. How was it she was flipping sides? Was the Holy Mother bipolar? And where did that leave him? He shrank into his bedclothes, feeling more lost and alone than ever before.

Then the Holy Mother seemed to ripple, to dissipate, and he was left staring only at the cold light of distant stars.

When Seth opened his eyes again, the stars were gone. He was once more staring at cinderblock walls painted an antiseptic, glossy aquamarine. The hospital bed stretched out in front of him, and he saw a pair of feet that he assumed were his, although he felt little attachment to them.

"Seth?" As he moved his head toward the sound, it felt like an overripe pumpkin, as if the insides moved slower than the outside, his brains sloshing sluggishly until they caught up. To his right, a woman was sitting in a chair near his bed. She looked familiar. Instinctively he smiled. Then he found her name. "Margaret?"

"Hello, Seth. How are you feeling?"

He tried to move his hands to his head, but was startled to discover they were bound to the bed frame with padded leather straps. "What...?" he began, but couldn't seem to formulate a question. Then he remembered. "Oh, yeah. I'm in jail. Am I still in jail?"

Margaret nodded. "My name isn't really Margaret, though, Seth. My name is Keira Sloane. I'm a special agent with CHS."

"You are?"

"Seth, you've suffered quite an injury, and you're on pain

medication. That's why everything seems a little bit woozy. I've asked them to back off the pain meds for a few hours so we can talk. Your head will feel clearer soon, but you'll most likely feel some pain, too. Do you understand?"

"Yeah," he said. His head was becoming clearer by the moment. And the pain in his chest kept time with it, the ache building in intensity. He blinked and looked around. A camera was set on a tripod to his left—a red light atop it was glowing.

Seth smacked his lips, and they felt dry. His throat hurt. "Can I have a drink?"

"Of course." Keira turned to a tray on wheels and poured water from a salmon-colored pitcher into a salmon-colored tumbler. She held it to his lips, and he slurped at it in a way that was functional but felt undignified. Cold wetness touched the left side of his chest where he'd dribbled.

"Thank you," he said. "Why does my throat hurt so bad?"

"You were intubated during surgery," Keira told him.

"Feels like something broke down there."

"It'll get better. Listen, I have some questions for you, Seth. Some of them might not be pleasant, but I need you to stay focused and tell me everything you can. As soon as we're done, we can raise your pain meds again. Okay?"

Seth nodded. The pain was severe, but he was relieved to have a clear head. He tried to sit up straighter, but it only made his chest wrench with painful spasms.

"Just lie back and relax," Keira commanded him.

He nodded, closing his eyes for a moment. "Ask."

"Seth, we have you on video behind an S-panel. We also found an S-panel key on your person when we picked you up. As you know, these are serious felonies, punishable by years in prison. Before we let the Attorney General throw the book at you, I want to hear your side of the story."

Seth opened his eyes and met hers. He blinked.

"Seth, why were you behind that S-panel?"

Seth said nothing. He swallowed. It hurt.

"A man was killed, Seth. A computer technician by the name of Harlan Paltier. He was married. He had two kids, both under seven years old. That family doesn't have a father anymore, and as far as I can see, it's because you were where you shouldn't have been. I want to know why you were there."

"I'm really sorry. He came after me," Seth said. "I-I-I was protecting myself."

"The man wasn't armed," Keira said.

"I wasn't either. He raised his radio—"

"You used his radio to crush his skull."

"It was self-defense."

"You can't claim self-defense if you are trespassing."

Seth wasn't sure that was true. It didn't sound right, but he knew next to nothing about the law.

"So once more," Keira said, her voice weary with feigned patience, "why were you there?"

Something in the intensity of her eyes pricked at him. The vision of the Holy Mother rushed back to him. She had been so angry, so cold, so utterly unlike every other encounter he had had with her. He grasped for possible reasons why he had evoked her wrath. Well, he had gotten caught, hadn't he? He wondered if that was it. The feeling of being the object of her displeasure evoked a very old feeling. It felt exactly like how he used to feel as a very young boy, being reminded in every sermon what a disappointment he was to God, how God was justly angry at him, at enmity with him, and would be, no matter how hard he tried to do better. He was flooded with feelings of futility, of being small and weak and cowering before unfathomable power intent on his annihilation. He shrank into his sheets, inarticulately hoping the bed would simply swallow him up and permit him some form of nonbeing. *What cruelty it is,* he thought, *to be born upon the earth, destined for damnation and helpless in the face of it. It would have been better to never have been born.*

"We also have video of you going into the PG&E building in Sacramento. And once again, we have video of you on the other side of the S-panel. Fortunately for you, you didn't kill anyone that time. But we still need to know: Why were you there?"

Seth tried to take a deep breath, but the pain in his chest prevented it. He forced himself to relax until the urgency to breathe deeply subsided.

"Does this have something to do with the Lodge?" Keira asked.

Seth's head jerked up.

"I've talked to Mr. Basil," Keira informed him. "And to Dr. Teasdale."

"You have?" Seth asked.

"I have. They were very forthcoming," she lied. "But I want to hear it from you."

He searched her face for a clue to her veracity, but she was unreadable. He very much doubted Mr. Basil or Dr. Teasdale would tell her anything, but she did have the full power of the state behind her. He hadn't seen either of them in days. What if...?

"I need you to talk to me, Seth," Keira said. "You need to help yourself before you take the blame for all of it."

Seth wondered at her words. She seemed to be implying that it would go easier on him if he implicated others in his illegal activity. That made sense. He'd seen almost every police procedural produced in the past fifty years. He knew how they worked. Was he willing to sacrifice himself for the movement? Of course—he proved that every time he went through an S-panel. He swallowed and said nothing.

Keira rolled her eyes and huffed. Then she pulled out her phone. She swiped away at its screen and then held it where he could see it. It emitted a cacophony of noise, loud brushes of a microphone, and rustlings of being held by hand. But the images were clear. He saw himself from behind, his buttocks clenching as he thrust himself into Sheila before the congregation.

Blood rose to his cheeks, and he looked away, suddenly feeling dizzy and very warm.

"Care to tell me what was going on there—besides the obvious, that is?" Keira asked.

"Where did you get that?" Seth asked.

"It's all over the internet. Let's see..." she peered at her screen again. "So far it's had 600,000 plays on ViewTube."

"Oh, shit," Seth said. If he could have slid down the bed any further, he would have.

"And that's not counting the other sites."

Seth shook his head. Suddenly, sacrificing himself didn't seem like a bad idea at all. The only problem was how to hasten it before he imploded with shame.

"That's nearly a million people staring at your cute little heinie."

"Stop," Seth said.

"Your friend Angie posted it."

Seth's eyes grew wide. "What?"

"And then she sent this to my boss."

"How could she...?"

"She did it because she believes you've gone off the deep end and she obviously loves you."

"How much did she tell you?"

"That doesn't matter. What matters is how much *you're* going to tell me."

Seth's eyes moved back and forth quickly. His pulse raced. He pulled at his restraints. He felt like a caged rat.

"Okay, okay. I'll talk to you," Seth said, hyperventilating. "Just...turn the camera off." He nodded at the tripod.

"So...off the record?" Keira asked.

Seth nodded.

"Okay, but depending on what you tell me, you may need to go on the record."

Seth nodded. He could cross that bridge if and when he came to it.

He watched as the special agent crossed the room and touched a button on the camera. The little red light went dark. Then she pulled a small moleskin notebook from her pocket and opened it. Withdrawing a small pen, she clicked it.

"Talk."

"Are you telling me...this spaceship is on a suicide mission?" Keira asked, looking up from her notebook, now filled with her indecipherable scribble.

Seth nodded. "Not suicide. It's only suicide if you kill yourself. It's murder...genocide, I guess. The people on earth are sending us to be killed. We're a sacrifice. We're supposed to...get eaten."

"By this monster god," Keira said, her voice betraying her incredulity.

"Yeah."

Keira cocked her head. She'd hoped to hear something she didn't know before, but she didn't expect...this. "Seth, do you know how insane this sounds?"

"Oh, absolutely," he said. "But that's the perfect cover. And it doesn't mean it isn't true."

Keira debated inwardly. Should she go hard-ass on the kid? If she'd caught even a whiff of guile, she would have, without even thinking about it. But she hadn't. Seth seemed completely sincere, contrite even. She'd always trusted her instincts—she'd trust them now.

"So your...missions, behind the S-panels. What were you trying to accomplish?"

"If we can't get someone to stop the ship, to turn it around, I guess...then we've got to find a way to do it ourselves." Seth met her eyes, almost pleading. "I mean, what would *you* do? I mean, if you believed what we believe? Wouldn't you try to save all these people? There are millions of us. Isn't protecting them your job? But you've been lied to, we all have. What you're doing is making sure that we fly right into the mouth of that monster."

Keira felt a chill burn down her back. She shuddered. She swallowed.

"Seth, I need to know where I can find Mr. Basil."

He shook his head. "I don't know. Sometimes he comes to the warehouse. Sometimes he calls, but it's always from a different number."

"Of course it is."

"Do you know who shot me?" Seth asked.

Keira nodded. "A Charles Fairworth."

Seth shook his head. "I never heard of him."

"Goes by the name of Nazz," Keira added.

Seth's eyes snapped open. "Nazz? He tried to kill me?"

"And he did, in fact, kill Jude Ash."

"Oh, my god. Poor Mr. Basil."

Keira narrowed one eye. "Why do you say that?"

"Because Nazz is his son."

Keira's jaw fell open. "What?" She composed herself and scrawled another note. "Are you sure?"

"Yeah. Nazz hated him. Mr. Basil...I think he hoped that if he kept him close, Nazz would...I don't know...grow up, get on board with the mission...something."

"This is very helpful, Seth. But you don't know where Mr. Basil is staying now? Or where Nazz is staying? It's imperative that we find him quickly."

"No. Nazz slept at the warehouse sometimes."

Keira rose, closed her notebook, and replaced it in her back pocket. "Seth, thank you for being so open with me. I'm going to go talk to my superiors."

Seth nodded, and his eyes focused on some far away image only he could see.

"I can't promise anything, but if it means anything to you...I don't think you're a murderer. It sounds like manslaughter to me. That's for the AG to decide, of course, but that's what I'm going to tell him."

Seth nodded, not looking at her. With a sad but encouraging smile, she left the room. She stopped to speak to the uniformed guard just outside the door. "No one in except doctors." The guard —a tall, beefy black man with kind eyes—nodded. She handed him her card. "And if anything happens or anyone suspicious comes by, call me immediately."

He nodded again. She turned on her heel and headed for the elevators.

All the way out to her car, her mind raced. The story he had told her was spinning around in her head, and she wasn't sure how to make sense of it. It was religious madness, of course, but like all religions it sought to provide a story that explained the tragic complexities of life. What shook her about this story is that it was the first one she had heard that adequately explained all that she had learned since her security upgrade. Schenck had certainly not provided a better one. "Need to know," he had said. It seemed to her that she needed to know why she was doing what she was doing, and perhaps even more importantly, for whom she was doing it.

The idea of being food for a demonic deity was delusional. But what if there was even a grain of truth to it? What if the purpose of the starship's journey was somehow nefarious? What if her superiors didn't want to tell her why they were hurtling through space because if she knew, she'd fight against it just as hard as these gnostics were? And maybe that was why it was a secret. Maybe if *anyone* knew, they'd revolt against it.

The drive back to the office passed in a blur. She wondered if the electricians knew why they did their jobs—or anyone who worked behind the façade. What did Schenck know? Did anyone in Homeland Security know why they were on a spaceship, or where they were going, or why? Or were they all just acting like Russian nesting dolls, each layer knowing only a bit more than the last? But wasn't that the way all intelligence systems worked? And she supposed that was just fine so long as the person at the center —the person or persons who actually knew the whole truth— were trustworthy and had their best interests at heart. And that had always been her operating assumption. But Seth had shaken that. It was the first time she had seriously considered that whoever was pulling the strings might not be pulling them in a noble or worthy direction. And here she was, a willing puppet, doing god knows what for god knows who for god knows why.

And suddenly, that just wasn't good enough anymore.

Once at her office, she rode the elevator up in a bit of a daze. How much should she tell Schenck? How much would he even want to hear? The doors parted and she headed for Schenck's office.

Somehow, he saw her and waved her in without bothering to look up from his papers.

She took her seat, feeling a gravity come over her that could have flattened a planet. She sat still until he finally shut the folder he was studying and put it aside. "Did he talk?"

"He did."

"Any of it useful?"

"He doesn't know where Terrance Basil is. He was a little shook up to discover that Charles Fairworth was the shooter."

"He knew him, then?"

"Yes. Says he was Basil's son."

The grey puffs that were Schenck's eyebrows elevated. "No shit?"

She nodded. "And chief, I know it's not our call, but for what it's worth, I don't think St. John committed murder. I think it was...maybe not self-defense, but definitely manslaughter."

"What makes you think so?"

"There was no connection between him and the victim. There was no motive. St. John was trespassing, he got caught, and he panicked. That's all."

"A person died during the commission of another crime."

"I understand that. As I said, for what it's worth."

"Did you figure out what he was doing Behind?"

"Mapping."

Scheck nodded. "For this terrorist group—"

"We don't have any evidence that the gnostics are a terrorist organization," Keira countered. "What have they destroyed? Who have they threatened?"

Schenck grunted. "Then what are they doing it for? Because they've discovered it's there? Like Mount Everest?"

Keira's hands tightened on the arms of her chair as panic rolled through her. How much should she say? "They know about the ship. They even know the name. And they've come up with an elaborate religious myth to explain it all."

"But you don't put any stock in it?" He was studying her. She shifted in her seat.

"As much as I put stock in any story involving gods, angels, demons, or leprechauns," she answered.

Schenck chuckled. "How is he? St. John?"

It occurred to her that any decent human being would have led with that question. But she hadn't volunteered that information, either. What did that say about her?

"He's in pain, but the shot was clean. He should be up and about in a few days."

"Let's get the AG in there as soon as possible and get an arraignment set up for as soon as he's out. I'm going to lobby for ROR."

"You're cutting him loose?" Keira asked, frowning.

"Of course. He has no home, other than that warehouse. We put a tracker chip in him, we'll always know where he is. And as far as we know, he's still an asset to them. He'll take us straight to the leaders."

WHAT IS SACRIFICE?

Sacrifice is a ritual practice that has played a significant role in various cultures, religions, and societies throughout history. It involves offering something of value, often an animal, food, or other valuable possessions, to a deity or higher power. The act of sacrifice is deeply rooted in religious and spiritual beliefs, and it serves as a means of communication, appeasement, gratitude, or seeking favor from the divine.

The concept of sacrifice can be traced back to ancient times, with evidence of sacrificial rituals found in archaeological sites around the world. Different cultures have employed diverse forms of sacrifice, ranging from blood sacrifices involving the slaughter of animals, to symbolic offerings of crops, wine, or other valuable items. The rituals associated with sacrifice often involve prayers, chants, incantations, or ceremonies performed by priests, shamans, or religious leaders.

The underlying reasons for sacrifice vary across cultures and religious traditions. Some believe that sacrifice is a way to establish a reciprocal relationship with the divine, expressing devotion and seeking blessings or protection in return. Sacrifice can also be seen as an act of atonement, where the offering is made to cleanse oneself or one's community from sins or transgressions. In certain belief systems, sacrifice is performed as a form of thanksgiving or celebration, expressing gratitude for divine providence or assistance.

While animal sacrifice has been practiced historically, many modern religious traditions have moved away from this form of sacrifice due to ethical considerations. Symbolic or non-violent forms of sacrifice, such as offering fruits, flowers, or symbolic representations, have gained prominence.

The significance and interpretation of sacrifice vary greatly across religious and cultural contexts. In some traditions, sacrifice is seen as a central pillar of worship, while in others it may have evolved or been replaced by alternative forms of devotion. The philosophical and theological justifications for sacrifice continue to be topics of scholarly inquiry and religious discourse.

It is important to note that the practice of sacrifice should be understood within its cultural and historical context. While it may seem foreign or unfamiliar to some, sacrifice has held deep meaning and significance for countless communities throughout human history, reflecting their beliefs, values, and understanding of the relationship between humanity and the divine.

CHAPTER TWENTY-TWO

The way was dangerous and difficult,
and I was very young to travel it...
I went straight to the serpent,
I dwelt in his abode,
waiting till he should lumber and sleep,
and I could take my pearl from him.
—*The Hymn of the Pearl**

---

* The Hymn of the Pearl survives as an interpolation into The Acts of Thomas. This quotation is taken from *Apocryphal Acts of the Apostles*, translated by William Wright (London: Williams and Norgate, 1871).

Do not suppose that the resurrection is an illusion
—it is no illusion, it is truth.
It is more proper to say that the world is illusion,
rather than the resurrection.
—*Treatise on the Resurrection**

T he corrections officer put Seth in the back of the car, then undid his handcuffs. To Seth's further surprise, Special Agent Keira Sloane slid into the driver's seat. Neither of them said a word until they pulled out of the parking lot.

"Where are we going?" Seth asked. The sky was overcast, but Seth felt grateful to see it—even if it was fake.

"I'm taking you home," Agent Sloane said.

Seth looked out the window. "I don't know where that is anymore." At one time, home was wherever Kush was. Then it was where Angie was. Now... He felt his throat thicken.

"I can take you to your apartment," the agent said, "or I can take you to the warehouse."

"Seems like Nazz can get to me in both places."

"Do you have any other ideas?"

He could go to his mother's. He shuddered at the thought of it. The idea of the demiurge looming over his shoulder at every moment was horrifying. Could he go to Becky's? He'd need to apologize. And Angie might still be there. He felt his jaw tighten as he remembered the intervention, their betrayal.

---

* Treatise on the Resurrection: Nag Hammadi Codex I, 4 translated by Malcolm Peel and Bentley Leyton, revised by Willis Barnestone, published in *The Gnostic Bible* (Boston, MA: Shambhala Publications, 2009).

"I'm going to take you to your apartment, then. You can make other arrangements."

Seth sighed. Nazz had tried to kill him twice now. Would the third time be the charm? He worried that it would be.

He watched the streets of San Jose pass in a blur. Only now and then did his brain register a familiar landmark. He caught motion out of the side of his eye. Agent Sloane tossed a manila envelope over the seat.

"What's this?" he asked.

"Your personal effects," she said.

He undid the metal clasp on the envelope and looked inside. There was his wallet, a few coins, his burner phone. He gasped when he saw the final item. He looked up, catching Agent Sloane's eyes in the rear-view mirror. He reached in and drew forth the S-panel key.

"Why?" he asked.

"Because at this point, I trust you more than I trust them," Agent Sloane said.

"But—"

"Look, Seth, just shut up and listen," she continued. "I don't think your story is true. It's too...mythological. But I'm not getting the truth from my higher-ups, either. Whoever you're working for, whatever this Mr. Basil is up to, it doesn't seem to be terrorism."

"No," Seth agreed.

"And I'm not a fan of secrecy."

"But you're—"

"Just relish the irony, will you?" Keira snapped. But he saw a hint of a smile in her eyes in the mirror. "I know I'm putting myself on the line, but...I think there are bigger things afoot than me. Or you, for that matter. So whatever it is you're really up to...I hope accountability is part of it."

Seth nodded.

"I'm taking a huge risk here, Seth."

"I get it," he said.

They rode in silence for several seconds. Then Seth said, "Didn't you have to register all this stuff? How did—"

"I pocketed the S-panel key before I turned in your effects. No one knows about it but me and you. My boss knows you have one, he just didn't know you had it on your person when we picked you up."

"Oh," Seth said.

"There's a price," she said.

"Price?" he asked.

"For you going scot-free," she said. "I want you to call me once a day. I want you to give me a report on all your activities and your whereabouts."

Seth felt his stomach sink into his legs. "Do I have to tell you everything?"

"You can keep the quality of your stools to yourself," Agent Sloane said. "But everything else...yes."

She pulled up to the curb. His curb. His building loomed over them, seeming empty and dark. Setting the brake, she turned in her seat to face him. "I'm serious, Seth. Every day. If you miss a day, we pick you up."

"And if I don't tell you everything?"

"We pick you up."

"And if I ditch my phone?" he asked.

"Then we find you. Then we pick you up." Her face was deadly serious.

He nodded.

"Call me tonight, then," she said. He nodded again and opened the car door. He got out and watched as the black sedan pulled away from the curb.

"Great," he said out loud. "Now I'm a double agent."

Seth opened the door to his apartment and then stood there. The late afternoon light was fading, and the walls were awash with shadows and grays. The lingering odor of old pizza boxes tickled his nose, even though the boxes were gone. He looked at the couch where he and Angie used to sit watching monster movies. He looked at the spot on the floor in front of the wall heater where Kush used to sprawl out, all four legs in the air. He felt his throat begin to swell.

There's nothing but loss here, the voice in his head said. *This place is an empty shell. It's dead.*

He sat heavily on the couch, his eyes seeking out the dust motes hanging on the last slivers of day. They floated dreamily, as if the day was not running out, as if the dying of the light was not imminent. He sighed and choked back a sob. He sniffed and wiped his eyes on the back of his hand.

He knew he was feeling sorry for himself. He didn't care. It suddenly occurred to him that, poor as he was, he had once been a rich man. He had once had friends, a girlfriend, a dog who loved him. He once had a job that he enjoyed, that he was damned good at. He could walk to the store and back without wondering whether someone was going to shoot at him. He didn't have the fate of forty million people weighing on him. And the slavering deity that haunted his dreams was a troublesome figment of his imagination, not a writhing, tentacled monster that was actually going to devour him and everything and everyone he had ever known.

He felt an overwhelming urge to run, to flee the ghosts of this place that had once been home. He felt tempted to go to Travis' house. Maybe he could catch a glimpse of his dog.

But he knew that was a bad idea. For one thing, it would only make him feel worse. For another, every moment he was in the open he was an easy target. Better to stay holed up, even if it was in a place haunted by memory.

His mind flashed on the intervention, that night when he was surrounded by his mother, Becky, Travis, and Angie. He heard Angie's voice trying to reason with him. Could it possibly be that she was right? Had he brought all of this on himself? Was everything the Lodge told him religious nonsense? He had fallen for it before. Had he been duped again? His mind flashed on one of his mother's stuffed rats, holding a sign that said, "Lean not on your own understanding." Perhaps he should have. Perhaps he should have leaned on Angie's.

But then there was the Behind. He knew it was there. He couldn't deny it. They *were* on a spaceship. He did believe that. But did that validate everything Dr. Robinson had told him? Had Dr. Teasdale reached into his most vulnerable parts and manipulated him? Had he been taken in by Mr. Basil's charisma?

He felt his head begin to spin. Then he felt his pocket vibrate. He pulled the burner phone from his pocket and noted a number he did not recognize. He flipped the phone open and pushed the green button. "Hello?"

"Mr. St. John," Mr. Basil's voice said, amidst some crackling. "How are you, my boy?"

Where to start? "I'm out of jail," he said.

"I'm so relieved to hear it."

"Nazz tried to kill me. Twice." He couldn't actually prove that Nazz had tried to poison him the first time, but he strongly suspected it. But there was no doubt about the fact that Jude was dead and that Seth himself had a hole in his shoulder.

"I'm so sorry." Seth couldn't tell if that was news to Mr. Basil or not. He decided he didn't have the energy to speculate. "My boy, we need to meet."

"I don't think that's a good idea," Seth said. "I'm pretty sure CHS is following me. I don't want them to...catch you."

"Yes, that's probably wise."

"Plus, I don't know what Nazz will try next. And...I'm sure you know this, but he's pretty angry at you. I mean, deep-seated anger. I wouldn't put it past him..." He let the thought remain unspoken.

"Yes, well, quite, quite," agreed Mr. Basil. "Perhaps it's best if we just talk like this."

Seth nodded, forgetting for the moment that this was not an audible response. He sighed heavily.

"How long has it been since you've had a good sleep?" Mr. Basil asked.

"Too long," Seth said. "It's hard to sleep in the jail. It's cold all the time."

"By all means, then, get some sleep. You'll need it."

Seth was about to ask him why, but decided it would come soon enough without his prompting. Besides, there was another question that seemed more pressing. "Mr. Basil, when I was in lockup, I tried to pray."

"Oh, yes?"

"I did everything just as I always did. I called on Sophia, and she came, but..." How to describe her? "She was angry. She seemed...there was a dark energy I've never felt before. It was horrible. Did I...what did I do wrong? Does she hate me now? Did I fuck up?"

Mr. Basil chuckled—actually chuckled. Seth felt his heart sink. "Oh, no, my dear boy, no. I'm so sorry that happened. That was not the Sophia you know, not the Holy Mother we love. You had the misfortune of running into Achamoth. You were in prison, so I have no doubt you were fearful, that your emotions were chaotic—"

"That's putting it mildly," Seth agreed.

"My guess is that your state of mind summoned her."

"And...who is Achamoth?"

"She is the unredeemed part of Sophia. When she was cut off from the Pleroma, she became Achamoth. When the Christ visited us in the time of the apostles, he redeemed the better part of her, returning her to communion with the One. That is the Holy Mother you have come to know. But a part of her still remains below, cut off, lost—"

"Achamoth," Seth said.

"Yes. And you are right. She is angry."

"Why didn't the Christ save her, too? Why didn't he save all of her?"

"That, my dear boy, is a mystery we do not have an answer for. All we know is that she is there...here...and in a way she is symbolic of all that is unreconciled."

"So, she's not mad at me?" Seth asked, feeling his throat tighten again. He was weepy, and he hated that.

"No, my son, our Holy Mother loves you desperately. Achamoth despises everything and all, because she is driven by pain and loss. One day, we hope, she will be reunited with our Mother, but that healing is still in the future, alas."

Seth didn't know how to feel about this new revelation. The already Byzantine mythology had just gotten a new wrinkle and it would take some time to get used to it.

Had Mr. Basil just called him "my son"? Seth didn't know what to make of that. He breathed into the phone but said nothing.

Finally, Mr. Basil broke the silence. "Seth? Seth, are you there?"

"Yeah. Yeah, I'm here."

"Listen, my boy. We have one more mission for you."

It was an odd way to put it. Mr. Basil did not say, "We have *another* mission for you," but "one more." Only one?

"Yes?"

"Are you up for it?"

Seth looked around the now mostly dark apartment. The air was becoming even thicker with ghosts.

It felt weird getting on the train to Sacramento with no other instructions. Seth had no idea where he was going, or what he was supposed to do when he arrived. A voice in his head told him it was an "exercise in trust," and he elected to be content with that.

But it was easier thought than done. His leg began to bounce, the first time in weeks, since the medication had really kicked in. He watched it dispassionately. He even got annoyed with it, as if it were someone else's leg. He sighed and turned to the window, resting his head against it, feeling the rumble of the tracks in his teeth.

He must have dozed off, because the next thing he knew, someone was sitting next to him. He saw hosiery in his peripheral vision, so he assumed it must be a woman. There was a dark blue backpack at her feet. He turned to give her a perfunctory smile, but then started.

"Dr. Teasdale!" he said.

"Shhhh," she put her index finger to her lips. "How are you, Seth?"

He wondered if he would ever see her again, after...

He looked down at his hands, which were rubbing together. He put them between his knees and squeezed his legs together. The pressure eased his anxiety somewhat. "I didn't expect..."

"I wanted to see you once more, before..."

He waited, but she didn't finish the sentence. He wondered how to interpret that. Before what? And why did she want to see him again? Was there a part of her that had feelings for him? Or was she just concerned for him from a professional point of view? Or was it something else?

It was something else. He felt his shoulders relax as the realization hit. "You're my contact."

"Yes," she said. "*And*, I wanted to see you again. To say goodbye. For now."

Seth felt a surge of vertigo. He took a deep breath and pressed his hands even harder between his knees until it passed.

"So...I meant it when I asked how you are. I wasn't just being polite." She smiled. It was a professional smile. That was disappointing.

"I'm...pretty freaked out," Seth confessed. "My life has completely fallen apart. I've been arrested. I've lost my dog. I've lost all my friends. I feel like I've done everything wrong." He felt his throat tighten and swallowed hard, determined not to cry.

"'Those who want to save their life will lose it,'" Dr. Teasdale quoted, "'and those who lose their life for my sake will find it.'"

It would have been something that might have sounded wise to him in the past, but at the moment it just seemed hollow.

"I know it's been hard, Seth," Dr. Teasdale said. "But we're almost at the end."

"What does that mean?"

"It means that our work is almost done...and our suffering is almost over, too. We will soon be released from our prison."

That sounded ominous. But then again, the entire gnostic worldview was ominous. When he had been initiated into the secrets, he had entered a much darker and more dangerous world than he had previously inhabited.

Dr. Teasdale handed him a piece of paper. There was an address on one side of it. He recognized it. "I'm going back—"

She put her finger to her lips and nodded. He returned to the paper. On the other side was a map, and again, it was familiar.

THE WHERE, THE WHO & THE WHAT • 627

Too familiar. He realized that he had drawn it. But there, in another hand, were details he had not recorded. He studied them.

"Memorize it," she said. "Once you get there, you won't have time to refer to it."

He did. Then he handed the paper back to her. "You might need this," she handed him an envelope.

"What's that?" he asked.

"A PG&E bill," she said with a shrug. "You never know. Oh, but you *will* need this." She handed him a key card on a lanyard. It had a picture on one side of a man Seth didn't recognize. Underneath the picture was a name: Trevor Milner. "It'll get you into the engine room."

"How did you get this?" Seth asked.

"We have our ways," she smiled at him. "Let's just say that Mr. Milner has called in sick."

"Won't he miss this and call it in?"

"That is not part of your job description," she said. He could tell she was trying for playful, but her levity rang hollow. "You have the address?" she asked.

He nodded, reciting to himself in his head just to be sure. It was there.

She put the paper away. "Good. This is it, Seth. We have every-thing riding on this bet."

"What am I doing?"

"You found the engines. It makes sense that the fuel is nearby. We knew about these holding tanks," she patted the pocket where she'd put the paper, "but we weren't sure what they were for. We do now."

She leaned over and dragged the backpack toward him. His eyes widened. "It's safe. Just treat it normally. You can even run with it."

"Is...it's a b—"

"Don't say it," she said.

628 • J.R. MABRY
He nodded. Looking around, he was glad to see that no one was sitting near them. Still, it would be good to be prudent.

“What do I do?”

“Just put it under the tank furthest to the north.”

“How is it...activated?”

“In order to...well, to do the job...it has to be activated at the moment fuel is being pumped to the engines. That way we get... results...in both directions. We’ll need it.”

“So the activator—”

“Is already in place in the engine room—which you discovered on your last mission.”

Seth stopped breathing as he realized the implications of this. “Are we just trying to stop it?”

“No, Seth.”

“We’re not going to turn around and go back to Earth?”

“No. We’ve run every scenario. This is the only one that has any hope of succeeding.”

“So...we’re just going to...die?”

“We are. After a fashion. But I prefer to think of it as us being released from this illusion. As *The Treatise on the Resurrection* says, ‘The world is an illusion.’”

“Oh my god,” Seth said. He turned and looked out of the window. He felt faint. High grasses rushed by at sixty miles per hour. In the distance, he could see the freeway running like an artery clotted with cars through the suave femininity of the valley.

“What if we don’t?”

“Then we die in about six months,” she said. “When we become food for the demiurge.”

“But then we’d have six more months,” he said. “What’s so bad about being food for the demiurge?”

“Oh, dear. Robinson has really fallen down on the job, hasn’t he?”

Seth shrank, feeling undercatechized for the first time in his life.

"If you don't eat, you die," she explained patiently. "If you eat, you are nourished and you live. It is no different for gods. They need their sacrifices to survive."

"That sounds so..."

"Anthropomorphic? Yes. But remember that the demiurge is a creature, not pure spirit. But there's another reason. If the sacrifice is delivered to the god, then the covenant has been honored, and his tyrannical reign over the Earth is extended for another millennium. Do you want that?"

"But what happens to the people on Earth if we don't...complete the sacrifice?"

"Then they have to face the truth. We have people there, too, of course. Maybe the world will be ready to hear. Maybe they will be ready to be free—for the first time in their history. But we can't worry about what they will do or won't do. Our only job is to give them a chance—to wake up, to move in another direction, to choose liberation over bondage. Let us hope our courage today is not in vain."

Speed-walking through the parking lot, Seth pulled the hood over his head and put his hands in the pockets of the sweater, fingering the key card and lanyard. He looked at the floor as he entered the revolving doors of the PG&E building. He set his face toward the elevators, fitting his thumbs through the straps of the heavy backpack and trying to find a more comfortable placement on his shoulders.

"You!" a voice called out. Seth kept walking. "Hey!" Seth stopped and looked around. A security person at a desk waved him over. He wondered if he'd been recognized from his last visit.

Had they known about his breach? Were they looking for him? Had face-recognition software already identified him as The Intruder?

He felt his pulse surge as he walked toward the desk. "Business?" the man asked. He was African American, taller than Seth, and a little older. To Seth's relief he looked more bored than suspicious.

"I've got a huge snafu with my bill," Seth said. "I'm sick of it. So I've made an appointment with a Ms.—" He pulled the envelope from his back pocket and unfolded it. He pulled the paper out and handed it to the security guard. "Trellis? Anyway, I don't want to be late."

The guard studied the paper and handed it back to him. He pointed toward the elevators. "Third floor. Hop hop!" The guard grinned.

Seth raised the paper as if it were a beer glass and he was offering a "cheers." Then he turned and headed toward the elevators again. He noticed he was sweating. He concentrated on his breathing and tried to calm himself.

Entering the elevators, he pushed the button for the top floor, waited three seconds, and pushed it again. The ride up was interrupted by a trickle of others riding from the second to the third floor. Eventually, he made it to the fourth floor and exited. It was the same empty office he'd seen before. Following the map in his head, he took the same path he had last time to the end of the hallway, and then to the right. He pulled his ski mask from his hoodie pocket and fitted it over his head. Taking the key in hand, he inserted it into the S-panel and turned it.

He opened the panel just wide enough to slip through and felt it catch on the backpack. He opened it a bit wider until the pack was free and then closed it again as quickly as possible. He felt for the click as it slid into place. He jogged down the corridor, turning left at the T.

His memory of the place was still vivid from his previous visit, and he felt none of his previous hesitation. Within minutes, the door to the engine room was before him. Getting past this particular barrier would be easier this time, and he was glad of it. With his left hand he felt for the lanyard and held it to the magnetic latch fixed above the door handle. A green light flickered, and he heard the catch release. He tried the handle, pushing it down and pulling it toward himself.

It opened.

Before going in, he looked through the narrow vertical window to make sure the room beyond was clear. It was. He pulled the door wider and went inside.

He didn't bother to look around. Instead, he headed directly for the engine bulwark as he had been instructed. Pulling the backpack strap from one arm, he let it swing off his other arm and caught it just before it hit the floor. It continued to swing as he walked, as quickly as he could, toward the bulwark. He remembered the map Dr. Teasdale had shown him and located the spot it indicated for the backpack placement. He swung the heavy pack into place, tucked under two massive metal ducts secured with bolts as large as his fist. He stepped back and admired his work. The backpack was hidden by the ducts from almost any angle except directly beneath them. He indulged in a deep breath of satisfaction, and turned.

Then he stopped. A person in a hazmat suit stood between him and the door. "Who the fuck are you?" came a muffled male voice. Without thinking, Seth put his head down and ran directly at the man. He had never played football, but images from games he'd seen flashed through his head as he plowed into the man, forcing him backward.

The man's awkward gloves pinwheeled as he tried to find his balance. His helmet hit the far wall with a loud clank, and Seth heard a muffled "Oaf" and a moan. One glove snatched at Seth's

632 • J.R. MABRY

632 • J.R. MABRY

head, but the thick glove found no purchase. Seth ducked, but this time the man used both gloves, taking Seth's head between them and pulling the stocking mask up and off.

Seth felt his hair standing up from the static electricity, but his appearance was the last thing on his mind. He lowered his shoulder and pushed the man against the wall as hard as he could again, then again. The man slid down the wall, groaning. Seth pulled the man's helmet free from its seal on the suit, twisting it up and off. Then, taking it in one hand, he swung it like a hammer, bashing the man's head, first on one side and then the other until the man stopped moving.

He stopped short of drawing blood. The last thing he needed was a mess, but it was clear he'd done the job. A voice in his head accused him of murder, but it was shushed by another voice that told him they'd all be dead soon, so what did it matter?

Looking around, Seth saw no one else. Grabbing the man by his suit shoulders, he dragged him toward the bulwark, and stuffed his still body out of sight, under the twin ducts, right next to the backpack. He wondered if the man's placement would affect the blast radius, but realized he knew nothing about such things and had more important matters to worry about.

He had done his job. Now he needed to get out of there.

He hit the release bar on the door and burst into the hallway, running full out. He tripped over his own feet, but didn't go down. Instead, he lurched to one side, put his hand out to steady himself against the wall of the corridor, and caught his balance. Then he ran again. Rounding the corner to the right, he started, when he nearly ran into a woman approaching the corner from the other direction.

He stopped, his eyes flashing about wildly, unable to think of anything to say. The last thing he needed was for the woman to sound an alarm. Would he need to kill her, too?

"Oh, it's *you*," the woman smiled and visibly relaxed.

For the first time he looked up at her face. She looked familiar, although he didn't know why. Then he knew. Her hair was long and blonde, she was slender, with an oval face. A brown birthmark about the size of a quarter marred her cheek.

"I thought I'd never get the chance to thank you," she said. "For what you did on the bus." She shifted awkwardly. "So...thank you. You didn't need to stand up to that troglodyte, but you did. You made him stop." She smiled shyly.

Seth's heart raced. So did his brain. He ran his fingers through his hair, unconsciously straightening it. "Oh...it was nothing."

"It wasn't nothing. Most people would have just looked the other way."

"Yeah, well...I was bullied as a kid, so I know how it feels. And yeah, people looked the other way. So...I couldn't, you know?"

"I do," she said. Only then did she seem to notice his disheveled appearance. "Um...are you supposed to be back here?"

Seth froze. He opened his mouth and something came out. "Uh...yeah. Sorry about running. I thought I was going to be late back from my break. You know, heh, third time and you're out." He made a gesture like a baseball umpire. She cocked her head and narrowed her eyes. He realized this was going to go sideways badly and soon.

He fumbled in his pocket and pulled out the lanyard and put it over his neck. "Damn, forgot this stupid thing. Sorry."

"You must be new here," she said.

"I am, yeah. And I already got two strikes."

"You must work for Newberg. He's a hard ass."

"You're telling me," Seth said, pushing his hands into his pockets.

"I should report this," she said.

"Oh?" Seth said, his heart leaping into his throat. "Oh. I wish... please don't. I need this job and Newberg is a fucking slavedriver."

"Well," she said. "I guess I owe you one."

Seth felt his bowels turn to jelly.

"See you around, hero," she said, pushing past him.

"See you around," Seth said.

Once she was around the corner, he felt his knees buckle. He steadied himself against the side of the wall and gasped to catch his breath. Then he walked unsteadily at a normal speed toward the S-panel.

WHAT IS APOTHEOSIS?

Apotheosis is a concept rooted in ancient religious and philosophical traditions that refers to the elevation of a person, typically a mortal, to a divine or godlike status. The term derives from the Greek words "apo" meaning "from" or "away" and "theos" meaning "god." Apotheosis is often depicted as a process or event in which an individual transcends the limitations of humanity and attains a higher spiritual or immortal state.

Throughout history, apotheosis has been a prominent theme in mythologies, folklore, and religious beliefs. In many polytheistic religions, gods and goddesses were often depicted as humans who had achieved apotheosis through extraordinary deeds, divine favor, or by fulfilling specific criteria. For example, in ancient Egyptian mythology, pharaohs were believed to ascend to a divine status upon death, becoming gods in the afterlife.

In the realm of philosophy and spirituality, apotheosis has been interpreted as a metaphorical or symbolic concept rather than a literal transformation. It represents the process of self-realization, enlightenment, or the attainment of a higher level of consciousness. In this context, apotheosis is often associated with the quest for transcendence, inner growth, and the union of the individual with the divine or universal consciousness.

The concept of apotheosis has also found its way into artistic expressions. In literature, apotheosis may be depicted as a climactic moment where a hero or protagonist achieves a godlike state, exemplifying ideals of courage, wisdom, or self-sacrifice.

Similarly, in visual arts, apotheosis is often depicted through allegorical or symbolic representations, with individuals being elevated, surrounded by divine beings or radiating divine light.

While the notion of apotheosis has historical and cultural significance, it is essential to differentiate it from literal claims of divinity or the supernatural. The concept serves primarily as a metaphorical or symbolic construct, offering insights into human aspirations for transcendence and the desire to connect with the divine or higher aspects of existence.

CHAPTER TWENTY-THREE

From the savior we radiate beams,
and we are held in his arms until our own sunset,
our death in this life. We are drawn to heaven by him,
like beams, by the sun, and nothing holds us down.
This is the resurrection of the spirit,
which swallows up the soul and the flesh.
—*Treatise on the Resurrection*[*]

S eth leaned his head against the window of his train car and watched the California countryside rush past. He heard the vibration of the wheels on the track in his skull, and it occurred to him that his bones were connected—through the window, through the wheels, through the rails—with the

---

[*] Treatise on the Resurrection: Nag Hammadi Codex I, 4 translated by Malcolm Peel and Bentley Leyton, revised by Willis Barnestone, published in *The Gnostic Bible* (Boston, MA: Shambhala Publications, 2009).

earth. *No, not the earth,* he thought, *the ship.* He sighed. *All of this is going to go away. This fake California...this train...these people...all of these people...millions of people.*

How soon before the bomb goes off? he wondered. How much time did he have—did any of them have? *I wonder if I have an hour?* If so, the last thing he would see is this train. *I wonder if I have two? If so...*

He thought of Kush, and his heart ached. But there was someone he needed to see more than Kush. He needed to see Angie.

He pulled his phone from his pocket and opened his messenger app. He pulled up her name, and the long string of messages between them appeared, going back for years. As he flipped through them, water came to his eyes. All the teasing, the planning, the news they shared dissolved into a blur. He wiped his eyes on the back of his hand and heaved a shuddering breath. Then he began to type with his thumbs.

I'm sorry. For everything. I need to see you. Soon.

His thumbs wavered over the screen as he read the message over and over again, trying to anticipate the many ways it might be received. "Fuck it," he said out loud, and hit *Send.*

He watched the screen, but nothing happened. He watched some more. Finally, he put the phone in his pocket. He nearly jumped thirty seconds later when it vibrated.

He yanked it from his pocket and read Angie's response: *Anytime. Anywhere.*

Seth nearly choked on a sob. He wiped his eyes again and typed, Diridon Amtrak. 3:30?

He waited. Then the answer came: *OK.*

Seth put his phone back in his pocket. He looked around and was relieved to see that no one was watching him. He buried his face in his hands and gave himself permission to cry.

After the tears passed, he had another thought. He pulled his phone out and typed one more message. *Bring Kush?*

S eth stepped off the platform and pulled up the hood of his sweatshirt. Stuffing his hands in his pockets, he wove his way through the departing passengers, through the station that reminded him of a California mission church, and out the front doors.

Angie was on the steps, holding Kush on a leash. She turned, saw him, and gave him a sad smile. Seth returned it and stepped down to her. She opened her arms to embrace him, but he knelt and rubbed his dog all over. Kush's yellow tail beat the air furiously, and he made ecstatic minileaps as he panted his joy. Finally, Seth stood and embraced Angie.

"What's up?" she asked, as if a lifetime had not passed since she had seen him last.

Seth's hood was still up. He looked around, biting his lip. "Not here," he said. He waved her after him and started walking. She and Kush caught up to him, and they speed-walked wordlessly past the bike rentals toward Cahill Park.

The late afternoon sun was still hot, and the park was brown and dusty, more weeds than grass, and more baked dirt than weeds.

"Where are we going?" Angie asked.

"I don't know," Seth replied. "Someplace...not so open."

"We could have sat in my car," Angie noted.

Since Seth didn't have a car, it hadn't been his first thought. It might have been a good option. But they were walking now, and the movement felt good.

Exiting the park, they kept going on San Fernando Street, past the convenience store. They turned right on Sunol, and once on the green, tree-lined street, Seth finally began to slow down. Small, older, well-kept houses surrounded them on all sides. Seth felt himself relax.

"Are you going to tell me what this is all about?" Angie asked.

Seth threw back his hood and gave her a pained smile. "I'm sorry," he said.

"For what?"

"For all the craziness. For throwing you out. For not being a better friend. For not...loving you better."

Angie stopped, and he watched her face work as if she were trying not to cry. She threw her arms around him and pressed her head into his chest. "I'm sorry too. I could have tried to under-stand what all this...gnosticism stuff meant for you."

Kush apparently decided he didn't like being left out of the affection, so he barked.

"It's okay. It *is* pretty weird."

"I'm glad you can see that," Angie said, muffled, into his chest.

"You're the best friend I've ever had," Seth said, his eyes welling. "I just wanted to say I'm sorry. And I love you. Before..."

"Before?"

"Before the ship blows up."

Angie stepped back, her red eyes narrow. "Ship? *The* ship? You mean the *spaceship*? The one that we're somehow *on*?"

"Yeah."

"It's going to blow up?"

"Yeah."

Angie cocked her head. Kush barked again. "And you know this...how?"

"Because I set the bomb."

"What the holy fuck, Seth?" She took a step back from him.

He looked up and saw that they were at the gates of the Shri Hanuman Temple. "C'mon, in here," he said. They went through the gate and into a courtyard surrounded by a number of buildings. Within sight of the street, but blessedly protected on three sides, Seth sat on a bench under an olive tree. A spray of bougainvillea decorated the facing wall.

"What bomb?" Angie asked.

"I can't tell you that. You'd need to report it. I just...need you to know that it could go off at any time."

"And take you and everyone else on this...ship...with it?"

"Yeah."

"So, what you're telling me is that you're a suicide bomber now? A religious fanatic suicide bomber? Is that right?"

"Well. I mean. I hadn't looked at it that way. I guess it *is* suicide. But I'll be taking everyone else out, too."

"Including me?"

"Well...yeah."

"Gee...thanks, buddy."

Seth said nothing.

"And Kush," Angie added.

Seth nodded.

"Look, Seth, I get why you're angry at me. But Kush? What did he do to deserve getting blown to smithereens?"

"Nothing. No one did anything. It's not a punishment," Seth said.

"You're not...lashing out at any political targets, then?" Angie asked.

"No."

Angie's forehead scrunched. "So...you're trying to make a point?"

"No."

"Then Jesus fucking Christ, dude, why are you blowing something up?"

"To stop the sacrifice."

"Sounds like we *are* the sacrifice," Angie said.

"I can see how it looks that way. But...listen. We can't feed the monster god."

Angie's face twisted, and he could see her effort at comprehension. "Jesus, Seth, is this about growing up in your fucked-up religion? Are you blowing something up in order to...I don't know, get back at God?"

Seth blinked. "Well, if you put it like that...yeah."

"You *do* need a 5150. I should have called a 5150 on you. Jesus, what the fuck was I thinking?"

"I'm not crazy."

"If you believe that blowing something up is going to strike a blow at God, or hurt God, or hurt God's widdow feewings, then yeah, that's the very definition of crazy."

"Look, Angie," Seth stood up again and began to pace. Kush panted and watched him move from left to right and back again. "If I'm right, then the bomb I set is going to blow up the whole world as we know it—"

"The ship," Angie said.

"Yes. And we'll stop the demiurge from...well, from being fed his sacrifice."

Angie opened her mouth to protest, but Seth held up his hand to stop her and continued. "But if you're right, the only thing that gets blown up is the Behind of a PG&E building."

"You're blowing up a PG&E building?" Angie's eyes grew wide. "That's like the holy of holies for electricians!"

Seth supposed it was. "But not the building itself. Only the Behind."

"Behind...what?"

"Behind the façade. Behind the illusion of the building—not the building itself."

"You lost me," Angie said.

"The S-panels don't lead to the power grid or anything, they lead to...the guts of the ship, behind the terrarium of what we think of as 'California.'"

Angie shook her head. "You're fucking delusional. Are there people in this...*behind*?"

"Sure. The people who work there."

"And when your bomb goes off, how many children are going to be without their mothers and fathers?"

"There won't be any children—"

"Because the whole ship is going to go boom," Angie said dryly.

"Yeah."

"If you're right," she corrected him. "If I'm right, we're going to have hundreds of orphaned children."

"I guess," Seth shrugged.

"Seth, what the fuck? You used to have a conscience!"

"I still have a conscience," Seth said.

"Could've fooled me," Angie said. "What PG&E building?"

"What?"

Angie flipped out her phone. "Which PG&E building did you hide the bomb in?"

Seth grabbed her phone from her and threw it to the ground. He stomped on it, shattering the glass.

"Holy fuck, Seth! My phone!"

"I can't have you ruin everything. You don't understand. Everything is at stake here. Especially for the people on Earth."

"'The people on Earth.' Jesus, listen to yourself!"

"I don't know how else to explain it to you," Seth said. "I've already told you way too much."

Angie's gaze jumped from his face to somewhere beyond him. "Who the fuck are you?" But before Seth could turn around, he felt a sharp pain in his shoulder and neck. His vision went fuzzy and his legs buckled. Dazed, he groaned, raised himself on one shoulder and opened his eyes just in time to see Nazz swing a large metal pipe at Angie's head. He missed and hit her shoulder. She went down with a howl, at which point Nazz hovered over her, raising the pipe again.

Struggling onto his elbow, Seth saw Angie covering her head protectively, until the pipe shattered the bones in her arms, leaving them little more than flaccid flaps of gore. Kush growled and circled him, punctuating the air with staccato bursts of aggression. Seth struggled to his feet and threw himself at Nazz.

The pipe connected with his ribs and Seth heard the sickening *thuck* of breaking bone. Turning in a circle, Nazz swung at the dog next, but Kush leaped up and backwards in a balletic move that Seth wouldn't have thought possible. The bar swooshed through empty air with such force that Seth both heard it and felt the wind of it. Kush continued to bark furiously, always keeping just beyond the reach of the weapon.

Seth staggered, clutching at his shattered ribs. The door of what must have been the ashram sanctuary opened and a man in saffron robes peered out, scowling his disapproval. He was bald and a single vertical ochre stripe adorned his forehead. He stepped clear of the door and waggled his head. "If you do not mind, sirs, we are in the middle of puja—" Then he saw the bloody pulp that was Angie and stopped, his mouth frozen open in horror. "Sirs, what is—"

Nazz spun toward the sound, drew his arm back, and sent the pipe spinning through the air. It hit the guru in the collarbone with such force that Seth heard it snap. The man toppled backwards. Nazz pulled a knife from his pocket and flicked it open. Grasping it firmly in his right hand, he stepped toward Seth, his head blocking the sun so all Seth could see was the shadow of him. "Daddy's favorite," Nazz said. "The favored son."

"Did you fucking kill her?" Seth asked, pointing at Angie.

"Oh, did I hurt your girlfriend?" Nazz sneered. "Didn't mean to hurt anyone *close* to you."

"Nazz, what the fuck have you done?"

"You're not the savior," Nazz said, waving the knife in the air. "Look how pathetic you are. Look how weak, how vulnerable you are. You're a disgrace."

"I never said I was anything else," Seth told him, and it was true.

"We're going to end this right now. Just you and me."

"Okay, but...you have a knife. It's not exactly a fair fight," Seth pointed out.

Looking beyond Nazz, Seth's eyes widened to see Angie scooting herself with her legs toward Nazz, her useless arms trailing at her sides along the brick of the courtyard.

"'Fair' isn't really your strong suit, is it?" Nazz accused. Seth had no idea what he was talking about. Then a wicked grin spread over Nazz' face, and he raised the knife, ready to strike.

"Dude, don't do this," Seth pleaded.

Nazz let loose with an ululation of triumph, raised the knife, and threw himself at Seth. He watched Angie lash out with one leg, hooking Nazz' foot just as he pounced. Nazz went down hard, the knife clattering away from his hand.

Seth rushed to Angie and knelt, but he didn't know where to touch her. He pushed the hair back out of her eyes and cradled her head in his palm. "Angie, I'm so sorry. I'll get help. I'll—"

Seth heard Kush before he saw him. Whipping his head toward the dog, he watched him in mid-flight leaping on Nazz' felled body. But Nazz was already rolling, had already snatched the knife up in his hand. Kush landed on the courtyard's brick where Nazz had just been and advanced on him, his growl becoming gnarled as it tangled with the spit oozing from his jowls.

But instead of rolling away from the dog, Seth was surprised to see Nazz roll toward him. In a flash, he buried the knife up to the hilt in the dog's neck. Kush exploded with a howl of rage and pain, dropping to the brick and wildly pawing at the knife with his front feet. Seth moved toward him, but Nazz was on his feet now. He snatched the knife from the dog's blood-matted fur and wiped the blade on his jeans.

Then he grinned. For all the bloodshed, for all the pain Nazz himself must be feeling, the only thing Seth could see on his face was the treacly joy of revenge. Step by step he came closer, swinging the knife through the air in wide, looping arcs so that Seth could hear it. Nazz was careful to step wide of Angie's kicking feet. Nazz kept coming until he was close enough for Seth to smell his breath.

Seth put his hands out to push Nazz away, but the knife flashed in front of him, opening oozing slits on his forearms. Seth began to back away, but Nazz kept pace with him, clearly enjoying every moment of the kill.

Seth felt something on the back of his calves, but too late to stop himself from tripping. He realized it was the bench, but any thought was instantly extinguished when his head made contact with the bricks. Snow washed over his vision, and his ears rang. He squeezed one eye open just enough to see Nazz raise his hand for the killing blow, then launch himself over the bench at Seth. Just then an explosion reverberated off the walls of the compound. The knife flew from Nazz' hand as the young man landed heavily on Seth.

Nazz' falling body knocked the wind from Seth, but he was able to push Nazz up and off him. There was a gaping socket of gore in the middle of Nazz's forehead, and his body lay limp on the bricks. Seth's eyes were wide and wild as he looked around for the source of the explosion. Special Agent Keira Sloane holstered her weapon and approached. She knelt by him. "Seth, don't move," she said. She pulled a walkie-talkie from her belt and called for a bus.

"Angie—is she?" He pointed to where Angie lay.

Keira rose and turned toward Angie. But before she could speak there was the sound of heavens rending, the roar of mighty winds, and the screaming of stars as the air was baptized with fire.

S eth rushed upward toward the crack in the hull. His mind flashed on the image he'd seen in a Chick tract about the rapture, where the bodies of Christians rose into the sky. But this was no rapture, or if it was, cars, mobile homes, animals, telephone poles, and everything else not fastened to the ground was being called to heaven. Seth felt the wind go out of him as he collided with a food truck. He managed to cling to its side mirror, and though he was not certain why it was comforting to do so— its heft managed to give him the illusion of solidity.

The journey up lasted mere seconds, however, before he had cleared the jagged tear in the outer hull and found the truck floating in free space. Enough air was still rushing out of the ship to breathe, but it was dissipating fast. The problem in the moment was not breathing but the bitter cold of space.

Seth watched the tear growing smaller below him as livestock, semis, boats, and people—so, so many people poured out of the crack. He realized he was now looking at the exterior of the *Cibus Dei* and marveled at its size. It was not the size of California, he knew, but it was the size of *his* California. It was home. And now it was going up in flames. Explosion after explosion wracked the length of its hull, erupting soundlessly with blinding bright flashes.

A new sensation gripped him as he realized he could no longer breathe. And then his blood began to boil. A moment later, he was looking down at what had, for the whole of his life, been his true home—his body. His hands swayed lazily, as if he were acting out the motions of some languid fan dance. His eyes were open, but they were sightless. For the first time in his life, it occurred to him that he was beautiful.

But Seth realized that his locus of consciousness was no longer entrapped in the suit of meat that floated before him. He was free. And he was still...something. He still had thoughts. He still had feelings. He still had will.

He tried to look at his hands, and he could see them—ghostly outlines that became clearer and more distinct as he concentrated on them. He tried to move and found that he could. By means of some unknown system of propulsion, he could go in whichever direction he pleased.

He dismissed his body with one final, sentimental glance, and then he swam away from it. In the corner of his vision, he detected something keeping pace with him. Looking over, he saw a small blur. Concentrating on it, it came into sharper focus. It was a dog. No, it was *his* dog. Not Kush's body, but his essence, recognizable and still irrepressible. He waved at him, and Kush, pumping his ghostly legs with crazy enthusiasm, came nearer.

Seth wondered if he could touch him. He reached down and felt a slight resistance before his hand passed through and into the dog's form. He retracted his hand until he felt the resistance again, feeling at the dog's circumference, petting him but clumsily slipping into the dog now and then.

Kush did not seem to mind. He gingerly patted the dog and then shifted his attention to the stream of detritus pouring from the ship. For all the horror of the moment, he felt calm. And then an image hit his mind with the force of revelation.

Angie.

If Kush had found him, he could find her. After all, they had been close together when the sky had cracked open. But had she already been dead? Should he be looking for her body or for her essence? *She would be dead by now either way,* he thought. Essence, then. He called her image more vividly to mind and, following his intuition, kicked off in a new direction, Kush at his heels.

He soared past speedboats tipping bow over stern in lazy circles, through a floating cloud of trash—plastic garbage bags orbiting an unseen sun like a ring of asteroids—toward a frozen concrete brontosaurus Seth recognized from atop a gas station in the California desert.

And then he found her. She spun without moving, and as he swam to her, he saw that what passed for her eyes were closed. Her arms were not shredded, but whole. He wondered if she could still be unconscious somehow. He collided with her, but instead of passing through her, was somehow able to scoop her up and carry her in his arms.

She lay limp, unmoving, but whatever luminescence gave Seth and Kush their own form was still bright in her. To his great relief, she began to stir.

Shhh, he thought at her. *Be still. Everything is fine.*

What the fuck? He heard her think back at him.

Looking down, he saw her eyes open and felt her essence jolt. *What is happening?* she asked.

Shhh. You're dead, he informed her.

I'm dead and everything is fine?

Yes, he thought at her. *Look, Kush is here. I'm here. You're here. The danger is over.*

And this is...heaven? This doesn't seem like heaven.

No. I think we're floating in outer space, Seth informed her.

Why are we doing that? Then she pointed at the *Cibus Dei. And what the fuck is that?*

That's the spaceship I was telling you about, he said.

For the first time, she looked at him. And he could see that she really saw him. He saw confusion and fear and resignation pass in quick succession. Then the essence of her eyes narrowed. *Is this where you tell me "I told you so"?*

He laughed then, and it would have been full-throated had he possessed a throat. But somehow the laugh still manifested, along with the joy of it. He was beginning to truly relax. *I would never,* he said.

Good thing. I'd have to wail on you, Angie thought at him.

I'd like to see you try, he shot back.

She moved her ghostly head back and forth. *I remember being hit with something—*

A metal pipe, Seth said. *Intended for me.*

I always thought I was the dangerous one, Angie marveled.

That made Seth laugh, too.

So what? Do we just...float? Angie asked. Kush was also looking up at him, and he seemed to be posing a similar question.

I think it's time to go home, Seth said.

He closed his eyes and felt his way toward warmth, toward peace, toward beauty, toward wholeness, toward...her. And when he opened his eyes, she was there.

Who the fuck is that? Angie asked.

That goddess you worship in your coven? Seth whispered. *That's who she really is.*

He felt Angie's ectoplasmic form wince and hug itself closer to him.

He still couldn't see the Holy Mother's face clearly, but he could tell she was distraught. *So much death,* she said, surveying the disintegrating ship.

Seth wanted to open his mouth to say, *It was your idea,* but thought better of it.

No, you're right. It was, she said. She turned back toward Seth, who was mildly horrified that she'd heard his thought.

I'm sorry. I meant no disrespect, he said.

It's all right, she said. *There's room for honesty between us.*

I'm glad to hear that, he said, visibly relieved.

Her dress waved as if a current was tugging it. He wondered

what kind of force was playing upon it. But if she heard that wondering, too, she did not address it. Instead she looked at Angie with what seemed like pity. Then she turned her gaze to Kush.

It's time to go home, Seth, she said.

To the Pleroma? he asked.

Yes. To the One.

I'm ready, he said.

You cannot bring them, you know.

Even though her words had no volume in space, they hit him like a thunderclap.

What?

You cannot bring them with you. Angie is not a Pneumatic. And your dog is but an animal, with no soul to speak of.

I see him just fine, Seth said.

Now she turned her pity on him. *I'm sorry, love.*

For the first time since death, Seth felt vertigo. The whole Milky Way galaxy seemed to be spinning, and he was not at the still center. He lowered his head into Angie's neck and wailed.

There was no sound, of course, but there was a wail just the same. Beside him, Seth heard Kush howl in his head.

Then I guess I'm not going either, Seth said.

Seth, think about what you're saying—

And you know what? Seth continued. *Neither should you. Not without her. Not without Achamoth. You shouldn't leave her here. She's...part of you.* And with that, he turned his back on the Holy Mother and faced the cold infinity of space. A few moments later, he looked behind him. Sophia was gone. He imagined her leading all the Pneumatics in a procession to some ethereal version of the pearly gates. In what passed for his head he heard, *O when the saints...come marching in...I want to be...in that number...*

But I'm not, he thought.

A hand stroked his face. He looked down at Angie, still somehow buoyed by his arms.

You should go, she said. *You were right. You earned this. I was the idiot, it turns out, against all odds. You...go take your big gnostic victory lap.*

He looked into her eyes, and despite her not having flesh anymore, clearly saw—more clearly than ever—her intelligence, her steel, her mystery, and her kindness.

No, he said. *My place is with you. It has always been with you. You and Kush. I left him behind before. I'm not going to do it again. And I'm not going to leave you again either. Not ever.*

God, you sure know what a girl wants to hear. Angie smiled. *If you had genitals, I'd be so tempted to fuck you—I mean, even if you do have* the *wrong genitals.*

No one is perfect, Seth admitted.

That's for sure, Angie agreed. She pointed toward a towering purple nebula. *Let's float...that way.*

It is *pretty over there,* Seth agreed.

You know you don't have to carry me, Angie said.

I kind of do. Not for you, for me.

Knock yourself out, then, she said. And they started moving.

Seth had no idea how fast they were moving, or for how long. He wondered what they would have to say to each other after a hundred years. He wondered if they could stop somewhere and maybe haunt a planet. The whole universe was before them, yet there seemed to be precious little to do.

And then Seth heard a marching band. It was in his head, of course, or what remained of his head. But it was loud, and it was glorious. He heard the banging of cymbals and blast of trumpets and the fluttering of piccolos.

He turned and looked all around him. And then he saw it. Her. Bigger, somehow. And for the first time, clearer. She was, in fact, in perfect focus. Distance didn't seem to be an obstacle, and he had no gauge to tell how far away she was, or how close. But he could see every line and every pore on her face.

She was beautiful, clad in a smart periwinkle uniform with dark blue piping. Atop her head was the jaunty cap of a majorette, with a purple plume jutting from its top. Her hair was silver and hung in a bouncy bob around her jawline. Her smile was bright as a star, and her teeth were perfect. Her white boots kicked to one side, then the other in dramatic, exaggerated movements. She spun her silver baton over her head, catching the starlight and refracting it to every corner of the galaxy in a rainbow spray of color.

Is that...the same person? Angie asked. *The Holy Mother?*

Yeah, Seth answered. But...more. He wondered how that could be true. And then he saw it. There was a mad ferocity in her grin. It was balanced by sobriety and tenderness, but it was there. *Achamoth,* Seth whispered. She had gone back for her. The redeemed Sophia had merged with the fallen Sophia. She had healed the split. She had become whole. She had become One. And now she was leading the band. She looked over to Seth. She winked. And she waved at him to follow. Then she turned her back and began to march away.

Thousands of souls gravitated toward her, their silvery outlines snaking toward her over a pattern of alternating void and star.

She looks familiar, Angie said.

She is familiar, Seth said.

How so?

Remember the Pride Parade? Remember the majorette? You wanted to be her? Seth prompted.

Oh yeah. Dude, do you think...?

I know, Seth confirmed. *Let's go together.*

She already told me no, Angie said. *But you should go.*

Let's both go, Seth said. *All three of us.*

But she—

She's different now. And even if Sophia would turn you away, Achamoth won't.

Acha-who?

Never mind, Seth said.

The majorette looked back and waved them on again.

Not without them, Seth thought at her.

We aren't whole without them, she thought back.

Seth felt punched in the gut. The logic was indisputable. The whole required everybody and everything. It turned the whole Hylic-Psychic-Pneumatic structure on its head. Seth realized that grace like that turned most religions on their heads.

He looked down at Angie, still cradled in his arms-that-did-not-tire. *What do you think?*

She looked at him with a love he'd always ached for. *Let's march in the parade,* she said.

Achamoth, which is translated "Sophia,"
and who I myself am,
and who the imperishable Sophia is
through whom you will be redeemed,
and all the children of The One Who Is—
these things they have known
and have hidden within them.
You are to hide these things within you,
and you are to keep silence.
—*The First Apocalypse of James*[*]

---

[*] "The First Apocalypse of James," translated by Wllliam R. Schoedel, from *The Nag Hammadi Library,* adapted for inclusive language by the author.

AUTHOR'S NOTE

This book came to me while I was napping, in that peaceful twilight-zone space between sleep and the waking world. It arrived all at once, fully formed, like an explosion. I got up instantly and started typing notes. It has taken me over a year to write it. I'm sorry it's so long.

Although the details of the story came quickly, the seeds of it were many years in gestation. I was raised in a loving, moderate Southern Baptist home (yes, there were such things as moderate Southern Baptists in the 1960s and 1970s). Nevertheless, I can recall sermons on the subject of hellfire from as early as I could sit up in a pew. We were the kind of churchgoers who were there three times a week (at least). Certainly we were there for Sunday school and Sunday worship, Sunday night worship, and Wednesday night prayer meetings. That's a lot of hellfire.

But things really heated up when I got to high school. We joined a church that was heavily influenced by Bob Jones and his particularly virulent strain of independent Baptist teaching. There was nothing moderate about this church—it was hardcore funda-mentalist. They had a great youth group, though, and that was

656 • AUTHOR'S NOTE

the draw for me. We were *very* involved, and while my whole family emerged from that experience with some significant wounds, I think I got the worst of it. The story Seth relates about the youth group meeting in Chapter Two? That really happened to me.

Suffice to say that I had some major healing to do after we left that church. In fact, I would say that I have spent the majority of my professional life trying to heal from the spiritual wounds inflicted by that church and its toxic teachings. After forty years of therapy, twenty-five years of spiritual direction, five years of Fundamentalists Anonymous, and a doctorate in philosophy and religion, I am very relieved to have found that healing. But it was not an easy road, and I'm not sure I would have made it without an assist from gnosticism.

In the late 1990s, *The Nag Hammadi Library* became my bedside reading and remained so for about five straight years. I didn't understand what drew me to those ancient heretical scriptures, but I felt compelled to read them and read them again. Eventually, the penny dropped. Gnosticism posits that the creator of this world is not the True God, but a tyrant and a pretender to the throne of heaven who longs to keep us humans enslaved and blind to our true situation. But there is another God, beyond that false god, who loves us and calls us to health and wholeness.

I came to understand that the god of fundamentalism was not the True God, but a demiurge intent on my destruction. This empowered me to let go of that destructive image of the divine and left me free to discover the true face of God. It was the beginning of true healing.

Along the way, many people helped midwife my spiritual rebirth. I am grateful to Dennis Rivers and Joan Morton, my first spiritual directors, for listening as I sorted my religious trash. I am grateful to my friends and parishioners at Grace North Church, who read these scriptures with me and discussed their meanings.

I am grateful to the United Church of Christ, which gave me a home large enough to hold me while my faith evolved and evolved again. I am grateful to Martin Luther, whose 775-page *Basic Theological Writings* turned me inside out spiritually, and gave Jesus back to me. And I am grateful to my dear wife, Lisa Fullam, for loving and supporting me in every way imaginable.

This was a painful book to write, and I struggled with it. But I needed to write it. I needed to explore the themes at the heart of gnosticism, and to revisit the roadmap to freedom that showed me the Way Out. To be clear, I am not a gnostic—in fact many would consider my theology boringly orthodox. But, like all good myth, I appreciate how gnosticism points to important truths. If this novel speaks to even one person wounded by a church, by church people, or by toxic teachings, it will all have been worth it.

All of the gnostic scripture quoted is real, and all of the teachings belong to actual gnostic schools—although not all to the same school. Mr. Basil's gnosticism is a bit of a hodgepodge, but it is mostly resonant with the Valentinian school. The ritual of the Bridal Chamber comes from Epiphanius' *Panarion*, in a section on the Borborites. I will grant that Epiphanius is not the most reliable narrator, since he is writing *against* gnostics, but the scene was simply too juicy to leave out. (Ahem.) It is for this reason that I have not capitalized "gnosticism" wherever it appears in this text (much to the consternation of my spell-check), since it is a broad category invented by 19th-century academics as a term of convenience and not actually a single tradition.

Quotations from *The Gospel of Thomas* and *The Gospel of Philip* are my own versions, constructed through the use of Coptic-English interlinears, and by comparing them with a variety of existing English translations. Other quotations are adapted from various translations, including *The Gnostic Bible*, *The Gnostic Scriptures*, and *The Nag Hammadi Library*. I adapted some of the Gnostic ritual texts from *Suppressed Prayers*. I have tried to refer-

658 · AUTHOR'S NOTE

ence all of the quotes I have used, and have indicated where I have adapted them.

I experimented with ChatGPT-4 to produce many of the *Liquipedia* entries. I thought an actual answerbot might capture the style better than I could, and it did not disappoint. Most entries required some tweaking, but I was amazed at how complete and well-written they were. Plus, it was fun. But please rest assured, all of the actual fiction is my own work.

To those who have read this and my other novels, thank you for reading my books and supporting me as a writer. It means the world to me.

J.R. Mabry
September 1, 2024
Hannacroix, NY